The Single Voice

AN ANTHOLOGY OF
CONTEMPORARY FICTION

The Single Voice

EDITED BY JEROME CHARYN

COLLIER BOOKS

COLLIER-MACMILLAN LTD., LONDON

Library of Congress Catalog Card Number: 69–15089

THIRD PRINTING 1970

The Macmillan Company
866 Third Avenue, New York, N.Y. 10022
Collier-Macmillan Canada Ltd., Toronto, Ontario

Printed in the United States of America

ACKNOWLEDGMENTS

The author and publisher wish to acknowledge and express their gratitude to the following for permission to reprint selections included in this anthology:

" 'The Christ' and His Teachings" from *Soul on Ice* by Eldridge Cleaver. Copyright © 1968 by Eldridge Cleaver. Used by permission of McGraw-Hill Book Company.

"Novotny's Pain" by Philip Roth. Copyright © 1962 by Philip Roth. Used by permission of Robert Lantz-Candida Donadio Literary Agency Inc.

"Death in Miami Beach" from *The Age of Happy Problems* by Herbert Gold. Copyright © 1952, 1954, 1957, 1958, 1959, 1960, 1961, 1962 by Herbert Gold. Used by permission of The Dial Press, Inc.

"No! In Thunder" from *No! In Thunder* by Leslie Fiedler. Copyright © 1960 by Leslie A. Fiedler. Used by permission of Beacon Press.

"V. in Love" from *V.* by Thomas Pynchon. Copyright © 1961, 1963 by Thomas Pynchon. Used by permission of J. B. Lippincott Company.

"The Guest" from *Criers and Kibitzers, Kibitzers and Criers* by Stanley Elkin. Copyright © 1965 by Stanley Elkin. Used by permission of Random House, Inc.

"Wobbilobby Mobbays" from *The Steagle* by Irvin Faust. Copyright © 1964, 1966 by Irvin Faust. Used by permission of Random House, Inc.

"White Days and Red Nights" from *Stop-Time* by Frank Conroy. Copyright © 1965, 1967 by Frank Conroy. All rights reserved. Used by permission of The Viking Press, Inc.

"Smolak" from *Henderson the Rain King* by Saul Bellow. Copyright © 1959 by Saul Bellow. Used by permission of The Viking Press, Inc.

iv

34186

CONTENTS

vii

INTRODUCTION

In the opening words of *The White Negro*, Norman Mailer eloquently defines the central madness and trauma of our time:

Probably we will never be able to determine the psychic havoc of the concentration camps and the atomic bomb upon the unconscious mind of almost everyone alive in these years. For the first time in civilized history, perhaps the first time in all of history, we have been forced to live with the suppressed knowledge that the smallest facets of our personality or the most minor projection of our ideas, or indeed the absence of ideas and the absence of personality could mean equally well that we might still be doomed to die as a cipher in some vast statistical operation in which our teeth would be counted, and our hair would be saved, but our death itself would be unknown, unhonored, and unremarked, a death which could not follow with dignity as a possible consequence to serious actions we had chosen, but rather a death by *deus ex machina* in a gas chamber or a radioactive city; and so if in the midst of civilization—that civilization founded upon the Faustian urge to dominate nature by mastering time, mastering the links of social cause and effect—in the middle of an economic civilization founded upon the confidence that time could indeed be subjected to our will, our psyche was subjected itself to the intolerable anxiety that death being causeless, life was causeless as well, and time deprived of cause and effect had come to a stop.

And it is hardly surprising that the best writers of postwar America should reflect upon, explore, mimic, parody, attack, and deny, though rarely ignore, this sense of dread: the terrible isolation, the fear of total destruction, and the dreamlike suspension of time. As Roland Barthes has noted in *Writing Degree Zero*, "Literature is no longer felt as a socially privileged mode of transaction," in tune with its own culture and history, but as a language that has turned in upon itself, that exists outside of history, "both as dream and menace." It is the language of hysteria.

The one writer who best anticipated the tone of postwar American fiction, who envisioned the nightmare that lies at the heart of the American dream, was Nathanael West. Tod Hackett, reacting to Homer Simpson's hysteria in *The Day of the Locust*, "sat down and tried to make sense out of what Homer had told him. A great deal of it was gibberish. Some of it, however, wasn't. He hit upon a key that helped him when he realized that a lot of it wasn't jumbled so much as timeless. The words went behind each other instead of after. What he had taken for long strings were really one thick word and not a sentence. In the same way several sentences were simultaneous and not a paragraph."

It is the "one thick word" of pained, frozen, obsessive language that characterizes some of the best writing of John Hawkes, Saul Bellow, William Gass, and Leonard Cohen, and the most recent writing of Philip Roth. Hawkes provides a startling metaphor for his own fiction when he speaks of the child Monica's nightmare screams in *The Lime Twig*: "There was a white thread hanging from the opened lips and it blew gently in the vibrations of the scream." This hanging white thread, caught within the nightmare of a terrified child, delicate, graceful, dancing toward its own extinction, is the very force of Hawkes' prose: a poetic, troubled language under grave pressure, amid chaos and terror.

Though Hawkes has his own private nightmare vision and sense of the grotesque, his concern with terror is hardly unique. Terror has become the dominant fictional mode of postwar America and is the force behind such writers as Joseph Heller, Thomas Pynchon, John Barth, Donald Barthelme, and Stanley Elkin, who have been popularly labeled, and at times scorned, as "black humorists." In *An Age of Enormity*, the late Isaac Rosenfeld wrote:

Terror is today the main reality because it is the model reality. The concentration camp is the model educational system and the model form of government. War is the model enterprise and the model form of community. These are abstract propositions, but even so they are obvious; when we fill them in with experience, they are overwhelming. Unfortunately, there is nothing else into which we can fit our experience—traditions are broken and culture is unavailable. A culture is dead when the experience of men has no place in it. Our culture is an empty form, standing for a continuity of experience which is now discontinued, for the reality and inviolability of human values that are everywhere violated and denied.

Accused of being brash, cruel, irrelevant, and antihuman by a generation of older critics stuck to the values and critical apparatus of thirty years ago, the black humorists, in refusing to buy the sentimental, supermarket humanism and homogenized morality of modern America, in forcing irrationality and illogic upon us, in reminding us that we are all part monkey and part fool, and that there is more truth in parody and caricature, in excess and madness, than in all the shopworn fiction devoted to character development and depth psychology, have shown themselves to be our most profound moralists, for they have not glossed over or denied the terror, the loneliness, and the perversity of human existence. Shorn of all values and fake humanism, Jacob Horner, in John Barth's *End of the Road*, understands that "existence not only precedes essence: in the case of human beings it defies essence." Benny Profane, the human yo-yo of Thomas Pynchon's *V.*, feels stranded "in the aisles of a bright, gigantic supermarket, his only function to want." V. is perhaps the most severe indictment of Western civilization ever written by an American. Europe, for Pynchon, has become "Baedeker land," a triumph of the inanimate, a self-sufficient landscape in which "statues talk" and "government buildings go mad." The European civil servants, who are bound to this landscape, are only "the lead weights of a fantastic clock, necessary to keep it in motion, to keep an ordered sense of history and time prevailing against chaos." And hovering over the world, in her various sizes, shapes, and manifestations, is V., the goddess of love *and* death; in a murderous, mechanical society, love and death have become interchangeable.

Whatever place the black humorists ultimately hold in our literature, they have, in our own time, forced us to examine the absurdities and contradictions of our own nature; they have shown us the brittleness of the human heart and have warned us of the emptiness we will have to endure in a society that has devoted itself to hate rather than love.

1 Stanley Elkin

Stanley Elkin has published two comic novels, Boswell (1964) and A Bad Man (1967), and a collection of shorter fiction, Criers and Kibitzers, Kibitzers and Criers (1966). He is an associate professor of English at Washington University in St. Louis, Missouri.

❖

THE GUEST

On Sunday, Bertie walked into an apartment building in St. Louis, a city where, in the past, he had changed trains, waited for buses, or thought about Klaff, and where, more recently, truckers dropped him, or traveling salesmen stopped their Pontiacs downtown just long enough for him to reach into the back seat for his trumpet case and get out. In the hallway he stood before the brass mail-boxed wall seeking the name of his friend, his friends' friend really, and his friends' friend's wife. The girl had danced with him at parties in the college town, and one night—he imagined he must have been particularly pathetic, engagingly pathetic— she had kissed him. The man, of course, patronized him, asked him questions that would have been more vicious had they been less naïve. He remembered he rather enjoyed making his long, patient answers. Condescension always brought the truth out of him. It was more appealing than indifference at least, and more necessary to him now. He supposed he didn't care for either of them, but he couldn't go further. He had to rest or he would die.

He found the name on the mailbox—Mr. and Mrs. Richard Preminger—the girl's identity, as he might have guessed, swallowed

1

up in the husband's. It was no way to treat women, he thought gallantly.

He started up the stairs. Turning the corner at the second landing, he saw a man moving cautiously downward, burdened by boxes and suitcases and loose bags. Only as they passed each other did Bertie, through a momentary clearing in the boxes, recognize Richard Preminger.

"Old man, old man," Bertie said.

"Just a minute," Preminger said, forcing a package aside with his chin. Bertie stood, half a staircase above him, leaning against the wall. He grinned in the shadows, conscious of his ridiculous fedora, his eye patch rakishly black against the soft whiteness of his face. Black-suited, tiny, white-fleshed, he posed above Preminger, dapper as a scholarly waiter in a restaurant. He waited until he was recognized.

"Bertie? Bertie? Let me get rid of this stuff. Give me a hand, will you?" Preminger said.

"Sure," Bertie said. "It's on my family crest. One hand washing the other. Here, wait a minute." He passed Preminger on the stairs and held the door for him. He followed him outside.

"Take the key from my pocket, Bertie, and open the trunk. It's the blue convertible."

Bertie put his hand in Preminger's pocket. "You've got nice thighs," he said. To irritate Preminger he pretended to try to force the house key into the trunk lock. Preminger stood impatiently behind him, balancing his heavy burdens. "I've been to Dallas, lived in a palace," Bertie said over his shoulder. "There's this great Eskimo who blows down there. Would you believe he's cut the best side ever recorded of 'Mood Indigo'?" Bertie shook the key ring as if it were a castanet.

Preminger dumped his load on the hood of the car and took the keys from Bertie. He opened the trunk and started to throw things into it. "Going somewhere?" Bertie asked.

"Vacation," Preminger said.

"Oh," Bertie said.

Preminger looked toward the apartment house. "I've got to go up for another suitcase, Bertie."

"Sure," Bertie said.

He went up the stairs behind Preminger. About halfway up he stopped to catch his breath. Preminger watched him curiously. He pounded his chest with his tiny fist and grinned weakly. "*Mea culpa*," he said. "Mea booze, Mea sluts. Mea pot. Me-o-mea."

"Come on," Preminger said.

They went inside and Bertie heard a toilet flushing. Through a hall, through an open door, he saw Norma, Preminger's wife, staring absently into the bowl. "If she moves them now you won't have to stop at God knows what kind of place along the road," Bertie said brightly.

Norma lifted a big suitcase easily in her big hands and came into the living room. She stopped when she saw Bertie. "Bertie! Richard, it's Bertie."

"We bumped into each other in the hall," Preminger said.

Bertie watched the two of them look at each other.

"You sure picked a time to come visiting, Bertie," Preminger said.

"We're leaving on our vacation, Bertie," Norma said.

"We're going up to New England for a couple of weeks," Preminger told him.

"We can chat for a little with Bertie, can't we, Richard, before we go?"

"Of course," Preminger said. He sat down and pulled the suitcase next to him.

"It's very lovely in New England." Bertie sat down and crossed his legs. "I don't get up there very regularly. Not my territory. I've found that when a man makes it in the Ivy League he tends to forget about old Bertie," he said sadly.

"What are you doing in St. Louis, Bertie?" Preminger's wife asked him.

"It's my Midwestern swing," Bertie said. "I've been down South on the southern sponge. Opened up a whole new territory down there." He heard himself cackle.

"Who did you see, Bertie?" Norma asked him.

"You wouldn't know her. A cousin of Klaff's."

"Were you living with her?" Preminger asked.

Bertie shook his finger at him. The Premingers stared glumly at each other. Richard rubbed the plastic suitcase handle. In a moment, Bertie thought, he would probably say, "Gosh, Bertie, you should have written. You should have let us know." He should have written! Did the Fuller Brush man write? Who would be home? Who *wouldn't* be on vacation? They were commandos, the Fuller Brush man and he. He was tired, sick. He couldn't move on today. Would they kill him because of their lousy vacation?

Meanwhile the Premingers weren't saying anything. They stared at each other openly, their large eyes in their large heads on their large necks largely. He thought he could wait them out. It was what he *should* do. It should have been the easiest thing in the world to wait out the Premingers, to stare them down. Who was he kidding? It wasn't his forte. He had no forte. *That* was his forte. He could already hear himself begin to speak.

"Sure," he said. "I almost married that girl. Klaff's lady cousin. The first thing she ever said to me was, 'Bertie, they never build drugstores in the middle of the block. Always on corners.' It was the truth. Well, I thought, this was the woman for me. One time she came out of the ladies' john of a Greyhound bus station and she said, 'Bertie, have you ever noticed how public toilets often smell like bubble gum?' That's what it was like all the time. She had all these institutional insights. I was sure we could make it together. It didn't work out." He sighed

Preminger stared at him, but Norma was beginning to soften. He wondered randomly what she would be like in bed. He looked coolly at her long legs, her wide shoulders. Like Klaff's cousin: institutional.

"Bertie, how are your eyes now?" she asked.

"Oh," he said, "still seeing double." He smiled. "Two for one. It's all right when there's something to look at. Other times I use the patch."

Norma seemed sad.

"I have fun with it," he said. "It doesn't make any difference which eye I cover. I'm ambidexterous." He pulled the black elastic band from his forehead. Instantly there were two large Richards, two large Normas. The Four Premingers like a troupe of Jewish acrobats. He felt surrounded. In the two living rooms his four hands fumbled with the two patches. He felt sick to his stomach.

He closed one eye and hastily replaced the patch. "I shouldn't try that on an empty stomach," he said.

Preminger watched him narrowly. "Gee, Bertie," he said finally, "maybe we could drop you some place."

It was out of the question. He couldn't get into a car again. "Do you go through Minneapolis, Minnesota?" he asked indifferently.

Preminger looked confused, and Bertie liked him for a moment. "We were going to catch the Turnpike up around Chicago, Bertie."

"Oh, Chicago," Bertie said. "I can't go back to Chicago yet." Preminger nodded.

"Don't you know anybody else in St. Louis?" Norma asked.

"Klaff used to live across the river, but he's gone," Bertie said.

"Look, Bertie . . ." Preminger said.

"I'm fagged," Bertie said helplessly, "locked out."

"Bertie," Preminger said, "do you need any money? I could let you have twenty dollars."

Bertie put his hand out mechanically.

"This is stupid," Norma said suddenly. "Stay here."

"Oh, well—"

"No, I mean it. Stay here. We'll be gone for two weeks. What difference does it make?"

Preminger looked at his wife for a moment and shrugged. "Sure," he said, "there's no reason you couldn't stay here. As a matter of fact you'd be doing us a favor. I forgot to cancel the newspaper, the milk. You'd keep the burglars off. They don't bother a place if it looks lived in." He put twenty dollars on the coffee table. "There might be something you need," he explained.

Bertie looked carefully at them both. They seemed to mean it. Preminger and his wife grinned at him steadily, relieved at how easily they had come off. He enjoyed the idea himself. At last he had a real patron, a real matron. "Okay," he said.

"Then it's settled," Preminger said, rising.

"It's all right?" Bertie said.

"Certainly it's all right," Preminger said. "What harm could you do?"

"I'm harmless," Bertie said.

Preminger picked up the suitcase and led his wife toward the door. "Have a good time," Bertie said, following them. "I'll watch things for you. Rrgghh! Rrrgghhhffff!"

Preminger waved back at him as he went down the stairs. "Hey," Bertie called, leaning over the banister, "did I tell you about that crazy Klaff? You know what nutty Klaff did out at U.C.L.A.? He became a second-story man." They were already down the stairs.

Bertie pressed his back against the door and turned his head slowly across his left shoulder. He imagined himself photographed from underneath. "Odd man in," he said. He bounded into the center of the living room. I'll bet there's a lease, he thought. I'll bet there's a regular lease that goes with this place. He considered this respectfully, a little awed. He couldn't remember ever having been in a place where the tenants actually had to sign a lease. In the dining room he turned on the chandelier lights. "Sure there's a lease," Bertie said. He hugged himself. "How the fallen are mighty," he said.

In the living room he lay down on the couch without taking off his shoes. He sat up and pulled them off, but when he lay down again he was uneasy. He had gotten out of the habit, living the way he did, of sleeping without shoes. In his friends' leaseless basements the nights were cold and he wore them for warmth. He put the shoes on again, but found that he wasn't tired any more. It was a fact that dependence gave him energy. He was never so alert as when people did him favors. It was having to be on your own that made you tired.

"Certainly," Bertie said to the committee, "it's scientific. We've suspected it for years, but until our researchers divided up the town of Bloomington, Indiana, we had no proof. What our people found in that community was that the orphans and bastards were sleepy and run down, while the housewives and people on relief were wide awake, alert, raring to go. We can't positively state the link yet, but we're fairly certain that it's something to do with dependency—in league perhaps with a particularly virulent form of gratitude. Ahem. Ahem."

As he lectured the committee he wandered around the apartment, touring from right to left. He crossed from the living room into the dining room and turned right into the kitchen and then right again into Preminger's small study. "Here's where all the magic happens," Bertie said, glancing at the contour chair near Preminger's desk. He went back into the kitchen. "Here's where all the magic happens," he said, looking at Norma's electric stove. He stepped into the dining room and continued on, passing Norma's paintings of picturesque side streets in Mexico, of picturesque side streets in Italy, of picturesque side streets in Puerto Rico, until he came to a door that led to the back sun parlor. He went through it and found himself in a room with an easel, with paints in sexy little tubes, with brushes, with palettes and turpentine and rags. "Here's where all the magic happens," Bertie said and walked around the room to another door. He opened it and was in the Premingers' master bedroom. He looked at the bed. "Here's where all the magic happens," he said. Through a door at the other end of the room was another small hall. On the right was the toilet. He went in and flushed it. It was one of those toilets with instantly renewable tanks. He flushed it again. And again. "The only kind to have," he said out of the side of his mouth, imagining a rental agent. "I mean, it's like this. Supposing the missus has diarrhea or something. You don't want to have to wait until the tank fills up. Or suppose you're sick. Or suppose you're giving a party and it's mixed company. Well, it's just corny to whistle to cover the noise, know what I mean? 'S jus' corny. On the other hand, you flush it once suppose you're not through, then what happens? There's the damn noise after the water goes down. What have you accomplished? This way"—he reached across and jiggled the little lever and then did it a second time, a third, a fourth—"you never have any embarrassing interim, what we in the trade call 'flush lag.'"

He found the guest bedroom and knew at once that he would never sleep in it, that he would sleep in the Premingers' big bed.

"Nice place you got here," he said when he had finished the tour.

"Dooing de woh eet ees all I tink of, what I fahting foe," the man from the Underground said. "Here ees eet fahrproof, air-condizione and safe from Nazis."

"Stay out of Volkswagens, kid," Bertie said.

He went back into the living room. He wanted music, but it was a cardinal principle with him never to blow alone. He would drink alone, take drugs alone, but somehow for him the depths of depravity were represented by having to play jazz alone. He had a vision of himself in a cheap hotel room sitting on the edge of an iron bedstead. Crumpled packages of cigarettes were scattered throughout the room. Bottles of gin were on top of the Gideon Bible, the Western Union blanks. His trumpet was in his lap. "Perfect," Bertie said. "Norma Preminger could paint it in a picture." He shuddered.

The phonograph was in the hall between the dining room and living room. It was a big thing, with the AM and the FM and the short wave and the place where you plugged in the color television when it was perfected. He found records in Preminger's little room and went through them rapidly. "Ahmad Jamahl, for Christ's sake." Bertie took the record out of its sleeve and broke it across his knee. He stood up slowly and kicked the fragments of the broken recording into a neat pile.

He turned around and scooped up as many of Preminger's recordings as he could carry and brought them to the machine. He piled them on indiscriminately and listened with visible, professional discomfort. He listened to *The New World Symphony*, to Beethoven's *Fifth*, to *My Fair Lady*. The more he listened the more he began to dislike the Premingers. When he could stand it no longer he tore the playing arm viciously away from the record and looked around him. He saw the Premingers' bookcase.

"I'll read," Bertie said.

He took down the Marquis de Sade and Henry Miller and Ronald Firbank and turned the pages desultorily. Nothing happened. He tried reading aloud in front of a mirror. He went back to the bookcase and looked for *The Egg and I* and *Please Don't Eat the Daisies*. The prose of a certain kind of bright housewife always made Bertie feel erotic. But the Premingers owned neither book. He browsed through Rachel Carson's *Silent Spring* with his fly unzipped, but he felt only a mild lasciviousness.

He went into their bedroom and opened the closet. He found a pair of Norma's shoes and put them on. Although he was no fetishist, he had often promised himself that if he ever had the opportunity he would see what it was like. He got into drag and walked around the apartment in Norma's high heels. All he experienced was a pain in his calves.

In the kitchen he looked into the refrigerator. There were some frozen mixed vegetables in the freezer compartment. "I'll starve first," Bertie said.

He found a Billie Holiday record and put it on the phonograph. He hoped that out in Los Angeles, Klaff was being beaten with rubber hoses by the police. He looked up at the kitchen clock. "Nine," he said. "Only seven in L.A. They probably don't start beating them up till later."

"Talk, Klaff," he snarled, "or we'll drag you into the Blood Room."

"Flake off, copper," Klaff said.

"That's enough of that, Klaff. Take that and that and that."

"*Bird lives!*" Bertie screamed suddenly, invoking the dead Charlie Parker. It was his code cry.

"Mama may have," Billie Holiday wailed, "Papa may have, but God Bless the child who's got his own, who—oo—zz—"

"Who—oo—zz," Bertie wailed.

"Got his own," Billie said.

"I'll tell him when he comes in, William," Bertie said.

He waited respectfully until Billie was finished and then turned off the music.

He wondered why so many people felt that Norman Mailer was the greatest living American novelist.

He sat down on the Premingers' coffee table and marveled at his being alone in so big and well-furnished an apartment. The Premingers were probably the most substantial people he knew. Though plenty of the others wanted to, Bertie thought bitterly, Preminger was the only one from the old crowd who might make it. Of course he was Jewish, and that helped. Some Jews swung pretty good, but he always suspected that in the end they would hold out on you. But then who wouldn't, Bertie wondered. Kamikaze pilots, maybe. Anyway, this was Bertie's special form of anti-Semitism and he cherished it. Melvin Gimpel, for example, his old roommate. Every time Melvin tried to kill himself by sticking his head in the oven he left the kitchen window open. One time he found Gimpel on his knees with his head on the oven door, oddly like the witch in Hansel and Gretel. Bertie closed the window and shook Gimpel awake.

"Mel," he yelled, slapping him. "*Mel.*"

"Bertie, go way. Leave me alone, I want to kill myself."

"Thank God," Bertie said. "Thank God I'm in time. When I found that window closed I thought it was all over."

"What, the window was closed? My God, was the *window* closed?"

> "Melvin Gimpel is so simple
> Thinks his nipple is a pimple,"

Bertie recited.

He hugged his knees, and felt again a wave of the nauseous sickness he had experienced that morning. "It's foreshadowing. One day as I am shoveling my walk I will collapse and die."

When the nausea left him he thought again about his situation. He had friends everywhere and made his way from place to place like an old-time slave on the Underground Railway. For all the pathos of the figure he knew he deliberately cut, there were always people to do him favors, give him money, beer, drugs, to nurse him back to his normal state of semi-invalidism, girls to kiss him in the comforting way he liked. This was probably the first time he had been alone in months. He felt like a dog whose master has gone away for the weekend. Just then he heard some people coming up the stairs and he growled experimentally. He went down on his hands and knees and scampered to the door, scratching it with his nails. "Rrrgghhf," he barked. "Rrgghhfff!" He heard whoever it was fumbling to open a door on the floor below him. He smiled. "Good dog," he said. "Good dog, goodog, gudug, gudugguduggudug."

He whined. He missed his master. A tear formed in the corner of his left eye. He crawled to a full-length mirror in the bathroom. "Ahh," he said. "Ahh." Seeing the patch across his eye, he had an inspiration. "Here, Patch," he called. "Come on, Patch." He romped after his own voice.

He moved beside Norma Preminger's easel in the sun parlor. He lowered his body carefully, pushing himself slightly backward with his arms. He yawned. He touched his chest to the wooden floor. He wagged his tail and then let himself fall heavily on one side. He pulled his legs up under him and fell asleep.

When Bertie awoke he was hungry. He fingered the twenty dollars in his pocket that Preminger had given him. He could order out. The light in the hall where the phone and phone books were was not good, so he tore "Restaurants" from the Yellow Pages and brought the sheets with him into the living room. Only two places delivered after one A.M. It was already one-thirty. He dialed the number of a pizza place across the city.

"Pal, bring over a big one, half shrimp, half mushroom. And two six-packs." He gave the address. The man explained that the truck had just gone out and that he shouldn't expect delivery for at least another hour and a half.

"Put it in a cab," Bertie said. "While Bird lives Bertie spends."

He took out another dozen or so records and piled them on the machine. He sat down on the couch and drummed his trumpet case with his fingers. He opened the case and fit the mouthpiece to the body of the horn. He put the trumpet to his lips and experienced the unpleasant shock of cold metal he always felt. He still thought it strange that men could mouth metal this way, ludicrous that his professional attitude should be a kiss. He blew a few bars in accompaniment to the record and then put the trumpet back in the case. He felt in the side pockets of the trumpet case and took out two pairs of dirty underwear, some handkerchiefs and three pairs of socks. He unrolled one of the pairs of socks and saw with pleasure that the drug was still there. He took out the bottle of carbon tetrachloride. This was what he cleaned his instrument with, and it was what he would use to kill himself when he had finally made the decision.

He held the bottle to the light. "If nothing turns up," he said, "I'll drink this. And to hell with the kitchen window."

The cab driver brought the pizza and Bertie gave him the twenty dollars.

"I can't change that," the driver said.

"Did I ask you to change it?" Bertie said.

"That's twenty bucks there."

"Bird lives. Easy come, easy go go go," Bertie said.

The driver started to thank him.

"Go." He closed the door.

He spread Norma Preminger's largest tablecloth over the dining-room table and then, taking china and silver from the big
breakfront, laid several place settings. He found champagne
glasses.

Unwrapping the pizza, he carefully plucked all the mushrooms
from it ("American mushrooms," he said. "Very square. No visions.") and laid them in a neat pile on the white linen. ("Many
mushloom," he said. "Mushloom crowd.") He poured some beer
into a champagne glass and rose slowly from his chair.

"Gentlemen," he said, "to the absent Klaff. May the police in
Los Angeles, California, beat his lousy ass off." He drank off all
the beer in one gulp and tossed the glass behind him over his
shoulder. He heard it shatter and then a soft sizzling sound.
Turning around, he saw that he had hit one of Norma's paintings
right in a picturesque side street. Beer dripped ignobly down a
donkey's leg. "Goddamn," Bertie said appreciatively, "*action
painting.*"

He ate perhaps a quarter of the pizza before rising from the
table, wiping the corner of his lips with a big linen napkin. "Gentlemen," he said. "I propose that the ladies retire to the bedroom
while we men enjoy our cigars and port and some good talk."

"I propose that we men retire to the bedroom and enjoy the
ladies," he said in Gimpel's voice.

"Here, here," he said in Klaff's voice. "Here, here. Good talk.
Good talk."

"If you will follow me, gentlemen," Bertie said in his own
voice. He began to walk around the apartment. "I have often been
asked the story of my life. These requests usually follow a personal favor someone has done me, a supper shared, a bed made
available, a ride in one of the several directions. Indeed, I have
become a sort of troubadour who does not sing so much as whine
for his supper. Most of you—"

"Whine is very good with supper," Gimpel said.

"Gimpel, my dear, why don't you run into the kitchen and
play?" Bertie said coolly. "Many of you may know the humble

beginnings, the sordid details, the dark Freudian patterns, and those of you who are my friends—"

Klaff belched.

"Those of you who are my *friends*, who do not run off to mix it up with the criminal element in the far West, have often wondered what will ultimately happen to me, to 'Poor Bertie' as I am known in the trade."

He unbuttoned his shirt and let it fall to the floor. In his undershirt he looked defenseless, his skin pale as something seen in moonlight. "Why, you wonder, doesn't he do something about himself, pull himself up by his bootstraps? Why, for example, doesn't he get his eyes fixed? Well, I've tried."

He kicked off his shoes. "You have all admired my bushy mustache. Do you remember that time two years ago I dropped out of sight for four months? Well, let me tell you what happened that time."

He took off his black pants. "I had been staying with Royal Randle, the distinguished philologist and drunk. You will recall what Royal, Klaff, Myers, Gimpel and myself once were to each other. Regular Whiffenpoofs we were. Damned from here to eternity. Sure, sure." He sighed. "You remember Randle's promises: 'It won't make any difference, Bertie. It won't make any difference, Klaff. It won't make any difference, fellas.' He married the girl in the muu-muu."

He was naked now except for his socks. He shivered once and folded his arms across his chest. "Do you know why the girl in the muu-muu married Randle?" He paused dramatically. *"To get at me, that's why!* The others she didn't care about. She knew even before I did what they were like. Even what *Klaff* was like. She knew they were corrupt, that they had it in them to sell me out, to settle down—that all anyone had to do was wave their deaths in front of them and they'd come running, that reason and fucking money and getting it steady would win again. But in me she recognized the real enemy, the last of the go-to-hell-god-damn-its. Maybe the first.

"They even took me with them on their honeymoon. At the time I thought it was a triumph for dependency, but it was just a trick, that's all. The minute they were married, this girl in the muu-muu was after Randle to do something about Bertie. And it wasn't 'Poor' Bertie this time. It was she who got me the appointment with the mayor. Do you know what His Honor said to me? 'Shave your mustache and I'll give you a job clerking in one of my supermarkets.' Christ, friends, do you know I *did* it? Well, I'm not made of stone. They had taken me on their honeymoon, for God's sake."

He paused.

"I worked in that supermarket *for three hours*. Clean-shaved. My mustache sacrificed as an earnest to the mayor. Well, I'm telling you, you don't know what square *is* till you've worked in a supermarket for three hours. They pipe in Mantovani. Mantovani! I cleared out for four months to raise my mustache again and to forget. What you see now isn't the original, you understand. It's all second growth, and believe me it's not the same."

He drew aside the shower curtain and stepped into the tub. He paused with his hand on the tap. "But I tell you this, friends. I would rather be a mustached bum than a clean-shaved clerk. I'll work. Sure I will. When they pay anarchists! When they subsidize the hip! When they give grants to throw bombs! When they shell out for gainsaying!"

Bertie pulled the curtain and turned on the faucet. The rush of water was like applause.

After his shower Bertie went into the second bedroom and carefully removed the spread from the cot. Then he punched the pillow and mussed the bed. "Very clever," he said. "It wouldn't do to let them think I never slept here." He had once realized with sudden clarity that he would never, so long as he lived, make a bed.

Then he went into the other bedroom and ripped the spread from the big double bed. For some time, in fact since he had first seen it, Bertie had been thinking about this bed. It was the biggest bed he would ever sleep in. He thought invariably in such terms. One cigarette in a pack would suddenly become distinguished in his mind as the best, or the worst, he would smoke that day. A homely act, such as tying his shoelaces, if it had occurred with unusual ease, would be remembered forever. This lent to his vision an oblique sadness, conscious as he was that he was forever encountering experiences which would never come his way again.

He slipped his naked body between the sheets, but no sooner had he made himself comfortable than he became conscious of the phonograph, still playing in the little hall. He couldn't hear it very well. He thought about turning up the volume, but he had read somewhere about neighbors. Getting out of bed, he moved the heavy machine through the living room, pushing it with difficulty over the seamed, bare wooden floor, trailing deep scratches. Remember not to walk barefoot there, he thought. At one point one of the legs caught in a loop of the Premingers' shag rug and Bertie strained to free it, finally breaking the thick thread and producing an interesting pucker along one end of the rug, not unlike the pucker in raised theatrical curtains. At last he had maneuvered the machine into the hall just outside the bedroom and plugged it in. He went back for the Billie Holiday recording he had heard earlier and put it on the phonograph. By fiddling with the machine, he fixed it so that the record would play all night.

Bertie got back into the bed. "Ah," he said, "the *sanctum sanctorum*." He rolled over and over from one side of the bed to the other. He tucked his knees into his chest and went under the covers. "It makes you feel kind of small and insignificant," he said.

"Ladies and gentlemen, this is Graham Macnamee speaking to you from the Cave of the Winds. I have made my way into the heart of this darkness to find my friend, Poor Bertie, who, as you know, entered the bed eight weeks ago. Bertie is with me now, and while there isn't enough light for me to be able to see his condition, his voice may tell us something about his physical state. Bertie, just what *is* the official record?"

"Well, Graham, some couples have been known to stick it out for seventy-five years. Of course, your average is much less than that, but still—"

"Seventy-five years."

"Seventy-five, yes sir. It's amazing, isn't it, Graham, when you come to think? All that time in one bed."

"It certainly is," Graham Macnamee said. "Do you think you'll be able to go the distance, Bert?"

"Who, me? No, no. A lot of folks have misunderstood my purpose in coming here. I'm rather glad you've given me the opportunity to clear that up. Actually my work here is scientific. This isn't a stunt or anything like that. I'm here to learn."

"Can you tell us about it, Bert?"

"Graham, it's been a fascinating experience, if you know what I mean, but frankly there are many things we still don't understand. *I* don't know why they do it. All that licit love, that regularity. Take the case of Richard and Norma, for example—and incidentally, you don't want to overlook the significance of that name 'Norma,' Norma/Normal, you see?"

"Say, I never thought of that."

"Well, I'm trained to think like that, Graham. In my work you have to."

"Say," Graham Macnamee said.

"Sure. Well, the thing is this, buddy, when I first came into this bed I felt the aura, know what I mean, the power. I think it's built into the mattress or something."

"Say."

"Shut your face, Graham, and let me speak, will you please? Well, anyway, you feel surrounded. Respectable. Love is made here, of course, but it's not love as we know it. There are things that must remain mysteries until we have more facts. I mean, Graham, checks could be cashed in this bed, for Christ's sake, credit cards honored. It's ideal for family reunions, high teas. Graham, it's the kind of place you wouldn't be ashamed to take your mother."

"Go to sleep, Bert," Graham Macnamee said.

"Say," Bertie said.

Between the third and fourth day of his stay in the Premingers' apartment Bertie became restless. He had not been outside the house since the Sunday he arrived, even to bring in the papers Preminger had told him about. (Indeed, it was by counting the papers that he knew how long he had been there, though he couldn't be sure, since he didn't know whether the Premingers had taken the Sunday paper along with them.) He could see them on the back porch through the window of Norma's sun parlor. With the bottles of milk they made a strange little pile. After all, he was not a caretaker; he was a guest. Preminger could bring in his own papers, drink his own damn milk. For the same reasons he had determined not even to answer the phone when it rang.

One evening he tried to call Klaff at the Los Angeles County Jail, but the desk sergeant wouldn't get him. He wouldn't even take a message.

Although he had not been outside since Sunday, Bertie had only a vague desire to leave the apartment. He weighed this against his real need to rest and his genuine pleasure in being alone in so big a place. Like the man in the joke who does not leave his Miami hotel room because it is costing him thirty-five dollars a day, Bertie decided he had better remain inside.

With no money left he was reduced to eating the dry, cold remainder of the pizza, dividing it mathematically into a week's provisions, like someone on a raft. (He actually fancied himself, not on a raft perhaps, but set alone and drifting on, say, the Queen Mary.) To supplement the pizza he opened some cans of soup he found in the pantry and drank the contents straight, without heating it or even adding water. Steadily he drank away at the Premingers' modest stock of liquor. The twelve cans of beer had been devoured by the second morning, of course.

After the second full day in the apartment his voices began to desert him. It was only with difficulty that he could manage his imitations, and only for short lengths of time. The glorious discussions that had gone on long into the night were now out of the question. He found he could not do Gimpel's voice any more, and even Klaff's was increasingly difficult and largely confined to his low, caressing obscenities. Mostly he talked with himself, although it was a real strain to keep up his end of the conversation, and it always made him cry when he said how pathetic he was and asked himself where do you go from here. Oh, to be like Bird, he thought. Not to have to be a bum. To ask, as it were, no quarter.

At various times during the day he would call out "Bird lives" in seeming stunning triumph. But he didn't believe it.

He watched a lot of television. "I'm getting ammunition," he said. "It's scientific."

Twice a day he masturbated in the Premingers' bed.

He settled gradually, then, into restlessness. He knew, of course, that he had it always in his power to bring himself back up to the heights he had known in those wonderful first two days. He was satisfied, however, not to use this power, and thought of himself as a kind of soldier, alone in a foxhole, in enemy territory, at night, at a bad time in the war, with one bullet in his pistol. Oddly, he derived more pride—and comfort, and a queer security—from this single bullet than others might have from whole cases of ammunition. It was his *strategic* bullet, the one he would use to get the big one, turn the tide, make the difference. The Premingers would be away two weeks. He would not waste his ammunition. Just as he divided the stale pizza, cherishing each piece as much for the satisfaction he took from possessing it during a time of emergency as for any sustenance it offered, so he enjoyed his knowledge that at any time he could recoup his vanishing spirits. He shared with the squares ("Use their own weapons to beat them, Bertie") a special pride in adversity, in having to do without, in having to expose whatever was left of his character to the narrower straits. It was strange, he thought seriously, it was the paradox of the world and an institutional insight that might have come right out of the mouth of that slut in Dallas, but the most peculiar aspect of the squares wasn't their lack of imagination or their bland bad taste, but their ability, like the wildest fanatics, like the furthest out of the furthest out, to cling to the illogical, finally untenable notion that they must have and have in order to live, at the same time that they realized that it was better not to have. What seemed so grand to Bertie, who admired all impossible positions, was that they believed both things with equal intensity, never suspecting for a moment any inconsistency. And here was Bertie, Bertie thought, here was Bertie inside their capitol, on the slopes of their mountains, on their smooth shores, who believed neither of these propositions, who believed in not having and in not suffering too, who yet realized the very same pleasure that they would in having and not using. It was the strangest thing that would ever happen to him, he thought.

"Are you listening, Klaff, you second-story fink?" Bertie yelled. "Do you see how your old pal is developing what is called character?"

And so, master of himself for once, he resolved—feeling what someone taking a vow feels—not to use the last of his drugs until the strategic moment of strategic truth.

That was Wednesday evening. By Thursday morning he had decided to break his resolution. He had not yielded to temptation, had not lain fitfully awake all night—indeed, his resolution had given him the serenity to sleep well—in the sweaty throes of withdrawal. There had been no argument or rationalization, nor had he decided that he had reached his limit or that this was the strategic moment he had been waiting for. He yielded as he always yielded: spontaneously, suddenly, unexpectedly, as the result neither of whim nor of calculation. His important decisions were almost always reached without his knowledge, and he was often as surprised as the next one to see what he was going to do—to see, indeed, that he was already doing it. (Once someone had asked him whether he believed in Free Will, and after considering this for a moment as it applied to himself, Bertie had answered "Free? Hell, it's positively *loose*.")

Having discovered his new intention, he was eager to realize it. As often as he had taken drugs (he never called it anything but drugs, never used the cute or obscene names, never even said "dope"; to him it was always "drugs," medicine for his spirit), they were still a major treat for him. "It's a rich man's game," he had once told Klaff, and then he had leaned back philosophically. "You know, Klaff, it's a good thing I'm poor. When I think of the snobbish ennui of your wealthy junkies, I realize that they don't know how to appreciate their blessings. God keep me humble, Klaff. Abstinence makes the heart grow fonder, a truer word was never spoken."

Nor did a drug ever lose its potency for him. If he graduated from one to another, it was not in order to recover some fading jolt, but to experience a new and different one. He held in contempt all those who professed disenchantment with the drugs they had been raised on, and frequently went back to rediscover the old pleasures of marijuana, as a sentimental father might chew some of his boy's bubble gum. "Loyalty, Gimpel," he exclaimed, "loyalty, do you know what *that* is?"

Bertie would and did try anything, though currently his favorite was mescaline for the visions it induced. Despite what he considered his eclectic tastes in these matters, there were one or two things he would not do, however. He never introduced any drug by hypodermic needle. This he found disgusting and, frankly, painful. He often said he could stand anything but pain and was very proud of his clear, unpunctured skin. "Not a mark on me," he would say, waving his arms like a professional boxer. The other thing he would not do was take his drugs in the presence of other users, for he found the company of addicts offensive. However, he was not above what he called "seductions." A seduction for him was to find some girl and talk her into letting him share his drugs with her. Usually it ended in their lying naked in a bed together, both of them serene, absent of all desire and what Bertie called "unclean thoughts."

"You know," he would say to the girl beside him, "I think that if all the world's leaders would take drugs and lie down on the bed naked like this without any unclean thoughts, the cause of world peace would be helped immeasurably. What do you think?"

"I think so too," she would say.

Once he knew he was going to take the drug, Bertie made his preparations. He went first to his trumpet case and took out the last small packet of powder. He opened it carefully, first closing all the windows so that no sudden draft could blow any of it away. This had once happened to a friend of his, and Bertie had never forgotten the warning.

"I am not one on whom a lesson is lost," Bertie said.

"You're okay, Bertie," a Voice said. "Go save France."

He placed the packet on the Premingers' coffee table and carefully spread the paper, exactly like the paper wrapper around a stick of chewing gum, looking almost lustfully at the soft, flat layer of ground white powder. He held out his hand to see how steady it was, and although he was not really shaky he did not trust himself to lift the paper from the table. He brought a water tumbler from the kitchen and gently placed it upside down on top of the powder. He was not yet ready to take it. Bertie was a man who postponed his pleasures as long as he possibly could; he let candy dissolve in his mouth and played with the threads on his tangerine before eating the fruit. It was a weakness in his character perhaps, but he laid it lovingly at the feet of his poverty.

He decided to wait until sundown to take the drug, reasoning that when it wore off, it would be early next morning and he would be ready for bed. Sleep was one of his pleasures too, and he approved of regularity in small things, taking a real pride in being able to keep hours. To pass the time until sundown he looked for something to do. First he found some tools and busied himself by taking Norma's steam iron apart. There was still time left after that, so he took a canvas and painted a picture. Because he did not know how to draw he simply covered the canvas first with one color and then with another, applying layer after layer of the paint thickly. Each block of color he made somewhat smaller than the last, so that the finished painting portrayed successive jagged margins of color. He stepped back and considered his work seriously.

"Well, it has texture, Bertie," Hans Hoffman said.

"Bertie," the Voice said suddenly, "I don't like to interrupt when you're working, but it's sundown."

"So it is," he said, looking up.

He went back into the living room and removed the tumbler. Taking up the paper in his fingers and creasing it as if he were a cowboy rolling a cigarette, Bertie tilted his head far back and inhaled the powder deeply. This part was always uncomfortable for him. "Ooo," he said, "the bubbles." He stuffed the last few grains up his nose with his fingers. "Waste not, want not," he said.

He sat down to wait. After half an hour in which nothing happened, Bertie became uneasy. "It's been cut," he said. "Sure, depend upon friends to do you favors." He was referring to the fact that the mescaline had been a going-away present from friends in Oklahoma City. He decided to give it fifteen more minutes. "Nothing," he said at last, disappointed. "Nothing."

The powder, as it always did, left his throat scratchy, and there was a bitter taste in his mouth. His soft palate prickled. He seized the water tumbler from the coffee table and walked angrily into the kitchen. He ran the cold water, then gargled and spit in the sink. In a few minutes the bitter taste and the prickly sensation subsided and he felt about as he had before he took the drug. He was conscious, however, of a peculiar smell, unpleasant, unfamiliar, nothing like the odor of rotting flowers he associated with the use of drugs. He opened a window and leaned out, breathing the fresh air. But as soon as he came away from the window, the odor was again overpowering. He went to see if he could smell it in the other rooms. When he had made his tour he realized that the stench must be coming from the kitchen. Holding his breath, he came back to see if he could locate its source. The kitchen was almost as Norma had left it. He had done no cooking, and although there were some empty soup and beer cans in the sink he knew they couldn't be causing the odor. He shrugged. Then he noticed the partially closed door to Preminger's study.

"Of course," Bertie said. "Whatever it is must be in there." He pushed the door open. In the middle of the floor were two blackish mounds that looked like dark sawdust. Bertie stepped back in surprise.

"Camel shit," he said. "My God, how did that get in here?" He went closer to investigate. "That's what it is, all right." He had never seen it before but a friend had, and had described it to him. This stuff fitted the description perfectly. He considered what to do.

"I can't leave it there," he said. He found a dustpan and a broom, and propping the pan against the leg of Preminger's chair, began to sweep the stuff up. He was surprised at how remarkably gummy it seemed. When he finished he washed the spot on the floor with a foaming detergent and stepped gingerly to the back door. He lifted the lid of the garbage can and shoved the broom and the contents of the dustpan and the dustpan itself into the can. Then he went to the bathroom and washed his hands.

In the living room he saw the Chinaman. "Jesus," Bertie said breathlessly.

The Chinaman lowered his eyes in a shy, almost demure smile. He said nothing, but motioned Bertie to sit in the chair across from him. Bertie, too frightened to disobey, sat down.

He waited for the Chinaman to tell him what he wanted. After an hour (he heard the chime clock strike nine times and then ten times), when the Chinaman still had not said anything, he began to feel a little calmer. Maybe he was just tired, Bertie thought,

and came in to rest. He realized that perhaps he and the Chinaman had more in common than had at first appeared. He looked
at the fellow in this new light and saw that he had been foolish to
fear him. The Chinaman was small, smaller even than Bertie. In
fact, he was only two feet tall. Perhaps what made him seem
larger was the fact that he was wrapped in wide, voluminous
white silk robes. Bertie stared at the robes, fascinated by the delicate filigree trim up and down their length. To see this closer he
stood up and walked tentatively toward the Chinaman.

The Chinaman gazed steadily to the front, and Bertie, seeing
no threat, continued toward him. He leaned down over the
Chinaman, and gently grasping the delicate lacework between
his forefinger and his thumb, drew it toward his eye. "May I?"
Bertie asked. "I know a good deal about this sort of thing."

The Chinaman lowered his eyes.

Bertie examined the weird symbols and designs, and although
he did not understand them, recognized at once their cabalistic
origin.

"Magnificent," Bertie said at last. "My God, the man hours
that must have gone into this. *The sheer craftsmanship!* That's
really a terrific robe you've got there."

The Chinaman lowered his eyes still further.

Bertie sat down in his chair again. He heard the clock strike
eleven and he smiled at the Chinaman. He was trying to be sympathetic, patient. He knew the fellow had his reasons for coming
and that in due time they would be revealed, but he couldn't
help being a little annoyed. First the failure of the drug and then
the camel shit on the floor and now this. However, he remained
very polite.

There was nothing else to do, so he concentrated on the Chinaman's face.

Then a strange thing happened.

He became aware, as he scrutinized the face, of some things he
hadn't noticed before. First he realized that it was the oldest face
he had ever seen. He knew that this face was old enough to have
looked on Buddha's. It was only *faintly* yellow, really, and he
understood with a sweeping insight that originally it must have
been white, as it still largely was, a striking, flat white, naked as

a sheet, bright as teeth, that its yellowness was an intrusion, the intruding yellowness of fantastic age, of pages in ancient books. As soon as he perceived this he understood the origin and mystery of the races. All men had at first been white; their different tints were only the shades of their different wisdoms. Of course, he thought. Of course. It's beautiful. Beautiful!

The second thing Bertie noticed was that the face seemed extraordinarily wise. The longer he stared at it the wiser it seemed. Clearly this was the wisest Chinaman, and thus the wisest man, in the history of the world. Now he was impatient for the Chinaman to speak, to tell him his secrets, but he also understood that so long as he was impatient the Chinaman would *not* speak, that he must become serene, as serene as the Chinaman himself, or else the Chinaman would go away. As this occurred to him the Chinaman smiled and Bertie knew he had been right. He was aware that if he just sat there, deliberately trying to become serene, nothing would happen. He decided that the best way to become serene was to ignore the Chinaman, to go on about his business as if the Chinaman weren't even there.

He stood up. "Am I getting warm?" Bertie asked.

The Chinaman lowered his eyes and smiled.

"Well, then," Bertie said, rubbing his hands, "let's see."

He went into the kitchen to see if there was anything he could do there to make him serene.

He washed out the empty cans of soup.

He strolled into the bedroom and made the bed. This took him an hour. He heard the clock strike twelve and then one.

He took a record off the machine, and starting from the center hole and working to the outer edge, counted all the ridges. This took him fourteen seconds.

He found a suitcase in one of the closets and packed all of Norma's underwear into it.

He got a pail of water and some soap and washed all the walls in the small bedroom.

It was in the dining room, however, that he finally achieved serenity. He studied Norma's pictures of side streets throughout the world and with sudden insight understood what was wrong with them. He took some tubes of white paint and with a brush worked over the figures, painting back into the flesh all their original whiteness. He made the Mexicans white, the Negroes white, feeling as he worked an immense satisfaction, the satisfaction not of the creator, nor even of the reformer, but of the restorer.

Swelling with serenity, Bertie went back into the living room and sat down in his chair. For the first time the Chinaman met his gaze directly, and Bertie realized that something important was going to happen.

Slowly, very slowly, the Chinaman began to open his mouth. Bertie watched the slow parting of the Chinaman's thin lips, the gleaming teeth, white and bright as fence pickets. Gradually the rest of the room darkened and the thinly padded chair on which Bertie sat grew incredibly soft. He knew that they had been transported somehow, that they were now in a sort of theater. The Chinaman was seated on a kind of raised platform. Meanwhile the mouth continued to open, slowly as an ancient drawbridge. Tiny as the Chinaman was, the mouth seemed enormous. Bertie gazed into it, seeing nothing. At last, deep back in the mouth, he saw a brief flashing, as of a small crystal on a dark rock suddenly illuminated by the sun. In a moment he saw it again, brighter now, longer sustained. Soon it was so bright that he had to force himself to look at it. Then the mouth went black. Before he could protest, the brightness was overwhelming again and he saw a cascade of what seemed like diamonds tumble out of the Chinaman's mouth. It was the Chinaman's tongue.

Twisting, turning over and over like magicians' silks pulled endlessly from a tube, the tongue continued to pour from the Chinaman's mouth. Bertie saw that it had the same whiteness as the rest of his face, and that it was studded with bright, beautiful jewels. On the tongue, long now as an unfurled scroll, were thick black Chinese characters. It was the secret of life, of the world, of the universe. Bertie could barely read for the tears of gratitude in his eyes. Desperately he wiped the tears away with his fists. He looked back at the tongue and stared at the strange words, realizing that he could not read Chinese. He was sobbing helplessly now because he knew there was not much time. The presence of the Chinaman gave him courage and strength and he *forced* himself to read the Chinese. As he concentrated it became easier, the characters somehow re-forming, translating themselves into a sort of decipherable Chinesey script, like the words "Chop Suey" on the neon sign outside a Chinese restaurant. He was breathless from his effort and the stunning glory of what was being revealed to him. Frequently he had to pause, punctuating his experience with queer little squeals. "Oh," he said. "Oh. Oh."

Then it was over.

He was exhausted, but his knowledge glowed in him like fire. "So *that's* it" was all he could say. "So *that's* it. So *that's* it."

Bertie saw that he was no longer in the theater. The Chinaman was gone and Bertie was back in the Premingers' living room. He struggled for control of himself. He knew it was urgent that he tell someone what had happened to him. Desperately he pulled open his trumpet case. Inside he had pasted sheets with the names, addresses and phone numbers of all his friends.

"Damn Klaff," he said angrily. "Damn Second-Story Klaff in his lousy jail."

He spotted Gimpel's name and the phone number of his boarding house in Cincinnati. Tearing the sheet from where it was pasted inside the lid, he rushed to the phone and placed the call. "Life and death," he screamed at Gimpel's bewildered landlady. "Life and death."

When Gimpel came to the phone Bertie began to tell him, coherently, but with obvious excitement, all that had happened. Gimpel was as excited as himself.

"Then the Chinaman opened his mouth and this tongue with writing on it came out."

"Yeah?" Gimpel said. "Yeah? Yeah?"

"Only it was in Chinese," Bertie shouted.

"Chinese," Gimpel said.

"But I could read it, Gimpel! *I could read it!*"

"I didn't know you could read Chinese," Gimpel said.

"It was the meaning of life."

"Yeah?" Gimpel said. "Yeah? What'd it say? What'd it say?"

"What?" Bertie said.

"What'd it say? What'd the Chink's tongue say was the meaning of life?"

"I forget," Bertie said and hung up.

He slept until two the next afternoon, and when he awoke he felt as if he had been beaten up. His tongue was something that did not quite fit in his mouth, and throughout his body he experienced a looseness of the bones, as though his skeleton were a mobile put together by an amateur. He groaned dispiritedly, his eyes still closed. He knew he had to get up out of the bed and take a shower and shave and dress, that only by making extravagant demands on it would his body give him any service at all. "You *will* make the Death March," he warned it ruthlessly.

He opened his eyes and what he saw disgusted him and turned his stomach. His eye patch had come off during the night and now there were two of everything. He saw one eye patch on one pillow and another eye patch on another pillow. Hastily he grabbed for it, but he had chosen the wrong pillow. He reached for the other eye patch and the other pillow, but somehow he had put out one of his illusory hands. It did not occur to him to shut one eye. At last, by covering all visible space, real or illusory, with all visible fingers, real or illusory—like one dragging a river —he recovered the patch and pulled it quickly over one of his heads.

He stood stunned in his hot shower, and then shaved, cutting his neck badly. He dressed.

"Whan 'e iz through his toilette, *Monsieur* will see how much better 'e feel," his valet said. He doubted it and didn't answer.

In the dining room he tried not to look at Norma's paintings, but could not help noticing that overnight many of her sunny side streets had become partial snow scenes. He had done that, he remembered, though he could not now recall exactly why. It seemed to have something to do with a great anthropological discovery he had made the night before. He finished the last of the pizza, gagging on it briefly.

Considering the anguish of his body, it suddenly occurred to him that perhaps he was hooked. Momentarily this appealed to his sense of the dramatic, but then he realized that it would be a terrible thing to have happen to him. He could not afford to be hooked, for he knew with a sense of calm sadness that his character could no more sustain the responsibility of a steady drug habit than it could sustain the responsibility of any other kind of pattern.

"Oh, what a miserable bastard I am," Bertie said.

In near-panic he considered leaving the Premingers' apartment immediately, but he knew that he was in no condition to travel. "You wouldn't make it to the corner," he said.

He felt massively sorry for himself. The more he considered it the more certain it appeared that he was hooked. It was terrible. Where would he get the money to buy the drugs? What would they do to his already depleted physical resources? "Oh, what a miserable bastard I am," he said again.

To steady himself he took a bottle of Scotch from the shelf in the pantry. Bertie did not like hard liquor. Though he drank a lot, it was beer he drank, or, when he could get them, the sweeter cordials. Scotch and bourbon had always seemed vaguely square to him. But he had already finished the few liqueurs that Preminger had, and now nothing was left but Scotch. He poured himself an enormous drink.

Sipping it calmed him—though his body still ached—and he considered what to do. If he was hooked, the first thing was to tell his friends. Telling his friends his latest failure was something Bertie regarded as a sort of responsibility. Thus his rare letters to them usually brought Bertie's intimates—he laughed at the word—nothing but bad news. He would write that a mistress had given him up, and, with his talent for mimicry, would set down her last long disappointed speech to him, in which she exposed in angry, honest language the hollowness of his character, his infinite weakness as a man, his vileness. When briefly he had turned to homosexuality to provide himself with funds, the first thing he did was write his friends about it. Or he wrote of being fired from bands when it was discovered how bad a trumpeter he really was. He spared neither himself nor his friends in his passionate self-denunciations.

Almost automatically, then, he went into Preminger's study and began to write all the people he could think of. As he wrote he pulled heavily at the whiskey remaining in the bottle. At first the letters were long, detailed accounts of symptoms and failures and dashed hopes, but as evening came on and he grew inarticulate he realized that it was more important—and, indeed, added to the pathos of his situation—for him just to get the facts to them.

"Dear Klaff," he wrote at last, "I am hooked. I am at the bottom, Klaff. I don't know what to do." Or "Dear Randle, I'm hooked. Tell your wife. I honestly don't know where to turn." And "Dear Myers, how are your wife and kids? Poor Bertie is hooked. He is thinking of suicide."

He had known for a long time that one day he would have to kill himself. It would happen, and even in the way he had imagined. One day he would simply drink the bottle of carbon tetrachloride. But previously he had been in no hurry. Now it seemed like something he might have to do before he had meant to, and what he resented most was the idea of having to change his plans.

He imagined what people would say.

"I let him down, Klaff," Randle said.

"Everybody let him down," Klaff said.

"Everybody let him down," Bertie said. "Everybody let him down."

Weeping, he took a last drink from Preminger's bottle, stumbled into the living room and passed out on the couch.

That night Bertie was awakened by a flashlight shining in his eyes. He threw one arm across his face defensively and struggled to sit up. So clumsy were his efforts that whoever was holding the flashlight started to laugh.

"Stop that," Bertie said indignantly, and thought, I have never been so indignant in the face of danger.

"You said they were out of town," a voice said. The voice did not come from behind the flashlight, and Bertie wondered how many there might be.

"Jesus, I thought so. Nobody's answered the phone for days. I never seen a guy so plastered. He stinks."

"Kill him," the first voice said.

Bertie stopped struggling to get up.

"Kill him," the voice repeated.

"What is this?" Bertie said thickly. "What is this?"

"Come on, he's so drunk he's harmless," the second voice said.

"Kill him," the first voice said again.

"You kill him," the second voice said.

The first voice giggled.

They were playing with him, Bertie knew. Nobody who did not know him could want him dead.

"Turn on the lights," Bertie said.

"Screw that," the second voice said. "You just sit here in the dark, sonny, and you won't get hurt."

"We're wasting time," the first voice said.

A beam from a second flashlight suddenly intersected the beam from the first.

"Say," Bertie said nervously, "it looks like the opening of a supermarket."

Bertie could hear them working in the dark, moving boxes, pulling drawers.

"Are you folks Negroes?" Bertie called. No one answered him. "I mean I dig Negroes, man—men. Miles. Jay Jay. Bird lives." He heard a closet door open.

"You are robbing the place, right? I mean you're actually stealing, aren't you? This isn't just a social call. Maybe you know my friend Klaff."

The men came back into the living room. From the sound of his footsteps Bertie knew one of them was carrying something heavy.

"I've got the TV," the first voice said.

"There are some valuable paintings in the dining room," Bertie said.

"Go see," the first voice said.

One of Norma's pictures suddenly popped out of the darkness as the man's light shone on it.

"Crap," the second voice said.

"You cats can't be all bad," Bertie said.

"Any furs?" It was a third voice, and it startled Bertie. Someone flashed a light in Bertie's face. "Hey, you," the voice repeated, "does your wife have any furs?"

"Wait a minute," Bertie said as though it were a fine point they must be made to understand, "you've got it wrong. This isn't my place. I'm just taking care of it while my friends are gone." The man laughed.

Now all three flashlights were playing over the apartment. Bertie hoped a beam might illuminate one of the intruders, but this never happened. Then he realized that he didn't want it to happen, that he was safe as long as he didn't recognize any of them. Suddenly a light caught one of the men behind the ear. "Watch that light. Watch that light," Bertie called out involuntarily.

"I found a trumpet," the second voice said.

"Hey, that's mine," Bertie said angrily. Without thinking, he got up and grabbed for the trumpet. In the dark he was able to get his fingers around one of the valves, but the man snatched it away from him easily. Another man pushed him back down on the couch.

"Could you leave the carbon tetrachloride?" Bertie asked miserably.

In another ten minutes they were ready to go. "Shouldn't we do something about the clown?" the third voice said.

"Nah," the second voice said.

They went out the front door.

Bertie sat in the darkness. "I'm drunk," he said after a while. "I'm hooked and drunk. It never happened. It's still the visions. The apartment is a vision. The darkness is. Everything."

In a few minutes he got up and wearily turned on the lights. Magicians, he thought, seeing even in a first glance all that they had taken. Lamps were gone, curtains. He walked through the apartment. The TV was gone. Suits were missing from the closets. Preminger's typewriter was gone, the champagne glasses, the silver. His trumpet was gone.

Bertie wept. He thought of phoning the police, but then wondered what he could tell them. The thieves had been in the apartment for twenty minutes and he hadn't even gotten a look at their faces.

Then he shuddered, realizing the danger he had been in. "Crooks," he said. "Killers." But even as he said it he knew it was an exaggeration. He had never been in any danger. He had the fool's ancient protection, his old immunity against consequence.

He wondered what he could say to the Premingers. They would be furious. Then, as he thought about it, he realized that this too was an exaggeration. They would not be furious. Like the thieves they would make allowances for him, as people always made allowances for him. They would forgive him; possibly they would even try to give him something toward the loss of his trumpet.

Bertie began to grow angry. They had no right to patronize him like that. If he was a clown it was because he had chosen to be. It was a way of life. Why couldn't they respect it? He should have been hit over the head like other men. How dare they forgive him? For a moment it was impossible for him to distinguish between the thieves and the Premingers.

Then he had his idea. As soon as he thought of it he knew it would work. He looked around the apartment to see what he could take. There was some costume jewelry the thieves had thrown on the bed. He scooped it up and stuffed it in his pockets. He looked at the apartment one more time and then got the hell out of there. "Bird lives," he sang to himself as he raced down the stairs. "He lives and lives."

It was wonderful. How they would marvel! He couldn't get away with it. Even the far West wasn't far enough. How they hounded you if you took something from them! He would be back, no question, and they would send him to jail, but first there would be the confrontation, maybe even in the apartment itself: Bertie in handcuffs, and the Premingers staring at him, not understanding and angry at last, and something in their eyes like fear.

2 Flannery O'Connor

*Flannery O'Connor was born in Savannah, Georgia, in 1925, and was edu-
cated at the Georgia State College for Women and the University of Iowa.
She died in 1964. Her novels are* Wise Blood *(1952) and* The Violent Bear
It Away *(1960). Critics generally agree that Flannery O'Connor's stories,
collected in* A Good Man Is Hard to Find *(1955) and* Everything That Rises
Must Converge *(1965), are among the very best short fiction of our time.*

◈

PARKER'S BACK

Parker's wife was sitting on the front porch floor, snapping beans.
Parker was sitting on the step, some distance away, watching her
sullenly. She was plain, plain. The skin on her face was thin and
drawn as tight as the skin on an onion and her eyes were grey
and sharp like the points of two icepicks. Parker understood why
he had married her—he couldn't have got her any other way—
but he couldn't understand why he stayed with her now. She
was pregnant and pregnant women were not his favorite kind.
Nevertheless, he stayed as if she had him conjured. He was
puzzled and ashamed of himself.

The house they rented sat alone save for a single tall pecan
tree on a high embankment overlooking a highway. At intervals
a car would shoot past below and his wife's eyes would swerve
suspiciously after the sound of it and then come back to rest on
the newspaper full of beans in her lap. One of the things she
did not approve of was automobiles. In addition to her other
bad qualities, she was forever sniffing up sin. She did not smoke
or dip, drink whiskey, use bad language or paint her face, and
God knew some paint would have improved it, Parker thought.

Her being against color, it was the more remarkable she had married him. Sometimes he supposed that she had married him because she meant to save him. At other times he had a suspicion that she actually liked everything she said she didn't. He could account for her one way or another; it was himself he could not understand.

She turned her head in his direction and said, "It's no reason you can't work for a man. It don't have to be a woman."

"Aw shut your mouth for a change," Parker muttered.

If he had been certain she was jealous of the woman he worked for he would have been pleased but more likely she was concerned with the sin that would result if he and the woman took a liking to each other. He had told her that the woman was a hefty young blonde; in fact she was nearly seventy years old and too dried up to have an interest in anything except getting as much work out of him as she could. Not that an old woman didn't sometimes get an interest in a young man, particularly if he was as attractive as Parker felt he was, but this old woman looked at him the same way she looked at her old tractor —as if she had to put up with it because it was all she had. The tractor had broken down the second day Parker was on it and she had set him at once to cutting bushes, saying out of the side of her mouth to the nigger, "Everything he touches, he breaks." She also asked him to wear his shirt when he worked; Parker had removed it even though the day was not sultry; he put it back on reluctantly.

This ugly woman Parker married was his first wife. He had had other women but he had planned never to get himself tied up legally. He had first seen her one morning when his truck broke down on the highway. He had managed to pull it off the road into a neatly swept yard on which sat a peeling two-room house. He got out and opened the hood of the truck and began to study the motor. Parker had an extra sense that told him when there was a woman nearby watching him. After he had leaned over the motor a few minutes, his neck began to prickle. He cast his eye over the empty yard and porch of the house. A woman he could not see was either nearby beyond a clump of honeysuckle or in the house, watching him out the window.

Suddenly Parker began to jump up and down and fling his hand about as if he had mashed it in the machinery. He doubled over and held his hand close to his chest. "God dammit!" he hollered. "Jesus Christ in hell! Jesus God Almighty damm! God dammit to hell!" he went on, flinging out the same few oaths over and over as loud as he could.

Without warning a terrible bristly claw slammed the side of his face and he fell backwards on the hood of the truck. "You don't talk no filth here!" a voice close to him shrilled.

Parker's vision was so blurred that for an instant he thought he had been attacked by some creature from above, a giant hawk-eyed angel wielding a hoary weapon. As his sight cleared, he saw before him a tall raw-boned girl with a broom.

"I hurt my hand," he said. "I HURT my hand." He was so incensed that he forgot that he hadn't hurt his hand. "My hand may be broke," he growled although his voice was still unsteady.

"Lemme see it," the girl demanded.

Parker stuck out his hand and she came closer and looked at it. There was no mark on the palm and she took the hand and turned it over. Her own hand was dry and hot and rough and Parker felt himself jolted back to life by her touch. He looked more closely at her. I don't want nothing to do with this one, he thought.

The girl's sharp eyes peered at the back of the stubby reddish hand she held. There emblazoned in red and blue was a tattooed eagle perched on a cannon. Parker's sleeve was rolled to the elbow. Above the eagle a serpent was coiled about a shield and in the spaces between the eagle and the serpent there were hearts, some with arrows through them. Above the serpent there was a spread hand of cards. Every space on the skin of Parker's arm, from wrist to elbow, was covered in some loud design. The girl gazed at this with an almost stupefied smile of shock, as if she had accidentally grasped a poisonous snake; she dropped the hand.

"I got most of my other ones in foreign parts," Parker said. "These here I mostly got in the United States. I got my first one when I was only fifteen year old."

"Don't tell me," the girl said, "I don't like it. I ain't got any use for it."

"You ought to see the ones you can't see," Parker said and winked.

Two circles of red appeared like apples on the girl's cheeks and softened her appearance. Parker was intrigued. He did not for a minute think that she didn't like the tattoos. He had never yet met a woman who was not attracted to them.

Parker was fourteen when he saw a man in a fair, tattooed from head to foot. Except for his loins which were girded with a panther hide, the man's skin was patterned in what seemed from Parker's distance—he was near the back of the tent, standing on a bench—a single intricate design of brilliant color. The man, who was small and sturdy, moved about on the platform, flexing his muscles so that the arabesque of men and beasts and flowers on his skin appeared to have a subtle motion of its own. Parker was filled with emotion, lifted up as some people are when the flag passes. He was a boy whose mouth habitually hung open. He was heavy and earnest, as ordinary as a loaf of bread. When the show was over, he had remained standing on the bench, staring where the tattooed man had been, until the tent was almost empty.

Parker had never before felt the least motion of wonder in himself. Until he saw the man at the fair, it did not enter his head that there was anything out of the ordinary about the fact that he existed. Even then it did not enter his head, but a peculiar unease settled in him. It was as if a blind boy had been turned so gently in a different direction that he did not know his destination had been changed.

He had his first tattoo some time after—the eagle perched on the cannon. It was done by a local artist. It hurt very little, just enough to make it appear to Parker to be worth doing. This was peculiar too for before he had thought that only what did not hurt was worth doing. The next year he quit school because he was sixteen and could. He went to the trade school for a while, then he quit the trade school and worked for six months in a garage. The only reason he worked at all was to pay for more tattoos. His mother worked in a laundry and could support him, but she would not pay for any tattoo except her name on a heart, which he had put on, grumbling. However, her name was Betty

Jean and nobody had to know it was his mother. He found out that the tattoos were attractive to the kind of girls he liked but who had never liked him before. He began to drink beer and get in fights. His mother wept over what was becoming of him. One night she dragged him off to a revival with her, not telling him where they were going. When he saw the big lighted church, he jerked out of her grasp and ran. The next day he lied about his age and joined the navy.

Parker was large for the tight sailor's pants but the silly white cap, sitting low on his forehead, made his face by contrast look thoughtful and almost intense. After a month or two in the navy, his mouth ceased to hang open. His features hardened into the features of a man. He stayed in the navy five years and seemed a natural part of the grey mechanical ship, except for his eyes, which were the same pale slate-color as the ocean and reflected the immense spaces around him as if they were a microcosm of the mysterious sea. In port Parker wandered about comparing the run-down places he was in to Birmingham, Alabama. Everywhere he went he picked up more tattoos.

He had stopped having lifeless ones like anchors and crossed rifles. He had a tiger and a panther on each shoulder, a cobra coiled about a torch on his chest, hawks on his thighs, Elizabeth II and Philip over where his stomach and liver were respectively. He did not care much what the subject was so long as it was colorful; on his abdomen he had a few obscenities but only because that seemed the proper place for them. Parker would be satisfied with each tattoo about a month, then something about it that had attracted him would wear off. Whenever a decent-sized mirror was available, he would get in front of it and study his overall look. The effect was not of one intricate arabesque of colors but of something haphazard and botched. A huge dissatisfaction would come over him and he would go off and find another tattooist and have another space filled up. The front of Parker was almost completely covered but there were no tattoos on his back. He had no desire for one anywhere he could not readily see it himself. As the space on the front of him for tattoos decreased, his dissatisfaction grew and became general.

After one of his furloughs, he didn't go back to the navy but remained away without official leave, drunk, in a rooming house in a city he did not know. His dissatisfaction, from being chronic and latent, had suddenly become acute and raged in him. It was as if the panther and the lion and the serpents and the eagles and the hawks had penetrated his skin and lived inside him in a raging warfare. The navy caught up with him, put him in the brig for nine months and then gave him a dishonorable discharge.

After that Parker decided that country air was the only kind fit to breathe. He rented the shack on the embankment and bought the old truck and took various jobs which he kept as long as it suited him. At the time he met his future wife, he was buying apples by the bushel and selling them for the same price by the pound to isolated homesteaders on back country roads.

"All that there," the woman said, pointing to his arm, "is no better than what a fool Indian would do. It's a heap of vanity." She seemed to have found the word she wanted. "Vanity of vanities," she said.

Well what the hell do I care what she thinks of it? Parker asked himself, but he was plainly bewildered. "I reckon you like one of these better than another anyway," he said, dallying until he thought of something that would impress her. He thrust the arm back at her. "Which you like best?"

"None of them," she said, "but the chicken is not as bad as the rest."

"What chicken?" Parker almost yelled.

She pointed to the eagle.

"That's an eagle," Parker said. "What fool would waste their time having a chicken put on themself?"

"What fool would have any of it?" the girl said and turned away. She went slowly back to the house and left him there to get going. Parker remained for almost five minutes, looking agape at the dark door she had entered.

The next day he returned with a bushel of apples. He was not one to be outdone by anything that looked like her. He liked women with meat on them, so you didn't feel their muscles, much less their old bones. When he arrived, she was sitting on the top step and the yard was full of children, all as thin and poor as herself; Parker remembered it was Saturday. He hated to be making up to a woman when there were children around, but it was fortunate he had brought the bushel of apples off the truck. As the children approached him to see what he carried, he gave each child an apple and told it to get lost; in that way he cleared out the whole crowd.

The girl did nothing to acknowledge his presence. He might have been a stray pig or goat that had wandered into the yard and she too tired to take up the broom and send it off. He set the bushel of apples down next to her on the step. He sat down on a lower step.

"Hep yourself," he said, nodding at the basket; then he lapsed into silence.

She took an apple quickly as if the basket might disappear if she didn't make haste. Hungry people made Parker nervous. He had always had plenty to eat himself. He grew very uncomfortable. He reasoned he had nothing to say so why should he say it? He could not think now why he had come or why he didn't go before he wasted another bushel of apples on the crowd of children. He supposed they were her brothers and sisters.

She chewed the apple slowly but with a kind of relish of concentration, bent slightly but looking out ahead. The view from the porch stretched off across a long incline studded with iron weed and across the highway to a vast vista of hills and one small mountain. Long views depressed Parker. You look out into space like that and you begin to feel as if someone were after you, the navy or the government or religion.

"Who them children belong to, you?" he said at length.

"I ain't married yet," she said. "They belong to momma." She said it as if it were only a matter of time before she would be married.

Who in God's name would marry her? Parker thought.

A large barefooted woman with a wide gap-toothed face appeared in the door behind Parker. She had apparently been there for several minutes.

"Good evening," Parker said.

The woman crossed the porch and picked up what was left of the bushel of apples. "We thank you," she said and returned with it into the house.

"That your old woman?" Parker muttered.

The girl nodded. Parker knew a lot of sharp things he could have said like "You got my sympathy," but he was gloomily silent. He just sat there, looking at the view. He thought he must be coming down with something.

"If I pick up some peaches tomorrow I'll bring you some," he said.

"I'll be much obliged to you," the girl said.

Parker had no intention of taking any basket of peaches back there but the next day he found himself doing it. He and the girl had almost nothing to say to each other. One thing he did say was, "I ain't got any tattoo on my back."

"What you got on it?" the girl said.

"My shirt," Parker said. "Haw."

"Haw, haw," the girl said politely.

Parker thought he was losing his mind. He could not believe for a minute that he was attracted to a woman like this. She showed not the least interest in anything but what he brought until he appeared the third time with two cantaloups. "What's your name?" she asked.

"O. E. Parker," he said.

"What does the O.E. stand for?"

"You can just call me O.E.," Parker said. "Or Parker. Don't nobody call me by my name."

"What's it stand for?" she persisted.

"Never mind," Parker said. "What's yours?"

"I'll tell you when you tell me what them letters are the short of," she said. There was just a hint of flirtatiousness in her tone and it went rapidly to Parker's head. He had never revealed the name to any man or woman, only to the files of the navy and the government, and it was on his baptismal record which he got at the age of a month; his mother was a Methodist. When the name leaked out of the navy files, Parker narrowly missed killing the man who used it.

"You'll go blab it around," he said.

"I'll swear I'll never tell nobody," she said. "On God's holy word I swear it."

Parker sat for a few minutes in silence. Then he reached for the girl's neck, drew her ear close to his mouth and revealed the name in a low voice.

"Obadiah," she whispered. Her face slowly brightened as if the name came as a sign to her. "Obadiah," she said.

The name still stank in Parker's estimation.

"Obadiah Elihue," she said in a reverent voice.

"If you call me that aloud, I'll bust your head open," Parker said. "What's yours?"

"Sarah Ruth Cates," she said.

"Glad to meet you, Sarah Ruth," Parker said.

Sarah Ruth's father was a Straight Gospel preacher but he was away, spreading it in Florida. Her mother did not seem to mind his attention to the girl so long as he brought a basket of something with him when he came. As for Sarah Ruth herself, it was plain to Parker after he had visited three times that she was crazy about him. She liked him even though she insisted that pictures on the skin were vanity of vanities and even after hearing him curse, and even after she had asked him if he was saved and he had replied that he didn't see it was anything in particular to save him from. After that, inspired, Parker had said, "I'd be saved enough if you was to kiss me."

She scowled. "That ain't being saved," she said.

Not long after that she agreed to take a ride in his truck. Parker parked it on a deserted road and suggested to her that they lie down together in the back of it.

"Not until after we're married," she said—just like that.

"Oh that ain't necessary," Parker said and as he reached for her, she thrust him away with such force that the door of the truck came off and he found himself flat on his back on the ground. He made up his mind then and there to have nothing further to do with her.

They were married in the County Ordinary's office because Sarah Ruth thought churches were idolatrous. Parker had no opinion about that one way or the other. The Ordinary's office was lined with cardboard file boxes and record books with dusty yellow slips of paper hanging on out of them. The Ordinary was an old woman with red hair who had held office for forty years and looked as dusty as her books. She married them from behind the iron-grill of a stand-up desk and when she finished, she said with a flourish, "Three dollars and fifty cents and till death do you part!" and yanked some forms out of a machine.

Marriage did not change Sarah Ruth a jot and it made Parker gloomier than ever. Every morning he decided he had had enough and would not return that night; every night he returned. Whenever Parker couldn't stand the way he felt, he would have another tattoo, but the only surface left on him now was his back. To see a tattoo on his own back he would have to get two mirrors and stand between them in just the correct position and this seemed to Parker a good way to make an idiot of himself. Sarah Ruth who, if she had had better sense, could have enjoyed a tattoo on his back, would not even look at the ones he had elsewhere. When he attempted to point out especial details of them, she would shut her eyes tight and turn her back as well. Except in total darkness, she preferred Parker dressed and with his sleeves rolled down.

"At the judgement seat of God, Jesus is going to say to you, 'What you been doing all your life besides have pictures drawn all over you?'" she said.

"You don't fool me none," Parker said, "you're just afraid that hefty girl I work for'll like me so much she'll say, 'Come on, Mr. Parker, let's you and me . . .'"

"You're tempting sin," she said, "and at the judgement seat of God you'll have to answer for that too. You ought to go back to selling the fruits of the earth."

Parker did nothing much when he was at home but listen to what the judgement seat of God would be like for him if he didn't change his ways. When he could, he broke in with tales of the hefty girl he worked for. "'Mr. Parker,'" he said she said, "'I hired you for your brains.'" (She had added, "So why don't you use them?")

"And you should have seen her face the first time she saw me without my shirt," he said. "'Mr. Parker,' she said, 'you're a walking panner-rammer!'" This had, in fact, been her remark but it had been delivered out of one side of her mouth.

Dissatisfaction began to grow so great in Parker that there was no containing it outside of a tattoo. It had to be his back. There was no help for it. A dim half-formed inspiration began to work in his mind. He visualized having a tattoo put there that Sarah Ruth would not be able to resist—a religious subject. He thought of an open book with HOLY BIBLE tattooed under it and an actual verse printed on the page. This seemed just the thing for a while; then he began to hear her say, "Ain't I already got a real Bible? What you think I want to read the same verse over and over for when I can read it all?" He needed something better even than the Bible! He thought about it so much that he began to lose sleep. He was already losing flesh—Sarah Ruth just threw food in the pot and let it boil. Not knowing for certain why he continued to stay with a woman who was both ugly and pregnant and no cook made him generally nervous and irritable, and he developed a little tic in the side of his face.

Once or twice he found himself turning around abruptly as if someone were trailing him. He had had a granddaddy who had ended in the state mental hospital, although not until he was seventy-five, but as urgent as it might be for him to get a tattoo, it was just as urgent that he get exactly the right one to bring Sarah Ruth to heel. As he continued to worry over it, his eyes took on a hollow preoccupied expression. The old woman he worked for told him that if he couldn't keep his mind on what he was doing, she knew where she could find a fourteen-year-old colored boy who could. Parker was too preoccupied even to be offended. At any time previous, he would have left her then and there, saying drily, "Well, you go ahead on and get him then."

Two or three mornings later he was baling hay with the old woman's sorry baler and her broken down tractor in a large field, cleared save for one enormous old tree standing in the middle of it. The old woman was the kind who would not cut down a large old tree because it was a large old tree. She had pointed it out to Parker as if he didn't have eyes and told him to be careful not to hit it as the machine picked up hay near it. Parker began at the outside of the field and made circles inward toward it. He had to get off the tractor every now and then and untangle the baling cord or kick a rock out of the way. The old woman had told him to carry the rocks to the edge of the field, which he did when she was there watching. When he thought he could make it, he ran over them. As he circled the field his mind was on a suitable design for his back. The sun, the size of a golf ball, began to switch regularly from in front to behind him, but he appeared to see it both places as if he had eyes in the back of his head. All at once he saw the tree reaching out to grasp him. A ferocious thud propelled him into the air, and he heard himself yelling in an unbelievably loud voice, "GOD ABOVE!"

He landed on his back while the tractor crashed upside-down into the tree and burst into flame. The first thing Parker saw were his shoes, quickly being eaten by the fire; one was caught under the tractor, the other was some distance away, burning by itself. He was not in them. He could feel the hot breath of the burning tree on his face. He scrambled backwards, till sitting, his eyes cavernous, and if he had known how to cross himself he would have done it.

His truck was on a dirt road at the edge of the field. He moved toward it, still sitting, still backwards, but faster and faster; half-way to it he got up and began a kind of forward-bent run from which he collapsed on his knees twice. His legs felt like two old rusted rain gutters. He reached the truck finally and took off in it, zigzagging up the road. He drove past his house on the embankment and straight for the city, fifty miles distant.

Parker did not allow himself to think on the way to the city. He only knew that there had been a great change in his life, a leap forward into a worse unknown, and that there was nothing he could do about it. It was for all intents accomplished.

The artist had two large cluttered rooms over a chiropodist's office on a back street. Parker, still barefooted, burst silently in on him at a little after three in the afternoon. The artist, who was about Parker's own age—twenty-eight—but thin and bald, was behind a small drawing table, tracing a design in green ink. He looked up with an annoyed glance and did not seem to recognize Parker in the hollow-eyed creature before him.

"Let me see the book you got with all the pictures of God in it," Parker said breathlessly. "The religious one."

The artist continued to look at him with his intellectual, superior stare. "I don't put tattoos on drunks," he said.

"You know me!" Parker cried indignantly. "I'm O. E. Parker! You done work for me before and I always paid!"

The artist looked at him another moment as if he were not altogether sure. "You've fallen off some," he said. "You must have been in jail."

"Married," Parker said.

"Oh," said the artist. With the aid of mirrors the artist had tattooed on the top of his head a miniature owl, perfect in every detail. It was about the size of a half-dollar and served him as a show piece. There were cheaper artists in town but Parker had never wanted anything but the best. The artist went over to a cabinet at the back of the room and began to look over some art books. "Who are you interested in?" he said, "saints, angels, Christs or what?"

"God," Parker said.

"Father, Son or Spirit?"

"Just God," Parker said impatiently. "Christ. I don't care. Just so it's God."

The artist returned with a book. He moved some papers off another table and put the book down on it and told Parker to sit down and see what he liked. "The up-t-date ones are in the back," he said.

Parker sat down with the book and wet his thumb. He began to go through it, beginning at the back where the up-to-date pictures were. Some of them he recognized—The Good Shepherd, Forbid Them Not, The Smiling Jesus, Jesus the Physician's Friend, but he kept turning rapidly backwards, and the pictures became less and less reassuring. One showed a gaunt green dead face streaked with blood. One was yellow with sagging purple eyes. Parker's heart began to beat faster and faster until it appeared to be roaring inside him like a great generator. He flipped the pages quickly, feeling that when he reached the one ordained, a sign would come. He continued to flip through until he had almost reached the front of the book. On one of the pages a pair of eyes glanced at him swiftly. Parker sped on, then stopped. His heart too appeared to cut off; there was absolute silence. It said as plainly as if silence were a language itself, GO BACK.

Parker returned to the picture—the haloed head of a flat stern

Byzantine Christ with all-demanding eyes. He sat there trembling; his heart began slowly to beat again as if it were being brought to life by a subtle power.

"You found what you want?" the artist asked.

Parker's throat was too dry to speak. He got up and thrust the book at the artist, opened at the picture.

"That'll cost you plenty," the artist said. "You don't want all those little blocks though, just the outline and some better features."

"Just like it is," Parker said, "just like it is or nothing."

"It's your funeral," the artist said, "but I don't do that kind of work for nothing."

"How much?" Parker asked.

"It'll take maybe two days' work."

"How much?" Parker said.

"On time or cash?" the artist asked. Parker's other jobs had been on time, but he had paid.

"Ten down and ten for every day it takes," the artist said.

Parker drew ten dollar bills out of his wallet; he had three left in.

"You come back in the morning," the artist said, putting the money in his own pocket. "First I'll have to trace that out of the book."

"No no!" Parker said. "Trace it now or gimme my money back," and his eyes blared as if he were ready for a fight.

The artist agreed. Any one stupid enough to want a Christ on his back, he reasoned, would be just as likely as not to change his mind the next minute, but once the work was begun he could hardly do so.

While he worked on the tracing, he told Parker to go wash his back at the sink with the special soap he used there. Parker did it and returned to pace back and forth across the room, nervously flexing his shoulders. He wanted to go look at the picture again but at the same time he did not want to. The artist got up finally and had Parker lie down on the table. He swabbled his back with ethyl chloride and then began to outline the head on it with his iodine pencil. Another hour passed before he took up his electric instrument. Parker felt no particular pain. In Japan he had had a tattoo of the Buddha done on his upper arm with ivory needles; in Burma, a little brown root of a man had made a peacock on each of his knees using thin pointed sticks, two feet long; amateurs had worked on him with pins and soot. Parker was usually so relaxed and easy under the hand of the artist that he often went to sleep, but this time he remained awake, every muscle taut.

At midnight the artist said he was ready to quit. He propped one mirror, four feet square, on a table by the wall and took a smaller mirror off the lavatory wall and put it in Parker's hands. Parker stood with his back to the one on the table and moved the other until he saw a flashing burst of color reflected from his back. It was almost completely covered with little red and blue and ivory and saffron squares; from them he made out the lineaments of the face—a mouth, the beginning of heavy brows, a straight nose, but the face was empty; the eyes had not yet been put in. The impression for the moment was almost as if the artist had tricked him and done the Physician's Friend.

"It don't have eyes," Parker cried out.

"That'll come," the artist said, "in due time. We have another day to go on it yet."

Parker spent the night on a cot at the Haven of Light Christian Mission. He found these the best places to stay in the city because they were free and included a meal of sorts. He got the last available cot and because he was still barefooted, he accepted a pair of second-hand shoes which, in his confusion, he put on to go to bed; he was still shocked from all that had happened to him. All night he lay awake in the long dormitory of cots with lumpy figures on them. The only light was from a phosphorescent cross glowing at the end of the room. The tree reached out to grasp him again, then burst into flame; the shoe burned quietly by itself; the eyes in the book said to him distinctly GO BACK and at the same time did not utter a sound. He wished that he were not in this city, not in this Haven of Light Mission, not in a bed by himself. He longed miserably for Sarah Ruth. Her sharp tongue and icepick eyes were the only comfort he could bring to mind. He decided he was losing it. Her eyes appeared soft and dilatory compared with the eyes in the book, for even though he could not summon up the exact look of those eyes, he could still feel their penetration. He felt as though, under their gaze, he was as transparent as the wing of a fly.

The tattooist had told him not to come until ten in the morning, but when he arrived at that hour, Parker was sitting in the dark hallway on the floor, waiting for him. He had decided upon getting up that, once the tattoo was on him, he would not look at it, that all his sensations of the day and night before were those of a crazy man and that he would return to doing things according to his own sound judgement.

The artist began where he left off. "One thing I want to know," he said presently as he worked over Parker's back, "why do you want this on you? Have you gone and got religion? Are you saved?" he asked in a mocking voice.

Parker's throat felt salty and dry. "Naw," he said, "I ain't got no use for none of that. A man can't save his self from whatever it is he don't deserve none of my sympathy." These words seemed to leave his mouth like wraiths and to evaporate at once as if he had never uttered them.

"Then why . . ."

"I married this woman that's saved," Parker said. "I never should have done it. I ought to leave her. She's done gone and got pregnant."

"That's too bad," the artist said. "Then it's her making you have this tattoo."

"Naw," Parker said, "she don't know nothing about it. It's a surprise for her."

"You think she'll like it and lay off you a while?"

"She can't hep herself," Parker said. "She can't say she don't like the looks of God." He decided he had told the artist enough of his business. Artists were all right in their place but he didn't like them poking their noses into the affairs of regular people. "I didn't get no sleep last night," he said. "I think I'll get some now."

That closed the mouth of the artist but it did not bring him any sleep. He lay there, imagining how Sarah Ruth would be struck speechless by the face on his back and every now and then this would be interrupted by a vision of the tree of fire and his empty shoe burning beneath it.

The artist worked steadily until nearly four o'clock, not stopping to have lunch, hardly pausing with the electric instrument except to wipe the dripping dye off Parker's back as he went along. Finally he finished. "You can get up and look at it now," he said.

Parker sat up but he remained on the edge of the table.

The artist was pleased with his work and wanted Parker to look at it at once. Instead Parker continued to sit on the edge of the table, bent forward slightly but with a vacant look. "What ails you?" the artist said. "Go look at it."

"Ain't nothing ail me," Parker said in a sudden belligerent voice. "That tattoo ain't going nowhere. It'll be there when I get there." He reached for his shirt and began gingerly to put it on.

The artist took him roughly by the arm and propelled him between the two mirrors. "Now *look*," he said, angry at having his work ignored.

Parker looked, turned white and moved away. The eyes in the reflected face continued to look at him—still, straight, all-demanding, enclosed in silence.

"It was your idea, remember," the artist said. "I would have advised something else."

Parker said nothing. He put on his shirt and went out the door while the artist shouted, "I'll expect all of my money!"

Parker headed toward a package shop on the corner. He bought a pint of whiskey and took it into a nearby alley and drank it all in five minutes. Then he moved on to a pool hall nearby which he frequented when he came to the city. It was a well-lighted barn-like place with a bar up one side and gambling machines on the other and pool tables in the back. As soon as Parker entered, a large man in a red and black checkered shirt hailed him by slapping him on the back and yelling, "Yeyyyyyy boy! O. E. Parker!"

Parker was not yet ready to be struck on the back. "Lay off," he said, "I got a fresh tattoo there."

"What you got this time?" the man asked and then yelled to a few at the machines. "O.E.'s got him another tattoo."

"Nothing special this time," Parker said and slunk over to a machine that was not being used.

"Come on," the big man said, "let's have a look at O.E.'s tattoo," and while Parker squirmed in their hands, they pulled up his shirt. Parker felt all the hands drop away instantly and his shirt fell again like a veil over the face. There was a silence in the pool room which seemed to Parker to grow from the circle around him until it extended to the foundations under the building and upward through the beams in the roof.

Finally some one said, "Christ!" Then they all broke into noise at once. Parker turned around, an uncertain grin on his face.

"Leave it to O.E.!" the man in the checkered shirt said. "That boy's a real card!"

"Maybe he's gone and got religion," someone yelled.

"Not on your life," Parker said.

"O.E.'s got religion and is witnessing for Jesus, ain't you, O.E.?" a little man with a piece of cigar in his mouth said wryly. "An o-riginal way to do it if I ever saw one."

"Leave it to Parker to think of a new one!" the fat man said.

"Yyeeeeeeyyyyyyy boy!" someone yelled and they all began to whistle and curse in compliment until Parker said, "Aaa shut up."

"What'd you do it for?" somebody asked.

"For laughs," Parker said. "What's it to you?"

"Why ain't you laughing then?" somebody yelled. Parker lunged into the midst of them and like a whirlwind on a summer's day there began a fight that raged amid overturned tables and swinging fists until two of them grabbed him and ran to the door with him and threw him out. Then a calm descended on the pool hall as nerve shattering as if the long barn-like room were the ship from which Jonah had been cast into the sea.

Parker sat for a long time on the ground in the alley behind the pool hall, examining his soul. He saw it as a spider web of facts and lies that was not at all important to him but which appeared to be necessary in spite of his opinion. The eyes that were now forever on his back were eyes to be obeyed. He was as certain of it as he had ever been of anything. Throughout his life, grumbling and sometimes cursing, often afraid, once in rapture, Parker had obeyed whatever instinct of this kind had come to him—in rapture when his spirit had lifted at the sight of the tattooed man at the fair, afraid when he had joined the navy, grumbling when he had married Sarah Ruth.

The thought of her brought him slowly to his feet. She would know what he had to do. She would clear up the rest of it, and she would at least be pleased. It seemed to him that, all along, that was what he wanted, to please her. His truck was still parked in front of the building where the artist had his place, but it was not far away. He got in it and drove out of the city and into the country night. His head was almost clear of liquor and he observed that his dissatisfaction was gone, but he felt not quite like himself. It was as if he were himself but a stranger to himself, driving into a new country though everything he saw was familiar to him, even at night.

He arrived finally at the house on the embankment, pulled the truck under the pecan tree and got out. He made as much noise as possible to assert that he was still in charge here, that his leaving her for a night without word meant nothing except it was the way he did things. He slammed the car door, stamped up the two steps and across the porch and rattled the door knob. It did not respond to his touch. "Sarah Ruth!" he yelled, "let me in."

There was no lock on the door and she had evidently placed the back of a chair against the knob. He began to beat on the door and rattle the knob at the same time.

He heard the bed springs screak and bent down and put his head to the keyhole, but it was stopped up with paper. "Let me in!" he hollered, bamming on the door again. "What you got me locked out for?"

A sharp voice close to the door said, "Who's there?"

"Me," Parker said, "O.E."

He waited a moment.

"Me," he said impatiently, "O.E."

Still no sound from inside.

He tried once more. "O.E.," he said, bamming the door two or three more times. "O. E. Parker. You know me."

There was a silence. Then the voice said slowly, "I don't know no O.E."

"Quit fooling," Parker pleaded. "You ain't got any business doing me this way. It's me, old O.E., I'm back. You ain't afraid of me."

"Who's there?" the same unfeeling voice said.

Parker turned his head as if he expected someone behind him to give him the answer. The sky had lightened slightly and there were two or three streaks of yellow floating above the horizon. Then as he stood there, a tree of light burst over the skyline.

Parker fell back against the door as if he had been pinned there by a lance.

"Who's there?" the voice from inside said and there was a quality about it now that seemed final. The knob rattled and the voice said peremptorily, "Who's there, I ast you?"

Parker bent down and put his mouth near the stuffed keyhole. "Obadiah," he whispered and all at once he felt the light pouring through him, turning his spider web soul into a perfect arabesque of colors, a garden of trees and birds and beasts.

"Obadiah Elihue!" he whispered.

The door opened and he stumbled in. Sarah Ruth loomed there, hands on her hips. She began at once, "That was no hefty blonde woman you was working for and you'll have to pay her every penny on her tractor you busted up. She don't keep insurance on it. She came here and her and me had us a long talk and I . . ."

Trembling, Parker set about lighting the kerosene lamp.

"What's the matter with you, wasting that keresene this near daylight?" she demanded. "I ain't got to look at you."

A yellow glow enveloped them. Parker put the match down and began to unbutton his shirt.

"And you ain't going to have none of me this near morning," she said.

"Shut your mouth," he said quietly. "Look at this and then I don't want to hear no more out of you." He removed the shirt and turned his back to her.

"Another picture," Sarah Ruth growled. "I might have known you was off after putting some more trash on yourself."

Parker's knees went hollow under him. He wheeled around and cried, "Look at it! Don't just say that! *Look* at it!"

"I done looked," she said.

"Don't you know who it is?" he cried in anguish.

"No, who is it?" Sarah Ruth said. "It ain't anybody I know."

"It's him," Parker said.

"Him who?"

"God!" Parker cried.

"God? God don't look like that!"

"What do you know how he looks?" Parker moaned. "You ain't see him."

"He don't *look*," Sarah Ruth said. "He's a spirit. No man shall see his face."

"Aw listen," Parker groaned, "this is just a picture of him."

"Idolatry!" Sarah Ruth screamed. "Idolatry! Enflaming yourself with idols under every green tree! I can put up with lies and vanity but I don't want no idolator in this house!" and she grabbed up the broom and began to thrash him across the shoulders with it.

Parker was too stunned to resist. He sat there and let her beat him until she had nearly knocked him senseless and large welts had formed on the face of the tattooed Christ. Then he staggered up and made for the door.

She stamped the broom two or three times on the floor and went to the window and shook it out to get the taint of him off it. Still gripping it, she looked toward the pecan tree and her eyes hardened still more. There he was—who called himself Obadiah Elihue—leaning against the tree, crying like a baby.

③ Vladimir Nabokov

Vladimir Nabokov was born in Russia in 1899. He has won distinction as a
lepidopterist and translator, as well as novelist. The Defense, Invitation to a
Beheading, and The Gift belong to his Russian period, and Pnin, Lolita,
Pale Fire, Speak, Memory, and the four-volume translation of Pushkin's
Eugene Onegin were produced during his twenty years of American residence.
Now living in Switzerland, he will soon complete Ada, his sixteenth novel.

Although it is one of Nabokov's best stories, "The Potato-Elf" is little
known. Nabokov has excluded it from his volumes of collected stories in
English, and it has never been anthologized. Written in Russian in 1929,
when Nabokov was thirty, it was included in The Return of Chorb: Stories
and Poems and published by an émigré press in Berlin in 1930. It appeared in
English in the December 1939 issue of Esquire, under Nabokov's pen name
of "Vladimir Sirin" (which he discarded the following year upon his emigra-
tion to America). "The Potato-Elf" marks Nabokov's first publication in an
American magazine.

◆

THE POTATO-ELF

I

His real name was Frederic Dobson. When he told his friend the
magician something of himself, he said:

". . . There was no one in Bristol who didn't know Dobson,
the tailor for children's clothes. He was my father. I feel proud
of that fact only out of stubbornness. I might add here that he
drank like a fish. Once, not long before I was born, my father,
who was staggering with drink, put a wax figure that had a silly,
cherub-like face and was dressed like a sailor, in my mother's bed.
The poor thing escaped having a miscarriage only by a miracle. . . .

You understand, of course, that I know all of this only by hearsay, but if the good people who informed me were telling the truth, here is the secret reason for me . . ."

And Fred Dobson suddenly, and with slow, gentle resignation made a little gesture with his tiny palms. The magician with his usual dreamy smile, stooped over and picked him up, and with a sigh put him on the top of a cabinet where the Potato-Elf obediently rolled himself up, began softly to sneeze and make a little whimpering noise.

He was twenty—he weighed about sixty-five pounds. He was only several inches taller than the famous Swiss dwarf, Zimmerman, who was called Prince Balthazar. Like his colleague, Zimmerman, Fred was very well built, and with the exception of the wrinkles on his round forehead and about his squinted eyes, and with his painfully tense air of seeming to have resisted growing up, the dwarf would have looked like a quiet eight-year-old boy. His hair, the color of damp straw, was sleeked down and separated with an even line of parting, which ran up the middle as if it were coming to some diplomatic agreement with the crown of his head. Fred had an easy carriage, he danced indifferently well, but his first manager decided to lend a heavy character to the name of Elf by adding a funny epithet to it after he had looked at the fleshy nose which the dwarf had inherited from his plethoric, sullen father.

The Potato-Elf, by virtue of his appearance alone, aroused a whirlwind of applause and laughter throughout the whole of England, and later throughout the main cities of the Continent. Unlike other dwarfs his nature was kind, docile. He became very much attached to the tiny pony, Snowdrop, on which he diligently trotted around the arena of a Dutch circus. And in Vienna he conquered the heart of a silly and gloomy Russian giant from Omsk, because, the first time he saw him, he stretched out his little arms, like a child, and pleaded to be allowed to sit in his hand.

He made his appearance usually not alone. So in Vienna the dwarf appeared together with the giant and walked around him with little mincing steps, very carefully dressed in striped trousers and smart-tailored, precise little coat, and carrying a huge roll of

music under his arm. He handed the giant his guitar. The latter
stood like a colossal doll and with a mechanical movement took
the instrument. His long Prince Albert looked as if it were carved
out of ebony, his high heels and shining topcoat increased the
height of the well-shaped, three hundred and sixty pound Siberian.
With his strong jaw jutting out, he would beat the strings with
his fingers. During the intermissions he always complained of
giddiness like a woman.

Fred became very fond of him, and even cried a little when the
separation came, because he became very easily attached to people.
His life was running in a circle as exactly and as monotonously as a
circus horse in an arena. Once in the darkness of the wings he
stumbled over a bucket of paint and softly plopped into it. For a
long time after he related this event as if it were something very
unusual.

So the dwarf traveled around the greater part of Europe, saved
money and sang with the silvery soprano of a eunuch. In German
theatres the audience ate sandwiches, and nuts on straw sticks,
and in Spanish theatres, sugared violets, and also nuts on straw
sticks.

Of the outside world he saw nothing. In his memory only was
always the same faceless abyss of the audience laughing at him,
and later, after the performance, the quiet, dreaming slope of a
cool night, which looks so blue when you leave the theatre.

Coming back to London he found a new partner, a magician
called Shock. Shock had a melodious voice, pale, fleshless hands,
and a chestnut-colored, wedge-shaped lock of hair which fell down
over his brow. He looked more like a poet than a magician and
demonstrated his tricks with a tender, quiet mournfulness, without any of the bustling chatter typical of his profession. The Potato-Elf assisted him in his act in a very comic fashion.

At the end of the act he would appear in the gallery with a
joyful cooing exclamation, although a minute before everyone
had seen how the magician had closeted him in a black case
which had stood in the center of the stage.

All this happened in one of those London theatres where one
sees acrobats who swing in the buzzing tremor of their trapeze,
foreign tenors (failures in their own countries), who sing folk

songs, ventriloquists in naval uniforms, bicyclists, and the inevitable clown eccentric who softly shuffles on the stage with his tiny derby, and waistcoat trailing on the floor.

II

During all this time Fred became somewhat somber, he sneezed continuously, soundlessly, and sadly, like a little Japanese dog. After not feeling any desire for a woman for months, the virginal dwarf would be overcome by piercing attacks of solitary love anguish, which would go away as unexpectedly as they would come over him. And again for a while he would pay no attention to the bare shoulders which gleamed whitely against the velvet enclosure of the boxes, nor to the little female acrobats, nor the Spanish dancer, whose gleaming haunches were revealed in all their nudeness for a brief precious minute when the orange down of her frilled skirt whirled gaily in the air.

"What you need is a female dwarf," said Shock with a preoccupied air, drawing a silver coin out of the dwarf's ear with a familiar gesture. The latter brushed his ear with his tiny hand, as if he were sweeping away a fly.

The same night when Fred's act was over and he was trotting along in the dimly lit corridor of the backstage, sneezing and grumbling, dressed in his tiny overcoat and derby, a bright streak of light suddenly flashed out as a door was thrown slightly ajar, and two voices called to him. The voices belonged to Zita and Arabella, sister acrobats who were at this moment half-undressed, showing their brown-skinned bodies. They had black hair and long, narrow blue eyes. Untidiness reigned in the dressing room filled with a theatrical disarray and the smell of perfume. On the dressing table were lying in disorder puffs, combs, a corrugated atomizer, hairpins in an empty candy box, and rouge sticks.

The sisters immediately proceeded to stun the dwarf with their loud chattering. They tickled and squeezed Fred, who, puffed up with dark pulsating blood, was looking askance and rolling like a ball between the quick nude arms which were teasing him. And when Arabella, playing, drew him to her and fell down backwards on the couch, Fred felt that he was losing his mind. He began to

wrestle and sniffle, and clutched her neck. Pushing him back,
she lifted her bare arm and he sprang back, slipped down, and
fastened his lips to her shaven, hot, slightly prickly armpit. The
other, Zita, dying with laughter, tried to pull him away by his
legs. The same minute the door opened noisily, and in came the
acrobats' partner, a Frenchman in white tights that looked like
marble. Silently and without any anger he grabbed the dwarf by
the scruff of the neck—one could only hear the crackling of his
starched collar as it was torn away from the collar button—lifted
him up into the air and threw him out of the room like a little
monkey. The door slammed shut.

The magician who was wandering about in the corridor, just
had time to notice the white gleam of a strong hand and the tiny
figure with its little paws drawn up as it flew through the air.

Fred was hurled painfully to the floor and lay there motionless.
He did not lose consciousness—he only became limp, staring
straight ahead, his teeth chattering.

"What rotten luck," said the magician, lifting him up from
the floor and touching the dwarf's round forehead with his gentle,
fragrant fingers. "I told you not to go in there, and now you've
got the thrashing you deserve. You really ought to have a female
dwarf."

Fred was silent—his eyes dilated.

"You'll have to sleep at my place tonight," decided Shock,
carrying the Elf in his arms on the way to the exit.

I I I

There was also a Madame Shock. She was a lady of indefinite
age, with dark eyes that looked slightly jaundiced. Her thinness,
her parchment-like skin, black, dried hair, her habit of blowing
smoke through her nostrils, her deliberate untidiness of dress and
coiffure were not particularly attractive to men; but no doubt attracted the magician, although actually he seemed to pay no attention to her at all, because as he was always preoccupied with his
hidden inventions, he seemed vacillating, remote when talking
about unimportant things; attentive and keen when he was thinking about his magic. Nora always stood on guard, because her
husband never lost a chance to play a trick on her, a small, un-

necessary one, but always refined and sly. It would happen like this:—at dinner he would amaze her with his unusual gluttony, juicily smacking his lips, sucking at the bones, again and again refilling his plate; and then he would go away looking sadly at his wife. Later the maid, chuckling into her apron, would say that Mr. Shock didn't even touch his dinner, because all of it was hidden under the table in three new pans.

Nora was the daughter of a distinguished artist who painted only horses, spotted dogs, and hunters in formal red riding clothes. Before her marriage she had lived in Chelsea, admired the smoky sunset about the Thames, painted, attended absurd meetings where the London Bohemia was present. There the ethereal eyes of a quiet, slender man noticed her, a man who spoke little, and was as yet unknown. One suspected that he was a lyrical poet. She was immediately captivated by him. The poet absent-mindedly became engaged to her, and the first day after the marriage he told her with a sad smile that he didn't know how to write poetry; and immediately during the conversation he turned an old alarm clock into a nickel pocket watch and the latter into a charming wrist watch which Nora had worn ever since.

She felt at heart that the magician Shock still, in some way, was a poet, but she could never become accustomed to the fact that every minute, under any circumstances, he practiced his art. It is hard to be happy when your husband is a mirage, a living trick, an illusion of all the five senses.

IV

Absent-mindedly Nora was tapping her nails against the glass of a fish bowl, where several goldfish, which looked as if they were carved out of orange peel, were gently breathing, when the door softly opened and Shock appeared on the threshold with his top hat awry, the chestnut-colored lock over his eyebrow, holding in his arm a huddled little figure.

Nora thought suddenly—a child—a foundling—He must have picked it up somewhere . . . Her dark eyes grew moist.

"We will have to adopt it," said Shock softly, waiting stiffly in the doorway.

The little figure suddenly became alive, mumbled, and began

shyly to scratch the starched bosom of the magician's shirt-front. Nora looked at the tiny shoes with their buckskin spats—at the derby . . .

"It isn't so easy to fool me," said she, laughing through her nose.

The magician looked at her reproachfully, then he put Fred down on the plush couch and covered him with a plaid robe.

"The acrobat bruised him," explained Shock, and he had to add, "he struck him in his little belly with a weight."

And Nora, kind-hearted like many a childless woman, felt such an especial sorrow that she almost cried. She started to mother the dwarf, got him something to eat, also some port, rubbed his forehead, his temples and the childish hollow back of his ears with an aromatic alcohol.

The next morning Fred awoke early, paced up and down the strange room, and, sneezing softly like a boy, seated himself on the wide window sill.

The drizzling, pleasant fog was washing the gray roofs. Somewhere far away, a garret window opened, and its glass caught the glitter of the morning sun.

Fred thought of yesterday's event. The laughing voices of the acrobats blended strangely with the feel of the aromatic, cool hands of Madame Shock. He had at first been offended, and then caressed by her, and he was a dwarf who became easily and passionately attached. He dreamed how he would some day save Nora from a coarse, strong man, a man like the Frenchman in the white tights. For no reason at all he remembered a fifteen-year-old female dwarf with whom he had once made some appearances. The female dwarf had a turned-up nose and was both unhealthy and evil by nature. She was introduced to the audience as Fred's fiancée, and he shuddered with disgust when he had to dance a clinging tango with her.

At eight o'clock the apartment came to life; the magician smiling absent-mindedly left the house, where, nobody knew; in the dining room it smelt wonderfully of fried bacon, which was lying in fragrant strips above the hot bubble of the eggs. With her hair carelessly arranged, Madame Shock appeared in a peignoir embroidered with sunflowers.

After lunch she gave Fred a perfumed cigarette, the end of which was covered with a red petal; and looking at him through half-veiled eyes, she made him tell her about himself. On such occasions Fred's voice became slightly deeper, he spoke slowly, carefully choosing his words, and this unexpected choice in his style of speaking, strange to say, suited him. With his head on one side, intent on what he was saying, he was sitting at Nora's feet. The latter was half-lying on the plush couch, revealing the pointed elbows of her bare, uplifted arms. After finishing his speech the dwarf fell silent, but he still kept gesticulating with his tiny hands as if he were still talking. His little black coat, his bowed face, his fleshy little nose, his yellow hair with its parting on the top of his head, vaguely touched her. Looking through her eyelashes, she tried to visualize that this was not a dwarf in front of her, but her imaginary son who was telling her how mistreated he was at school. Stretching out her hand, Nora softly stroked his head, and the same minute, through some unexplainable combination of ideas, she dreamed of something more, which was both revengeful and curious.

Feeling her moving fingers in his hair, the dwarf stiffened and suddenly began to lick his lips quickly in silence. Cocking his eyes to one side, he could not tear his gaze from the green pom-pom on Madame Shock's slipper.

And suddenly, absurdly, and delightfully—everything became motion.

V

On this dove-colored, sunny August afternoon, London looked especially beautiful.

Every single day of the year is given to only one man; to the most happy one. All others use this day, enjoying the sun, or being angry with the rain, but never knowing to whom this day really belongs, and this ignorance on their part is very pleasant to the lucky one, and he laughs at them. No one can foresee which day will be his, what trifle he will remember eternally—the rippling of light along the water, or the fluttering of a maple leaf—and often it so happens that he will recognize his day only among days already long past.

Almighty God gave Fred Dobson, a dwarf in mouse-colored spats, this merry August day which began with a soft whistle and the opening of a flashing window frame. Children who came back from a walk, related to their parents, breathlessly, and with amazement, that they saw a dwarf in a derby and striped trousers, carrying a cane and a pair of yellow gloves in his hands.

After passionately saying good-bye to Nora who was expecting guests, the Potato-Elf came out on the broad smooth street that was drenched with sun and immediately he knew that the entire town was created for him alone. A merry chauffeur pushed down the iron flag of the meter with a resounding click, the street flew away and Fred repeatedly slipped off the leather seat laughing continuously, and cooing to himself.

He got out at the entrance to Hyde Park and without paying attention to the curious looks, trotted along past the green folding chairs, the fountain, past the huge rhododendron bushes. Horsemen were flying past, lightly galloping, their boots creaking, the slender mouths of their horses tinkling with the bits.

The dwarf had a complete feeling of freedom and ease. Nora had seen him off with such a hasty tenderness—she had laughed so emotionally—it looked to him as if she were afraid that her old father who usually came to lunch, would begin to suspect something, having surprised a strange man in her house.

The same day one saw him everywhere—in the park where a rosy-cheeked nurse in a starched bonnet, who was pushing a perambulator, offered him a ride in it—for no reason at all—in the halls of the British Museum, on the living stairs which crept slowly out of the depths of the subway—in an exclusive shop where only men's handkerchiefs are sold—and on top of a bus where some kind hands had helped him up.

And then he became tired, dizzy from moving and from the glitter; he felt disquiet from the continuously laughing looks. He felt that he had to justify this broad feeling of freedom, of pride and happiness which still stayed with him.

When, feeling hungry, he entered a familiar little restaurant which was patronized by all kind of performers, and where his presence excited no attention, he realized, after he looked over the guests—the old dull clown who was already drunk, the Frenchman, his enemy, who gave him a friendly nod—he realized quite clearly that he would never again appear on the stage.

The restaurant was dark, as usual in the afternoon. The dull clown who looked like a ruined banker, and the acrobat, so strangely awkward in a coat, were silently playing at dominoes. A Spanish dancer, alone at a table in a corner, crossed her legs. There were seven or eight people unknown to Fred.

And suddenly at a distance in the twilight gloom of the restaurant, Fred recognized the slender profile of the magician, who was softly talking to a fat old gentleman. Fred had not counted on meeting the magician, who never visited saloons, and in general he had forgotten his existence. Now he felt so sorry for poor Shock, that at first he decided to keep everything from him; but he thought anyway that Nora didn't know how to deceive and would probably tell her husband even today—"I fell in love with Fred Dobson—I am leaving you . . ." and then this conversation would be so unpleasant, difficult that he should make it easier for her. He was her knight—he was proud of her love, and even though he was sorry for Shock he would have to grieve him.

Meanwhile, the waiter brought him an order of kidney pie and a stone bottle of ginger beer. The dwarf saw from afar how the chestnut lock on the magician's forehead gleamed with gold light, how his tender, fragrant fingers went from light to shadow. His companion in talk got up, hitched up his belt under his coat, and giving Shock a flattering smile, accompanied him to the coat rack. The fat fellow jammed his hat down on his head and left the restaurant. The door banged.

"Shock!" called the Potato-Elf, paddling his feet under the table.

Shock came over. On his way he pensively took a lighted cigar out of his vest pocket, inhaled, blew out some smoke and put it back. Nobody knew how he did it.

"Shock," said the dwarf, whose nose had become very red from the ginger beer, "I must speak to you—it's very important."

The magician sat next to him, slouching on one elbow, his head on his hand.

"You don't have a headache?" he asked indifferently.

Fred wiped his lips with his napkin; he didn't know quite how to begin in order to keep from hurting his friend too much.

"Tonight I am appearing with you for the last time," said the magician. "That American is taking me away—I think the prospects look pretty good."

"Listen, Shock," said the dwarf, crumbling some bread, and starting to fumble for the necessary words. "There now, be brave, Shock. I love your wife . . . Today when you went away . . . I . . . with her . . . we both . . . she . . ."

"But I am a bad sailor," said the magician thoughtfully, "and it takes a week to Boston. Sometime ago I sailed to India, and later I felt the way my leg does when it goes to sleep."

Fred, becoming crimson, was rubbing his little fist against the tablecloth. The magician was laughing softly at his own thoughts, and later said:

"Did you want to tell me something, little friend?"

The dwarf looked into his ethereal eyes and shook his head in confusion.

"No, no . . . nothing . . . it's impossible to talk to you."

Shock stretched out his hand. Evidently he wanted to flip a coin out of the dwarf's ear, but for the first time after many years of masterly magic, the coin unsteadily fell out ahead of time.

The magician caught it and got up.

"And I don't think I'll have dinner here," he said, examining the top of the dwarf's head with curiosity. "I don't like it here."

Fred, puffed up and silent, was eating a baked apple.

"He didn't want to listen. Well, it's his lookout," thought Fred, sighing with relief, and deciding that Nora would explain everything anyway.

A little later he asked for some paper, and started to write her a letter. It ended like this: "Now you realize that I cannot go on with my former existence. How would you feel, knowing that every night the people are laughing at your chosen one? Tomorrow I am tearing up my contract and leaving. I will write you again as soon as I find a peaceful little spot, where after your divorce, we will love each other, my Nora."

So ended the swift day which was given to the dwarf in mouse-colored spats.

V I

London was carefully growing dark. The street noises blended into a soft musical rumbling, as if someone had suddenly stopped playing and still kept his foot on the pedal. The black leaves of the linden trees stood out against the transparent sky like aces of spades. In some places, at the bend of a street, or between two mournful towers, the fire of the sunset appeared like a vision.

The magician always went home for dinner, and to change into his professional evening clothes, later to go straight to the theatre. That night Nora awaited him with special impatience, trembling with evil joy, happy in the knowledge that now she too had her mystery. The dwarf, himself, she didn't want to remember. The dwarf was an unpleasant little worm.

The lock of the entrance door clicked thinly. As it often happens when you know that you have cheated someone, the face of the magician appeared new, almost strange to her. Giving her a nod, he somehow shamefully and sadly lowered his eyelids. Silently he sat down at the table opposite her. Nora looked at his light gray suit in which he appeared more slender, more intangible than ever, and her eyes gleamed with hot triumph. The evil little impish smile trembled in the corner of her mouth.

She asked, enjoying the carelessness of her question:

"How is your dwarf? I thought you'd bring him with you."

"I didn't see him today," answered Shock, starting to eat. Suddenly he remembered something. He took out a phial and cautiously drawing out the cork with a squeak, bent it over a little glass filled with wine.

Nora thought irritably—he is going to play a trick now. The wine will become a vivid blue, or transparent as water—but the color of the wine remained unchanged. Shock, who caught her look, gave her a vague smile.

"Some drops—for my indigestion," he explained. A thoughtful look passed over his face.

"You're lying as usual," said Nora. "There is nothing the matter with your stomach."

The magician laughed softly, then he coughed in a business-like manner and gulped the wine.

"Eat for heaven's sake," said Nora. "Everything is getting cold."

She thought maliciously: "Oh, if he only knew! You will never know. From now on my power lies in this."

The magician was eating silently. Suddenly he made a wry face, pushed away the plate and started to speak. As usual he did not look into his wife's eyes, but a little above her, and his voice was soft and resonant. He related how today he was at the King's in Windsor, where he was engaged to entertain the little dukes in their velvet jackets and lace collars. He was describing it pictur-esquely and easily imitating the people he saw, and laughing, nod-ding his head a little to one side.

"I let a flock of white pigeons out of a top hat," he said.

"And the dwarf's little hands were moist, and you are telling lies," mentally added Nora.

". . . and you know those pigeons started to fly around the queen. She shooed them away and smiled to be polite."

The magician got up, stumbled forward a little, softly pressed against the edge of the table with two fingers, and said as if ending his tale:

"I feel bad, Nora. Just now I took poison. You shouldn't be un-true to me."

His throat swelled, and pressing his handkerchief to his lips he quickly went from the room.

Nora got up swiftly, knocking a silver knife off a plate with her long amber beads.

"All on purpose," she thought maliciously. "He wants to scare me—to torture me. No, my friend, it won't work. You'll see!"

She was vexed that Shock had guessed her secret so easily. But now anyway she would have a reason for unburdening to him, to yell to him that she hated him, that she despised him with all her heart, that he wasn't a human being, but a rubber ghost, that she couldn't bear to live with him any longer—that—

The magician was sitting on his bed, bent in two, and painfully gritting his teeth, but he attempted to smile when Nora dashed into the bedroom.

"So I am supposed to believe all this," she said gasping for breath. "No, this is the end of your tricks. I can cheat, too. Oh, how repulsive you are to me—how laughable your unsuccessful tricks are to me."

Shock, with a bewildered smile on his face, tried to get up from the bed, but the soles of his shoes slipped against the carpet. Nora stopped, trying to think what else she could yell at him that was insulting.

"Don't—if I—pardon me—" Shock breathed with difficulty.

The veins on his forehead swelled, he shriveled, his throat rattled. His moist hair lock trembled, and the handkerchief which he convulsively pressed to his mouth became swollen with dark blood.

"Stop playing the fool," Nora stamped her foot.

He straightened up, pale as wax, and threw his handkerchief into the corner.

"Stop, Nora—I don't understand—it is my last trick—I won't do it any more."

His terrible, shining face became painfully disfigured. He swayed, then fell back on the bed, his head dropping behind him.

Nora approached, and looked at him, knitting her brows. Shock was lying with his eyes closed, his clenched teeth squeaking. When she bent over him, his eyelids trembled, his look was glazed as if he didn't recognize his wife, and then suddenly he recognized her, and in his eyes there flashed a moist beam of tenderness and suffering.

And suddenly Nora realized that she loved him more than anything in the world. And horror and sorrow took hold of her like a whirlwind. She ran in circles around the room, for no reason at all poured some water into a glass, left it on the washstand, flew back to her husband, who lifted himself a little off the bed, and pressing the end of the sheet to his lips, trembled and emitted a low moan, dilating his insensible eyes, already veiled with death. Then she wrung her hands, dashed to the next room where the telephone stood, dialed endlessly, got the wrong number, called again—her breath sobbing and her fist hammering the little table.

And when she finally heard the doctor's voice, she screamed that her husband had poisoned himself, that he was dying—all the while passionately sobbing into the mouthpiece—then replaced the receiver crookedly and rushed back to the bedroom.

The magician, smoothly shaven, dressed in a white waistcoat and well-pressed black trousers, stood in front of the mirror, and with his arms upraised was methodically arranging his tie. Seeing Nora in the mirror, he smiled at her absent-mindedly without turning his head, and whistling softly, put the finishing touches to the black silk ends.

VII

Drowsy, the little town in the north of England, appeared so quiet that it looked as if someone had forgotten it in the midst of the foggy, dewy fields, where the little town seemed to sleep forever. There was a post office, a bicycle store, two or three tobacco shops with red and blue signs, an old gray church surrounded by grave-stones which were covered by the shadow of the enormous chestnut tree. Along the single street, there were green fences, little gardens, small brick houses on which ivy trellises grew slant-wise. One of these little houses was rented to a certain F. Dobson whom no one had seen face to face, except the doctor, and the doctor did very little talking in general. Mr. Dobson apparently never went out of the house, and his housekeeper, a severe, fat woman who had formerly had a job in an insane asylum, answered the casual questions of the neighbors by saying that Mr. Dobson was an old paralytic who was destined to live in half twilight and quiet. He was forgotten the same year that he arrived in Drowsy Town—he became something unnoticed, but everyone accepted him in good faith, as they did the unknown bishop whose stone image was standing so long in a niche above the entrance to the church. Apparently the mysterious old man had a grandchild—a quiet, blond boy who sometimes came out of Mr. Dobson's house at dusk, with small, shy steps. But it happened so seldom that nobody could say definitely whether it was always the same boy or or another one—and the twilight was blue and foggy, making everything hazy. So the dreamy, incurious residents of the little town missed the fact that the pretended grandson of the paralytic did not grow as the years passed, and that his flaxen hair was nothing but a beautifully made little wig. Because the Potato-Elf started to grow bald the first year of his new life, and soon his head became so smooth and shiny that severe Anna, his housekeeper, had a desire once in a while to clasp this funny roundness. In other respects he changed little, only perhaps his little belly became fuller, and the crimson threads looked transparent on his dark, puffed-up nose which he powdered when he dressed as a boy. Besides, Anna and the doctor knew that the heart attacks from which the dwarf suffered would come to no good.

He lived peacefully unnoticed in his three rooms, subscribed to a library, and three or four times a week got new books, mostly novels, bought a black yellow-eyed cat, because he was scared to death of mice which scurried by in the evening as if they were playing with kindle wood in the corner behind the cupboard. He ate a good deal, especially sweet things—sometimes he would even jump up in the middle of the night and trot across the cold floor, feeling the chill on his little feet, so tiny and grotesque in his long shirt, and run into the pantry for chocolate cookies like a little boy. Always, with increasing infrequency, he would remember his first love and his first terrible days in Drowsy Town.

However, inside his desk among thin, carefully folded posters, he still kept a sheet of flesh-colored writing paper with a watermark in the shape of a dragon, which was covered with almost illegible handwriting. On this paper was written:

"Dear Mr. Dobson: I also received your second letter in which you invite me to D. I am afraid there was a terrible misunderstanding. Try to pardon and forget me. Tomorrow my husband and I are leaving for America and will probably not be back for a long time. I don't know what more I can tell you, my poor Fred."

That was the time when the first heart attack took place. A mild, bewildered look remained in his eyes since that day. And for many days he used to pace up and down, swallowing tears and waving his trembling little hand in front of his face.

And then Fred began to forget. He started to love this cosiness, until now unknown to him. The blue flames above the coals in the fireplace, the dusty vases on the rounded shelves, an etching between the windows which depicted a St. Bernard with a flask around his neck and a weakened traveler on a black cliff. He seldom remembered his former life. Only once in awhile he dreamed that the starry sky became full of the swinging trapeze, and then he was locked in a black box and heard through its walls Shock's resonant, indifferent voice, and couldn't find the trap door on the stage, suffocated by the murky, sticky gloom, and the magician's voice became sadder, and more and more remote, until it finally dissolved. And Fred would awake on his broad bed with a moan, in the quiet dark bedroom where it smelled slightly of lavender; and choking and pressing his little fist to his hammering heart he would look for a long time at a pale spot in the window shade.

As the years passed, the painful desire for a woman's love would sigh in him more and more seldom, as if Nora had suddenly taken out of his body all the passion which used to torture him in the past. However, there would be some days, some vague spring evenings, when the dwarf shyly dressed up in short pants and covering his baldness with the little blond wig, left the house to go out and become a part of the twilight; and trotting along a little path in the fields, he would suddenly stop and look with a troubled, uneasy air at a motionless couple of lovers, who were clasped languidly against the fence under a shower of blossoming blackberry bushes. And then this too passed away, and he stopped seeing people entirely. The only one who came was the gray-haired doctor with piercing black eyes. Sitting opposite Fred at a chessboard with curiosity and delight, he was looking at the soft little hand, the bull-dog face of the dwarf, who, thinking about his move, was wrinkling his brow.

Eight years passed; it was Sunday morning. On the table a jug of cocoa, which was covered over with a cloth that resembled the head of a parrot, was waiting for Fred. The sunny, greenish light from the apple trees was streaming into the windows, and the fat Anna was dusting off the lid of a little pianola, on which the dwarf sometimes played waltzes.

Fred, still sleepy, with checkered house slippers on his bare feet, and dressed in a little black robe with a yellow cord, entered the room. He stared at the table, blinking from the glare, smoothing his baldness with his hand. Anna left for church. Fred, sucking in his lips and pouting them, approached the picture section of the Sunday paper, examined at great length the prizewinning puppets, the Russian ballerina who was bent down in the attitude of an agonized swan, the top hat and the large snout of a financier who had cheated somebody. Under the table the cat twisted her back and rubbed herself against his bare ankle. He drank the cocoa and got up, yawning—he had had a very bad night. Never had his heart tormented him so, and now he felt too lazy to dress. His legs became unpleasantly chilled. He crept into an armchair near the window and curled himself up into a little heap, and sat without thinking about anything. The cat stretched herself next to him, opening a tiny, rosy mouth.

A bell tinkled in the ante-room.

"The doctor," thought Fred indifferently, and remembering that Anna was in church he went to open it himself.

The sun poured through the door. A tall woman all in black stood on the threshold. Fred jumped back, muttering something; and drawing his robe more closely about himself, he dashed back to his rooms. During the flight he lost one of his slippers and had no time to pick it up, feeling he had to hide quickly so that it couldn't be seen that he was a dwarf. Breathing rapidly, he stopped in the middle of the drawing room. "Oh, if I had only banged the door shut!" Who could be visiting him? It was some sort of a mistake . . .

And suddenly he distinctly heard the noise of approaching steps. He flung himself out of the drawing room into the bedroom and wanted to lock himself in, but there was no key. In the drawing room his other slipper was lying imposingly on the carpet.

"It is terrible," said Fred, stopping to get his wind and listening.

Steps approached the drawing room. Then with a light moan, the dwarf ran to the clothes closet. Oh, if he could only hide himself!

A voice, undoubtedly familiar, called his name, and the door opened.

"Fred, why are you so afraid of me?"

The dwarf, bare-footed, his bald head covered with sweat,

stiffened against the closet, still holding onto the latch. He remembered very vividly the orange fish in the glass bowl.

She had become unhealthily older in all these years. There were olive-colored shadows under her eyes, and more distinctly than ever the dark fuzz stood out above her upper lip. From her black hair, from the severe folds of her black dress, there emanated something dusty and mournful.

"I never thought," began Fred, slowly, looking at her askance.

Nora took him by the shoulders and turned him towards the light, began to examine his features with greedy and sad eyes. The dwarf, confused, blinked, painfully feeling sorry that he was without his wig—amazed at Nora's emotion. He had stopped thinking about her so long ago that he felt nothing now except sorrow and wonder. Nora closed her eyes, still holding him by the shoulders and then pushing the dwarf back slightly, turned towards the window.

Fred cleared his throat.

"I lost sight of you entirely. Tell me—how is Shock?"

"He is still performing tricks," answered Nora, absent-mindedly. "We just returned recently from America."

Not removing her hat, she sat in an armchair near the window, still looking at Fred with a strange intensity.

"It means that Shock . . ." said the dwarf quickly, feeling uneasy under her glance—

"Is still the same," said Nora, not taking her shining eyes from his face, and starting to take off and crumple her shiny black gloves which had a white lining.

"It is possible that she again . . . ?" thought the dwarf abruptly. In his thoughts he saw again with rushing swiftness—the bowl with the fish—the smell of eau de cologne—the emerald pom-pom on the slipper.

Nora got up. The gloves fell on the floor like two little black balls.

"The garden is small but it has apple trees," said Fred, still puzzled. "Is it possible that I could ever have—she is quite yellow —with a mustache—and why is she doing so much sighing?"

"But I seldom go out," slightly swinging himself as he sat in a chair, rubbing his little knees.

"Fred," said Nora. "Do you know why I came to see you?"

She came closer to him. Fred, with a guilty smile, slipped out of the chair, trying to escape.

Then she said very softly, "I had a son from you."

The dwarf stiffened, staring at the tiny window which was reflected on the blue cup. A timid, amazed smile started to play around the corner of his mouth, became broader, illuminated his cheeks with a lavender flush.

"My—son—"

And immediately he understood everything—all the meaning of life—all his long anguish—the spot on the cup.

Slowly he raised his eyes. Nora was seated sideways on a chair, sobbing loudly. The glass head of her hat pin shone like a tear. The cat, tenderly purring, was rubbing itself against her legs.

The dwarf jumped down towards her, remembering the novel he had recently read.

"But don't be afraid—don't be afraid," he said. "I am so happy."

She looked at him through a mist of tears, wanted to explain something, swallowed, saw with what tender and joyful light the dwarf was dreaming and then did not explain anything. She got up, and quickly she picked up the sticky black balls of gloves.

"Well, now I know—nothing more is necessary . . . I am going."

A sudden idea pierced through Fred's mind.

His trembling happiness mingled with a feeling of shame. Pulling the cord of his robe tighter about him, he asked:

"And how is he? He isn't—"

"No, no—he is as big as other boys," said Nora quickly, and started to weep again.

Fred dropped his eyes.

"I would like to see him."

He gaily added: "Oh, I understand. He mustn't know that I am like this. But maybe you will arrange . . ."

"Yes, certainly, certainly," said Nora quickly, almost dryly, going towards the door. "We will arrange it somehow. I have to be going—train—it takes twenty minutes to walk to the station."

Turning back in the doorway, she fixed her eyes heavily and greedily upon Fred's face for the last time. The sun was trembling

on his bald head. His ears looked transparently pink. He understood nothing in his amazement and happiness. And when she
left, Fred was still standing in the center of the room for a long
time, holding himself together carefully as if afraid that he would
spill his full heart. He tried to visualize his son and could only
visualize himself, dressed as a schoolboy with a blond wig. Somehow he transferred his appearance to his son. He stopped feeling
that he was a dwarf.

He saw how he would enter a house, meet his son—with poignant pride he would smooth his light hair—and later, together
with him and Nora—silly goose, to think that he would take the
boy—they would go into the street and on the street . . . Fred
slapped his thighs.

He had forgotten to ask Nora the address.

And then there began something crazy—something incoherent.
He rushed to the bedroom, began to dress, hurrying terribly. He
put on all his best clothes—a starched shirt, striped trousers, a
coat made some time ago in Paris—always smiling, breaking his
nails in the chinks of the tight drawers. Twice he had to sit
down, his heart became so swollen and palpitating, and again he
jumped into the room, looking for the derby which he hadn't worn
for so long, and finally he looked into the mirror where a well-
shaped, middle-aged gentleman, severely and dandily dressed,
flashed back at him. Fred ran down the stairs to the entrance, full
of a new blinding idea: To go to London with Nora; he would
have time to catch her and have a look at his son tonight.

The broad dusty road ran straight to the station. It was deserted
as usual on Sunday. Unexpectedly a boy came suddenly around the
corner, holding a cricket mallet. He was the first to notice the
dwarf. He slapped himself on the top of his colored cap, looking
at Fred's disappearing back and at the flashing mouse-colored
spats.

And immediately from God knows where, other boys appeared,
and open-mouthed, started running after the dwarf. He was going
faster all the time, looking at his gold watch, smiling and excited.
He felt slightly nauseated by the sun. And the group of boys grew
larger and larger. The infrequent passers-by stopped in amazement.
Far away some chimes sang out sonorously. The sleepy town came

to life and suddenly started to laugh uncontrollably, as if this laughter had been secreted for years.

Not able to quiet his impatience, the Potato-Elf started to run. One of the boys rushed in front of him, peeped into his face—another yelled something with a crude throaty voice. Fred ran, choking from the dust, and suddenly it seemed to him that all of the boys in the crowd pursuing him were his merry, pink-cheeked, well-built sons, and he was smiling in perplexity—and kept running and coughing, trying to forget his heart which was bursting his chest with a burning wedge.

A bicyclist was riding near him on gleaming wheels, cupping his fist to his mouth like a megaphone, cheering him along as they do at races. Women came out on the stoops of their houses, squinting in the sun, laughing loudly, pointing out the running dwarf to one another. All the dogs in town awoke—the parishioners in the stuffy church were unwillingly listening to the barking and the provoking tallyhos. And the crowd running after the dwarf became larger and larger. The people thought all this was a wonderful trick advertising a circus, or that someone was shooting a picture. Fred began to stumble—there was a buzzing in his ears—the collar button was piercing his throat—he had nothing to breathe with. The moan of laughter, of yelling, the clatter of running feet deafened him—but now through a sweaty mist he saw a black dress in front of him. Nora was slowly walking beside a brick wall in the beams of the sun. Now she turned around and stopped. The dwarf ran to her and clasped the folds of her skirt . . .

With a smile of happiness he looked up at her from below, tried to say something, and raising his eyebrows with amazement, he collapsed to the pavement. The crowd was breathing noisily all around.

Someone, understanding that this was not all a joke, bent over the dwarf, whistled softly and took off his cap. Nora looked indifferently on Fred's tiny little body which resembled a crumpled black glove. She was shoved this way and that. Someone took her by the elbow.

"Let me alone," said Nora feebly. "I know nothing about this . . . My son died a short time ago . . ."

4 Alfred Appel, Jr.

*Alfred Appel, Jr., has taught at Columbia and Stanford. He is presently an
assistant professor of English at Northwestern, where he directs the Freshman
Humanities Program. He has completed an annotated edition of Lolita, is
editing a collection of Nabokov essays for Prentice-Hall's Twentieth Century
Views series, and is completing a critical study of Nabokov for New Directions.*

❖

NABOKOV'S PUPPET SHOW*

Now in his seventieth year, Vladimir Nabokov is suddenly upon
us. Of course, he was here all along, but *Lolita* (1955) was the
first of his books in English to attract wide attention, though
too much of that was of an extraliterary sort. *Lolita*'s American
publication in 1958 brought fame to Lolita, not Nabokov. Although praised by influential critics, *Lolita* was treated as a kind
of miracle of spontaneous combustion, for Nabokov's œuvre was
like an iceberg, the massive body of his Russian novels, stories,
plays, and poems remaining untranslated and out of sight, lurking
beneath the visible peaks of *Lolita* and *Pnin* (1957). But in the
eleven years since Putnam published *Lolita*, eighteen Nabokov
titles have appeared, including seven works translated from the
Russian, three out-of-print novels, two collections of stories, *Pale
Fire* (1962), the monumental four-volume translation of Pushkin's *Eugene Onegin* (1964), and *Speak, Memory: An Autobiography Revisited* (1966), a considerably revised and expanded ver-

---

*This essay originally appeared in two parts in *The New Republic*, January
14 and 21, 1967, as a review of *Speak, Memory*. A few minor changes have
been made.

sion of the memoir first issued in 1951 as *Conclusive Evidence.* The publication of *The Exploit* (1932), now being translated by his son Dmitri, will leave untranslated only Nabokov's first novel, *Mashenka* (1926).

This extraordinary outburst of Nabokovia highlights the resolute and indomitable spirit of the man who published his masterpieces, *Lolita* and *Pale Fire*, at the age of 56 and 62, respectively. Nabokov endured the exigencies of being an émigré writer when the Western world only seemed interested in his inferior Soviet contemporaries, and has emerged not only as a major Russian writer, but as the most important living American novelist. No doubt some academic pigeonholers still worry about Nabokov's nationality and where to "place" him, but John Updike solved this synthetic problem when he described Nabokov as "the best writer of English prose at present holding American citizenship." Not since Henry James, an émigré in his own right, has an American citizen created so formidable a corpus of work.

Nabokov was born in 1899, the same year as Hemingway and Hart Crane, a year before Thomas Wolfe. One doesn't readily think of him as their contemporary, and this fact serves to underscore a familiar and saddening story about American letters, and to emphasize Nabokov's signal achievement. One hesitates to sustain a vocabulary better suited for a General Motors account report, but in total output, Nabokov surpasses Faulkner, the only other major American writer of the modern period whose work threatens to occupy a full shelf, and even Dreiser, that veritable writing machine. To find a comparable verbal felicity in our literature, one has to go back to Melville and Hawthorne, but the poetic order of Nabokov's virtuoso prose, the joy and the exactitude with which every sentence seems to have been composed, finally places him beyond comparison.

Nabokov's pronounced antipathy to Freud and the novel of society will continue to alienate some critics, but there is a reason for the delay in achieving his proper status more basic than the unavailability of his books or his failure to conform to some accepted school or *Zeitgeist* pattern: readers trained on the tenets of formalist criticism have simply not known what to make of works which resist the search for ordered mythic and symbolic "levels of meaning," and depart completely from post-Jamesian requisites for the "realistic" or "impressionistic" novel—that a fiction be the impersonal product of a pure aesthetic impulse, a self-contained illusion of reality rendered from a consistently held point of view and through a central intelligence from which all authorial comment has been exorcised. Quite the opposite happens in Nabokov's fiction: his art is artifice or nothing, and the fantastic, a-realistic, and involuted forms toward which even his earliest fictions evolve make it clear that Nabokov has always gone his own way, and it has not been the way of the novel's Great Tradition according to F. R. Leavis. But Nabokov's present eminence signals a radical shift in opinions about the novel and the novelists' ethical responsibilities. A future historian of the novel may one day claim that it was Nabokov, more than any novelist now living, who kept alive an exhausted art form not only by demonstrating new possibilities for it, but by reminding us, through his example, of the variegated aesthetic resources of his great forebears, such as Sterne, and the Joyce who was a parodist rather than a symbolist.

The new edition of *Speak, Memory* affords an opportunity to make some general remarks about Nabokov's art which, however admired it may be, is almost never considered on its own terms. A compulsive exegete could devote several hundred pages to an elucidation of the literary allusions in *Lolita* and *Pale Fire* and yet fail to identify Nabokov's fundamental concerns and methods. *Speak, Memory* goes surprisingly far in helping to introduce them.

The 1951 version of *Speak, Memory* has been widely read in a paperback edition, but its readers may be assured that the revisited memoir is indispensable, its more than one hundred new pages and many important revisions increasing its cumulative power considerably. The new edition is also much enhanced by eighteen illustrations of Nabokov, his family, and his butterflies. These are not mere ancillary documents, and several present striking juxtapositions: Nabokov in a rowboat as a handsome, white-garbed 21-year-old Cambridge undergraduate, an open-shirted Russian Romantic by way of Rupert Brooke; then an unposed shot taken only nine years later but showing a much older-looking man, a decade of exile behind him, concentration creasing his forehead as he writes *The Defense* (1930), his third novel. Nabokov has also drawn the endpapers for the new edition: a map of the Nabokov lands and a butterfly (not identified, it is, rightly, *Parnassius mnemosyne*; in fact, *Speak Mnemosyne* was his first choice for a title).

Like the first edition, the augmented *Speak, Memory* spans the first 40 years of Nabokov's life—one half of them spent in Russia, the other in exile in England, Germany, and France—stopping with his departure for America in 1940. Its researches into the history of his distinguished family extend back to the 15th century, and Chapter Three, which once featured eccentric Uncle Ruka, who at his death in 1916 bequeathed to young Nabokov his lands and the equivalent of a few million dollars, has now been doubled in length in order to accommodate as much of the family tree as possible. Chapter Fourteen provides history of a different sort. It in part deals with Russian émigré existence in Berlin and Paris (1922–1939), spectral worlds in which Nabokov supported himself through translations, lessons in English and tennis, and, fittingly, the first Russian crossword puzzles, which he composed for a daily émigré paper. He re-creates émigré literary life most vividly in *The Gift* (1938), but Bunin, Aldanov, Kuprin, Marina Tsvataev, and other émigré writers pass through *Speak, Memory* too quickly, and some readers will wish that Chapter Fourteen had grown in proportion to Chapter Three, especially since there is only one full-length study of the émigré period (by Gleb Struve, available only in Russian). Yet it is the very paucity of such documentary material that points to the excellence and rare purity of *Speak, Memory*: like Nabokov's fiction, its landscape is ultimately inward, and the memories which provide Nabokov with conclusive evidence of his having existed do not derive from the kind of high-toned gossip which so many literary memoirists confuse with significant personal experience.

Although *Speak, Memory* proliferates with names and faces, its most revelatory passages concern solitary moments, and describe the torture and rapture and sense of timelessness experienced in the hunting of rare butterflies and the composition of poems or chess problems. But its sunniest pages are inspired by the memories which "belong to the harmonious world of a perfect childhood," and Nabokov re-creates this lost world with an affecting tenderness and exuberance: summers on country estates; winters in St. Petersburg; trips on the Nord-Express; Biarritz and the Riviera; a succession of governesses and tutors; the warmth and gaiety of large family gatherings; the elegant appurtenances of an Anglophile household—all belonging, as they say, to a vanished era, and as such, making *Speak, Memory* an important social record, among other things, though its author might not consider this a recommendation.

The rich and aristocratic Nabokovs were not the "White Russian" stock figures of Western liberal demonology—all monocles, Fabergé snuffboxes, and reactionary opinions—but rather a family with a long tradition of high culture and public service. Nabokov's grandfather was Minister of Justice under two Tsars and implemented the court reforms, while Nabokov's father adds a special resonance to the nostalgic memoirs of his apolitical son, since he tragically epitomizes the final efforts of the non-Soviet intelligentsia to create a democratic society in Russia. By education a lawyer, he lectured at the Imperial School of Jurisprudence, was an editor of liberal newspapers, a foe of anti-Semitism, an authority on Dickens, and a prolific journalist and scholar of law who wrote several books and thousands of articles, including "The Blood Bath of Kishinev," a famous protest against the 1903 pogrom. "At an official banquet in 1904," writes his son, "he refused to drink the Tsar's health. He is said to have coolly advertised in the papers his court uniform for sale." Deprived of his title by imperial decree, he "resolutely plunged into antidespotic labors." He was fined by the government for the fiery articles he wrote about the Beiliss trial (Maurice Samuel mentions him several times in his fine book on the Beiliss case, *Blood Accusation*—coincidentally published at the same time as Malamud's *The Fixer*—and quotes from Nabokov's reportage). A leader of the liberal opposition party (the Kadets), he was elected to the first parliament (Duma), went to prison for issuing a revolutionary manifesto, served in the provisional government after the 1917 Revolution, and then escaped to the Crimea, where he was Minister of Justice in the regional government. In 1919 he went into exile, co-editing a

liberal émigré daily in Berlin until his death in 1922 (age, 52), at a
political meeting, when he was shot while trying to shield the
speaker from two monarchist assassins. Mr. D. J. Enright, com-
menting on *Speak, Memory* in *The New York Review of Books*
(November 3, 1966), carefully avoids mentioning any of the above,
and decides that Nabokov "loved and admired" his father not
for his liberalism, but for the snobbery made possible by his wealth
and position. Thus the morality of reviewing.

What Nabokov in the afterword to *Lolita* calls his "second-
rate brand of English" has never been more virtuoso than in
Speak, Memory. Utilizing as many of the devices of poetry as
prose can accommodate, he unfolds his memories in a rich, shimmering style that in its most ecstatic moments is nothing less than
enchanting. When he is writing about those he loves most, the
welling prose will build to a final crescendo, as at the end of
Chapter One, when he describes "the national [tossing] ordeal"
with which the villagers would honor his father after he had been
called from the dining-room table and had successfully mediated
a local dispute or granted a subsidy:

From my place at table I would suddenly see through one of the
west windows a marvelous case of levitation. There, for an instant,
the figure of my father in his wind-rippled white summer suit would
be displayed, gloriously sprawling in midair, his limbs in a curiously
casual attitude, his handsome, imperturbable features turned to the
sky. Thrice, to the mighty heave-ho of his invisible tossers, he would
fly up in this fashion, and the second time he would go higher than
the first and then there he would be, on his last and loftiest flight,
reclining, as if for good, against the cobalt blue of the summer noon,
like one of those paradisiac personages who comfortably soar, with
such a wealth of folds in their garments, on the vaulted ceiling of a
church while below, one by one, the wax tapers in mortal hands light
up to make a swarm of minute flames in the mist of incense, and
the priest chants of eternal repose, and funeral lilies conceal the face
of whoever lies there, among the swimming lights, in the open coffin.

Effects such as these, abundant in *Speak, Memory*, are not a
matter of "fine writing"—that vaguely pejorative designation, carrying with it suggestions of a hollow eloquence, a disparity between a high style and mean subject—for they rise inexorably out
of Nabokov's deepest promptings.

Although the above quotation is also in the 1951 *Speak, Memory*, there were surprisingly few sustained passages about his father in that first version. This fact, coupled with the short biography of him which Nabokov has added to Chapter Nine, suggests how difficult it has been for him to write about his father, and reveals an especially poignant dimension of the new book which may not immediately be apparent. The nine new pages on his father are informative enough. His memory bolstered by a recently reclaimed family scrapbook, Nabokov coolly details his father's exemplary career, but as the declarative sentences fall into place, one soon realizes that Nabokov's feelings for his father are so profound that, 45 years after his assassination, they still threaten to overwhelm him, and the emotion seems to well up behind the fortress of facts. At one point he interrupts a very short passage about his father's manuscripts to say "I am taking two hours now to describe a two-minute run of his flawless handwriting." These new pages, unadorned and low-keyed, contrast starkly with the sonorous, evocative pages against which they are set, making the biography of his father a very moving experience in an unexpected way.

The first chapter's crescendo ending defines a structural pattern consistent throughout *Speak, Memory*. In spite of Nabokov's indifference to music of any kind, he describes the use memory makes of "innate harmonies" and "wandering tonalities," its resolution of "jangling chords," and the overriding design of *Speak, Memory* is intricately contrapuntal. Each of its fifteen chapters sounds a major motif, and the titles which they bore in their initial appearance as magazine pieces summarize these motifs best: "Portrait of My Mother"; "My English Education"; "Butterflies"; "Exile," and so forth (see Nabokov's Foreword). These "bright blocks of perception" follow a rough chronology in time, but weaving through them in almost rhythmical associative progressions are separate out-of-sequence themes which, when followed and apprehended by the autobiographer, reduce time to a convenient abstraction. Every chapter moves, in varying degrees, toward a recapitulation of its intertwining thematic lines, a full orchestration that in its closing moment reaches for a plangent chord—an incandescent, summary image.

Because consciousness is virtually an optical instrument to Nabokov, his efforts to recapture the past are something vividly seen. The struggle takes place before the reader, who shares with the memoirist that exhilarating instant when Mnemosyne obeys Nabokov's injunction, and the isolated, dimly remembered moments—mute images which have been fading in and out of focus —suddenly coalesce and come to life, releasing a cascade of reverberating sounds and sights, as at the end of Chapter Eight when, after resurrecting a large family outing, Nabokov hears "beyond the river, behind the rhythmic trees, the confused and enthusiastic hullabaloo of bathing young villagers, like a background of wild applause"—as though the bathers were a concord of witnesses to Nabokov's bravura performance, the memory feat which includes his bedazzling re-creation of them.

In addition to its qualities as a memoir, *Speak, Memory* serves, along with Chapter Five in *Gogol* (1944), as the ideal introduction to Nabokov's art, for some of the most lucid criticism of Nabokov is found in his own books. His most overtly parodic novels spiral in upon themselves and provide their own commentary; sections of *The Gift and The Real Life of Sebastian Knight* (1941) limpidly describe the narrative strategies of later novels. Nabokov's preoccupations are perhaps best projected by bringing together the opening and closing sentences of *Speak, Memory*: "The cradle rocks above an abyss, and common sense tells us that our existence is but a brief crack of light between two eternities of darkness." At the end of the book, he describes how he and his wife first perceived, through the stratagems thrown up to confound the eye, the ocean liner waiting to take them and their son to America: "It was most satisfying to make out among the jumbled angles of roofs and walls, a splendid ship's funnel, showing from behind the clothesline as something in a scrambled picture—Find What the Sailor Has Hidden—that the finder cannot unsee once it has been seen." *The Eye* is well-titled; the apprehension of "reality" (a word that Nabokov says must always have quotes around it) is first of all a miracle of vision, and our existence is a sequence of attempts to unscramble the "pictures" glimpsed in that "brief crack of light." Both art and nature are to Nabokov "a game of intricate enchantment and deception," and

the process of reading and rereading his novels is a game of perception, like those which E. H. Gombrich writes about in *Art and
Illusion*—everything is *there*, in sight (no symbols lurking in
murky depths), but one must penetrate the *trompe l'oeil*, which
eventually reveals something totally different from what one had
expected. This is how Nabokov seems to envision the game of life
and the effect of his novels: each time a "scrambled picture" has
been discerned "the finder cannot unsee" it; consciousness has
been expanded or created.

The word "game" commonly denotes frivolity and an escape
from the exigencies of the world, but Nabokov confronts the void
by virtue of his play-concept. His "game of worlds" (to quote
John Shade in *Pale Fire*) proceeds within the terrifyingly immu-
table limits defined by the "two eternities of darkness," and is a
search for order—for "some kind/Of correlated pattern in the
game"—which demands the full consciousness of its players. The
author and the reader are the "players," and when in *Speak,
Memory* Nabokov describes the composition of chess problems he
is also telescoping his fictional practices. If one responds to the
author's "false scents" and "specious lines of play," best effected
by parody, and believes, say, that Humbert's confession is "sin-
cere" and that he exorcises his guilt, or that the narrator of *Pnin*
is really perplexed by Pnin's animosity toward him, or that a Nabokov book is an illusion of a reality proceeding under the natural
laws of our world, then one has not only lost the game to the
author, but most likely is not faring too well in the "game of
worlds," one's own unscrambling of pictures.

Speak, Memory rehearses the major themes of Nabokov's
fiction: the confrontation of death; the withstanding of exile; the
search for complete consciousness and the "free world of timelessness." In the first chapter, he writes, "I have journeyed back in
thought—with thought hopelessly tapering off as I went—to remote regions where I groped for some secret outlet only to discover that the prison of time is spherical and without exits." Nabokov's protagonists live in claustrophobic, cell-like rooms, and
Humbert, Cincinnatus in *Invitation to a Beheading* (1936), and
Krug in *Bend Sinister* (1947) are all indeed imprisoned. The

struggle to escape from this spherical prison (Krug is Russian for "circle") assumes many forms throughout Nabokov, and his own desperate and sometimes ludicrous attempts, as described in *Speak, Memory*, are variously parodied in the poltergeist machinations of *The Eye*, Hazel Shade's involvement with "a domestic ghost" and her spirit-writing in the haunted barn in *Pale Fire*, and "The Vane Sisters" (in *Nabokov's Quartet* [1966]), where an acrostic in the final paragraph reveals that two vivid images from the story's opening paragraphs were dictated by the dead Vane sisters.

Although *Speak, Memory* clearly illuminates the self-parodic content of Nabokov's fiction, no one has fully recognized the aesthetic implications of these transmutations, or the extent to which Nabokov has consciously projected his own life in his fiction. To be sure, this is dangerous talk, easily misunderstood. Of course Nabokov does not write the kind of thinly disguised transcription of personal experience which too often passes for fiction. But it is crucial to an understanding of his art to realize how often his novels are improvisations on an autobiographic theme, and in *Speak, Memory* Nabokov good-naturedly anticipates his critics: "The future specialist in such dull literary lore as autoplagiarism will like to collate a protagonist's experience in my novel *The Gift* with the original event." Further on, he comments on his habit of bestowing "treasured items" from his past on his characters, but it is more than mere "items" that Nabokov has transmogrified in the "artificial world" of his novels, as a dull specialist discovers by comparing Chapters Eleven and Thirteen of *Speak, Memory* with *The Gift*, or, since it is Nabokov's overriding subject, by comparing the attitudes toward exile expressed in *Speak, Memory* with the treatment of it in his fiction. The reader of his memoir learns that Nabokov's great-grandfather explored and mapped Nova Zembla (where Nabokov's River is named after him), and in *Pale Fire* Kinbote believes himself to be the exiled King of Zembla. His is both a fantastic vision of Nabokov's opulent past, entertained by a madman, and of a poet's irreparable loss, expressed by Nabokov in 1945: "Beyond the seas where I have lost a sceptre,/I hear the neighing of my dappled nouns" ("An Evening of Russian Poetry"). Nabokov's avatars do not grieve for "lost banknotes." Their circumstances, though exacerbated by adversity, are not exclusive to the émigré. Exile is a correlative for all human loss, and Nabokov records with infinite tenderness the constrictions the heart must suffer; even in his most parodic novels, such as *Lolita*, he makes audible through all the playfulness a cry of pain. "Pity," says John Shade, "is the password." Nabokov's are emotional and spiritual exiles, turned back upon themselves, trapped by their obsessive memories and desires in a solipsistic "prison of mirrors" in which they cannot distinguish the glass from themselves (to use another prison trope, drawn from the story "The Assistant Producer" [1943], in *Nabokov's Dozen* [1958]).

The transcendence of solipsism is a central concern in Nabokov. He recommends no "escape," and there is an unmistakable moral resonance in his treatment of the theme; it is only at the outset of *Lolita* that Humbert can say that he had Lolita "Safely solipsized." The coldly unromantic scrutiny which his exiles endure is often overlooked by critics.

In *Pnin*, the gentle addlepated professor is seen in a new and harsh light in the final chapter, when the narrator assumes control and makes it clear that he is inheriting Pnin's job but not, he would hope, his existence. John Shade asks us to pity "the exile, the old man/Dying in a motel," and we do, but in the Commentary, Kinbote says that a "king who sinks his identity in the mirror of exile is guilty of [a regicide]." "The past is the past," Lolita tells Humbert at the end of the novel, when he asks her to relive what had always been inexorably lost. As a book about the spell exerted by the past, *Lolita* is Nabokov's own parodic answer to his previous book, the first edition of *Speak, Memory*. Mnemosyne is now seen as a black muse, nostalgia as a grotesque *cul-de-sac*. *Lolita* is the last book one would offer as "autobiographical," but even in its totally created form it connects with the deepest reaches of Nabokov's soul. Like the poet Fyodor in *The Gift*, Nabokov could say that while he keeps everything "on the very brink of parody . . . there must be on the other hand an abyss of seriousness, and I must make my way along this narrow ridge between my own truth and a caricature of it."

An autobiographic theme submitted to the imagination thus takes on a new life: frozen in art, halted in space, now timeless, it can be lived with. When the clownish Gradus assassinates John Shade by mistake, in a novel published 40 years after Nabokov's father was similarly murdered, one may remember the butterfly which the seven-year-old Nabokov caught and then lost, but which was "finally overtaken and captured, after a 40-year race, on an immigrant dandelion . . . near Boulder." One recognizes how art makes life possible for Nabokov, and why he calls *Invitation to a Beheading* a "violin in a void." His art records a constant process of *becoming*—the evolution of the artist's self through artistic creation—and the cycle of insect metamorphosis is Nabokov's controlling metaphor for the process, provided by a lifetime of biological investigations which established in his mind "links between butterflies and the central problems of nature." Significantly, a butterfly or moth will often appear at the end of a Nabokov novel, when the artistic "cycle" of that book is complete.

Speak, Memory only reinforces what is suggested by Nabokov's visibly active participation in the life of his fiction, as in *Invitation to a Beheading* when Cincinnatus strains to look out of his barred window, and sees on the prison wall the telling inscription, "You cannot see anything. I tried it too," written in the neat, recognizable hand of the "prison director"—that is, the author—whose intrusions involute the book, and deny it any reality except that of "book." Nabokov's remarks on Gogol help to define this involution. "All reality is a mask," he writes, and Nabokov's own narratives are masques, stagings of Nabokov's inventions rather than re-creations of the naturalistic world, and since the latter is what most readers expect and demand of fiction, many still do not understand what Nabokov is doing. They are not accustomed to "the allusions to something else behind the crudely painted scenes," where the "real plots behind the obvious ones are taking place." There are thus two "plots" in all of Nabokov's fiction: the characters in the book and the consciousness of the creator above it—the "real plot" which is visible in the "gaps" and "holes" in the narrative. These are best described in *Speak, Memory*, when

Nabokov discusses "the loneliest and most arrogant" of the émigré writers, Sirin (his émigré pen-name): "The real life of his books flowed in his figures of speech, which one critic [Nabokov?] has compared to windows giving upon a contiguous world . . . a rolling corollary, the shadow of a train of thought." The contiguous world is the mind and spirit of the author, whose identity, psychic survival, and "manifold awareness" is ultimately both the subject and the product of the book. In whatever way they are opened, the "windows" always reveal that "the poet (sitting in a lawn chair, at Ithaca, N. Y.) is the nucleus" of everything.

From its birth in *King, Queen, Knave* (1928), to its full maturation in *Invitation to a Beheading* (1936), to its apotheosis in the "involute abode" of *Pale Fire* (1962), the strategy of involution has determined the structure and meaning of Nabokov's novels. One must always be aware of the imprint of "that master thumb," to quote Frank Lane in *Pale Fire*, "that made the whole involuted boggling thing one beautiful straight line," for only then does it become possible to see how the "obvious plots" spiral in and out of the "real" ones. Not including autobiographic themes, the involution is achieved in six basic ways, all closely interrelated, but schematized here for the sake of clarity:

PARODY

As willful artifice, parody provides the main basis for Nabokov's involution, the "springboard for leaping into the highest region of serious emotion," as the narrator of *The Real Life of Sebastian Knight* says of Knight's novels. Because its referents are either other works of art or itself, parody denies the possibility of a naturalistic fiction. Only an authorial sensibility can be responsible for the texture of parody and self-parody; it is a verbal vaudeville, a series of literary impersonations performed by the author. When Nabokov calls a character or even a window shade "a parody," it is in the sense that his creation can possess no other "reality." In a novel such as *Lolita*, which has the fewest "gaps" and is seemingly his most realistic of any novel after *Despair* (1934), the involution is sustained by the parody and the verbal patterning.

COINCIDENCE

Speak, Memory is filled with examples of Nabokov's love of coincidence. Because they are drawn from his life, these incidents demonstrate how Nabokov's imagination responds to coincidence, using it in his fiction to trace the pattern of a life's design, to achieve shattering interpenetrations of space and time. Humbert goes to live in Charlotte Haze's house at 342 Lawn Street; he and Lolita inaugurate their illicit cross-country tour in room 342 of The Enchanted Hunters hotel; and in one year on the road they register in 342 motels and hotels. Given the endless mathematical combinations possible, the numbers seem to signal his entrapment by McFate (to use Humbert's personification). But they are also a patent, purposeful contrivance, like the copy of the 1946 *Who's Who in the Limelight* which Humbert would have us believe he found in the prison library on the night previous to his writing the chapter we are now reading. The yearbook not only prefigures the novel's action, but under Lolita's mock-entry of "Dolores Quine," we are informed that she "Made New York debut in 1904 in *Never Talk to Strangers*"—and in the closing paragraph of the novel, almost three hundred pages later, Humbert advises the absent Lolita, "Do not talk to strangers," a detail that exhibits extraordinary narrative control for an allegedly unrevised, first draft confessional, written during 56 chaotic days. Clearly, "Someone else is in the know," to quote a mysterious voice that interrupts the narration of *Bend Sinister*. It is no coincidence when coincidences extend from book to book. Creations from one "reality" continually turn up in another: the imaginary writer Pierre Delalande is quoted in *The Gift*, and provides the epigraph for *Invitation to a Beheading* (inadvertently omitted from the paperback edition); Pnin and another character mention "Vladimir Vladimirovich" and dismiss his entomology as an affectation; "Hurricane Lolita" is mentioned in *Pale Fire*, and Pnin is glimpsed in the university library. Mythic or prosaic names and certain fatidic numbers recur with slight variation in many books, carrying no burden of meaning whatsoever other than the fact that someone beyond the work is repeating them, that they are all part of one master pattern.

PATTERNING

Nabokov's passion for chess, language, and lepidoptery has inspired the most elaborately involuted patterning in his work. Like the games implemented by parody, the puns, anagrams, and spoonerisms all reveal the controlling hand of the logomachist; thematically, they are appropriate to the prison of mirrors. Chess motifs are woven into several narratives, and even in *The Defense* (1930), a most naturalistically ordered early novel, the chess patterning points to forces beyond Grandmaster Luzhin's comprehension ("Thus toward the end of Chapter Four an unexpected move is made by me in a corner of the board," writes Nabokov in the Foreword). The importance of the lepidopteral motif has already been suggested, and it spirals freely in and out of Nabokov's books: in *Invitation to a Beheading*, just before he is scheduled to die, Cincinnatus gently strokes a giant moth; in *Pale Fire*, a butterfly alights on John Shade's arm the minute before he is killed; and at the end of *Bend Sinister*, the masked author intrudes and suspends the "obvious plot" and, as the book closes, he looks out of the window and decides, as a moth twangs against the screen, that it is "A good night for mothing." *Bend Sinister* was published in 1947, and it is no accident that in Nabokov's next novel (1955), Humbert meets Lolita back in 1947, thus sustaining the author's "fictive time" without interruption, enabling him to pursue that moth's lovely diurnal Double through the substratum of the new novel in the most fantastic butterfly hunt of his career. "I confess I do not believe in time," writes Nabokov at the end of the ecstatic butterfly chapter in *Speak, Memory*. "I like to fold my magic carpet, after use, in such a way as to superimpose one part of the pattern upon another."

THE WORK WITHIN THE WORK

The self-referential devices in Nabokov, mirrors inserted into the book at oblique angles, are clearly of the author's making since no point of view within the fiction could possibly account for the dizzying inversions which they create. The course of *The Real Life of Sebastian Knight*, which purports to be an attempt to gather material for a proposed literary biography of the narrator's half-brother but ends by obfuscating even the narrator's identity, is refracted in Knight's first novel, *The Prismatic Bezel*, "a rollicking parody of the setting of a detective tale." Like an Elizabethan play within a play, Quilty's play within *Lolita*, *The Enchanted Hunters*, offers a "message" that can be taken seriously as a commentary on the progression of the entire novel, and *Who's Who in the Limelight* and the class list of the Ramsdale School magically mirror the action taking place around them, including, by implication, the writing of *Lolita*. The a-novelistic components of *Pale Fire*—Foreword, Poem, Commentary, and Index—create a mirror-lined labyrinth of involuted cross-references, a closed cosmos that only can be of the author's making, rather than the product of an "unreliable" narrator. *Pale Fire* realizes the ultimate possibilities of works within works, already present 24 years earlier in the literary biography that serves as the fourth chapter of *The Gift*. If it is disturbing to discover that the characters in *The Gift* are also the readers of Chapter Four, it is because this suggests, as Jorge Luis Borges says of the play within *Hamlet*, "that if the characters of a fictional work can be readers or spectators, we, its readers or spectators, can be fictitious."

THE STAGING OF THE NOVEL

Nabokov wrote the screenplay of *Lolita*, as well as nine plays in Russian, including one of his several forays into science fiction, *The Waltz Invention* (1938), which was translated and published in 1966. It is not surprising, then, that his novels should proliferate with "theatrical" effects that serve his play-spirit exceedingly well. Problems of identity can be investigated poetically by trying on and discarding a series of masks. Moreover, what better way to demonstrate that everything in a book is being manipulated than by seeming to stage it? In *Invitation to a Beheading*, "A Summer thunderstorm, simply yet tastefully staged, was performed outside." When Quilty finally dies in *Lolita*, Humbert says, "This was

the end of the ingenious play staged for me by Quilty," and in
Laughter in the Dark (1932), "The stage manager whom Rex
had in view was an elusive, double, triple, self-reflecting Proteus."
Nabokov the protean impersonator is always a masked presence in
his fiction: as impresario, scenarist, director, warden, dictator, landlord, actor, and even as bit player (the seventh Hunter in Quilty's
play within *Lolita*, a Young Poet who insists that everything in
the play is his invention)—to name only a few of the disguises
he has donned as a secret agent who moves among his own creations like Prospero in *The Tempest*. Shakespeare is very much an
ancestor, and the creaking, splintering noises made by the stage-
setting as it disintegrates at the end of *Invitation to a Beheading*
is Nabokov's version of the snapping of Prospero's wand, and his
speech to the players ("Our revels now are ended. These our
actors,/ As I foretold you, were all spirits and/ Are melted into
air, thin air"; IV. i).

AUTHORIAL VOICE

All the involuted effects spiral into the authorial voice—"an
anthropomorphic deity impersonated by me," Nabokov calls it—
which intrudes continually in all of his novels after *Despair*, most
strikingly at the end, when it completely takes over the book
(*Lolita* is a notable exception). It is this "deity" who is responsible for everything: who begins a narrative only to stop and retell
the passage differently; halts a scene to "rerun" it on the chapter's
screen, or turns a reversed lantern slide around to project it
properly; intrudes to give stage directions, to compliment or exhort
the actors, to have a prop moved; who reveals that the characters
have "cotton-padded bodies" and are the author's puppets, that
all is a fiction; and who widens the "gaps" and "holes" in the
narrative until it breaks apart at "the end," when the vectors are
removed, the cast of characters is dismissed, and even the fiction
fades away, at most leaving behind an imprint on space in the
form of the "deity's" précis of "an old-fashioned [stage] melodrama" he may one day write, and which describes *Pale Fire*, the
book we've just finished reading.

The vertiginous conclusion of a Nabokov novel calls for a complicated response which many readers, after a lifetime of realistic novels, are incapable of making. Children, however, are aware of other possibilities, as their art reveals. My own children, then three and six years old, reminded me of this three summers ago when they inadvertently demonstrated that, unless they change, they will be among Nabokov's ideal readers. One afternoon, my wife and I built them a puppet theatre. After propping the theatre on the top edge of the living room couch, I crouched down behind it and began manipulating the two hand puppets in the theatre above me. The couch and the theatre's scenery provided good cover, enabling me to peer over the edge and watch the children immediately become engrossed in the show, and then virtually mesmerized by my improvised little story that ended with a patient father spanking an impossible child. But the puppeteer, carried away by his story's violent climax, knocked over the entire theatre, which clattered onto the floor, collapsing into a heap of cardboard, wood, and cloth—leaving me crouched, peeking out at the room, my head now visible over the couch's rim, my puppeted hands, with their naked wrists, poised in mid-air. For several moments my children remained in their open-mouthed trance, still in the story, staring at the space where the theatre had been, not seeing me at all. Then they did the kind of double-take that a comedian might take a lifetime to perfect, and began to laugh uncontrollably, in a way I had never seen before, and not so much at my clumsiness, which was nothing new, but rather at those moments of total involvement in a non-existent world, and at what its collapse implied to them about the authenticity of the larger world, and their daily efforts to order it and their own fabricated illusions. They were laughing too over their sense of what the vigorous performance had meant to me, but they saw how easily they could be tricked and their trust belied, and the shrillness of their laughter finally suggested that they recognized the frightening implications of what had happened, and that only laughter could steel them in their new awareness.

When in 1966 I visited Vladimir Nabokov for four days in Montreux, Switzerland, to interview him for *Wisconsin Studies* and in regard to my critical study of his work, I told him about this incident, and how for me it defined literary involution and the response which he hoped to elicit from his readers at "the end" of a novel. "Exactly, exactly," he said as I finished. "You must put that in your book."

By parodying the reader's complete, self-indulgent identification with a character, which in its mindlessness limits consciousness, Nabokov is able to create the detachment necessary for a multi-form, spatial view of his novels. The reader of *Pale Fire* then may see that the fatuous locutions in annotator Kinbote's monstrously presumptive analysis of Shade's poem inform but one of four distinctive voices in a shifting sequence of "serial selves": the self seen by the world, a construct whose assumed name and distracting scholarly labors conceal the terror and despair experienced by another self, Botkin, who "live[s] like Timon in his cave," and whose anguished voice every so often surfaces through the unintentional comedy of Kinbote's compensatory, royal ravings —to plea, "Dear Jesus, do something," or moan, "Migraine again worse today," or debate with its anagrammatic self the efficacy or means of suicide. And at the end of *Pale Fire*, the "voices" are all absorbed by the authorial voice which, by suspending the fiction altogether and *then* providing an Index, demonstrates the author's command of the book, and his outdistancing of Botkin's "nightfall of the mind." From the Index, the reader moves to a global view of the novel. Seen from all sides, its four dimensions of sensory perception, memory, imagination, and death are perceived as instantaneous: Botkin, Kinbote, King Charles, and, surrounding their "death-padded life," Gradus, a jet-propelled Angel of Death—an idea and an actuality who casts his shadow across the entire book, its creations and creator. The "two plots" in Nabokov's puppet show are thus made plainly visible, describing the total design of his work, which reveals that in novel after novel his characters try to escape from Nabokov's prison of mirrors, engaging in a struggle toward a self-awareness that only their creator has achieved by creating them—an involuted process which connects his art with his life, and clearly indicates that the author himself is not in this prison, but is its creator, and is *above* it, in control of a book, as in one of those Saul Steinberg drawings (greatly admired by Nabokov) in which a man is seen to be drawing the very line that gives him "life," in the fullest sense. But the process of Nabokov's involution, the global perspective which he invites us to share with him in a novel such as *Pale Fire*, is best described in *Speak, Memory,* Chapter Fifteen, when Nabokov comments on the disinclination of

. . . physicists to discuss the outside of the inside, the whereabouts of the curvature; for every dimension presupposes a medium within which it can act, and if, in the spiral unwinding of things, space warps into something akin to time, and time, in its turn, warps into something akin to thought, then, surely, another dimension follows —a special Space maybe, not the old one, we trust, unless spirals become vicious circles again.

The ultimate detachment of an "outside" view of a novel inspires our wonder and enlarges our potential for compassion because, "in the spiral unwinding of things," such compassion is extended to include the mind of an author whose deeply humanistic art affirms man's ability to confront and order chaos.

5 Leonard Cohen

Poet, novelist, songwriter, and singer Leonard Cohen was born in Montreal and was graduated from McGill University in 1955. His second novel, Beautiful Losers (1966), is one of the liveliest books of the postwar era and is perhaps the first truly revolutionary novel.

❖

CHARLES AXIS
(FROM *BEAUTIFUL LOSERS*)

I will explain how F. got his extraordinary body. Once again I will explain it to myself. HOW JOE'S BODY BROUGHT HIM *FAME* INSTEAD OF *SHAME*: headline on the back of an American comic which we both read one afternoon when we were thirteen. We were sitting on some trunks in an unused solarium on the third floor of the orphanage, a glass-roofed room dark as any other because of the soot deposited by a badly placed chimney—we often hid here. JOE'S BODY was the concern of an ad for a muscle-building course. His triumph is traced in seven cartoon panels. Can I recall?

1. Joe is skeletal. His legs are piteous sticks. His red bathing suit is the baggy boxer type. His voluptuous girl friend is with him. Her thighs are thicker than his. The calm sea beyond contrasts with Joe's ordeal. A man with a grand physique is humiliating him. We cannot see the torturer's face, but the girl informs Joe that the man is a well-known local nuisance.

2. A tiny sail has appeared on the horizon. We see the bully's face. We appreciate his beery chest. The girl friend has drawn up

her knees and is wondering why she ever dated this no-assed weakling. Joe has been pulled to his feet by the bully and now must sustain a further insult.

3. The sail is gone. Some minuscule figures play ball at the edge of the sea. Seagulls appear. An anguished Joe stands beside the girl he is losing. She has put on her white sunhat and has turned her tits from him. She answers him over her right shoulder. Her body is massive and maternal, low-breasted. Somehow we have an impression of stretched muscles in her abdomen.

JOE: The big bully! I'll get even some day.

HER: Oh, don't let it *bother* you, little boy!

4. Joe's room, or the remains of it. A cracked picture hangs askew on the green wall. A broken lamp is in motion. He is kicking a chair over. He wears a blue blazer, tie, white ducks. He clenches his fist, a clawlike articulation from a wrist thin as a bird leg. The girl friend lies in some panel of the imagination snuggling in the bully's armpit, winking out a thousand shameful anecdotes about Joe's body.

JOE: Darn it! I'm sick and tired of being a scarecrow! Charles Axis says he can give me a REAL body. All right! I'll gamble a stamp and get his FREE book.

5. LATER. Could this be Joe? He flexes a whole map of jigsaw muscles before his dresser mirror.

JOE: Boy! It didn't take Axis long to do this for me! What MUSCLES! That bully won't shove me around again!

Is this the same red bathing suit?

6. The beach. The girl has come back. She is having a good time. Her body is relaxed and hips have appeared. Her left hand is raised in a gesture of surprised delight as her vision of Joe undergoes a radical transformation. Joe has just thrown a punch which lands in an electrical blaze on the bully's chin, knocking him off balance, knitting his eyebrows with amazed pain. Beyond we have the same white strand, the same calm sea.

JOE: What! You here again? Here's something I owe you!

7. The girl touches Joe's memorable biceps with her right hand. Her left shoulder and left arm are obscured by Joe's massive chest but we know that she has shoved it down the back of his tight red bathing suit and is working with his testicles.

HER: Oh, Joe! You ARE a real man after all!

AN ATTRACTIVE GIRL SITTING ON THE SAND NEARBY: GOSH! What a build!

THE ENVIOUS MAN BESIDE HER: He's already famous for it!

Joe stands there in silence, thumbs hooked in the front of his bathing suit, looking at his girl, who leans lasciviously against him. Four thick black words appear in the sky and they radiate spears of light. None of the characters in the panel seems aware of the celestial manifestation exploding in terrific silence above the old marine landscape. HERO OF THE BEACH is the sky's announcement.

F. studied the ad for a long time. I wanted to get on with what we had come for, the scuffling, the dusty caresses, the comparison of hair, the beauty of facing a friend and binding two cocks in my hands, one familiar and hungry, one warm and strange, the flash along the whole length. But F.'s eyes were wet, his lips trembling as he whispered:

—Those words are always in the sky. Sometimes you can see them, like a daytime moon.

The afternoon darkened over the soot-layered glass roof. I waited silently for F.'s mood to change and I suppose I fell asleep, for I started at the sound of scissors.

—What are you clipping out there, F.?

—Charles Axis thing.

—You going to send away?

—Bet your fucking life.

—But it's for thin guys. We're fat.

—Shut your fucking face.

—We're fat, F.

—Smack! Wham! Pow!

—Fat.

—Socko! Sok! Bash!

—Fat fat fat fat fat fat fat!

I lit a stolen match and we both huddled over the comic which had fallen to the floor. At the right-hand side of the ad there is an actual photo of the man who holds the title "The World's Most Flawlessly Formed Man." Oh! I remember! In a flawless bathing suit he stands on the clip-away coupon.

—But look at him, F., the guy's got no hair.

—But *I* have hair. *I* have hair.

His hands are fists, his smile is Florida, he does not look serious, he doesn't really care about us, maybe he is even a little fat.

—Just inspect this photo, F. The guy is soft in the gut.

—He's fat, all right.

—But—

—He's fat. He understands the fat. Use your eyes! Look at his face. Now look at Plastic Man's face. Charles Axis wants to be our uncle. He is one of us slobs who dwells pages behind Plastic Man. But can't you see that he has made his peace with Plastic Man? With Blue Beetle? With Captain Marvel? Can't you see that he believes in the super-world?

—F., I don't like it when your eyes get shiny like that.

—The Fat! The Fat! He's one of us! Charles Axis is on our side! He's with us against Blue Beetle and Ibis and Wonder Woman!

—F., you're talking funny again.

—Charles Axis has an address in New York, look, 405 West 34th St., New York 1! Don't you think he knows about Krypton? Don't you see him suffering on the outer limits of the Bat Cave? Has anyone ever lived so close to fantastic imaginary muscles?

—F.!

—Charles Axis is all compassion, he's our sacrifice! He calls the thin but he means both the fat and the thin; he calls the thin because it is worse to be fat than thin; he calls the thin so that the fat can hear and come and not be named!

—Get away from that window!

—Charles! Charles! Charles! I'm coming, I'm coming to be with you at the sad edge of the spirit world!

—F.! Uppercut! Sok! Thud!

—Puff! *#\#! Sob! Thank you, my friend, I guess you kinda saved my life.

That was the last time I ever equaled F. in a physical contest. He gave Charles Axis fifteen minutes a day in the privacy of his room. Fat fell away or turned to muscle, he increased his chest measurement, he was not ashamed to strip for sports. Once on the beach a huge man in a very white bathing suit kicked sand in his face as we sat sunbathing on a small towel. F. merely smiled. The huge man stood there, hands on hips, then he performed a little hop and jump, like a soccer kickoff, and kicked sand in his face once again.

—Hey! I cried: Quit kicking that sand in our faces! F., I whispered: That man is the worst nuisance on the beach.

The bully ignored me completely. He seized F.'s thick hard wrist in his own massive fist and yanked F. to a standing position.

—Listen here, he snarled, I'd smash your face . . . only you're so skinny you might dry up and blow away.

—Why did you let him shove you around?

F. sat down meekly as the man strode away.

—That was Charles Axis.

—But that man is the worst nuisance on the beach.

⑥ Saul Bellow

Saul Bellow was born in Lachine, Quebec, in 1915 and grew up in Chicago. He served in the merchant marine during World War II. He has published six novels—Dangling Man (1944), The Victim (1947), The Adventures of Augie March (1953), Seize the Day (1956), Henderson the Rain King (1959), and Herzog (1964). Never cruel, Bellow is one of the few writers of our time who has managed to combine in his work great wit, intelligence, and pathos. The late Richard Chase said of Bellow's Henderson: "Once he is in Africa, we see him in episodes which make us think him the momentary equal, for tragicomic madness, for divine insanity, of the greatest heroes of comic fiction."

◈

SMOLAK
(FROM *HENDERSON THE RAIN KING*)

Romilayu started to protest, but I held the creature to me, hearing its tiny snarl and pricked in the chest by its claws. "The king would want me to take it along," I said. "Look, he's got to survive in some form. Can't you see?" The moonlit horizon was extremely clear. It had the effect of making me feel logical. Light was released over us from the summits of the mountains. Thirty miles of terrain opened before us, the path of our flight. I suppose that Romilayu could have pointed out to me that this animal was the child of my enemy who had deprived me of Dahfu. "Well, so look," I said, "I didn't kill that guy. So if I spared him . . . Romilayu, let's not stand here and gab. I can't leave the animal behind and I won't. Look," I said, "I can carry it in my helmet. I don't need it at night." As a matter of fact the night breeze was doing my fever good.

Romilayu gave in to me, and we started our flight, leaping through the shadows of the moon up the side of the ravine. We put the hopo between ourselves and the town, and headed into the mountains, on a straight course for Baventai. I ran behind with the cub, and all that night we did double time, so that by sunrise we had about twenty miles behind us.

Without Romilayu I couldn't have lasted two of the ten days that it took to reach Baventai. He knew where the water was and which roots and insects we could eat. After the yams gave out, as they did on the fourth day, we had to forage for grubs and worms. "You could be a survival instructor for the Air Force," I told him. "You'd be a jewel to them," I also said to him. "So at last I'm living on locusts, like Saint John. 'The voice of one that crieth in the wilderness.'" But we had this lion, which had to be fed and cared for. I doubt whether any such handicap was ever seen before. I had to mince grubs and worms with the knife in my palm and make a paste, and I fed the little creature by hand. During the day, when I had to have the helmet, I carried the cub under my arm, and sometimes I led him on the leash. He slept in the helmet, too, with my wallet and passport, teething on the leather and in the end devouring most of it. I then carried my documents and the four one-thousand-dollar bills inside my jockey shorts.

From gaunt cheeks, my whiskers grew in various colors, and during most of the trek I was demented and raving. I would sit and play with the cub, whom I named Dahfu, while Romilayu foraged. I was too simple in the head to help him. Nevertheless, in many essential matters my mind was very clear and even fine or delicate. As I ate the cocoons and the larvae and ants, crouching in the jockey shorts with the lion lying under me for shade, I spoke oracles and sang—yes, I remembered many songs from nursery and school, like "Fair do-do," "Pierrot," "Malbrouck s'en va-t'en guerre," "Nut Brown Maiden," and "The Spanish Guitar," while I fondled the animal, which had made a wonderful adjustment to me. He rolled between my feet and scratched my legs. Although on a diet of worms and grubs he could not have been very healthy. I feared and Romilayu hoped that the animal would die. But we were lucky. We had the spears and Romilayu killed a few birds. I am pretty sure we killed a bird of prey that had got too near and that we feasted on it.

And on the tenth day (as Romilayu told me afterward, for I had lost count) we came to Baventai, sitting parched on its rocks, but not so parched as we were. The walls were white as eggs, and the brown Arabs in their clothes and muffles watched us arise from the sterile road, myself greeting everyone with two fingers for victory, like Churchill, and giving a cracked, crying, black-throated laugh of survival, holding out the cub Dahfu by the scruff to all those head-swathed and silent men, and the women who revealed only eyes, and the black herdsmen with sunny fat melting from their hair. "Get the band. Get the music," I was saying to them all.

Pretty soon I folded, but I made Romilayu promise to look out for the little animal. "This is Dahfu to me," I said. "Don't let anything happen, please, Romilayu. It would ruin me now. I can't threaten you, old fellow," I said. "I'm too weak, and I can only beg."

Romilayu said I shouldn't worry. At least he told me, "Wo-kay, sah."

"I can beg," I said to him. "I'm not what I thought I was."

"One thing, Romilayu . . ." I was in a native house and lying on a bed while he, squatting beside me, took the animal from my arms. "Is it promised? Between the beginning and the end, is it promised?"

"Whut promise, sah?"

"Well, I mean something *clear*. Isn't it promised? Romilayu, I suppose I mean the reason—*the* reason. It may be postponed until the last breath. But there is justice. I believe there is justice, and that much is promised. Though I am not what I thought."

Romilayu was about to console me, but I said to him, "You don't have to give me consolation. Because the sleep is burst, and I've come to myself. It wasn't the singing of boys that did it," I said. "What I'd like to know is why this has to be fought by everybody, for there is nothing that's struggled against so hard as coming-to. We grow these sores instead. Burning sores, fertile sores." I held the lion on my breast, the child of our murderous enemy. Because of my weakness and fatigue, I was reduced to grimacing at Romilayu. "Don't let me down, old pal," was what I tried to say.

Then I let him take the animal from me and I slept for a while and had dreams, or I didn't sleep but lay on the cot in somebody's house, and those were not dreams but hallucinations. One thing however I kept saying to myself and telling Romilayu, and this was that I had to get back to Lily and the children; I would never feel right until I saw them, and especially Lily herself. I developed a bad case of homesickness. For I said, What's the universe? Big. And what are we? Little. I therefore might as well be at home where my wife loves me. And even if she only seemed to love me, that too was better than nothing. Either way, I had tender feelings toward her. I remembered her in a variety of ways; some of her sayings came back to me, like one should live for this and not for that; not evil but good, not death but life, and all the rest of her theories. But I suppose it made no difference what she said, I wouldn't be kept from loving her even by her preaching. Frequently Romilayu came up to me, and in the worst of my delirium his black face seemed to me like shatter-proof glass to which everything had been done that glass can endure.

"Oh, you can't get away from rhythm, Romilayu," I recall saying many times to him. "You just can't get away from it. The left hand shakes with the right hand, the inhale follows the exhale, the systole talks back to the diastole, the hands play patty-cake, and the feet dance with each other. And the seasons. And the stars, and all of that. And the tides, and all that junk. You've got to live at peace with it, because if it's going to worry you, you'll lose. You can't win against it. It keeps on and on and on. Hell, we'll never get away from rhythm, Romilayu. I wish my dead days would quit bothering me and leave me alone. The bad stuff keeps coming back, and it's the worst rhythm there is. The repetition of a man's bad self, that's the worst suffering that's ever been known. But you can't get away from regularity. But the king said I should change. I shouldn't be an agony type. Or a Lazarus type. The grass should be my cousins. Hey, Romilayu, not even Death knows how many dead there are. He could never run a census. But these dead should go. They make us think of them. That is their immortality. In us. But my back is breaking. I'm loaded down. It isn't fair—what about the grun-tu-molani?"

He showed me the little creature. It had survived all the hardships and was thriving like anything.

So after several weeks in Baventai, beginning to recover, I said to my guide, "Well, kid, I suppose I'd better get moving while the cub is still small. I can't wait till he grows into a lion, can I? It will be a job to get him back to the States even if he's half grown."

"No, no. You too sick, sah."

And I said, "Yes, the flesh is not in such hot shape. But I will beat this rap. It's merely some disease. Otherwise, I'm well."

Romilayu was much opposed but I made him take me in the end to Baktale. There I bought a pair of pants and the missionary let me have some sulfa until my dysentery was under control. That took a few days. After this I slept in the back of the jeep with the lion cub under a khaki blanket, while Romilayu drove us to Harar, Ethiopia. That took six days. And in Harar I made Romilayu a few hundred dollars' worth of presents. I filled the jeep with all sorts of stuff.

"I was going to stop over in Switzerland and visit my little daughter Alice," I said. "My youngest girl. But I guess I don't look well, and there's no use frightening the kid. I'd better do it another time. Besides, there's the cub."

"You tek him home?"

"Where I go he goes," I said. "And Romilayu, you and I will get together again one day. The world is not so loose any more. You can locate a man, provided he stays alive. You have my address. Write to me. Don't take it so hard. Next time we meet I may be wearing a white coat. You'll be proud of me. I'll treat you for nothing."

"Oh, you too weak to go, sah," said Romilayu. "I 'fraid to leave you go."

I took it every bit as hard as he did.

"Listen to me, Romilayu, I'm unkillable. Nature has tried everything. It has thrown the book at me. And here I am."

He saw, however, that I was feeble. You could have tied me up with a ribbon of haze.

And after we had said good-by, finally, for good, I realized that he still dogged my steps and kept an eye on me from a distance as I went around Harar with the cub. My legs quaked, my beard was like the purple sage, and I was sightseeing in front of the old King Menelik's palace, accompanied by the lion, while bushy Romilayu, fear and anxiety in his face, watched from around the corner to make sure I didn't collapse. For his own good I paid no attention to him. When I boarded the plane he still was observing me. It was the Khartoum flight and the lion was in a wicker basket. The jeep was beside the airstrip and Romilayu was in it, praying at the wheel. He held together his hands like giant crayfish and I knew he was doing his utmost to obtain safety and well-being for me. I cried, "Romilayu!" and stood up. Several of the passengers seemed to think I was about to overturn the small plane. "That black fellow saved my life," I said to them.

However, we were now in the air, flying over the shadows of the heat. I then sat down and brought out the lion, holding him in my lap.

In Khartoum I had a hassel with the consular people about arrangements. There was quite a squawk about the lion. They said there were people who were in the business of selling zoo animals in the States, and they told me if I didn't go about it in the right way the lion would have to be in quarantine. I said I was willing to go to a vet and get some shots, but I told them, "I'm in a hurry to get home. I've been sick and I can't stand any delay." The guys said they could see for themselves that I had been through quite a bit. They tried to pump me about my trip, and asked how I had lost all my stuff. "It's none of your lousy business," I said. "My passport is okay, isn't it? And I've got dough. My great-grandfather was head of your crummy outfit, and he was no cold-storage, Ivy League, button-down, broken-hipped civilian like you. All you fellows are just the same. You think U.S. citizens are dummies and morons. Listen, all I want from you is to expedite— Yes, I saw a few things in the interior. Yes, I did. I have had a look into some of the fundamentals, but don't expect me to tickle your idle curiosity. I wouldn't talk even to the ambassador, if he asked me."

They didn't like this. I had the staggers in their office. The lion was on the fellows' desk and knocked down their stapler and nipped them through the clothes. They got rid of me the fastest way they could, and I flew into Cairo that same evening. There

I called Lily on the transatlantic phone. "It's me, baby," I cried. "I'm coming home Sunday." I knew she must be pale and going paler, purer and purer in the face as she always did under great excitement, and that her lips must have moved five or six times before she could get out a word. "Baby, I'm coming home," I said. "Speak clearly, don't mumble now." "Gene!" I heard, and after that the waves of half the world, the air, the water, the earth's vascular system, came in between. "Honey, I aim to do better, can you hear? I've had it now." Of what she said I could make out no more than two or three words. Space with its weird cries came between. I knew she was speaking about love; her voice thrilled, and I guessed she was moralizing and calling me back. "For a big broad you sound very tiny," I kept saying. She could hear me all right. "Sunday, Idlewild. Bring Donovan," I said. This Donovan is an old lawyer who was a trustee of my father's estate. He must be eighty now. I thought I might need his legal help on account of the lion.

This was Wednesday. On Thursday we flew to Athens. I thought I should see the Acropolis. So I hired a car and a guide, but I was too ill and in too much confusion to take in very much of it. The lion was with us, on a leash, and except for the suntans I had bought in Baktale I was dressed as in Africa, same helmet, same rubber shoes. My beard had grown out considerably; on one side it gushed out half white but with many streaks of blond, red, black, and purple. The embassy people had suggested a shave to make identification easier from the passport. But I did not take their advice. As far as the Acropolis went, I saw something on the heights, which was yellow, bonelike, rose-colored. I realized it must be very beautiful. But I couldn't get out of the automobile, and the guide didn't even suggest it. Altogether he said very little, almost nothing; however, his eyes showed what he thought. "There are reasons for it all," I said to him.

On Friday I got to Rome. I bought a corduroy outfit, burgundy colored, and an alpine hat with Bersagliere feathers, plus a shirt and underpants. Except to buy this stuff I didn't leave my room. I wasn't eager to make a show of myself on the Via Veneto walking the cub on a leash.

On Saturday we flew again by way of Paris and London, which

was the only arrangement I could make. To see either place again
I had no curiosity. Or any other place, for that matter. For me
the best part of the flight was over water. I couldn't seem to get
enough of it, as if I had been dehydrated—the water, combing
along, endless, the Atlantic, deep. But the depth made me happy.
I sat by the window, in the clouds. The sea was thickened by the
late, awful, air-blind, sea-blanched sun. We were carried over the
calm swarm of the water, the lead-sealed but expanding water, the
heart of the water.

Other passengers were reading. Personally, I can't see that.
How can you sit in a plane and be so indifferent? Of course, they
weren't coming from mid-Africa like me; they weren't discontinu-
ous with civilization. They arose from Paris and London into the
skies with their books. But I, Henderson, with my glowering face,
with corduroy and Bersagliere feathers—the helmet was inside the
wicker basket with the cub, as I figured he needed a familiar object
to calm him on this novel, exciting trip—I couldn't get enough of
the water, and of these upside-down sierras of the clouds. Like
courts of eternal heaven. (Only they aren't eternal, that's the
whole thing; they are seen once and never seen again, being
figures and not abiding realities; Dahfu will never be seen again,
and presently I will never be seen again; but every one is given
the components to see: the water, the sun, the air, the earth.)

The stewardess offered me a magazine to calm me down, seeing
how overwrought I was. She was aware that I had the lion cub
Dahfu in the baggage compartment, as I had ordered chops and
milk for him, and there was a certain inconvenience about my
going back and forth constantly and prowling around the rear of
the plane. She was an understanding girl, and finally I told her
what it was all about, that the lion cub was important to me, and
that I was bringing him home to my wife and children. "It's a
souvenir of a very dear friend," I said. It was also an enigmatic
form of that friend, I might have tried to explain to this girl. She
was from Rockford, Illinois. Every twenty years or so the earth
renews itself in young maidens. You know what I mean? Her
cheeks had the perfect form that belongs to the young; her hair
was kinky gold. Her teeth were white and posted on every approach. She was all sweet corn and milk. Blessings on her hips.

Blessings on her thighs. Blessings on her soft little fingers which were somewhat covered by the cuffs of her uniform. Blessings on that rough gold. A wonderful little thing; her attitude was that of a pal or playmate, as is common with Midwestern young women. I said, "You make me think of my wife. I haven't seen her in months."

"Oh? How many months?" she said.

That I couldn't tell her, for I didn't know the date. "Is it about September?" I asked.

Astonished, she said, "Honestly, don't you know? It'll be Thanksgiving next week."

"So late! I missed out on enrollment. I'll have to wait until next semester. You see, I got sick in Africa and had a delirium and lost count of time. When you go in deep you run that risk, you know that, don't you, kid?"

She was amused that I called her kid.

"Do you go to school?"

"Instead of coming to ourselves," I said, "we grow all kinds of deformities and enormities. At least something can be done for those. You know? While we wait for the day?"

"Which day, Mr. Henderson?" she said, laughing at me.

"Haven't you ever heard the song?" I said. "Listen, and I'll sing you a little of it." We were back at the rear of the plane where I was feeding the animal Dahfu. I sang, "And who shall abide the day of His coming (the day of His coming)? And who shall stand when He appeareth (when He appeareth)?"

"That is Handel?" she said. "That's from Rockford College."

"Correct," I said. "You are a sensible young woman. Now I have a son, Edward, whose wits were swamped by all that cool jazz. . . . I slept through my youth," I went on as I was feeding the lion his cooked meat. "I slept and slept like our first-class passenger." Note: I must explain that we were on one of those stratocruisers with a regular stateroom, and I had noticed the stewardess going in there with steak and champagne. The fellow never came out. She told me he was a famous diplomat. "I guess he just has to sleep, it's costing so much," I commented. "If he has insomnia it'll be a terrible let-down to a man in his position. You know why I'm impatient to see my wife, miss? I'm eager to know how it will be now that the sleep is burst. And the children, too. I love them very much—I think."

"Why do you say think?"

"Yes, I think. We'll have to see. You know we're a very funny family for picking up companions. My son Edward had a chimpanzee who was dressed in a cowboy suit. Then in California he and I nearly took a little seal into our lives. Then my daughter brought home a baby. Of course we had to take it away from her. I hope she will consider this lion as a replacement. I hope I can persuade her."

"There's a little kid on the plane," said the stewardess. "He'd probably adore the lion cub. He looks pretty sad."

And I said, "Who is it?"

"Well, his parents were Americans. There's a letter around his neck that tells the story. The kid doesn't speak English at all. Only Persian."

"Go on," I said to her.

"The father worked for oil people in Persia. The kid was raised by Persian servants. Now he's an orphan and going to live with grandparents in Carson City, Nevada. At Idlewild I'm supposed to turn him over to somebody."

"Poor little bastard," I said. "Why don't you bring him, and we'll show him the lion."

So she fetched the boy. He was very white and wore short pants with strap garters and a little dark green sweater. He was a black-haired boy, like my own. This kid went to my heart. You know how it is when your heart drops. Like a fall-bruised apple in the cold morning of autumn. "Come here, little boy," I said, and reached for the child's hand. "It's a bad business," I told the stewardess, "to ship a little kid around the world alone." I took the cub Dahfu and gave it to him. "I don't think he knows what it is—he probably imagines it's a kitty."

"But he likes it."

As a matter of fact the animal did lighten the boy's melancholy, and so we let them play. And when we went back to our seats I kept him with me and tried to show him pictures in the magazine. I gave him his dinner, and at night he fell asleep in my lap, and I had to ask the girl to keep her eye on the lion for me—I couldn't move now. She said he was asleep, too.

And during this leg of the flight, my memory did me a great favor. Yes, I was granted certain recollections and they have made a sizable difference to me. And after all, it's not all to the bad to have had a long life. Something of benefit can be found in the past. First I was thinking, Take potatoes. They actually belong to the deadly nightshade family. Next I thought, Actually, pigs don't have a monopoly on grunting, either.

This reflection made me remember that after my brother Dick's death I went away from home, being already a big boy of about sixteen, with a mustache, a college freshman. The reason why I left was that I couldn't bear to see the old man mourn. We have a beautiful house, a regular work of art. The foundations are of stone and three feet thick; the ceilings are eighteen feet. The windows are twelve, and start at the floor, so that the light fills everything through that kind of marred old-fashioned glass. There's a peace that even I haven't been able to destroy, in those old rooms. Only one thing is wrong: the joint isn't modern. It's not like the rest of life at all, and therefore it's misleading. And as far as I was concerned, Dick could have had it. But the old man, gushing white beard from all his face, he made me feel our family line had ended with Dick up in the Adirondacks when he shot at the pen and plugged the Greek's coffee urn. Dick also was a curly-headed man with broad shoulders, like the rest of us. He was drowned in the wild mountains, and now my dad looked at me and despaired.

An old man, disappointed, of failing strength, may try to reinvigorate himself by means of anger. Now I understand it. But I couldn't see it at sixteen, when we had a falling out. I was working that summer wrecking old cars, cutting them up for junk with the torch. I was lord and master of the wrecked cars, at a place about three miles from home. It did me good to work in this wrecking yard. That summer I did nothing but dismantle cars. I was grease and rust all over and scalded and dazzled with the cutting torch, and I made mountains of fenders and axles and car innards. On the day of Dick's funeral, I went to work, too. And

in the evening, when I washed myself in the back of the house
under the garden hose, I was gasping as the chill water rushed
over my head, and the old man came out on the back porch, in
the dark green of the vines. By the side was a neglected orchard
which later I cut down. The water blurted over me. It was cold
as outer space. Fiercely, the old man started to yell at me. The
hose bubbled on my head while inside I was hotter than the
cutting torch that I took to all those old death cars from the
highway. My father in his grief swore at me. I knew he meant it
because he put aside his customary elegance of words. He cursed,
I guess, because I didn't comfort him.

So I went away. I hitchhiked to Niagara Falls. I reached Niagara and stood looking in. I was entranced by the crash of the
water. Water can be very healing. I went on the *Maid of the
Mists*, the old one, since burned, and through the Cave of the
Winds, and the rest of it. And then I went on up to Ontario
and picked up a job in an amusement park. This was most of all
what I recalled on the plane, with the head of the American-
Persian child on my lap, the North Atlantic leading its black life
beneath us as the four propellers were fanning us homeward.

It was Ontario, then, though I don't remember which part of
the province. The park was a fairground, too, and Hanson, the
guy in charge, slept me in the stables. There the rats jumped
back and forth over my legs at night, and fed on oats, and the
watering of the horses began at daybreak, in the blue light that
occurs at the end of darkness in the high latitudes. The Negroes
came to the horses at this blue time of the night, when the damp
was heavy.

I worked with Smolak. I almost had forgotten this animal,
Smolak, an old brown bear whose trainer (also Smolak; he had
been named for him) had beat it with the rest of the troupe and
left him on Hanson's hands. There was no need of a trainer.
Smolak was too old and his master had dusted him off. This
ditched old creature was almost green with time and down to his
last teeth, like the pits of dates. For this shabby animal Hanson
had thought up a use. He had been trained to ride a bike, but
now he was too old. Now he could feed from a dish with a rabbit;
after which, in a cap and bib, he drank from a baby bottle while

he stood on his hind legs. But there was one more thing, and this was where I came in. There was a month yet to the end of the season, and every day of this month Smolak and I rode on a roller coaster together before large crowds. This poor broken ruined creature and I, alone, took the high rides twice a day. And while we climbed and dipped and swooped and swerved and rose again higher than the Ferris wheels and fell, we held on to each other. By a common bond of despair we embraced, cheek to cheek, as all support seemed to leave us and we started down the perpendicular drop. I was pressed into his long-suffering, age-worn, tragic, and discolored coat as he grunted and cried to me. At times the animal would wet himself. But he was apparently aware I was his friend and he did not claw me. I took a pistol with blanks in case of an assault; it never was needed. I said to Hanson, as I recall, "We're two of a kind. Smolak was cast off and I am an Ishmael, too." As I lay in the stable, I would think about Dick's death and about my father. But most of the time I lived not with horses but with Smolak, and this poor creature and I were very close. So before pigs ever came on my horizon, I received a deep impression from a bear. So if corporeal things are an image of the spiritual and visible objects are renderings of invisible ones, and if Smolak and I were outcasts together, two humorists before the crowd, but brothers in our souls—I enbeared by him, and he probably humanized by me—I didn't come to the pigs as a tabula rasa. It only stands to reason. Something deep already was inscribed on me. In the end, I wonder if Dahfu would have found this out for himself.

Once more. Whatever gains I ever made were always due to love and nothing else. And as Smolak (mossy like a forest elm) and I rode together, and as he cried out at the top, beginning the bottomless rush over those skimpy yellow supports, and up once more against eternity's blue (oh, the stuff that has been done within this envelope of color, this subtle bag of life-giving gases!) while the Canadian hicks were rejoicing underneath with red faces, all the nubble-fingered rubes, we hugged each other, the bear and I, with something greater than terror and flew in those gilded cars. I shut my eyes in his wretched, time-abused fur. He held me in his arms and gave me comfort. And the great thing is that he didn't blame me. He had seen too much of life, and somewhere in his huge head he had worked it out that for creatures there is nothing that ever runs unmingled.

Lily will have to sit up with me if it takes all night, I was thinking, while I tell her all about this.

As for this kid resting against me, bound for Nevada with nothing but a Persian vocabulary—why, he was still trailing his cloud of glory. God knows, I dragged mine on as long as I could till it got dingy, mere tatters of gray fog. However, I always knew what it was.

"Well, look at you two," said the hostess, meaning that the kid also was awake. Two smoothly gray eyes moved at me, greatly expanded into the whites—new to life altogether. They had that new luster. With it they had ancient power, too. You could never convince me that *this was for the first time.*

"We are going to land for a while," said the young woman.

"The hell you say. Have we crept up on New York so soon? I told my wife to meet me in the afternoon."

"No, it's Newfoundland, for fuel," she said. "It's getting on toward daylight. You can see that, can't you?"

"Oh, I'm dying to breathe some of this cold stuff we've been flying through," I said. "After so many months in the Torrid Zone. You get what I mean?"

"I guess you'll have an opportunity," said the girl.

"Well, let me have a blanket for this child. I'll give him a breath of fresh air, too."

We started to slope and to go in, at which time there was a piercing red from the side of the sun into the clouds near the sea's surface. It was only a flash, and next gray light returned, and cliffs in an ice armor met with the green movement of the water, and we entered the lower air, which lay white and dry under the gray of the sky.

"I'm going to take a walk. Will you come with me?" I said to the kid. He answered me in Persian. "Well, it's okay," I said. I held out the blanket, and he stood on the seat and entered it. Wrapping him, I took him in my arms. The stewardess was going in to that invisible first-class passenger with coffee.

"All set? Why, where's your coat?" she asked me.

"That lion is all the baggage that I have," I said. "But that's all right. I'm country bred. I'm rugged."

So we were let out, this kid and I, and I carried him down from the ship and over the frozen ground of almost eternal winter, drawing breaths so deep they shook me, pure happiness, while the cold smote me from all sides through the stiff Italian corduroy with its broad wales, and the hairs on my beard turned spiky as the moisture of my breath froze instantly. Slipping, I ran over the ice in those same suede shoes. The socks were rotting within and crumbled, as I had never got around to changing them. I told the kid, "Inhale. Your face is too white from your orphan's troubles. Breathe in this air, kid, and get a little color." I held him close to my chest. He didn't seem to be afraid that I would fall with him. While to me he was like medicine applied, and the air, too; it also was a remedy. Plus the happiness that I expected at Idlewild from meeting Lily. And the lion? He was in it, too. Laps and laps I galloped around the shining and riveted body of the plane, behind the fuel trucks. Dark faces were looking from within. The great beautiful propellers were still, all four of them. I guess I felt it was my turn now to move, and so went running—leaping, leaping, pounding, and tingling over the pure white lining of the gray Arctic silence.

7 Jorge Luis Borges

Jorge Luis Borges was born in Buenos Aires in 1899 and was educated in Geneva. Poet, translator, and fiction writer, Borges is best known to English readers for his Ficciones (1962) and is, as Anthony Kerrigan suggests, "probably . . . the most succinct writer of this century."

❖

PIERRE MENARD, AUTHOR
OF DON QUIXOTE

Translated by Anthony Bonner   *To Silvina Ocampo*

The *visible* works left by this novelist are easily and briefly enumerated. It is therefore impossible to forgive the omissions and additions perpetrated by Madame Henri Bachelier in a fallacious catalogue that a certain newspaper, whose Protestant tendencies are no secret, was inconsiderate enough to inflict on its wretched readers—even though they are few and Calvinist, if not Masonic and circumcised. Menard's true friends regarded this catalogue with alarm, and even with a certain sadness. It is as if yesterday we were gathered together before the final marble and the fateful cypresses, and already Error is trying to tarnish his Memory. . . . Decidedly, a brief rectification is inevitable.

I am certain that it would be very easy to challenge my meager authority. I hope, nevertheless, that I will not be prevented from mentioning two important testimonials. The Baroness de Bacourt (at whose unforgettable *vendredis* I had the honor of becoming acquainted with the late lamented poet) has seen fit to approve these lines. The Countess de Bagnoregio, one of the most refined minds in the Principality of Monaco (and now of Pittsburgh, Pennsylvania, since her recent marriage to the international philanthropist Simon Kautsch who, alas, has been so slandered by the victims of his disinterested handiwork) has sacrificed to "truth and death" (those are her words) that majestic reserve which distinguishes her, and in an open letter published in the magazine *Luxe* also grants me her consent. These authorizations, I believe, are not insufficient.

I have said that Menard's *visible* lifework is easily enumerated. Having carefully examined his private archives, I have been able to verify that it consists of the following:

a) A symbolist sonnet which appeared twice (with variations) in the magazine *La Conque* (the March and October issues of 1899).

b) A monograph on the possibility of constructing a poetic vocabulary of concepts that would not be synonyms or periphrases of those which make up ordinary language, "but ideal objects created by means of common agreement and destined essentially to fill poetic needs" (Nîmes, 1901).

c) A monograph on "certain connections or affinities" among the ideas of Descartes, Leibnitz and John Wilkins (Nîmes, 1903).

d) A monograph on the *Characteristica Universalis* of Leibnitz (Nîmes, 1904).

e) A technical article on the possibility of enriching the game of chess by means of eliminating one of the rooks' pawns. Menard proposes, recommends, disputes, and ends by rejecting this innovation.

f) A monograph on the *Ars Magna Generalis* of Ramón Lull (Nîmes, 1906).

g) A translation with prologue and notes of the *Libro de la invención y arte del juego del axedrez* by Ruy López de Segura (Paris, 1907).

h) The rough draft of a monograph on the symbolic logic of George Boole.

i) An examination of the metric laws essential to French prose, illustrated with examples from Saint-Simon (*Revue des langues romanes*, Montpellier, October, 1909).

j) An answer to Luc Durtain (who had denied the existence of such laws) illustrated with examples from Luc Durtain (*Revue des langues romanes*, Montpellier, December, 1909).

k) A manuscript translation of the *Aguja de navegar cultos* of Quevedo, entitled *La boussole des précieux*.

l) A preface to the catalogue of the exposition of lithographs by Carolus Hourcade (Nîmes, 1914).

m) His work, *Les problèmes d'un problème* (Paris, 1917), which takes up in chronological order the various solutions of the famous problem of Achilles and the tortoise. Two editions of this book have appeared so far; the second has as an epigraph Leibnitz' advice "Ne craignez point, monsieur, la tortue," and contains revisions of the chapters dedicated to Russell and Descartes.

n) An obstinate analysis of the "syntactic habits" of Toulet (*N.R.F.*, March, 1921). I remember that Menard used to declare that censuring and praising were sentimental operations which had nothing to do with criticism.

o) A transposition into Alexandrines of *Le Cimetière marin* of Paul Valéry (*N.R.F.*, January, 1928).

p) An invective against Paul Valéry in the *Journal for the Suppression of Reality* of Jacques Reboul. (This invective, it should be stated parenthetically, is the exact reverse of his true opinion of Valéry. The latter understood it as such, and the old friendship between the two was never endangered.)

q) A "definition" of the Countess of Bagnoregio in the "victorious volume"—the phrase is that of another collaborator, Gabriele d'Annunzio—which this lady publishes yearly to rectify the inevitable falsifications of journalism and to present "to the world and to Italy" an authentic effigy of her person, which is so exposed (by reason of her beauty and her activities) to erroneous or hasty interpretations.

r) A cycle of admirable sonnets for the Baroness de Bacourt (1934).

s) A manuscript list of verses which owe their effectiveness to punctuation.*

Up to this point (with no other omission than that of some

---

*Madame Henri Bachelier also lists a literal translation of a literal translation done by Quevedo of the *Introduction à la vie dévote* of Saint Francis of Sales. In Pierre Menard's library there are no traces of such a work. She must have misunderstood a remark of his which he had intended as a joke.

vague, circumstantial sonnets for the hospitable, or greedy, album of Madame Henri Bachelier) we have the *visible* part of Menard's works in chronological order. Now I will pass over to that other part, which is subterranean, interminably heroic, and unequalled, and which is also—oh, the possibilities inherent in the man!—inconclusive. This work, possibly the most significant of our time, consists of the ninth and thirty-eighth chapters of Part One of *Don Quixote* and a fragment of the twenty-second chapter. I realize that such an affirmation seems absurd; but the justification of this "absurdity" is the primary object of this note.*

Two texts of unequal value inspired the undertaking. One was that philological fragment of Novalis—No. 2005 of the Dresden edition—which outlines the theme of *total* identification with a specific author. The other was one of those parasitic books which places Christ on a boulevard, Hamlet on the Cannebière and Don Quixote on Wall Street. Like any man of good taste, Menard detested these useless carnivals, only suitable—he used to say—for evoking plebeian delight in anachronism, or (what is worse) charming us with the primary idea that all epochs are the same, or that they are different. He considered more interesting, even though it had been carried out in a contradictory and superficial way, Daudet's famous plan: to unite in one figure, Tartarin, the Ingenious Gentleman and his squire. . . . Any insinuation that Menard dedicated his life to the writing of a contemporary *Don Quixote* is a calumny of his illustrious memory.

He did not want to compose another *Don Quixote*—which would be easy—but *the Don Quixote*. It is unnecessary to add that his aim was never to produce a mechanical transcription of the original; he did not propose to copy it. His admirable ambition was to produce pages which would coincide—word for word and line for line—with those of Miguel de Cervantes.

"My intent is merely astonishing," he wrote me from Bayonne on December 30th, 1934. "The ultimate goal of a theological or metaphysical demonstration—the external world, God, chance, universal forms—are no less anterior or common than this novel which I am now developing. The only difference is that philoso-

---

*I also had another, secondary intent—that of sketching a portrait of Pierre Menard. But how would I dare to compete with the golden pages the Baroness de Bacourt tells me she is preparing, or with the delicate and precise pencil of Carolus Hourcade?

phers publish in pleasant volumes the intermediary stages of their work and that I have decided to lose them." And, in fact, not one page of a rough draft remain to bear witness to this work of years.

The initial method he conceived was relatively simple: to know Spanish well, to re-embrace the Catholic faith, to fight against Moors and Turks, to forget European history between 1602 and 1918, and to be Miguel de Cervantes. Pierre Menard studied this procedure (I know that he arrived at a rather faithful handling of seventeenth-century Spanish) but rejected it as too easy. Rather because it was impossible, the reader will say! I agree, but the undertaking was impossible from the start, and of all the possible means of carrying it out, this one was the least interesting. To be, in the twentieth century, a popular novelist of the seventeenth seemed to him a diminution. To be, in some way, Cervantes and to arrive at *Don Quixote* seemed to him less arduous—and consequently less interesting—than to continue being Pierre Menard and to arrive at *Don Quixote* through the experiences of Pierre Menard. (This conviction, let it be said in passing, forced him to exclude the autobiographical prologue of the second part of *Don Quixote*. To include this prologue would have meant creating another personage—Cervantes—but it would also have meant presenting *Don Quixote* as the work of this personage and not of Menard. He naturally denied himself such an easy solution.) "My undertaking is not essentially difficult," I read in another part of the same letter. "I would only have to be immortal in order to carry it out." Shall I confess that I often imagine that he finished it and that I am reading *Don Quixote*—the entire work—as if Menard had conceived it? Several nights ago, while leafing through Chapter XXVI—which he had never attempted—I recognized our friend's style and, as it were, his voice in this exceptional phrase: *the nymphs of the rivers, mournful and humid Echo.* This effective combination of two adjectives, one moral and the other physical, reminded me of a line from Shakespeare which we discussed one afternoon:

Where a malignant and turbaned Turk . . .

Why precisely *Don Quixote*, our reader will ask. Such a preference would not have been inexplicable in a Spaniard; but it undoubtedly was in a symbolist from Nîmes, essentially devoted to Poe, who engendered Baudelaire, who engendered Mallarmé, who engendered Valéry, who engendered Edmond Teste. The letter quoted above clarifies this point. "*Don Quixote*," Menard explains, "interests me profoundly, but it does not seem to me to have been—how shall I say it—inevitable. I cannot imagine the universe without the interjection of Edgar Allan Poe

Ah, bear in mind this garden was enchanted!

or without the *Bateau ivre* or the *Ancient Mariner*, but I know that I am capable of imagining it without *Don Quixote*. (I speak, naturally, of my personal capacity, not of the historical repercussions of these works.) *Don Quixote* is an accidental book, *Don Quixote* is unnecessary. I can premeditate writing, I can write it, without incurring a tautology. When I was twelve or thirteen years old I read it, perhaps in its entirety. Since then I have reread several chapters attentively, but not the ones I am going to undertake. I have likewise studied the *entremeses*, the comedies, the *Galatea*, the exemplary novels, and the undoubtedly laborious efforts of *Pérsiles y Sigismunda* and the *Viaje al Parnaso*. . . . My general memory of *Don Quixote*, simplified by forgetfulness and indifference, is much the same as the imprecise, anterior image of a book not yet written. Once this image (which no one can deny me in good faith) has been postulated, my problems are undeniably considerably more difficult than those which Cervantes faced. My affable precursor did not refuse the collaboration of fate; he went along composing his immortal work a little *à la diable*, swept along by inertias of language and invention. I have contracted the mysterious duty of reconstructing literally his spontaneous work. My solitary game is governed by two polar laws. The first permits me to attempt variants of a formal and psychological nature; the second obliges me to sacrifice them to the 'original' text and irrefutably to rationalize this annihilation. . . . To these artificial obstacles one must add another congenital one. To compose *Don Quixote* at the beginning of the seventeenth century was a reasonable, necessary and perhaps inevitable undertaking; at the beginning of the twentieth century it is almost impossible. It is not in vain that three hundred years have passed, charged with the most complex happenings—among them, to mention only one, that same *Don Quixote*."

In spite of these three obstacles, the fragmentary *Don Quixote* of Menard is more subtle than that of Cervantes. The latter indulges in a rather coarse opposition between tales of knighthood and the meager, provincial reality of his country; Menard chooses as "reality" the land of Carmen during the century of Lepanto and Lope. What Hispanophile would not have advised Maurice Barrès or Dr. Rodríguez Larreta to make such a choice! Menard, as if it were the most natural thing in the world, eludes them. In his work there are neither bands of gypsies, conquistadors, mystics, Philip the Seconds, nor autos-da-fé. He disregards or proscribes local color. This disdain indicates a new approach to the historical novel. This disdain condemns *Salammbô* without appeal.

It is no less astonishing to consider isolated chapters. Let us examine, for instance, Chapter XXXVIII of Part One "which treats of the curious discourse that Don Quixote delivered on the subject of arms and letters." As is known, Don Quixote (like Quevedo in a later, analogous passage of *La hora de todos*) passes judgment against letters and in favor of arms. Cervantes was an old soldier, which explains such a judgment. But that the *Don Quixote* of Pierre Menard—a contemporary of *La trahison des clercs* and Bertrand Russell—should relapse into these nebulous sophistries! Madame Bachelier has seen in them an admirable and typical subordination of the author to the psychology of the hero; others (by no means perspicaciously) a *transcription* of Don Quixote; the Baroness de Bacourt, the influence of Nietzsche. To this third interpretation (which seems to me irrefutable) I do not know if I would dare to add a fourth, which coincides very well with the divine modesty of Pierre Menard: his resigned or ironic habit of propounding ideas which were the strict reverse of those he preferred. (One will remember his diatribe against Paul Valéry in the ephemeral journal of the superrealist Jacques Reboul.) The text of Cervantes and that of Menard are verbally identical, but the second is almost infinitely richer. (More ambiguous, his detractors will say; but ambiguity is a richness.) It is a revelation to compare the *Don Quixote* of Menard with that of Cervantes. The latter, for instance, wrote (*Don Quixote*, Part One, Chapter Nine):

. . . la verdad, cuya madre es la historia, émula del tiempo, depósito de las acciones, testigo de lo pasado, ejemplo y aviso de lo presente, advertencia de lo por venir.

[. . . truth, whose mother is history, who is the rival of time, depository of deeds, witness of the past, example and lesson to the present, and warning to the future.]

Written in the seventeenth century, written by the "ingenious layman" Cervantes, this enumeration is a mere rhetorical eulogy of history. Menard, on the other hand, writes:

. . . la verdad, cuya madre es la historia, émula del tiempo, depósito de las acciones, testigo de lo pasado, ejemplo y aviso de lo presente, avertencia de lo por venir.

[. . . truth, whose mother is history, who is the rival of time, depository of deeds, witness of the past, example and lesson to the present, and warning to the future.]

History, mother of truth; the idea is astounding. Menard, a contemporary of William James, does not define history as an investigation of reality, but as its origin. Historical truth, for him, is not what took place; it is what we think took place. The final clauses—example and lesson to the present, and warning to the future—are shamelessly pragmatic.

Equally vivid is the contrast in styles. The archaic style of Menard—in the last analysis, a foreigner—suffers from a certain affectation. Not so that of his precursor, who handles easily the ordinary Spanish of his time.

There is no intellectual exercise which is not ultimately useless. A philosophical doctrine is in the beginning a seemingly true description of the universe; as the years pass it becomes a mere chapter—if not a paragraph or a noun—in the history of philosophy. In literature, this ultimate decay is even more notorious. "Don Quixote," Menard once told me, "was above all an agreeable book; now it is an occasion for patriotic toasts, grammatical arrogance and obscene deluxe editions. Glory is an incomprehension, and perhaps the worst."

These nihilist arguments contain nothing new; what is unusual is the decision Pierre Menard derived from them. He resolved to outstrip that vanity which awaits all the woes of mankind; he undertook a task that was complex in the extreme and futile from the outset. He dedicated his conscience and nightly studies to the repetition of a pre-existing book in a foreign tongue. The number of rough drafts kept on increasing; he tenaciously made corrections and tore up thousands of manuscript pages.* He did not permit them to be examined, and he took great care that they would not survive him. It is in vain that I have tried to reconstruct them.

I have thought that it is legitimate to consider the "final" *Don Quixote* as a kind of palimpsest, in which should appear traces—tenuous but not undecipherable—of the "previous" handwriting of our friend. Unfortunately, only a second Pierre Menard, inverting the work of the former, could exhume and rescuscitate these Troys. . . .

"To think, analyze and invent," he also wrote me, "are not anomalous acts, but the normal respiration of the intelligence. To glorify the occasional fulfillment of this function, to treasure ancient thoughts of others, to remember with incredulous amazement that the *doctor universalis* thought, is to confess our languor or barbarism. Every man should be capable of all ideas, and I believe that in the future he will be."

Menard (perhaps without wishing to) has enriched, by means of a new technique, the hesitant and rudimentary art of reading: the technique is one of deliberate anachronism and erroneous attributions. This technique, with its infinite applications, urges us to run through the *Odyssey* as if it were written after the *Aeneid*, and to read *Le jardin du Centaure* by Madame Henri Bachelier as if it were by Madame Henri Bachelier. This technique would fill the dullest books with adventure. Would not the attributing of *The Imitation of Christ* to Louis Ferdinand Céline or James Joyce be a sufficient renovation of its tenuous spiritual counsels?

Nîmes

1939

---

*I remember his square-ruled notebooks, the black streaks where he had crossed out words, his peculiar typographical symbols and his insect-like handwriting. In the late afternoon he liked to go for walks on the outskirts of Nîmes; he would take a notebook with him and make a gay bonfire.

$\mathcal{8}$ Joseph Heller

Joseph Heller was born in Brooklyn in 1923 and attended New York, Columbia, and Oxford universities. Published in 1961, Catch-22 is one of the most popular novels of the 1960s. Heller claims to "have no hobbies, no recreations. I hate sports. I hate gardening and walking. I don't go to movies or the theatre or watch television. What I do like is lying down. My best thinking is done going into or coming out of naps."

❖

SNOWDEN
(FROM *CATCH-22*)

"Cut," said a doctor.

"You cut," said another.

"No cuts," said Yossarian with a thick, unwieldy tongue.

"Now look who's butting in," complained one of the doctors. "Another county heard from. Are we going to operate or aren't we?"

"He doesn't need an operation," complained the other. "It's a small wound. All we have to do is stop the bleeding, clean it out and put a few stitches in."

"But I've never had a chance to operate before. Which one is the scalpel? Is this one the scalpel?"

"No, the other one is the scalpel. Well, go ahead and cut already if you're going to. Make the incision."

"Like this?"

"Not there, you dope!"

"No incisions," Yossarian said, perceiving through the lifting fog of insensibility that two strangers were ready to begin cutting him.

"Another county heard from," complained the first doctor sarcastically. "Is he going to keep talking that way while I operate on him?"

"You can't operate on him until I admit him," said a clerk.

"You can't admit him until I clear him," said a fat, gruff colonel with a mustache and an enormous pink face that pressed down very close to Yossarian and radiated scorching heat like the bottom of a huge frying pan. "Where were you born?"

The fat, gruff colonel reminded Yossarian of the fat, gruff colonel who had interrogated the chaplain and found him guilty. Yossarian stared up at him through a glassy film. The cloying scents of formaldehyde and alcohol sweetened the air.

"On a battlefield," he answered.

"No, no. In what state were you born?"

"In a state of innocence."

"No, no, you don't understand."

"Let me handle him," urged a hatchet-faced man with sunken acrimonious eyes and a thin, malevolent mouth. "Are you a smart aleck or something?" he asked Yossarian.

"He's delirious," one of the doctors said. "Why don't you let us take him back inside and treat him?"

"Leave him right here if he's delirious. He might say something incriminating."

"But he's still bleeding profusely. Can't you see? He might even die."

"Good for him!"

"It would serve the finky bastard right," said the fat, gruff colonel. "All right, John, let's speak out. We want to get to the truth."

"Everyone calls me Yo-Yo."

"We want you to co-operate with us, Yo-Yo. We're your friends and we want you to trust us. We're here to help you. We're not going to hurt you."

"Let's jab our thumbs down inside his wound and gouge it," suggested the hatchet-faced man.

Yossarian let his eyes fall closed and hoped they would think he was unconscious.

"He's fainted," he heard a doctor say. "Can't we treat him now before it's too late? He really might die."

"All right, take him. I hope the bastard does die."

"You can't treat him until I admit him," the clerk said.

Yossarian played dead with his eyes shut while the clerk admitted him by shuffling some papers, and then he was rolled away slowly into a stuffy, dark room with searing spotlights overhead in which the cloying smell of formaldehyde and sweet alcohol was even stronger. The pleasant, permeating stink was intoxicating. He smelled ether too and heard glass tinkling. He listened with secret, egotistical mirth to the husky breathing of the two doctors. It delighted him that they thought he was unconscious and did not know he was listening. It all seemed very silly to him until one of the doctors said,

"Well, do you think we should save his life? They might be sore at us if we do."

"Let's operate," said the other doctor. "Let's cut him open and get to the inside of things once and for all. He keeps complaining about his liver. His liver looks pretty small on this X ray."

"That's his pancreas, you dope. This is his liver."

"No it isn't. That's his heart. I'll bet you a nickel this is his liver. I'm going to operate and find out. Should I wash my hands first?"

"No operations," Yossarian said, opening his eyes and trying to sit up.

"Another county heard from," scoffed one of the doctors indignantly. "Can't we make him shut up?"

"We could give him a total. The ether's right here."

"No totals," said Yossarian.

"Another county heard from," said a doctor.

"Let's give him a total and knock him out. Then we can do what we want with him."

They gave Yossarian total anesthesia and knocked him out. He woke up thirsty in a private room, drowning in ether fumes. Colonel Korn was there at his bedside, waiting calmly in a chair in his baggy, wool, olive-drab shirt and trousers. A bland, phlegmatic smile hung on his brown face with its heavy-bearded cheeks, and he was buffing the facets of his bald head gently with the palms of both hands. He bent forward chuckling when Yossarian awoke, and assured him in the friendliest tones that the deal they had made was still on if Yossarian didn't die. Yossarian vomited, and

Colonel Korn shot to his feet at the first cough and fled in disgust, so it seemed indeed that there was a silver lining to every cloud, Yossarian reflected, as he drifted back into a suffocating daze. A hand with sharp fingers shook him awake roughly. He turned and opened his eyes and saw a strange man with a mean face who curled his lip at him in a spiteful scowl and bragged,

"We've got your pal, buddy. We've got your pal."

Yossarian turned cold and faint and broke into a sweat.

"Who's my pal?" he asked when he saw the chaplain sitting where Colonel Korn had been sitting.

"Maybe I'm your pal," the chaplain answered.

But Yossarian couldn't hear him and closed his eyes. Someone gave him water to sip and tiptoed away. He slept and woke up feeling great until he turned his head to smile at the chaplain and saw Aarfy there instead. Yossarian moaned instinctively and screwed his face up with excruciating irritability when Aarfy chortled and asked how he was feeling. Aarfy looked puzzled when Yossarian inquired why he was not in jail. Yossarian shut his eyes to make him go away. When he opened them, Aarfy was gone and the chaplain was there. Yossarian broke into laughter when he spied the chaplain's cheerful grin and asked him what in the hell he was so happy about.

"I'm happy about you," the chaplain replied with excited candor and joy. "I heard at Group that you were very seriously injured and that you would have to be sent home if you lived. Colonel Korn said your condition was critical. But I've just learned from one of the doctors that your wound is really a very slight one and that you'll probably be able to leave in a day or two. You're in no danger. It isn't bad at all."

Yossarian listened to the chaplain's news with enormous relief. "That's good."

"Yes," said the chaplain, a pink flush of impish pleasure creeping into his cheeks. "Yes, that is good."

Yossarian laughed, recalling his first conversation with the chaplain. "You know, the first time I met you was in the hospital. And now I'm in the hospital again. Just about the only time I see you lately is in the hospital. Where've you been keeping yourself?"

The chaplain shrugged. "I've been praying a lot," he confessed. "I try to stay in my tent as much as I can, and I pray every time Sergeant Whitcomb leaves the area, so that he won't catch me."

"Does it do any good?"

"It takes my mind off my troubles," the chaplin answered with another shrug. "And it gives me something to do."

"Well, that's good, then, isn't it?"

"Yes," agreed the chaplain enthusiastically, as though the idea had not occurred to him before. "Yes, I guess that is good." He bent forward impulsively with awkward solicitude. "Yossarian, is there anything I can do for you while you're here, anything I can get you?"

Yossarian teased him jovially. "Like toys, or candy, or chewing gum?"

The chaplain blushed again, grinning self-consciously, and then turned very respectful. "Like books, perhaps, or anything at all. I wish there was something I could do to make you happy. You know, Yossarian, we're all very proud of you."

"Proud?"

"Yes, of course. For risking your life to stop that Nazi assassin. It was a very noble thing to do."

"What Nazi assassin?"

"The one that came here to murder Colonel Cathcart and Colonel Korn. And you saved them. He might have stabbed you to death as you grappled with him on the balcony. It's a lucky thing you're alive."

Yossarian snickered sardonically when he understood. "That was no Nazi assassin."

"Certainly it was. Colonel Korn said it was."

"That was Nately's girl friend. And she was after me, not Colonel Cathcart and Colonel Korn. She's been trying to kill me ever since I broke the news to her that Nately was dead."

"But how could that be?" the chaplain protested in livid and resentful confusion. "Colonel Cathcart and Colonel Korn both saw him as he ran away. The official report says you stopped a Nazi assassin from killing them."

"Don't believe the official report," Yossarian advised dryly. "It's part of the deal."

"What deal?"

"The deal I made with Colonel Cathcart and Colonel Korn. They'll let me go home a big hero if I say nice things about them to everybody and never criticize them to anyone for making the rest of the men fly more missions."

The chaplain was appalled and rose halfway out of his chair. He bristled with bellicose dismay. "But that's terrible! That's a shameful, scandalous deal, isn't it?"

"Odious," Yossarian answered, staring up woodenly at the ceiling with just the back of his head resting on the pillow. "I think 'odious' is the word we decided on."

"Then how could you agree to it?"

"It's that or a court-martial, Chaplain."

"Oh," the chaplain exclaimed with a look of stark remorse, the back of his hand covering his mouth. He lowered himself into his chair uneasily. "I shouldn't have said anything."

"They'd lock me in prison with a bunch of criminals."

"Of course. You must do whatever you think is right, then." The chaplain nodded to himself as though deciding the argument and lapsed into embarrassed silence.

"Don't worry," Yossarian said with a sorrowful laugh after several moments had passed. "I'm not going to do it."

"But you must do it," the chaplain insisted, bending forward with concern. "Really, you must. I had no right to influence you. I really had no right to say anything."

"You didn't influence me." Yossarian hauled himself over onto his side and shook his head in solemn mockery. "Christ, Chaplain! Can you imagine that for a sin? Saving Colonel Cathcart's life! That's one crime I don't want on my record."

The chaplain returned to the subject with caution. "What will you do instead? You can't let them put you in prison."

"I'll fly more missions. Or maybe I really will desert and let them catch me. They probably would."

"And they'd put you in prison. You don't want to go to prison."

"Then I'll just keep flying missions until the war ends, I guess. Some of us have to survive."

"But you might get killed."

"Then I guess I won't fly any more missions."

"What will you do?"

"I don't know."

"Will you let them send you home?"

"I don't know. Is it hot out? It's very warm in here."

"It's very cold out," the chaplain said.

"You know," Yossarian remembered, "a very funny thing happened—maybe I dreamed it. I think a strange man came in here before and told me he's got my pal. I wonder if I imagined it."

"I don't think you did," the chaplain informed him. "You started to tell me about him when I dropped in earlier."

"Then he really did say it. 'We've got your pal, buddy,' he said. 'We've got your pal.' He had the most malignant manner I ever saw. I wonder who my pal is."

"I like to think that I'm your pal, Yossarian," the chaplain said with humble sincerity. "And they certainly have got me. They've got my number and they've got me under surveillance, and they've got me right where they want me. That's what they told me at my interrogation."

"No, I don't think it's you he meant," Yossarian decided. "I think it must be someone like Nately or Dunbar. You know, someone who was killed in the war, like Clevinger, Orr, Dobbs, Kid Sampson or McWatt." Yossarian emitted a startled gasp and shook his head. "I just realized it," he exclaimed. "They've got all my pals, haven't they? The only ones left are me and Hungry Joe." He tingled with dread as he saw the chaplain's face go pale. "Chaplain, what is it?"

"Hungry Joe was killed."

"God, no! On a mission?"

"He died in his sleep while having a dream. They found a cat on his face."

"Poor bastard," Yossarian said, and began to cry, hiding his tears in the crook of his shoulder. The chaplain left without saying good-bye. Yossarian ate something and went to sleep. A hand shook him awake in the middle of the night. He opened his eyes and saw a thin, mean man in a patient's bathrobe and pajamas who looked at him with a nasty smirk and jeered,

"We've got your pal, buddy. We've got your pal."

Yossarian was unnerved. "What the *hell* are you talking about?" he pleaded in incipient panic.

"You'll find out, buddy. You'll find out."

Yossarian lunged for his tormentor's throat with one hand, but the man glided out of reach effortlessly and vanished into the corridor with a malicious laugh. Yossarian lay there trembling with a pounding pulse. He was bathed in icy sweat. He wondered who his pal was. It was dark in the hospital and perfectly quiet. He had no watch to tell him the time. He was wide-awake, and he knew he was a prisoner in one of those sleepless, bedridden nights that would take an eternity to dissolve into dawn. A throbbing chill oozed up his legs. He was cold, and he thought of Snowden, who had never been his pal but was a vaguely familiar kid who was badly wounded and freezing to death in the puddle of harsh yellow sunlight splashing into his face through the side gunport when Yossarian crawled into the rear section of the plane over the bomb bay after Dobbs had beseeched him on the intercom to help the gunner, please help the gunner. Yossarian's stomach turned over when his eyes first beheld the macabre scene; he was absolutely revolted, and he paused in fright a few moments before descending, crouched on his hands and knees in the narrow tunnel over the bomb bay beside the sealed corrugated carton containing the first-aid kit. Snowden was lying on his back on the floor with his legs stretched out, still burdened cumbersomely by his flak suit, his flak helmet, his parachute harness and his Mae West. Not far away on the floor lay the small tail gunner in a dead faint. The wound Yossarian saw was in the outside of Snowden's thigh, as large and deep as a football, it seemed. It was impossible to tell where the shreds of his saturated coveralls ended and the ragged flesh began.

There was no morphine in the first-aid kit, no protection for Snowden against pain but the numbing shock of the gaping wound itself. The twelve syrettes of morphine had been stolen from their case and replaced by a cleanly lettered note that said: "What's good for M & M Enterprises is good for the country. Milo Minderbinder." Yossarian swore at Milo and held two aspirins out to ashen lips unable to receive them. But first he hastily drew a tourniquet around Snowden's thigh because he could not think what else to do in those first tumultuous moments when his senses were in turmoil, when he knew he must act competently at once and feared he might go to pieces completely. Snowden watched him steadily, saying nothing. No artery was spurting, but Yossarian pretended to absorb himself entirely into the fashioning of a tourniquet, because applying a tourniquet was something he did know how to do. He worked with simulated skill and composure, feeling Snowden's lackluster gaze resting upon him. He recovered possession of himself before the tourniquet was finished and loosened it immediately to lessen the danger of gangrene. His mind was clear now, and he knew how to proceed. He rummaged through the first-aid kit for scissors.

"I'm cold," Snowden said softly. "I'm cold."

"You're going to be all right, kid," Yossarian reassured him with a grin. "You're going to be all right."

"I'm cold," Snowden said again in a frail, childlike voice. "I'm cold."

"There, there," Yossarian said, because he did not know what else to say. "There, there."

"I'm cold," Snowden whimpered. "I'm cold."

"There, there. There, there."

Yossarian was frightened and moved more swiftly. He found a pair of scissors at last and began cutting carefully through Snowden's coveralls high up above the wound, just below the groin. He cut through the heavy gabardine cloth all the way around the thigh in a straight line. The tiny tail gunner woke up while Yossarian was cutting with the scissors, saw him, and fainted again. Snowden rolled his head to the other side of his neck in order to stare at Yossarian more directly. A dim, sunken light glowed in his weak and listless eyes. Yossarian, puzzled, tried not to look at him. He began cutting downward through the coveralls along the inside seam. The yawning wound—was that a tube of slimy bone he saw running deep inside the gory scarlet flow behind the twitching, startling fibers of weird muscle?—was dripping blood in several trickles, like snow melting on eaves, but viscous and red, already thickening as it dropped. Yossarian kept cutting through the coveralls to the bottom and peeled open the severed leg of the garment. It fell to the floor with a plop, exposing the hem of khaki undershorts that were soaking up blotches of blood on one side as though in thirst. Yossarian was stunned at how waxen and ghastly Snowden's bare leg looked, how loathsome, how lifeless and esoteric the downy, fine, curled blond hairs on his odd, white shin and calf. The wound, he saw now, was not nearly as large as a football, but as long and wide as his hand, and too raw and deep to see into clearly. The raw muscles inside twitched like live hamburger meat. A long sigh of relief escaped slowly through Yossarian's mouth when he saw that Snowden was not in danger of dying. The blood was already coagulating inside the wound, and it was simply a matter of bandaging him up and keeping him calm until the plane landed. He removed some packets of sulfanilamide from the first-aid kit. Snowden quivered when Yossarian pressed against him gently to turn him up slightly on his side.

"Did I hurt you?"

"I'm cold," Snowden whimpered. "I'm cold."

"There, there," Yossarian said. "There, there."

"I'm cold. I'm cold."

"There, there. There, there."

"It's starting to hurt me," Snowden cried out suddenly with a plaintive, urgent wince.

Yossarian scrambled frantically through the first-aid kit in search of morphine again and found only Milo's note and a bottle of aspirin. He cursed Milo and held two aspirin tablets out to Snowden. He had no water to offer. Snowden rejected the aspirin with an almost imperceptible shake of his head. His face was pale and pasty. Yossarian removed Snowden's flak helmet and lowered his head to the floor.

"I'm cold," Snowden moaned with half-closed eyes. "I'm cold."

The edges of his mouth were turning blue. Yossarian was petrified. He wondered whether to pull the rip cord of Snowden's parachute and cover him with the nylon folds. It was very warm in the plane. Glancing up unexpectedly, Snowden gave him a wan, cooperative smile and shifted the position of his hips a bit so that Yossarian could begin salting the wound with sulfanilamide. Yossarian worked with renewed confidence and optimism. The plane bounced hard inside an air pocket, and he remembered with a start that he had left his own parachute up front in the nose. There was nothing to be done about that. He poured envelope after envelope of the white crystalline powder into the bloody oval wound until nothing red could be seen and then drew a deep, apprehensive breath, steeling himself with gritted teeth as he touched his bare hand to the dangling shreds of drying flesh to tuck them up inside the wound. Quickly he covered the whole wound with a large cotton compress and jerked his hand away. He smiled nervously when his brief ordeal had ended. The actual contact with the dead flesh had not been nearly as repulsive as he had anticipated, and he found excuse to caress the wound with his fingers again and again to convince himself of his own courage.

Next he began binding the compress in place with a roll of gauze. The second time around Snowden's thigh with the bandage, he spotted the small hole on the inside through which the piece of flak had entered, a round, crinkled wound the size of a quarter with blue edges and a black core inside where the blood had crusted. Yossarian sprinkled this one with sulfanilamide too and continued unwinding the gauze around Snowden's leg until the compress was secure. Then he snipped off the roll with the scissors and slit the end down the center. He made the whole thing fast with a tidy square knot. It was a good bandage, he knew, and he sat back on his heels with pride, wiping the perspiration from his brow, and grinned at Snowden with spontaneous friendliness.

"I'm cold," Snowden moaned. "I'm cold."

"You're going to be all right, kid," Yossarian assured him, patting his arm comfortingly. "Everything's under control."

Snowden shook his head feebly. "I'm cold," he repeated, with eyes as dull and blind as stone. "I'm cold."

"There, there," said Yossarian, with growing doubt and trepidation. "There, there. In a little while we'll be back on the ground and Doc Daneeka will take care of you."

But Snowden kept shaking his head and pointed at last, with just the barest movement of his chin, down toward his armpit. Yossarian bent forward to peer and saw a strangely colored stain seeping through the coveralls just above the armhole of Snowden's flak suit. Yossarian felt his heart stop, then pound so violently he found it difficult to breathe. Snowden was wounded inside his flak suit. Yossarian ripped open the snaps of Snowden's flak suit and heard himself scream wildly as Snowden's insides slithered down to the floor in a soggy pile and just kept dripping out. A chunk of flak more than three inches big had shot into his other side just underneath the arm and blasted all the way through, drawing whole mottled quarts of Snowden along with it through the gigantic hole in his ribs it made as it blasted out. Yossarian screamed a second time and squeezed both hands over his eyes. His teeth were chattering in horror. He forced himself to look again. Here was God's plenty, all right, he thought bitterly as he stared—liver, lungs, kidneys, ribs, stomach and bits of the stewed tomatoes Snowden had eaten that day for lunch. Yossarian hated stewed tomatoes and turned away dizzily and began to vomit, clutching his burning throat. The tail gunner woke up while Yossarian was vomiting, saw him, and fainted again. Yossarian was limp with exhaustion, pain and despair when he finished. He turned back weakly to Snowden, whose breath had grown softer and more rapid, and whose face had grown paler. He wondered how in the world to begin to save him.

"I'm cold," Snowden whimpered. "I'm cold."

"There, there," Yossarian mumbled mechanically in a voice too low to be heard. "There, there."

Yossarian was cold, too, and shivering uncontrollably. He felt goose pimples clacking all over him as he gazed down despondently at the grim secret Snowden had spilled all over the messy floor. It was easy to read the message in his entrails. Man was matter, that was Snowden's secret. Drop him out a window and he'll fall. Set fire to him and he'll burn. Bury him and he'll rot, like other kinds of garbage. The spirit gone, man is garbage. That was Snowden's secret. Ripeness was all.

"I'm cold," Snowden said. "I'm cold."

"There, there," said Yossarian. "There, there." He pulled the rip cord of Snowden's parachute and covered his body with the white nylon sheets.

"I'm cold."

"There, there."

⑨ Thomas Pynchon

Thomas Pynchon was born in Glen Cove, Long Island, in 1937 and studied at Cornell University. Perhaps the most brilliant young writer in America today, Pynchon has published two novels, V. *(1963) and* The Crying of Lot 49 *(1966).*

❖

V. IN LOVE
(FROM *V.*)

I

The clock inside the Gare du Nord read 11:17: Paris time minus five minutes, Belgian railway time plus four minutes, mid-Europe time minus 56 minutes. To Mélanie, who had forgotten her traveling clock—who had forgotten everything—the hands might have stood anywhere. She hurried through the station behind an Algerian-looking facteur who carried her one embroidered bag lightly on his shoulder, who smiled and joked with customs officials being driven slowly to frenzy by a beseeching mob of English tourists.

By the cover of Le Soleil, the Orleanist morning paper, it was 24 July 1913. Louis Philippe Robert, duc d'Orleans, was the current Pretender. Certain quarters of Paris raved under the heat of Sirius, were touched by its halo of plague, which is nine light-years from rim to center. Among the upper rooms of a new middle-class home in the 17th arrondissement, Black Mass was held every Sunday.

Mélanie l'Heuremaudit was driven away down the rue La Fayette in a noisy auto-taxi. She sat in the exact center of the seat,

while behind her the three massive arcades and seven allegorical
statues of the Gare slowly receded into a lowering, pre-autumn sky.
Her eyes were dead, her nose French: the strength there and about
the chin and lips made her resemble the classical rendering of
Liberty. In all, the face was quite beautiful except for the eyes,
which were the color of freezing rain. Mélanie was fifteen.

Had fled from school in Belgium as soon as she received the
letter from her mother, with 1500 francs and the announcement
that her support would continue, though all Papa's possessions
had been attached by the court. The mother had gone off to tour
Austria-Hungary. She did not expect to see Mélanie in the forsee-
able future.

Mélanie's head ached, but she didn't care. Or did, but not
where she was, here present as a face and a ballerina's figure on the
bouncing back seat of a taxi. The driver's neck was soft, white:
wisps of white hair straggled from under the blue stocking cap.
On reaching the intersection with the Boulevard Haussmann, the
car turned right up rue de la Chaussée d'Antin. To her left rose
the dome of the Opéra, and tiny Apollo, with his golden lyre . . .

"Papa!" she screamed.

The driver winced, tapped the brake reflexively. "I am not your
father," he muttered.

Up into the heights of Montmarte, aimed for the most dis-
eased part of the sky. Would it rain? The clouds hung like
leprous tissue. Under that light the color of her hair reduced to
neutral browns, buffs. Let down the hair reached halfway over her
buttocks. But she wore it high with two large curls covering her
ears, tickling the sides of her neck.

Papa had a strong bald skull and a brave mustache. Evenings
she would come softly into the room, the mysterious place walled
in silk where he and her mother slept. And while Madeleine
combed the hair of Maman in the other room, Mélanie lay on the
wide bed beside him, while he touched her in many places, and
she squirmed and fought not to make a sound. It was their game.
One night there had been heat lightning outside, and a small
night bird had lit on the windowsill and watched them. How long
ago it seemed! Late summer, like today.

This had been at Serre Chaude, their estate in Normandy, once the ancestral home of a family whose blood had long since turned to a pale ichor and vaporized away into the frosty skies over Amiens. The house, which dated from the reign of Henri IV, was large but unimpressive, like most architecture of the period. She had always wanted to slide down the great mansard roof: begin at the top and skid down the first gentle slope. Her skirt would fly above her hips, her black-stockinged legs would writhe matte against a wilderness of chimneys, under the Norman sunlight. High over the elms and the hidden carp pools, up where Maman could only be a tiny blotch under a parasol, gazing at her. She imagined the sensation often: the feeling of roof-tiles rapidly sliding beneath the hard curve of her rump, the wind trapped under her blouse teasing the new breasts. And then the break: where the lower, steeper slope of the roof began, the point of no return, where the friction against her body would lessen and she would accelerate, flip over to twist the skirt—perhaps rip it off, be done with it, see it flutter away, like a dark kite!—to let the dovetailed tiles tense her nipple-points to an angry red, see a pigeon clinging to the eaves just before flight, taste the long hair caught against her teeth and tongue, cry out . . .

The taxi stopped in front of a cabaret in the rue Germaine Pilon, near Boulevard Clichy. Mélanie paid the fare and was handed her bag from the top of the cab. She felt something which might be the beginning of the rain against her cheek. The cab drove away, she stood before Le Nerf in an empty street, the flowered bag without gaiety under the clouds.

"You believed us after all." M. Itague stood, half-stooping holding the handle of the traveling bag. "Come, fétiche, inside. There's news."

On the small stage, which faced a dining room filled only with stacked tables and chairs, and lit by uncertain August daylight, came the confrontation with Satin.

"Mlle. Jarretière"; using her stage name. He was short and heavily built: the hair stuck out in tufts from each side of his head. He wore tights and a dress shirt, and directed his eyes parallel to a line connecting her hip-points. The skirt was two years old, she was growing. She felt embarrassed.

"I have nowhere to stay," she murmured.

"Here," announced Itague, "there's a back room. Here, until we move."

"Move?" She gazed at the raving flesh of tropical blossoms decorating her bag.

"We have the Théâtre de Vincent Castor," cried Satin. He spun, leaped, landed atop a small stepladder.

Itague grew excited, describing L'Enlèvement des Vierges Chinoises—Rape of the Chinese Virgins. It was to be Satin's finest ballet, the greatest music of Vladimir Porcépic, everything formidable. Rehearsals began tomorrow, she'd saved the day, they would have waited until the last minute because it could only be Mélanie, La Jarretière, to play Su Feng, the virgin who is tortured to death defending her purity against the invading Mongolians.

She had wandered away, to the edge of stage right. Itague stood in the center, gesturing, declaiming: while enigmatic on the stepladder, stage left, perched Satin, humming a music-hall song.

A remarkable innovation would be the use of automata, to play Su Feng's handmaidens. "A German engineer is building them," said Itague. "They're lovely creatures: one will even unfasten your robes. Another will play a zither—although the music itself comes from the pit. But they move so gracefully! Not like machines at all."

Was she listening? Of course: part of her. She stood awkwardly on one leg, reached down and scratched her calf, hot under its black stocking. Satin watched hungrily. She felt the twin curls moving restless against her neck. What was he saying? Automata . . .

She gazed up at the sky, through one of the room's side windows. God, would it ever rain?

Her room was hot and airless. Asprawl in one corner was an artist's lay figure, without a head. Old theater posters were scattered on the floor and bed, tacked to the wall. She thought once she heard thunder rumbling from outside.

"Rehearsals will be here," Itague told her. "Two weeks before the performance we move into the Théâtre de Vincent Castor, to get the feel of the boards." He used much theater talk. Not long ago he'd been a bartender near Place Pigalle.

Alone, she lay on the bed, wishing she could pray for rain. She was glad she couldn't see the sky. Perhaps certain of its tentacles already touched the roof of the cabaret. Someone rattled the door. She had thought to lock it. It was Satin, she knew. Soon she heard the Russian and Itague leave together by the back door.

She may not have slept: her eyes opened to the same dim ceiling. A mirror hung on the ceiling directly over the bed. She hadn't noticed it before. Deliberately she moved her legs, leaving her arms limp at her sides, till the hem of the blue skirt had worked high above the tops of the stockings. And lay gazing at the black and tender white. Papa had said, "How pretty your legs are: the legs of a dancer." She could not wait for the rain.

She rose, in a near-frenzy, removed blouse, skirt and undergarments and moved swiftly to the door, wearing only the black stockings and white buck tennis shoes. Somewhere on the way she managed to let down her hair. In the next room she found the costumes for L'Enlèvement des Vierges Chinoises. She felt her hair, heavy and almost viscous along the length of her back and tickling the tops of her buttocks as she knelt beside the large box and searched for the costume of Su Feng.

Back in the hot room she quickly removed shoes and stockings, keeping her eyes closed tight until she had fastened her hair in back with the spangled amber comb. She was not pretty unless she wore something. The sight of her nude body repelled her. Until she had drawn on the blond silk tights, embroidered up each leg with a long, slender dragon; stepped into the slippers with the cut steel buckles, and intricate straps which writhed up halfway to her knees. Nothing to restrain her breasts: she wrapped the underskirt tightly around her hips. It fastened with thirty hooks and eyes from waist to thigh-top, leaving a fur-trimmed slit so that she could dance. And finally, the kimono, translucent and dyed rainbowlike with sunbursts and concentric rings of cerise, amethyst, gold and jungly green.

She lay back once more, hair spread above her on the pillowless mattress, breath taken by her own beauty. If Papa could see her.

The lay figure in the corner was light and carried easily to the bed. She raised her knees high and—interested—saw her calves in the mirror crisscross over the small of its plaster back. Felt the coolness of the figure's flanks against the nude-colored silk, high on her thighs, hugged it tight. The neck top, jagged and flaking off, came to her breasts. She pointed her toes, began to dance horizontal, thinking of how her handmaidens would be.

Tonight there would be a magic-lantern show. Itague sat outside L'Ouganda, drinking absinthe and water. The stuff was supposed to be aphrodisiac but it affected Itague the opposite. He watched a Negro girl, one of the dancers, adjusting her stocking. He thought of francs and centimes.

There weren't many. The scheme might succeed. Porcépic had a name among the avant-garde in French music. Opinion in the city was violently divided: once the composer had been loudly insulted in the street by one of the most venerable of the Post-Romantics. Certainly the man's personal life wasn't one to endear many prospective patrons, either. Itague suspected him of smoking hashish. And there was the Black Mass.

"The poor child," Satin was saying. The table in front of him was nearly covered with empty wine glasses. The Russian moved them from time to time, blocking out the choreography to l'Enlè-vement. Satin drank wine like a Frenchman, Itague thought: never outright falling-down drunk. But growing more unstable, more nervous, as his chorus of hollow glass dancers grew. "Does she know where her father's gone?" Satin wondered aloud, looking off into the street. The night was windless, hot. Darker than Itague could ever remember it. Behind them the small orchestra began to play a tango. The Negro girl arose and went inside. To the south, the lights along the Champs Élysées picked out the underbelly of a nauseous-yellow cloud.

"With the father deserted," said Itague, "she's free. The mother doesn't care."

The Russian looked up, sudden. A glass fell over his table.

"—or nearly free."

"Fled to the jungles, I understand," Satin said. A waiter brought more wine.

"A gift. What had he ever given before? Have you seen the child's furs, her silks, the way she watches her own body? Heard the noblesse in the way she speaks? He gave her all that. Or was he giving it all to himself, by way of her?"

"Itague, she certainly could be the most giving—"

"No. No, it is merely being reflected. The girl functions as a mirror. You, that waiter, the chiffonnier in the next empty street she turns into: whoever happens to be standing in front of the mirror in the place of that wretched man. You will see the reflection of a ghost."

"M. Itague, your late readings have convinced you—"

"I said ghost," Itague answered softly. "Its name is not l'Heuremaudit, or l'Heuremaudit is only one of its names. That ghost fills the walls of this café and the streets of this district, perhaps every one of the world's arrondissements breathes its substance. Cast in the image of what? Not God. Whatever potent spirit can mesmerize the gift of irreversible flight into a grown man and the gift of self-arousal into the eyes of a young girl, his name is unknown. Or if known then he is Yahweh and we are all Jews, for no one will ever speak it." Which was strong talk for M. Itague. He read La Libre Parole, had stood among the crowds to spit at Captain Dreyfus.

The woman stood at their table, not waiting for them to rise, merely standing and looking as if she'd never waited for anything.

"Will you join us," said Satin eagerly. Itague looked far to the south, at the hanging yellow cloud which hadn't changed its shape.

She owned a dress shop in the rue du Quatre-Septembre. Wore tonight a Poiret-inspired evening dress of crepe Georgette the color of a Negro's head, beaded all over, covered with a cerise tunic which was drawn in under her breasts, Empire style. A harem veil covered the lower part of her face and fastened behind to a tiny hat riotous with the plumage of equatorial birds. Fan with amber stick, ostrich feathers, silk tassel. Sand-colored stockings, clocked exquisitely on the calf. Two brilliant-studded tortoise-shell pins through her hair; silver mesh bag, high-buttoned kid shoes with patent leather at the toe and French heel.

Who knew her "soul," Itague wondered, glancing sideways at the Russian. It was her clothes, her accessories, which determined her, fixed her among the mobs of tourist ladies and putains that filled the street.

"Our prima ballerina has arrived today," said Itague. He was always nervous around patrons. As bartender he'd seen no need to be diplomatic.

"Mélanie l'Heuremaudit," his patroness smiled. "When shall I meet her?"

"Any time," Satin muttered, shifting glasses, keeping his eyes on the table.

"Was there objection from the mother?" she asked.

The mother did not care, the girl herself, he suspected, did not care. The father's flight had affected her in some curious way. Last year she'd been eager to learn, inventive, creative. Satin would have his hands full this year. They would end up screaming at each other. No: the girl wouldn't scream.

The woman sat, lost in watching the night, which enveloped them like a velvet teaser-curtain. Itague, for all his time in Montmartre, had never seen behind it to the bare wall of the night. But had this one? He scrutinized her, looking for some such betrayal. He'd observed the face some dozen times. It had always gone through conventional grimaces, smiles, expressions of what passed for emotion. The German could build another, Itague thought, and no one could tell them apart.

The tango still played: or perhaps a different one, he hadn't been listening. A new dance, and popular. The head and body had to be kept erect, the steps had to be precise, sweeping, graceful. It wasn't like the waltz. In that dance was room for an indiscreet billow of crinolines, a naughty word whispered through mustaches into an ear all ready to blush. But here no words, no deviating: simply the wide spiral, turning about the dancing floor, gradually narrowing, tighter, until there was no motion except for the steps, which led nowhere. A dance for automata.

The curtain hung in total stillness. If Itague could have found its pulleys or linkage, he might make it stir. Might penetrate to the wall of the night's theater. Feeling suddenly alone in the wheeling, mechanical darkness of la Ville-Lumière, he wanted to cry, Strike! Strike the set of night and let us all see. . . .

The woman had been watching him, expressionless, poised like one of her own mannequins. Blank eyes, something to hang a Poiret dress on. Porcépic, drunk and singing, approached their table.

The song was in Latin. He'd just composed it for a Black Mass to be held tonight at his home in Les Batignolles. The woman wanted to come. Itague saw this immediately: a film seemed to drop from her eyes. He sat forlorn, feeling as if that most feared enemy of sleep had entered silently on a busy night, the one person whom you must come face to face with someday, who asks you, in the earshot of your oldest customers, to mix a cocktail whose name you have never heard.

They left Satin shuffling empty wine-glasses, looking as if to-night, in some tenantless street, he would murder.

Mélanie dreamed. The lay figure hung half off the bed, its arms stretched out, crucified, one stump touching her breast. It was the sort of dream in which, possibly, the eyes are open: or the last vision of the room is so reproduced in memory that all details are perfect, and the dreamer is unclear whether he is asleep or awake. The German stood over the bed watching her. He was Papa, but also a German.

"You must turn over," he repeated insistently. She was too embarrassed to ask why. Her eyes—which somehow she was able to see, as if she were disembodied and floating above the bed, perhaps somewhere behind the quicksilver of the mirror—her eyes were slanted Oriental: long lashes, spangled on the upper lids with tiny fragments of gold leaf. She glanced sideways at the lay figure. It had grown a head, she thought. The face was turned away. "To reach between your shoulderblades," said the German. What does he look for there, she wondered.

"Between my thighs," she whispered, moving on the bed. The silk was dotted with the same gold, like sequins. He placed his hand under her shoulder, turned her. The skirt twisted on her thighs: she saw their two inner edges blond and set off by the muskrat skin on the slit of the skirt. The Mélanie in the mirror watched sure fingers move to the center of her back, search, find a small key, which he began to wind.

"I got you in time," he breathed. "You would have stopped, had I not . . ."

The face of the lay figure had been turned toward her, all the time. There was no face.

She woke up, not screaming, but moaning as if sexually aroused.

Itague was bored. This Black Mass had attracted the usual complement of nervous and blasé. Porcépic's music was striking, as usual; highly dissonant. Lately he had been experimenting with African polyrhythms. Afterward Gerfaut the writer sat by a window, discoursing on how for some reason the young girl—adolescent or younger—had again become the mode in erotic fiction. Gerfaut had two or three chins, sat erect and spoke pedantically, though he had only Itague for an audience.

Itague didn't really want to talk with Gerfaut. He wanted to watch the woman who had come with them. She sat now in a side pew with one of the acolytes, a little sculptress from Vaugirard. The woman's hand, gloveless, and decorated only with a ring, stroked the girl's temple as they spoke. From the ring there sprouted a slender female arm, fashioned in silver. The hand was cupped, and held the lady's cigarette. As Itague watched she lit another: black paper, gold crest. A small pile of stubs lay scattered beneath her shoes.

Gerfaut had been describing the plot of his latest novel. The heroine was one Doucette, thirteen and struggled within by passions she could not name.

"A child, and yet a woman," Gerfaut said. "And a quality of something eternal about her. I even confess to a certain leaning of my own that way. La Jarretière . . ."

The old satyr.

Gerfaut at length moved away. It was nearly morning. Itague's head ached. He needed sleep, needed a woman. The lady still smoked her black cigarettes. The little sculptress lay, legs curled up on the seat, head pillowed against her companion's breasts. The black hair seemed to float like a drowned corpse's hair against the cerise tunic. The entire room and the bodies inside it—some twisted, some coupled, some awake—the scattered Hosts, the black furniture, were all bathed in an exhausted yellow light, filtered through rain clouds which refused to burst.

The lady was absorbed in burning tiny holes with the tip of her cigarette, through the skirt of the young girl. Itague watched as the pattern grew. She was writing ma fétiche, in black-rimmed holes. The sculptress wore no lingerie. So that when the lady finished the words would be spelled out by the young sheen of the girl's thighs. Defenseless? Itague wondered briefly.

II

The next day the same clouds were over the city, but it did not rain. Mélanie had awakened in the Su Feng costume, excited as soon as her eyes recognized the image in the mirror, knowing it hadn't rained. Porcépic showed up early with a guitar. He sat on the stage and sang sentimental Russian ballads about willow trees, students getting drunk and going off on sleigh-rides, the body of his love floating belly up in the Don. (A dozen young gathered round the samovar to read novels aloud: where had youth gone?) Porcépic, nostalgic, snuffled over his guitar.

Mélanie, looking newly scrubbed and wearing the dress she'd arrived in, stood behind him, hands over his eyes, and caroled harmony. Itague found them that way. In the yellow light, framed by the stage, they seemed like a picture he'd seen somewhere once. Or perhaps it was only the melancholy notes of the guitar, the subdued looks of precarious joy on their faces. Two young people conditionally at peace in the dog days. He went into the bar and began chipping away at a large block of ice; put the chips into an empty champagne bottle and filled the bottle with water.

By noon the dancers had arrived, most of the girls seemingly deep in a love affair with Isadora Duncan. They moved over the stage like languid moths, gauzy tunics fluttering limp. Itague guessed half the men were homosexual. The other half dressed that way: foppish. He sat at the bar and watched as Satin began the blocking.

"Which one is she?" The woman again. In Montmartre, 1913, people materialized.

"Over there with Porcépic."

She hurried over to be introduced. Vulgar, thought Itague, and then amended it at once to "uncontrollable." Perhaps? A little. La Jarretière stood there only gazing. Porcépic looked upset, as if they'd had an argument. Poor, young, pursued, fatherless. What would Gerfaut make of her? A wanton. In body if he could; in the pages of a manuscript most certainly. Writers had no moral sense.

Porcépic sat at the piano, playing Adoration of the Sun. It was a tango with cross-rhythms. Satin had devised some near-impossible movements to go with it. "It cannot be danced," screamed a young man, leaping from the stage to land, belligerent, in front of Satin.

Mélanie had hurried off to change to her Su Feng costume. Lacing on her slippers she looked up and saw the woman, leaning in the doorway.

"You are not real."

"I . . ." Hands resting dead on her thighs.

"Do you know what a fetish is? Something of a woman which gives pleasure but is not a woman. A shoe, a locket . . . une jarretière. You are the same, not real but an object of pleasure."

Mélanie could not speak.

"What are you like unclothed? A chaos of flesh. But as Su Feng, lit by hydrogen, oxygen, a cylinder of lime, moving doll-like in the confines of your costume . . . You will drive Paris mad. Women and men alike."

The eyes would not respond. Not with fear, desire, anticipation. Only the Mélanie in the mirror could make them do that. The woman had moved to the foot of the bed, ring hand resting on the lay figure. Mélanie darted past her, continued on toes and in twirls to the wings; appeared on stage, improvising to Porcépic's lackadaisical attack on the piano. Outside thunder could be heard, punctuating the music at random.

It was never going to rain.

The Russian influence in Porcépic's music was usually traced to his mother, who'd been a milliner in St. Petersburg. Porcépic now, between his hashish dreams, his furious attacks on the grand piano out in Les Batignolles, fraternized with a strange collection of Russian expatriates led by a certain Kholsky, a huge and homicidal tailor. They were all engaged in clandestine political activity, they spoke volubly and at length of Bakunin, Marx, Ulyanov.

Kholsky entered as the sun fell, hidden by yellow clouds. He drew Porcépic into an argument. The dancers dispersed, the stage emptied until only Mélanie and the woman remained. Satin produced his guitar; Porcépic sat on the piano, and they sang revolutionary songs. "Porcépic," grinned the tailor, "you'll be surprised one day. At what we will do."

"Nothing surprises me," answered Porcépic. "If history were cyclical, we'd now be in a decadence, would we not, and your projected Revolution only another symptom of it."

"A decadence is a falling-away," said Kholsky. "We rise."

"A decadence," Itague put in, "is a falling-away from what is human, and the further we fall the less human we become. Because we are less human, we foist off the humanity we have lost on inanimate objects and abstract theories."

The girl and the woman had moved away from the stage's one overhead light. They could hardly be seen. No sound came from up there. Itague finished the last of the ice water.

"Your beliefs are non-human," he said. "You talk of people as if they were point-clusters or curves on a graph."

"So they are," mused Kholsky, dreamy-eyed. "I, Satin, Porcépic may fall by the wayside. No matter. The Socialist Awareness grows, the tide is irresistible and irreversible. It is a bleak world we live in, M. Itague; atoms collide, brain cells fatigue, economies collapse and others rise to succeed them, all in accord with the basic rhythms of History. Perhaps she is a woman; women are a mystery to me. But her ways are at least measurable."

"Rhythm," snorted Itague, "as if you listened to the jitterings and squeaks of a metaphysical bedspring." The tailor laughed, delighted, like a great fierce child. Acoustics of the room gave his mirthfulness a sepulchral ring. The stage was empty.

"Come," said Porcépic. "To L'Ouganda," Satin on a table danced absently to himself.

Outside they passed the woman, holding Mélanie by the arm. They were headed toward the Métro station; neither spoke. Itague stopped at a kiosk to buy a copy of La Patrie, the closest one could get to an anti-Semitic newspaper in the evening. Soon they had vanished down the Boulevard Clichy.

As they descended the moving stairs, the woman said, "You are afraid." The girl didn't answer. She still wore the costume, covered now with a dolman wrap which looked expensive and was, and which the woman approved of. She bought them first-class tickets.

Closeted in the suddenly-materialized train, the woman asked: "Do you only lie passive then, like an object? Of course you do. It is what you are. Une fétiche." She pronounced the silent e's, as if she were singing. Air in the Métro was close. The same as outside. Mélanie studied the tail of the dragon on her calf.

After some time had passed the train climbed to ground level. Mélanie may have noticed they were crossing the river. To her left she saw the Eiffel Tower, quite near. They were crossing the Pont de Passy. At the first stop on the Left Bank the woman arose. She'd not left off clutching Mélanie's arm. Out on the street they began to walk, bearing southwest, into the district of Grenelle: a landscape of factories, chemical works, iron foundries. They were alone in the street. Mélanie wondered if the woman indeed lived among factories.

They walked for what seemed a mile: arrived, finally, at a loft building, in which only the third floor was occupied, by a manu-facturer of belts. They climbed narrow stairs, flight after flight. The woman lived on the top floor. Mélanie, though a dancer and strong-legged, now showed signs of exhaustion. When they arrived at the woman's rooms, the girl lay down without invitation on a large pouf in the center of the room. The place was decorated African and oriental: black pieces of primitive sculpture, lamp in the shape of a dragon, silks, Chinese red. The bed was a great four-poster. Mélanie's wrap had fallen away: her legs, blond and bedragoned, lay unmoving half on the pouf, half on the oriental rug. The woman sat down beside the girl, resting her hand lightly on Mélanie's shoulder, and began to talk.

If we've not already guessed, "the woman" is, again, the lady V. of Stencil's mad time-search. No one knew her name in Paris.

Not only was she V., however, but also V. in love. Herbert Stencil was willing to let the key to his conspiracy have a few of the human passions. Lesbianism, we are prone to think in this Freudian period of history, stems from self-love projected on to some other human object. If a girl gets to feeling narcissist, she will also sooner or later come upon the idea that women, the class she belongs to, are not so bad either. Such may have been the case with Mélanie, though who could say: perhaps the spell of incest at Serre Chaude was an indication that her preferences merely lay outside the usual, exogamous-heterosexual pattern which prevailed in 1913.

But as for V.—V. in love—the hidden motives, if there were any, remained a mystery to all observers. Everyone connected with the production knew what was going on; but because intelligence of the affair remained inside a circle inclined toward sadism, sacrilege, endogamy and homosexuality anyway, there was little concern, and the two were let alone, like young lovers. Mélanie showed up faithfully at all rehearsals and as long as the woman wasn't enticing her away from the production—which, apparently, she had no intention of doing, being a patroness—Itague for one couldn't have cared less.

One day the girl arrived at Le Nerf accompanied by the woman and wearing schoolboy's clothing: tight black trousers, a white shirt, a short black jacket. Moreover, her head—all her thick buttock-length hair—had been shorn. She was nearly bald; and but for the dancer's body no clothes could conceal, she might have been a young lad playing hooky. There was, fortunately, a long black wig in the costume box. Satin greeted the idea with enthusiasm. Su Feng would appear in the first act with hair, in the second without: having been tortured anyway by Mongolians. It would shock the audience, whose tastes, he felt, were jaded.

At every rehearsal, the woman sat at a rear table, watching, silent. All her attention was concentrated on the girl. Itague tried at first to engage her in conversation; but failed and went back to La Vie Heureuse, Le Rire, Le Charivari. When the company moved to the Théâtre de Vincent Castor, she followed like a faithful lover. Mélanie continued dressing transvestite for the street. Speculation among the company was that a peculiar inversion had taken place: since an affair of this sort generally involves one dominant and one submissive, and it was clear which one was which, the woman should have appeared in the clothing of an aggressive male. Porcépic, to the amusement of all, produced at L'Ouganda one evening a chart of the possible combinations the two could be practicing. It came out to 64 different sets of roles, using the subheadings "dressed as," "social role," "sexual role." They could both for example be dressed as males, both have dominant social roles and strive for dominance sexually. They could be dressed different-sexed and both be entirely passive, the game then being to trick the other into making an aggressive move. Or any of 62 other combinations. Perhaps, Satin suggested, there were also inanimate mechanical aids. This, it was agreed, would confuse the picture. At one point someone suggested that the woman might actually be a transvestite to begin with, which made things even more amusing.

But what actually was going on at the loft in Grenelle? Each mind at L'Ouganda and among the troupe at the Théâtre Vincent Castor had conjured up a different scene; machines of exquisite torture, bizarre costuming, grotesque movements of muscle under flesh.

How disappointed they all would have been. Had they seen the skirt of the little sculptress-acolyte from Vaugirard, heard the pet-name the woman had for Mélanie, or read—as had Itague— in the new science of the mind, they would have known that certain fetishes never have to be touched or handled at all; only seen, for there to be complete fulfillment. As for Mélanie, her lover had provided her with mirrors, dozens of them. Mirrors with handles, with ornate frames, full-length and pocket mirrors came to adorn the loft wherever one turned to look.

V. at the age of thirty-three (Stencil's calculation) had found love at last in her peregrinations through (let us be honest) a world if not created then at least described to its fullest by Karl Baedeker of Leipzig. This is a curious country, populated only by a breed called "tourists." Its landscape is one of inanimate monu-ments and buildings; near-inanimate barmen, taxi-drivers, bellhops, guides: there to do any bidding, to various degrees of efficiency, on receipt of the recommended baksheesh, pourboire, manica, tip. More than this it is two-dimensional, as is the Street, as are the pages and maps of those little red handbooks. As long as the Cook's, Travellers' Clubs and banks are open, the Distribution of Time section followed scrupulously, the plumbing at the hotel in order ("No hotel," writes Karl Baedeker, "can be recommended as first-class that is not satisfactory in its sanitary arrangements, which should include an abundant flush of water and a supply of proper toilette paper"), the tourist may wander anywhere in this coordinate system without fear. War never becomes more

serious than a scuffle with a pickpocket, one of "the huge army . . .
who are quick to recognize the stranger and skilful in taking
advantage of his ignorance"; depression and prosperity are reflected only in the rate of exchange; politics are of course never
discussed with the native population. Tourism thus is suprana-
tional, like the Catholic Church, and perhaps the most absolute
communion we know on earth: for be its members American, German, Italian, whatever, the Tour Eiffel, Pyramids, and Campanile
all evoke identical responses from them; their Bible is clearly written and does not admit of private interpretation; they share the
same landscapes, suffer the same inconveniences; live by the same
pellucid time-scale. They are the Street's own.

The lady V., one of them for so long, now suddenly found
herself excommunicated; bounced unceremoniously into the null-
time of human love, without having recognized the exact moment
as any but when Mélanie entered a side door to Le Nerf on Porcépic's arm and time—for a while—ceased. Stencil's dossier has
it on the authority of Porcépic himself, to whom V. told much
of their affair. He repeated none of it then, neither at L'Ouganda
nor anywhere else: only to Stencil, years later. Perhaps he felt
guilty about his chart of permutations and combinations, but to
this extent at least he acted like a gentleman. His description of
them is a well-composed and ageless still-life of love at one of its
many extremes: V. on the pouf, watching Mélanie on the bed;
Mélanie watching herself in the mirror; the mirror-image perhaps contemplating V. from time to time. No movement but
a minimum friction. And yet one solution to a most ancient
paradox of love: simultaneous sovereignty yet a fusing-together.
Dominance and submissiveness didn't apply; the pattern of three
was symbiotic and mutual. V. needed her fetish, Mélanie a mirror,
temporary peace, another to watch her have pleasure. For such
is the self-love of the young that a social aspect enters in: an
adolescent girl whose existence is so visual observes in a mirror
her double; the double becomes a voyeur. Frustration at not being
able to fragment herself into an audience of enough only adds
to her sexual excitement. She needs, it seems, a real voyeur to
complete the illusion that her reflections are, in fact, this audience.
With the addition of this other—multiplied also, perhaps, by

mirrors—comes consummation: for the other is also her own double. She is like a woman who dresses only to be looked at and talked about by other women: their jealousy, whispered remarks, reluctant admiration are her own. They are she.

As for V., she recognized—perhaps aware of her own progression toward inanimateness—the fetish of Mélanie and the fetish of herself to be one. As all inanimate objects, to one victimized by them, are alike. It was a variation on the Porpentine theme, the Tristan-and-Iseult theme, indeed, according to some, the single melody, banal and exasperating, of all Romanticism since the Middle Ages: "the act of love and the act of death are one." Dead at last, they would be one with the inanimate universe and with each other. Love-play until then thus becomes an impersonation of the inanimate, a transvestism not between sexes but between quick and dead; human and fetish. The clothing each wore was incidental. The hair shorn from Mélanie's head was incidental: only an obscure bit of private symbolism for the lady V. perhaps, if she were in fact Victoria Wren, having to do with her time in the novitiate.

If she were Victoria Wren, even Stencil couldn't remain all unstirred by the ironic failure her life was moving toward, too rapidly by that prewar August ever to be reversed. The Florentine spring, the young entrepreneuse with all spring's hope in her virtù, with her girl's faith that Fortune (if only her skill, her timing held true) could be brought under control; that Victoria was being gradually replaced by V.; something entirely different, for which the young century had as yet no name. We all get involved to an extent in the politics of slow dying, but poor Victoria had become intimate also with the Things in the Back Room.

If V. suspected her fetishism at all to be part of any conspiracy leveled against the animate world, any sudden establishment here of a colony of the Kingdom of Death, then this might justify the opinion held in the Rusty Spoon that Stencil was seeking in her his own identity. But such was her rapture at Mélanie's having sought and found her own identity in her and in the mirror's soulless gleam that she continued unaware, off-balanced by love; forgetting even that although the Distribution of Time here on pouf, bed and mirrors had been abandoned, their love was in its way only another version of tourism; for as tourists bring into the world as it has evolved part of another, and eventually create a parallel society of their own in every city, so the Kingdom of Death is served by fetish-constructions like V.'s, which represent a kind of infiltration.

What would have been her reaction, had she known? Again, an ambiguity. It would have meant, ultimately, V.'s death: in a sudden establishment here, of the inanimate Kingdom, despite all efforts to prevent it. The smallest realization—at any step: Cairo, Florence, Paris—that she fitted into a larger scheme leading eventually to her personal destruction and she might have shied off, come to establish eventually so many controls over herself that she became—to Freudian, behaviorist, man of religion, no matter—a purely determined organism, an automaton, constructed, only quaintly, of human flesh. Or by contrast, might have reacted against the above, which we have come to call Puritan, by journeying even deeper into a fetish-country until she became entirely and in reality—not merely as a love-game with any Mélanie—an inanimate object of desire. Stencil even departed from his usual ploddings to daydream a vision of her now, at age seventy-six: skin radiant with the bloom of some new plastic; both eyes glass but now containing photoelectric cells, connected by silver electrodes to optic nerves of purest copper wire and leading to a brain exquisitely wrought as a diode matrix could ever be. Solenoid relays would be her ganglia, servo-actuators move her flawless nlyon limbs, hydraulic fluid be sent by a platinum heart-pump through butyrate veins and arteries. Perhaps—Stencil on occasion could have as vile a mind as any of the Crew—even a complex system of pressure transducers located in a marvelous vagina of polyethylene; the variable arms of their Wheatstone bridges all leading to a single silver cable which fed pleasure-voltages direct to the correct register of the digital machine in her skull. And whenever she smiled or grinned in ecstasy there would gleam her crowning feature: Eigenvalue's precious dentures.

Why did she tell so much to Porcépic? She was afraid, she said, that it wouldn't last; that Mélanie might leave her. Glittering world of the stage, fame, foul-mind's darling of a male audience: the woe of many a lover. Porcépic gave her what comfort he could.

He was under no delusions about love as anything but transitory, he left all such dreaming to his compatriot Satin, who was an idiot anyway. Sad-eyed, he commiserated with her: what else should he've done? Pass moral judgment? Love is love. It shows up in strange displacements. This poor woman was racked by it. Stencil however only shrugged. Let her be a lesbian, let her turn to a fetish, let her die: she was a beast of venery and he had no tears for her.

The night of the performance arrived. What happened then was available to Stencil in police records, and still told, perhaps, by old people around the Butte. Even as the pit orchestra tuned up there was loud argument in the audience. Somehow the performance had taken on a political cast. Orientalism—at this period showing up all over Paris in fashions, music, theater—had been connected along with Russia to an international movement seeking to overthrow Western civilization. Only six years before a newspaper had been able to sponsor an auto-race from Peking to Paris, and enlist the willing assistance of all the countries between. The political situation these days was somewhat darker. Hence, the turmoil which erupted that night in the Théâtre Vincent Castor.

Before the first act was barely under way, there came catcalls and uncouth gestures from the anti-Porcépic faction. Friends, already calling themselves Porcépiquistes, sought to suppress them. Also present in the audience was a third force who merely wanted quiet enough to enjoy the performance and naturally enough tried to silence, prevent or mediate all disputes. A three-way wrangle developed. By intermission it had degenerated into near-chaos.

Itague and Satin screamed at each other in the wings, neither able to hear the other for the noise out in the audience. Porcépic sat by himself in a corner, drinking coffee, expressionless. A young ballerina, returning from the dressing room, stopped to talk. "Can you hear the music?" Not too well, she admitted. "Dommage. How does La Jarretière feel?" Mélanie knew the dance by heart, she had perfect rhythm, she inspired the whole troupe. The dancer was ecstatic in her praise: another Isadora Duncan! Porcépic shrugged, made a moue. "If I ever have money again," more to himself than to her, "I'll hire an orchestra and dance company for my own amusement and have them perform L'Enlèvement. Only to see what the work is like. Perhaps I will catcall too." They laughed sadly with one another, and the girl passed on.

The second act was even noisier. Only toward the end were the attentions of the few serious onlookers taken entirely by La Jarretière. As the orchestra, sweating and nervous, moved baton-driven into the last portion, Sacrifice of the Virgin, a powerful, slow-building seven-minute crescendo which seemed at its end to've explored the furthest possible reaches of dissonance, tonal color and (as Le Figaro's critic put it next morning) "orchestral barbarity," light seemed all at once to be reborn behind Mélanie's rainy eyes and she became again the Norman dervish Porcépic remembered. He moved closer to the stage, watching her with a kind of love. An apocryphal story relates that he vowed at that moment never to touch drugs again, never to attend another Black Mass.

Two of the male dancers, whom Itague had never left off calling Mongolized fairies, produced a long pole, pointed wickedly at one end. The music, near triple-forte, could be heard now above the roaring of the audience. Gendarmes had moved in at the rear entrances, and were trying ineffectually to restore order. Satin, next to Porcépic, one hand on the composer's shoulder, leaned forward, shaking. It was a tricky bit of choreography, Satin's own. He'd got the idea from reading an account of an Indian massacre in America. While two of the other Mongolians held her, struggling and head shaven, Su Feng was impaled at the crotch on the point of the pole and slowly raised by the entire male part of the company, while the females lamented below. Suddenly one of the automaton handmaidens seemed to run amok, tossing itself about the stage. Satin moaned, gritted his teeth. "Damn the German," he said, "it will distract." The conception depended on Su Feng continuing her dance while impaled, all movement restricted to one point in space, an elevated point, a focus, a climax.

The pole was now erect, the music four bars from the end. A terrible hush fell over the audience, gendarmes and combatants all turned as if magnetized to watch the stage. La Jarretière's movements became more spastic, agonized: the expression on the normally dead face was one which would disturb for years the dreams of those in the front rows. Porcépic's music was now almost deafening: all tonal location had been lost, notes screamed out simultaneous and random like fragments of a bomb: winds, strings, brass and percussion were indistinguishable as blood ran down the pole, the impaled girl went limp, the last chord blasted out, filled the theater, echoed, hung, subsided. Someone cut all the stage lights, someone else ran to close the curtain.

It never opened. Mélanie was supposed to have worn a protective metal device, a species of chastity belt, into which the point of the pole fit. She had left it off. A physician in the audience had been summoned at once by Itague as soon as he saw the blood. Shirt torn, one eye blackened, the doctor knelt over the girl and pronounced her dead.

Of the woman, her lover, nothing further was seen. Some versions tell of her gone hysterical backstage, having to be detached forcibly from Mélanie's corpse; of her screaming vendetta at Satin and Itague for plotting to kill the girl. The coroner's verdict, charitably, was death by accident. Perhaps Mélanie, exhausted by love, excited as at any première, had forgotten. Adorned with so many combs, bracelets, sequins, she might have become confused in this fetish-world and neglected to add to herself the one inanimate object that would have saved her. Itague thought it was suicide, Satin refused to talk about it, Porcépic suspended judgment. But they lived with it for many years.

Rumor had it that a week or so later the lady V. ran off with one Sgherraccio, a mad Irredentist. At least they both disappeared from Paris at the same time; from Paris and as far as anyone on the Butte could say, from the face of the earth.

10 Grace Paley

Grace Paley was born in the Bronx in 1922 and attended Hunter College and New York University. Her first collection of stories, The Little Disturbances of Man, was published in 1959 and reissued in 1968. Of Mrs. Paley's writing Philip Roth has said: "Grace Paley has deep feelings, a wild imagination, and a style whose toughness and bumpiness arise not out of exasperation with the language, but the daring and heart of a genuine writer of prose."

❖

IN TIME WHICH MADE A MONKEY OF US ALL

No doubt that is Eddie Teitelbaum on the topmost step of 1434, a dark-jawed, bossy youth in need of repair. He is dredging a cavity with a Fudgsicle stick. He is twitching the cotton in his ear. He is sniffing and snarling and swallowing spit because of rotten drainage. But he does not give a damn. Physicalities aside, he is only knee-deep so far in man's inhumanity; he is reconciled to his father's hair-shirted Jacob, Itzik Halbfunt; he is resigned to his place in this brick-lined Utrillo which runs east and west, flat in the sun, a couple of thousand stoop steps. On each step there is probably someone he knows. For the present, no names.

Now look at the little kids that came in those days to buzz at his feet. That is what they did, they gathered in this canyon pass, rumbling at the knee of his glowering personality. Some days he heeded them a long and wiggily line which they followed up and down the street, around the corner, and back to 1434.

On dark days he made elephants, dogs, rabbits, and long-tailed mice for them out of pipe cleaners. "You can also make a neat

ass cleaner this way," he told them for a laugh, which turned their
mothers entirely against him. Well, he was a poor sloppy bastard
then, worked Saturdays, Sundays, summers, and holidays, no union
contract in his father's pet shop. But penny-wise as regards the
kids, he was bubble-gum foolish, for bubble gum strengthens the
jaw. He never worried about teeth but approved of dentures and,
for that matter, all prostheses.

In the end, man will probably peel his skin (said Eddie) to
favor durable plastics, at which time, kaput the race problem. A
man will be any color he chooses or translucent too, if the shape
and hue of intestines can be made fashionable. Eddie had lots of
advance information which did not turn a hair of his head, for
he talked of the ineluctable future; but all his buddies, square or
queer, clever and sentimental, pricked their ears in tears.

He also warned them of the spies who peeked from windows
or plopped like stones on the street which was the kids' by all
unentailed rights. Mrs. Goredinsky, head spy the consistency of
fresh putty, sat on an orange crate every morning, her eye on the
door of 1434. Also Mrs. Green, Republican poll watcher in November—the rest of the year she waited in her off-the-street doorway, her hand trembling, her head turning one way, then the
other.

"Tennis, anyone?" asked Carl Clop, the super's son.

"Let her live," said Eddie, marking time.

Then one day old Clop, the super, rose from the cellar, scrambling the kids before him with the clatter of bottle tops. He took
a stance five steps below Eddie, leaned on his broom, and prepared to make conversation.

"What's the matter, son?" he asked. "Where's your pals?"

"Under the kitchen table," said Eddie. "They got juiced on
apricot nectar."

"Go on, Eddie; you got an in. Who's the bum leaves Kleenex
in the halls?"

"I don't know. Goredinsky has a cold for months."

"Aah, her, what you got against her, a old pot of cabbage
soup? You always make a remark on her."

Out of a dark window in second-floor front a tiny voice sang
to the tune of "My Country, 'tis of Thee":

"Mrs. Goredinsky was a spy
Caught by the FBI.
Tomorrow she will die—
Won't that be good?"

"Get a load of that, Clop," said Eddie. "Nobody has any privacy around here, you notice? Listen to me, Clop, in the country in superbia, every sonofabitch has a garage to tinker in. On account of that, great ideas, brilliant inventions come from out of town. Why the hell shouldn't we produce as fine minds as anybody else?"

Now Eddie was just helping Clop out, talkwise, maintaining relations with authority, so to speak. He would have ended the conversation right then and there, since at that moment he was in the mental act of inventing a cockroach segregator, a device which would kill only that cockroach which emigrated out of its pitchy crack into the corn flakes of people. If properly conceived and delicately contrived, all the other cockroaches would be left alone to gum up the lathes and multiply and finally inherit the entire congressional district. Why not?

"Not so dumb," said Mr. Clop. "Privacy." Then he let Eddie have a bewhiskered, dead-eye, sideways leer. "What you need privacy for, you? To stick it into girls?"

No reply.

Clop retrieved the conversation. "So that's how it goes, that's how they get ahead of us, the farmers. What do you know? How come someone don't figure it out, to educate you kids up a little, especially in summer? The city's the one pays the most taxes. Anyway, what the hell you do on the stoop all day? How come Carl hangs out in front of Michailovitch, morning noon night, every tme I look up? Come on, get the hell off the stoop here, you Teitelbaum," he yelled. "Stupids. Stick the Kleenex in your pocket." He gave Eddie a splintery whisk with the broom. He turned away, frowning, thinking. "Go 'way, bums," he mumbled at two loitering infants, maybe four years old.

Nevertheless, Clop was a man of grave instinct, a serious man. Three days later he offered Eddie the key to the bicycle and carriage room of 1436, the corner and strategic building.

"For thinking up inventions," said Clop. "What are we, animals?" He went on to tell that he was proud to be associated with scientific research. So many boys were out bumming, on the tramp, tramp, tramp. Carl, his own son, looked bad, played poker day and night under the stairs with Shmul, the rabbi's son, a Yankee in a skullcap.* Therefore, Clop begged Eddie to persuade Carl to do a little something in his line of thinking and follow-through. He really liked science very much, Mr. Clop said, but needed a little encouragement, since he had no mother.

"O.K., O.K." Eddie was willing. "He can help me figure out a rocket to the moon."

"The moon?" Mr. Clop asked. He peeked out the cellar window at a piece of noonday sky.

Right before Eddie's mirage-making eyes for his immediate use was a sink, electricity, gas outlets, and assorted plumbing pipes. What else is basic to any laboratory? Do you think that the Institute for Advanced Studies started out any stronger than that, or all the little padlocked cyclotron houses? The beginning of everything is damp and small, but wide-armed oaks—according to myth, legend, and the folk tales of the people—from solitary acorns grow.

Eddie's first chore was the perfection of the cockroach segregator. At cost plus 6 per cent, he trailed some low-voltage wire all around local kitchen baseboards, which immediately returned to its gummy environment under the linoleum the cockroach which could take a hint. It electrocuted the stubborn fools not meant by Darwin anyway to survive.

There was nothing particularly original in this work. Eddie would be the first to concede that he had been thinking about the country and cows all summer, as well as barbed wire, and had simply applied recollected knowledge to the peculiar conditions of his environment.

"What a hell of a summer this is turning into," said Carl, plucking a bug off the lab's wire. "I mean, we ought to have some fun too, Eddie. How about it? I mean, if we were a club, we would be more well rounded."

"Everyone wants fun," said Eddie.

"I don't mean real fun," said Carl. "We could be a science

*Yankee in a Skullcap: My Day & Night in the East Bronx, Shmul Klein, Mitzvah Press club. But just you and me— No, I'm sick of that crap. Get some more guys in. Make it an organization, Eddie."

"Why not?" said Eddie, anxious to get to work.

"Great. I've been thinking of some names. How's . . . Advanseers . . . Get it?"

"Stinks."

"I thought of a funny one . . . like on those little cards. How about The Thimkers?"

"Very funny."

Carl didn't press it. "All right. But we have to get some more members."

"Two," said Eddie, thinking a short laugh.

"Well, O.K. But, Eddie, what about girls? I mean, after all, women have the vote a long time. They're doctors and . . . What about Madame Curie? There's others."

"Please, Carl, lay off. We got about thirteen miles of wire left. I got to figure out something."

Carl couldn't stop. He liked girls all around him, he said. They made him a sunny, cheerful guy. He could think of wonderful witticisms when they were present. Especially Rita Niskov and Stella Rosenzweig.

He would like to go on, describing, as an example, the Spitz twins, how they were so top-heavy but with hips like boys. Hadn't Eddie seen them afloat at the Seymour Street Pool, water-winged by their airtight tits?

Also darling little Stella Rosenzweig, like a Vassar girl despite being only in third-term high. When you danced with her, you could feel something like pinpricks, because although she was little she was extremely pointed.

Eddie was absolutely flipped by a ground swell of lust just before lunch. To save himself, he coldly said, "No, no. No girls. Saturday nights they can come over for a little dancing, a little petting. Fix up the place. No girls in the middle of the week."

He promised, however, to maintain an open line between Carl and the Spitz twins by recruiting for immediate membership their brother Arnold. That was a lucky, quiet choice. Arnold needed a corner in which to paint. He stated that daylight would eventually disappear and with it the myths about northlight. He

founded in that dark cellar a school of painters called the Light
Breakers, who still work together in a loft on East Twenty-ninth
Street under two 25-watt bulbs.

On Carl's recommendation Shmul Klein was ingathered, a
great fourth hand, but Eddie said no card tables. Shmul had the
face of an unentrammeled guy. Did he make book after school?
No, no, he said, rumors multiplied: the truth was single.

He was a journalist of life, as Eddie was a journeyman in
knowledge. When questioned about his future, he would guess
that he was destined to trip over grants, carrying a fearsome load
of scholarships on his way to a soft job in advertising, using a
fraction of his potential.

Well, there were others, of course, who glinted around, seeking
membership under the impression that a neighborhood cat house
was being established. Eddie laughed and pointed to a market
glutted by individual initiative, not to mention the way the bottom has fallen out of the virgin as moral counterweight.

It took time out of Eddie to be a club. Whole afternoons and
weekends were lost for public reasons. The boys asked him to
hold open meetings so that the club's actual disposition would be
appreciated by the parents of girls. Eddie talked then on "The
Dispersal of the Galaxies and the Conservation of Matter." Carl
applauded twice, in an anarchy of enthusiasm. Mr. Clop listened,
was impressed, asked what he could do for them, and then tied
their wattage into Mrs. Goredinsky's meter.

Eddie offered political lectures, too, as these are times which, if
man were human, could titillate his soul. From the four-by-six
room which Eddie shared with Itzik Halbfunt, his father's monkey, he saw configurations of disaster revise the sky before anyone
even smelled smoke.

"Who was the enemy?" he asked, to needle a little historicity
into his clubmates. "Was it the People of the Sea? Troy? Rome?
The Saracens? The Huns? The Russians? The colonies in Africa,
the stinking proletariat? The hot owners of capital?"

Typically he did not answer. He let them weave these broad
questions on poor pinheaded looms while he slipped into Michailovitch's for a celery tonic.

He shared his profits from the cockroach segregator with the
others. This way they took an interest and were courteous enough

to heed his philosophic approach, as did the clients to whom he pointed out a human duty to interfere with nature as little as possible except for food-getting (survival), a seminal tragedy which obtains in the wild forests as well.

Reading, thinking on matters beyond the scope of the physical and chemical sciences carried his work from the idealistic cockroach segregator to a telephone dial system for people on relief within a ten-block radius—and finally to the well-known War Attenuator, which activated all his novitiate lab assistants but featured his own lonely patience.

"Eddie, Eddie, you take too much time," said his father. "What about us?"

"You," said Eddie.

How could he forget his responsibilities at the Teitelbaum Zoo, a pet shop where three or four mutts, scabby with sawdust, slept in the window? A hundred gallons of goldfish were glassed inside, four canaries singing tu-wit-tu-wu—all waited for him to dump the seeds, the hash, the mash into their dinner buckets. Poor Itzik Halbfunt, the monkey from Paris, France, waited too, nibbling his beret. Itzik looked like Mr. Teitelbaum's uncle who had died of Jewishness in the epidemics of '40, '41. For this reason he would never be sold. "Too bad," is an outsider's comment, as a certain local Italian would have paid maybe $45 for that monkey.

In sorrow Mr. Teitelbaum had turned away forever from his neighbor, man, and for life, then, he squinted like a cat and hopped like a bird and drooped like a dog. Like a parrot, all he could say and repeat when Eddie made his evening break was, "Eddie, don't leave the door open, me and the birds will fly away."

"If you got wings, Papa, fly," said Eddie. And that was Eddie's life for years and years, from childhood on: he shoveled dog shit and birdseed, watching the goldfish float and feed and die in a big glass of water far away from China.

One Monday morning in July, bright and hot and early, Eddie called the boys together for assignments in reconnaissance and mapping. Carl knew the basement extremely well, but Eddie wanted a special listing of doors and windows, their conditions established. There were three buildings involved in this series,

1432, 1434, 1436. He requested that they keep a diary in order to arrive at viable statistics on how many ladies used the laundry facilities at what hours, how hot the hot water generally was at certain specific times.

"Because we are going to work with gases now. Gas expands, compresses, diffuses, and may be liquefied. If there is any danger involved at any point, I will handle it and be responsible. Just don't act like damn fools. I promise you," he added bitterly, "a lot of fun."

He asked them to develop a little competence with tools. Carl as the son of Clop, plumber, electrician, and repairman, was a happy, aggressive teacher. In the noisy washing-machine hours of morning, under Carl's supervision, they drilled barely visible holes in the basement walls and pipe-fitted long-wear rubber tubes. The first series of tests required a network of delicate ducts.

"I am the vena cava and the aorta," Eddie paraphrased. "Whatever goes from me must return to me. You be the engineers. Figure out the best way to nourish all outlying areas."

By "nourish," Shmul pointed out, he really meant "suffocate."

On the twenty-ninth of July they were ready. At 8:13 A.M. the first small-scale, small-area test took place. At 8:12 A.M., just before the moment of pff,* all the business of the cellars was being transacted—garbage transferred from small cans into large ones; early wide-awake grandmas, rocky with insomnia, dumped wash into the big tubs; boys in swimming trunks rolled baby carriages out into the cool morning. A coal truck arrived, shifted, backed up across the sidewalk, stopped, shoved its black ramp into one sooty cellar window, and commenced to roar.

Mr. Clop's radio was loud. As he worked, rolling the cans, hoisting them with Carl's help up the wooden cellar steps, arguing with the coalmen about the right of way, he listened to the news. He wanted to know if the sun would roll out, flashy as ever; if there was a chance for rain, as his brother grew tomatoes in Jersey.

At 8:13 A.M. the alarm clock in the laboratory gave the ringing word. Eddie touched a button in the substructure of an ordinary

*The Moment of Pff: An Urban Boyhood, Shmul Klein, Mitzvah Press

glass coffeepot, from whose spout two tubes proceeded into the wall. A soft hiss followed: the coffeepot steamed and clouded and cleared.

Forty seconds later Mr. Clop howled, "Jesus, who farted?" although the smell was not quite like that at all, Eddie the concoctor knew. It was at least *meant* to be greener, skunkier, closer to the deterrents built into animals and flowers, but stronger. He was informed immediately of a certain success by the bellows of the coal delivery men, the high cries of the old ladies.

Satisfied, Eddie touched another button, this at the base of Mrs. Spitz's reconstructed vacuum cleaner. The reverse process used no more than two minutes. The glass clouded, the spout was stoppered, the genie returned.

Eddie knew it would take the boys a little longer to get free of their observation posts and the people who were observing them. During that speck of time his heart sank as hearts may do after a great act of love. He suffered a migraine from acceding desolation. When Carl brought excited news, he listened sadly, for what is life? he thought.

"God, great!" cried Carl. "History-making! Crazee! Eddie, Eddie, a mystery! No one knows how what where . . ."

"Yet," Eddie said. "You better quiet down, Carl."

"But listen, Eddie, nobody can figure it out," said Carl. "How long did it last? It ended before that fat dope, Goredinsky, got out of our toilet. She was hollering and pulling up her bloomers and pulling down her dress. I watched from the door. It laid me sidewise. She's not even supposed to use that toilet. It's ours."

"Yeh," said Eddie.

"Wait a minute, wait a minute, listen. My father kept saying, 'Jesus dear, did I forget to open an exhaust someplace? Jesus dear, what did I do? Did I wreck up the flues? Tell me, tell me, give me a hint!'"

"Your father's a very nice old guy," Eddie said coldly.

"Oh, I know that," said Carl.

"Wonderful head," said Arnold, who had just entered.

"Look at my father," Eddie said, taking the dim and agitated view. "Look at him, he sits in that store, he doesn't shave, maybe twice a week. Sometimes he doesn't move an hour or two. His nose drips, so the birds know he's living. That lousy sonofabitch, he used to be a whole expert on world history, he supports a stinking zoo and that filthy monkey that can't even piss straight." . . . Bitterness for his cramped style and secondhand pants took his breath away. So he laughed and let them have the facts. "You know, my old man was so hard up just before he got married and he got such terrific respect for women (he respects women, let me tell you) that you know what he did? He snuck into the Bronx Zoo and he rammed it up a chimpanzee there. You're surprised, aren't you! Listen to me, they shipped that baby away to France. If my father'd've owned up, we'd've been rich. It makes me sore to think about. He'd've been the greatest bug-gerer in recorded history. He'd be wanted in pigsties and stud farms. They'd telegraph him a note from Irkutsk to get in on those crazy cross-pollination experiments. What he could do to winter wheat! That cocksucker tells everyone he went over to Paris to see if his cousins were alive. He went over to get my big brother Itzik. To bring him home. To aggravate my mother and me."

"Aw . . ." said Carl.

"So that's it," said Shmul, a late reporter, playing alongside Eddie. "That's how you got so smart. Constant competition with an oddball sibling . . . Aha . . ."

"Please," said Arnold, his sketch pad wobbly on his knee. "Please, Eddie, raise your arms like that again, like you just did when you were mad. It gives me an idea."

"Jerks," said Eddie, and spat on the spotless laboratory floor. "A bunch of jerks."

Still and all, the nineteenth-century idea that progress is immanent is absolutely correct. For his sadness dwindled and early August was a time of hard work and glorious conviviality. The mystery of the powerful nontoxic gas from an unknowable source remained. The boys kept their secret. Outsiders wondered. They knew. They swilled Coke like a regiment which has captured all the enemy pinball machines without registering a single tilt.

Saturday nights at the lab were happy, ringing with 45 r.p.m.'s, surrounded by wonderful women. All kinds of whistling adventures were recorded by Shmul. . . . He had it all written down: how one night Mr. Clop wandered in looking for fuses and found Arnold doing life sketches of Rita Niskov. She held a retort over one breast in order to make technical complications for Arnold, who was ambitious. "Keep it up, keep it up, son," mumbled Clop, to whom it was all a misunderstanding.

And another night Blanchie Spitz took off everything but her drawers and her brassière and because of a teaspoon of rum in a quart and a half of Coke decided to do setting-up exercises to the tune of the "Nutcracker Suite." "Ah, Blanchie," said Carl, nearly nauseous with love, "do me a belly dance, baby." "I don't know what a belly dance is, Carl," she said, and to the count of eight went into a deep knee bend. Arnold lassoed her with Rita's skirt, which he happened to have in his hand. He dragged Blanchie off to a corner, where he slapped her, dressed her, asked her what her fee was and did it include relatives, and before she could answer he slapped her again, then took her home, Rita's skirt flung over one shoulder. This kind of event will turn an entire neighborhood against the most intense chronology of good works. Rita's skirt, hung by a buttonhole, fluttered for two days from the iron cellar railing and was unclaimed. Girls, Shmul editorialized in his little book, live a stone-age life in a blown-glass cave.

Eddie had to receive most of this chattery matter from Shmul. The truth is that Eddie did not take frequent part in the festivities, as Saturday was his father's movie night. Mr. Teitelbaum would have closed the shop, but the manager of the Loew's refused to sell Itzik a ticket. "Show me," said Mr. Teitelbaum, "where it says no monkeys." "Please," said the manager, "this is my busy night." Itzik had never been alone, for although he was a brilliant monkey, in the world of men he is dumb. "Ach," said Mr. Teitelbaum, "you know what it's like to have a monkey for a pet? It's like raising up a moron. You get very attached, no matter what, and very tied down."

"Still and all, things are picking up around here," said Carl.

About a week after the unpleasant incident with the girls (which eventually drove the entire Niskov family about six blocks uptown where they were unknown), Eddie asked for an off-schedule meeting. School was due to begin in three weeks, and he was determined to complete the series which would prove his War Attenuator marketable among the nations.

"Don't exaggerate," said Shmul. "What we have here is a big smell."

"Non-toxic," Eddie pointed out. "No matter how concentrated, non-toxic. Don't forget that, Klein, because that's the beauty of it. An instrument of war that will not kill. Imagine that."

"O.K.," he said. "I concede. So?"

"Shmul, you got an eye. What did the people do during the last test? Did they choke? Did their eyes run? What happened?"

"I already told you, Eddie. Nothing happened. They only ran. They ran like hell. They held their noses and they tore out the door and a couple of kids crawled up the coal ramp. Everybody gave a yelp and then ran."

"What about your father, Carl?"

"Oh, for Christ's sake, if I told you once, I told you twenty times, he got out fast. Then he stood on the steps, holding his nose and figuring who to pass the buck to."

"Well, that's what I mean, boys. It's the lesson of the cockroach segregator. The peaceful guy who listens to the warning of his senses will survive generations of defeat. Who needs the inheritance of the louse with all that miserable virulence in his nucleic acid? Who? I haven't worked out the political strategy altogether, but our job here, anyway, is just to figure out the technology.

"O.K., now the rubber tubes have to be extended up to the first and second floor of 1432, 1434, 1436—the three attached buildings. Do not drill into Michailovitch on the corner, as this could seep into the ice cream containers and fudge and stuff, and I haven't tested out all comestibles. If you work today and tomorrow, we should be done by Thursday. On Friday the test goes forward; by noon we ought have all reports and know what we have. Any questions? Carl, get the tools, you're in charge. I have to fix this goddamn percolater and see what the motor's like. We'll meet on Friday morning. Same time—7:30 A.M."

Then Eddie hurried back to the shop to clean the bird cages which he had forgotten about for days because of the excitement in his mind. Itzik offered him a banana. He accepted. Itzik peeled

it for him, then got a banana for himself. He threw the peels
into the trash can, for which Eddie kissed him on his foolish face.
He jumped to Eddie's shoulder to tease the birds. Eddie did not
like him to do this, for those birds will give you psittacosis (said
Eddie) if you aggravate them too much. This is an untested hypothesis, but it makes sense; as you know, people who loathe you
will sneeze in your face when their mucous membranes are most
swollen or when their throat is host to all kinds of cocci.

"Don't, Itzikel," he said gently, and put the monkey down.
Then Itzik hung from Eddie's shoulder by one long arm, eating
the banana behind his back. "That's how I like to see you," said
Mr. Teitelbaum when he looked into the shop. "Once in a while
anyway."

Eddie was near the end of a long summer's labor. He could
bear being peaceful and happy.

On Friday morning Carl, Arnold, and Shmul waited outside.
They had plenty of bubble gum and lollipops in which Eddie
had personally invested. They were responsible for maintaining
equilibrium among the little children who might panic. They
also had notebooks, and in these reports each boy was expected
to cover only one building.

Inside, Eddie played a staccato note on the button under the
percolator. After that it was very simple. People poured from the
three buildings. Tenants on the upper floors, which were not
involved, poked their heads out the windows because of the commotion. The controls were so fine that they had gotten only the
barest whiff and had assumed it to be the normal smell of morning rising from the cracked back of the fish market three blocks
east.

Eddie had agreed not to leave the laboratory until reports
came in from the other boys. He was perplexed when half an
hour had passed and they did not appear. There wasn't even a
book to read. So he busied himself disconnecting his home-con-
structed appliances, funneling the residue powder into a paper
envelope which he kept in his back pocket. Suddenly he worried
about everyone. What could happen to Itsy Bitsy Michailovitch,
who sat outside his father's store spinning a yo-yo and singing a
no-song to himself all day? He was in fact a goddamn helpless
idiot. What about Mrs. Spitz, who would surely stop to put her

corset on and would faint away and maybe crack her skull on a piece of rococo mahogany? What about heart failure in people over forty? What about the little Susskind kids? They were so wild, so baffled out of sense, they might jump into the dumbwaiter shaft.

He was scrubbing the sink, trying to uproot his miserable notions, when the door opened. Two policemen came in and put their hands on him. Eddie looked up and saw his father. Their eyes met and because of irrevocable pain, held. That was the moment (said Shmul, later on after that and other facts) that Eddie fell headfirst into the black heart of a deep depression. This despair required all his personal attention for years.

No one could make proper contact with him again, to tell him the news. Did he know that he had caused the death of all his father's stock? Even the three turtles, damn it, every last minnow, even the worms that were the fishes' Sunday dinner had wriggled their last. The birds were dead at the bottom of their clean cages.

Itzik Halbfunt lay in a coma from which he would not recover. He lay in Eddie's bed on Eddie's new mattress, between Eddie's sheets. "Let him die at home," said Mr. Teitelbaum, "not with a bunch of poodles at Speyer's."

He caressed his scrawny shoulder that was itchy and furry and cried, "Halbfunt, Halbfunt, you were my little friend."

No matter how lovingly a person or a doctor rapped at the door to Eddie's mind, Eddie refused to say "come in." Carl Clop called loudly, taking a long distance, local stop, suburban train several times to tell Eddie that it was really he who had thought it would be wonderful to see old Teitelbaum run screaming with hysterical Itzik. For the pleasure this sight would give, Carl had connected the rubber tubes to a small vent between the basement of 1436 and the rear of the pet shop. He had waited at the corner and, sure enough, they had come at last, Mr. Teitelbaum running and Itzik gasping for breath. Clop's bad luck, said Clop, to have a son who wasn't serious.

Eddie was remanded to the custody of Dr. Scott Tully, director of A Home For Boys, in something less than three weeks. The police impounded Shmul's notebooks but learned only literary things about faces and the sex habits of adolescent boys. Also found was an outline of a paper Eddie had planned for the antivivisectionist press, describing his adventures as a self-prepared subject for the gas tolerance experiments. It was entitled NO GUINEA PIG FRONTS FOR ME. As any outsider can judge, this is an insane idea.

Eddie was cared for at A Home For Boys by a white-frocked attendant, cross-eyed and muscle-bound, with strong canines oppressing his lower lip, a nose neatly broken and sloppily joined. This was Jim Sunn and he was kind to Eddie. "Because he's no trouble to me, Mr. Teitelbaum, he's a good boy. If he opens his eyes wide, I know he wants to go to the bathroom. He ain't crazy, Mr. Teitelbaum, he just got nothing to say right now, is all. I seen a lot of cases, don't you worry."

Mr. Teitelbaum didn't have too much to say himself, and this made him feel united with Eddie. He came every Sunday and sat with him in silence on a bench in the garden behind A Home; in bad weather they met in the parlor, a jolly rectangle scattered with small hooked rugs. They sat for one hour opposite one another in comfortable chairs, peaceful people, then Eddie opened his eyes wide and Jim Sunn said, "O.K. Let's go, buddy. Shut-eye don't hurt the kings of the jungle. Bears hibernate." Mr. Teitelbaum stood on his tiptoes and enfolded Eddie in his arms. "Sonny, don't worry so much," he said, then went home.

This situation prevailed for two years. One cold winter day Mr. Teitelbaum had the flu and couldn't visit. "Where the hell's my father?" Eddie growled.

That was the opener. After that Eddie said other things. Before the week had ended, Eddie said. "I'm sick of peppers, Jim. They give me gas."

A week later he said, "What's the news? Long Island sink yet?"

Dr. Tully had never anticipated Eddie's return. ("Once they go up this road, they're gone," he had confided to the newspapermen.) He invited a consultant from a competing but friendly establishment. He was at last able to give Eddie a Rorschach, which restored his confidence in his original pessimism.

"Let him have more responsibility," the consultant suggested, which they did at once, allowing him because of his background to visit the A Home For Boys' Zoo. He was permitted to fondle a rabbit and tease two box turtles. There was a fawn, caged and sick. Also a swinging monkey, but Eddie didn't bat an eyelash.

That night he vomited. "What's with the peppers, Jimmy? Can't that dope cook? Only with peppers?"

Dr. Tully explained that Eddie was now a helper. As soon as there was a vacancy, he would be given sole responsibility for one animal. "Thank God," Mr. Teitelbaum said. "A dumb animal is a good friend."

At last a boy was cured, sent home to his mother; a vacancy existed. Dr. Tully considered this a fortunate vacancy, for the cured boy had been in charge of the most popular snake in the zoo. The popularity of the snake had made the boy very popular. The popularity of the boy had increased his self-confidence; he had become vice-president of the Boys' Assembly; he had acquired friends and sycophants, he had become happy, cured, and had been returned to society.

On the very first day Eddie proved his mettle. He cleaned the cage with his right hand, holding the snake way out with his left. He had many admirers immediately.

"When you go home, could I have the job?" asked a very pleasant small boy who was only mildly retarded, but some father was willing to lay out a fortune because he was ashamed. "I'm not going anywhere, sonny," said Eddie. "I like it here."

On certain afternoons, shortly after milk and cookies, Eddie had to bring a little white mouse to his snake. He slipped the mouse into the cage, and that is why this snake was so popular: the snake did not eat the mouse immediately. At four o'clock the boys began to gather. They watched the mouse cowering in the corner. They watched the lazy snake wait for his hungry feelings to tickle him all along his curly interior. Every now and then he hiked his spine and raised his head, and the boys breathed hard. Sometime between four-thirty and six o'clock he would begin to slither aimlessly around the cage. The boys laid small bets on the time, winning and losing chunks of chocolate cake or a handful of raisins. Suddenly, but without fuss (and one had to be really watching), the snake stretched his long body, opened his big mouth, and gulped the little live mouse, who always went down squeaking.

Eddie could not disapprove, because this was truly the nature of the snake. But he pulled his cap down over his eyes and turned away.

Jimmy Sunn told him at supper one night, "Guess what I heard. I heard you're acquiring back your identity. Not bad."

"My identity?" asked Eddie.

A week later Eddie handed in a letter of resignation. He sent a copy to his father. The letter said: "Thank you, Dr. Tully. I know who I am. I am no mouse killer. I am Eddie Teitelbaum, the Father of the Stink Bomb, and I am known for my Dedication to Cause and my Fearlessness in the Face of Effect. Do not bother me any more. I have nothing to say. Sincerely."

Dr. Tully wrote a report in which he pointed with pride to his consistent pessimism in the case of Eddie Teitelbaum. This was considered remarkable, in the face of so much hope, and it was remembered by his peers.

While Eddie was making the decision to go out of his mind as soon as possible, other decisions were being made elsewhere. Mr. Teitelbaum, for instance, decided to die of grief and old age—which frequently overlap—and that was the final decision for all Teitelbaums. Shmul sat down to think and was disowned by his father.

Arnold ran away to East Twenty-ninth Street, where he built up a lovely bordello of naked oils at considerable effort and expense.

But Carl, the son of Clop, had tasted with Eddie's tongue. He went to school and stayed for years in order to become an atomic physicist for the Navy. Nowadays on the 8:07 Carl sails out into the hophead currents of our time, fights the undertow with little beep-beep signals. He has retained his cheerful disposition and for this service to the world has just received a wife who was washed out of the Rockettes for being too beautiful.

The War Attenuator has been bottled weak under pressure. It is sometimes called Teitelbaum's Mixture, and its ingredients have been translated into Spanish on the label. It is one of the greatest bug killers of all time. Unfortunately it is sometimes hard on philodendrons and old family rubber plants.

Mrs. Goredinsky still prefers to have her kitchen protected by the Segregator. An old-fashioned lady, she drops in bulk to her knees to scrub the floor. She cannot help seeing the cockroach caught and broiled in his own juice by the busy A.C. She flicks the cockroach off the wall. She smiles and praises Eddie.

11 John Hawkes

John Hawkes was born in Stamford, Connecticut, in 1925, and was educated at Harvard University. He is an associate professor of English at Brown University. His novels are The Cannibal (1949), The Beetle Leg (1951), The Goose on the Grave and The Owl (1954), The Lime Twig (1961), and Second Skin (1964). Leslie Fiedler has called Hawkes "a Gothic novelist . . . one who makes terror rather than love the center of his work, knowing all the while, of course, that there can be no terror without the hope for love and love's defeat."

❖

HENCHER
(FROM *THE LIME TWIG*)

Have you ever let lodgings in the winter? Was there a bed kept waiting, a corner room kept waiting for a gentleman? And have you ever hung a cardboard in the window and, just out of view yourself, watched to see which man would stop and read the hand-lettering on your sign, glance at the premises from roof to little sign—an awkward piece of work—then step up suddenly and hold his finger on your bell? What was it you saw from the window that made you let the bell continue ringing and the bed go empty another night? Something about the eyes? The smooth white skin between the brim of the bowler hat and the eyes?

Or perhaps you yourself were once the lonely lodger. Perhaps you crossed the bridges with the night crowds, listened to the tooting of the river boats and the sounds of shops closing on the far side. Perhaps the moon was behind the cathedral. You walked in the cathedral's shadow while the moon kept shining on three girls ahead. And you followed the moonlit girls. Or followed a woman carrying a market sack, or followed a slow bus high as a house with a saint's stone shadow on its side and smoke coming out from between the tires. Then a turn in the street and broken glass at the foot of a balustrade and you wiped your forehead. And standing still, shoes making idle noise on the smashed glass, you took the packet from inside your coat, unwrapped the oily paper, and far from the tall lamp raised the piece of hot white fish to your teeth.

You must have eaten with your fingers. And you were careful not to lick your lips when you stepped out into the light once more and felt against your face the air waves from the striking of the clock high in the cathedral's stone. The newspaper—it was folded to the listings of single rooms—fell from your coat pocket when you drank from the bottle. But no matter. No need for the rent per week, the names of streets. You were walking now, peering in the windows now, looking for the little signs. How bloody hard it is to read hand-lettering at night. And did your finger ever really touch the bell?

I wouldn't advise Violet Lane—there is no telling about the beds in Violet Lane—but perhaps in Dreary Station you have already found a lodging good as mine, if you were once the gentleman or if you ever took a tea kettle from a lady's hands. A fortnight is all you need. After a fortnight you will set up your burner, prepare hot water for the rubber bottle, warm the bottom of the bed with the bag that leaks round its collar. Or you will turn the table's broken leg to the wall, visit the lavatory in your robe, drive a nail or two with the heel of your boot. After a fortnight they don't evict a man. All those rooms—number twenty-eight, the one the incendiaries burned on Ash Wednesday, the final cubicle that had iron shutters with nymphs and swans and leaves—all those rooms were vacancies in which you started growing fat or first found yourself writing to the lady in the *Post* about salting breast of chicken or sherrying eggs. A lodger is a man who does not forget the cold drafts, the snow on the window ledge, the feel of his knees at night, the taste of a mutton chop in a room in which he held his head all night.

It was from Mother that I learned my cooking.

They were always turning Mother out onto the street. Our pots, our crockery, our undervests, these we kept in cardboard boxes, and from room to empty room we carried them until the strings wore out and her garters and medicines came through the holes. Our boxes lay in spring rains, they gathered snow. Troops, cabmen, bobbies passed them moldering and wet on the street. Once, dried out at last and piled high in a dusty hall, our boxes were set afire. Up narrow stairs and down we carried them, over steps with spikes that caught your boot heels and into small premises still rank with the smells of dead dog or cat. And out of her greasy bodice the old girl paid while I would be off to the unfamiliar lavatory to fetch a pull of tea water in our black pot.

"Here's home, Mother," I would say.

Then down with the skirt, down with the first chemise, off with the little boots. And, hands on the last limp bows: "You may manipulate the screen now, William." It was always behind the boxes, a screen like those standing in theater dressing rooms or in the wards of hospitals, except that it was horsehair brown and filled with holes from her cigarette. And each time we changed our rooms, whether in the morning or midday or dusk, I would set up the screen first thing and behind it Mother would finish stripping to the last scrap of girded rag—the obscene bits of makeshift garb poor old women carry next their skin—and after discarding that would wrap herself in the tawny dressing gown and lie straight upon the single bed while I worked at the burner's pale and rubbery flame. And beyond our door and before the tea was in the cup, we would hear the footsteps, the cheap bracelet tinkling a moment at the glass, would hear the cold fingers lifting down the sign.

Together we took our lodgings, together we went on the street. Fifteen years of circling Dreary Station, she and I, of discovering footprints in the bathtub or a necktie hanging from the toilet chain, or seeing flecks of blood in the shaving glass. Fifteen years with Mother, going from loft to loft in Highland Green, Pinky Road—twice in Violet Lane—and circling all that time the gilded cherubim big as horses that fly off the top of the Dreary Station itself.

If you live long enough with your mother you will learn to

cook. Your flesh will know the feel of cabbage leaves, your bare hands will hold everything she eats. Out of the evening paper you will prepare each night your small and tidy wad of cartilage, raw fat, cold and dusty peels and the mouthful—still warm—which she leaves on her plate. And each night as softly as you can, wiping a little blood off the edge of the apron, you will carry your paper bundle down the corridor and into the coldness and falling snow where you will deposit it, soft and square, just under the lid of the landlady's great pail of slops. Mother wipes her lips with your handkerchief and you set the rest of the kidneys on the sooty and frozen window ledge. You cover the burner with its flowered cloth and put the paring knife, the spoon, the end of bread behind the little row of books. There is a place for the pot in the drawer beside the undervests.

In one of the alleys off Pinky Road I remember a little boy who wore black stockings, a shirt ripped off the shoulder, a French sailor's hat with a red pompom. The whipping marks were always fresh on his legs and one cheekbone was blue. A flying goose darkened the mornings in that alley off Pinky Road, the tar buildings were slick with gray goose slime. After the old men and apprentices had left for the high bridges and little shops the place was empty and wet and dead as a lonely dockyard. Then behind the water barrel you could see the boy and his dog.

Each morning when the steam locomotives began shrieking out of Dreary Station the boy knelt on the stones in the leakage from the barrel and caught the puppy by its jowls and rolled its fur and rubbed its ears between his fingers. Alone with the tar doors dripping and the petrol and horse water drifting down the gutters, the boy would waggle the animal's fat head, hide its slow shocked eyes in his hands, flop it upright and listen to its heart. His fingers were always feeling the black gums or the soft wormy little legs or quickly freeing and pulling open the eyes so that he, the thin boy, could stare into them. No fields, sunlight, larks—only the stoned alley like a footpath on a quay down which a black ship might come sailing if the wind held, and down beneath the mists coming off the dead steeple-cocks the boy with the poor dog in his arms and loving his close scrutiny of the nicks in its ears, tiny channels over the dog's brain, pictures he could find on its purple tongue, pearls he could discover between the claws. Love is a long close scrutiny like that. I loved Mother in the same way.

I see her: it is just before the end; she is old; I see her through the red light of my glass of port. See the yellow hair, the eyes drying up in the corners. She laughs and jerks her head but the mouth is open, and that is what I see through the glass of port: the laughing lips drawn round a stopper of darkness and under the little wax chin a great silver fork with a slice of bleeding meat that rises slowly, slowly, over the dead dimple in the wax, past the sweat under the first lip, up to the level of her eyes so she can take a look at it before she eats. And I wait for the old girl to choke it down.

But there is a room waiting if you can find it, there is a joke somewhere if you can bring it to your lips. And my landlord, Mr. Banks, is not the sort to evict a man for saying a kind word to his wife or staying in the parlor past ten o'clock. His wife, Margaret, says I was a devoted son.

Yes, devoted. I remember fifteen years of sleeping, fifteen years of smelling cold shoes in the middle of the night and waiting, wondering whether I smelled smoke down the hallway to the toilet or smelled smoke coming from the parlor that would burn like hay. I think of the whipped boy and his dog abed with him and that's what devotion is: sleeping with a wet dog beneath your pillow or humming some childish tune to your mother the whole night through while waiting for the plaster, the beams, the glass, the kidneys on the sill to catch fire. Margaret's estimation of my character is correct. Heavy men are most often affectionate. And I, William Hencher, was a large man even then.

"Don't worry about it, Hencher," the captain said. "We'll carry you out if we have to." On its cord the bulb was circling round his head, and across the taverns and walls and craters of Dreary Station came the sirens and engines of the night. Sometimes, at the height of it, the captain and his man—an ex-corporal with rotten legs who wore a red beret and was given to fainting in the hall—went out to walk in the streets, and I would watch them go and wait, watch the searchlights fix upon the wounded cherubim like giants caught naked in the sky, until I heard them

swearing in the hall again and, from the top of the stair, an unfamiliar voice crying, "Shut the door. Oh, for the love of bleeding
Hell, come shut the door."

We were so close to the old malevolent station that I could
hear the shifting of the sandbags piled round it and could hear
the locomotives shattering into bits of iron. And one night
wouldn't a cherubim's hand or arm or curly head come flying
down through our roof? Some dislodged ball of saintly brass palm
or muscle or jagged neck find its target in Lily Eastchip's house?
But I wasn't destined to die with a fat brass finger in my belly.

To think that Mr. and Mrs. Banks—Michael and Margaret—
were only children then, as small and crouching and black-eyed
as the boy with the French sailor's hat and the dog. It is a pity
I did not know them then: somehow I would have cared for
them.

Such things don't want forgetting. When they anchored a
barrage balloon over number twenty-eight—how long it was since
we had been evicted from that room—and when the loft in Highland Green had burned Ash Wednesday, and during those days
when the water would curl a horse's lip and somebody's copy of
The Vicar of Wakefield was run over by a fire truck outside my
door, why then there was plenty of soot and scum the memory
could not let go of.

There was Lily Eastchip with bird feathers round her throat
and a dusty rag up the tiny pearl lacing of her sleeve; there was
the captain dishonorably mustered from the forces; there was the
front of our narrow lodging which the firemen kept hosing down
for luck; there was the pink slipper left caught by its heel in the
stairway rungs and hanging toe first into the dark of that dry
plaster hall. And there were our boxes with broken strings, piled
in the hallway and rising toward the slipper, all the cartons I
had not the heart to drag to Mother's room. So I see the pasty
corporal—Sparrow was his name—rubbing together the handles
of his canes, I see Miss Eastchip serving soup, I see Mother's
dead livid face. And I shall always see the bomber with its bulbous
front gunner's nest flattened over the cistern in the laundry court.

Margaret remembers none of it and Mr. Banks, her husband,
is not a talker. But Miss Eastchip's brother went down in his

spotter's steeple, tin hat packed red with embers and both feet in the enormous boots burning with a gas-blue flame. Lily got word of it the eve he fell and with the duster hanging down her wrist and the tears on her cheek she looked as if someone had touched a candle to her nightdress in the dark of our teatime. She stood behind the captain's chair whispering, "That's the end for me, the end for me," while the bearer of the news merely sat for a moment, teacup rattling in the saucer and helmet gripped between his knees.

"Well, sorry to bring distressing information," the warden had said. "You'd better keep the curtains on good tonight. We're in for it, I'm afraid."

A pale snow was coming down when he passed my window—a black square-shouldered man—and I saw the dark shape of him and the gleam off the silvery whistle caught in his teeth. Somebody laid the cold table, and far-off we heard the first dull boom and breath, as if they had blown out a candle as tall as St. George's spire.

"Good night, Hencher. . . ."

"Good night, Captain. Mother gave you the salts for Lily, did she?"

"She did. And—Hencher—if anything uncommon occurs in the night, you can always give me a signal on the pipes."

"I'll just do that, Captain. It's good of you."

Mother got the covers to her chin and, lights off, blackout drawn aside, I sat watching to see the aircraft shoot out the eyes of the cherubim who, beyond sifting snow, and triangulated, now and then, by flooding white shafts of light, hugged each other atop the Dreary Station dome. I held my cheeks. I listened to the old girl's chamber pot—she had stuffed it with jewelry and glass buttons and an ostrich plume—that rolled about beneath the bed. Missing one front wheel, a tiny tar-painted lorry passed in dreadful crawl and the bare hub of its broken axle screeched and sent off sparks against the stones. And all through that blistering snowy night my hands were drenching the angora white yarn of a tasseled shawl, twisting it like a young girl's lock of hair.

When engines shook the night beyond the nymphs and apple

leaves in the filigreed shutters of my window, I began suddenly to smell it: not the stench of rafters burning, not the vaporized rubber stench that stayed about the street for days after the hit on the garage of Autorank, Limited, but only a faint live smell of worn carpet or paper or tissue being singed within the lodging house itself. And I fancied it was coming round the edges of my door—the odor of smoke—and I held to the arms of my chair and slowly breathed into my lungs that smoke.

"Are you awake?" I said.

She sat up with the nightdress slanting down her flesh.

"You'd better put your wrapper on, old girl."

She sat there startled by the light of a flare that was plainly going to land in old John's chimney across the way. I could see her game face and I squeezed on the slippers and squeezed the shawl.

"Don't you smell the smoke? The house is going up," I said. "Do you want to burn?"

"It's only the kettle, William. . . ." And she was grinning, one foot was trying to escape the sheet. They were running with buckets across the way at John's.

"You look, William, you tell me what it is. . . ."

"Out of that bed now, and we'll just have a look together."

Then I pulled open the door and there was the hallway dry and dark as ever, the slipper still hooked on the stair, the one faint bulb swinging round and round on its cord. But our boxes were burning. The bottom of the pile was sunk in flame, hot crabbing flame orange and pale blue in the draft from the door and the sleeve of a coat of mine was crumbling and smoking out of a black pasty hole.

Mother began to cough and pull at my hand—the smoke was mostly hers and thick, and there is no smudge as black as that from burning velveteen and stays and packets of cheap face powder—and then she cried, "Oh, William, William." I saw the pile lean and dislodge a clump of cinders while at the same moment I heard a warden tapping on the outside door with his torch and heard him call through the door: "All right in there?"

I could taste my portion of the smoke; the banging on the door grew louder. Now they were flinging water on old John's roof, but Mother and I were in an empty hall with only our own fire to care about.

"Can't you leave off tugging on me, can't you?" But before I could close my robe she was gone, three or four steps straight into the pile to snatch the stays and an old tortoise-shell fan from out of the fire.

"Mum!"

But she pulled, the boxes toppled about her, the flames shot high as the ceiling. While a pink flask of ammonia she had saved for years exploded and hissed with the rest of it.

From under the pall I heard her voice: "Look here, it's hardly singed at all, see now? Hardly singed . . ." Outside footfalls, and then the warden: "Charlie, you'd better give us a hand here, Charlie. . . ."

On hands and knees she was trying to crawl back to me, hot sparks from the fire kept settling on her arms and on the thin silk of her gown. One strap was burned through suddenly, fell away, and then a handful of tissue in the bosom caught and, secured by the edging of charred lace, puffed at its luminous peak as if a small forced fire, stoked inside her flesh, had burst a hole through the tender dry surface of my mother's breast.

"Give us your shoulder here, Charlie . . . lend a heave!"

And even while I grunted and went at her with robe outspread, she tried with one hand to pluck away her bosom's fire. "Mother," I shouted, "hold on now, Mother," and knelt and got the robe round her—mother and son in a single robe—and was slapping the embers and lifting her back toward the bed when I saw the warden's boot in the door and heard the tooting of his whistle. Then only the sound of dumping sand, water falling, and every few minutes the hurried crash of an ax head into our smothered pile.

At dawn I returned to the charcoal of the hall and met the captain in corduroy jacket and wearing a gun and holster next his ribs. For a moment we stood looking at the scorch marks on the lath and the high black reach of extinguished flames. The captain ran his toe through the ashes.

"How is your mother, Hencher? A bit hard on her, wasn't it?"

"She won't say, of course, though the pain must be considerable. . . ."

"Well, Hencher," rattling tin and glass in his pocket, "give me a call on the pipes if it gets worse. I happen to have a needle and a few drops in an ampule can relieve all that."

"Oh, she'll do quite nicely, I'm sure. . . ."

But the blisters did not go down. They were small, translucent, membranous and tough all over her body, and no matter how often I dressed them with marge from Lily's kitchen they retained their bulbous density. And even today I smell them: smell the skin, smell the damp sheets I wrapped her in, smell that room turned infirmary. I smell that house.

For after a decade it is the same house, a different landlord—Michael Banks now, not poor grieving Lily—but the same house, the one in the middle of Corking Street not five minutes east of the station. Refurbished, an electric buzzer at the door, three flats instead of beds for lodgers, and a spirit shop where John's house stood—from the peaked garret to the electric buzzer it is the exact same place. I know it well. A lodger is forever going back to the pictures in black bead frames, back to the lost slipper, or forever coming round to pay respects when you think you've seen the last of him, or to tell you—stranger as far as you know—that his was the cheek that left the bloody impression in your looking glass. "My old girl died on these premises, Mr. Banks," looking over his shoulder, feeling the wall, and he had to take me in. And then it was home again for William when I found the comforter with hearts on it across my bed. Now there are orange deck chairs in the laundry court, and sitting out with a sack of beans on my stomach and hearing the sounds of the wireless from Annie's window, still through half-shut eyes I see the shadow of the bomber that once filled the court.

Sometimes I wake in the night, very late in the still night, and go sit in the lavatory and run the water and smoke half a thin cigar until there is nothing to feel, nothing to hear except Margaret turning over or the cat pacing my step in the parlor. I see the cherubim safely lit, I wipe my hands, I sleep.

I waited three weeks before signaling the captain on the pipes, and then I beat at them with my slipper until I threw it across the room and found the warden's torch in the covers and, after the blow that smashed the glass, fetched the captain with loud strokes on first the hot water pipe and then the cold. Together they came, captain and corporal, while the pipes still shivered up the wall. I looked away when I saw the captain pulling out the plunger.

"You ain't going to give my stuff to her?" said Sparrow. "Not to the old woman, are you? I'd sooner you give a jab to this fat man here. . . ."

I trembled then.

"No use giving my stuff to her," said Sparrow, the corporal.

And then in the dark: "She'll do now, Hencher. I'd get a little sleep if I were you."

But it was not sleep I wanted. I fastened the robe, tied the white shawl round my throat. "Good night, old girl," I whispered and went out of the door, flinging an end of the shawl aside flier fashion. It was cold; I walked beneath the black supports and timbers of a burned city, and how often I had made passage through the length of Lily Eastchip's corridor, carried my neat square of dinner garbage past the parlor when Mother and I first joined that household and ate alone. No garbage now. Only the parlor with pinholes in the curtain across the window and a pile of clothing and several candles in the fireplace; only the hallway growing more and more narrow at the end; only the thought that, behind the screen, I had left Mother comfortable and that to-night, this night, I was going to stand bareheaded in the laundry court and breathe, watch the sky, hear what I could of the cries coming from Violet Lane, from the oil-company docks, the Mall. When I found the bolt and pulled it, squeezed out of that black entrance with a hand to my throat, I expected to see the boy dancing with his dog.

The light snow fell, tracers went straight up from behind the garret that faced me across the court, I noticed a pink reflection in the sky west of the station. The airplanes were bombing Highland Green. I saw the humps of dead geraniums and a wooden case of old stout bottles black and glistening against a shed. I had not moved, I felt the snow wet on my shoulders and on the rims of my ears.

Large, brown, a lifeless airplane returning, it was one of our own and I saw it suddenly approach out of the snow perhaps a hundred feet above the garret and slow as a child's kite. Big and blackish-brown with streaks of ice across the nose, which was beginning to rise while the tail sank behind in the snow, it was simply there, enormous and without a trace of smoke, the engines dead and one aileron flapping in the wind. And ceasing to climb, ceasing to move, a vast and ugly shape stalled against the snow up there, the nose dropped and beneath the pilot's window I saw the figure of a naked woman painted against the bomber's pebbly surface. Her face was snow, something back of her thigh had sprung a leak and the thigh was sunk in oil. But her hair, her long white head of hair was shrieking in the wind as if the inboard engine was sucking the strands of it.

Her name was Reggie's Rose and she was sitting on the black pack of a parachute.

Dipped, shuddered, banged up and down for a moment—I could see the lifted rudder then, swinging to and fro above the tubular narrowing of its fuselage—and during that slapping glide the thick wings did not fall, no frenzied hand wiped the pilot's icy windscreen, no tiny torch switched on to prove this final and outrageous landfall. It made no sound, but steepened its glide, then slowed again with a kind of gigantic deranged and stubborn confidence and pushed on, shedding the snow, as if after the tedium of journey there would be a mere settling, rolling to silence, with a drink and hot sandwiches for her crew. And I myself fell down next to Lily Eastchip's garbage tin, in darkness drove my cheek among the roots of her dead bushes. Through the dressing robe and bedroom silks the heat of my body dissolved the snow. I was wet and waited for the blow of a flying gyroscope compass or propeller blade.

Or to be brushed to death by a wing, caught beneath cold tons of the central fuselage, or surely sprayed by petrol and burned alive: tasting those hard white rubber roots I wondered whether the warden and his friend Charlie would hear the crash. And

tightening, biting to the sour heart of the root, I saw the bomber
in its first shapeless immensity and thought I could hold it off—
monstrous, spread-winged, shadowy—hold it off with my out-
stretched arms eternally or at least until I should escape by Lily's
door.

The warden must have heard the crash. His Charlie must have
heard the crash.

Something small and round struck suddenly against my side.
When again I made out the sounds from the far corner—the
steady firing of the guns—I breathed, rolled, sat with my back
to the wall. My fingers found the painful missile, only a hard
tuft of wool blown loose from inside a pilot's boot or torn from
the shaggy collar of his flying coat. The snow was falling, still
the sky was pink from the bombing of Highland Green. But no
whistles, no wardens running: a single window smashed on the
other side of the court and a woman began shrieking for her husband. And again there was only silence and my belly trembling.

I took one step, another. Then there were the high dark sides
of the intact bomber and the snow was melting on the iron. I
reached the first three-bladed propeller—the two bottom sweeps
of steel were doubled beneath the cowling—and for a moment
I leaned against it and it was like touching your red cheek to a
stranded whale's fluke when, in all your coastal graveyard, there
was no witness, no one to see. I walked round the bubble of the
nose—that small dome set on edge with a great crack down the
middle—and stood beneath the artistry of Reggie's Rose. Her leg
was long, she sat on her parachute with one knee raised. In the
knee cap was a half-moon hole for a man's boot, above it another,
and then a hand grip just under the pilot's door. So I climbed
up poor Rose, the airman's dream and big as one of the cherubim,
and snatched at the high door which, sealed in the flight's vacuum,
sucked against its fitting of rust and rubber and sprang open.

I should have had a visored cap, leather coat, gauntlets. But,
glancing once at the ground, poised in the snow over Rose's
hair, I tugged, entered head first the forward cabin.

The cabin roof as well as the front gunner's dome was cracked
and a little snow fell steadily between the seats. In the dark I sat
with my hands on the half wheel and slippers resting on the

jammed pedals, my head turning to see the handles, rows of knobs, dials with needles all set at zero, boxes and buttons and toggle switches and loop of wire and insulated rings coming down from the roof. In this space I smelled resin and grease and lacquer and something fatty that made me groan.

I tried to work the pedals, turn the wheel. I could not breathe. When suddenly from a hook between two cylinders next to my right hand I saw a palm-shaped cone of steel and took it up, held it before my face—a metal kidney trimmed round the edges with a strip of fur—I looked at it, then lowered my head and pressed my nose and mouth into its drawn cup. My breath came free. The inhalation was pure and deep and sweet. I smelled tobacco and a cheap wine, was breathing out of the pilot's lungs.

Cold up here. Cold up here. Give a kiss to Rose.

Surely it was Reggie's breath—the tobacco he had got in an Egyptian NAAFI, his cheap wine—frozen on the slanting translucent glass of the forward cabin's windows. Layer overlapping icy layer of Reggie's breath. And I clapped the mask back on its hook, turned a wheel on the cylinder. Leaning far over, sweating, I thrust my hands down and pushed them back along the aluminum trough of floor and found the bottle. Then I found something else, something cool and round to the skin, something that had rested there behind my heels all this while. I set the bottle on top of the wireless box—I heard the sounds of some strange brass anthem coming from the earphones—and reached for that black round shape, carefully and painfully lifted it and cradled it in my lap.

The top of the flying helmet was a perfect dome. Hard, black, slippery. And the flaps were large. On the surface all the leather of that helmet was soft—if you rubbed it—and yet bone hard and firm beneath the hand's polishing. There were holes for wire plugs, bands for the elastic of a pair of goggles, some sort of worn insignia on the front. A heavy wet leather helmet large enough for me. I ran my fingernail across the insignia, picked at a blemish, and suddenly I leaned forward, turned the helmet over, looked inside. Then I lifted the helmet, gripped it steadily at arm's length—I was sitting upright now, upright and staring at the polished thing I held—and slowly raised it high and twisting it, hitching it down from side to side, settled the helmet securely on my own smooth head. I extended my hands again and took the wheel.

"How's the fit, old girl?" I whispered. "A pretty good fit, old girl?" And I turned my head as far to the right as I was able, so that she might see how I—William Hencher—looked with my bloody coronet in place at last.

Give a kiss to Rose.

Between 3 and 4 A.M. on the night she died—so many years ago—that's when I set out walking with my great black coat that made the small children laugh, walking alone or sometimes joining the crowds and waiting under the echoes of the dome and amid the girders and shattered skylight of Dreary Station to see another trainload of our troops return. So many years ago. And I had my dreams; I had my years of walking to the cathedral in the moonlight.

"My old girl died on these premises, Mr. Banks."

And then all the years were gone and I recognized that house, that hall, despite the paint and plaster and the cheap red carpet they had tacked on the parlor floor. I paid him in advance, I did, and he put the money in his trouser pocket while Margaret went to lift their awkward sign out of the window. Fresh paint, fresh window glass, new floorboards here and here: to think of the place not gutted after all but still standing, the house lived in now by those with hardly a recollection of the nightly fires. Cheery, new, her dresses in one of the closets and his hat by the door. But one of his four rooms was mine, surely mine, and I knew I'd smell the old dead odor of smoke if only I pushed my face close enough to those shabby walls.

Here's home, old girl, here's home.

So I spent my first long night in the renovated room, and I dared not spend that night in the lavatory but smoked my cigars in bed. Sitting up in bed, smoking, thinking of my mother all night long. And then there was the second night and I ventured into the hallway. There was the third night and in the darkened cubicle I listened to the far bells counting two, three, four o'clock in the morning and all that time—thinking now of

comfort, tranquillity, and thinking also of their two clasped hands
—I wondered what I might do for them. The bells were slow in
counting, the water dripped. And suddenly it was quite clear
what I could do for them, for Michael and his wife.

I hooked the lavatory door. Then I filled the porcelain sink,
and in darkness smelling of lavender and greasy razor blades I
immersed my hands up to the wrists, soaked them silently. I dried
them on a stiff towel, pushing the towel between my fingers again
and again. I wiped the top of my head until it burned. Then I
used his talc, showed my teeth in the glass, straightened the robe.
I took up the pink-shelled hair brush for a moment but replaced
it. And off to the kitchen and then on boards that made tiny
sounds, walking with a heavy man's sore steps, noticing a single
lighted window across the court.

It grew cold and before dawn I left the kitchen once: only to
pull the comforter off my bed. Again in the kitchen and on Margaret's wooden stool I sat with the comforter hooded round my
head and shoulders, sat waiting for the dawn to come fishing up
across the chimney pots and across that dirty gable in the apex of
which a weathered muse's face was carved. When I heard the
dog barking in the flat upstairs, when water started running in the
pipes behind the wall, and a few river gulls with icy feathers
hovered outside the window, and light from a sun the color of
some guardsman's breast warmed my hooded head and arms and
knees—why then I got off the stool, began to move about. Wine
for the eggs, two pieces of buttered toast, two fried strips of
mackerel, a teapot small as an infant's head and made of iron and
boiling—it was a tasteful tray, in one corner decorated with a few
pinched violet buds I tore from the plant that has always grown
on Margaret's window shelf. I looked round, made certain the jets
were off, thought to include a saucer of red jam, covered the hot
salted portions with folded table napkins. Then I listened. I
heard nothing but the iron clock beating next to the stove and a
boot landing near the dog upstairs.

The door was off the latch and they were sleeping. I turned and
touched it with my hip, my elbow, touched it with only a murmur.
And it swung away on smooth hinges while I watched and listened
until it came up sharply against the corner of a little cane chair.

They lay beneath a single sheet and a single sand-colored blanket, and I saw that on his thin icy cheeks Banks had grown a beard in the night and that Margaret—the eyelids defined the eyes, her lips were dry and brown and puffy—had been dreaming of a nice picnic in narrow St. George's Park behind the station. Behind each silent face was the dream that would collect slack shadows and tissues and muscles into some first mood for the day. Could I not blow smiles onto their nameless lips, could I not force apart those lips with kissing? One of the gulls came round from the kitchen and started beating the glass.

"Here's breakfast," I said, and pushed my knees against the footboard.

For a moment the vague restless dreams went faster beneath those two faces. Then stopped suddenly, quite fixed in pain. Then both at once they opened their eyes and Banks' were opalescent, quick, the eyes of a boy, and Margaret's eyes were brown.

"It's five and twenty past six," I said. "Take the tray now, one of you. Tea's getting cold. . . ."

Banks sat up and smiled. He was wearing an undervest, his arms were naked and he stretched them toward me. "You're not a bad sort, Hencher," he said. "Give us the tray!"

"Oh, Mr. Hencher," I heard the warm voice, the slow sounds in her mouth, "you shouldn't have gone to the trouble. . . ."

It was a small trouble. And not long after—a month or a fortnight perhaps—I urged them to take a picnic, not to the sooty park behind the station but farther away, farther away to Landingfield Battery, where they could sit under a dead tree and hold their poor hands. And while they were gone I prowled through the flat, softened my heart of introspection: I found her small tube of cosmetic for the lips and, in the lavatory, drew a red circle with it round each of my eyes. I had their bed to myself while they were gone. They came home laughing and brought a postal card of an old pocked cannon for me.

It was the devil getting the lipstick off.

But red circles, giving your landlord's bed a try, keeping his flat to yourself for a day—a man must take possession of a place if it is to be a home for the waiting out of dreams. So we lead our lives, keep our privacy in Dreary Station, spend our days grubbing at the rubber roots, pausing at each other's doors. I still fix them breakfast now and again and the cherubim are still my monument. I have my billet, my memories. How permanent some transients are at last. In a stall in Dreary Station there is a fellow with vocal cords damaged during the fire who sells me chocolates, and I like to talk to him; sometimes I come across a gagger lying out cold in the snow, and for him I have a word; I like to talk to all the unanswering children of Dreary Station. But home is best.

I hear Michael in the bath, I whet Margaret's knives. Or it is 3 or 4 A.M. and I turn the key, turn the knob, avoid the empty goldfish bowl that catches the glitter off the street, feel the skin of my shoes going down the hallway to their door. I stand whispering our history before that door and slowly, so slowly, I step behind the screen in my own dark room and then, on the edge of the bed and sighing, start peeling the elastic sleeves off my thighs. I hold my head awhile and then I rub my thighs until the sleep goes out of them and the blood returns. In my own dark room I hear a little bird trying to sing on the ledge where the kidneys used to freeze.

Smooth the pillow, pull down the sheets for me. Thinking of Reggie and the rest of them, can I help but smile?

I can get along without you, Mother.

12 Philip Roth

Philip Roth was born in 1933 in Newark, New Jersey, and educated at Bucknell University and the University of Chicago. His works of fiction include Goodbye, Columbus (1959), Letting Go (1962), When She Was Good (1967), and Portnoy's Complaint (1969), one of the funniest and most poignant works of fiction of our time.

❖

NOVOTNY'S PAIN

In the early months of the Korean War, a young man who had been studying to be a television cameraman in a night school just west of the Loop in Chicago was drafted into the Army and almost immediately fell ill. He awoke one morning with a pain on the right side of his body, directly above the buttock. When he rolled over, it was as though whatever bones came together inside him there were not meeting as they should. The pain, however, was not what had awakened him; his eyes always opened themselves five minutes before the appearance in the barracks of the Charge of Quarters. Though there was much of Army life that he had to grit his teeth to endure, he did not have to work at getting up on time; it simply happened to him. When it was necessary to grit his teeth, he gritted them and did what he was told. In that way, he was like a good many young men who suffered military life alongside him or had suffered it before him. His sense of shame was strong, as was his sense of necessity; the two made him dutiful.

Also, he was of foreign extraction, and though his hard-working family had not as yet grown fat off the fat of the land, it was nevertheless in their grain to feel indebted to this country. Perhaps if they had been a little fatter they would have felt less indebted. As it was, Novotny believed in fighting for freedom, but because what he himself wanted most from any government was that it should let him alone to live his life. His patriotism, then— his commitment to wearing this republic's uniform and carrying this republic's gun—was seriously qualified by his feeling of confinement and his feeling of loss, both of which were profound.

When the C.Q. got around to Novotny's bed that morning, he did not shine his flashlight into the soldier's eyes; he simply put a hand to his arm and said, "You better get yourself up, young trooper." Novotny was appreciative of this gentleness, and though, as he stepped from his bunk, the pain across his back was momentarily quite sharp, he met the day with his usual decision. Some mornings, making the decision required that he swallow hard and close his eyes, but he never failed to make it: *I am willing.* He did not know if any of those around him had equivalent decisions to make, because he did not ask. He did not mull much over motive. People were honest or dishonest, good or bad, himself included.

After dressing, he moved off with four others to the mess hall, where it was their turn to work for the day. It was still dark, and in the barracks the other recruits slept on. The previous day, the entire company had marched fifteen miserable miles with full packs, and then, when it was dark, they had dropped down on their stomachs and fired at pinpoints of light that flickered five hundred yards away and were supposed to be the gunfire of the enemy. Before they had climbed into trucks at midnight, they were ordered to attention and told in a high, whiny voice by their captain, a National Guardsman recently and unhappily called back to duty, that only one out of every fifty rounds they had fired had hit the targets. This news had had a strong effect upon the weary recruits, and the trucks had been silent all the way to the barracks, where it had been necessary for them to clean their rifles and scrape the mud from their boots before they flung themselves onto the springs of their bunks for a few hours' rest.

At the mess hall, the K.P.s were each served two large spoonfuls of Army eggs and a portion of potatoes. The potatoes had not been cooked long enough, and the taste they left on the palate was especially disheartening at such an early hour, with no light outdoors and a cold wind blowing. But Novotny did not complain. For one thing, he was occupied with finding a comfortable position in which to sit and eat—he had the pain only when he twisted the wrong way. Besides, the food was on his tray to give him strength, not pleasure. Novotny did not skip meals, no matter how ill-prepared they were, for he did not want to lose weight and be unequal to the tasks assigned him.

Before entering the Army, Novotny had worked for several years as an apprentice printer with a company that manufactured telephone books in Chicago. It had turned out to be dull work, and because he considered himself a bright and ambitious young man, he had looked around for a night school where he might learn a job with a future. He had settled on television, and for over a year he had been attending classes two evenings a week. He had a girl friend and a mother, to both of whom he had a strong attachment; his girl friend he loved, his mother he took care of. Novotny did not want to cause any trouble. On the other hand, he did not want to be killed. With his girl friend, he had been a man of passion; he dreamed of her often. He was thrifty, and had four hundred dollars in a savings account in the First Continental Bank on LaSalle Street in Chicago. He knew for a fact that he had been more adept at his work than anyone else in his television course. He hated the Army because nothing he did there was for himself.

The labors of the K.P.s began at dawn, and at midnight—light having come and gone—they were still at it. The cooks had ordered the men around all day until five in the afternoon, when the Negro mess sergeant showed up. He hung his Eisenhower jacket on a hook, rolled up the sleeves of his shirt, and said, "As there is a regimental inspection tomorrow morning, we will now get ourselves down to the fine points of housecleaning, gentlemens." The K.P.s had then proceeded to scrub the mess hall from floor to ceiling, inside and out.

A little after midnight, while Novotny was working away at the inside of a potato bin with a stiff brush and a bucket of hot, soapy water, the man working beside him began to cry. He said the sergeant was never going to let them go to sleep. The sergeant would be court-martialed for keeping them up like this. They would all get weak and sick. All Novotny knew of the fellow beside him was that his name was Reynolds and that he had been to college. Apparently, the mess sergeant only knew half that much, but that was enough; he came into the storeroom and saw Reynolds weeping into the empty potato bins. "College boy," he said, "wait'll they get you over in Korea." The sergeant delivered his words standing over them, looking down, and for the moment Novotny stopped feeling sorry for himself.

When the scrubbing was finished, Novotny and Reynolds had to carry back the potatoes, which were in garbage cans, and dump them into the bins. Reynolds began to explain to Novotny that he had a girl friend whom he was supposed to have called at ten-thirty. For some reason, Reynolds said, his not having been able to get to a phone had made him lose control. Novotny had, till then, been feeling superior to Reynolds. For all his resenting of the stupidity that had made them scrub out bins one minute so as to dump dirty potatoes back into them the next, he had been feeling somewhat in league with the sergeant. Now Reynolds' words broke through to his own unhappiness, and he was about to say a kind word to his companion when the fellow suddenly started crying again. Reynolds threw his hand up to cover his wet cheeks and dropped his end of the can. Novotny's body stiffened; with a great effort he yanked up on the can so that it wouldn't come down on Reynolds' toes. Pain cut deep across the base of Novotny's spine.

Later, he limped back to the barracks. He got into bed and counted up the number of hours he had spent scrubbing out what hadn't even needed to be scrubbed. At a dollar and a quarter an hour, he would have made over twenty dollars. Nineteen hours was as much night-school time as he had been able to squeeze into three weeks. He had known Rose Anne, his girl, for almost a year, but never had he spent nineteen consecutive hours in her company. Though once they had had twelve hours. . . . He had driven in his Hudson down to Champaign, where she was a freshman at the University of Illinois, and they had stayed together, in the motel room he had rented, from noon to midnight, not even going out for meals. He had driven her back to her dormitory, his shoe-laces untied and wearing no socks. Never in his life had he been so excited.

The following week, he had been drafted.

After completing his eight weeks of basic training, Novotny was given a week's leave. His first evening home, his mother prepared a large meal and then sat down opposite him at the table and watched him eat it. After dinner, he stood under the hot shower for twenty minutes, letting the water roll over him. In his bed-room, he carefully removed the pins from a new white-on-white shirt and laid it out on the bedspread, along with a pair of Argyles, a silver tie clasp, cufflinks, and his blue suit. He polished his shoes—not for the captain's pleasure, but for his own—and chose a tie. Then he dressed for his date as he had learned to dress for a date from an article he had read in a Sunday picture magazine, while in high school, that he kept taped to the inside of his closet door. He had always collected articles having to do with how to act at parties, or dances, or on the job; his mother had never had any reason not to be proud of Novotny's behavior. She kissed him when he left the house, told him how handsome he looked, and then tears moved over her eyes as she thanked him for the government checks—for always having been a good son.

Novotny went to a movie with Rose Anne, and afterward he drove to the forest preserve where they remained until 2 A.M. In bed, later, he cursed the Army. He awoke the following morn-ing to find that the pain, which had not troubled him for some weeks, had returned. It came and went through the next day and the following night, when once again he saw Rose Anne. Two days later, he visited the family doctor, who said Novotny had strained a muscle, and gave him a diathermy treatment. On their last night together, Rose Anne said that if writing would help, she would write not just twice a day, as was her habit, but three times a day, even four. In the dark of the forest preserve, she told Novotny that she dreamed about his body; in the dark, he told her that he dreamed of hers.

He left her weeping into a Kleenex in her dim front hallway, and drove home in a mood darker than any he had ever known.

He would be killed in Korea and never see Rose Anne again, or his mother. And how unfair—for he *had* been a good son. Following his father's death, he had worked every day after school, plus Wednesday nights and Saturdays. When he had been drafted, he had vowed he would do whatever they told him to do, no matter how much he might resent it. He had kept his mouth shut and become proficient at soldiering. The better he was at soldiering, the better chance he had of coming out alive and in one piece. But that night when he left Rose Anne, he felt he had no chance at all. He would leave some part of his body on the battlefield, or come home to Rose Anne in a box. Good as he had been—industrious, devoted, stern, sacrificing—he would never have the pleasure of being a husband, or a television cameraman, or a comfort to his mother in her old age.

Five days after his return to the post—where he was to receive eight weeks of advanced infantry training, preparatory to being shipped out—he went on sick call. He sat on a long bench in the barren waiting room, and while two sullen prisoners from the stockade mopped the floor around his feet, he had his temperature taken. There were thirteen men on sick call, and they all watched the floor being washed and held thermometers under their tongues. When Novotny got to see the medic, who sat outside the doctor's office, he told him that every time he twisted or turned or stepped down on his right foot, he felt a sharp pain just above the buttock on the right side of his body. Novotny was sent back to duty with three inches of tape across his back, and a packet of APC pills.

At mail call the following morning, Novotny received a letter from Rose Anne unlike any he had ever received from her before. It was not only that her hand was larger and less controlled than usual; it was what she said. She had written down, for his very eyes to see, all those things she dreamed about when she dreamed about his body. He saw, suddenly, scenes of passion that he and she were yet to enact, moments that would not merely repeat the past but would be even deeper, even more thrilling. Oh Rose Anne—how had he found her?

Novotny's company spent the afternoon charging around with

fixed bayonets—crawling, jumping up, racing ahead, through fences, over housetops, down into trenches—creaming murderously all the while. At one point, leaping from a high wall, Novotny almost took his eye out with his own bayonet; he had been dreaming of his beautiful future.

The next morning, he walked stiffly to sick call and asked to see the doctor. When, in response to a question, he said it was his back that hurt him, the medic who was interviewing him replied sourly, "Everybody's back hurts." The medic told Novotny to take off his shirt so that he could lay on a few more inches of tape. Novotny asked if he could please see the doctor for just a minute. He was informed that the doctor was only seeing men with temperatures of a hundred or more. Novotny had no temperature, and he returned to his unit, as directed.

On the seventh weekend, with only one more week of training left, Novotny was given a seventy-two-hour pass. He caught a plane to Chicago and a bus to Champaign, carrying with him only a small ditty bag and Rose Anne's impassioned letter. Most of Friday, most of Saturday, and all day Sunday, Rose Anne wept, until Novotny was more miserable than he had ever imagined a man could be. On Sunday night, she held him in her arms and he proceeded to tell her at last of how he had been mistreated by the medic; till then he had not wanted to cause her more grief than she already felt. She stroked his hair while he told how he had not even been allowed to see a doctor. Rose Anne wept and said the medic should be shot. They had no right to send Novotny to Korea if they wouldn't even look after his health here at home. What would happen to him if his back started to act up in the middle of a battle? How could he take care of himself? She raised many questions—rational ones, irrational ones, but none that Novotny had not already considered himself.

Novotny traveled all night by train so as to be back at the base by reveille. He spent most of the next day firing a Browning automatic, and the following morning, when he was to go on K.P., he could not even lift himself from his bed, so cruel was the pain in his back.

In the hospital, the fellow opposite Novotny had been in a wheelchair for two years with osteomyelitis. Every few months, they shortened his legs; nevertheless, the disease continued its slow ascent. The man on Novotny's right had dropped a hand grenade in basic training and blown bits of both his feet off. Down at the end of Novotny's aisle lay a man who had had a crate full of ammunition tip off a truck onto him, and the rest of the men in the ward, many of whom were in the hospital to learn to use prosthetic devices, had been in Korea.

The day after Novotny was assigned to the ward, the man the crate had fallen on was wheeled away to be given a myelogram. He came back to the ward holding his head in his hands. As soon as Novotny was able to leave his bed, he made his way over to this fellow's bed, and because he had heard that the man's condition had been diagnosed as a back injury, he asked him how he was feeling. He got around to asking what a myelogram was, and why he had come back to the ward holding his head. The fellow was talkative enough, and told him that they had injected a white fluid directly into his spine and then X-rayed him as the fluid moved down along the vertebrae, so as to see if the spinal discs were damaged. He told Novotny that apparently it was the stuff injected into him that had given him the headache, but then he added that, lousy as he had felt, he considered himself pretty lucky. He had heard of cases, he said, where the needle had slipped. Novotny had himself heard of instances where doctors had left towels and sponges inside patients, so he could believe it. The man said that all the needle had to do was go off by a hairbreadth and it would wind up in the tangle of nerves leading into the spine. Two days later, two damaged discs were cut out of the man with the injured back, and three of his vertebrae were fused together. All through the following week he lay motionless in his bed.

One evening earlier, while Novotny was still restricted to bed, he had been visited by Reynolds. Reynolds had come around to say good-bye; the entire outfit was to be flown out the next day. Since Reynolds and Novotny hardly knew each other, they had been silent after Reynolds spoke of what was to happen to him and the others the following day. Then Reynolds had said that Novotny was lucky to have developed back trouble when he did; he wouldn't have minded a touch of it himself. Then he left.

When Novotny was out of bed and walking around, X-rays

were taken of his back, and the doctors told him they showed no sign of injury or disease; there was a slight narrowing of the inter-vertebral space between what they referred to on the pictures as L-1 and L-2, but nothing to suggest damage to the disc—which was what Novotny had worked up courage to ask them about. The doctors took him into the examination room and bent him forward and backward. They ran a pin along his thigh and calf and asked if he felt any sensation. They laid him down on a table and, while they slowly raised his leg, asked if he felt any pain. When his leg was almost at a ninety-degree angle with his body, Novotny thought that he did feel his pain—he did, most certainly, remember the pain, and remembered the misery of no one's taking it seriously but himself. Then he thought of all the men around him who hobbled on artificial limbs during the day and moaned in their beds at night, and he said nothing. Consequently, they sent him back to duty.

He was shunted into an infantry company that was in its seventh week of advanced training. Two days before the company was to be shipped out, he awoke in the morning to discover that the pain had returned. He was able to limp to sick call, where he found on duty the unsympathetic medic, who, almost immediately upon seeing Novotny, began to unwind a roll of three-inch tape. Novotny raised an objection, and an argument ensued, which was settled when the doctor emerged from behind his door. He ordered Novotny into his office and had him strip. He told him to bend forward and touch his toes. Novotny tried, but could come only to within a few inches of them. The doctor looked over Novotny's medical record and then asked if he expected the Army to stand on its head because one soldier couldn't touch his toes. He asked him what he expected the Army to do for him. The doctor said there were plenty of G.I.s with sore backs in Korea. And with worse. Plenty worse.

Though the pain diminished somewhat during the day, it re-turned the next morning with increased severity. Novotny could by this time visualize his own insides—he saw the bone as white, and the spot where the pain was located as black. At breakfast, he changed his mind three times over, then went off to the first sergeant to ask permission to go on sick call. He had decided finally that if he did not go and have the condition taken care of within the next few days it would simply get worse and worse; surely there would be no time for medical attention, no proper facilities, while they were in transit to Korea. And, once in Korea, those in charge would surely be even more deaf to his complaints than they were here; there they would be deafened by the roar of cannons. The first sergeant asked Novotny what the matter was this time, and he answered that his back hurt. The first sergeant said what the medic had said the first day: "Everybody's back hurts." But he let him go.

At sick call, the doctor sat Novotny down and asked him what *he* thought was wrong with him. What the suffering soldier had begun to think was that perhaps he had cancer or leukemia. It was really in an effort to minimize his complaint that he said that maybe he had a slipped disc. The doctor said that if Novotny had slipped a disc he wouldn't even be able to walk around. Novotny suddenly found it difficult to breathe. What had he done in life to deserve this? What had he done, from the day he had grown out of short pants, but everything that was asked of him? He told the doctor that all he knew was that he had a pain. He tried to explain that taping it up didn't seem to work; the pain wasn't on the surface but deep inside his back. The doctor said it was deep inside his head. When the doctor told him to go back to duty like a man, Novotny refused.

Novotny was taken to the hospital, and to the office of the colonel in charge of orthopedics. He was a bald man with weighty circles under his eyes and a very erect carriage, who looked to have lived through a good deal. The colonel asked Novotny to sit down and tell him about the pain. Novotny, responding to a long-suffering quality in the man that seemed to him to demand respect, told him the truth: he had rolled over one morning during his basic training, and there it had been, deep and sharp. The colonel asked Novotny if he could think of anything at all that might have caused the pain. Novotny recounted what had happened on K.P. with Reynolds. The doctor asked if that had occurred before the morning he had awakened with the pain, or after it. Novotny admitted that it was after. But surely, he added, that must have aggravated the pain. The doctor said that that did not clear up the problem of where the pain had come from in the first place. He reminded Novotny that the X-rays showed nothing. He ordered Novotny to take off his hospital blues and stretch out on the examination table. By this time, of course, Novotny knew all the tests by heart; once, in fact, he anticipated what he was about to be asked to do, and the colonel gave him a strange look.

When the doctor was finished, he told Novotny that he had a lumbosacral strain with some accompanying muscle spasm. Nothing more. It was what they used to call a touch of lumbago. Novotny stood up to leave, and the colonel informed him that when he was released from the hospital he would have to appear at a summary court-martial for having refused to obey the doctor's order to return to duty. Novotny felt weak enough to faint. He was suddenly sorry he had ever opened his mouth. He was ashamed. He heard himself explaining to the colonel that he had refused to obey only because he had felt too sick to go back to duty. The colonel said it was for a trained doctor to decide how sick or well Novotny was. But, answered Novotny—hearing the gates to the stockade slamming shut behind him, imagining prison scenes so nasty even he couldn't endure them—but the doctor had made a mistake. As the colonel said, he *did* have a lumbosacral strain, and muscle spasm, too. In a steely voice, the colonel told him that there were men in Korea who had much worse. That was the statement to which Novotny had no answer; it was the statement that everyone finally made to him.

When they put him in traction, he had further premonitions of his court-martial and his subsequent internment in the stockade. He, Novotny, who had never broken a law in his life. What was happening? Each morning, he awoke at the foot of the bed, pulled there by the weights tied to his ankles and hanging to the floor. His limbs and joints ached day in and day out from being stretched. More than once, he had the illusion of being tortured for a crime he had not committed, although he knew that the traction was therapeutic. At the end of a week, the weights were removed and he was sent to the physical-therapy clinic, where he received heat treatments and was given a series of exercises to perform. Some days, the pain lessened almost to the point of disappearing. Other days, it was as severe as it had ever been. Then he believed that they would have to cut him open, and it would be the doctor at sick call who would be court-martialed instead of himself. When the pain was at its worst, he felt vindicated; but then, too, when it was at its worst he was most miserable.

He was only alone when he was in the bathroom, and it was there that he would try to bend over and touch his toes. He repeated and repeated this, as though it were a key to something. One day, thinking himself alone, he had begun to strain toward his toes when he was turned around by the voice of the osteomyelitis victim, who was sitting in the doorway in his wheelchair. "How's your backache, buddy?" he said, and wheeled sharply away. Everybody in the ward somehow knew bits of Novotny's history; nobody, nobody knew the whole story.

Nobody he didn't know liked him; and he stopped liking those he did know. His mother appeared at the hospital two weeks after his admittance. She treated him like a hero, leaving with him a shoebox full of baked goods and a Polish sausage. He could not bring himself to tell her about his court-martial; he could not disappoint her—and that made him angry. He was even glad to see her go, lonely as he was. Then, the following weekend, Rose Anne arrived. Everybody whistled when she walked down the ward. And he was furious at her—but for what? For being so desirable? So perfect? They argued, and Rose Anne went back to Champaign, bewildered. That night, the Negro fellow next to Novotny, who had lost his right leg in the battle of Seoul, leaned over the side of his bed and said to him, with a note in his voice more dreamy than malicious, "Hey, man, you got it made."

The next day, very early, Novotny went to the hospital library and searched the shelves until he found a medical encyclopedia. He looked up "slipped disc." Just as he had suspected, many of his own symptoms were recorded there. His heart beat wildly as he read of the difficulties of diagnosing a slipped disc, even with X-rays. Ah yes, only the myelogram was certain. He read on and on, over and over, symptoms, treatments, and drugs. One symptom he read of was a tingling sensation that ran down the back of the leg and into the foot, caused by pressure of the herniated disc on a nerve. The following morning, he awoke with a tingling sensation that ran down the back of his right leg and into his foot. Only momentarily was he elated; then it hurt.

On his weekly ward rounds, the colonel, followed by the nurse and the resident, walked up to each bed and talked to the patient; everyone waited his turn silently, as in formation. The colonel examined stumps, incisions, casts, prosthetic devices, and then asked each man how he felt. When he reached Novotny, he asked him to step out of bed and into the aisle, and there he had him reach down and touch his toes. Novotny tried, bending and bending. Someone in the ward called out, "Come on, Daddy, you can do it." Another voice called, "Push, Polack, *push*"—and then it seemed to him that all the patients in the ward were shouting and laughing, and the colonel was doing nothing to restrain them. "Ah, wait'll they get you in Korea"—and then suddenly the ward was silent, for Novotny was straightening up, his face a brilliant red. "I can't do it, sir," he said. "Does your back feel better?" the colonel asked. "Yes, sir." "Do you think we should send you back to duty?" "I've had a tingling sensation down the back of my right leg," Novotny said. "So?" the colonel asked. The ward was silent; Novotny decided not to answer.

In the afternoon, Novotny was called to the colonel's office. He walked there without too much difficulty—but then it was not unusual for the pain to come and go and come back again, with varying degrees of severity. Sometimes the cycle took hours, sometimes days, sometimes only minutes. It was enough to drive a man crazy.

In the colonel's office, Novotny was told that he was going to get another chance. Novotny was too young, the colonel said, not to be extended a little forgiveness for his self-concern. If he went back to duty, the charges against him would be dismissed and there would be no court-martial. The colonel said that with a war on there was nothing to be gained by putting a good soldier behind bars. The colonel let Novotny know that he was impressed by his marksmanship record, which he had taken the trouble to look up in the company files.

When it was Novotny's turn to speak, he could only think to

ask if the colonel believed the tingling sensation in his leg meant nothing at all. The colonel, making it obvious that it was patience he was displaying, asked Novotny what *he* thought it meant. Novotny said he understood it to be a symptom of a slipped disc. The colonel asked him how he knew that, and Novotny—hesitating only a moment, then going on with the truth, on and on with it—said that he had read it in a book. The colonel, his mouth turning down in disgust, asked Novotny if he was that afraid of going to Korea. Novotny did not know what to answer; he truly had not thought of it that way before. The colonel then asked him if he ever broke out in a cold sweat at night. Novotny said no—the only new symptom he had was the tingling in the leg. The colonel brought a fist down on his desk and told Novotny that the following day he was sending him over to see the psychiatrist. He could sit out the rest of the war in the nuthouse.

What to do? Novotny did not know. It was not a cold but a hot sweat that he was in all through dinner. In the evening, he walked to the Coke machine in the hospital basement, as lonely as he had ever been. A nurse passed him in the hall and smiled. She thought he was sick. He drank his Coke, but when he saw two wheelchairs headed his way he turned and moved up the stairs to the hospital library. He began to perspire again, and then he set about looking through the shelves for a book on psychology. Since he knew as little about psychology as he did about medicine, he had to look for a very long time. He did not want to ask for the help of the librarian, even though she was a civilian. At last he was able to pick out two books, and he sat down on the floor between the stacks, where nobody could see him.

Much of what he read he did not completely follow, but once in a while he came upon an anecdote, and in his frustration with the rest of the book, he would read that feverishly. He read of a woman in a European country who had imagined that she was pregnant. She had swelled up, and then, after nine months, she had had labor pains—but no baby. Because it had all been in her imagination. *Her imagination had made her swell up!* Novotny read this over several times. He was respectful of facts, and believed what he found in books. He did not believe that a man would take the time to sit down and write a book so as to tell other people lies.

When he walked back to the ward, his back seemed engulfed in flames. It was then that he became absorbed in the fantasy of reaching inside himself and cutting out of his body the offending circle of pain. He saw himself standing over his own naked back and twisting down on an instrument that resembled the little utensil that is sold in dime stores to remove the core of a grapefruit. In his bed, he could not find a position in which the pain could be forgotten or ignored. He got up and went to the phone booth, where he called long distance to Rose Anne. He could barely prevent himself from begging her to get on a plane and fly down to him that very night. And yet—the darkness, his fright, his fatigue were taking their toll—if it wasn't his back that was causing the pain, was it Rose Anne? Was he being punished for being so happy with her? Were they being punished for all that sex? Unlike his mother, he was not the kind of Catholic who believed in Hell; he was not the kind who was afraid of sex. All he wanted was his chance at life. That was all.

In the washroom, before he returned to bed, he tried to touch his toes. He forced himself down and down and down until his eyes were cloudy from pain and his fingers had moved to within an inch of the floor. But he could not keep his brain from working, and he did not know what to think. If a woman could imagine herself to be in labor, then for him, too, anything was possible. He leaned over the sink and looked into the mirror. With the aid of every truthful cell in his pained body, he admitted to his own face that he was—yes, he was—frightened of going to Korea. Terribly frightened. But wasn't everybody? He wondered if nothing could be wrong with him. He wondered if nothing he knew was so.

The next day, the psychiatrist asked Novotny if he felt nervous. He said he didn't. The psychiatrist asked if he had felt nervous before he had come into the Army. Novotny said no, that he had been happy. He asked if Novotny was afraid of high places, and if he minded being in crowds; he asked if he had any brothers and sisters, and which he liked better, his mother or his father.

Novotny answered that his father was dead. He asked which Novotny had liked better before his father died. Novotny did not really care to talk about this subject, particularly to someone he didn't even know, but he had decided to be as frank and truthful with the psychiatrist as it was still possible for him to be—at least, he meant to tell him what he *thought* was the truth. Novotny answered that his father had been lazy and incompetent, and the family was finally better off with him gone. The psychiatrist then asked Novotny about Rose Anne. Novotny was frank. He asked Novotny if his back hurt when he was being intimate with Rose Anne. Novotny answered that sometimes it did and sometimes it didn't. He asked Novotny if, when it did hurt, they ceased being intimate. Novotny dropped his head. It was with a searing sense that some secret had been uncovered, something he himself had not even known, that he admitted that they did not. He simply could not bring himself, however, to tell the psychiatrist what exactly they did do when Novotny's back was at its worst. He said quickly that he planned to marry Rose Anne—that he had always known he would marry her. The psychiatrist asked where the couple would live and Novotny said with his mother. When he asked Novotny why, Novotny said because he had to take care of her, too.

The psychiatrist made Novotny stand up, close his eyes, and try to touch the tips of his index fingers together. While Novotny's eyes were closed, the psychiatrist leaned forward and, in a whisper, asked if Novotny was afraid of dying. The weight of all that he had been put through in the past weeks came down upon the shoulders of the young soldier. He broke down and admitted to a fear of death. He began to weep and to say that he didn't want to die. The psychiatrist asked him if he hated the Army, and he admitted that he did.

The psychiatrist's office was across the street from the main hospital, in the building the colonel had called the nuthouse. Novotny, full of shame, was led out of the building by an attendant with a large ring of keys hooked to his belt; he had to unlock three doors before Novotny got out to the street. He went out the rear door, just in sight of a volleyball game that was

being played within a wire enclosure at the back of the building.
To pull himself together before returning to the hostile cripples
in the ward, Novotny watched the teams bat the ball back and
forth over the net, and then he realized that they were patients
who spent their days and nights inside the building from which
he had just emerged. It occurred to him that the doctors were
going to put him into the psychiatric hospital. Not because he
was making believe he had a pain in his back—which, he had come
to think, was really why they had been going to put him in the
stockade—but precisely because he was not making believe. He
was feeling a pain for which there was no cause. He had a terrible
vision of Rose Anne having to come here to visit him. She was
only a young girl, and he knew that it would frighten her so much
to be led through three locked doors that he would lose her. He
was about to begin to lose things.

He pulled himself straight up—he had been stooping—and
clenched his teeth and told himself that in a certain number of
seconds the pain would be gone for good. He counted to thirty,
and then took a step. He came down upon his right foot with only
half his weight, but the pain was still there, so sharp that it made
his eyes water. The volleyball smashed against the fence through
which he was peering, and, trying to walk as he remembered
himself walking when he was a perfectly healthy young man, a
man with nothing to fear—a man, he thought, who had not even
begun to know of all the confusion growing up inside him—he
walked away.

The colonel had Novotny called to his office the following day.
The night before, Novotny had got little sleep, but by dawn he
had reached a decision. Now, though he feared the worst, he
marched to the colonel's office with a plan of action held firmly in
mind. When Novotny entered, the colonel asked him to sit down,
and proceeded to tell him of his own experiences in the Second
World War. He had flown with an airborne division at a time
when he was only a little more than Novotny's age. He had
jumped from a plane over Normandy and broken both his legs,
and then been shot in the chest by a French farmer for a reason
he still did not understand. The colonel said that he had returned
from Korea only a week before Novotny had entered the hospital.

He wished that Novotny could see what the men there were going through—he wished Novotny could be a witness to the bravery and the courage and the comradery, and, too, to the misery and suffering. The misery of our soldiers and of those poor Koreans! He was not angry with Novotny personally; he was only trying to tell him something for his own good. Novotny was too young to make a decision that might disgrace him for the rest of his life. He told the young soldier that if he walked around with that back of his for a few weeks, if he just stopped *thinking* about it all the time, it would be as good as new. That, in actual fact, it was almost as good as new right now. He said that Novotny's trouble was that he was a passive-aggressive.

Novotny's voice was very thin when he asked the colonel what he meant. The colonel read to him what the psychiatrist had written. It was mostly the answers that Novotny had given to the psychiatrist's questions; some of it had to do with the way Novotny had sat, and the tone of his voice, and certain words he had apparently used. In the end, the report said that Novotny was a passive-aggressive and recommended he be given an administrative separation from the Army, and the appropriate discharge. Novotny asked what that meant. The colonel replied that the appropriate discharge as far as he was concerned was "plain and simple"; he took down a book of regulations from a shelf behind him, and after flipping past several pages read to Novotny in a loud voice. " 'An undesirable discharge is an administrative separation from the service under conditions other than honorable. It is issued for unfitness, misconduct, or security reasons.' " He looked up, got no response, and, fiery-eyed, read further. " 'It is recognized that all enlisted personnel with behavior problems cannot be rehabilitated by proper leadership and/or psychiatric assistance. It is inevitable that a certain percentage of individuals entering the service subsequently will demonstrate defective moral habits, irresponsibility, inability to profit by experience—' " He paused to read the last phrase again, and then went on—" 'untrustworthiness, lack of regard for the rights of others, and inability to put off pleasures and impulses of the moment.' " He engaged Novotny's eye. " 'Often,' " he said, returning to the regulation, " 'these individuals show poor performance despite intelligence, superficial charm, and a readiness to promise improvement. The effective leader is able to rehabilitate only the percentage of persons with behavior problems who are amenable to leadership.'" He stopped. "You can say that again," he mumbled, and pushed the book forward on his desk so that it faced Novotny. "Unfitness, soldier," he said, tapping his finger on the page. "It's what we use to get the crackpots out—bed-wetters, homos, petty thieves, malingerers, and so on." He waited for Novotny to take in the page's contents, and while he did, the colonel made it clear that such a discharge followed a man through life. Novotny, raising his head slightly, asked again what a passive-aggressive was. The colonel looked into his eyes and said, "Just another kind of coward."

What Novotny had decided in bed the night before was to request a myelogram. Of course, there lived still in his imagination the man who had said that all the needle had to do was be off by a hairbreadth; he was convinced, in fact, that something like that was just what would happen to him, given the way things had begun to go in his life. But though such a prospect frightened him, he did not see that he had any choice. The truth had to be known, one way or the other. But when the colonel finished and waited for him to speak, he remained silent.

"What do you have against the Army, Novotny?" the colonel asked. "What makes you so special?"

Novotny did not mention the myelogram. Why *should* he? Why should he have to take so much from people when he had an honest-to-God pain in his back? He was not imagining it, he was not making it up. He had practically ruptured himself when Reynolds had dropped the end of the can of potatoes. Maybe he had only awakened with a simple strain that first morning, but trying to keep the can from dropping on Reynolds' toes, he had done something serious to his back. That all the doctors were unable to give a satisfactory diagnosis did not make his pain any less real.

"You are a God-damned passive-aggressive, young man, what do you think of that?" the colonel said.

Novotny did not speak.

"You know how many people in America have low back pain?" the colonel demanded. "Something like fifteen per cent of the adult population of this country has low back pain—and what do you think they do, quit? Lay down on the job? What do you think a man does who has a family and responsibilities—stop supporting them? You know what your trouble is, my friend? You think life owes you something. You think something's coming to you. I spotted you right off, Novotny. You're going to get your way in this world. Everybody else can go to hell, just so long as you have your way. Imagine if all those men in Korea, if they all gave in to every little ache and pain. Imagine if that was what our troops had done at Valley Forge, or Okinawa. Then where would we all be? Haven't you ever heard of self-sacrifice? The average man, if you threatened him with this kind of discharge, would do just about anything he could to avoid it. But not you. Even if you have a pain, haven't you got the guts to go ahead and serve like everybody else? Well, answer me, yes or no?"

But Novotny would not answer. All he had done was answer people and tell them the truth, and what had it got him? What good was it, being good? What good was it, especially if at bottom you were bad anyway? What good was it, acting strong, if at bottom you were weak and couldn't be strong if you wanted to? With the colonel glaring across at him, the only solace Novotny had was to think that nobody knew any more about him than he himself did. Whatever anybody chose to call him didn't really mean a thing.

"Ah, get out of my sight," the colonel said. "People like you make me sick. Go ahead, join the bed-wetters and the queers. Get the hell out of here."

Within six days, the Army had rid itself of Novotny. It took Novotny, however, a good deal more than six days to rid himself of infirmity, if he can be said ever to have rid himself of infirmity —or, at least, the threat of infirmity. During the next year, he missed days of work and evenings of night school, and spent numerous weekends on a mattress supported by a bed board, where he rested and nursed away his pain. He went to one doctor who prescribed a set of exercises, and another who prescribed a steel brace, which Novotny bought but found so uncomfortable that he finally had to stick it away in the attic, though it had cost forty-five dollars. Another doctor, who had been recommended to him, listened to his story, then simply shrugged his shoulders; and still another told Novotny what the colonel had—that many Americans had low back ailments, that they were frequently of unknown origin, and that he would have to learn to live with it.

That, finally was what he tried to do. Gradually, over the years, the pain diminished in severity and frequency, though even today he has an occasional bad week, and gets a twinge if he bends the wrong way or picks up something he shouldn't. He is married to Rose Anne and is employed as a television cameraman by an educational channel in Chicago. His mother lives with him and his wife in Park Forest. For the most part, he leads a quiet, ordinary sort of life, though his attachment to Rose Anne is still marked by an unusual passion. When the other men in Park Forest go bowling on Friday nights, Novotny stays home, for he tries not to put strains upon his body to which he has decided it is not equal. In a way, all the awfulness of those Army days has boiled down to that—no bowling. There are nights, of course, when Novotny awakens from a dead sleep to worry in the dark about the future. What will happen to him? What won't? But surely those are questions he shares with all men, sufferers of low back pain and non-sufferers alike. Nobody has ever yet asked to see his discharge papers, so about that the colonel was wrong.

13 William H. Gass

William H. Gass was born in Fargo, North Dakota, in 1924, and educated at Kenyon College, Ohio Wesleyan, and Cornell. He has published a collection of stories, In the Heart of the Heart of the Country (1968), and a novel, Omensetter's Luck (1966). He is a professor of philosophy at Purdue University.

❖

IN THE HEART OF THE HEART
OF THE COUNTRY

A PLACE

So I have sailed the seas and come . . .

to B . . .

a small town fastened to a field in Indiana. Twice there have been twelve hundred people here to answer to the census. The town is outstandingly neat and shady, and always puts its best side to the highway. On one lawn there's even a wood or plastic iron deer.

You can reach us by crossing a creek. In the spring the lawns are green, the forsythia is singing, and even the railroad that guts the town has straight bright rails which hum when the train is coming, and the train itself has a welcome horning sound.

Down the back streets the asphalt crumbles into gravel. There's Westbrook's, with the geraniums, Horsefall's, Mott's. The sidewalk shatters. Gravel dust rises like breath behind the wagons. And I am in retirement from love.

WEATHER

In the Midwest, around the lower Lakes, the sky in the winter is heavy and close, and it is a rare day, a day to remark on, when the sky lifts and allows the heart up. I am keeping count, and as I write this page, it is eleven days since I have seen the sun.

MY HOUSE

There's a row of headless maples behind my house, cut to free the passage of electric wires. High stumps, ten feet tall, remain, and I climb these like a boy to watch the country sail away from me. They are ordinary fields, a little more uneven than they should be, since in the spring they puddle. The topsoil's thin, but only moderately stony. Corn is grown one year, soybeans another. At dusk starlings darken the single tree—a larch—which stands in the middle. When the sky moves, fields move under it. I feel, on my perch, that I've lost my years. It's as though I were living at last in my eyes, as I have always dreamed of doing, and I think then I know why I've come here: to see, and so to go out against new things—oh god how easily—like air in a breeze. It's true there are moments—foolish moments, ecstasy on a tree stump—when I'm all but gone, scattered I like to think like seed, for I'm the sort now in the fool's position of having love left over which I'd like to lose; what good is it now to me, candy ungiven after Halloween?

A PERSON

There are vacant lots on either side of Billy Holsclaw's house. As the weather improves, they fill with hollyhocks. From spring through fall, Billy collects coal and wood and puts the lumps and pieces in piles near his door, for keeping warm is his one work. I see him most often on mild days sitting on his doorsill in the sun. I notice he's squinting a little, which is perhaps the reason he doesn't cackle as I pass. His house is the size of a single garage, and very old. It shed its paint with its youth, and its boards are a warped and weathered gray. So is Billy. He wears a short lumpy faded black coat when it's cold, otherwise he always goes about in the same loose, grease-spotted shirt and trousers. I suspect his galluses were yellow once, when they were new.

WIRES

These wires offend me. Three trees were maimed on their account, and now these wires deface the sky. They cross like a fence in front of me, enclosing the crows with the clouds. I can't reach in, but like a stick, I throw my feelings over. What is it that offends me? I am on my stump, I've built a platform there and the wires prevent my going out. The cut trees, the black wires, all the beyond birds therefore anger me. When I've wormed through a fence to reach a meadow, do I ever feel the same about the field?

THE CHURCH

The church has a steeple like the hat of a witch, and five birds, all doves, perch in its gutters.

MY HOUSE

Leaves move in the windows. I cannot tell you yet how beautiful it is, what it means. But they do move. They move in the glass.

POLITICS

. . . for all those not in love.

I've heard Batista described as a Mason. A farmer who'd seen him in Miami made this claim. He's as nice a fellow as you'd ever want to meet. Of Castro, of course, no one speaks.

For all those not in love there's law: to rule . . . to regulate . . . to rectify. I cannot write the poetry of such proposals, the poetry of politics, though sometimes—often—always now—I am in that uneasy peace of equal powers which makes a State; then I communicate by passing papers, proclamations, orders, through my bowels. Yet I was not a State with you, nor were we both together any Indiana. A squad of Pershing Rifles at the moment, I make myself Right Face! Legislation packs the screw of my intestines. Well, king of the classroom's king of the hill. You used to waddle when you walked because my sperm between your legs was draining to a towel. Teacher, poet, folded lover—like the politician, like those drunkards, ill, or those who faucet-off while pissing heartily to preach upon the force and fullness of that stream, or pause from vomiting to praise the purity and passion of their puke—I chant, I beg, I orate, I command, I sing—

> Come back to Indiana—not too late!
>   (Or will you be a ranger to the end?)
> Good-bye . . . Good-bye . . . oh, I shall always wait
>   You, Larry, traveler—
>   stranger,
>   son,
>   —my friend—

my little girl, my poem by heart, my self, my childhood.

But I've heard Batista described as a Mason. That dries up my pity, melts my hate. Back from the garage where I have overheard it, I slap the mended fender of my car to laugh, and listen to the metal stinging tartly in my hand.

PEOPLE

Their hair in curlers and their heads wrapped in loud scarves, young mothers, fattish in trousers, lounge about in the speedwash, smoking cigarettes, eating candy, drinking pop, thumbing magazines, and screaming at their children above the whir and rumble of the machines.

At the bank a young man freshly pressed is letting himself in with a key. Along the street, delicately teetering, many grandfathers move in a dream. During the murderous heat of summer, they perch on window ledges, their feet dangling just inside the narrow shelf of shade the store has made, staring steadily into the street. Where their consciousness has gone I can't say. It's not in the eyes. Perhaps it's diffuse, all temperature and skin, like an infant's, though more mild. Near the corner there are several large overalled men employed in standing. A truck turns to be weighed on the scales at the Feed and Grain. Images drift on the drugstore window. The wind has blown the smell of cattle into town. Our eyes have been driven in like the eyes of the old men. And there's no one to have mercy on us.

VITAL DATA

There are two restaurants here and a tearoom. two bars. one bank, three barbers, one with a green shade with which he blinds his window. two groceries. a dealer in Fords. one drug, one hardware, and one appliance store. several that sell feed, grain, and farm equipment. an antique shop. a poolroom. a laundromat. three doctors. a dentist. a plumber. a vet. a funeral home in elegant repair the color of a buttercup. numerous beauty parlors which open and shut like night-blooming plants. a tiny dime and department store of no width but several floors. a hutch, homemade, where you can order, after lying down or squirming in, furniture that's been fashioned from bent lengths of stainless tubing, glowing plastic, metallic thread, and clear shellac. an American Legion Post and a root beer stand. little agencies for this and that: cosmetics, brushes, insurance, greeting cards and garden produce—anything—sample shoes—which do their business out of hats and satchels, over coffee cups and dissolving sugar. a factory for making paper sacks and pasteboard boxes that's lodged in an old brick building bearing the legend OPERA HOUSE, still faintly golden, on its roof. a library given by Carnegie. a post office. a school. a railroad station. fire station. lumberyard. telephone company. welding shop. garage . . . and spotted through the town from one end to the other in a line along the highway, gas stations to the number five.

EDUCATION

In 1833, Colin Goodykoontz, an itinerant preacher with a name from a fairytale, summed up the situation in one Indiana town this way:

Ignorance and her squalid brood. A universal dearth of intellect. Total abstinence from literature is very generally practiced. . . . There is not a scholar in grammar or geography, or a *teacher capable* of *instructing* in them, to my knowledge. . . . Others are supplied a few months of the year with the most antiquated & unreasonable forms of teaching reading, writing & cyphering. . . . Need I stop to remind you of the host of loathsome reptiles such a stagnant pool is fitted to breed! Croaking jealousy; bloated bigotry; coiling suspicion; wormish blindness; crocodile malice!

Things have changed since then, but in none of the respects mentioned.

BUSINESS

One side section of street is blocked off with sawhorses. Hard, thin, bitter men in blue jeans, cowboy boots and hats, untruck a dinky carnival. The merchants are promoting themselves. There will be free rides, raucous music, parades and coneys, pop, popcorn, candy, cones, awards and drawings, with all you can endure of pinch, push, bawl, shove, shout, scream, shriek, and bellow. Children pedal past on decorated bicycles, their wheels a blur of color, streaming crinkled paper and excited dogs. A little later there's a pet show for a prize—dogs, cats, birds, sheep, ponies, goats—none of which wins. The whirlabouts whirl about. The Ferris wheel climbs dizzily into the sky as far as a tall man on tiptoe might be persuaded to reach, and the irritated operators measure the height and weight of every child with sour eyes to see if they are safe for the machines. An electrical megaphone repeatedly trumpets the names of the generous sponsors. The following day they do not allow the refuse to remain long in the street.

MY HOUSE, THIS PLACE AND BODY

I have met with some mischance, wings withering, as Plato says obscurely, and across the breadth of Ohio, like heaven on a table, I've fallen as far as the poet, to the sixth sort of body, this house in B, in Indiana, with its blue and gray bewitching windows, holy magical insides. Great thick evergreens protect its entry. And I live *in*.

Lost in the corn rows, I remember feeling just another stalk, and thus this country takes me over in the way I occupy myself when I am well . . . completely—to the edge of both my house and body. No one notices, when they walk by, that I am brimming in the doorways. My house, this place and body, I've come in mourning to be born in. To anybody else it's pretty silly: love. Why should I feel a loss? How am I bereft? She was never mine; she was a fiction, always a golden tomgirl, barefoot, with an adolescent's slouch and a boy's taste for sports and fishing, a figure out of Twain, or worse, in Riley. Age cannot be kind.

There's little hand-in-hand here . . . not in B. No one touches except in rage. Occasionally girls will twine their arms about each other and lurch along, school out, toward home and play. I dreamed my lips would drift down your back like a skiff on a river. I'd follow a vein with the point of my finger, hold your bare feet in my naked hands.

THE SAME PERSON

Billy Holsclaw lives alone—how alone it is impossible to fathom. In the post office he talks greedily to me about the weather. His head bobs on a wild flood of words, and I take this violence to be a measure of his eagerness for speech. He badly needs a shave, coal dust has layered his face, he spits when he speaks, and his fingers pick at his tatters. He wobbles out in the wind when I leave him, a paper sack mashed in the fold of his arm, the leaves blowing past him, and our encounter drives me sadly home to poetry—where there's no answer. Billy closes his door and carries coal or wood to his fire and closes his eyes, and there's simply no way of knowing how lonely and empty he is or whether he's as vacant and barren and loveless as the rest of us are—here in the heart of the country.

WEATHER

For we're always out of luck here. That's just how it is—for instance in the winter. The sides of the buildings, the roofs, the limbs of the trees are gray. Streets, sidewalks, faces, feelings—they are gray. Speech is gray, and the grass where it shows. Every flank and front, each top is gray. Everything is gray: hair, eyes, window glass, the hawkers' bills and touters' posters, lips, teeth, poles and metal signs—they're gray, quite gray. Cars are gray. Boots, shoes, suits, hats, gloves are gray. Horses, sheep, and cows, cats killed in the road, squirrels in the same way, sparrows, doves, and pigeons, all are gray, everything is gray, and everyone is out of luck who lives here.

A similar haze turns the summer sky milky, and the air muffles your head and shoulders like a sweater you've got caught in. In the summer light, too, the sky darkens a moment when you open your eyes. The heat is pure distraction. Steeped in our fluids, miserable in the folds of our bodies, we can scarcely think of anything but our sticky parts. Hot cyclonic winds and storms of dust crisscross the country. In many places, given an indifferent push, the wind will still coast for miles, gathering resource and edge as it goes, cunning and force. According to the season, paper, leaves, field litter, seeds, snow, fill up the fences. Sometimes I think the land is flat because the winds have leveled it, they blow so constantly. In any case, a gale can grow in a field of corn that's as hot as a draft from hell, and to receive it is one of the most dismaying experiences of this life, though the smart of the same wind in winter is more humiliating, and in that sense even worse. But in the spring it rains as well, and the trees fill with ice.

PLACE

Many small Midwestern towns are nothing more than rural slums, and this community could easily become one. Principally during the first decade of the century, though there were many earlier instances, well-to-do farmers moved to town and built fine homes to contain them in their retirement. Others desired a more social life, and so lived in, driving to their fields like storekeepers to their businesses. These houses are now dying like the bereaved who inhabit them; they are slowly losing their senses—deafness, blindness, forgetfulness, mumbling, an insecure gait, an uncontrollable trembling has overcome them. Some kind of Northern Snopes will occupy them next: large-familied, Catholic, Democratic, scrambling, vigorous, poor; and since the parents will work in larger, nearby towns, the children will be loosed upon themselves and upon the hapless neighbors much as the fabulous Khan loosed his legendary horde. These Snopes will undertake makeshift repairs with materials that other people have thrown away; paint halfway round their house, then quit; almost certainly maintain an ugly loud cantankerous dog and underfeed a pair of cats to keep the rodents down. They will collect piles of possibly useful junk in the back yard, park their cars in the front, live largely leaning over engines, give not a hoot for the land, the old community, the hallowed ways, the established clans. Weakening widow ladies have already begun to hire large rude youths from families such as these to rake and mow and tidy the grounds they will inherit.

PEOPLE

In the cinders at the station boys sit smoking steadily in darkened cars, their arms bent out the windows, white shirts glowing behind the glass. Nine o'clock is the best time. They sit in a line facing the highway—two or three or four of them—idling their engines. As you walk by a machine may growl at you or a pair of headlights flare up briefly. In a moment one will pull out, spinning cinders behind it, to stalk impatiently up and down the dark streets or roar half a mile into the country before returning to its place in line and pulling up.

MY HOUSE, MY CAT, MY COMPANY

I must organize myself. I must, as they say, pull myself together, dump this cat from my lap, stir—yes, resolve, move, do. But do what? My will is like the rosy dustlike light in this room: soft, diffuse, and gently comforting. It lets me do . . . anything . . . nothing. My ears hear what they happen to; I eat what's put before me; my eyes see what blunders into them; my thoughts are not thoughts, they are dreams. I'm empty or I'm full . . . depending; and I cannot choose. I sink my claws in Tick's fur and scratch the bones of his back until his rear rises amorously. Mr. Tick, I murmur, I must organize myself. I must pull myself together. And Mr. Tick rolls over on his belly, all ooze.

I spill Mr. Tick when I've rubbed his stomach. Shoo. He steps away slowly, his long tail rhyming with his paws. How beautifully he moves, I think; how beautifully, like you, he commands his loving, how beautifully he accepts. So I rise and wander from room to room, up and down, gazing through most of my forty-one windows. How well this house receives its loving too. Let out like Mr. Tick, my eyes sink in the shrubbery. I am not here; I've passed the glass, passed second-story spaces, flown by branches, brilliant berries, to the ground, grass high in seed and leafage every season; and it is the same as when I passed above you in my aged, ardent body; it's, in short, a kind of love; and I am learning to restore myself, my house, my body, by paying court to gardens, cats, and running water, and with neighbors keeping company.

Mrs. Desmond is my right-hand friend; she's eighty-five. A thin white mist of hair, fine and tangled, manifests the climate of her mind. She is habitually suspicious, fretful, nervous. Burglars break in at noon. Children trespass. Even now they are shaking the pear tree, stealing rhubarb, denting lawn. Flies caught in the screens and numbed by frost awake in the heat to buzz and scrape the metal cloth and frighten her, though she is deaf to me, and consequently cannot hear them. Boards creak, the wind whistles across the chimney mouth, drafts cruise like fish through the hollow rooms. It is herself she hears, her own flesh failing, for only death will preserve her from those daily chores she climbs like stairs, and all that anxious waiting. Is it now, she wonders. No? Then: is it now?

We do not converse. She visits me to talk. My task to murmur. She talks about her grandsons, her daughter who lives in Delphi, her sister or her husband—both gone—obscure friends—dead—obscurer aunts and uncles—lost—ancient neighbors, members of her church or of her clubs—passed or passing on; and in this way she brings the ends of her life together with a terrifying rush: she is a girl, a wife, a mother, widow, all at once. All at once—appalling—but I believe it; I wince in expectation of the clap. Her talk's a fence—a shade drawn, window fastened, door that's locked —for no one dies taking tea in a kitchen; and as her years compress and begin to jumble, I really believe in the brevity of life; I sweat in my wonder; death is the dog down the street, the angry gander, bedroom spider, goblin who's come to get her; and it occurs to me that in my listening posture I'm the boy who suffered the winds of my grandfather with an exactly similar politeness, that I am, right now, all my ages, out in elbows, as angular as badly stacked cards. Thus was I, when I loved you, every man I could be, youth and child—far from enough—and you, so strangely ambiguous a being, met me, heart for spade, play after play, the whole run of our suits.

Mr. Tick, you do me honor. You not only lie in my lap, but you remain alive there, coiled like a fetus. Through your deep nap, I feel you hum. You are, and are not, a machine. You are alive, alive exactly, and it means nothing to you—much to me. You are a cat—you cannot understand—you are a cat so easily. Your nature is not something you must rise to. You, not I, live in: in house, in skin, in shrubbery. Yes. I think I shall hat my head with a steeple; turn church; devour people. Mr. Tick, though, has a tail he can twitch, he need not fly his Fancy. Claws, not metrical schema, poetry his paws; while smoothing . . . smoothing . . . smoothing roughly, his tongue laps its neatness. O Mr. Tick, I know you; you are an electrical penis. Go on now, shoo. Mrs. Desmond doesn't like you. She thinks you will tangle yourself in her legs and she will fall. You murder her birds, she knows, and walk upon her roof with death in your jaws. I must gather myself together for a bound. What age is it I'm at right now, I wonder. The heart, don't they always say, keeps the true time. Mrs. Desmond is knocking. Faintly, you'd think, but she pounds. She's brought me a cucumber. I believe she believes I'm a woman. Come in, Mrs. Desmond, thank you, be my company, it looks lovely, and have tea. I'll slice it, crisp, with cream, for luncheon, each slice as thin as me.

POLITICS

O all ye isolate and separate powers, Sing! Sing, and sing in such a way that from a distance it will seem a harmony, a Strindberg play, a friendship ring . . . so happy—happy, happy, happy—as

here we go hand in handling, up and down. Our union was a
singing, though we were silent in the songs we sang like single
notes are silent in a symphony. In no sense sober, we barber-
shopped together and never heard the discords in our music or
saw ourselves as dirty, cheap, or silly. Yet cats have worn out
better shoes than those thrown through our love songs at us.
Hush. Be patient—prudent—politic. Still, Cleveland killed you,
Mr. Crane. Were you not politic enough and fond of being
beaten? Like a piece of sewage, the city shat you from its stern
three hundred miles from history—beyond the loving reach of
sailors. Well, I'm not a poet who puts Paris to his temple in his
youth to blow himself from Idaho, or—fancy that—Missouri. My
god, I said, this is my country, but must my country go so far as
Terre Haute or Whiting, go so far as Gary?

When the Russians first announced the launching of their
satellite, many people naturally refused to believe them. Later
others were outraged that they had sent a dog around the earth.
I wouldn't want to take that mutt from out that metal flying
thing if he's still living when he lands, our own dog catcher said;
anybody knows you shut a dog up by himself to toss around the
first thing he'll be setting on to do you let him out is bite somebody.

This Midwest. A dissonance of parts and people, we are a
consonance of Towns. Like a man grown fat in everything but
heart, we overlabor; our outlook never really urban, never rural
either, we enlarge and linger at the same time, as Alice both
changed and remained in her story. You are blond. I put my hand
upon your belly; feel it tremble from my trembling. We always
drive large cars in my section of the country. How could you be
a comfort to me now?

MORE VITAL DATA

The town is exactly fifty houses, trailers, stores, and miscellaneous
buildings long, but in places no streets deep. It takes on width
as you drive south, always adding to the east. Most of the dwell-
ings are fairly spacious farm houses in the customary white, with
wide wraparound porches and tall narrow windows, though there

are many of the grander kind—fretted, scalloped, turreted, and decorated with clapboards set at angles or on end, with stained-glass windows at the stair landings and lots of wrought iron full of fancy curls—and a few of these look like castles in their rarer brick. Old stables serve as garages now, and the lots are large to contain them and the vegetable and flower gardens which, ultimately, widows plant and weed and then entirely disappear in. The shade is ample, the grass is good, the sky a glorious fall violet; the apple trees are heavy and red, the roads are calm and empty; corn has sifted from the chains of tractored wagons to speckle the streets with gold and with the russet fragments of the cob, and a man would be a fool who wanted, blessed with this, to live anywhere else in the world.

EDUCATION

Buses like great orange animals move through the early light to school. There the children will be taught to read and warned against Communism. By Miss Janet Jakes. That's not her name. Her name is Helen something—Scott or James. A teacher twenty years. She's now worn fine and smooth, and has a face, Wilfred says, like a mail-order ax. Her voice is hoarse, and she has a cough. For she screams abuse. The children stare, their faces blank. This is the thirteenth week. They are used to it. You will all, she shouts, you will all draw pictures of me. No. She is a Mrs.—someone's missus. And in silence they set to work while Miss Jakes jabs hairpins in her hair. Wilfred says an ax, but she has those rimless tinted glasses, graying hair, an almost dimpled chin. I must concentrate. I must stop making up things. I must give myself to life; let it mold me: that's what they say in *Wisdom's Monthly Digest* every day. Enough, enough—you've been at it long enough; and the children rise formally a row at a time to present their work to her desk. No, she wears rims; it's her chin that's dimpleless. Well, it will take more than a tablespoon of features to sweeten that face. So she grimly shuffles their sheets, examines her reflection crayoned on them. I would not dare . . . allow a child . . . to put a line around me. Though now and then she smiles like a nick in the blade, in the end these drawings depress her. I could not bear it—how can she ask?—that anyone . . . draw me. Her anger's lit. That's why she does it: flame. There go her eyes; the pink in her glasses brightens, dims. She is a pumpkin, and her rage is breathing like the candle in. No, she shouts, no—the cartoon trembling—no, John Mauck, John Stewart Mauck, this will not do. The picture flutters from her fingers. You've made me too muscular.

I work on my poetry. I remember my friends, associates, my students, by their names. Their names are Maypop, Dormouse, Upsydaisy. Their names are Gladiolus, Callow Bladder, Prince and Princess Oleo, Hieronymus, Cardinal Mummum, Mr. Fitchew, The Silken Howdah, Spot. Sometimes you're Tom Sawyer, Huckleberry Finn; it is perpetually summer; your buttocks are my pillow; we are adrift on a raft; your back is our river. Sometimes you are Major Barbara, sometimes a goddess who kills men in battle, sometimes you are soft like a shower of water; you are bread in my mouth.

I do not work on my poetry. I forget my friends, associates, my students, and their names: Gramophone, Blowgun, Pickle, Serenade . . . Marge the Barge, Arena, Uberhaupt . . . Doctor Dildoe, The Fog Machine. For I am now in B, in Indiana: out of job and out of patience, out of love and time and money, out of bread and out of body, in a temper, Mrs. Desmond, out of tea. So shut your fist up, bitch, you bag of death; go bang another door; go die, my dearie. Die, life-deaf old lady. Spill your breath. Fall over like a frozen board. Gray hair grows from the nose of your mind. You are a skull already—*memento mori*—the foreskin retracts from your teeth. Will your plastic gums last longer than your bones, and color their grinning? And is your twot still hazel-hairy, or are you bald as a ditch? . . . bitch . . . . . . bitch . . . . bitch. I wanted to be famous, but you bring me age —my emptiness. Was it *that* which I thought would balloon me above the rest? Love? where are you? . . . love me. I want to rise so high, I said, that when I shit I won't miss anybody.

BUSINESS

For most people, business is poor. Nearby cities have siphoned off all but a neighborhood trade. Except for feed and grain and farm supplies, you stand a chance to sell only what one runs out to buy. Chevrolet has quit, and Frigidaire. A locker plant has left its afterimage. The lumberyard has been, so far, six months about its going. Gas stations change hands clumsily, a restaurant becomes available, a grocery closes. One day they came and knocked the cornices from the watch repair and pasted campaign posters on the windows. Torn across, by now, by boys, they urge you still to vote for half an orange beblazoned man who as a whole one failed two years ago to win at his election. Everywhere, in this manner, the past speaks, and it mostly speaks of failure. The empty stores, the old signs and dusty fixtures, the debris in alleys, the flaking paint and rusty gutters, the heavy locks and sagging boards: they say the same disagreeable things. What do the sightless windows see, I wonder, when the sun throws a passerby against them? Here a stair unfolds toward the street—dark, rickety, and treacherous—and I always feel, as I pass it, that if I just went carefully up and turned the corner at the landing, I would find myself out of the world. But I've never had the courage.

THAT SAME PERSON

The weeds catch up with Billy. In pursuit of the hollyhocks, they rise in coarse clumps all around the front of his house. Billy has to stamp down a circle by his door like a dog or cat does turning round to nest up, they're so thick. What particularly troubles me is that winter will find the weeds still standing stiff and tindery to take the sparks which Billy's little mortarless chimney spouts. It's true that fires are fun here. The town whistle, which otherwise only blows for noon (and there's no noon on Sunday), signals the direction of the fire by the length and number of its blasts, the volunteer firemen rush past in their cars and trucks, houses empty their owners along the street every time like an illustration in a children's book. There are many bikes, too, and barking dogs, and sometimes—halleluiah—the fire's right here in town—a vacant lot of weeds and stubble flaming up. But I'd rather it weren't Billy or Billy's lot or house. Quite selfishly I want him to remain the way he is—counting his sticks and logs, sitting on his sill in the soft early sun—though I'm not sure what his presence means to me . . . or to anyone. Nevertheless,

I keep wondering whether, given time, I might not someday find a figure in our language which would serve him faithfully, and furnish his poverty and loneliness richly out.

WIRES

Where sparrows sit like fists. Doves fly the steeple. In mist the wires change perspective, rise and twist. If they led to you, I would know what they were. Thoughts passing often, like the starlings who flock these fields at evening to sleep in the trees beyond, would form a family of paths like this; they'd foot down the natural height of air to just about a bird's perch. But they do not lead to you.

> Of whose beauty it was sung
> She shall make the old man young.

They fasten me.

If I walked straight on, in my present mood, I would reach the Wabash. It's not a mood in which I'd choose to conjure you. Similes dangle like baubles from me. This time of year the river is slow and shallow, the clay banks crack in the sun, weeds surprise the sandbars. The air is moist and I am sweating. It's impossible to rhyme in this dust. Everything—sky, the cornfield, stump, wild daisies, my old clothes and pressless feelings—seem fabricated for installment purchase. Yes. Christ. I am suffering a summer Christmas; and I cannot walk under the wires. The sparrows scatter like handfuls of gravel. Really, wires are voices in thin strips. They are words wound in cables. Bars of connection.

WEATHER

I would rather it were the weather that was to blame for what I am and what my friends and neighbors are—we who live here in the heart of the country. Better the weather, the wind, the pale dying snow . . . the snow—why not the snow? There's never much really, not around the lower Lakes anyway, not enough to boast about, not enough to be useful. My father tells how the snow in the Dakotas would sweep to the roofs of the barns in the old days, and he and his friends could sled on the crust that would form because the snow was so fiercely driven. In Bemidji trees have been known to explode. That would be something—if the trees in Davenport or Francisville or Carbondale or Niles were to go blam some winter—blam! blam! blam! all the way down the gray, cindery, snow-sick streets.

A cold fall rain is blackening the trees or the air is like lilac and full of parachuting seeds. Who cares to live in any season but his own? Still I suspect the secret's in this snow, the secret of our sickness, if we could only diagnose it, for we are all dying like the elms in Urbana. This snow—like our skin it covers the country. Later dust will do it. Right now—snow. Mud presently. But it is snow without any laughter in it, a pale gray pudding thinly spread on stiff toast, and if that seems a strange description, it's accurate all the same. Of course soot blackens everything, but apart from that, we are never sufficiently cold here. The flakes as they come, alive and burning, we cannot retain, for if our temperatures fall, they rise promptly again, just as, in the summer, they bob about in the same feckless way. Suppose though . . . suppose they were to rise some August, climb and rise, and then hang in the hundreds like a hawk through December, what a desert we could make of ourselves—from Chicago to Cairo, from Hammond to Columbus—what beautiful Death Valleys.

PLACE

I would rather it were the weather. It drives us in upon ourselves —an unlucky fate. Of course there is enough to stir our wonder anywhere; there's enough to love, anywhere, if one is strong enough, if one is diligent enough, if one is perceptive, patient, kind enough—whatever it takes; and surely it's better to live in the country, to live on a prairie by a drawing of rivers, in Iowa or Illinois or Indiana, say, than in any city, in any stinking fog of human beings, in any blooming orchard of machines. It ought to be. The cities are swollen and poisonous with people. It ought to be better. Man has never been a fit environment for man—for rats, maybe, rats do nicely, or for dogs or cats and the household beetle.

And how long the street is, nowadays. These endless walls are fallen to keep back the tides of earth. Brick could be beautiful but we have covered it gradually with gray industrial vomits. Age does not make concrete genial, and asphalt is always—like America—twenty-one, until it breaks up in crumbs like stale cake. The brick, the asphalt, the concrete, the dancing signs and garish posters, the feed and excrement of the automobile, the litter of its inhabitants: they compose, they decorate, they line our streets, and there is nowhere, nowadays, our streets can't reach.

A man in the city has no natural thing by which to measure himself. His parks are potted plants. Nothing can live and remain free where he resides but the pigeon, starling, sparrow, spider, cockroach, mouse, moth, fly and weed, and he laments the existence of even these and makes his plans to poison them. The zoo? There is the zoo. Through its bars the city man stares at the great cats and dully sucks his ice. Living, alas, among men and their marvels, the city man supposes that his happiness depends on establishing, somehow, a special kind of harmonious accord with others. The novelists of the city, of slums and crowds, they call it love—and break their pens.

Wordsworth feared the accumulation of men in cities. He foresaw their "degrading thirst after outrageous stimulation," and some of their hunger for love. Living in a city, among so many, dwelling in the heat and tumult of incessant movement, a man's affairs are touch and go—that's all. It's not surprising that the novelists of the slums, the cities, and the crowds, should find that sex is but a scratch to ease a tickle, that we're most human when we're sitting on the john, and that the justest image of our life is in full passage through the plumbing.

> That man, immur'd in cities, still retains
> His inborn inextinguishable thirst
> Of rural scenes, compensating his loss
> By supplemental shifts, the best he may.

Come into the country, then. The air nimbly and sweetly recommends itself unto our gentle senses. Here, growling tractors tear the earth. Dust roils up behind them. Drivers sit jouncing under bright umbrellas. They wear refrigerated hats and steer by looking at the tracks they've cut behind them, their transistors blaring. Close to the land, are they? good companions to the soil? Tell me: do they live in harmony with the alternating seasons?

It's a lie of old poetry. The modern husbandman uses chemicals from cylinders and sacks, spike-ball-and-claw machines, metal sheds, and cost accounting. Nature in the old sense does not matter. It does not exist. Our farmer's only mystical attachment is to parity. And if he does not realize that cows and corn are simply different kinds of chemical engine, he cannot expect to make a go of it.

It isn't necessary to suppose our cows have feelings; our neighbor hasn't as many as he used to have either; but think of it this way a moment, you can correct for the human imputations later: how would it feel to nurse those strange tentacled calves with their rubber, glass, and metal lips, their stainless eyes?

PEOPLE

Aunt Pet's still able to drive her car—a high square Ford—even though she walks with difficulty and a stout stick. She has a watery gaze, a smooth plump face despite her age, and jet black hair in a bun. She has the slowest smile of anyone I ever saw, but she hates dogs, and not very long ago cracked the back of one she cornered in her garden. To prove her vigor she will tell you this, her smile breaking gently while she raises the knob of her stick to the level of your eyes.

HOUSE, MY BREATH AND WINDOW

My window is a grave, and all that lies within it's dead. No snow is falling. There's no haze. It is not still, not silent. Its images are not an animal that waits, for movement is no demonstration. I have seen the sea slack, life bubble through a body without a trace, its spheres impervious as soda's. Downwound, the whore at wagtag clicks and clacks. Leaves wiggle. Grass sways. A bird chirps, pecks the ground. An auto wheel in penning circles keeps its rigid spokes. These images are stones; they are memorials. Beneath this sea lies sea: god rest it . . . rest the world beyond my window, me in front of my reflection, above this page, my shade. Death is not so still, so silent, since silence implies a falling quiet, stillness a stopping, containing, holding in; for death is time in a clock, like Mr. Tick, electric . . . like wind through a windup poet. And my blear floats out to visible against the glass, befog its country and bespill myself. The mist lifts slowly from the fields in the morning. No one now would say: the Earth throws back its covers; it is rising from sleep. Why is the feeling foolish? The image is too Greek. I used to gaze at you so wantonly your body blushed. Imagine: wonder: that my eyes could cause such flowering. Ah, my friend, your face is pale, the weather cloudy; a street has been felled through your chin, bare trees do nothing, houses take root in their rectangles, a steeple stands up in your head. You speak of loving; then give me a kiss. The pane is cold. On icy mornings the fog rises to greet me (as you always did); the barns and other buildings, rather than ghostly, seem all the more substantial for looming, as if they grew in themselves while I watched (as you always did). Oh my approach, I suppose, was like breath in a rubber monkey. Nevertheless, on the road along the Wabash in the morning, though the trees are sometimes obscured by fog, their reflection floats serenely on the river, reasoning the banks, the sycamores in French rows. Magically, the world tips. I'm led to think that only those who grow down live (which will scarcely win me twenty-five from *Wisdom's Monthly Digest*), but I find I write that only those who live down grow; and what I write, I hold, whatever I really know. My every word's inverted, or reversed—or I am. I held you, too, that way. You were so utterly provisional, subject to my change. I could inflate your bosom with a kiss, disperse your skin with gentleness, enter your vagina from within, and make my love emerge like a fresh sex. The pane is cold. Honesty is cold, my inside lover. The sun looks, through the mist, like a plum on the tree of heaven, or a bruise on the slope of your belly. Which? The grass crawls with frost. We meet on this window, the world and I, inelegantly, swimmers of the glass; and swung wrong way round to one another, the world seems in. The world—how grand, how monumental, grave and deadly, that word is: the world, my house and poetry. All poets have their inside lovers. Wee penis does not belong to me, or any of this foggery. It is *his* property which he's thrust through what's womanly of me to set down this. These wooden houses in their squares, gray streets and fallen sidewalks, standing trees, your name I've written sentimentally across my breath into the whitening air, pale birds: they exist in me now because of him. I gazed with what intensity . . . A bush in the excitement of its roses could not have bloomed so beautifully as you did then. It was a look I'd like to give this page. For that is poetry: to bring within about, to change.

POLITICS

Sports, politics, and religion are the three passions of the badly educated. They are the Midwest's open sores. Ugly to see, a source of constant discontent, they sap the body's strength. Appalling quantities of money, time, and energy are wasted on them. The rural mind is narrow, passionate, and reckless on these matters. Greed, however shortsighted and direct, will not alone account for it. I have known men, for instance, who for years have voted squarely against their interests. Nor have I ever noticed that their surly Christian views prevented them from urging forward the smithereening, say, of Russia, China, Cuba, or Korea. And they tend to back their country like they back their local team: they have a fanatical desire to win; yelling is their forte; and if things go badly, they are inclined to sack the coach. All in all, then, Birch is a good name. It stands for the bigot's stick, the wild-child-tamer's cane.

Forgetfulness—is that their object?

Oh, I was new, I thought. A fresh start: new cunt, new climate, and new country—there you were, and I was pioneer, and had no history. That language hurts me, too, my dear. You'll never hear it.

FINAL VITAL DATA

The Modern Homemakers' Demonstration Club. The Prairie Home Demonstration Club. The Night-outers' Home Demonstration Club. The IOOF, FFF, VFW, WCTU, WSCS, 4-H, 40 and 8, Psi Iota Chi, and PTA. The Boy and Girl Scouts, Rainbows, Masons, Indians and Rebekah Lodge. Also the Past Noble Grand Club of the Rebekah Lodge. As well as the Moose and the Ladies of the Moose. The Elks, the Eagles, the Jaynettes

and the Eastern Star. The Women's Literary Club, the Hobby
Club, the Art Club, the Sunshine Society, the Dorcas Society,
the Pythian Sisters, the Pilgrim Youth Fellowship, the American
Legion, the American Legion Auxiliary, the American Legion
Junior Auxiliary, the Gardez Club, the Bridge for Fun Club, the
What-can-you-do? Club, the Get Together Club, the Coterie
Club, the Worthwhile Club, the Let's Help Our Town Club,
the No Name Club, the Forget-me-not Club, the Merry-go-round
Club . . .

EDUCATION

Has a quarter disappeared from Paula Frosty's pocket book?
Imagine the landscape of that face: no crayon could engender it;
soft wax is wrong; thin wire in trifling snips might do the trick.
Paula Frosty and Christopher Roger accuse the pale and splotchy
Cheryl Pipes. But Miss Jakes, I saw her. Miss Jakes is so extremely
vexed she snaps her pencil. What else is missing? I appoint you a
detective, John: search her desk. Gum, candy, paper, pencils,
marble, round eraser—whose? A thief. I can't watch her all the
time, I'm here to teach. Poor pale fossetted Cheryl, it's determined, can't return the money because she took it home and
spent it. Cindy, Janice, John, and Pete—you four who sit around
her—you will be detectives this whole term to watch her. A thief.
In all my time. Miss Jakes turns, unfists, and turns again. I'll
handle you, she cries. To think. A thief. In all my years. Then
she writes on the blackboard the name of Cheryl Pipes and beneath that the figure twenty-five with a large sign for cents. Now
Cheryl, she says, this won't be taken off until you bring that
money out of home, out of home straight up to here, Miss Jakes
says, tapping her desk.
Which is three days.

ANOTHER PERSON

I was raking leaves when Uncle Halley introduced himself to me.
He said his name came from the comet, and that his mother had
borne him prematurely in her fright of it. I thought of Hobbes,
whom fear of the Spanish Armada had hurried into birth, and

so I believed Uncle Halley to honor the philosopher, though Uncle Halley is a liar, and neither the one hundred twenty-nine nor the fifty-three he ought to be. That fall the leaves had burned themselves out on the trees, the leaf lobes had curled, and now they flocked noisily down the street and were broken in the wires of my rake. Uncle Halley was himself (like Mrs. Desmond and history generally) both deaf and implacable, and he shooed me down his basement stairs to a room set aside there for stacks of newspapers reaching to the ceiling, boxes of leaflets and letters and programs, racks of photo albums, scrapbooks, bundles of rolled-up posters and maps, flags and pennants and slanting piles of dusty magazines devoted mostly to motoring and the Christian ethic. I saw a bird cage, a tray of butterflies, a bugle, a stiff straw boater, and all kinds of tassels tied to a coat tree. He still possessed and had on display the steering lever from his first car, a linen duster, driving gloves and goggles, photographs along the wall of himself, his friends, and his various machines, a shell from the first war, a record of "Ramona" nailed through its hole to a post, walking sticks and fanciful umbrellas, shoes of all sorts (his baby shoes, their counters broken, were held in sorrow beneath my nose—they had not been bronzed, but he might have them done someday before he died, he said), countless boxes of medals, pins, beads, trinkets, toys, and keys (I scarcely saw—they flowered like jewels from his palms), pictures of downtown when it was only a path by the railroad station, a brightly colored globe of the world with a dent in Poland, antique guns, belt buckles, buttons, souvenir plates and cups and saucers (I can't remember all of it —I won't), but I recall how shamefully, how rudely, how abruptly, I fled, a good story in my mouth but death in my nostrils; and how afterward I busily, righteously, burned my leaves as if I were purging the world of its years. I still wonder if this town—its life, and mine now—isn't really a record like the one of "Ramona" that I used to crank around on my grandmother's mahogany Victrola through lonely rainy days as a kid.

THE FIRST PERSON

Billy's like the coal he's found: spilled, mislaid, discarded. The sky's no comfort. His house and his body are dying together. His windows are boarded. And now he's reduced to his hands. I suspect he has glaucoma. At any rate he can scarcely see, and weeds his yard of rubble on his hand and knees. Perhaps he's a surgeon cleansing a wound or an ardent and tactile lover. I watch, I must say, apprehensively. Like mine-war detectors, his hands graze in circles ahead of him. Your nipples were the color of your eyes. Pebble. Snarl of paper. Length of twine. He leans down closely, picks up something silvery, holds it near his nose. Foil? cap? coin? He has within him—what, I wonder? Does he know more now because he fingers everything and has to sniff to see? It would be romantic cruelty to think so. He bends the down on your arms like a breeze. You wrote me: something is strange when we don't understand. I write in return: I think when I loved you I fell to my death.

Billy, I could read to you from Beddoes; he's your man perhaps; he held with dying, freed his blood of its arteries; and he said that there were many wretched love-ill fools like me lying alongside the last bone of their former selves, as full of spirit and speech, nonetheless, as Mrs. Desmond, Uncle Halley and the Ferris wheel, Aunt Pet, Miss Jakes, Ramona or the megaphone; yet I reverse him finally, Billy, on no evidence but braggadocio, and I declare that though my inner organs were devoured long ago, the worm which swallowed down my parts still throbs and glows like a crystal palace.

Yes, you were younger. I was Uncle Halley, the museum man and infrequent meteor. Here is my first piece of ass. They weren't so flat in those days, had more round, more juice. And over here's the sperm I've spilled, nicely jarred and clearly labeled. Look at this tape like lengths of intestine where I've stored my spew, the endless worm of words I've written, a hundred million emissions or more: oh I was quite a man right from the start; even when unconscious in my cradle, from crotch to cranium, I was erectile tissue; though mostly, after the manner approved by Plato, I had intercourse by eye. Never mind, old Holsclaw, you are blind. We pull down darkness when we go to bed; put out like Oedipus the actually offending organ, and train our touch to lies. All cats are gray, says Mr. Tick; so under cover of glaucoma you are sack gray too, and cannot be distinguished from a stallion.

I must pull myself together, get a grip, just as they say, but I feel spilled, bewildered, quite mislaid. I did not restore my house to its youth, but to its age. Hunting, you hitch through the hollyhocks. I'm inclined to say you aren't half the cripple I am, for there is nothing left of me but mouth. However, I resist the impulse. It is another lie of poetry. My organs are all there, though it's there where I fail—at the roots of my experience. Poet of the spiritual, Rilke, weren't you? yet that's what you said. Poetry, like love, is—in and out—a physical caress. I can't tolerate any more of my sophistries about spirit, mind, and breath. Body equals being, and if your weight goes down, you are the less.

HOUSEHOLD APPLES

I knew nothing about apples. Why should I? My country came in my childhood, and I dreamed of sitting among the blooms like the bees. I failed to spray the pear tree too. I doubled up under them at first, admiring the sturdy low branches I should have pruned, and later I acclaimed the blossoms. Shortly after the fruit formed there were falls—not many—apples the size of goodish stones which made me wobble on my ankles when I walked about the yard. Sometimes a piece crushed by a heel would cling on the shoe to track the house. I gathered a few and heaved them over the wires. A slingshot would have been splendid. Hard, an unattractive green, the worms had them. Before long I realized the worms had them all. Even as the apples reddened, lit their tree, they were being swallowed. The birds preferred the pears, which were small—sugar pears I think they're called—with thick skins of graying green that ripen on toward violet. So the fruit fell, and once I made some applesauce by quartering and paring hundreds; but mostly I did nothing, left them, until suddenly, overnight it seemed, in that ugly late September heat we often have in Indiana, my problem was upon me.

My childhood came in the country. I remember, now, the flies on our snowy luncheon table. As we cleared away they would settle, fastidiously scrub themselves and stroll to the crumbs to feed where I would kill them in crowds with a swatter. It was quite a game to catch them taking off. I struck heavily since I didn't mind a few stains; they'd wash. The swatter was a square of screen bound down in red cloth. It drove no air ahead of it to give them warning. They might have thought they'd flown headlong into a summered window. The faint pink dot where they had died did not rub out as I'd supposed, and after years of use our luncheon linen would faintly, pinkly, speckle.

The country became my childhood. Flies braided themselves on the flypaper in my grandmother's house. I can smell the bakery and the grocery and the stables and the dairy in that small Dakota town I knew as a kid; knew as I dreamed I'd know your body, as I've known nothing, before or since; knew as the flies knew, in the honest, unchaste sense: the burned house, hose-wet, which drew a mist of insects like the blue smoke of its smolder, and gangs of boys, moist-lipped, destructive as its burning. Flies have always impressed me; they are so persistently alive. Now they were coating the ground beneath my trees. Some were ordinary flies; there were the large blue-green ones; there were swarms of fruit flies too, and the red-spotted scavenger beetle; there were a few wasps, several sorts of bees and butterflies—checkers, sulphurs, monarchs, commas, question marks—and delicate dragonflies . . . but principally houseflies and horseflies and bottleflies, flies and more flies in clusters around the rotting fruit. They loved the pears. Inside, they fed. If you picked up a pear, they flew, and the pear became skin and stem. They were everywhere the fruit was: in the tree still—apples like a hive for them—or where the fruit littered the ground, squashing itself as you stepped . . . there was no help for it. The flies droned, feasting on the sweet juice. No one could go near the trees; I could not climb; so I determined at last to labor like Hercules. There were fruit baskets in the barn. Collecting them and kneeling under the branches, I began to gather remains. Deep in the strong rich smell of the fruit, I began to hum myself. The fruit caved in at the touch. Glistening red apples, my lifting disclosed, had families of beetles, flies, and bugs, devouring their rotten undersides. There were streams of flies; there were lakes and cataracts and rivers of flies, seas and oceans. The hum was heavier, higher, than the hum of the bees when they came to the blooms in the spring, though the bees were there, among the flies, ignoring me—ignoring everyone. As my work went on and juice covered my hands and arms, they

would form a sleeve, black and moving, like knotty wool. No
caress could have been more indifferently complete. Still I rose
fearfully, ramming my head in the branches, apples bumping
against me before falling, bursting with bugs. I'd snap my hand
sharply but the flies would cling to the sweet. I could toss a whole
cluster into a basket from several feet. As the pear or apple lit,
they would explosively rise, like monads for a moment, window-
less, certainly, with respect to one another, sugar their harmony.
I had to admit, though, despite my distaste, that my arm had
never been more alive, oftener or more gently kissed. Those hundreds of feet were light. In washing them off, I pretended the
hose was a pump. What have I missed? Childhood is a lie of
poetry.

THE CHURCH

Friday night. Girls in dark skirts and white blouses sit in ranks
and scream in concert. They carry funnels loosely stuffed with
orange and black paper which they shake wildly, and small mega-
phones through which, as drilled, they direct and magnify their
shouting. Their leaders, barely pubescent girls, prance and shake
and whirl their skirts above their bloomers. The young men,
leaping, extend their arms and race through puddles of amber
light, their bodies glistening. In a lull, though it rarely occurs,
you can hear the squeak of tennis shoes against the floor. Then
the yelling begins again, and then continues; fathers, mothers,
neighbors joining in to form a single pulsing ululation—a cry of
the whole community—for in this gymnasium each body becomes
the bodies beside it, pressed as they are together, thigh to thigh,
and the same shudder runs through all of them, and runs toward
the same release. Only the ball moves serenely through this daz-
zling din. Obedient to law it scarcely speaks but caroms quietly
and lives at peace.

BUSINESS

It is the week of Christmas and the stores, to accommodate the
rush they hope for, are remaining open in the evening. You can
see snow falling in the cones of the street lamps. The roads are

filling—undisturbed. Strings of red and green lights droop over the principal highway, and the water tower wears a star. The windows of the stores have been bedizened. Shamelessly they beckon. But I am alone, leaning against a pole—no . . . there is no one in sight. They're all at home, perhaps by their instruments, tuning in on their evenings, and like Ramona, tirelessly playing and replaying themselves. There's a speaker perched in the tower, and through the boughs of falling snow and over the vacant streets, it drapes the twisted and metallic strains of a tune that can barely be distinguished—yes, I believe it's one of the jolly ones, it's "Joy to the World." There's no one to hear the music but myself, and though I'm listening, I'm no longer certain. Perhaps the record's playing something else.

14 Ivan Gold

Ivan Gold was born in New York City in 1932 and was graduated from Columbia College in 1953. His first collection of stories, Nickel Miseries, was published in 1963.

❖

A CHANGE OF AIR

PROLOGUE

Bobbie Bedner at the age of nineteen during the course of three warm August days and nights lost not her virginity which she had long before misplaced in the back of an automobile but the memory of it, and almost, along with this, the capacity to remember. What she knew when she awoke on the first of the August mornings was that on such a fine sunny morning one had to be completely out of one's head to go to work in a button factory what with a hundred better nicer cleaner things to do, and damn her mother and the button factory, she would go for a long walk out of doors or maybe to a movie. What she knew as well (but not as loudly) as her not going to work was exactly where she was going and why. But what she did not know . . . what she could not possibly know when she got on the bus (which passed one park and two movie houses on its journey along an avenue of New York's lower East Side, but which also stopped almost directly outside the clubroom of the silk-jacketed Werewolves, membership thirty-five, and many friends) was that when she returned home seventy-two hours later, she would do so minus her underwear, the greater part of her emotional stability, her future in the button factory, and eleven pounds.

For the two or three young men of her acquaintance whom she expected to find in the clubroom at this early hour (they living there, being otherwise unhoused and temporarily unemployed) she found in the clubroom, running win, place, and show in a fabulous, all-night, seven-man stud poker game, and consequently filled to overflowing with philanthropy (love for one's fellow man). She walked in boldly, then hesitated, seeing seven card players and three hecklers, ten in all, counted on Tony, Frank, and Fat Andy for the protection she thought she wanted, found them extremely interested in her presence, but averse to any plan of action which did not include their intimates at the card table, who were now poorer (and they richer) by three hundred dollars. Decided finally, persuaded by Frank's embraces and the uniqueness (ten of them—why not the hecklers too—on the same day) of the prospect, communicated her decision by her slightly hysterical laugh, running crazily up the scale and halfway down, and thereby set out to make East Side of New York (and possibly national) history.

For . . . although unrecorded in the Werewolves' minutes, or in any other written source (ignoring the possibility that one or more of the half-dozen or so twelve- to fifteen-year-old young men she devirginized during the three-day period was sentimental enough to keep a diary), it is proved beyond any doubt by an unchallengeable number of oral affirmations that Bobbie Bedner (although expressing some desire to leave about four o'clock of the same afternoon when the situation seemed to be getting out of hand) nevertheless was taken, or rather had, one hundred and sixty times during seventy hours by a total of fifty-three persons (the entire membership of the Werewolves, their younger brothers and friends) of all nationalities and sizes, slept a grand total of seven hours during the three days and nights, consumed a bottle of milk, two of beer, a number of pretzels and a ham sandwich, called her mother on the evening of the first day to assure her that everything was under control and (it was Friday) she was spending the night at a friend's house and did not know exactly when she would be home, and returned home two and one-half days later when one of the Werewolves, preparing to make the trip for the third time, suddenly and concernedly noticed how peaked she was. They put her on a bus at eight o'clock on Monday morning, thoughtfully providing her with carfare, warning her to keep it quiet which they did not have to do since she truly bore them no animosity, and she returned home, eleven pounds less of her, to her mother and to the police who had preceded her by only twenty minutes, and fainted in the doorway.

When she awoke, tight-lipped, in a hospital, heard the doctor proclaim to the police and nurse the girl has suffered an ordeal, been without food and raped many times, laughed her crazy laugh, and had to say you screwy sawbones you it wasn't rape and how many times and laughed the crazy laugh for many minutes at the doctor's guess of thirty the nurse's forty the police's fifty, told them how many times (having kept a careful count), told them laughing crazily it was all her own idea and she might have a go at it again, but worth less than nothing to the forces of law and order in the names and places department.

They sent her away. They had to. Her mother wrung her hands, cursed her God and the memory of her husband. They sent her away for two years. When she returned from Rehabilitation School she had regained the eleven pounds and five additional. There were other, apparently deeper changes.

Franklin Cripple DeTorres, carrying himself well at five foot-seven, absolutely sound of limb and body, derived his middle name, twenty-five cents, and a good part of his reputation as a result of an encounter in (and with) a subway. Always sure of himself, acutely conscious of his heritage—Puerto Rico (for his birth and the year afterward), New York and bravery—never more so than at five A.M. on a liquored Sunday morning. Cripple (Crip to his friends) conjectured aloud on the fate of his foot provided he left it where it was, hanging over the parapet above the tracks, a void soon to be filled by an incoming subway train.

His friends, not realizing the full extent of his courage, liking him and wishing (in good spirits) to create the opportunity to apply to him a large number of defamatory epithets (which they would be in a position to do when he snatched his foot out of danger), offered (one of them did) the sum of twenty-five cents to the soon-to-be-martyred if he left his foot there until and after the train arrived. It was not the money which decided him, but the attitude which prompted its offer. Placing his foot up to the heel (with which he clutched the edge of the parapet for support) over the parapet, Cripple waited. The train came. He did not even flinch, not until the train (with its agonized conductor) hit him, and then he did not flinch but fell down parallel to the tracks, landing on his elbows, the foot which earned him the name the money the reputation seemingly unhurt, and shouted very loudly, unhysterically, but with great conviction, get me to the hospital.

His ten weeks in the hospital he found dull but not unbearable, being able to leaf through the books previously stolen from the bookstore where he stockclerked, being always interested in culture, and favored daily by visits from his friends, the entire membership of the Werewolves, most calling his act of bravery the stupidest thing anyone had ever done, but all admiring, and the six weeks after that when he walked with an ever-lessening limp were just that, six weeks, so he suffered nothing finally except the money he did not make (more than compensated for by the quarter which he had framed and hung in the Werewolves' clubroom threatening death and other penalties to anyone who removed it), and he gained a name which it seemed to outsiders should offend him, until they learned the manner of its origination.

On the day Bobbie Bedner did not go to work, Frank Cripple DeTorres won one hundred and forty dollars. It was the largest longest most expensive poker game ever played in the Werewolf clubroom, it was the most money he had ever won, and although by no means feeling guilty (perhaps even seeing a way to call a halt to the contest before his luck began to change), Cripple, when he saw her walk in, felt that the least he could do for the boys he had taken over was to get them to the slut as long as she happened to be around. He was the first on line, then, as the affair began to mushroom (something he did not foresee but which did not make any difference), thirty-first and again one hundred and sixth. He was sorry to hear (he did not hear, but deduced from her absence) that the girl had been sent to a reformatory.

When the Werewolves disbanded (after a police raid which

led to the twelve Werewolves present at the club spending some time at headquarters, and the two of them identified by the badly battered grocery proprietor remaining after the others were allowed to leave) Cripple devoted himself to intellectual pursuits, spending most of his evenings at Gelber's Chess Club on Seventeenth Street. He went usually with Joe Muneco, or met him there. They were the only two young men (except for occasional visits from Joe's friends) in what was otherwise a storm center for the old. Together, these two, they either beat (they played well) or talked down every old man in the place.

A problem to Early Environmentalists (the key to personality lies in the first three or five or nine or eleven years), *Joseph Muneco* (of whom they had never heard) spent the first three years of his life running around the streets of San Juan, Puerto Rico, the next fourteen years escaping policemen (for playing stickball on New York City streets and mugging usually close-to-penniless passersby), then, being expelled from three high schools (for non-attendance of classes and smoking marijuana), finally happening across a novel by Thomas Wolfe, impressed enough to read this author's entire works, discovering James Joyce, and in his twentieth year, and his fourth high school, becoming the editor (and first prize winner in a national short story contest) of his high school literary magazine.

Made many friends in this high school (at home on all intellectual strata), fell in love with and was loved by the editor of the high school newspaper (a Jewish girl of orthodox parents who were destined to object to their daughter's keeping company with a Gentile, and with a Spanish Gentile, and with one who looked so typically and unhealthily Spanish), went to a city college (his girl and he), saw the girl every day and on Saturday nights, and devoted the rest of his social time alternately to Cripple (alone or with mutual acquaintants, members of the long-defunct Werewolves) and to his other high school friends (the last high school), cream of the intellectual crop, the boys who read the books, who thought about writing them (as he did—although he only thought), and who by fairly frequent remarks pertaining to his dual heritage (the literate hoodlum, and variants, with lots of laughter, although he had for a long time now adhered to the straight and narrow path) contributed to the growth of his impassioned unusual campaign of self-justification.

Impassioned unusual campaign of self-justification . . . not with his girl Anne, with whom he was in love; nor with Cripple and with these friends with whom he fitted in so perfectly that there was no need of it; but with the others . . .

With *Phillip Zand*, literary critic until his junior year at college, thinking now of psychology, seeing it as a back door to the world he didn't live in; a great reader and a great listener to music, and a self-styled neurotic, finding himself replete with wrong things to say (to women), and not enough women to say them to; not pretty, but (not that this mattered) not as unpretty as he thought he was, weakly contemptuous of the others, his close circle of friends, in the only regions where he was qualified to be contemptuous, books and music, finding them in these regions, although reasonably well informed, nevertheless with sufficient (for the purposes of ridicule) misinformation . . .

With *Lee Miller*, a college man, sporadically read in Schopenhauer, Nietzsche, and Philip Wylie, with some Havelock Ellis (being interested in sex); contentious but without a conciliatory delivery (far from it; always unpleasant, not going out of his way to be unpleasant, but being that way because it came easiest), with the result that among his group of friends, he had no friend; cherubic in appearance (and thus with a number of conquests to his credit which Phil Zand—by no means accidentally—was forever hearing about, but still . . .), a lecher at nineteen, being famed (and given no peace) for the most amazing collection of pornographic snapshots and literature perhaps ever assembled, delighting in lending certain parts of his collection to Phil since he knew what he used them for, a good but strange mind; a flair for chess, a match for Joe Muneco, a terrific and serious rivalry building between them, a result of and a further prod to mutual dislike . . .

With *Benjamin Brock*, the only one of them attending a college which it required money to attend, assuming therefore a certain superiority in the quality of his education, never having to mention the felt superiority for them to know that it was there; doubting especially (again tacitly, or if not tacitly, then blatantly in jest) Muneco's claim to higher understanding (Joe having not written since the days of his high school triumphs—Ben writing all the time—two long years ago, unable to take his typewriter out of pawn, and besides, being busy—with his girl and with Cripple —being happy), Muneco feeling Ben's doubts, and the doubts of the others, knowing the realm of the intellect to be his as well as (if not more than) theirs, but feeling it always necessary to prove it to them, and so . . .

Joseph Muneco's impassioned unusual campaign of self-justification, the utilization of a phenomenal memory, an almost photographic memory, committing to it the equivalent of three large volumes of verse, from Sappho to Cummings, and considerable prose, quoting some part of his repertoire at the least provocation, creating his own provocation, irrelevant (the quoting) to anything occurring or even said in his immediate environment, but illustrating to Phil and to Lee and to Ben and to anyone else around that he, Joseph Muneco, had a sizable portion of the world's literature at his fingertips, had the best that man's mind has yet created stored (with an understanding of it, if anyone pursued the matter) in his memory, that he, Joseph Muneco was, whatever else he might also be, an intellectual.

With this and these in mind, we can begin the story.

THE STORY

Gelber's Chess Club was partly that. More, it was a place to play cards and a place to stay, on cold winter nights and dull summer ones. In the back of the club, away from the two windows overlooking Seventeenth Street, was a small room with a stove in which Mrs. Gelber made and sold coffee and sandwiches. The long, large room which was the club was divided by common consent into the section for chess players and for card players; there were the few benches in the chess player section for those who wished to sleep, to think, or to read the paper. On the door of the club was a sign reading FOR MEMBERS ONLY and inside the club a sign said MEMBERSHIP DUES, ONE DOLLAR A YEAR. Neither of these mattered. Gelber was friendly, did not need the money, and owned the building. The signs were put up at the insistence of his wife and Gelber neither desired to, nor did he, reinforce them. The club had been on Seventeenth Street for twenty-two years, and although the faces changed, at intervals, the mean age of the members did not. The men at the club—and they were all men aside from Gelber's wife—averaged fifty-five years of age. If not for the presence of Joseph Muneco and Franklin DeTorres, who came often enough to necessitate their inclusion in any mathematical calculations, the average age of the members of Gelber's Chess Club would have been fifty-seven.

Frank DeTorres was talking to Joe Muneco.

"Okay Ace," he said. "Push the pawn. Before the place closes, Ace. I guarantee the safety of the pawn move."

Frank had arrived at 11 o'clock and had played chess with the old men. He won more than he lost and enjoyed his conversation and the reactions to it. At one o'clock Joe Muneco walked in, earlier than usual for a Saturday night, but his girl had gotten sick and he took her home early, leaving her a block from where she lived in case one of her parents happened to be looking from the window. Meeting her on Saturday nights was no problem since she had a job ushering at concerts in a school auditorium in his neighborhood, and he could meet her afterward, at nine-thirty. On this Saturday night she became ill and he took her home. When he got to the club, he and Frank DeTorres played chess. Muneco was the better of the two but against each other they played carelessly, and games were not won or lost in accord with their ability.

At DeTorres' remark, Joe became angry for the three old men who made up his audience.

"Take it easy, Ace," he said. "Any time you want to play three seconds a move, you let me know, Ace. The pawn move is for the fushas. I give you this." He moved his bishop along its diagonal. One of the old men grunted approval and smiled a toothless smile. Frank addressed him.

"Doesn't he play like a master?" he said. "He is a true Morphy in the way he plays this game. I admire your manipulation of the pieces, Ace," he said to Joe. He looked swiftly at the board and made his move. "Try this one," he said.

Joe guffawed. "Swish, Ace," he said, swooping down upon De-Torres' unprotected queen, removing it, and upsetting four or five pieces on both sides of the board.

"I didn't see, Ace," Frank said, beginning to smile. Two of the old men laughed. The third yawned noisily and moved toward one of the benches leaning against the wall.

Frank resigned. He began to set up his pieces in preparation for another game. At one-thirty Phil Zand and Lee Miller walked in. They had gone to a movie, had coffee, and come to the chess club looking for Joe Muneco. They knew that he could be found here on Sunday mornings at this time after taking his girl home.

"Watch him!" Joe said agitatedly to Phil, glancing momentarily at Lee, as the two came over and sat down. "You shouldn't have taken him off the leash. He's liable to rape small boys."

"No need," Lee said. "I was refreshed last night. A very sweet young thing I met at a dance. How's Anne?"

The query might have been solicitous, but it was very poorly placed. Suddenly Muneco was no longer amusing or amused.

"She's all right," he said, looking at Lee. "Unless you just killed her by mentioning her name."

Lee laughed. He laughed unpleasantly, the only way he knew how.

"I thought you had signed a non-aggression pact," Phil said.

"Only verbal," Joe said. "It can be busted at any time."

"What's new?" Frank said to Phil.

"I'm glad you asked," Phil said. "My profession. I'm going to be a psychologist."

"That's nice," Frank said. "We are in need of psychologists. But you've got to gain weight if you want to be healthy enough to pursue your studies. You're very thin, in spite of your weight-lifting."

Phil laughed.

" 'I am thy father's spirit,' " Joe said. " 'Doomed for a certain term to walk the night, and for the day confined to fast in fires, till the foul crimes done in my days of nature are burnt and purged away. But that I am forbid,' " he said, " 'to tell the secrets of my prison-house, I could a tale unfold whose lightest word would harrow up thy soul,' checkmate Ace," he said.

"You're a genius, Muneco," Lee said, sitting in the chair Frank had just vacated. Frank visited Mrs. Gelber for some coffee.

"You didn't like that?" Joe inquired. "Maybe you'd prefer an excerpt from Krafft-Ebing. 'George K., longshoreman, locked in the embraces of Mollie F., housewife suffering from vaginismus, found it difficult to extricate . . .' "

"No moves back," Lee said, making his first move.

"Make it touch move," Joe said, unsmiling. "Better than that we measure the Galvanic Skin Response. If I catch you thinking about a piece, you got to move it."

"Agreed," Lee said.

Phil laughed: at their seriousness, and at the incongruity which it seemed to him the technical term had in Muneco's mouth.

"What do you know about the Galvanic Skin Response?" he said.

"Nothing," Joe said. "Now that you're a psychologist I know nothing about the Galvanic Skin Response. Just as when previously you were a literary critic I knew nothing about literature. And as in consequence of your large record collection, I know nothing about music. If I ever again say anything implying I know anything at all about psychology, may I suffer excruciating pain."

"Okay," Phil laughed. "I'm sorry. You're an intellectual."

Frank returned with his coffee. He knew these two, Lee and Phil, and also Ben, because of their friendship with Joe Muneco. They had graduated from high school with Joe three years ago, and he had continued seeing them, about once a week, since then. They were not particularly interesting, Frank thought, although they were supposed to be bright, and he guessed that this was what Joe saw in them. He could talk to them in Joe's presence, but doubted if he could find anything to say to them under other circumstances. These never arose since he ran into them only when he was with Muneco. Now he returned with the coffee and he saw skinny Phil leaning on the table, his hair mussed, smiling at Muneco, and it struck him what a particularly dull life Phil must lead.

"Hey Phil, you still got it?" he said.

"Got what?"

"Your chastity. Last time I heard, you had still got it."

"Still got it," Phil said, smiling ruefully, but resignedly, as if talking about an amputated arm.

"I can't understand it, Ace," Frank said. "What's the good of going to college if they don't teach you about life? That's why I didn't go to college, because they had no courses in screwing."

"That's right, Ace," Joe mumbled, engrossed in the game.

"You should have gone," Lee said. "You're a great loss to the academic world."

Frank had begun to understand that the things Lee said in jest were no different in tone from the things he said when he was being nasty. It was just the way he talked, everything seeming an insult. He thought for a moment, and decided from the context that Lee was jesting.

"I appreciate this," Frank said.

Frank sat down to kibitz the game, and Phil read the Sunday *Times*. If no one else arrived and even if someone else did, they would spend an hour or two at the chess club, then go downstairs and across the street into the all-night cafeteria (it was too cold in January for the groups to gather in Union Square Park), spend some time there over their coffee, and then go home at four or five o'clock in the morning. They would take Phil, who became tired before anyone else, and who lived the greatest distance (fourteen blocks) from Seventeenth Street, home first, then would walk three blocks uptown to where Lee lived; and finally walk back to the chess club, and three blocks beyond it, to the street on which Frank and Joe lived, in adjoining tenement buildings.

But Ben Brock arrived. Even this wouldn't have made any difference, for Ben Brock often arrived without noticeably disturbing the Saturday night ritual. But Ben Brock arrived with the family car, which meant, if nothing else, that they would all be driven home. It meant however enough more than that on this Saturday night to change the entire texture of the evening.

"Okay," he said, when he saw them around the chess table. "Drop everything. The bus awaits. Let me take you away from all this."

"You park it in the hallway?" Joe said.

"Stop, I can't stand the irony," Ben said. "The car is parked downstairs, three picas from the curb. How many times do I have to tell you, Muneco, I can park a car?"

"Perhaps," Joe said. "As soon as Krafft-Ebing here resigns his lost game."

"Lost game!" Lee said, angrily incredulous. "You talk like a chess player," he said. "But rather than destroy your ego, I agree to a ride in Brock's convertible."

"Anything," Phil said, "for a change of scenery."

Frank sat behind a board, set up the pieces, and beckoned to an old man who sat, half dozing, on a bench. The old man smiled and came toward him.

"Spot me a rook, Kurtz," Frank said.

The old man smiled. "Why not both?" he said. He sat down opposite Frank.

"Hey Crip, you coming?" Joe said to him.

"You college men go for a ride in the car," Frank said. "Driving . . ." (he groped for the cliché) ". . . exerts no appeal on me. I'm gonna teach Kurtz here how to play this game." The others were already outside and down the one landing to the street.

"Okay Ace," Joe said. "Castle early and open up a rook file. I'll see you." He turned and walked toward the door.

"So long Ace," Frank said.

The car was riding north, along First Avenue, toward Forty-second Street.

"Are we going to Times Square?" Phil said.

"If that's what you want," Ben said. "Although I was going to drive you down to Miami. It's time you phony authors and literary critics and psychologists and perverts learned that the East Side of New York is not the center of the world."

"How do you know that?" Joe said.

"Hearsay," Ben said. "But it sounds logical."

"We'll go to Miami next time," Phil yawned. "I've got to wake up early tomorrow."

On the corner of Twenty-sixth Street Ben stopped for a light. Muneco, sitting up front, glanced from the window. "Hey," he said suddenly. Ben, following Joe's eye, saw a figure turn the corner of Twenty-sixth Street and walk out of his range of vision. "Was that Barbara Bedner?" Joe said.

"I don't know," Ben said. "Shall we find out?"

"Who's Barbara Bedner?" Phil said.

"What difference does it make?" Lee said. "It's a girl's name."

The light changed and Ben turned the corner. "I've told you about her," Joe said, peering from the window. The street was dark and he could not be sure. "That's the girl they sent up for the impairment of everybody's morals. The record holder. I didn't know they'd let her out."

"Is it her?" Ben said, slowing down a few yards behind the girl.

"I can't tell," Joe said.

The girl turned off and walked up to a stoop leading to the entrance of a building.

"Well you'd better find out if you're going to find out," Lee said.

Joe opened his window.

"Barbara," he called. "Is that Bobbie Bedner?"

The girl turned, startled. It was late at night and she had not heard the car turn the corner. She saw the car but could not see who was inside. The car was a 1950 model, a red convertible. Ben and his father had washed and polished it that same day. It looked like a new car. Bobbie Bedner came, looking very curious, down the stairs and up to the open window.

"Hello," Joe said cheerfully. "I thought it was you. Do you remember me?"

"Yeah," Bobbie said, smiling blankly. "Yeah, I remember you. What's your name?"

Joe grinned. "Joe," he said. "I used to belong to the Werewolves. Remember the Werewolves?"

Bobbie grinned innocently back at him. "Yeah, I remember," she said. "How is everybody? How's Fat Andy?"

"He's fine," Joe said. "He got caught with a stolen car. He won't be around for a while."

"Gee, that's a shame," Bobbie said, meaning it. She laughed. "How's Tony?" she asked.

"I haven't seen him around," Joe said. "I think he's in the

army. But where have you been all this while?" he asked her, knowing she would lie, anxious to see how badly. "I haven't seen you for a long time."

Bobbie giggled. "Oh, I been away. I just got back to New York last week."

"You live in this house?" Lee said to her.

For the first time she took notice of the other occupants of the car.

"Yeah," she said, wary, but not unfriendly. Then to Joe: "Who are your friends?"

"Shall I introduce you?" Joe said. She nodded, laughing.

"Bobbie Bedner," Joe said. "This is Brock, the driver and part-owner of the car. This is Miller," and he gestured toward the back of the car, "consultant in pornography, and this is Zand, who is interested in people."

Bobbie laughed, taking her cue from his tone. "What are you doing out so late?" she said. "Just driving around?"

"Yeah," Lee said, anxious to make his presence felt. "How about you?"

"I went to a dance," Bobbie said. "At the Twenty-eighth Street Y."

"Did you have a nice time?" Lee said.

"Not so bad," Bobbie said, laughing.

There was a pause. Ben thought he might as well. She was standing there with her hand resting on the edge of the lowered window.

"Would you like to go for a ride?" he said.

Bobbie laughed uncertainly. "I don't know," she said. "My mother expected me home early, and it's late already."

"So," Joe said, "if it's late already it won't hurt if you come in a little later. Come on," he said persuasively, "we'll go for a ride."

"Where are you going?" the girl asked.

"We don't know," Ben said drily. "That's what makes it so exciting. We might go almost anywhere. Maybe you can help find us a destination."

The girl stood there, her hand on the window. Joe opened the door suddenly and beckoned to her. "Come on," he said. "Any place you say. When you're ready to come back, we'll bring you back."

"It's a nice car," she said.

Joe laughed. He reached out his hand and pulled her one step closer to the car. Then he let go and moved closer to Brock, making room for her. Bobbie Bedner laughed and got into the car.

Ben backed the car to the corner and they were back on First Avenue. He rode to Fourteenth Street and stopped for a light.

"You're looking well," Joe said. "You're looking much better than when I saw you last."

"Yeah," Bobbie said. "I gained a lot of weight."

She had changed. She had gotten into the car, but it wasn't as easy as it once would have been. Joe decided to let DeTorres find out how matters stood with the girl. Although he could have done so, his friends might interpret his efforts as illustrating a lack of sensibility. Or it might give them something to laugh about.

"Drive back to the club," Joe said. "We'll pick up Cripple."

"What club?" Bobbie asked alarmedly. "Who's Cripple?"

"Just a chess club," Joe said soothingly. "You remember Cripple. That's Frank, Frank DeTorres. You remember Frank, don't you?"

"What do you want to see him for?" Bobbie said.

"We don't want to see him," Joe said. "We just thought after all this time, he would be glad to see you. He won't hurt you."

Bobbie laughed. "I know he won't hurt me," she said. "I just thought we were going for a ride."

"We will," Ben said, knowing what was on Muneco's mind. "Just as soon as we pick up Frank."

He turned left on Seventeenth Street, pulled up in front of Gelber's Chess Club, and parked the car.

Frank was happy to have Muneco back and happier still when he saw who was with him. The presence of Bobbie Bedner, he felt sure, would liven up the evening. He thought immediately of his pigeon coop and its steam-heating. When Ben Brock came upstairs, after parking the car, he found Frank and Joe seated near the window, Frank talking earnestly to Bobbie, and Lee and Phil standing some distance away leaning against a chess table. He walked over to these two.

"Set 'em up," he said to Lee. "You can have the white pieces."

"I'll have to beat you in five moves," Lee apologized. "Don Juan is operating, and I don't know how long we'll be here."

"If he's got to operate," Ben said, "you may be here a long time. If this girl is the girl she's cracked up to be she should be on her hands and knees begging for it."

Joe came over.

"How does it look?" Lee said.

"I don't know," Joe said. "Frank is trying to get her to go to his place but she doesn't like pigeon coops."

"Ask her about bar-bell clubs," Phil said. "I've got the key to the club. There won't be anyone up there this time of night."

"I'll keep you posted," Joe said. He walked back to Frank and the girl.

"Your move," Lee said.

Ben looked at him. "I can't understand your hanging around, Miller," he said to him, "in the hope of laying a broad who has already been on intimate terms with everyone in the neighborhood. Haven't you got any standards?"

"Very funny," Lee said. "In this respect I'm like you. When it comes to women, anywhere and anytime."

"Are you looking forward to this prospect?" Ben said to Phil.

"Why not?" Phil said.

"Hell," Ben said, "you've had it so long you might as well save it for your wife. Listen to me," he said earnestly, "and don't throw yourself away on this harlot. Somewhere, there's a sweet, young, innocent girl who has been ordained by heaven to . . ."

"Balls to you," Phil said.

Muneco returned.

" 'The outlook wasn't brilliant for the Mudville nine that day,' " Joe began, with every intention of completing the poem.

"Can it," Ben said. "What's the latest?"

"She met a psychiatrist in reform school," Joe said. "He told her the reason she did what she did was her father died when she was six years old and she missed male attention. She agrees with his diagnosis and she's turning over a new leaf."

"You mean all the psychiatrist did was tell her?" Phil asked professionally.

"I don't know," Joe said. "She's been away for two years. Maybe she underwent intensive therapy. Whatever happened, she's metamorphosized."

"So?" Lee said.

"We're going to take her downstairs, try to soften her up," Joe said. "Give me the keys to the car," he said to Ben.

"You going somewhere?" Lee said suspiciously.

"Hey," Muneco laughed, taking the keys from Ben. "You think we'd run out on you, Miller? We can't leave you. This whole party is in Phil's honor. After Phil lays her we're going to nail her over his fireplace for a trophy." He jingled the keys at DeTorres and walked to the door. Frank got up, took the girl by the hand, and followed Muneco. She went without protesting but she did not look happy.

"Does Cripple have a driver's license?" Lee said.

Ben nodded.

"If those guys pull anything," Lee said, "I'm going to make Muneco pay for it."

"You wouldn't tell his mother, would you?" Ben said.

"No," Lee said. "I'll tell his girl. I'll call his girl and let her know how Muneco spends his Saturday nights." He looked toward the window. Phil, following his glance, walked over and looked out.

"The car's still there," Phil said. "Save your money."

"Your move," Ben said.

Lee moved.

"How long we going to wait here?" he said.

"Give them five more minutes," Ben said.

Phil walked over and looked out the window.

"Hey Zand," Ben called to him.

"What?"

"You're basing your life on a lie," Ben said. "You want to become a clinical psychologist. You want to help the maladjusted. Now here is this girl who has been abnormal, at least quantitatively, but has since been returned to normalcy by a practicing psychiatrist. Instead of trying to keep her there you're party to a scheme whose aim is to tear down her defenses and re-sink her in the morass of abnormality."

He looked sternly at Phil; then disgustedly shook his head.

"Look," Phil said. "Better her than me. She's neurotic from too much of it and I'm neurotic from too little. It's her or me. And I've got my career at stake."

"He thinks it's the panacea," Lee sneered. "Once he gets laid, he's solved all his problems. What an idiot."

"Okay," Ben said. "I resign. Let's go downstairs."

They got up and put on their coats. "Hey, Kurtz," Ben called to the old man who had been sitting on a bench watching them. "A lineup. Anybody else, we're charging two-fifty. For you, a buck and a half. How about it?"

The old man coughed up some phlegm and spit it into a handkerchief. He was unimpressed. "If I couldn't do better," he said, standing and stretching himself, "I'd shoot myself."

The three left the club.

Ben looked in at the back window of the car. Joe and Frank were in the front seat with the girl between them. Frank had his arm around the girl and was bending over her. Ben motioned the others to wait. After a while the girl worked an arm free from behind her and pushed Frank's face away. Ben walked to the side of the car and knocked on the window. Muneco opened the door.

"Come on in," he said. "We'll go for a ride."

Lee and Phil got into the back of the car. Ben squeezed into the driver's seat. There were four people in the front of the car. Joe moved over, making room for Ben, at the same time pushing Bobbie closer to Frank. Frank was talking into her ear.

"What's the matter baby? Don't you want to kiss me? Just a little kiss?"

"No-o," the girl said, indicating that she had said it many times before. Frank leaned over her and kissed her. After a great many seconds had passed she pushed his face away.

"I don't know what's happened to the way you kiss," Frank said to her. "It's not like you used to. Who ever heard of a girl kissing with her mouth closed?"

"I don't want to kiss you," Bobbie said primly.

"Two years ago," Frank said, "I wouldn't kiss you. I would screw you. That's more fun, isn't it? What's happened to you in two years?"

"I told you," Bobbie said laughing. Her laugh was heavy, like her voice, and unsteady, but it was not the way she used to laugh. "I don't do that anymore."

"For nobody?"

Bobbie laughed. "I don't know," she said. "But not for you."

"I'm truly sorry to hear that," Frank said. "I guess I'll go home and go to bed. Drive me home, Brock," he said. He leaned over the girl.

Ben made a right turn on Third Avenue and drove to Twentieth Street. He stopped once for a light. On Twentieth a sanitation truck was double parked and he slowed down to squeeze past it. During all this time, Frank, using all his art, was kissing the girl.

"You're home," Ben said.

"Yeah," Frank said. "We're home. Come on," he said to the girl. "We'll go upstairs to the pigeon coop and have a party."

"No," Bobbie said. "I don't like pigeon coops."

"Do you like parties?" Joe said.

"Not that kind," she said, laughing slyly.

"Look," Frank said. "Look what I got for you." He took her hand and pulled it to him, but she wrenched it free.

"I don't want it," she said, annoyed. "Leave me alone."

Ben became slightly annoyed by the proceedings. Not by the proceedings as much as by their lack of success.

"All right Frank, you drew a blank," he said. "We forgive you. If you can't convince this girl, she cannot be convinced. Go to bed." He looked at Bobbie. "I'll drive you home."

"Okay," Frank said. "But I don't know what's happened to this girl. She goes away for a short time and comes back with a whole new system of values. It's something for you college men to figure out."

He got out of the car.

"Don't give up the ship," he said. "A little patience. If this girl is Bobbie Bedner you should lay her before daybreak. I'm going to get some sleep."

The girl laughed as Frank turned his back and walked away. "Don't believe him," she said confidentially. "I don't do any of those things. He's just talking." She directed this primarily at Brock in whom she had mistaken the annoyance with DeTorres' methods for sympathy. Joe smiled. Ben started the car.

"Who's going home first?" he said.

"Home?" The girl was indignant. "I thought we were going for a ride."

"You still want to go for a ride?" Ben said.

"Sure. Let's go to Coney Island."

"No," Joe said to her. "Let's go lift some weights. Phil has the key to his bar-bell club."

The girl laughed. "Ah, die young," she said pleasantly. She recognized that the only serious threat had been Frank, and he was gone. She relaxed now, and looked forward to a good time being chauffeured around.

"You can drive me home," Phil said, seeing the futility of remaining. "I've got to wake up early tomorrow."

"How about you, Miller?" Ben said.

"No hurry," Lee said. "As a matter of fact you can take me home after you drop her off."

The girl laughed. "You ain't gonna miss nothin'," she said.

Joe laughed. "You're a dead pigeon, Miller," he said. "Even this dumb broad reads you like a book. You're shallower than a wading pool."

"That's extremely funny, Muneco," Lee said.

"I'm not a dumb broad," Bobbie said good-naturedly.

"Then what are you a dumb?" Joe said.

"Oh, die young," the girl said.

"Where would you like to go besides Coney Island?" Ben said.

"What's the matter with Coney Island?"

"There is nothing open and nobody in Coney Island in January," Ben explained patiently. "So I suggest you suggest something else."

"Let's go where there's excitement," Bobbie said. "Maybe we can see a fight somewhere."

"We have just the thing for you," Joe said. "Take her to Brooklyn," he said to Ben.

"That's right," Ben said. "Brooklyn's a wild town."

"What's so wild about Brooklyn?" the girl said.

"Everything goes positively smash in Brooklyn," Ben said. "There's a fight on every street corner. Trunk murders take place in front of your eyes. Also, there's a little cafeteria right across the bridge where we sometimes sober up after a devil-may-carish Saturday night."

"What's his name?" Bobbie said to Joe.

"That's Brock," Joe said. "Author and professional chauffeur. Why, do you like him?"

Bobbie laughed. "He's all right," she said.

"Brock has made a conquest," Lee called from the back of the car.

"I guess you're not interested," Joe said. "Maybe we should drive you home."

"Maybe you should," Lee said. "As a matter of fact, I'm sure you should. I've got a date tomorrow night with this girl I just met. I can use some sleep."

"You poor kid, I'll bet she knocks all hell out of you," Ben said.

Ben turned left, a block before the bridge which led to Brooklyn, and brought the car back to First Avenue. He left Paul on the corner of Third Street, and drove Lee to his home on Sixth Street between First and Second Avenues. He was tired, and got to thinking of the difficulty he would have in finding a parking space.

"Who's next?" he said.

He looked at Bobbie, who was about to protest.

"My old man gets up early in the morning," he lied. "He needs the car to get to work. I've got to bring it back before six o'clock."

"Gee," the girl said. "Your father works on Sundays?"

"Yeah," Ben said. "He's a preacher."

"Gee, that's tough," the girl said.

"Take me home first," Joe said, winking at Ben. "She said she likes you. Don't you like him, Bobbie?"

"Yeah, I like him," Bobbie said. "But I just wanted to drive around."

"You first," Ben said to her. He drove her home.

She got out of the car and turned toward them.

"Well, so long," she said. She laughed suddenly. "I had a very nice time."

"Glad to hear it," Joe said. "We must get together sometime and do the whole thing over again."

Ben leaned over and waved to her. "So long Bobbie," he said.

"Bye-bye Brock," she said. "It was nice meeting you." She walked up the stoop and was gone, into the building.

They sat there for a while, not talking.

"A hundred per cent American girl," Ben said finally. "I'm convinced you had her pegged wrong."

"A hundred and sixty times," Joe said absently, "in three days. That must have been one hell of a psychiatrist."

"He wasn't an East Side boy," Ben said, shaking his head. "He performed a great disservice to an entire neighborhood. He dissolved the last trace of communal endeavor to which we could proudly point."

"Yeah," Joe said, leaning back on the seat, his hands locked behind his head. "Drive around to Seventeenth Street. What we've got to do now is get some coffee."

15 John Barth

John Barth was born in 1930 in Cambridge, Maryland, and was educated at Johns Hopkins University. He is a professor of English at the State University of New York at Buffalo. Master of his own blend of black comedy, Barth has written four bitter, robust, and highly intelligent novels, The Floating Opera (1956), End of the Road (1958), The Sot-Weed Factor (1960), and Giles Goat-Boy (1966), and a collection of short, experimental fiction, Lost in the Funhouse (1968).

❖

THE LAW
(FROM *THE FLOATING OPERA*)

That will-o'-the wisp, the law: where shall I begin to speak of it? Is the law the legal rules, or their interpretations by judges, or by juries? Is it the precedent or the present fact? The norm or the practice? I think I'm not interested in what the law is.

Surely, though, I am curious about things that the law can be made to do, but this disinterestedly, without involvement. A child encounters a toy tractor, winds it up, and sets it climbing over a book. The tractor climbs well. The child puts another book here, so, and angles the first. The tractor surmounts them, with difficulty. The child opens the pages of the first book, leans the second obliquely against it, and places his shoe behind the two. The tractor tries, strains, spins, whirrs, and falls like a turtle on its back, treads racing uselessly. The child moves on to his crayons and picture puzzles, no expression on his face. I don't know what you mean, sir, when you speak of justice.

It may be that, like Capt. Osborn, you have come to believe that I have opinions about everything, absurd ones at that. Very well. But of most things about which people hold some sort of opinion, I have none at all, except by implication. What I mean is this: the law, for example, prescribes certain things that shall not be done, or certain ways in which things shall be done, but of most specific human acts it has nothing to say one way or the other. Yet these extralegal acts, or most of them, are certainly influenced and conditioned, implicitly, by the laws pertaining to other things. People, for example, aren't allowed to kill us while we're performing our extralegal acts. In the same way, though I have no opinion one way or the other on whether suicide, for instance, is a sin, I have certain opinions on a few things that made it possible for me to contemplate suicide in 1937, and actually to resolve to destroy myself.

All right. I have no general opinions about the law, or about justice, and if I sometimes set little obstacles, books and slants, in the path of the courts, it is because I'm curious, merely, to see what will happen. On those occasions when the engine of the law falls impotently sprawling, I make a mental note of it, and without a change of expression, go on to my boat or my *Inquiry*. Winning or losing litigations is of no concern to me, and I think I've never made a secret of that fact to my clients. They come to me, as they come before the law, because *they* think they have a case. The law and I are uncommitted.

One more thing, before I explain the contest over Harrison Mack Senior's will: if you have followed this chapter so far, you might sensibly ask, "Doesn't your attitude—which is, after all, irresponsible—allow for the defeat, even the punishment, of the innocent, and at times the victory of the guilty? And does this not concern you?" It does indeed allow for the persecution of innocence—though perhaps not so frequently as you might imagine. And this persecution *concerns* me, in the sense that it holds my attention, but not especially in the sense that it bothers me. Under certain circumstances, to be explained later, I am not averse to pillorying the innocent, to throwing my stone, with the crowd, at some poor martyr. Irresponsibility, yes: I affirm, I insist upon my basic and ultimate irresponsibility. Yes indeed.

It did not deeply concern me, as I said before, whether Harrison received his inheritance or not, though I stood to profit by some fifty thousand dollars or more if he did. In any world but ours, the case of the Mack estate would be fantastic; even in ours, it received considerable publicity from the Maryland press.

Old man Mack, whom I've come to admire tremendously though I never met him, died in 1935, after years of declining physical and mental health. He left a large estate: stock in the Mack Pickle Co. amounting to 58 per cent of the total shares, and worth perhaps two million dollars in fairly good times; stock in various other business concerns, some more prosperous than others; a large house in Ruxton, another in West Palm Beach, and cottages in Nova Scotia and Maryland (including the one I was seduced in); extensive farmlands, especially cucumber farms, the crop from which was bought by the Mack Pickle Co.; perhaps a hundred thousand dollars in cash; assorted automobiles, cabin cruisers, horses, and dogs, and, through the majority stockholdings, the potential presidency of the pickle company, which office carried a salary of twenty-five thousand dollars a year. It was, undeniably, an estate that many people would consider worth going to court about.

Now of the several characteristics of Harrison père, three were important to the case: he was in the habit of using his wealth as a club to keep his kin in line; he was, apparently, addicted to the drawing up of wills; and, especially in his last years, he was obsessively jealous of the products of his mind and body, and permitted none to be destroyed.

You perhaps recall my saying that when I first met Harrison Junior, in 1925, he was undergoing an attack of communism, and had been disinherited as a result? It seems that disinheritance, or the threat of it, was the old man's favorite disciplinary measure, not only for his son, but also for his wife. When young Harrison attended Dartmouth rather than Johns Hopkins; when he studied journalism rather than business; when he became a communist rather than a Republican; he was disinherited until such time as he mended his ways. When Mother Mack went to Europe rather than to West Palm Beach; when she chose sparkling burgundy over highballs, Dulaney Valley over Ruxton, Roosevelt and Garner over Hoover and Curtis; she was disinherited until such time as she recanted her heresies.

All these falls from and reinstatements to grace, of course, required emendations of Father Mack's will, and a number of extrafamiliar circumstances also demanded frequent revision of his bequests. His country club admits someone he doesn't like: the club must be disinherited. A pickle-truck driver runs down a state policeman checking on overloaded vehicles: the driver must be defended in court and provided for explicitly in the will. After the old man's death, when his safe was opened, a total of seventeen complete and distinct testamentary instruments was found, chronologically arranged, each beginning with a revocation of the preceding one. He hadn't been able to throw any of his soul-children into the fire.

Now this situation, though certainly unusual, would in itself have presented no particular problem of administration, because the law provides that where there are several wills, the last shall be considered representative of the testator's real intentions, other things being equal. And each of these wills explicitly revoked the preceding one. But alas, with Mr. Mack all other things weren't equal. Not only did his physical well-being deteriorate in his last years, through arthritis to leukemia to the grave; his sanity deteriorated also, gradually, along the continuum from relative normalcy through marked eccentricity to jibbering idiocy. In the first stages he merely inherited and disinherited his relatives and his society; in the second he no longer went to work, he required entertainment as well as care from his nurses, and he allowed nothing of his creation—including hair- and nail-clippings, urine, feces, and wills—to be thrown away; in the last stages he could scarcely move or talk, had no control whatever over his bodily functions, and recognized no one. To be sure, the stages were not dramatically marked, but blended into one another imperceptibly.

Of the seventeen wills (which represented by no means all the wills Mack had written, merely those written since he acquired his mania for preserving things), only the first two were composed during the time when the old man's sanity was pretty much indisputable; that is, prior to 1933. The first left about half the estate to Harrison Junior and the other half to Mother Mack, provided it could not be demonstrated to the court that she had drunk any sparkling burgundy since 1920. This one was dated 1924. The other, dated 1932, left about half the estate to Mrs. Mack unconditionally and the rest to Harrison, provided it could not be demonstrated to the court that during a five-year probationary period, 1932–37, Harrison had done, written, or said anything that could reasonably be construed as evidence of communist sympathies. This clause, incidentally, ran through most of the subsequent testaments as well.

Of the other fifteen documents, ten were composed in 1933 and 1934, years when the testator's sanity was open to debate. The last five, all written in the first three months of 1935, could be established without much difficulty, in court, as being the whims of a lunatic: one left everything to Johns Hopkins University on condition that the University's name be changed to Hoover College (the University politely declined); others bequeathed the whole shebang to the Atlantic Ocean or the A.F.L.

Luckily for the majesty of Maryland's law, there were only two primary and four secondary contestants for the estate. Elizabeth Sweetman Mack, the testator's widow, was interested in having Will #6, a product of late 1933, adjudged the last testament: it bequeathed her virtually the entire estate, on the sparkling-burgundy condition described above. Harrison Junior preferred #8, the fruit of early 1934; it bequeathed *him* virtually the whole works, on the clean-skirts condition also described above. Misses Janice Kosko, Shirley Mae Greene, and Berenice Silverman, registered nurses all, who had attended old Mack during the first, second, and third stages, respectively, of his physical invalidity, liked Wills #3, 9, and 12, in that order: therein, apparently, their late employer provided them remuneration for services beyond the line of duty. The final contestant was the pastor of the Macks' neighborhood church: in Will #13 the bulk of the estate was to pass to that church, with the express hope that the richer and more influential organized religion became, the sooner it would be cast off by the people.

It was an edifying spectacle. Mrs. Mack retained Messrs. Dugan, Froebel & Kemp, of Baltimore, to defend her legal rights; her son retained Andrews, Bishop, & Andrews, of Cambridge; the nurses and the minister retained separate attorneys. Everyone was a little afraid to carry the thing to court immediately, and for several months there was a welter of legal nonsense, threats, and counterthreats, among the six firms involved. Five of us joined forces to oust the clergyman from the sweepstakes—it was enough for the three nurses to agree that Mack was definitely insane by the time Will #13 was composed. A month later, by pretty much the same technique, Misses Kosko and Greene induced Miss Silverman to withdraw, on the solemnly contracted condition that should either of them win, she would get 20 per cent of the loot. Then, in a surprise maneuver, Bill Froebel, of Dugan, Froebel & Kemp, produced sworn affidavits from two Negro maids of the Mack household, to the effect that they had seen Miss Greene indulging in "unnatural and beastly" practices with the deceased—the practices were described in toothsome detail—and suggested to that young lady that, should she not decide the contest wasn't worth the trouble, he would release the affidavits to the newspapers. I never learned for certain whether the affidavits were true or false, but in either case they were effective: the additional attraction of several thousand dollars, payable when Mrs. Mack won the case, induced Miss Greene to seek her happiness outside the courts.

The field was cleared, then, in 1936, of half the entries, before the race even began. Only Miss Kosko, Harrison Junior, and Mrs. Mack remained. Each of them, of necessity, must attempt to prove two things: that Father Mack was still legally sane when the will of their choice was written, and that by the time the subsequent wills were written, he no longer could comprehend what he was about. On this basis, Miss Kosko, I should say, had the strongest case, since her will (dated February 1933) was the earliest of the three. But love was her undoing: she retained as her attorney her boy friend, a lad fresh out of law school, none too bright. After our initial out-of-court sparring I was fairly confident that he was no match for either Froebel or myself, and when, late in 1936, he refused on ethical grounds a really magnanimous bribe from Froebel, I was certain.

And sure enough, when the first swords clashed in Baltimore Probate Court, in May of 1936, Froebel was able, with little trouble, to insinuate that the young lawyer was an ass; that the nurse Miss Kosko was a hussy out to defraud poor widows of their honest legacies by seducing old men in their dotage; that Mrs. Mack, out of the kindness of her bereaved heart, had already offered the trollop a gratuity more munificent than she deserved (this news was ruled out as incompetent evidence, of course); and that even to listen tolerantly to such ill-concealed avariciousness was a tribute to the patience and indulgence of long-suffering judges. In addition, Froebel must have offered some cogent arguments, for surrogate courts, even in Baltimore, are notoriously competent, and the judge ruled in his favor. When Froebel then offered Miss Kosko another settlement, considerably smaller than the first, the young barrister accepted it humbly, coming as it did on the heels of his defeat, and didn't even think of appealing the judgment until it was too late.

Then, in June of the same year, Froebel filed suit for Mrs. Mack, charging flatly that Mr. Mack had been of unsound mind when he wrote Will #8, Harrison's will, and never again regained his sanity. If the court so ruled, then Mrs. Mack's will, #6, would become the authentic testamentary instrument, since Miss Kosko was out of the running. If the court ruled against him, then our document, #8, would automatically revoke his.

There was not much difference between Mack's mental state in late 1933 and his mental state in early 1934. I introduced statements from Misses Kosko and Greene that in both years he required them to save the contents of his bedpan in dill-pickle jars, which were then stored in the wine cellar, and I got the impression that the judge—a staid fellow—believed Mack had been insane from the beginning. The newspapers, too, expressed the opinion that there was no particular evidence on either side, and that, besides, it was a disgraceful thing for a mother and her son to squabble so selfishly. All the pressure was for out-of-court settlement on a fifty-fifty basis, but both Harrison and his mother—who had never especially liked each other—refused, on the advice of their attorneys. Froebel thought he could win, and wanted the money; I thought I could win, and wanted to see.

Will #6, remember, gave all the estate to Mrs. Mack, provided she hadn't tasted sparkling burgundy since 1920. Our will

left the money and property to Harrison, if he had steered clear of
Moscow since 1932, and in addition, bequeathed to Mrs. Mack
the several hundred pickle jars just mentioned. Both documents
included the extraordinary provision that, should the separate conditions not be fulfilled, the terms were to be reversed.

Froebel's arguments, essentially, were two: (1) That a man
has not necessarily lost his business sense if he provides once for a
complete reversal of bequests, of the sort seen in Will #6, assuming he is really dead set against sparkling burgundy; but then to
reverse himself completely in the space of a few months indicates
that something has snapped in his head, since there were no
dramatic external changes to account for the new will. (2) That
the bequest of the pickle jars appeared in no wills before #8, and
in all the wills from #8 through #16, and that such a bequest is
evidence tending to show that Mack no longer understood the
nature of his estate.

"Not necessarily," I suggested. "Suppose he didn't love his
wife?"

"Ah," Froebel replied quickly, "but he left the pickle jars to a
different person each time, not to Mrs. Mack every time."

"But remember," I said, "he saved the mess because he liked
it; the bequest of it, then, is an act of love. Would you call love
insane?"

"Indeed not," Froebel answered. "But if he'd loved her, he'd
have given her the property as well as the—excrement."

"No indeed," I countered. "Remember that in one will he
bequeathed all his money to the church because he disliked the
church. Couldn't the bequest to my client be such an act, and
the bequest to yours the real gift?"

"It could indeed," Froebel grinned. "Will you say that that's
the case?"

"No, I shan't," I said. "I merely suggested the possibility."

"And in doing so," Froebel declared, "you suggest the possibility that Will Number Eight is as insane as Will Number Thirteen, the church will you mentioned. Anyone who bequeaths three
millions of dollars as a punishment, I suggest, is out of perspective."

Oh, Bill Froebel was a lawyer. When it came to impromptu

legal sophistry, he and I had no equals at the Maryland Bar.

My arguments were (1) that the inclusion of the pickle jars was hardly sufficient evidence of a sudden loss of understanding, when Mack had been collecting them since Will #3 or 4; (2) that therefore the testator was either sane when he composed both instruments or insane when he composed them; (3) that if he was sane both times, Will #8 was official; (4) that if insane both times, some earlier will was official and must be brought forward, or otherwise Mack could be deemed to have died intestate (in which case Harrison would get all the money, Mrs. Mack retaining only dower).

The judge, Frank Lasker of the Baltimore bench, agreed. Froebel appealed the decision through the Court of Appeals to the Maryland Supreme Court, and both appellate courts affirmed the lower court's judgment. It seemed as if Harrison were a wealthy man: all that remained was to wait until January of 1937—the end of his probationary period—and then to demonstrate that Harrison had kept clear of communist sympathy since 1932. He assured me that nothing could be suggested which could be called fellow-traveling, even remotely. Froebel threatened for a while to institute a new suit, in favor of Will #2, but nothing came of his threat.

The final test was in the form of a hearing. Harrison and I appeared at the Baltimore courthouse early in January; Judge Lasker read the terms of Will #8 and declared that if no one present could offer evidence of such sympathies as were therein interdicted, he was prepared to declare the matter settled and to order the will executed. Froebel then appeared, much to my surprise, and announced that he had such evidence, enough to warrant the reversal of bequests provided for by our will, and was ready to offer it to the court.

"You told me there wasn't anything," I reminded Harrison, who had turned white.

"I swear there isn't!" he whispered back, but nevertheless he began perspiring and trembling a little. I sat back to see what Froebel had cooked up.

"What will you attempt to prove?" the Judge asked him.

"That as recently as last year, your honor, while his poor father was in the grave—perhaps speeded there (who knows?) by his son's regrettable irresponsibility—that just last year, your honor, this son, who is now so eager to take from his mother what is rightfully hers, was aiding and abetting actively, with large gifts of money, that doctrine against which his father's entire life was such an eloquent argument; confident, I doubt not, that he could conceal his surreptitious Bolshevism until such time as he was in a position to devote the whole of the Mack estate toward overthrowing the way of life that made its accumulation possible!"

Froebel was a past master of the detached noun clause: judge and spectators were stirred.

"For heaven's sake!" Harrison whispered. "You don't think he means my Spanish donations!"

"If you were silly enough to make any, then I daresay he does," I replied, appalled anew at Harrison's innocence.

And indeed, the "Spanish donations" were precisely what Froebel had in mind. He offered in evidence photostated checks, four of them, for one thousand dollars each, made out to an American subscription agency representing the Spanish Loyalist government. They were dated March 10, May 19, September 2, and October 7, and all were signed *Harrison A. Mack, Jr.*

Judge Lasker examined the photostats and frowned. "Did you write these checks?" he asked Harrison, passing the pictures to him.

"Of course!" Harrison yelled. "What the hell's that—"

"Order!" suggested the Judge. "Aren't you aware that the Loyalist movement is run by the Communist Party? Directed from the Kremlin?"

"Aw, come on!" Harrison pleaded, until I poked him and he sat down.

"May I point out," Froebel continued blandly, "that not only is a gift to the Loyalists in essence a gift to Moscow, but this particular subscription agency is a Party organization under FBI surveillance. A man may donate to the Loyalists through honest, if vague, liberalism, I daresay; but one doesn't send checks to this subscription outfit unless one is sympathetic with the Comintern. Young Mr. Mack, like too many of our idle aristocrats, is, I fear, a blue blood with a Red heart."

I believe it was this final metaphor that won Froebel the judgment. I saw the newspaper people virtually doff their hats in tribute, and scribble the immortal words for the next editions of their papers. Even the Judge smiled benignly upon the trope: I could see that it struck him square in the prejudices, and found a welcome there.

There was some further discussion, but no one listened closely; everyone was repeating to himself, with a self-satisfied smile, that too many young aristocrats are blue bloods with Red hearts. *Blue bloods with Red hearts!* How could mere justice cope with poetry? Men, I think, are ever attracted to the *bon mot* rather than the *mot juste*, and judges, no less than other men, are often moved by considerations more aesthetic than judicial. Even I was not a little impressed, and regretted only that we had no jury to be overwhelmed by such a purple plum from the groves of advocacy. *A blue blood with a Red heart!* How brandish reasonableness against music? Should I hope to tip the scales with puny logic, when Froebel had Parnassus in his pan? In vain might I warn Judge Lasker that, through the press, all America was watching, and Europe as well, for his decision.

"My client, a lover of freedom and human dignity," I declared, "made his contributions to the oppressed Loyalists as a moral obligation, proper to every good American, to fight those rebels who would crush the independence of the human spirit, and trample liberty under hobnailed boots! How can you charge him with advocating anarchy and violent overthrow, when in a single year he gives four thousand dollars to support the Spanish Government against those who would overthrow it?"

And on I went for some minutes, trying to make capital out of the Spanish confusion, wherein the radicals were the *status quo* and the reactionaries the rebels. It was an admirable bit of casuistry, but I knew my cause was lost. Only Froebel, I think, had ears for my rhetoric; the rest of the room was filled with *blue bloods with Red hearts*.

And Judge Lasker, as I think I mentioned, was famously conservative. Though by no means a fascist himself—he was probably uncommitted in the Spanish revolution—he epitomized the unthinking antagonism of his class toward anything pinker than the blue end of the spectrum: a familiar antagonism that used to infuriate me when, prior to 1924, I was interested in such things as social justice. When finally he ruled, he ruled in Froebel's favor.

"It does not matter whether there is a difference between the Moscow and Madrid varieties of communism," he declared, "or whether the Court or anyone else approves or disapproves of the defendant's gifts or the cause for which they were intended. The fact is that the subscription agency involved is a communist organization under government surveillance, and a gift to that agency is a gift to communism. There can be no question of the donor's sympathy with what the agency represented, and what it represented was communism. The will before me provides that should such sympathy be demonstrated, as it has been here, the terms of the document are to be reversed. The Court here orders such a reversal."

Well, we were poor again. Harrison went weak, and when I offered him a cigar he came near to vomiting.

"It's incredible!" he croaked, actually perspiring from the shock of it.

"Do you give up?" I asked him. "Or shall I appeal?"

He clutched at the hope. "Can we appeal?"

"Sure," I said. "Don't you see how unlogical Lasker's reasoning is?"

"Unlogical! It was so logical it overwhelmed me!"

"Not at all. He said the subscription agency was sympathetic to communism. You give money to the agency; therefore you're sympathetic to communism. It's like saying that if you give money to a Salvation Army girl who happens to be a vegetarian you're sympathetic to vegetarians. The communists support the Loyalists; you support the Loyalists; therefore you're a communist."

Harrison was tremendously relieved, but so weak he could scarcely stand. He laughed shortly.

"Well! That puts us back in the race, doesn't it? Ha, I'd thought there for a while—Christ, Toddy, you've saved my ass again! Damned judge! We've got it now, boy!"

I shook my head, and he went white again.

"What the hell's wrong?"

"I'll appeal," I said, "but we'll lose again, I guess."

"How's that? Lose again!" He laughed, and sucked in his breath.

"Forget about the logic," I said. "Nobody really cares about the logic. They make up their minds by their prejudices about Spain. I think you'd have lost here even without Froebel's metaphor. I'd have to talk Lasker into liberalism to win the case."

I went on to explain that of the seven judges of the Court of Appeals who would review the decision, three were Republicans with a pronounced anti-liberal bias, two were fairly liberal Democrats, one was a reactionary "Southern Democrat," more anti-liberal than the Republicans, and the seventh, an unenthusiastic Democrat, was relatively unbiased.

"I know them all," I said. "Abrams, Moore, and Stevens, the Republicans, will vote against you. Forrester, the Southern Democrat, would vote for you if it were a party issue, but it's not; he'll go along with the Republicans. Stedman and Barnes, the liberals, will go along with you, and I think Haddaway will too, because he likes me and because he dislikes Lasker's bad logic."

"But hell, that's four to three!" Harrison cried. "That means I lose!"

"As I said."

"How about the Maryland Supreme Court?"

"That's too much to predict," I said. "I don't know that they've declared themselves on Spain, and I don't know them personally. But they've affirmed almost every important verdict of the Court of Appeals in three years."

Harrison was crushed. "It's unjust!"

I smiled. "You know how these things are."

"Aw, but what the hell!" He shook his head, tapped his feet impatiently, pursed his lips, sighed in spasms. I expected him to faint, but he held on tightly, though he could scarcely talk. The truth was, of course, that it is one thing—an easy thing—to give what Cardinal Newman calls "notional" assent to a proposition such as "There is no justice"; quite another and more difficult matter to give it "real" assent, to learn it stingingly, to the heart, through involvement. I remember hoping that Harrison was strong enough at least to be educated by his expensive loss.

I appealed the judgment of the Court.

"Just to leave the door open," I explained. "I might think of something."

That evening, before I left Baltimore with Harrison, we had dinner at Bill Froebel's club, as his guests. I praised his inspiration, and he my logic-twisting. Harrison was morose, and although he drank heavily, he refused to join in the conversation. He couldn't drive home. On the way, he would clutch my arm and groan, "Three million bucks, Toddy!"

I looked coldly at him.

"Hell, man," he protested, "I know what you're thinking, but you should know me better. I don't want the money like another man might, just to go crazy on. Think what we could do on three million bucks, the three of us!"

It was the first time since Jane and I had resumed our affair in 1935 that Harrison had spoken again of "the three of us," as he had used to do.

"A million apiece?" I asked. "Or a joint account?"

Harrison felt the bristles and flinched, and all the way home he felt constrained to pretend that the loss of three million dollars touched his philosophical heart not at all. I watched the effort from the corner of my eye, and marveled sadly at his disorientation.

Finally he broke down, as we were crossing the Choptank River bridge, pulling into Cambridge. The water was white-capped and cold-looking. Dead ahead, at the end of the boulevard that the bridge ran onto, Morton's Marvelous Tomatoes, Inc., spread its red neon banner across the sky, and I smiled. The town lights ran in a flat string along the water's edge, from Hambrooks Bar Lighthouse, flashing on the right, to the Macks' house in East Cambridge, its ground-floor windows still lit, where Jane was waiting.

"I give up, Toddy," he said tersely; "I'm no philosopher. I can't say I wouldn't have been happy at one time without the money—I *did* get myself disinherited a few times, you know. But once it came so close and seemed so sure—"

"What is it?" I snapped.

"Ah, Christ—Janie and I had plans." He choked on his plans. "How the hell can I say it? I just don't feel like living any more."

"You *what?*" I sneered. "What'll you do—hang yourself in the cellar? There's a twentypenny nail right there, in a joist—you'll find it. It's already been broken in. And I know an undertaker who can turn black faces white again."

"All right, all right," Harrison said. "I don't care what you think. I said I'm no philosopher."

"Forget about philosophy," I said. "You don't lack philosophy; you lack guts. I suppose you're going to ask me to marry Jane afterwards, so the two of us can remember you? You're wallowing, Harrison. It's swinish."

"I'm weak, Toddy," he said. "I can't help it. Don't think I'm not ashamed of it."

"Then cut it out."

"You can't just cut it out," Harrison protested, and I sensed that he was growing stronger. "I'm past believing that people can change."

"You don't want to cut it out."

"Sure I do. It doesn't matter whether I do or not; I can't do it. I'm weak in some ways, Toddy. You don't understand that."

I flicked my cigarette out of the ventilator in a shower of sparks. We were off the bridge then, coasting along the dual highway in the Macks' big automobile.

"I know what weakness is. But you make your own difficulties, Harrison. It's hard because you never thought of it as easy. Listen. An act of will is the easiest thing there is—so easy it's laughable how people make mountains of it."

Harrison had by this time actually put aside the idea of his loss and was following the thought.

"You know better," he said. "You can't discount psychology."

"I'm not saying anything about psychology," I maintained. "Psychology doesn't interest me. We act as if we could choose, and so we can, in effect. All you have to do to be strong is stop being weak."

"Impossible."

"You never tried it."

Nor, alas, did he want to just then: I could see that plainly enough. We went into the house for a last drink. Jane had heard the news, of course, by telephone, and she cried awhile. I told her flatly that I had no sympathy for either of them while they behaved like that.

"What would you do, damn it!" she cried impatiently.

I laughed. "I've never lost three million bucks," I said, "but I'll tell you what I did once, after Dad hanged himself for losing a few thousand."

I told them then, for the first time, the story of my adventures with Col. Henry Morton—which story, reader, I'll pause to tell you, too, sooner or later, but not just now. I had decided that I didn't want Harrison to brood over his money: he wasn't ready to be strong of his own choosing yet, apparently, and so I opened the way toward turning him into a cynic, in emulation of me. He was ripe for it anyhow, it seemed to me, and even the one story might do the trick.

There's little need for weakness, reader: you are freer, perhaps, than you'd be comfortable knowing.

As I left, Jane asked me: "You don't have anything up your sleeve, Toddy?"

"I shan't commit myself," I said. "But Harrison might as well believe he's out three million bucks, at least for a while."

"What will he do?" she asked anxiously. "Did he say anything to you coming home?"

"He'll grow stronger or hang himself," I predicted. "If he grows stronger it won't matter to him whether he gets the money or not, really, and then I wouldn't mind seeing him get it. If he kills himself over it, I'll be just as glad he's dead, frankly. Sissies make me uncomfortable. That goes for you, too. You're not ready for three million bucks yet. You don't deserve it."

Then I left. I suppose if *I* ever lost three million dollars I'd holler like a stuck hero. Or perhaps not: one really can't tell until the thing is upon one.

Well, the will case dropped out of the papers then; the Court of Appeals wouldn't hear the appeal for at least six months, though I doubted that they'd wait much longer than that. In the meantime, Lizzie Mack, Harrison's mother, couldn't use up the old man's estate (except for running expenses for the house), though it was temporarily hers.

I conducted, during the next few months, a rather intensive

investigation into the characters of the appellate court judges—
my findings confirmed my original estimate of the situation. As
far as one with much information could guess, the decision would
be four to three for Lizzie if the hearing were held when tentatively scheduled.

And if it weren't? I considered that question, sitting in my
office, staring at my staring-wall opposite the desk. What advantage was there in delay, if any? And how could one delay the
appeal? The advantage was negative: that is, I was certain of
defeat if there were no delay; if there were any, I might very
possibly still be defeated, but there would be more time for
something to turn up. So, I suppose, a condemned man snatches
at a day's reprieve, still hoping for a god on wires to fetch him
off, and on the very gibbet, his neck roped, pleads eye-to-sky for
the saving car. Who knows? Perhaps, hooded and dropped, he yet
awaits in a second's agony for God's hands on him, till the noose
cracks neck and hope in one sick snap. To be sure, ours was but a
matter of money, but the principle was the same. By September
the Loyalists might be winning, or it might become dangerous
over here to like the fascists, the way Hitler was behaving. By
October Franco might win, and the poor crushed Loyalists be
pitied, then when they were no longer a threat. Anything could
happen to swing one more vote our way. November was an off-
year election month: perhaps some party issue would ally John
Forrester, the reactionary Democrat, with his more liberal col-
leagues. Perhaps—

I smiled, moved my feet off the desk, and went to the file.
I looked up each of the judges, checking the length of their
incumbencies and the number of years in office remaining to
each.

"Ah, Freddie Barnes, you old whoremonger," I cooed; "so
you're up to the post again this year, are you?"

That fact mattered little, since Roosevelt was going great
guns and Barnes was a popular figure in Maryland: he'd be
re-elected without difficulty. Of the other Democrats, Forrester
had two years to go, Haddaway had four, and Stedman had
six. I checked the Republicans: Abrams had two years yet;
Stevens, six; Moore—

"Well, well, well!" I grinned. "You rascal, Rollo! Time to run again, eh?"

Mrs. Lake, at my request, spent the rest of her afternoon telephoning various Baltimorians for me, some eminent and some shady, some honest and some flexible, some friendly and some employable. By quitting time I was one of perhaps seven people who knew as a fact, beyond puny speculation, that Judge Rollo Moore, despite the backing of Maryland republicanism, was going to lose his coming election by a well-insured margin to Joseph Singer, who, bless his heart, was a chronic if somewhat fuzzy liberal—a man after Harrison's own heart.

We would win, by God, almost certainly, if we could hold off the appeal until November! No, until January of 1938, after the new officeholders had been sworn in. Nearly a year! I racked my brain, in my thorough but unenthusiastic way, to think of some stalling maneuver, but of the few I could imagine, none was satisfactory. What I needed was something diverting, something tenuous and intricate, that I could go on complicating indefinitely, if need be. Nothing crude would do: my maneuver, whatever it was, must be subtle even if its motives were clear to the professional eye, or else I should lose the respect, and possibly the vote, of men like Judge Haddaway, for instance, whose decisions were more influenced by such things as the symmetry and logical elegance of a brief than by more mundane considerations like the appellant's politics.

Ah, nonsense, there was nothing. The months passed; it was spring; August and judgment would soon be upon us. Harrison sweated but kept silent. Jane wept a little, and sometimes failed to come to my room when I expected her, but kept silent. They were learning; they were strengthening, or else they were naïve enough to have some canine faith in me. At least they kept silent about it, though I often caught them looking at me intently, at supper or wherever. In fact, they often stared at me, and sometimes didn't even notice when I noticed them.

As for me, I stared at my wall. I have in my office, opposite the desk, a fine staring-wall, a wall that I keep scrupulously clear for staring purposes, and I stared at it. I stared at it through February, March, April, and May, and through the first week of June, without reading on its empty surface a single idea.

Then, on the very hot June 17th of 1937, our Mrs. Lake, who is as a rule a model of decorum, came sweating decorously into my office with a paper cup of iced coffee for me, set it decorously on my desk, accepted my thanks, dropped a handkerchief on the floor as she turned to leave, bent decorously down to retrieve it, and most undaintily—oh, most indecorously,—broke wind, virtually in my coffee.

"Oh, excuse me!" she gasped, and blushed, and fled. But ah, the fart hung heavy in the humid air, long past the lady's flight. It hung, it lolled, it wisped; it miscegenated with the smoke of my cigar, caressed the beading oil on the skin of my nose, lay obscenely on the flat of my desk, among my briefs and papers. It was everywhere, but I had learned, even then, to live with nature and my fellow animals. I didn't flinch; I didn't move. Through its dense invisible presence I regarded my oracular wall, and this time fruitfully.

"By God, now!" I cried.

I heard a small sound in the outer office.

"Mrs. Lake!" I rushed to my door. "Where's all the crap?"

"Oh, Mr. Andrews!" she wailed, and buried her face in her arms. Harry Bishop and Jimmy Andrews peered skeptically from their doorways.

"No!" I said, patting Mrs. Lake furiously on the head. "No, I mean old man Mack's pickle jars. Where've they been all this time? Where does Lizzie keep them?"

"I don't know," Mrs. Lake sniffed, wiping her eyes.

"What was it?" I hurried back to my file, began pushing things around, and finally found the inventory of the Mack estate. "One hundred twenty-nine bottles of it, in the wine cellar!"

"Well," remarked Mr. Bishop, and returned to his work. Jimmy Andrews hung around to see what was up.

"Call 'Stacia," I said to Mrs. Lake, "No, hell no, don't. I'll run up to Baltimore." I looked at my watch. "Will you run me to the bus, Jim? I bet I can catch the four o'clock."

"Sure," Jimmy said. He drove insanely; I made the bus with two minutes to spare, and was soon off to Baltimore.

Eustacia Callader was an old Negro servant in the Mack household, whom I'd met during the course of the litigation. She had virtually raised Harrison Junior and was quietly on our side in the

contest over the estate, though she grasped little of the contro-
versy. She it was whom I sought now. Arriving in Baltimore four
hours later, I stopped in a drugstore to buy envelopes and stamps,
and then took a taxi out to Ruxton, getting out at the driveway
of the Mack house. The sun had just set, and I actually hid myself on the grounds in the rear of the house—it was all quite
theatrical—and waited, I suppose, for 'Stacia to come out of the
kitchen for something. An unlikely plan, but then my whole
scheme, my suspicion, was unlikely: when the great Negro woman
did, as a matter of fact, come out just forty-five minutes later. en
route to the garbage cans down by the big garage, I took her
appearance as a good omen. Following her out of earshot of the
house, I approached her.

"Lord 'a mercy, Mister Andrews!" she chuckled enormously.
"What y'all doin' up here? Come see Lizzie?"

" 'Stacia, listen," I whispered urgently. "I've got a five-buck
question." I gave her the five, and she giggled helplessly.

"Where does Lizzie keep the old man's fertilizer?" I asked.
"Is it still in the wine cellar?"

"De fertilize'?" 'Stacia chortled. "What fertilize'?" She laughed
so hard that I knew she didn't understand.

"The crap, 'Stacia," I demanded. "How does Lizzie feel about
all those bottles of crap?"

"Oh, *dat's* what you mean de fertilize'!"

"A hundred and twenty-nine jars of it," I said. "Used to be in
the wine cellar. Are they still there?"

When 'Stacia regained control of her risibility, she admitted
that she didn't know, but she promised to find out and tell me.
I gave her a buss on the cheek and took up lodgings in a clump
of forsythia bushes near the garbage cans, while 'Stacia returned
to the house to question the other servants who lived in. I was
prepared, if it should prove necessary, to bribe somebody heavily
to destroy those pickle jars for me secretly, but I didn't look
forward to taking that step, since it opened the way for blackmail.
Still, it seemed highly unlikely to me that Mrs. Mack had ordered
them removed herself, although it was exactly that possibility
which had occurred to me on the occasion of Mrs. Lake's *faux
pas.*

I was pleasantly surprised, then, when three hours later—it was after midnight—'Stacia lumbered back with the announcement that though the bottles were indeed still in the wine cellar, Mrs. Mack had observed last week to R. J. Collier, the gimpy, dusty old fellow who tended the gardens, that the seals on the jars were apparently not airtight, and had mentioned the possibility of someday disposing of the collection. Indeed, 'Stacia verified that with the coming of hot weather the jars had begun to smell noticeably, and that the odor was creeping up occasionally to the ground floor. Two days before, R. J. Collier had taken it upon himself to pile the whole stack into the far corner of the wine cellar and to cover it with a wet tarpaulin, hoping thereby to check the bouquet, but his experiment had yielded no apparent results. Mrs. Mack was growing annoyed. R. J. Collier had, that very day, broached the suggestion that his late employer's singular remains be put to work around the flower gardens—the zinnia beds, especially, could use the nourishment, he declared. All the servants considered the suggestion more touching than tactless, and I, too, sensed a seed of poetry in the gardener's practicality. But Lizzie had remained noncommittal.

"Listen, 'Stacia," I said, "you mustn't say a word about the pickle jars, or about me being here. I'm going to give you ten dollars, honey—"

"Hoo, Mister Andrews!"

"—here, ten bucks. Now I want you to keep a close watch on those jars. Make sure you know everything that Liz or R. J. Collier or anybody else does to them. Look. I'm giving you all these envelopes with stamps on them. They're addressed to me, so keep them hidden, and there's paper inside. Now, then, every time even one of those bottles is moved from where it is now, you write to me and tell me. Understand?"

'Stacia giggled and shook and grunted, but I was fairly sure she understood.

"For Christ's sake don't say a word," I cautioned her again. "If everything turns out right, Harrison will give you a brand-new car. A yellow roadster, he'll buy you. Okay?"

'Stacia could scarcely stand for laughing. But she stuck the envelopes deep between her endless bosoms and rumbled off to the house, shaking her head at my derangement. I walked out to the road and hiked two miles to a telephone. Next day I was back in my office, smoking cigars and staring at my wall. I didn't bother to tell Harrison anything about my trip—perhaps nothing would come of it after all.

And except for the infrequent parries with Charley Parks, the attorney next door, over our automobile suit—you'll recall I mentioned it earlier?—I had done nothing else, no work at all on any case, since then: nearly a week. I was waiting for 'Stacia's letter, and thinking steadily about possible alternative plans of action. I'd decided to sit thus until July 1. If nothing had happened to the jars by then, I'd take the risk of bribing R. J. Collier to destroy some of them.

Then, this morning, there was 'Stacia's letter, one of the self-addressed envelopes I'd given her. It could contain anything from nonsense to the key to three million dollars, and it was merely as a disciplinary exercise that I'd postponed reading it until after I'd read the other letters and the handbill, and had called Marvin Rose. But I shan't exact such discipline from you, reader. Here is the letter:

Mr. Andrew. Mrs. Mack, has put pickle jars in grenhouse. R. J. Coler, has put on zinas. Eustacia M. Callader. R. J. Coler, has put 27 bottles on zinas. Eustacia M. Callader.

I put the letter in the dossier with the other documents pertaining to the Mack will case, returned the dossier to the file, and locked the filing cabinets. For nearly two hours I stared at my wall, and then I left the office to stroll uptown for my appointment with Marvin.

A good morning's work, reader: I opened a few letters and put one in the file. An excellent morning's work for one's last morning on earth, I should say.

My friend Harrison is three million dollars richer for it.

16 Leonard Michaels

Leonard Michaels teaches at the University of California, Davis. His first collection of stories, Going Places, *was published in 1969.*

❖

CITY BOY

"Phillip," she said, "this is crazy."

I didn't agree or disagree. She wanted some answer. I bit her neck. She kissed my ear. It was nearly three in the morning. We had just returned. The apartment was dark and quiet. We were on the living room floor and she repeated, "Phillip, this is crazy." Her crinoline broke under us like cinders. Furniture loomed all around in the darkness—settee, chairs, a table with a lamp. Pictures were cloudy blotches drifting above. But no lights, no things to look at, no eyes in her head. She was underneath me and warm. The rug was warm, soft as mud, deep. Her crinoline cracked like sticks. Our naked bellies clapped together. Air fired out like farts. I took it as applause. The chairs smirked and spit between their feet. The chandelier clicked giddy teeth. The clock ticked as if to split its glass. "Phillip," she said, "this is crazy." A little voice against the grain and power. Not enough to stop me. Yet once I had been a man of feeling. We went to concerts, walked in the park, trembled in the maid's room. Now in the foyer, a flash of hair and claws. We stumbled to the living room floor. She said, "Phillip, this is crazy." Then silence, except in my head where a conference table was set up, ashtrays scattered about. Priests, ministers and rabbis were rushing to take seats. I wanted their opinion, but came. They vanished. A voice lingered, faintly crying, "You could mess up the rug, Phillip, break something . . ." Her fingers pinched my back like ants. I expected a remark to kill good death. She said nothing. The breath in her nostrils whipped mucus. It cracked in my ears like flags. I dreamed we were in her mother's Cadillac, trailing flags. I heard her voice before I heard the words. "Phillip, this is crazy. My parents are in the next room." Her cheek jerked against mine, her breasts were knuckles in my nipples. I burned. Good death was killed. I burned with hate. A rabbi shook his finger, "You shouldn't hate." I lifted on my elbows, sneering in pain. She wrenched her hips, tightened muscles in belly and neck. She said, "Move." It was imperative to move. Her parents were thirty feet away. Down the hall between Utrillos and Vlamincks, through the door, flick the light and I'd see them. Maybe like us, Mr. Cohen adrift on the missus. Hair sifted down my cheek. "Let's go to the maid's room," she whispered. I was reassured. She tried to move. I kissed her mouth. Her crinoline smashed like sugar. Pig that I was, I couldn't move. The clock ticked hysterically. Ticks piled up like insects. Muscles lapsed in her thighs. Her fingers scratched on my neck as if looking for buttons. She slept. I sprawled like a bludgeoned pig, eyes open, loose lips. I flopped into sleep, in her, in the rug, in our scattered clothes.

Dawn hadn't shown between the slats in the blinds. Her breathing sissed in my ear. I wanted to sleep more, but needed a cigarette. I thought of the cold avenue, the lonely subway ride. Where could I buy a newspaper, a cup of coffee? This was crazy, dangerous, a waste of time. The maid might arrive, her parents might wake. I had to get started. My hand pushed along the rug to find my shirt, touched a brass lion's paw, then a lamp cord.

A naked heel bumped wood.

She woke, her nails in my neck. "Phillip, did you hear?" I whispered, "Quiet." My eyes rolled like Milton's. Furniture loomed, whirled. "Dear God," I prayed, "save my ass." The steps ceased. Neither of us breathed. The clock ticked. She trembled. I pressed my cheek against her mouth to keep her from talking. We heard pajamas rustle, phlegmy breathing, fingernails scratching hair. A voice, "Veronica, don't you think it's time you sent Phillip home?"

A murmur of assent started in her throat, swept to my cheek, fell back drowned like a child in a well. Mr. Cohen had spoken. He stood ten inches from our legs. Maybe less. It was impossible to tell. His fingernails grated through hair. His voice hung in the dark with the quintessential question. Mr. Cohen, scratching his crotch, stood now as never in the light. Considerable. No tool of his wife, whose energy in business kept him eating, sleeping, overlooking the park. Pinochle change in his pocket four nights a week. But were they his words? Or was he the oracle of Mrs. Cohen, lying sleepless, irritated, waiting for him to get me out? I didn't breathe. I didn't move. If he had come on his own he would leave without an answer. His eyes weren't adjusted to the dark. He couldn't see. We lay at his feet like worms. He scratched, made smacking noises with his mouth.

The question of authority is always with us. Who is responsible for the triggers pulled, buttons pressed, the gas, the fire? Doubt banged my brain. My heart lay in the fist of intellect, which squeezed out feeling like piss out of kidneys. Mrs. Cohen's voice demolished doubt, feeling, intellect. It ripped from the bedroom.

"For God's sake, Morris, don't be banal. Tell the schmuck to go home and keep his own parents awake all night, if he has any."

Veronica's tears slipped down my cheeks. Mr. Cohen sighed, shuffled, made a strong voice. "Veronica, tell Phillip . . ." His foot came down on my ass. He drove me into his daughter. I drove her into his rug.

"I don't believe it," he said.

He walked like an antelope, lifting hoof from knee, but stepped down hard. Sensitive to the danger of movement, yet finally impulsive, flinging his pot at the earth in order to cross it. His foot brought me his weight and character, a hundred fifty-five pounds of stomping *schlemiel,* in a mode of apprehension so primal we must share it with bugs. Let armies stomp me to insensate pulp —I'll yell "Cohen" when he arrives.

Veronica squealed, had a contraction, fluttered, gagged a shriek,

squeezed, and up like a frog out of the hand of a child I stood
spread-legged, bolt naked, great with eyes. Mr. Cohen's face was
eyes in my eyes. A secret sharer. We faced each other like men
accidentally met in hell. He retreated flapping, moaning, "I will
not believe it one bit."

Veronica said, "Daddy?"

"Who else you no good bum?"

The rug raced. I smacked against blinds, glass broke and I
whirled. Veronica said, "Phillip," and I went off in streaks, a
sparrow in the room, here, there, early American, baroque and
rococo. Veronica wailed, "Phillip." Mr. Cohen screamed, "I'll kill
him." I stopped at the door, seized the knob. Mrs. Cohen yelled
from the bedroom, "Morris, did something break? Answer me."

"I'll kill that bastid."

"Morris, if something broke you'll rot for a month."

"Mother, stop it," said Veronica. "Phillip, come back."

The door slammed. I was outside, naked as a wolf.

I needed poise. Without poise the street was impossible. Blood
shot to my brain, thought blossomed. I'd walk on my hands.
Beards were fashionable. I kicked up my feet, kicked the elevator
button, faced the door and waited. I bent one elbow like a knee.
The posture of a clothes model, easy, poised. Blood coiled down
to my brain, weeds bourgeoned. I had made a bad impression.
There was no other way to see it. But all right. We needed a new
beginning. Everyone does. Yet how few of us know when it
arrives. Mr. Cohen had never spoken to me before; this was a
breakthrough. There had been a false element in our relationship.
It was wiped out. I wouldn't kid myself with the idea that he
had nothing to say. I'd had enough of his silent treatment. It was
worth being naked to see how mercilessly I could think. I had
his number. Mrs. Cohen's, too. I was learning every second. I
was a city boy. No innocent shitkicker from Jersey. I was the A
train, the Fifth Avenue bus. I could be a cop. My name was
Phillip, my style New York City. I poked the elevator button
with my toe. It rang in the lobby, waking Ludwig. He'd come
for me, rotten with sleep. Not the first time. He always took me
down, walked me through the lobby and let me out on the

avenue. Wires began tugging him up the shaft. I moved back, conscious of my genitals hanging upside down. Absurd consideration; we were both men one way or another. There were social distinctions enforced by his uniform, but they would vanish at the sight of me. "The unaccommodated thing itself." "Off ye lendings!" The greatest play is about a naked man. A picture of Lear came to me, naked, racing through the wheat. I could be cool. I thought of Ludwig's uniform, hat, whipcord collar. It signified his authority. Perhaps he would be annoyed, in his authority, by the sight of me naked. Few people woke him at such hours. Worse, I never tipped him. Could I have been so indifferent month after month? In a crisis you discover everything. Then it's too late. Know yourself, indeed. You need a crisis every day. I refused to think about it. I sent my mind after objects. It returned with the chairs, settee, table and chandelier. Where were my clothes? I sent it along the rug. It found buttons, eagles stamped in brass. I recognized them as the buttons on Ludwig's coat. Eagles, beaks like knives, shrieking for tips. Fuck'm, I thought. Who's Ludwig? A big coat, a whistle, white gloves and a General MacArthur hat. I could understand him completely. He couldn't begin to understand me. A naked man is mysterious. But aside from that, what did he know? I dated Veronica Cohen and went home late. Did he know I was out of work? That I lived in a slum downtown? Of course not.

Possibly under his hat was a filthy mind. He imagined Veronica and I might be having sexual intercourse. He resented it. Not that he hoped for the privilege himself, in his coat and soldier hat, but he had a proprietary interest in the building and its residents. I came from another world. *The* other world against which Ludwig defended the residents. Wasn't I like a burglar sneaking out late, making him my accomplice? I undermined his authority, his dedication. He despised me. It was obvious. But no one thinks such thoughts. It made me laugh to think them. My genitals jumped. The elevator door slid open. He didn't say a word. I padded inside like a seal. The door slid shut. Instantly, I was ashamed of myself, thinking as I had about him. I had no right. A better man than I. His profile was an etching by Dürer.

Good peasant stock. How had he fallen to such work? Existence precedes essence. At the controls, silent, enduring, he gave me strength for the street. Perhaps the sun would be up, birds in the air. The door slid open. Ludwig walked ahead of me through the lobby. He needed new heels. The door of the lobby was half a ton of glass, encased in iron vines and leaves. Not too much for Ludwig. He turned, looked down into my eyes. I watched his lips move.

"I vun say sumding. Yur bisniss vot you do. Bud vy you mek her miserable? Nod led her slip. She has beks unter her eyes."

Ludwig had feelings. They spoke to mine. Beneath the uniform, a man. Essence precedes existence. Even rotten with sleep, thick, dry bags under his eyes, he saw, he sympathized. The discretion demanded by his job forbade anything tangible, a sweater, a hat. "Ludwig," I whispered, "you're all right." It didn't matter if he heard me. He knew I said something. He knew it was something nice. He grinned, tugged the the door open with both hands. I slapped out onto the avenue. I saw no one, dropped to my feet and glanced back through the door. Perhaps for the last time. I lingered, indulged a little melancholy. Ludwig walked to a couch in the rear of the lobby. He took off his coat, rolled it into a pillow and lay down. I had never stayed to see him do that before, but always rushed off to the subway. As if I were indifferent to the life of the building. Indeed, like a burglar. I seized the valuables and fled to the subway. I stayed another moment, watching good Ludwig, so I could hate myself. He assumed the modest, saintly posture of sleep. One leg here, the other there. His good head on his coat. A big arm across his stomach, the hand between his hips. He made a fist and punched up and down.

I went down the avenue, staying close to the buildings. Later I would work up a philosophy. Now I wanted to sleep, forget. I hadn't the energy for moral complexities: Ludwig cross-eyed, thumping his pelvis in such a nice lobby. Mirrors, glazed pots, rubber plants ten feet high. As if he were generating all of it. As if it were part of his job. I hurried. The buildings were on my left, the park on my right. There were doormen in all the buildings; God knows what was in the park. No cars were moving. No people in sight. Streetlights glowed in a receding sweep down to Fifty-ninth Street and beyond. A wind pressed my face like Mr. Cohen's breath. Such hatred. Imponderable under any circumstances, a father cursing his daughter. Why? A fright in the dark? Freud said things about fathers and daughters. It was too obvious, too hideous. I shuddered and went more quickly. I began to run. In a few minutes I was at the spit-mottled steps of the subway. I had hoped for vomit. Spit is no challenge for bare feet. Still, I wouldn't complain. It was sufficiently disgusting to make me live in spirit. I went down the steps flatfooted, stamping, elevated by each declension. I was a city boy, no mincing creep from the sticks.

A Negro man sat in the change booth. He wore glasses, a white shirt, black knit tie and a silver tie clip. I saw a mole on his right cheek. His hair had spots of grey, as if strewn with ashes. He was reading a newspaper. He didn't hear me approach, didn't see my eyes take him in, figure him out. Shirt, glasses, tie—I knew how to address him. I coughed. He looked up.

"Sir, I don't have any money. Please let me through the turnstile. I come this way every week and will certainly pay you the next time."

He merely looked at me. Then his eyes flashed like fangs. Instinctively, I guessed what he felt. He didn't owe favors to a white man. He didn't have to bring his allegiance to the transit authority into question for my sake.

"Hey, man, you naked?"

"Yes."

"Step back a little."

I stepped back.

"You're naked."

I nodded.

"Get your naked ass the hell out of here."

"Sir," I said, "I know these are difficult times, but can't we be reasonable? I know that . . ."

"Scat, mother, go home."

I crouched as if to dash through the turnstile. He crouched, too. It proved he would come after me. I shrugged, turned back toward the steps. The city was infinite. There were many other subways. But why had he become so angry? Did he think I was a bigot? Maybe I was running around naked to get him upset. His anger was incomprehensible otherwise. It made me feel like a bigot. First a burglar, then a bigot. I needed a cigarette. I could hardly breathe. Air was too good for me. At the top of the steps, staring down, stood Veronica. She had my clothes.

"Poor, poor," she said.

I said nothing. I snatched my underpants and put them on. She had my cigarettes ready. I tried to light one, but the match failed. I threw down the cigarette and the matchbook. She retrieved them as I dressed. She lit the cigarette for me and held my elbow to help me keep my balance. I finished dressing, took the cigarette. We walked back toward her building. The words "thank you" sat in my brain like driven spikes. She nibbled her lip.

"How are things at home?" My voice was casual and morose, as if no answer could matter.

"All right," she said, her voice the same as mine. She took her tone from me. I liked that sometimes, sometimes not. Now I didn't like it. I discovered I was angry. Until she said that I had no idea I was angry. I flicked the cigarette into the gutter and suddenly I knew why. I didn't love her. The cigarette sizzled in the gutter. Like truth. I didn't love her. Black hair, green eyes, I didn't love her. Slender legs. I didn't. Last night I had looked at her and said to myself, "I hate communism." Now I wanted to step on her head. Nothing less than that would do. If it was a perverted thought, then it was a perverted thought. I wasn't afraid to admit it to myself.

"All right? Really? Is that true?"

Blah, blah, blah. Who asked those questions? A zombie; not Phillip of the foyer and rug. He died in flight. I was sorry, sincerely sorry, but with clothes on my back I knew certain feelings would not survive humiliation. It was so clear it was thrilling. Perhaps she felt it, too. In any case she would have to accept it. The nature of the times. We are historical creatures. Veronica and I were finished. Before we reached her door I would say deadly words. They'd come in a natural way, kill her a little. Veronica, let me step on your head or we're through. Maybe we're through, anyway. It would deepen her looks, give philosophy to what was only charming in her face. The dawn was here. A new day. Cruel, but change is cruel. I could bear it. Love is infinite and one.

Women are not. Neither are men. The human condition. Nearly unbearable.

"No, it's not true," she said.

"What's not?"

"Things aren't all right at home."

I nodded intelligently, sighed, "Of course not. Tell me the truth, please. I don't want to hear anything else."

"Daddy had a heart attack."

"Oh God," I yelled. "Oh God, no."

I seized her hand, dropped it. She let it fall. I seized it again. No use. I let it fall. She let it drift between us. We stared at one another. She said, "What were you going to say? I can tell you were going to say something."

I stared, said nothing.

"Don't feel guilty, Phillip. Let's just go back to the apartment and have some coffee."

"What can I say?"

"Don't say anything. He's in the hospital and my mother is there. Let's just go upstairs and not say anything."

"Not say anything. Like moral imbeciles go slurp coffee and not say anything? What are we, nihilists or something? Assassins? Monsters?"

"Phillip, there's no one in the apartment. I'll make us coffee and eggs . . ."

"How about a roast beef? Got a roast beef in the freezer?"

"Phillip, he's my father."

We were at the door. I rattled. I was in a trance. This was life. Death!

"Indeed, your father. I'll accept that. I can do no less."

"Phillip, shut up. Ludwig."

The door opened. I nodded to Ludwig. What did he know about life and death? Give him a uniform and a quiet lobby— that's life and death. In the elevator he took the controls. "Always got a hand on the controls, eh Ludwig?"

Veronica smiled in a feeble, grateful way. She liked to see me get along with the help. Ludwig said, "Dots right."

"Ludwig has been our doorman for years, Phillip. Ever since I was a little girl."

"Wow," I said.

"Dots right."

The door slid open. Veronica said, "Thank you, Ludwig." I said, "Thank you, Ludwig."

"Vulcum."

"Vulcum? You mean, 'welcome'? Hey, Ludwig, how long you been in this country?"

Veronica was driving her key into the door.

"How come you never learned to talk American, baby?"

"Phillip, come here."

"I'm saying something to Ludwig."

"Come here right now."

"I have to go, Ludwig."

"Vulcum."

She went directly to the bathroom. I waited in the hallway between Vlamincks and Utrillos. The Utrillos were pale and flat. The Vlamincks were thick, twisted and red. Raw meat on one wall, dry stone on the other. Mrs. Cohen had an eye for contrasts. I heard Veronica sob. She ran water in the sink, sobbed, sat down, peed. She saw me looking and kicked the door shut.

"At a time like this . . ."

"I don't like you looking."

"Then why did you leave the door open? You obviously don't know your own mind."

"Go away, Phillip. Wait in the living room."

"Just tell me why you left the door open."

"Phillip, you're going to drive me nuts. Go away. I can't do a damn thing if I know you're standing there."

The living room made me feel better. The settee, the chandelier full of teeth and the rug were company. Mr. Cohen was everywhere, a simple, diffuse presence. He jingled change in his pocket, looked out the window and was happy he could see the park. He took a little antelope step and tears came into my eyes. I sat among his mourners. A rabbi droned platitudes: Mr. Cohen was generous, kind, beloved by his wife and daughter. "How much did he weigh?" I shouted. The phone rang.

Veronica came running down the hall. I went and stood at her side when she picked up the phone. I stood dumb, stiff as a hatrack. She was whimpering, "Yes, yes . . ." I nodded my head yes, yes, thinking it was better than no, no. She put the phone down.

"It was my mother. Daddy's all right. Mother is staying with him in his room at the hospital and they'll come home together tomorrow."

Her eyes looked at mine. At them as if they were as flat and opaque as hers. I said in a slow, stupid voice, "You're allowed to do that? Stay overnight in a hospital with a patient? Sleep in his room?" She continued looking at my eyes. I shrugged, looked down. She took my shirt front in a fist like a bite. She whispered. I said, "What?" She whispered again, "Fuck me." The clock ticked like crickets. The Vlamincks spilled blood. We sank into the rug as if it were quicksand.

17 Tommaso Landolfi

Hailed as "the Italian Kafka," Tommaso Landolfi has published several volumes of stories in Italy during the past thirty years. A collected one-volume edition of his stories, Racconti, appeared in 1961.

❖

GOGOL'S WIFE

Translated by Wayland Young

At this point, confronted with the whole complicated affair of Nikolai Vassilevitch's wife, I am overcome by hesitation. Have I any right to disclose something which is unknown to the whole world, which my unforgettable friend himself kept hidden from the world (and he had his reasons), and which I am sure will give rise to all sorts of malicious and stupid misunderstandings? Something, moreover, which will very probably offend the sensibilities of all sorts of base, hypocritical people, and possibly of some honest people too, if there are any left? And finally, have I any right to disclose something before which my own spirit recoils, and even tends toward a more or less open disapproval?

But the fact remains that, as a biographer, I have certain firm obligations. Believing as I do that every bit of information about so lofty a genius will turn out to be of value to us and to future generations, I cannot conceal something which in any case has no hope of being judged fairly and wisely until the end of time. Moreover, what right have we to condemn? Is it given to us to know, not only what intimate needs, but even what higher and wider ends may have been served by those very deeds of a lofty genius which perchance may appear to us vile? No indeed, for we understand so little of these privileged natures. "It is true," a great man once said, "that I also have to pee, but for quite different reasons."

But without more ado I will come to what I know beyond doubt, and can prove beyond question, about this controversial matter, which will now—I dare to hope—no longer be so. I will not trouble to recapitulate what is already known of it, since I do not think this should be necessary at the present stage of development of Gogol studies.

Let me say it at once: Nikolai Vassilevitch's wife was not a woman. Nor was she any sort of human being, nor any sort of living creature at all, whether animal or vegetable (although something of the sort has sometimes been hinted). She was quite simply a balloon. Yes, a balloon; and this will explain the perplexity, or even indignation, of certain biographers who were also the personal friends of the Master, and who complained that, although they often went to his house, they never saw her and "never even heard her voice." From this they deduced all sorts of dark and disgraceful complications—yes, and criminal ones too. No, gentlemen, everything is always simpler than it appears. You did not hear her voice simply because she could not speak, or to be more exact, she could only speak in certain conditions, as we shall see. And it was always, except once, in tête-à-tête with Nikolai Vassilevitch. So let us not waste time with any cheap or empty refutations but come at once to as exact and complete a description as possible of the being or object in question.

Gogol's so-called wife was an ordinary dummy made of thick rubber, naked at all seasons, buff in tint, or as is more commonly said, flesh-colored. But since women's skins are not all of the same color, I should specify that hers was a light-colored, polished skin, like that of certain brunettes. It, or she, was, it is hardly necessary to add, of feminine sex. Perhaps I should say at once that she was capable of very wide alterations of her attributes without, of course, being able to alter her sex itself. She could sometimes appear to be thin, with hardly any breasts and with narrow hips more like a young lad than a woman, and at other times to be excessively well-endowed or—let us not mince matters

—fat. And she often changed the color of her hair, both on her head and elsewhere on her body, though not necessarily at the same time. She could also seem to change in all sorts of other tiny particulars, such as the position of moles, the vitality of the mucous membranes and so forth. She could even to a certain extent change the very color of her skin. One is faced with the necessity of asking oneself who she really was, or whether it would be proper to speak of a single "person"—and in fact we shall see that it would be imprudent to press this point.

The cause of these changes, as my readers will already have understood, was nothing else but the will of Nikolai Vassilevitch himself. He would inflate her to a greater or lesser degree, would change her wig and her other tufts of hair, would grease her with ointments and touch her up in various ways so as to obtain more or less the type of woman which suited him at that moment. Following the natural inclinations of his fancy, he even amused himself sometimes by producing grotesque or monstrous forms; as will be readily understood, she became deformed when inflated beyond a certain point or if she remained below a certain pressure.

But Gogol soon tired of these experiments, which he held to be "after all, not very respectful" to his wife, whom he loved in his own way—however inscrutable it may remain to us. He loved her, but which of these incarnations, we may ask ourselves, did he love? Alas, I have already indicated that the end of the present account will furnish some sort of an answer. And how can I have stated above that it was Nikolai Vassilevitch's will which ruled that woman? In a certain sense, yes, it is true; but it is equally certain that she soon became no longer his slave but his tyrant. And here yawns the abyss, or if you prefer it, the Jaws of Tartarus. But let us not anticipate.

I have said that Gogol obtained with his manipulations more or less the type of woman which he needed from time to time. I should add that when, in rare cases, the form he obtained perfectly incarnated his desire, Nikolai Vassilevitch fell in love with it "exclusively," as he said in his own words, and that this was enough to render "her" stable for a certain time—until he fell out of love with "her." I counted no more than three or four of these violent passions—or, as I suppose they would be called today, infatuations—in the life (dare I say in the conjugal life?) of the great writer. It will be convenient to add here that a few years after what one may call his marriage, Gogol had even given a name to his wife. It was Caracas, which is, unless I am mistaken, the capital of Venezuela. I have never been able to discover the reason for this choice: great minds are so capricious!

Speaking only of her normal appearance, Caracas was what is called a fine woman—well built and proportioned in every part. She had every smallest attribute of her sex properly disposed in the proper location. Particularly worthy of attention were her genital organs (if the adjective is permissible in such a context). They were formed by means of ingenious folds in the rubber. Nothing was forgotten, and their operation was rendered easy by various devices, as well as by the internal pressure of the air.

Caracas also had a skeleton, even though a rudimentary one. Perhaps it was made of whalebone. Special care had been devoted to the construction of the thoracic cage, of the pelvic basin and of the cranium. The first two systems were more or less visible in accordance with the thickness of the fatty layer, if I may so describe it, which covered them. It is a great pity that Gogol never let me know the name of the creator of such a fine piece of work. There was an obstinacy in his refusal which was never quite clear to me.

Nikolai Vassilevitch blew his wife up through the anal sphincter with a pump of his own invention, rather like those which you hold down with your two feet and which are used today in all sorts of mechanical workshops. Situated in the anus was a little one-way valve, or whatever the correct technical description would be, like the mitral valve of the heart, which, once the body was inflated, allowed more air to come in but none to go out. To deflate, one unscrewed a stopper in the mouth, at the back of the throat.

And that, I think, exhausts the description of the most note-worthy peculiarities of this being. Unless perhaps I should mention the splendid rows of white teeth which adorned her mouth and the dark eyes which, in spite of their immobility, perfectly simulated life. Did I say simulate? Good heavens, simulate is not the word! Nothing seems to be the word, when one is speaking

of Caracas! Even these eyes could undergo a change of color, by
means of a special process to which, since it was long and tire-
some, Gogol seldom had recourse. Finally, I should speak of her
voice, which it was only once given to me to hear. But I cannot
do that without going more fully into the relationship between
husband and wife, and in this I shall no longer be able to answer
to the truth of everything with absolute certitude. On my conscience I could not—so confused, both in itself and in my memory,
is that which I now have to tell.

Here, then, as they occur to me, are some of my memories.

The first and, as I said, the last time I ever heard Caracas
speak to Nikolai Vassilevitch was one evening when we were
absolutely alone. We were in the room where the woman, if I
may be allowed the expression, lived. Entrance to this room was
strictly forbidden to everybody. It was furnished more or less in
the Oriental manner, had no windows and was situated in the
most inaccessible part of the house. I did know that she could
talk, but Gogol had never explained to me the circumstances
under which this happened. There were only the two of us, or
three, in there. Nikolai Vassilevitch and I were drinking vodka
and discussing Butkov's novel. I remember that we left this topic,
and he was maintaining the necessity for radical reforms in the
laws of inheritance. We had almost forgotten her. It was then
that, with a husky and submissive voice, like Venus on the nuptial
couch, she said point-blank: "I want to go poo poo."

I jumped, thinking I had misheard, and looked across at her.
She was sitting on a pile of cushions against the wall; that evening
she was a soft, blonde beauty, rather well-covered. Her expression
seemed commingled of shrewdness and slyness, childishness and
irresponsibility. As for Gogol, he blushed violently and, leaping on
her, stuck two fingers down her throat. She immediately began
to shrink and to turn pale; she took on once again that lost and
astonished air which was especially hers, and was in the end reduced to no more than a flabby skin on a perfunctory bony arma-
ture. Since, for practical reasons which will readily be divined,
she had an extraordinarily flexible backbone, she folded up almost
in two, and for the rest of the evening she looked up at us from
where she had slithered to the floor, in utter abjection.

All Gogol said was: "She only does it for a joke, or to annoy me, because as a matter of fact she does not have such needs." In the presence of other people, that is to say of me, he generally made a point of treating her with a certain disdain.

We went on drinking and talking, but Nikolai Vassilevitch seemed very much disturbed and absent in spirit. Once he suddenly interrupted what he was saying, seized my hand in his and burst into tears. "What can I do now?" he exclaimed. "You understand, Foma Paskalovitch, that I loved her?"

It is necessary to point out that it was impossible, except by a miracle, ever to repeat any of Caracas' forms. She was a fresh creation every time, and it would have been wasted effort to seek to find again the exact proportions, the exact pressure, and so forth, of a former Caracas. Therefore the plumpish blonde of that evening was lost to Gogol from that time forth forever; this was in fact the tragic end of one of those few loves of Nikolai Vassilevitch, which I described above. He gave me no explanation; he sadly rejected my proffered comfort, and that evening we parted early. But his heart had been laid bare to me in that outburst. He was no longer so reticent with me, and soon had hardly any secrets left. And this, I may say in parenthesis, caused me very great pride.

It seems that things had gone well for the "couple" at the beginning of their life together. Nikolai Vassilevitch had been content with Caracas and slept regularly with her in the same bed. He continued to observe this custom till the end, saying with a timid smile that no companion could be quieter or less importunate than she. But I soon began to doubt this, especially judging by the state he was sometimes in when he woke up. Then, after several years, their relationship began strangely to deteriorate.

All this, let it be said once and for all, is no more than a schematic attempt at an explanation. About that time the woman actually began to show signs of independence or, as one might say, of autonomy. Nikolai Vassilevitch had the extraordinary impression that she was acquiring a personality of her own, indecipherable perhaps, but still distinct from his, and one which slipped through his fingers. It is certain that some sort of continuity was established between each of her appearances—between all those brunettes, those blondes, those redheads and auburn-headed girls, between those plump, those slim, those dusky or snowy or golden beauties, there was a certain something in common. At the beginning of this chapter I cast some doubt on the propriety of considering Caracas as a unitary personality; nevertheless I myself could not quite, whenever I saw her, free myself of the impression that, however unheard of it may seem, this was fundamentally the same woman. And it may be that this was why Gogol felt he had to give her a name.

An attempt to establish in what precisely subsisted the common attributes of the different forms would be quite another thing. Perhaps it was no more and no less than the creative afflatus of Nikolai Vassilevitch himself. But no, it would have been too singular and strange if he had been so much divided off from himself, so much averse to himself. Because whoever she was, Caracas was a disturbing presence and even—it is better to be quite clear—a hostile one. Yet neither Gogol nor I ever succeeded in formulating a remotely tenable hypothesis as to her true nature; when I say formulate, I mean in terms which would be at once rational and accessible to all. But I cannot pass over an extraordinary event which took place at this time.

Caracas fell ill of a shameful disease—or rather Gogol did—though he was not then having, nor had he ever had, any contact with other women. I will not even try to describe how this happened, or where the filthy complaint came from; all I know is that it happened. And that my great, unhappy friend would say to me: "So, Foma Paskalovitch, you see what lay at the heart of Caracas; it was the spirit of syphilis."

Sometimes he would even blame himself in a quite absurd manner; he was always prone to self-accusation. This incident was a real catastrophe as far as the already obscure relationship between husband and wife, and the hostile feelings of Nikolai Vassilevitch himself, were concerned. He was compelled to undergo long-drawn-out and painful treatment—the treatment of those days—and the situation was aggravated by the fact that the disease in the woman did not seem to be easily curable. Gogol deluded himself for some time that, by blowing his wife up and down and furnishing her with the most widely divergent aspects, he could obtain a woman immune from the contagion, but he was forced to desist when no results were forthcoming.

I shall be brief, seeking not to tire my readers, and also because what I remember seems to become more and more confused. I shall therefore hasten to the tragic conclusion. As to this last, however, let there be no mistake. I must once again make it clear that I am very sure of my ground. I was an eyewitness. Would that I had not been!

The years went by. Nikolai Vassilevitch's distaste for his wife became stronger, though his love for her did not show any signs of diminishing. Toward the end, aversion and attachment struggled so fiercely with each other in his heart that he became quite stricken, almost broken up. His restless eyes, which habitually assumed so many different expressions and sometimes spoke so sweetly to the heart of his interlocutor, now almost always shone with a fevered light, as if he were under the effect of a drug. The strangest impulses arose in him, accompanied by the most senseless fears. He spoke to me of Caracas more and more often, accusing her of unthinkable and amazing things. In these regions I could not follow him, since I had but a sketchy acquaintance with his wife, and hardly any intimacy—and above all since my sensibility was so limited compared with his. I shall accordingly restrict myself to reporting some of his accusations, without reference to my personal impressions.

"Believe it or not, Foma Paskalovitch," he would, for example, often say to me: "Believe it or not, *she's aging!*" Then, unspeakably moved, he would, as was his way, take my hands in his. He also accused Caracas of giving herself up to solitary pleasures, which he had expressly forbidden. He even went so far as to charge her with betraying him, but the things he said became so extremely obscure that I must excuse myself from any further account of them.

One thing that appears certain is that toward the end Caracas, whether aged or not, had turned into a bitter creature, querulous, hypocritical and subject to religious excess. I do not exclude the possibility that she may have had an influence on Gogol's moral position during the last period of his life, a position which is sufficiently well known. The tragic climax came one night quite unexpectedly when Nikolai Vassilevitch and I were celebrating his silver wedding—one of the last evenings we were to spend together. I neither can nor should attempt to set down what it was that led to his decision, at a time when to all appearances he was resigned to tolerating his consort. I know not what new events had taken place that day. I shall confine myself to the facts; my readers must make what they can of them.

That evening Nikolai Vassilevitch was unusually agitated. His distaste for Caracas seemed to have reached an unprecedented intensity. The famous "pyre of vanities"—the burning of his manuscripts—had already taken place; I should not like to say whether or not at the instigation of his wife. His state of mind had been further inflamed by other causes. As to his physical condition, this was ever more pitiful, and strengthened my impression that he took drugs. All the same, he began to talk in a more or less normal way about Belinsky, who was giving him some trouble with his attacks on the *Selected Correspondence*. Then suddenly, tears rising to his eyes, he interrupted himself and cried out: "No. No. It's too much, too much. I can't go on any longer," as well as other obscure and disconnected phrases which he would not clarify. He seemed to be talking to himself. He wrung his hands, shook his head, got up and sat down again after having taken four or five anxious steps round the room. When Caracas appeared, or rather when he went in to her later in the evening in her Oriental chamber, he controlled himself no longer and began to behave like an old man, if I may so express myself, in his second childhood, quite giving way to his absurd impulses. For instance, he kept nudging me and winking and senselessly repeating: "There she is, Foma Paskalovitch; there she is!" Meanwhile she seemed to look up at us with a disdainful attention. But behind these "mannerisms" one could feel in him a real repugnance, a repugnance which had, I suppose, now reached the limits of the endurable. Indeed . . .

After a certain time Nikolai Vassilevitch seemed to pluck up courage. He burst into tears, but somehow they were more manly tears. He wrung his hands again, seized mine in his, and walked up and down, muttering: "That's enough! We can't have any more of this. This is an unheard of thing. How can such a thing be happening to me? How can a man be expected to put up with this?"

He then leapt furiously upon the pump, the existence of which he seemed just to have remembered, and, with it in his hand, dashed like a whirlwind to Caracas. He inserted the tube in her anus and began to inflate her. . . . Weeping the while, he shouted like one possessed: "Oh, how I love her, how I love her, my poor, poor darling! . . . But she's going to burst! Unhappy Caracas, most pitiable of God's creatures! But die she must!"

Caracas was swelling up. Nikolai Vassilevitch sweated, wept and pumped. I wished to stop him but, I know not why, I had not the courage. She began to become deformed and shortly assumed the most monstrous aspect; and yet she had not given any signs of alarm—she was used to these jokes. But when she began to feel unbearably full, or perhaps when Nikolai Vassilevitch's intentions became plain to her, she took on an expression of bestial amazement, even a little beseeching, but still without losing that disdainful look. She was afraid, she was even committing herself to his mercy, but still she could not believe in the immediate approach of her fate; she could not believe in the frightful audacity of her husband. He could not see her face because he was behind her. But I looked at her with fascination, and did not move a finger.

At last the internal pressure came through the fragile bones at the base of her skull, and printed on her face an indescribable rictus. Her belly, her thighs, her lips, her breasts and what I could see of her buttocks had swollen to incredible proportions. All of a sudden she belched, and gave a long hissing groan; both these phenomena one could explain by the increase in pressure, which had suddenly forced a way out through the valve in her throat. Then her eyes bulged frantically, threatening to jump out of their sockets. Her ribs flared wide apart and were no longer attached to the sternum, and she resembled a python digesting a donkey. A donkey, did I say? An ox! An elephant! At this point I believed her already dead, but Nikolai Vassilevitch, sweating, weeping and repeating: "My dearest! My beloved! My best!" continued to pump.

She went off unexpectedly and, as it were, all of a piece. It

was not one part of her skin which gave way and the rest which
followed, but her whole surface at the same instant. She scattered
in the air. The pieces fell more or less slowly, according to their
size, which was in no case above a very restricted one. I distinctly
remember a piece of her cheek, with some lip attached, hanging
on the corner of the mantelpiece. Nikolai Vassilevitch stared at
me like a madman. Then he pulled himself together and, once
more with furious determination, he began carefully to collect
those poor rags which once had been the shining skin of Caracas,
and all of her.

"Good-by, Caracas," I thought I heard him murmur, "Good-
by! You were too pitiable!" And then suddenly and quite
audibly: "The fire! The fire! She too must end up in the fire."
He crossed himself—with his left hand, of course. Then, when
he had picked up all those shriveled rags, even climbing on the
furniture so as not to miss any, he threw them straight on the
fire in the hearth, where they began to burn slowly and with an
excessively unpleasant smell. Nikolai Vassilevitch, like all Russians,
had a passion for throwing important things in the fire.

Red in the face, with an inexpressible look of despair, and yet
of sinister triumph too, he gazed on the pyre of those miserable
remains. He had seized my arm and was squeezing it convulsively.
But those traces of what had once been a being were hardly well
alight when he seemed yet again to pull himself together, as if
he were suddenly remembering something or taking a painful
decision. In one bound he was out of the room.

A few seconds later I heard him speaking to me through the
door in a broken, plaintive voice: "Foma Paskalovitch, I want you
to promise not to look. *Golubchik*, promise not to look at me
when I come in."

I don't know what I answered, or whether I tried to reassure
him in any way. But he insisted, and I had to promise him, as if
he were a child, to hide my face against the wall and only turn
round when he said I might. The door then opened violently and
Nikolai Vassilevitch burst into the room and ran to the fireplace.

And here I must confess my weakness, though I consider it
justified by the extraordinary circumstances. I looked round before
Nikolai Vassilevitch told me I could; it was stronger than me. I

was just in time to see him carrying something in his arms, something which he threw on the fire with all the rest, so that it suddenly flared up. At that, since the desire to see had entirely mastered every other thought in me, I dashed to the fireplace. But Nikolai Vassilevitch placed himself between me and it and pushed me back with a strength of which I had not believed him capable. Meanwhile the object was burning and giving off clouds of smoke. And before he showed any sign of calming down there was nothing left but a heap of silent ashes.

The true reason why I wished to see was because I had already glimpsed. But it was only a glimpse, and perhaps I should not allow myself to introduce even the slightest element of uncertainty into this true story. And yet, an eyewitness account is not complete without a mention of that which the witness knows with less than complete certainty. To cut a long story short, that something was a baby. Not a flesh and blood baby, of course, but more something in the line of a rubber doll or a model. Something, which, to judge by its appearance, could have been called *Caracas' son.*

Was I mad too? That I do not know, but I do know that this was what I saw, not clearly, but with my own eyes. And I wonder why it was that when I was writing this just now I didn't mention that when Nikolai Vassilevitch came back into the room he was muttering between his clenched teeth: "Him too! Him too!"

And that is the sum of my knowledge of Nikolai Vassilevitch's wife. In the next chapter I shall tell what happened to him afterwards, and that will be the last chapter of his life. But to give an interpretation of his feelings for his wife, or indeed for anything, is quite another and more difficult matter, though I have attempted it elsewhere in this volume, and refer the reader to that modest effort. I hope I have thrown sufficient light on a most controversial question and that I have unveiled the mystery, if not of Gogol, then at least of his wife. In the course of this I have implicitly given the lie to the insensate accusation that he ill-treated or even beat his wife, as well as other like absurdities. And what else can be the goal of a humble biographer such as the present writer but to serve the memory of that lofty genius who is the object of his study?

18 Jerome Charyn

Jerome Charyn's fourth novel, American Scrapbook, was published in 1969.
He teaches at Lehman College of the City University of New York.

◈

THE MAN WHO GREW YOUNGER

Bernstein, the translator, warily climbed the first of the forty-nine
steps that led to Misha's room: he was on the lookout for spiders
and rats. He stopped after the twenty-fifth step and removed a
lumpy handkerchief from his vest pocket. "Misha, Misha," he
mumbled plaintively to himself, and, holding his swollen hand
against his chest, he checked his heartbeat. A long furrow appeared
at the back of his bald head. Bernstein was convinced that he
was going to die before he reached the forty-ninth step. He cursed
himself for associating with publishers and poets. And he peti-
tioned the devil to destroy the stairway.

He knocked timidly on Misha's door. Bernstein was not worried. He knew that if he waited long enough Misha would let
him in. And so, to while away the time, he started talking to
himself. He hurled prolific curses at Misha, and Popkin the publisher, and then cursed himself for not being a haberdasher. He
envisioned himself boiling Misha and Popkin, Pushkin and Peretz,
Gogol and Sholem Aleichem in a huge blackened pot. The door
opened suddenly, and Misha's bloodless face startled Bernstein.
His untrimmed mustache and deeply cloven chin reminded Bernstein of some sinister Jack of Spades he had once seen in a deck
of hand-painted cards belonging to a one-eyed Armenian.

"So?" Bernstein said. "Are you letting me in or not?" and then he shuffled past Misha. Six or seven black penholders stood in a cracked jar on the desk near the door. A bottle of ink with a rubber plug and a single penpoint were stationed near the jar. A notebook with irregularly-lined paper sat on a narrow bench behind the desk. Bernstein hovered around Misha's steam pipe and slowly warmed his hands. Near the steam pipe was a toilet with a chipped seat and a huge wooden basin that Misha used for a bathtub. Bernstein's jaw dropped suddenly and he moved away from the steam pipe. "Bandit," he called out, and he chased a cockroach across the room. Misha removed the plug from the ink bottle and selected a penholder. The cockroach eluded Bernstein, and he sat on the toilet seat and brooded for a moment. The sound of Misha's pen scratching the notebook paper roused him, and he placed his elbows on his knees and rocked back and forth on the toilet seat. He waited for Misha's pen to stop moving, but the scratching sound continued. "Misha, I talked again to Popkin. Misha . . ."

He clapped his knees together. "Misha, I'm sixty-seven years old. Can I go out now and look for a job?" He complained to the steam pipe. "A chance comes along once in a lifetime and he says no!" Then he stared darkly at Misha and started rocking again. "Sure, you can afford to be particular. You at least have Rosalie the Widow to look after you. But not everyone can be a poet. I don't have a widow to wash for me my underwear. After all . . . Misha!"

Misha's stooped back shielded him from Bernstein's onslaught, and he continued to lean over the desk and write. Bernstein decided to attack him from another position. He was not desperate; he knew that Misha was vulnerable. So he stood up and walked around the desk. Misha's face hardened, but the hand that held the pen trembled slightly. Bernstein gripped the edge of the desk and glared at Misha. The penholders rattled in the cracked jar.

"Forty years I worked with you, Misha. Forty years. I was for you an agent, a friend, a translator, a father!" He held out the swollen fingers of his left hand. "For five years I went to night school just to learn English so I could translate for you your stories and your poems. You remember, Misha, how I would run over to Henry Street in the snow or in the rain without galoshes or a scarf or a coat, and with my grammar book under my shirt, so it shouldn't get wet. I did it for me, Misha, eh? For me! Sure, when they saw you sitting in Ratner's or the Royale, everybody said, 'Misha Dubrinoff, the Yiddish Lermontov!' And they all laughed at me. They saw me with my grammar book, and they called me *Yeshiva bucher*. After all, who needed Broadway when you had Second Avenue? And I warned you, and Shmulka, and Boris. Wait, I said, wait. In ten years everybody will move away from Delancey Street and then only the bedbugs and the lice will have the time to read your poems and your plays. So I wasn't a hundred percent right. It took thirty years instead of ten! Misha . . ."

Misha placed his pen on the table and closed the ink bottle. Bernstein pressed his perspiring face closer to him. "For twenty years I'm running after Popkin. 'Popkin,' I tell him, 'I know you publish books only in English. Who can blame you? After all, you're a businessman. So let me, I'll translate five or ten of Misha's stories, put them in a book, and I give you my personal guarantee that I will sell for you myself ten thousand copies. What, Misha is the king of Delancey Street. They worship him!' 'No,' he says, 'no. Who needs Yiddish poets!' 'Popkin, with my translation he'll be another Shakespeare.' 'One Shakespeare,' he says, 'is enough.' So I send him letters, and notes, and telegrams, I call him on the telephone three times every week, I curse him, I threaten him, but it does me no good. They see me come near his office and they lock the doors. He threatens yet to call the police. And then, all of a sudden, everybody is reading Peretz and Bashevis Singer, and it becomes fashionable to print Yiddish poets, and now he's the one who sends telegrams and notes. Misha, I know, I know he's a low life, but a publisher is a publisher!"

Bernstein produced three crumpled letters from his vest pocket. "Here, Misha, read for yourself." He placed the letters one at a time on the table. Misha walked away from the table and stood near the toilet seat. Bernstein's temples pounded; he expected a heart attack or a stroke. He clasped his hands and calmed himself.

"Misha. Do I have to walk around for the rest of my life with one suit to my name? Misha, do it, do it for me!" He shuffled blindly toward the toilet seat, banging his shoulder against the steam pipe. "Misha, if not for you I could have become a haberdasher, like my sister's husband. With my own store and everything. But I stuck instead with you. . . ." Bernstein watched Misha's shoulders slump, and he continued his attack. "Sure, I could have married Fritzie, the baker's daughter, and by now I would be living in Riverdale with two Buicks and a Siamese cat. But who needs Riverdale? Misha, I'm asking from you something so terrible? . . . I'm trying to help you! With Popkin, who knows, you could even win a Pulitzer Prize! Give me the green light. Misha, yes?"

"No."

Bernstein checked his heartbeat hastily and dropped down on the toilet seat. He was trying to regroup his forces for another attack. He stalled for a moment. "So give me at least a reason."

"I don't have to give out reasons. No is no."

"Misha. One reason."

The cleft in Misha's chin deepened and his nostrils flared.

"If Popkin wants me, let him publish the stories I'm writing now, not the stories I wrote thirty years ago."

"Misha, who can understand the stories you're writing now? I mean it! Now you write riddles, not stories. Cows that talk in ten languages, men who grow younger instead of older, women who go around naked day and night. Can you blame Popkin if he doesn't like them? You don't even bother to write sentences any more! Misha, honest to God, last week it took me three days to translate one line. I don't understand the stories in Yiddish, so how can I write them over in English?"

"Then let Popkin hire another translator!"

Bernstein stared dumbly at the steam pipe and mumbled to himself. "For forty years I work for him and now he says Popkin should find another translator." He closed his eyes and rocked back and forth on the toilet seat with a demonic half-broken rhythm; the hinges began to creak. One of the penholders fell out of the jar and rolled toward the edge of the table. Bernstein quieted the toilet seat and shamefully opened one eye. Misha placed a package in his lap. Bernstein's fingers clutched the package incredulously.

"Go already!" Misha said. "Burn together with Popkin."

Bernstein tried to mask his emotion. "Misha, are you sure you didn't leave out any of the old stories. Popkin wants all of them."

Misha lifted Bernstein off the toilet seat and carried him toward the door. Bernstein, cradled in Misha's arms, held the package against his chest. Misha put him down near the door.

"Bernstein, I never asked you to be my translator."

"I know," Bernstein said wistfully, "that's my fate."

Misha pushed him outside the door. "Misha, you won't regret it. You'll see. Stick with me, Misha, and you'll never go wrong." The door closed, but Bernstein kept talking. Then he paused and knocked on the door with one finger. "Misha?" He knocked again. "Misha? . . . Don't worry. Leave everything to me. I'll make sure that Popkin takes the story about the man who grows younger. I'll finish translating it tonight."

Bernstein gripped the banister with his left hand. And for the first time in his life the forty-nine steps did not gall him.

"Misha, Misha, Misha."

Rosalie the Widow stacked the empty Pepsi-Cola bottles in even rows near the steam pipe, and then, with one sweeping motion, dusted and washed Misha's toilet seat. Rosalie's washcloth was ubiquitous. Misha retreated behind his desk; he was in no mood to have his ears and his armpits scrubbed.

Rosalie cursed him. "Pig." Misha eyed her washcloth and remained behind his desk. She removed his books from the floor, dusted them, and paying no attention whatsoever to author or title, she arranged them on the shelf that her own brother, Itzie, had made for Misha. Misha despised the shelf. But he knew that if the shelf disappeared his life would be in danger. Itzie Himmelfarb was the sheriff of Delancey Street. When Bilka Bendelson terrorized the entire East Side thirty years ago, Itzie organized every butcher from Ludlow Street to East Broadway. And one day in June Itzie and his butcher army marched on Bilka's Second

Avenue headquarters, and drove Bilka and his stooges out of the East Side for good.

Rosalie put her washcloth on top of the shelf, and for the first time Misha allowed himself to relax, and even dared to light a cigarette.

"Misha," Rosalie said, "so?"

Misha pretended that he was working. But he knew that there was no real way of avoiding her.

"How long will I have to remain a widow?"

Rosalie picked up her washcloth again, and Misha dropped his cigarette.

"Misha," she said, "Itzie wants an answer. Five years is time enough. . . . Misha, remember, I have property."

"I know."

"Five offers I had last week. Five. Everybody wants to marry me. Misha, honest to God, Rabbi Gershenson is ready to divorce his wife."

Misha laughed for Rosalie's sake.

"Misha, how long can I wait? Give me already an answer. Yes or no."

Misha tried to avoid both Scylla and Charybdis. "No," and Itzie would be up in a minute and throw him off the roof. "Yes," and he would have to put up with Rosalie's washcloth day and night in this world and the next. But the constant agony of "maybe" was becoming for Misha a fate worse than Scylla and Charybdis combined.

"Misha," Rosalie said, "yes or no."

Misha glared at the Pepsi-Cola bottles stacked near the steam pipe. "No," he said, first to himself, and then to Rosalie. He had to tell her again before she would believe him. She folded her washcloth.

"Wait," she said, "wait. Leads a widow on for five years. Wait. You expect Itzie to stand around while his sister is disgraced? . . . Misha, I'm thinking now only of you. Maybe you should reconsider."

The cleft in Misha's chin deepened, and Rosalie knew that Misha's "no" was final. She felt a pain in her chest and started to cry. "Bum, bastard," she said. "A poet I had to pick! Itzie warned me not to wait around. He'll knock nails in your head for what you did to me. Nails."

From Misha's desk she stole the aluminum lamp with the retractable neck that she had given to him for his fifty-seventh birthday. She tore the lamp's shade and broke the retractable neck, and after depositing the remnants of the lamp on top of the shelf she sneezed and left.

The broken neck of the lamp kept swinging jauntily over the sides of the shelf and seemed to perform for Misha. He knew that it would be useless to hide or barricade the door, and so he sat and waited for Itzie. After searching through the shelf he found a battered copy of Sholem Aleichem's stories, and sitting at his desk, he began to read.

When Misha heard the doorknob rattle he put down the book. His knees were knocking, and he chided himself for being afraid. For a moment he even wished that he had stalled Rosalie at least a little while longer. He might have packed his books and moved uptown. But no matter where he had gone—Parkchester, Scarsdale, or Tel Aviv—Himmelfarb would have found him in the end. He smiled philosophically to himself and waited for Itzie to break down the door. The doorknob stopped rattling. Faintly, almost inaudibly, he heard someone call his name. He knew who was standing outside his room.

Bernstein kept wheezing. "Who can climb steps any more?" Misha unbuttoned the collar of Bernstein's shirt, brought him a glass of cognac, and then bolted the door. Bernstein was crying.

"Misha," he said, "Popkin refused us." He sought Misha's toilet seat. "Refused us. 'Popkin,' I said, 'take ten of the old and one of the new.' 'No,' he says. He changed his mind. He's no longer interested in Yiddish writers. Just like a whore. Now Mexican poets are in fashion. Misha, I begged him. 'Popkin, Popkin, take "The Man Who Grew Younger," you can't go wrong. Let ten years go by and it will be a classic. Popkin, I'm giving you my guarantee.' Classics he doesn't need. Only Mexican writers." He stumbled across the room, narrowly missing the steam pipe and the Pepsi-Cola bottles, and finally found the toilet seat. "Misha, are you listening to me or not?"

"What, what?"

"The deal with Popkin is off. We can't even worm from him a cent. You, you're a lucky man. You still have Rosalie."

Misha's lips shaped an ironic smile. "No more Rosalie. I packed her in."

Bernstein rocked his head in disbelief. "Misha, you gave up a gold mine. The woman is worth a fortune. Gershenson told me himself. He knows her finances. . . . Is this a Misha! Worse than a child. Misha, I mean it, without me you would be lost altogether. Forget about Rosalie! How will you handle Himmelfarb?" Bernstein, absorbed in Misha's sorrows, sucked his lip. "Misha, I have a plan. I'll take Rosalie off your hands. Sure, for you I'll make the sacrifice. You think that will satisfy Itzie, hah?" He drew his knees together and answered his own question. "What's the use, a *zhlub* like that, he'll fracture your head together with mine."

Bernstein clutched his chest; his lips turned ashen and his eyebrows twitched. Misha strode across the room and gripped Bernstein's hand. Then he stooped, lifted Bernstein gently, and brought him over to the bed. Bernstein's eyebrows stopped twitching. Misha covered him with a blanket. "See," Bernstein said, raising his chest wearily, "see. If it's not the heart then it's the liver. Misha, maybe I should go home?"

"Stay."

"So where will you sleep?"

"What, the bed is not big enough for two?"

"Misha, you know me. I snore. And I talk all the time when I sleep. Misha, I'll rest here for a little while and then I'll go."

"Bernstein, you have to make such a big production out of staying in a bed. Do, do whatever you want. But remember, you won't find an escalator outside my door."

Bernstein envisioned himself tumbling down Misha's forty-nine steps, and his lips turned ashen again. "Misha, maybe you're right. I'll stay here tonight. Misha, why are you standing by the door? Are you expecting somebody?"

"I'm expecting Itzie."

"Itzie," Bernstein said, "I almost forgot." He pulled away the blanket. "Misha, let's stay better at my place."

"My place, your place. He'll find me just the same."

"Misha, maybe we should go to Mexico? I mean it."

Misha covered Bernstein again. "Go, sleep. You give me headaches with your speeches."

Bernstein sat glumly for a moment.

"Misha—"

"What?"

"Don't worry about Itzie. I'll talk to him. Itzie listens to me. 'Itzie,' I'll tell him, 'What's fair is fair. There's no obligation on Misha's part. Where's the contract? The rabbi was never called in. Misha never promised to marry her. But it's his misfortune. Rosalie is a jewel. And she has bonds yet and two houses in Brownsville. Itzie, believe me, Rosalie is better off. Misha's no bargain. The man never worked a day in his life. Let him *drai* someone else's *kop* with his poetry.' Misha, what do you think? He'll listen to me or not?"

Misha stood near the steam pipe. Bernstein kept counseling Itzie, Misha, and himself. "You'll see. All right, I'm not the Baal Shem, but I know how to talk. And if Itzie brings Rosalie with him, I'll take her over to the toilet seat and talk to her privately. 'Rosalie,' I'll say, 'live and laugh. You should be glad he's giving you your release. . . .'"

"Go to sleep."

Bernstein hid under the blanket.

"Misha?"

Misha raised his arms despairingly.

"What does he say, your man, your man who grows younger all the time? *'The world is a shithouse.'* The man is a lunatic, but honest to God, he's a hundred percent right. A shithouse!" Bernstein clapped his knees. "Nobody, not Chekhov, not Tolstoy, not Babel, not Gogol, not Sholem Aleichem, nobody writes a story like Misha Dubrinoff."

Bernstein's chin dropped onto his sunken chest. He slept quietly.

Misha kept vigil near the toilet seat.

"Bastards," Bernstein cried out in his sleep, "bastards. Popkin, listen to me!"

Misha approached the bed. He gripped Bernstein's hand.

Bernstein opened one eye. "Misha, did he come yet, the *zhlub?*"

"No."

"Don't worry, Misha. I know how to handle him. Don't worry. You'll see. Itzie listens to me. Misha, should I run home and get my balalaika? My balalaika could bring over the devil to our side. Misha, you know it. Misha, you think he'll come? Maybe we should both run over to the precinct. There we'll be safe. Misha, maybe he won't come. Maybe Rosalie forgot to tell him. Misha, what do you think?"

"He'll be here. If not now, then later. If not today, then tomorrow. This I can guarantee."

Bernstein humped his back. "So what can we do? We'll wait for him."

They sat in the dark. Bernstein cursed Itzie and Popkin. Misha watched the door.

19 Donald Barthelme

Donald Barthelme was born in Philadelphia and grew up in Texas. He has published a highly original short novel, Snow White (1967), and two collections of stories, Come Back, Dr. Caligari (1964) and Unspeakable Practices, Unnatural Acts (1968).

❖

THE INDIAN UPRISING

We defended the city as best we could. The arrows of the Comanches came in clouds. The war clubs of the Comanches clattered on the soft, yellow pavements. There were earthworks along the Boulevard Mark Clark and the hedges had been laced with sparkling wire. People were trying to understand. I spoke to Sylvia. "Do you think this is a good life?" The table held apples, books, long-playing records. She looked up. "No."

Patrols of paras and volunteers with armbands guarded the tall, flat buildings. We interrogated the captured Comanche. Two of us forced his head back while another poured water into his nostrils. His body jerked, he choked and wept. Not believing a hurried, careless, and exaggerated report of the number of casualties in the outer districts where trees, lamps, swans had been reduced to clear fields of fire we issued entrenching tools to those who seemed trustworthy and turned the heavy-weapons companies so that we could not be surprised from that direction. And I sat there getting drunker and drunker and more in love and more in love. We talked.

"Do you know Fauré's 'Dolly'?"

"Would that be Gabriel Fauré?"

"It would."

"Then I know it," she said. "May I say that I play it at certain times, when I am sad, or happy, although it requires four hands."

"How is that managed?"

"I accelerate," she said, "ignoring the time signature."

And when they shot the scene in the bed I wondered how you felt under the eyes of the cameramen, grips, juicers, men in the mixing booth: excited? stimulated? And when they shot the scene in the shower I sanded a hollow-core door working carefully against the illustrations in texts and whispered instructions from one who had already solved the problem. I had made after all other tables, one while living with Nancy, one while living with Alice, one while living with Eunice, one while living with Marianne.

Red men in waves like people scattering in a square startled by something tragic or a sudden, loud noise accumulated against the barricades we had made of window dummies, silk, thoughtfully planned job descriptions (including scales for the orderly progress of other colors), wine in demijohns, and robes. I analyzed the composition of the barricade nearest me and found two ashtrays, ceramic, one dark brown and one dark brown with an orange blur at the lip; a tin frying pan; two-litre bottles of red wine; three-quarter-litre bottles of Black & White, aquavit, cognac, vodka, gin, Fad #6 sherry; a hollow-core door in birch veneer on black wrought-iron legs; a blanket, red-orange with faint blue stripes; a red pillow and a blue pillow; a woven straw wastebasket; two glass jars for flowers; corkscrews and can openers; two plates and two cups, ceramic, dark brown; a yellow-and-purple poster; a Yugoslavian carved flute, wood, dark brown; and other items. I decided I knew nothing.

The hospitals dusted wounds with powders the worth of which was not quite established, other supplies having been exhausted early in the first day. I decided I knew nothing. Friends put me in touch with a Miss R., a teacher, unorthodox they said, excellent they said, successful with difficult cases, steel shutters on the windows made the house safe. I had just learned via an International Distress Coupon that Jane had been beaten up by a dwarf in a bar on Tenerife but Miss R. did not allow me to speak of it.

"You know nothing," she said, "you feel nothing, you are locked in a most savage and terrible ignorance, I despise you, my boy, mon cher, my heart. You may attend but you must not attend now, you must attend later, a day or a week or an hour, you are making me ill. . . ." I nonevaluated these remarks as Korzybski instructed. But it was difficult. Then they pulled back in a feint near the river and we rushed into that sector with a reinforced battalion hastily formed among the Zouaves and cabdrivers. This unit was crushed in the afternoon of a day that began with spoons and letters in hallways and under windows where men tasted the history of the heart, cone-shaped muscular organ that maintains circulation of the blood.

But it is you I want now, here in the middle of this Uprising, with the streets yellow and threatening, short, ugly lances with fur at the throat and inexplicable shell money lying in the grass. It is when I am with you that I am happiest, and it is for you that I am making this hollow-core door table with black wrought-iron legs. I held Sylvia by her bear-claw necklace. "Call off your braves," I said. "We have many years left to live." There was a sort of muck running in the gutters, yellowish, filthy stream suggesting excrement, or nervousness, a city that does not know what it has done to deserve baldness, errors, infidelity. "With luck you will survive until matins," Sylvia said. She ran off down the Rue Chester Nimitz, uttering shrill cries.

Then it was learned that they had infiltrated our ghetto and that the people of the ghetto instead of resisting had joined the smooth, well-coördinated attack with zipguns, telegrams, lockets, causing that portion of the line held by the I.R.A. to swell and collapse. We sent more heroin into the ghetto, and hyacinths, ordering another hundred thousand of the pale, delicate flowers. On the map we considered the situation with its strung-out inhabitants and merely personal emotions. Our parts were blue and their parts were green. I showed the blue-and-green map to Sylvia. "Your parts are green," I said. "You gave me heroin first a year ago," Sylvia said. She ran off down George C. Marshall Allée, uttering shrill cries. Miss R. pushed me into a large room painted white (jolting and dancing in the soft light, and I was excited! and there were people watching!) in which there were two chairs.

I sat in one chair and Miss R. sat in the other. She wore a blue dress containing a red figure. There was nothing exceptional about her. I was disappointed by her plainness, by the bareness of the room, by the absence of books.

The girls of my quarter wore long blue mufflers that reached to their knees. Sometimes the girls hid Comanches in their rooms, the blue mufflers together in a room creating a great blue fog. Block opened the door. He was carrying weapons, flowers, loaves of bread. And he was friendly, kind, enthusiastic, so I related a little of the history of torture, reviewing the technical literature quoting the best modern sources, French, German, and American, and pointing out the flies which had gathered in anticipation of some new, cool color.

"What is the situation?" I asked.

"The situation is liquid," he said. "We hold the south quarter and they hold the north quarter. The rest is silence."

"And Kenneth?"

"That girl is not in love with Kenneth," Block said frankly. "She is in love with his coat. When she is not wearing it she is huddling under it. Once I caught it going down the stairs by itself. I looked inside. Sylvia."

Once I caught Kenneth's coat going down the stairs by itself but the coat was a trap and inside a Comanche who made a thrust with his short, ugly knife at my leg which buckled and tossed me over the balustrade through a window and into another situation. Not believing that your body brilliant as it was and your fat, liquid spirit distinguished and angry as it was were stable quantities to which one could return on wires more than once, twice, or another number of times I said: "See the table?"

In Skinny Wainwright Square the forces of green and blue swayed and struggled. The referees ran out on the field trailing chains. And then the blue part would be enlarged, the green diminished. Miss R. began to speak. "A former king of Spain, a Bonaparte, lived for a time in Bordentown, New Jersey. But that's no good." She paused. "The ardor aroused in men by the beauty of women can only be satisfied by God. That is very good (it is Valéry) but it is not what I have to teach you, goat, muck, filth, heart of my heart." I showed the table to Nancy. "See the table?"

She stuck out her tongue red as a cardinal's hat. "I made such a table once," Block said frankly. "People all over America have made such tables. I doubt very much whether one can enter an American home without finding at least one such table, or traces of its having been there, such as faded places in the carpet." And afterward in the garden the men of the 7th Cavalry played Gabrieli, Albinoni, Marcello, Vivaldi, Boccherini. I saw Sylvia. She wore a yellow ribbon, under a long blue muffler. "Which side are you on," I cried, "after all?"

"The only form of discourse of which I approve," Miss R. said in her dry, tense voice, "is the litany. I believe our masters and teachers as well as plain citizens should confine themselves to what can safely be said. Thus when I hear the words *pewter, snake, tea, Fad #6 sherry, serviette, fenestration, crown, blue* coming from the mouth of some public official, or some raw youth, I am not disappointed. Vertical organization is also possible," Miss R. said, "as in

> pewter
> snake
> tea
> Fad #6 sherry
> serviette
> fenestration
> crown
> blue.

I run to liquids and colors," she said, "but you, you may run to something else, my virgin, my darling, my thistle, my poppet, my own. Young people," Miss R. said, "run to more and more unpleasant combinations as they sense the nature of our society. Some people," Miss R. said, "run to conceits or wisdom but I hold to the hard, brown, nutlike word. I might point out that there is enough aesthetic excitement here to satisfy anyone but a damned fool." I sat in solemn silence.

Fire arrows lit my way to the post office in Patton Place where members of the Abraham Lincoln Brigade offered their last, exhausted letters, postcards, calendars. I opened a letter but inside was a Comanche flint arrowhead played by Frank Wedekind in an elegant gold chain and congratulations. Your earring rattled against my spectacles when I leaned forward to touch the soft, ruined place where the hearing aid had been. "Pack it in! Pack it in!" I urged, but the men in charge of the Uprising refused to listen to reason or to understand that it was real and that our water supply had evaporated and that our credit was no longer what it had been, once.

We attached wires to the testicles of the captured Comanche. And I sat there getting drunker and drunker and more in love and more in love. When we threw the switch he spoke. His name, he said, was Gustave Aschenbach. He was born at L—, a country town in the province of Silesia. He was the son of an upper official in the judicature, and his forebears had all been officers, judges, departmental functionaries. . . . And you can never touch a girl in the same way more than once, twice, or another number of times however much you may wish to hold, wrap, or otherwise fix her hand, or look, or some other quality, or incident, known to you previously. In Sweden the little Swedish children cheered when we managed nothing more remarkable than getting off a bus burdened with packages, bread and liver-paste and beer. We went to an old church and sat in the royal box. The organist was practicing. And then into the graveyard next to the church. *Here lies Anna Pedersen, a good woman.* I threw a mushroom on the grave. The officer commanding the garbage dump reported by radio that the garbage had begun to move.

Jane! I heard via an International Distress Coupon that you were beaten up by a dwarf in a bar on Tenerife. That doesn't sound like you, Jane. Mostly you kick the dwarf in his little dwarf groin before he can get his teeth into your tasty and nice-looking leg, don't you, Jane? Your affair with Harold is reprehensible, you know that, don't you, Jane? Harold is married to Nancy. And there is Paula to think about (Harold's kid), and Billy (Harold's other kid). I think your values are peculiar, Jane! Strings of language extend in every direction to bind the world into a rushing, ribald whole.

And you can never return to felicities in the same way, the brilliant body, the distinguished spirit recapitulating moments that occur once, twice, or another number of times in rebellions, or water. The rolling consensus of the Comanche nation smashed our inner defenses on three sides. Block was firing a greasegun from the upper floor of a building designed by Emery Roth & Sons. "See the table?" "Oh, pack it in with your bloody table!" The city officials were tied to trees. Dusky warriors padded with their forest tread into the mouth of the mayor. "Who do you want to be?" I asked Kenneth and he said he wanted to be Jean-Luc Godard but later when time permitted conversations in large, lighted rooms, whispering galleries with black-and-white Spanish rugs and problematic sculpture on calm, red catafalques. The sickness of the quarrel lay thick in the bed. I touched your back, the white, raised scars.

We killed a great many in the south suddenly with helicopters and rockets but we found that those we had killed were children and more came from the north and from the east and from other places where there are children preparing to live. "Skin," Miss R. said softly in the white, yellow room. "This is the Clemency Committee. And would you remove your belt and shoelaces." I removed my belt and shoelaces and looked (rain shattering from a great height the prospects of silence and clear, neat rows of houses in the subdivisions) into their savage black eyes, paint, feathers, beads.

20 Leo E. Litwak

Leo E. Litwak was born in Detroit in 1924 and was educated at Wayne and Columbia universities. He has published two novels, To the Hanging Gardens (1964) and In O'Brien's House (1969). The Solitary Life of Man is one of the most widely anthologized stories of the past ten years.

❖

THE SOLITARY LIFE OF MAN

Melford Kuhn had done his duty and with courage. He had received a Silver Star for carrying a wounded buddy a thousand yards while under fire from a pillbox. He mocked the decoration. He cursed brass hats. He disdained all that was rear echelon. He was judged to be the most effective platoon sergeant in the company. This judgment was the buttress of his pride.

There were a few truths that had so affected him that all else seemed irrelevant. A shell fragment has a trajectory defined by its initial velocity and direction and the successive forces impressed upon it. Flesh and bone were not impressive forces. The fragment could act as bullet, knife, cleaver, bludgeon. It could punch, shear, slice, crush, tear. It could be surgical in its precision or make sadistic excess seem unimaginative.

And what happened to brass-hat zeal when the brain was exposed, when guts unfolded, when a flayed stump drooled blood? Didn't the lieutenant turn away from Morgan's shredded stump, mumbling, "I can't. Oh, no!"? Kuhn fixed the tourniquet. Yet they became zealots again when the dying was a few days past and they were in the company of their brother officers and they could begin the falsification of history which proposed heroes and cowards and right action and blunders.

He had learned that the dread of dying is a knife that hacks at all sentiments and kills those which have no validity. He scorned those who approached combat from the perspective of honor, ambition, and the other sentiments of gallantry which flourish when there is no risk of dying.

He felt that ignorance had been pared away from him until only the core of truth was left. The more imminent death became, the narrower was his focus, until now, after two years of combat, he had reached hard fact. Not country, not family, not buddies, but only he himself was relevant. And as his focus narrowed, he became more taciturn, less concerned with the vanities which depended on a wider community.

He loathed Solomon. Solomon was a supply sergeant, assigned to battalion headquarters, who had no reason for being at the front. He should have been two miles back, in a village already secured, nicely housed, nicely fed, profiting from the German obsequiousness which made everything available to acquisitive hands. Solomon was forty-five, a swarthy, big-nosed man, his face creased, tall, gaunt, with a gentle manner. He was dressed like a soldier, yet Kuhn regarded him as a caricature of a soldier. His clothes were glistening new issue, and he used all the tricks of dressing which the combat soldier learns through necessity. He wore a field jacket over his wool sweater, OD trousers tucked into combat boots, a knit wool cap under his helmet liner and steel helmet. Solomon, with his pious talk, his admiration for heroes, his fear of cowardice, his flagrant sympathizing, had become intolerable to Kuhn. Solomon used the sanctimonious language which charmed officers back in battalion headquarters, but he had no flair for the bitter invective which the GI recognized as the language of a friend.

The platoon was assembled, ready to mount the truck. The company jeep arrived with a galvanized can filled with hot coffee. The men lined up and dipped into the coffee with their canteen cups. It was a chill morning, and Solomon stood at the rear of the line, his arms wrapped around his chest, his hands tucked into his armpits.

"Solomon—" Kuhn waved him over to his side and walked him out of earshot of the others. "What are you doing here, Solomon?"

Solomon smiled, misunderstanding Kuhn's intention. "I think I should take my chances with the rest of the boys, Mel. Let them have their coffee first."

"That's damn nice of you. You could be sitting down to breakfast back in battalion."

"It weighs on my conscience, Mel, that I should be safe while the boys up here take all the risks."

"This isn't a club for healthy consciences. I'm not interested in your conscience. There isn't one of us who wouldn't be back in battalion if he had the chance. All you're doing up here, Solomon, is taking someone's coffee."

Solomon shivered. He pulled one arm free and shrugged with it. "You're right. I'll go without coffee."

"Solomon! We're going to take a village this morning. Suppose we have trouble? What do you do, Solomon?"

"What I can do I don't know. But whatever you want I should do, I'll try."

"I've got no job for you." He wanted to snarl, "Stop cringing, Stupid!" Instead he glared his dislike. "Rodansky tells me you bother him with your kraut pitying. How come you're giving Rodansky trouble?"

Solomon rubbed his eyes. He wore OD wool gloves with leather palms. He was more than twenty years older than Kuhn. "Rodansky is bothered by the German boy. I know he's bothered. So he didn't offend me."

"I don't care if you're offended. You're no problem of mine. I care about my platoon. And you're just trouble for me. I don't want you around, Solomon."

Solomon nodded. "I'll ride back with the jeep. I apologize, Mel."

Kuhn walked away from him.

Rodansky had been on guard duty the day before. He had heard a noise in the bushes at the edge of the platoon area. He had challenged, then had fired, and Kuhn had found him standing beside the dying man. The German lay behind a bush, his arms extending through it. He wore a great-coat. His wool cap had fallen off. His hair was in the midst of the bush, an abundant, dirty yellow. He wasn't armed, and Kuhn rolled him over. The German wheezed through his chest.

"I told him to put up his hands. 'Hands auf,' I said."

"What a mess. He's a kid."

The boy was already soggy gray. The slug had hit at an angle, swerved within the compass of the chest, and his heart was bared. "Warum hast du—" Neither Kuhn nor Rodansky understood German and they did not respond to the boy's muttering.

Kuhn straightened up as others in the platoon joined them. "He won't last till the aid station. Leave him here. Is the medic around? It doesn't make any difference."

Then Solomon came up, gasping with fear, blanching when he heard the moans. He fell to his knees beside the boy and touched his face. He listened to the muttering. "He wants to know why did we shoot." Solomon looked up, asking the question in his own right. "He says he wanted to surrender. 'Wir haben nicht gewissen,'" he explained to the boy, his voice trembling with compassion. "He wants to know if he's dying."

"He's dead, Solomon! Tell him he's dead. Tot," Rodansky shouted at the boy. "Kraut tot!"

"Nein," Solomon said in turn. He told the boy they would soon have him in a hospital. "Wir haben nicht gewissen," he concluded in hopeless apology.

A few weeks before, twelve men from the platoon had been killed in front of a pillbox. There had been considerable variety in their deaths. They'd been zeroed in by eighty-eights. The GIs had swallowed these deaths as part of the nourishment of combat whose grotesqueries provisioned their daily fare.

Rodansky caught Solomon's arm as they left the boy to the medic.

"What the hell you doing in the army, Solomon—an old man like you? Why aren't you back with the girls, getting the dough, saluting the flag? What are you here for, Solomon?"

Solomon was still shocked by the sight of the naked heart beating in a sheath of slime. His face mirrored the open-mouthed pallor of the dying German.

He raised his arms waist high and let them flop. He repeated

this gesture several times before answering Rodansky. "He asked
is he dying. He came to surrender. Why did we shoot, he wants
to know. He's maybe only sixteen. The poor boy!"

"Poor boy!"

"It doesn't matter to me all of a sudden that he's German. His
chest was breathing, Harry. Did you hear it? Ah! I wish we didn't
shoot. It's a pity, a pity, Rodansky."

Though they had recently come from a reserve area where
shower facilities were available, Rodansky hadn't washed or shaved.
His helmet was set low on his forehead, and he peered from
under it like a man taking a cautious look in the midst of a
barrage. He released his grip on Solomon's arm to squeeze his
rifle with both hands. He shook the rifle at Solomon, his lips
twisting for an adequate expression of his outrage. "I shot, you
old bastard, not you! You bastard! We fight your wars and then
you come around and preach!"

It was clear that he meant the "you" generically. Solomon
revealed his identity with every shrug, with every anecdote, with
his intonation, with his liberal use of such notions as Pity and
Justice, with his faithful attendance at Saturday services.

Kuhn shared Rodansky's loathing for this old man who pre-
sumed to give them lessons in sentiment when he was so little
experienced in the passion that proved integrity, the fear of death.
The following morning he ordered Solomon back to the rear.

They had come so fast into Germany that they passed through
villages still entrucked, leaving the security of the area to the
reserve companies that followed. The widely spaced convoy rattled
down poor country roads, claiming a new segment of Germany
with each turn of the wheels. The Germans who lined the streets
cheered the convoy with the enthusiasm of the liberated. When
the soldiers dismounted and formed squads to scour a village,
they found the Germans more tractable than any ally. "*Nach
kirche!*" the GIs shouted. The Germans took up the cry and
without further urging streamed to church where they were instructed by the military government. The town was left in the
hands of the GIs. These were irreverent hands, not limited by
any law. They stripped watches from the grinning Germans. They
ransacked the German houses for guns and cameras and silver and

food. The Germans yielded their homes to GI boots which trampled their linens and muddied their beds. The women were cheerful offerings to appease the conqueror. Good food, good servants, good plumbing, good women, they were a magnificent fee to conquer. Kuhn despised them. Good cameras, good watches, good pistols, they were as good to Kuhn as any European. Kuhn had a Luger, a Leica, a fine Swiss watch.

Ahead of them, beyond the reach of GI boots, there was law supported by a seemingly death-defying ardor. There was German law and German pride ahead of them. Ahead of them were boasts that the German spirit would endure death rather than humiliation. Behind them they left a disordered mob prepared to sacrifice everything German and human to preserve themselves. Without urging, the Germans denied all that they had been and betrayed any compatriot whose betrayal benefited them.

Kuhn had so far not failed himself. He had not lost himself in the solvent of dread. He had made trembling legs advance. He had made his panicked hands obey him. He had refused to be overwhelmed by fatigue. Whatever beliefs he possessed he was sure of, since they had endured. Yet his victories had not relieved him from oppression. He was more and more oppressed. Instead of being restored by the intervals between hazards, he spent the time anticipating future catastrophes. He didn't know the extent of his endurance. He feared that moment when his courage would fail him and he would act badly.

As the truck bore them across a German valley, he scanned the sky for aircraft. He studied the roadside for cover. He planned his escape from the truck. The sky was too clear, the land too hilly, the opportunities for ambuscade unsettling. He didn't rely on the scouting jeeps to discover snipers. He only trusted his own vision. He tried imagining the city of Helo where they were to dismount and assemble for an assault. He wondered whether the Germans would be supported by tanks and artillery, whether they would be yielding or would resist.

The banter of the GIs irritated him. He considered their ability to forget hazards a kind of amnesia, fortunate if one could settle for something other than truth. The men were crammed on benches that ran the length of the truck on both sides. They squatted on the floor. They pressed together, shoulders and hips joined, knees against backs, rifles held between legs, loosened helmet straps clanging against steel with each toss of the truck.

"—outside of Triers, remember?" Reilly summoned his buddies to hear the anecdote. "That pillbox with the railroad tunnel?" He and Rodansky had left their squad to check a farmhouse. It was a place with an inner court and a ripe compost pile and pigs and chickens and Russian laborers. Rodansky found a book filled with sketches. These showed a man and woman going all out for love. Various attitudes were sketched in provocative detail. The farm wife entered. Rodansky looked at her, then at the sketchbook. "This is you?" He held up the book and tapped his finger on the woman depicted. The farm wife nodded. "This is me!" Rodansky shouted, pointing to the man. He threw off his harness, dropped his rifle on the table, and pursued her into the bedroom.

Rodansky admitted his conquest and in response to their urging detailed it. He was filled with a charge that raised him mile high. "She didn't run no further than that bed. All feathers it was, so she sunk out of sight with her legs poking up. We didn't get past page one. It's lucky for me there was a war on."

What perhaps the men most admired was Rodansky's ability to forget the pillbox where a few hours previously they had lost an entire squad. Rodansky was able to lust when only terror seemed appropriate. He made places and people who were strange to the GIs less intimidating by humbling them. He'd had limey women in England, Frog and Belgian girls, fräuleins—and in circumstances which seemed to rule out any passion but fear. Once he'd disappeared into a cellar with a fräulein while they struggled for a village. Machine guns directed tracers at the GIs from the high ground beyond. They could see Tiger tanks maneuvering on the hillside for a counterattack. And afterwards what they remembered of that village was, not the GI and German dead, not their panic when it seemed that the enemy tanks would assault them, but Rodansky taking a recess from war in order to satisfy an appetite they were delighted had survived.

Kuhn saw in this eagerness to return to manageable passions a betrayal of experience which he attributed not only to GIs, but to allies and enemies everywhere, and above all to those who remained in the rear echelons, never risking death. Instead of being readied for disaster by his relaxing intermissions, Rodansky was becoming untrustworthy. He bitched too much, he talked too much. He failed to tend himself when they were in reserve. And Kuhn believed that if fear hadn't predominated, Rodansky could have taken the German boy prisoner.

The convoy ascended a steep hill. From the crest they looked down upon a valley. The day was clear, and they were able to view a dozen villages, each centered around a church, ringed first with plowed fields and then with forest. The wind came from the east and brought a piney smell and a vague sound which seemed composed of church bells, the lowing of cattle, the barking of dogs, but nothing of war. Across the valley, straggling beneath the distant hills was the city of Helo. No tanks were visible, no Germans, there was no sound of artillery, no machine-gun staccato to presage resistance ahead. On the left, some two miles distant, they observed another column, preceding them toward Helo. The information was passed back that B and C Companies of their battalion would take the city, with small resistance expected, and that their company would follow in reserve.

The men were jubilant. This was a fine big city that had been spared air raids, and they were getting it peacefully. What novelties in bedding, what steals in cameras, what city fräuleins were available? They relished the chickens they would gut; hams, sausages, preserves they would loot; wine from cellars; and finally sleep.

They dismounted six miles from Helo with orders to sweep the area before the city. Kuhn's platoon controlled a sector three hundred yards wide, consisting mainly of open field and farmhouses. He broke the platoon into squads, instructing the squad leaders to keep track of their men. "There's a crossroads about three miles from here. We'll assemble there in two hours. Keep moving. Call me if there's any trouble."

The mission was uneventful. Kuhn reached the assembly point with time to spare. The day had warmed sufficiently to make the march uncomfortable. Chester Grove, the platoon messenger, accompanied Kuhn. Grove was a farmer from Oklahoma, a lumpish man who admired Kuhn. He nervously broached topics which he hoped would interest Kuhn.

"If we get it now, Sarge, when it's almost over, what a joke."

"It's a long way from over."

"It's been a couple weeks since we run into artillery. Everyone's relaxed. I tell you, Sarge, you can be trained for a lot of things. Experience makes you better if you want to be an athlete or a farmer or for screwing. You get smarter reading books. There's a lot of things where practice makes perfect. But, Sarge, when I hear a shell I don't have the nerve I first had. I figure that every time I wasn't killed I was in luck and there's only so much luck a man has before the cards change."

The squads arrived, Reilly's squad reporting last. The men sprawled along the roadside, munching at K-rations and food looted in the course of the march.

"Everybody here?"

"Rodansky ain't showed up," Reilly reported. "Give him a few minutes, Sarge. He'll be along."

"Where is he?"

"You know old Rodansky, Sarge. He could find himself a woman and a bed Sunday morning in church."

"Where is he?"

"Back in that farmhouse." Reilly pointed to a farmhouse in a grove of trees, half a mile from the assembly point.

"He's got five more minutes." When the five minutes passed, Kuhn nodded. "Okay, Reilly. Let's get him."

Plodding and sour-faced, there were a few buddy indiscretions Reilly wouldn't forgive. He might regret excess in killing, cowardice, gold-bricking, but so long as it was family that was in error he was tolerant. The broadness of his view did not extend beyond the family of buddies.

"Old Rodansky, when he's on tail, it takes a direct hit from a eighty-eight to get him off."

"I'll get him off."

"Take it easy, Sarge. Harry's okay."

"You think this war is a joke, Reilly?"

They walked directly into the kitchen. Rodansky's rifle was on a counter near a tile oven. His field jacket, hung with grenades, lay on a chair.

Kuhn shouted for Rodansky. He walked to the door beside the oven and kicked it. "Rodansky! Come out of there!"

Reilly caught his arm. "Hold on, Sarge. He'll come."

Kuhn shoved the door open. The room was dark. There was a burst of motion from the high bed. Rodansky scrambled from the bed, gripping his pants. He came toward the light, fumbling with his belt, his shirt undone, blinking, stunned, a sweaty smell accompanying him. The woman crouched on the other side of the bed.

"That's a lousy trick, Kuhn. It's no skin off your nose. What are you getting so goddam GI for?"

Kuhn struggled with a murderous impulse he didn't understand. "I catch you again leaving your rifle around like that and I'll bust the hell out of you."

"Bust me. I'm a PFC."

"I can bust you good, Rodansky. You know what I mean? You want to push harder and find out?"

Kuhn hurried back to the platoon without waiting for Reilly and Rodansky.

C Company had the outskirts of Helo. A tank man pissed from a doorway, his free hand gripping a bottle of wine. Chemical mortars had fired the bordering houses, and no efforts were made to stop the burning. B Company had sequestered an entire block, and the men of B Company had already cashed in on the available bounty.

Instead of approaching the heart of town, the reserve company was directed along its periphery. For a moment, peering down a winding street, they glimpsed a sizable plaza that promised the amenities of city life they had long missed. They were marched through a residential area, then to a dirt road, and soon the city was on their left, open field on their right, and it was evident they were not intended to share the fortunes of the other companies in the battalion.

In an open field, two miles beyond the city, they came to barracks enclosed with barbed wire. There were three buildings that formed a U-shape. The buildings were mere boxes, with small windows covered with steel mesh. The ground surrounding the buildings was hard clay.

The prospect was barren, and Kuhn shared the general dismay. The battalion jeep was at the entrance to the compound. A group of officers huddled around the jeep while the company halted. The captain and platoon leaders conferred with the major. Solomon was with them. He waved to Kuhn.

Kuhn's platoon was detached from the company and entered the grounds where they assembled around their officer. The rest of the company returned to the city.

"We're only going to be here a few hours. We have to make Brumberg by morning. We go by truck. There'll be hot chow. Get some rest, boys." Lieutenant Gordon was a ruddy-cheeked man of twenty-five, his natural stoutness trimmed down by rigorous living. "Now, about this place—I'm not going to give you the usual crap about looting and fraternizing. I know what goes on. This is a *Lager*. The middle barracks there has thirty women in it —Hungarians. These girls have had a very rough time. Stay away from them. They think the GI is something different, and I want them thinking that way when we leave. Sergeant!" He summoned Kuhn. "Sergeant, I want you to put out a guard detail for the women's barracks. Any man caught fraternizing I'll court-martial."

There were wooden bunks in the long room. A potbellied stove was in the center of the room, firewood heaped behind it. The men flung down their rifles, helmets, and harness. They sprawled in their bunks on bare springs.

Kuhn waited for them to settle down before assigning details. He felt dizzy and knew the dizziness to precede a blackout. These periods of amnesia had become frequent. Dread settled on him like a fog and, sometimes for several moments, he couldn't distinguish his place, his role, his purpose. He nerved himself to endure these moments. He took off his helmet and swabbed his forehead with his wool cap. Their names tumbled across his tongue, and he scanned the barracks but couldn't find the faces to fit the names. Then slowly their faces merged with the fog. He felt as distant from them as if they had been background to a dream. He couldn't pluck out the sense of their words. He fumbled for his detail book and turned the pages. The headings were

senseless, there was no clue in the words recorded. He felt nauseated but was determined not to reveal his panic and continued
turning the pages. Rebel, Reilly, Rodansky. Grove, Nelson,
Schultz The words became a rhythm which was compulsively
reiterated.

"Mel, Mel." The blackout lasted a few seconds. He was not
detected. Solomon gripped his sleeve. "Can I talk to you, Mel? In
private? A few seconds? Are you busy?"

The smiling, seamed face was in focus.

"Rebel, your squad takes the first tour of guard duty. Let's
make it till eleven. Nelson, from eleven to three. Schultz, from
three if we need your squad. One post in front, one in back."

He followed Solomon into the yard. The jeep had left. The
yard was empty. The sun was already low over the plowed fields.
They could hear the distant motors in the city, the heavy rumble
of tanks, a faraway shout.

"They're Jewish girls, Melford. Yesterday, before the Germans
left, they cut off their hair and marched them naked through the
streets. They're lucky they are alive. They come from a village,
Mel, where all the Jews are dead except these girls. The Germans
made them whores."

"What do you want from me, Solomon?"

"In two days it's Pesach—Passover—Mel. Tonight, while we're
still here, I want that you and I should help these girls to cele-
brate their luck. I want we should have a meal which we can pretend is a seder."

The sun was covered by the clouds rolling in from the horizon.
Long shadows spread from the forest across the furrows of the
encompassing fields. The forest hadn't been cleared of enemies.
Germans, by-passed by their column, might now be waiting at
the edge of the forest. The road to Helo went through the forest,
and Kuhn was to be briefed at company headquarters in Helo.
There were rumors that Brumberg, their next objective, was a
focus of resistance. He had to get to town before dark to secure
the password.

"I want you to meet the girls, Kuhn. It will give them a real
pleasure."

"What time is it?"

"It's four o'clock. I have permission from the major to hold a seder, Mel. These poor kids. There are some of them babies yet—fifteen, sixteen."

"I got troubles without you around, Solomon. What do you want? A seder?"

Rebel came out to begin the first tour of duty. "Where shall I dig in, Sarge?"

"In back. Near the wire."

Solomon caught his arm, and Kuhn shoved him away. "Don't touch me, you jerk."

But his single-mindedness brooked no offense. "It's not a question do I annoy you or do you like me or are you worried. The question has to do with these girls. I don't ask any big sacrifice from you, like to give up your life. I only ask you to be a little decent to some girls who, because you are a Jew—even if it annoys you—they would feel some pleasure to meet you."

"You're what annoys me, Solomon."

"Do you so much value yourself, Kuhn, that you can't take a little time for these poor girls?"

"Get off my back." He left Solomon abruptly and returned to the barracks. He told Reilly to take over the platoon while he and Grove went to headquarters for the briefing.

Rodansky lay on his bunk, still harnessed, his knees raised, his arms folded across his chest, his eyes closed.

Reilly accompanied Kuhn to the barbed-wire gate. "How about these gals, Sarge?"

"You heard the lieutenant. They're off-limits."

"What he don't know won't hurt him."

"It'll hurt you, Reilly. It's my orders you listen to. Stay away from them. I hold you responsible, Reilly. You're in charge. Don't get smart."

"What the hell. We're moving out in a few hours."

"I'm telling you straight. I'll break you, Reilly. Don't give me any of that buddy business. No screwing around. Get it?"

Reilly winked. "Got it."

Lately, Kuhn had sensed resistance among the men. He felt eyes

following him, averted when he turned. They were handling him
as they did officers, accepting orders with sardonic geniality, grins
becoming smirks.

"I'll make it a point to check, Reilly."

There was no part of army life which was natural to Kuhn.
He had no flair for communal living. He had early discovered that
his efforts to establish himself as a buddy made him foolish. He
could only pretend sympathy and when the pretense wearied him
his antipathy showed.

Forests were strange to him. Initially he had not been able to
orient himself in forests. He was not familiar with forest sounds,
had poor vision in the murkiness of the forest gloom. There were
men who could walk confidently in the dark. They could discrimi-
nate sounds and know when to be easy and when to be tense.
They could relax vigilance. A snapped twig, a sensed motion,
danger felt, and without doing violence to their nerves, they were
again prepared. But to Kuhn, all sounds were ominous. He had
no sense for danger and was always on guard. He feared the infiltration of enemies and he couldn't take advantage of lulls. Yet
Kuhn had mastered his natural disadvantages and by never yielding to terror he had established himself as the equal of any soldier
in the company.

The pines leaned together across the road. Kuhn and Grove
advanced into pockets of gloom, the only sound being the gravel
scattered by their boots. Kuhn held his carbine ready, bracing
against panic whenever they approached an area of darkness. He
felt himself vulnerable to any violence. If a German should leap
from the forest, he would turn and run. He would abandon
Grove. If captured, he would beg. He clicked off the safety of his
carbine and hunched his shoulders.

He was trembling when finally they were past the forest and
had entered the town.

"Maybe we'll get a ride back," Grove suggested.

"They don't run a taxi service."

Cobbled streets twisted up the hill toward the church. Half-
timbered houses fronted solidly on the narrow streets, their upper
stories cantilevered. The gutters were strewn with wires laid by the
Signal Corps. The intersections were placarded with directions

indicating the various units in the area. MPs supervised traffic
at intersections. Convoys of trucks rolled through. The front which
had been at Helo a few hours previously was already several miles
beyond.

Company headquarters were located in the main square which
centered about the church. Market stalls, shuttered and locked,
fringed the square. The area was being used as a motor-pool and
was crowded with trucks and jeeps. There were no civilians in
sight, and the soldiers who were not attending to their vehicles
were rummaging for loot.

The captain briefed them on the coming objective. Brumberg
was defended by twelve batteries of German artillery. This was,
perhaps, a sizable element of the remaining enemy resistance.
Their company was to participate in a task force that included
tanks, TDs, and air support. They had earned this privilege by
virtue of their great record. The captain was proud. The lieu-
tenants were proud.

Kuhn loathed himself after a session with the officers. A gen-
tlemanly jargon was in common use. The noncoms, as well as the
officers, lent themselves to a collegiate view of war. Even Kuhn
while in the company of officers was impressed by their vision of
combat. They had seen what shell fragments could do. They had
smelled blood and knew that it was a fecal smell. They had seen
how the perspective of a dying man narrows until it is confined
to himself. And yet they could still approach combat with collegiate sentiments. They ate well. They drank the best of Scotch,
served from German tumblers. They were established in the
mayor's residence and handsomely bedded. Kuhn withdrew from
the party spirit that prevailed. He saw them as a spic-and-span
hazing crew with a boy-scout ardor for protocol and a sophomoric
concern for reputation.

The major, who had joined the briefing, approached Kuhn.
"How's my boy Solomon doing, Sergeant? You keep an eye on
that old man, hear?" The charge was confided with the easy bon-
hommie that a master—a decent paternalistic master—has for his
underlings. He was a ruddy, bulky, senatorial type, his uniform
tailored to fit his bulk, his polished, stiff bearing a mark of his
caste. "I love that big-hearted sonofagun. He found himself some

Jewish girls who were treated very badly. And Solomon—well he
couldn't have been more concerned if it was him the krauts tortured. We could do with more like Solomon." He held Kuhn's
elbow and spoke confidentially: "By the way, Sergeant, I've fixed
a little surprise for Solomon. Some of the mail has arrived from
Division, and the chaplain has sent up some Jewish flat bread—
matzos—and I sent it on to your outfit together with the hot
chow. The old man will get a kick out of it. See that he's taken
care of, Sergeant. Right?" He squeezed Kuhn's elbow.

The password was Easter Bunny.

The twilight was well advanced when they started back toward
the platoon. It was chill again, and Kuhn shivered in his woolens
which were still damp from sweating. They left the town. The
moment they were on the country road the clamor of motors and
rummaging GIs diminished. They entered the forest. Grove
walked down the center of the road, his rifle clanking against his
canteen, the sling of his rifle slapping against the buckles of his
harness. Kuhn listened to him chew the chicken leg he had taken
from the officer's mess. He used both hands to hold the leg, his
head jerking back as he tugged at the meat. He flung the bone
away and wiped his hands on his trousers. He belched, then
reached into the pocket of his field jacket for a chocolate bar.
He stripped the paper, crumpled it into a ball, flung it into the
underbrush beside the road. Kuhn was dizzy with expectation of a
bullet. He felt like a target.

"You pig!"

"What?"

"Quiet!"

"I was just eating, Sarge."

"They can hear you eating in Berlin. Where did you learn
to eat, on your pig farm? You'll bring every kraut in ten miles."

"There're no krauts around."

"You're not getting me killed, Grove. This is enemy territory.
How do you know this forest is secure? There are twelve batteries
of kraut artillery at Brumberg. Brumberg is only ten miles from
here."

"I won't eat then. If my eating is going to lose the war, okay,
I won't eat."

"Whisper, Stupid! This isn't an officer's club."

"You're making more noise than me, Sarge."

"Shut up and let's move."

They trudged on opposite sides of the road, less concerned now with possible ambushes than with their hatred of each other. Kuhn listened to Grove's muttering, realized his own childishness, and yet couldn't restrain his loathing for this and all other buddies. He felt himself dying in a stupid war among stupid men whose understanding was confined to what sex and stomach could sense.

"Twelve batteries—they're honored."

Grove steamed with the insult. "You'd think you was General Patton. Who the hell are you to tell me how to eat? I can eat any damn way I please. I was the only friend you had in this platoon. With the friends you got, it ain't kraut shrapnel you have to worry about. Sonofabitch. They better section-eight you before you crack wide open."

They were still far from the barracks when they heard the party. It was night, and the windows hadn't been completely blacked out, and cracks of light sprayed over the plain.

"We move out in three hours and they're screwing up! I warned Reilly!"

The guard was near the door. It was Rebel. He was so intent upon the sounds from the barracks that he didn't observe their approach.

"*Hands auf*, you jerk! Put down that rifle. If I was a kraut you'd be a dead man and so would everyone else in this platoon. This isn't your post, Rebel. I could court-martial you, Stupid. What the hell's going on?"

"Solomon brought them in, Sarge. He said it was okay. He said he'd take responsibility. The major give him permission."

"Who's running this outfit, me or Solomon!"

"It ain't my fault, Sarge."

"The password is Easter Bunny. Got it? We're moving out in three hours. We're joining Task Force Onaway. We've been volunteered. There's twelve batteries of kraut artillery at Brumberg. You feel like kicking your heels, Rebel?"

"How come us, Sarge? Why don't they give some other company the chance?"

"We're honored, Stupid. What's the password?"

"Easter Bunny."

A long table had been constructed from planks fitted over sawhorses. There were candles on the table. Mess kits had been placed in front of the seated women. Hot chow was presented in huge GI pots. The women were shawled. They wore knee-length smocks, half-sleeved, open-throated. They were pallid and puffy-faced, an unhealthy taint that was as much the color of apathy as the consequence of poor food and imprisonment. Dead men had this color. Bodies moldering in trenches had this smell.

Yet now they could laugh. Now they felt no pain. Now they were ready to forget the several hundred krauts who had mounted them. So newly rescued from terror, could their equilibrium be so quickly restored? Kuhn shrank from the sight of them. How could they laugh? How could they respond to the buddy teasing? How could they live after their complete humiliation? They had given everything away.

The men stood behind them, helping with the preparations for the feast. They beckoned Kuhn to share the fun. "Climb in, Sarge. There's room for everybody."

"Grab a matzo, Sarge. Good old Solomon—"

Solomon beamed. Solomon, with his brood of chicks, thought he was among gentlemen.

"Reilly! What did I tell you!"

"Solomon's got orders from the major. I figured you was out-ranked, Sarge."

"I saw the lights a mile away. Is this what you call a blackout?"

"It ain't hardly dark."

"Clear out these women. I don't want any more screwing around. We move out in three hours."

"That's three hours. That's not now."

"I said, clear them out, Reilly," he slowly advised.

"What's the pitch? We're nice boys. These are friendly gals. What's eating you, Kuhn?"

"Twelve batteries of kraut artillery. That's what's eating me. Come morning we'll be at Brumberg."

"I'll be there, Kuhn, and so will the boys. Meantime, I don't see any artillery. Maybe I'll get kilt in the morning. Right now I'm not getting kilt."

"Melford!" Solomon shouted. "My friend! I want you to meet someone." He beckoned Kuhn with both hands, speaking excitedly to the woman beside him.

"Melford, I want you to meet Leona." In German he told Leona that Kuhn was the Jewish sergeant he had told her about. All the women turned to watch the introduction.

She was the only one not shawled. Her straight black hair was cropped at the neck. Leaning on her elbows, puffing a cigarette, she had seemed a beauty across the room—a dark, slim woman, great-eyed, fine-featured. But up close the ravage was apparent. The skin was jaundiced, and the face was dry and brittle. The swollen cords of her throat traced her gauntness. Her sprawled legs exhibited the welts of lice bites. There was a sore on her lower lip.

"It is a year now since I see a Jewish man," she told him in a rasping voice. She arose to greet him. She didn't bother to find out whether he would accept the identity she imposed on him. She came to him with the stiff gait of a pregnant woman, her arms half raised, and walked up in reach of the embrace she expected.

He was so strongly repelled by her that it required a physical effort to remain in her presence. She seemed to him fouled by all the abuse she had suffered. Her walk was infirm. The broadness of her hips, the puffy ankles were an unnatural contrast to the bony shoulders and skinny arms. The musty smell which repelled him seemed to have its source in her scabs and her welts. That she was still a young woman made her seem even more repellent. What hadn't she allowed to happen to her? What hadn't she endured in order to avoid death? Dared she claim him as kin? Face him as her equal?

"Everyone's had it tough." He stood his distance.

"Solomon has much praised you to us."

"Solomon is sometimes foolish. Solomon is a big talker. Pardon me, Leona, but now I have to talk to Solomon. I have to speak privately."

He took Solomon outside and when the door was closed, seized him and slammed him against the barrack wall. Solomon's helmet fell across his forehead. He lost his balance and grabbed Kuhn's arm.

"Mel!"

"I hate the way you smile, Solomon! I hate the way you wiggle on your belly to get laughs. I hate you for all the asses you've kissed. I hate you for being so stupid!"

"Because I'm a Jew maybe?" Solomon hissed, gasping under the hand that pinned him to the wall. "You hate me because I'm a Jew, Kuhn?"

"In three hours we go for a ride. At the end of the ride we get out and walk. And while we walk we get killed. The man ahead, the man behind, they get killed. Their bellies open. Their legs tear off. Their heads explode. That's what I concentrate on, Solomon. That's the important thing. And you, Smiley, you Fat-lips, you Big-heart—you drag your ass up here where it doesn't belong and you clap your head and say, 'Poor little kraut who doesn't have a chest—' You come up here and hunt out Jews and you say, 'Okay! Let's stop everything, boys, let's be nice to the Jew girls. They've had it so bad, take pity. Pity the poor Jews who are whores.' And you know what the boys think of you, Solomon? Who is this old jerk with the clean uniform and good food in his belly who comes up here and says, 'Time out, let's take pity.' Pity? What's that word? They use it back in headquarters? Those gentlemen back there, the ones who tell us we have the honor to get killed? They use words like honor, too, don't they, Solomon?"

He shook Solomon while he spoke. He clutched the lapels of Solomon's field jacket, and the old man gasped and choked, his head wobbling as he submitted to what appeared to him a murderous assault. His lips slackened, white showed in his eyes, his face was gray with shock, he embraced Kuhn's hands with his own.

"You want to kill me?" he hissed.

Kuhn felt the trembling hands on his own and tightened his grip.

"I'm old enough to be your father," Solomon said as if amazed. "Is this the way you treat me?"

"What have you ever learned, you bastard!" But suddenly he couldn't endure the terror in Solomon's eyes. He pushed Solomon against the wall once more and dropped his hands.

"Are you a Hitler or a God you can treat me like this? What gives you the power?"

Kuhn felt drugged in the aftermath of violence. He looked at Solomon as if he could see there the reflection of himself, see his brutishness mirrored there, see reflected in the older man's disillusionment his own deterioration.

"I learned how it is about dying," Kuhn muttered. "I learned what is bullshit. What I learned you have no idea of. Why are you so surprised, Stupid? Don't you know what the world is like?"

Solomon breathed deeply, his seamed face now resolute. "Don't be too proud, Kuhn," he answered hoarsely. "Don't think you only have felt what no one else has felt. There is always someone has had it worse."

"Have your seder, Solomon. But stay away from me. Stay away from me and stay away from this platoon."

He did not respond to the bitter dignity of Solomon's defiance. "It's not only your war, Kuhn."

Toward the east, in the direction of Brumberg, the sky pulsed from dark to lightening white. This was the artillery preparation of Brumberg. The damp chill pinched his toes and shivered his thighs. He raised the collar of his field jacket. It required intense listening to discern the pervasive bass rumble of the distant shelling. The furrows in the field seemed to writhe and twist after steady scanning. Clots of gloom separated from the forest wall and merged with the field. There was laughter in the barracks behind him. They were snug in their lighted room, warmed by the stove, guarded front and rear by entrenched GIs. But what was this one drop of light contrasted with the great puddle of darkness in which they were immersed?

When Solomon left, Kuhn felt the darkness swarm over him. It pressed a bubble of loneliness that rose from his guts to his throat. He despairingly summoned his exhausted pride to suppress this gas of pity.

He was close to tears when Rodansky came around the corner, followed by the girl. She was no more than seventeen. Shawled, her form distorted by the poor-fitting smock, there was still no mistaking her beauty. There was an idiot innocence in her eyes, as though she had preserved herself from further defeat by withdrawing her awareness from all that her body had suffered. She clutched Rodansky's arm when she saw Kuhn. She cowered at the sight of him.

Rodansky was in a fever, tensed from head to toe, his eyes darting in quest of escape. He jerked to a halt and spread out his arms to stop the girl when he saw Kuhn. His fear showed. He stood his ground, nerving himself for punishment. "Okay . . . so what are you going to do about it?"

He was strangely saddened by Rodansky's terror. Was his effort to find release of such pathetic consequence that he could now turn pale at the sight of Kuhn?

"There's kraut artillery waiting for us, Rodansky."

"You can wait for it, Kuhn. I don't ask any favors. At least I got my kicks in."

"Take the girl in, Rodansky. Get some chow. We move out in two hours."

Rodansky guided the girl into the barracks. She followed him docilely, averting her face as she passed Kuhn.

A flare ignited with a hiss, turning the sky greenish-white. It was the first of a series of flares aimed toward Brumberg. Planes flew overhead toward Brumberg. In front of him, the forest appeared in silhouette, the trees as sharply defined as paper cutouts. He remained frozen after the darkness again settled.

He had to clean his carbine, get the ammo distributed, receive the final briefing from the lieutenant. But until his loneliness was relieved, no action was possible.

Solomon was seated at the head of the table. He addressed both the seated girls and the standing GIs. Kuhn went to the opposite end of the table and sat by Leona. He did not reject her hand which gripped his under the table.

Somehow Solomon had made a congregation of his audience. There was pious intensity in their listening.

"—so that is why tonight we talk about the meaning of this day. And to make this meaning clear is why I ask why this night is different from all other nights. It has to do when our people were in Egypt. They were slaves."

21 Tadeusz Borowski

Tadeusz Borowski was born in Zytomierz, Poland, in 1922. Imprisoned in Auschwitz and Dachau from 1943 to 1945, he published two volumes of poetry and three collections of concentration-camp stories before taking his own life in 1951.

◈

THIS WAY FOR THE GAS, LADIES AND GENTLEMEN

All of us walk around naked. The delousing is finally over and our striped suits are back from the tanks of Cyclone B solution, an efficient killer of lice in clothing and of men in gas chambers. Only the inmates in the blocks cut off from ours by the "Spanish goats"* still have nothing to wear. But all the same, all of us walk around naked: the heat is unbearable. The camp has been sealed off tight. Not a single prisoner, not one solitary louse, can sneak through the gate. The labour Kommandos have stopped working. All day, thousands of naked men shuffle up and down the roads, cluster around the squares, or lie against the walls and on top of the roofs. We have been sleeping on plain boards, since our mattresses and blankets are still being disinfected. From the rear blockhouses we have a view of the F.K.L.—*Frauen Konzentration Lager;* there too the delousing is in full swing. Twenty-eight thousand women have been stripped naked and driven out of the

*Crossed wooden beams wrapped in barbed wire.

349

barracks. Now they swarm around the large yard between the blockhouses.

The heat rises, the hours are endless. We are without even our usual diversion: the wide roads leading to the crematoria are empty. For several days now, no new transports have come in. Part of "Canada"* has been liquidated and detailed to a labour Kommando—one of the very toughest—at Harmenz. For there exists in the camp a special brand of justice based on envy: when the rich and mighty fall, their friends see to it that they fall to the very bottom. And Canada, our Canada, which smells not of maple forests but of French perfume, has amassed great fortunes in diamonds and currency from all over Europe.

Several of us sit on the top bunk, our legs dangling over the edge. We slice the neat loaves of crisp, crunchy bread. It is a bit coarse to the taste, the kind that stays fresh for days. Sent all the way from Warsaw—only a week ago my mother held this white loaf in her hands . . . dear Lord, dear Lord . . .

We unwrap the bacon, the onion, we open a can of evaporated milk. Henri, the fat Frenchman, dreams aloud of the French wine brought by the transports from Strasbourg, Paris, Marseille . . . Sweat streams down his body.

"Listen, mon ami, next time we go up on the loading ramp, I'll bring you real champagne. You haven't tried it before, eh?"

"No. But you'll never be able to smuggle it through the gate, so stop teasing. Why not try and 'organize' some shoes for me instead—you know, the perforated kind, with a double sole, and what about that shirt you promised me long ago?"

"Patience, patience. When the new transports come, I'll bring all you want. We'll be going on the ramp again!"

"And what if there aren't any more 'cremo' transports?" I say spitefully. "Can't you see how much easier life is becoming around here: no limit on packages, no more beatings? You even write letters home . . . One hears all kind of talk, and, dammit, they'll run out of people!"

---

*"Canada" designated wealth and well-being in the camp. More specifically, it referred to the members of the labour gang, or Kommando, who helped to unload the incoming transports of people destined for the gas chambers.

"Stop talking nonsense." Henri's serious fat face moves rhythmically, his mouth is full of sardines. We have been friends for a long time, but I do not even know his last name. "Stop talking nonsense," he repeats, swallowing with effort. "They can't run out of people, or we'll starve to death in this blasted camp. All of us live on what they bring."

"All? We have our packages . . ."

"Sure, you and your friend, and ten other friends of yours. Some of you Poles get packages. But what about us, and the Jews, and the Russkis? And what if we had no food, no 'organization' from the transports, do you think you'd be eating those packages of yours in peace? We wouldn't let you!"

"You would, you'd starve to death like the Greeks. Around here, whoever has grub, has power."

"Anyway, you have enough, we have enough, so why argue?"

Right, why argue? They have enough, I have enough, we eat together and we sleep on the same bunks. Henri slices the bread, he makes a tomato salad. It tastes good with the commissary mustard.

Below us, naked, sweat-drenched men crowd the narrow barracks aisles or lie packed in eights and tens in the lower bunks. Their nude, withered bodies stink of sweat and excrement; their cheeks are hollow. Directly beneath me, in the bottom bunk, lies a rabbi. He has covered his head with a piece of rag torn off a blanket and reads from a Hebrew prayer book (there is no shortage of this type of literature at the camp), wailing loudly, monotonously.

"Can't somebody shut him up? He's been raving as if he'd caught God himself by the feet."

"I don't feel like moving. Let him rave. They'll take him to the oven that much sooner."

"Religion is the opium of the people," Henri, who is a Communist and a *rentier*, says sententiously. "If they didn't believe in God and eternal life, they'd have smashed the crematoria long ago."

"Why haven't you done it then?"

The question is rhetorical; the Frenchman ignores it.

"Idiot," he says simply, and stuffs a tomato in his mouth.

Just as we finish our snack, there is a sudden commotion at the door. The Muslims* scurry in fright to the safety of their bunks, a messenger runs into the Block Elder's shack. The Elder, his face solemn, steps out at once.

"Canada! *Antreten!* But fast! There's a transport coming!"

"Great God!" yells Henri, jumping off the bunk. He swallows the rest of his tomato, snatches his coat, screams "*Raus*" at the men below, and in a flash is at the door. We can hear a scramble in the other bunks. Canada is leaving for the ramp.

"Henri, the shoes!" I call after him.

"*Keine Angst!*" he shouts back, already outside.

I proceed to put away the food. I tie a piece of rope around the suitcase where the onions and the tomatoes from my father's garden in Warsaw mingle with Portuguese sardines, bacon from Lublin (that's from my brother), and authentic sweetmeats from Salonica. I tie it all up, pull on my trousers, and slide off the bunk.

"*Platz!*" I yell, pushing my way through the Greeks. They step aside. At the door I bump into Henri.

"*Was ist los?*"

"Want to come with us on the ramp?"

"Sure, why not?"

"Come along then, grab your coat! We're short of a few men. I've already told the Kapo," and he shoves me out of the barracks door.

We line up. Someone has marked down our numbers, someone up ahead yells, "March, march," and now we are running towards the gate, accompanied by the shouts of a multilingual throng that is already being pushed back to the barracks. Not everybody is lucky enough to be going on the ramp . . . We have almost reached the gate. *Links, zwei, drei, vier! Mützen ab!* Erect, arms stretched stiffly along our hips, we march past the gate briskly, smartly, almost gracefully. A sleepy S.S. man with a large pad in his hand checks us off, waving us ahead in groups of five.

"*Hundert!*" he calls after we have all passed.

---

*"Muslim" was the camp name for a prisoner who had been destroyed physically and spiritually, and who had neither the strength nor the will to go on living—a man ripe for the gas chamber.

"*Stimmt!*" comes a hoarse answer from out front.

We march fast, almost at a run. There are guards all around, young men with automatics. We pass camp II B, then some deserted barracks and a clump of unfamiliar green—apple and pear trees. We cross the circle of watchtowers and, running, burst on to the highway. We have arrived. Just a few more yards. There, surrounded by trees, is the ramp.

A cheerful little station, very much like any other provincial railway stop: a small square framed by tall chestnuts and paved with yellow gravel. Not far off, beside the road, squats a tiny wooden shed, uglier and more flimsy than the ugliest and flimsiest railway shack; farther along lie stacks of old rails, heaps of wooden beams, barracks, parts, bricks, paving stones. This is where they load freight for Birkenau: supplies for the construction of the camp, and people for the gas chambers. Trucks drive around, load up lumber, cement, people—a regular daily routine.

And now the guards are being posted along the rails, across the beams, in the green shade of the Silesian chestnuts, to form a tight circle around the ramp. They wipe the sweat from their faces and sip out of their canteens. It is unbearably hot; the sun stands motionless at its zenith.

"Fall out!"

We sit down in the narrow streaks of shade along the stacked rails. The hungry Greeks (several of them managed to come along, God only knows how) rummage underneath the rails. One of them finds some pieces of mildewed bread, another a few half-rotten sardines. They eat.

"*Schweinedreck*," spits a young, tall guard with corn-coloured hair and dreamy blue eyes. "For God's sake, any minute you'll have so much food to stuff down your guts, you'll bust!" He adjusts his gun, wipes his face with a handkerchief.

"Hey you, fatso!" His boot lightly touches Henri's shoulder. "*Pass mal auf*, want a drink?"

"Sure, but I haven't got any marks," replies the Frenchman with a professional air.

"*Schade*, too bad."

"Come, come, Herr Posten, isn't my word good enough any more? Haven't we done business before? How much?"

"One hundred. *Gemacht?*"

"*Gemacht.*"

We drink the water, lukewarm and tasteless. It will be paid for by the people who have not yet arrived.

"Now you be careful," says Henri, turning to me. He tosses away the empty bottle. It strikes the rails and bursts into tiny fragments. "Don't take any money, they might be checking. Anyway, who the hell needs money? You've got enough to eat. Don't take suits, either, or they'll think you're planning to escape. Just get a shirt, silk only, with a collar. And a vest. And if you find something to drink, don't bother calling me. I know how to shift for myself, but you watch your step or they'll let you have it."

"Do they beat you up here?"

"Naturally. You've got to have eyes in your ass. *Arschaugen.*"

Around us sit the Greeks, their jaws working greedily, like huge human insects. They munch on stale lumps of bread. They are restless, wondering what will happen next. The sight of the large beams and the stacks of rails has them worried. They dislike carrying heavy loads.

"*Was wir arbeiten?*" they ask.

"*Niks. Transport kommen, alles Krematorium, compris?*"

"*Alles verstehen,*" they answer in crematorium Esperanto. All is well—they will not have to move the heavy rails or carry the beams.

In the meantime, the ramp has become increasingly alive with activity, increasingly noisy. The crews are being divided into those who will open and unload the arriving cattle cars and those who will be posted by the wooden steps. They receive instructions on how to proceed most efficiently. Motor cycles drive up, delivering S.S. officers, bemedalled, glittering with brass, beefy men with highly polished boots and shiny, brutal faces. Some have brought their briefcases, others hold thin, flexible whips. This gives them an air of military readiness and agility. They walk in and out of the commissary—for the miserable little shack by the road serves as their commissary, where in the summertime they drink mineral water, *Studentenquelle,* and where in winter they can warm up with a glass of hot wine. They greet each other in the state-approved way, raising an arm Roman fashion, then shake hands cordially, exchange warm smiles, discuss mail from home, their children, their families. Some stroll majestically on the ramp. The silver squares on their collars glitter, the gravel crunches under their boots, their bamboo whips snap impatiently.

We lie against the rails in the narrow streaks of shade, breathe unevenly, occasionally exchange a few words in our various tongues, and gaze listlessly at the majestic men in green uniforms, at the green trees, and at the church steeple of a distant village.

"The transport is coming," somebody says. We spring to our feet, all eyes turn in one direction. Around the bend, one after another, the cattle cars begin rolling in. The train backs into the station, a conductor leans out, waves his hand, blows a whistle. The locomotive whistles back with a shrieking noise, puffs, the train rolls slowly alongside the ramp. In the tiny barred windows appear pale, wilted, exhausted human faces, terror-stricken women with tangled hair, unshaven men. They gaze at the station in silence. And then, suddenly, there is a stir inside the cars and a pounding against the wooden boards.

"Water! Air!"—weary, desperate cries.

Heads push through the windows, mouths gasp frantically for air. They draw a few breaths, then disappear; others come in their place, then also disappear. The cries and moans grow louder.

A man in a green uniform covered with more glitter than any of the others jerks his head impatiently, his lips twist in annoyance. He inhales deeply, then with a rapid gesture throws his cigarette away and signals to the guard. The guard removes the automatic from his shoulder, aims, sends a series of shots along the train. All is quiet now. Meanwhile, the trucks have arrived, steps are being drawn up, and the Canada men stand ready at their posts by the train doors. The S.S. officer with the briefcase raises his hand.

"Whoever takes gold, or anything at all besides food, will be shot for stealing Reich property. Understand? *Verstanden?*"

"*Jawohl!*" we answer eagerly.

"*Also los!* Begin!"

The bolts crack, the doors fall open. A wave of fresh air rushes inside the train. People . . . inhumanly crammed, buried under incredible heaps of luggage, suitcases, trunks, packages, crates, bundles of every description (everything that had been their past and was to start their future). Monstrously squeezed together, they have fainted from heat, suffocated, crushed one another. Now they push towards the open doors, breathing like fish cast out on the sand.

"Attention! Out, and take your luggage with you! Take out everything. Pile all your stuff near the exits. Yes, your coats too. It is summer. March to the left. Understand?"

"Sir, what's going to happen to us?" They jump from the train on to the gravel, anxious, worn-out.

"Where are you people from?"

"Sosnowiec-Będzin. Sir, what's going to happen to us?" They repeat the question stubbornly, gazing into our tired eyes.

"I don't know. I don't understand Polish."

It is the camp law: people going to their death must be deceived to the very end. This is the only permissible form of charity. The heat is tremendous. The sun hangs directly over our heads, the white, hot sky quivers, the air vibrates, an occasional breeze feels like a sizzling blast from a furnace. Our lips are parched, the mouth fills with the salty taste of blood, the body is weak and heavy from lying in the sun. Water!

A huge, multicoloured wave of people loaded down with luggage pours from the train like a blind, mad river trying to find a new bed. But before they have a chance to recover, before they can draw a breath of fresh air and look at the sky, bundles are snatched from their hands, coats ripped off their backs, their purses and umbrellas taken away.

"But please, sir, it's for the sun, I cannot . . ."

"Verboten!" one of us barks through clenched teeth. There is an S.S. man standing behind your back, calm, efficient, watchful.

"Meine Herrschaften, this way, ladies and gentlemen, try not to throw your things around, please. Show some goodwill," he says courteously, his restless hands playing with the slender whip.

"Of course, of course," they answer as they pass, and now they walk alongside the train somewhat more cheerfully. A woman reaches down quickly to pick up her handbag. The whip flies, the woman screams, stumbles, and falls under the feet of the surging crowd. Behind her, a child cries in a thin little voice "Mamele!" —a very small girl with tangled black curls.

The heaps grow. Suitcases, bundles, blankets, coats, handbags that open as they fall, spilling coins, gold, watches; mountains of bread pile up at the exits, heaps of marmalade, jams, masses of meat, sausages; sugar spills on the gravel. Trucks, loaded with people, start up with a deafening roar and drive off amidst the wailing and screaming of the women separated from their children, and the stupefied silence of the men left behind. They are the ones who had been ordered to step to the right—the healthy and the young who will go to the camp. In the end, they too will not escape death, but first they must work.

Trucks leave and return, without interruption, as on a monstrous conveyor belt. A Red Cross van drives back and forth, back and forth, incessantly: it transports the gas that will kill these people. The enormous cross on the hood, red as blood, seems to dissolve in the sun.

The Canada men at the trucks cannot stop for a single moment, even to catch their breath. They shove the people up the steps, pack them in tightly, sixty per truck, more or less. Near by stands a young, cleanshaven "gentleman," an S.S. officer with a notebook in his hand. For each departing truck he enters a mark; sixteen gone means one thousand people, more or less. The gentleman is calm, precise. No truck can leave without a signal from him, or a mark in his notebook: *Ordnung muss sein.* The marks swell into thousands, the thousands into whole transports, which afterwards we shall simply call "from Salonica," "from Strasbourg," "from Rotterdam." This one will be called "Sosnowiec-Będzin." The new prisoners from Sosnowiec-Będzin will receive serial numbers 131–2—thousand, of course, though afterwards we shall simply say 131–2, for short.

The transports swell into weeks, months, years. When the war is over, they will count up the marks in their notebooks— all four and a half million of them. The bloodiest battle of the war, the greatest victory of the strong, united Germany. *Ein Reich, ein Volk, ein Führer*—and four crematoria.

The train has been emptied. A thin, pock-marked S.S. man peers inside, shakes his head in disgust and motions to our group, pointing his finger at the door.

"*Rein.* Clean it up!"

We climb inside. In the corners amid human excrement and abandoned wrist-watches lie squashed, trampled infants, naked little monsters with enormous heads and bloated bellies. We carry them out like chickens, holding several in each hand.

"Don't take them to the trucks, pass them on to the women," says the S.S. man, lighting a cigarette. His cigarette lighter is not working properly; he examines it carefully.

"Take them, for God's sake!" I explode as the women run from me in horror, covering their eyes.

The name of God sounds strangely pointless, since the women and the infants will go on the trucks, every one of them, without exception. We all know what this means, and we look at each other with hate and horror.

"What, you don't want to take them?" asks the pock-marked S.S. man with a note of surprise and reproach in his voice, and reaches for his revolver.

"You mustn't shoot, I'll carry them." A tall, grey-haired woman takes the little corpses out of my hands and for an instant gazes straight into my eyes.

"My poor boy," she whispers and smiles at me. Then she walks away, staggering along the path. I lean against the side of the train. I am terribly tired. Someone pulls at my sleeve.

"*En avant*, to the rails, come on!"

I look up, but the face swims before my eyes, dissolves, huge and transparent, melts into the motionless trees and the sea of people . . . I blink rapidly: Henri.

"Listen, Henri, are we good people?"

"That's stupid. Why do you ask?"

"You see, my friend, you see, I don't know why, but I am furious, simply furious with these people—furious because I must be here because of them. I feel no pity. I am not sorry they're going to the gas chamber. Damn them all! I could throw myself at them, beat them with my fists. It must be pathological, I just can't understand . . ."

"Ah, on the contrary, it is natural, predictable, calculated. The ramp exhausts you, you rebel—and the easiest way to relieve your hate is to turn against someone weaker. Why, I'd even call it healthy. It's simple logic, *compris?*" He props himself up comfortably against the heap of rails. "Look at the Greeks, they know how to make the best of it! They stuff their bellies with anything they find. One of them has just devoured a full jar of marmalade."

"Pigs! Tomorrow half of them will die of the shits."

"Pigs? You've been hungry."

"Pigs!" I repeat furiously. I close my eyes. The air is filled with ghastly cries, the earth trembles beneath me, I can feel sticky moisture on my eyelids. My throat is completely dry.

The morbid procession streams on and on—trucks growl like mad dogs. I shut my eyes tight, but I can still see corpses dragged from the train, trampled infants, cripples piled on top of the dead, wave after wave . . . freight cars roll in, the heaps of clothing, suitcases and bundles grow, people climb out, look at the sun, take a few breaths, beg for water, get into the trucks, drive away. And again freight cars roll in, again people . . . The scenes become confused in my mind—I am not sure if all of this is actually happening, or if I am dreaming. There is a humming inside my head; I feel that I must vomit.

Henri tugs at my arm.

"Don't sleep, we're off to load up the loot."

All the people are gone. In the distance, the last few trucks roll along the road in clouds of dust, the train has left, several S.S. officers promenade up and down the ramp. The silver glitters on their collars. Their boots shine, their red, beefy faces shine. Among them there is a woman—only now I realize she has been here all along—withered, flat-chested, bony, her thin, colourless hair pulled back and tied in a "Nordic" knot; her hands are in the pockets of her wide skirt. With a rat-like, resolute smile glued on her thin lips she sniffs around the corners of the ramp. She detests feminine beauty with the hatred of a woman who is herself repulsive, and knows it. Yes, I have seen her many times before and I know her well: she is the commandant of the F.K.L. She has come to look over the new crop of women, for some of them, instead of going on the trucks, will go on foot—to the concentration camp. There our boys, the barbers from Zauna, will shave their heads and will have a good laugh at their "outside world" modesty.

We proceed to load the loot. We lift huge trunks, heave them on to the trucks. There they are arranged in stacks, packed tightly. Occasionally somebody slashes one open with a knife, for pleasure or in search of vodka and perfume. One of the crates falls open; suits, shirts, books drop out on the ground . . . I pick up a small, heavy package. I unwrap it—gold, about two handfuls, bracelets, rings, brooches, diamonds . . .

"Gib hier," an S.S. man says calmly, holding up his briefcase already full of gold and colourful foreign currency. He locks the case, hands it to an officer, takes another, an empty one, and stands by the next truck, waiting. The gold will go to the Reich.

It is hot, terribly hot. Our throats are dry, each word hurts. Anything for a sip of water! Faster, faster, so that it is over, so that we may rest. At last we are done, all the trucks have gone. Now we swiftly clean up the remaining dirt: there must be "no trace left of the Schweinerei." But just as the last truck disappears behind the trees and we walk, finally, to rest in the shade, a shrill whistle sounds around the bend. Slowly, terribly slowly, a train rolls in, the engine whistles back with a deafening shriek. Again weary, pale faces at the windows, flat as though cut out of paper, with huge, feverishly burning eyes. Already trucks are pulling up, already the composed gentleman with the notebook is at his post, and the S.S. men emerge from the commissary carrying briefcases for the gold and money. We unseal the train doors.

It is impossible to control oneself any longer. Brutally we tear suitcases from their hands, impatiently pull off their coats. Go on, go on, vanish! They go, they vanish. Men, women, children. Some of them know.

Here is a woman—she walks quickly, but tries to appear calm. A small child with a pink cherub's face runs after her and, unable to keep up, stretches out his little arms and cries: "Mama! Mama!"

"Pick up your child, woman!"

"It's not mine, sir, not mine!" she shouts hysterically and runs on, covering her face with her hands. She wants to hide, she wants to reach those who will not ride the trucks, those who will go on foot, those who will stay alive. She is young, healthy, good-looking, she wants to live.

But the child runs after her, wailing loudly: "Mama, mama, don't leave me!"

"It's not mine, not mine, no!"

Andrei, a sailor from Sevastopol, grabs hold of her. His eyes are glassy from vodka and the heat. With one powerful blow he knocks her off her feet, then, as she falls, takes her by the hair and pulls her up again. His face twitches with rage.

"Ah, you bloody Jewess. So you're running from your own child! I'll show you, you whore!" His huge hand chokes her, he lifts her in the air and heaves her on to the truck like a heavy sack of grain.

"Here! And take this with you, bitch!" and he throws the child at her feet.

"*Gut gemacht*, good work. That's the way to deal with degenerate mothers," says the S.S. man standing at the foot of the truck. "*Gut, gut, Russki.*"

"Shut your mouth," growls Andrei through clenched teeth, and walks away. From under a pile of rags he pulls out a canteen, unscrews the cork, takes a few deep swallows, passes it to me. The strong vodka burns the throat. My head swims, my legs are shaky, again I feel like throwing up.

And suddenly, above the teeming crowd pushing forward like a river driven by an unseen power, a girl appears. She descends lightly from the train, hops on to the gravel, looks around inquiringly, as if somewhat surprised. Her soft, blonde hair has fallen on her shoulders in a torrent, she throws it back impatiently. With a natural gesture she runs her hands down her blouse, casually straightens her skirt. She stands like this for an instant, gazing at the crowd, then turns and with a gliding look examines our faces, as though searching for someone. Unknowingly, I continue to stare at her, until our eyes meet.

"Listen, tell me, where are they taking us?"

I look at her without saying a word. Here, standing before me, is a girl, a girl with enchanting blonde hair, with beautiful breasts, wearing a little cotton blouse, a girl with a wise, mature look in her eyes. Here she stands, gazing straight into my face, waiting. And over there is the gas chamber: communal death, disgusting and ugly. And over in the other direction is the concentration camp: the shaved head, the heavy Soviet trousers in sweltering heat, the sickening, stale odour of dirty, damp female bodies, the animal hunger, the inhuman labour, and later the same gas chamber, only an even more hideous, more terrible death . . .

Why did she bring it? I think to myself, noticing a lovely gold watch on her delicate wrist. They'll take it away from her anyway.

"Listen, tell me," she repeats.

I remain silent. Her lips tighten.

"I know," she says with a shade of proud contempt in her voice, tossing her head. She walks off resolutely in the direction of the trucks. Someone tries to stop her; she boldly pushes him aside and runs up the steps. In the distance I can only catch a glimpse of her blonde hair flying in the breeze.

I go back inside the train; I carry out dead infants; I unload luggage. I touch corpses, but I cannot overcome the mounting, uncontrollable terror. I try to escape from the corpses, but they are everywhere: lined up on the gravel, on the cement edge of the ramp, inside the cattle cars. Babies, hideous naked women, men twisted by convulsions. I run off as far as I can go, but immediately a whip slashes across my back. Out of the corner of my eye I see an S.S. man, swearing profusely. I stagger forward and run, lose myself in the Canada group. Now, at last, I can once more rest against the stack of rails. The sun has leaned low over the horizon and illuminates the ramp with a reddish glow; the shadows of the trees have become elongated, ghostlike. In the silence that settles over nature at this time of day, the human cries seem to rise all the way to the sky.

Only from this distance does one have a full view of the inferno on the teeming ramp. I see a pair of human beings who have fallen to the ground locked in a last desperate embrace. The man has dug his fingers into the woman's flesh and has caught her clothing with his teeth. She screams hysterically, swears, cries, until at last a large boot comes down over her throat and she is silent. They are pulled apart and dragged like cattle to the truck. I see four Canada men lugging a corpse: a huge, swollen female corpse. Cursing, dripping wet from the strain, they kick out of their way some stray children who have been running all over the ramp, howling like dogs. The men pick them up by the collars, heads, arms, and toss them inside the trucks, on top of the heaps. The four men have trouble lifting the fat corpse on to the car, they call others for help, and all together they hoist up the mound of meat. Big, swollen, puffed-up corpses are being collected from all over the ramp; on top of them are piled the invalids, the smothered, the sick, the unconscious. The heap seethes, howls, groans. The driver starts the motor, the truck begins rolling.

"Halt! Halt!" an S.S. man yells after them. "Stop, damn you!"

They are dragging to the truck an old man wearing tails and a band around his arm. His head knocks against the gravel and pavement; he moans and wails in an uninterrupted monotone: *"Ich will mit dem Herrn Kommandanten sprechen—*I wish to speak with the commandant . . ."* With senile stubbornness he keeps repeating these words all the way. Thrown on the truck, trampled by others, choked, he still wails: *"Ich will mit dem . . ."*

"Look here, old man!" a young S.S. man calls, laughing jovially. "In half an hour you'll be talking with the top commandant! Only don't forget to greet him with a *Heil Hitler!"*

Several other men are carrying a small girl with only one leg. They hold her by the arms and the one leg. Tears are running down her face and she whispers faintly: "Sir, it hurts, it hurts . . ." They throw her on the truck on top of the corpses. She will burn alive along with them.

The evening has come, cool and clear. The stars are out. We lie against the rails. It is incredibly quiet. Anaemic bulbs hang from the top of the high lamp-posts; beyond the circle of light stretches an impenetrable darkness. Just one step, and a man could vanish for ever. But the guards are watching, their automatics ready.

"Did you get the shoes?" asks Henri.

"No."

"Why?"

"My God, man, I am finished, absolutely finished!"

"So soon? After only two transports? Just look at me, I . . . since Christmas, at least a million people have passed through

my hands. The worst of all are the transports from around Paris
—one is always bumping into friends."

"And what do you say to them?"

"That first they will have a bath, and later we'll meet at the
camp. What would you say?"

I do not answer. We drink coffee with vodka; somebody opens
a tin of cocoa and mixes it with sugar. We scoop it up by the
handful, the cocoa sticks to the lips. Again coffee, again vodka.

"Henri, what are we waiting for?"

"There'll be another transport."

"I'm not going to unload it! I can't take any more."

"So, it's got you down? Canada is nice, eh?" Henri grins indul-
gently and disappears into the darkness. In a moment he is back
again.

"All right. Just sit here quietly and don't let an S.S. man see
you. I'll try to find you your shoes."

"Just leave me alone. Never mind the shoes." I want to sleep.
It is very late.

Another whistle, another transport. Freight cars emerge out
of the darkness, pass under the lamp-posts, and again vanish in
the night. The ramp is small, but the circle of lights is smaller.
The unloading will have to be done gradually. Somewhere the
trucks are growling. They back up against the steps, black, ghostlike, their searchlights flash across the trees. Wasser! Luft! The
same all over again, like a late showing of the same film: a volley
of shots, the train falls silent. Only this time a little girl pushes
herself halfway through the small window and, losing her balance,
falls out onto the gravel. Stunned, she lies still for a moment, then
stands up and begins walking around in a circle, faster and faster,
waving her rigid arms in the air, breathing loudly and spasmodi-
cally, whining in a faint voice. Her mind has given way in the
inferno inside the train. The whining is hard on the nerves: an
S.S. man approaches calmly, his heavy boot strikes between her
shoulders. She falls. Holding her down with his foot, he draws
his revolver, fires once, then again. She remains face down, kicking the gravel with her feet, until she stiffens. They proceed to
unseal the train.

I am back on the ramp, standing by the doors. A warm, sickening smell gushes from inside. The mountain of people filling the car almost halfway up to the ceiling is motionless, horribly tangled, but still steaming.

"*Ausladen!*" comes the command. An S.S. man steps out from the darkness. Across his chest hangs a portable searchlight. He throws a stream of light inside.

"Why are you standing about like sheep? Start unloading!" His whip flies and falls across our backs. I seize a corpse by the hand; the fingers close tightly around mine. I pull back with a shriek and stagger away. My heart pounds, jumps up to my throat. I can no longer control the nausea. Hunched under the train I begin to vomit. Then, like a drunk, I weave over to the stack of rails.

I lie against the cool, kind metal and dream about returning to the camp, about my bunk, on which there is no mattress, about sleep among comrades who are not going to the gas tonight. Suddenly I see the camp as a haven of peace. It is true, others may be dying, but one is somehow still alive, one has enough food, enough strength to work . . .

The lights on the ramp flicker with a spectral glow, the wave of people—feverish, agitated, stupefied people—flows on and on, endlessly. They think that now they will have to face a new life in the camp, and they prepare themselves emotionally for the hard struggle ahead. They do not know that in just a few moments they will die, that the gold, money, and diamonds which they have so prudently hidden in their clothing and on their bodies are now useless to them. Experienced professionals will probe into every recess of their flesh, will pull the gold from under the tongue and the diamonds from the uterus and the colon. They will rip out gold teeth. In tightly sealed crates they will ship them to Berlin.

The S.S. men's black figures move about, dignified, business-like. The gentleman with the notebook puts down his final marks, rounds out the figures: fifteen thousand.

Many, very many, trucks have been driven to the crematoria today.

It is almost over. The dead are being cleared off the ramp and piled into the last truck. The Canada men, weighed down under a load of bread, marmalade and sugar, and smelling of perfume and fresh linen, line up to go. For several days the entire camp will live off this transport. For several days the entire camp will talk about "Sosnowiec-Będzin." "Sosnowiec-Będzin" was a good, rich transport.

The stars are already beginning to pale as we walk back to the camp. The sky grows translucent and opens high above our heads —it is getting light.

Great columns of smoke rise from the crematoria and merge up above into a huge black river which very slowly floats across the sky over Birkenau and disappears beyond the forests in the direction of Trzebinia. The "Sosnowiec-Będzin" transport is already burning.

We pass a heavily armed S.S. detachment on its way to change guard. The men march briskly, in step, shoulder to shoulder, one mass, one will.

"*Und morgen die ganze Welt . . .*" they sing at the top of their lungs.

"*Rechts ran!* To the right march!" snaps a command from up front. We move out of their way.

22 Eldridge Cleaver

Eldridge Cleaver, Minister of Information of the Black Panther Party and author of Soul on Ice (1968), was the 1968 candidate of the Peace and Freedom Party for the President of the United States.

◈

"THE CHRIST" AND HIS TEACHINGS
(FROM *SOUL ON ICE*)

Folsom Prison,
September 10, 1965

My first awareness of Thomas Merton came in San Quentin, back in (I believe) 1959–60. During that time, a saint walked the earth in the person of one Chris Lovdjieff. He was a teacher at San Quentin and guru to all who came to him. What did he teach? Everything. It is easier just to say he taught Lovdjieff and let it go at that. He himself claimed to be sort of a disciple of Alan W. Watts, whom he used to bring over to Q to lecture us now and then on Hinduism, Zen Buddhism, and on the ways the peoples of Asia view the universe. I never understood how "The Christ" (as I used to call Lovdjieff, to his great sorrow and pain) could sit at Watts' feet, because he always seemed to me more warm, more human, and possessed of greater wisdom than Watts displayed either in his lectures or his books. It may be that I received this impression from having been exposed more to Lovdjieff than to Watts. Yet there was something about Watts that reminded me of a slick advertisement for a labor-saving de-

vice, aimed at the American housewife, out of the center page of
Life magazine; while Lovdjieff's central quality seemed to be pain,
suffering, and a peculiar strength based on his understanding of
his own helplessness, weakness, and need. Under Lovdjieff I
studied world history, Oriental philosophy, Occidental philosophy, comparative religion, and economics. I could not tell one
class from the other—neither could the other students and neither,
I believe, could Lovdjieff. It was all Lovdjieff.

The walls of his classrooms were covered with cardboard
placards which bore quotations from the world's great thinkers.
There were quotes from Japanese, Eskimos, Africans, Hopi Indians, Peruvians, Voltaire, Confucius, Lao-tse, Jesus Christ, Moses,
Mohammed, Buddha, Rabbi Hillel, Plato, Aristotle, Marx, Lenin,
Mao Tse-tung, Zoroaster—and Thomas Merton, among others.
Once Lovdjieff gave a lecture on Merton, reading from his works
and trying to put the man's life and work in context. He seemed
desperately to want us to respect Merton's vocation and choice
of the contemplative life. It was an uphill battle because a prison
is in many ways like a monastery. The convicts in Lovdjieff's class
hated prison. We were appalled that a free man would voluntarily
enter prison—or a monastery. Let me say it right out: we thought
Merton was some kind of nut. We thought the same thing about
Lovdjieff. My secret disgust was that in many ways I was nothing
but a monk, and how I loathed that view of myself!

I was mystified by Merton and I could not believe in his
passionate defense of monkhood. I distrusted Lovdjieff on the
subject of Thomas Merton. My mind heard a special pleading in
his voice. In his ardent defense of Merton, Lovdjieff seemed to be
defending himself, even trying to convince himself. One day
Lovdjieff confided to us that he had tried to be a monk but
couldn't make it. He made it, all right, without even realizing it.
San Quentin was his monastery. He busied himself about the
prison as though he had a special calling to minister to the
prisoners. He was there day and night and on Saturdays, without
fail. The officials would sometimes have to send a guard to his
class to make him stop teaching, so the inmates could be locked
up for the night. He was horror-stricken that they could make
such a demand of him. Reluctantly, he'd sit down heavily in his

seat, burdened by defeat, and tell us to go to our cells. Part of the power we gave him was that we would never leave his class unless he himself dismissed us. If a guard came and told us to leave, he got only cold stares; we would not move until Lovdjieff gave the word. He got a secret kick out of this little victory over his tormentors. If, as happened once, he was unable to make it to the prison because his car had a blowout, he'd be full of apologies and pain next day.

Lovdjieff had extracted from me my word that I would some day read Merton for myself—he did not insist upon any particular time, just "some day." Easy enough. I gave my promise. In 1963, when I was transferred from San Quentin to Folsom for being an agitator, they put me in solitary confinement. The officials did not deem it wise, at that time, to allow me to circulate among the general inmate population. I had evolved a crash program which I would immediately activate whenever I was placed in solitary: stock up on books and read, read, read; do calisthenics and forget about the rest of the world. I had learned the waste and futility of worry. (Years ago, I had stopped being one of those convicts who take a little calendar and mark off each day.) When I asked for books to read in this particular hole, a trustee brought me a list from which to make selections. On the list I was delighted to see Merton's *The Seven Storey Mountain*, his autobiography. I thought of Lovdjieff. Here was a chance to fulfill my promise.

I was tortured by that book because Merton's suffering, in his quest for God, seemed all in vain to me. At the time, I was a Black Muslim chained in the bottom of a pit by the Devil. Did I expect Allah to tear down the walls and set me free? To me, the language and symbols of religion were nothing but weapons of war. I had no other purpose for them. All the gods are dead except the god of war. I wished that Merton had stated in secular terms the reasons he withdrew from the political, economic, military, and social system into which he was born, seeking refuge in a monastery.

Despite my rejection of Merton's theistic world view, I could not keep him out of the room. He shouldered his way through the door. Welcome, Brother Merton. I give him a bear hug. Most impressive of all to me was Merton's description of New York's black ghetto—Harlem. I liked it so much I copied out the heart of it in longhand. Later, after getting out of solitary, I used to keep this passage in mind when delivering Black Muslim lectures to other prisoners. Here is an excerpt:

Here in this huge, dark, steaming slum, hundreds of thousands of Negroes are herded together like cattle, most of them with nothing to eat and nothing to do. All the senses and imagination and sensibilities and emotions and sorrows and desires and hopes and ideas of a race with vivid feelings and deep emotional reactions are forced in upon themselves, bound inward by an iron ring of frustration: the prejudice that hems them in with its four insurmountable walls. In this huge cauldron, inestimable natural gifts, wisdom, love, music, science, poetry are stamped down and left to boil with the dregs of an elementally corrupted nature, and thousands upon thousands of souls are destroyed by vice and misery and degradation, obliterated, wiped out, washed from the register of the living, dehumanized.

What has not been devoured, in your dark furnace, Harlem, by marijuana, by gin, by insanity, hysteria, syphilis?

For a while, whenever I felt myself softening, relaxing, I had only to read that passage to become once more a rigid flame of indignation. It had precisely the same effect on me that Elijah Muhammad's writings used to have, or the words of Malcolm X, or the words of any spokesman of the oppressed in any land. I vibrate sympathetically to any protest against tyranny.

But I want to tell more about Lovdjieff—The Christ.

Chris Lovdjieff had a profound mind and an ecumenical education. I got the impression that the carnage of World War II, particularly the scientific, systematic approach to genocide of the Nazi regime, had been a traumatic experience from which it was impossible for him to recover. It was as if he had seen or experienced something which had changed him forever, sickened his soul, overwhelmed him with sympathy and love for all mankind. He hated all restraints upon the human mind, the human spirit, all blind believing, all dogmatic assertion. He questioned everything.

I was never sure of just what was driving him. That he was driven there could be no doubt. There was a sense of unreality about him. It seemed that he moved about in a mist. The atmosphere he created was like the mystic spell of Khalil Gibran's poetry. He seemed always to be listening to distant music, or silent voices, or to be talking in a whisper to himself. He loved silence and said that it should only be broken for important communications, and he would expel students from his classes for distracting the others by chatting idly in the back rows. In his classes he was a dictator. He enforced certain rules which brooked no deviation—no smoking in his classroom at any time, before class, during class, at recess, or even when school was out; no talking in Lovdjieff's class unless it was pertinent to the subject at hand; no eating or chewing gum in his classroom; no profanity. Simple rules, perhaps, but in San Quentin they were visionary, adventurous, audacious. The Christ enforced them strictly. The other teachers and the guards wondered how he got away with it. We students wondered why we enthusiastically submitted to it. The Christ would look surprised, as if he did not understand, if you asked him about it. If one of the other teachers forgot and came into Lovdjieff's classroom smoking, he was sent hopping. The same went for prison guards. I can still see the shocked expression of a substitute teacher who, coming into Lovdjieff's room during recess smoking a pipe, was told: "Leave this room!"

When you came to Lovdjieff's classes, you came to learn. If you betrayed other motives, "Get out of here this minute!"—without malice but without equivocation. He was a magnet, an institution. He worked indefatigably. His day started when the school bell rang at 8 A.M. Often he would forego lunch to interview a few students and help them along with their schoolwork or personal problems. He never ceased complaining because the officials refused to allow him to eat lunch in the mess hall with the prisoners. Had they given him a cell he would have taken it. After lunch, he'd teach until 3 P.M. When night school convened at 6 P.M., The Christ would be there, beaming, radiating, and he'd teach passionately until 10 P.M. Then, reluctantly, he'd go home to suffer in exile until school opened next day. On Saturdays he'd be there bright and early to teach—Lovdjieff. He would have come on Sundays too, only the officials put their foot down and refused to hear of it. The Christ settled for a Sunday evening radio program of two hours which he taped for broadcast to the prisoners.

His classes were works of art. He made ancient history contemporary by evoking the total environment—intellectual, social, political, economic—of an era. He breathed life into the shattered ruins of the past. Students sat entranced while The Christ performed, his silver-rimmed glasses reflecting the light in eye-twinkling flashes.

He dressed like a college boy, betraying a penchant for simple sweaters and plain slacks of no particular distinction. He burned incense in his classroom when he lectured on religion, to evoke a certain mood. He was drawn to those students who seemed most impossible to teach—old men who had been illiterate all their lives and set in their ways. Lovdjieff didn't believe that anyone or anything in the universe was "set in its ways." Those students who were intelligent and quickest to learn he seemed reluctant to bother with, almost as if to say, pointing at the illiterates and speaking to the bright ones: "Go away. Leave me. You don't need me. These others do."

Jesus wept. Lovdjieff would weep over a tragic event that had taken place ten thousand years ago in some forgotten byway in the Fertile Crescent. Once he was lecturing on the ancient Hebrews. He was angry with them for choosing to settle along the trade routes between Egypt and Mesopotamia. He showed how, over the centuries, time and time again, these people had been invaded, slaughtered, driven out, captured, but always to return.

"What is it that keeps pulling them back to this spot!" he exclaimed. He lost his breath. His face crumbled, and he broke down and wept. "Why do they insist on living in the middle of that—that [for once, I thought meanly, The Christ couldn't find a word] that—that—Freeway! They have to sit down in the center of the Freeway! That's all it is—look!" He pointed out the trade routes on the map behind his desk, then he sat down and cried uncontrollably for several minutes.

Another time, he brought tape-recorded selections from Thomas Wolfe's *Look Homeward Angel*. The Christ wept all through the tape.

The Christ could weep over a line of poetry, over a single

image in a poem, over the beauty of a poem's music, over the fact that man can talk, read, write, walk, reproduce, die, eat, eliminate—over the fact that a chicken can lay an egg.

Once he lectured us all week on Love. He quoted what poets had said of Love, what novelists had said of Love, what playwrights had said of Love. He played tapes of Ashley Montagu on Love. Over the weekend, each student was to write an essay on his own conception of Love, mindful to have been influenced by what he had been listening to all week long. In my essay I explained that I did not love white people. I quoted Malcom X:

How can I love the man who raped my mother, killed my father, enslaved my ancestors, dropped atomic bombs on Japan, killed off the Indians and keeps me cooped up in the slums? I'd rather be tied up in a sack and tossed into the Harlem River first.

Lovdjieff refused to grade my paper. He returned it to me. I protested that he was being narrow-minded and dogmatic in not understanding why I did not love white people simply because he himself was white. He told me to talk with him after class.

"How can you do this to me?" he asked.

"I've only written the way I feel," I said.

Instead of answering, he cried.

"Jesus wept," I told him and walked out.

Two days later, he returned my essay—ungraded. There were instead spots on it which I realized to be his tears.

Although Lovdjieff's popularity among the prisoners continued to soar and the waiting lists for his classes grew longer and longer, prison authorities banned his radio program. Then they stopped him from coming in on Saturdays. Then they stopped him from teaching night school. Then they took away his pass and barred him from San Quentin.

23 Frank Conroy

Frank Conroy was born in New York in 1936. Stop-Time, his first book, was published in 1967.

◈

WHITE DAYS AND RED NIGHTS
(FROM *STOP-TIME*)

Jean and my mother had weekend jobs as wardens at the South-bury Training School, a Connecticut state institution for the feeble-minded. Every Friday afternoon we drove out deep in the hills to an old cabin they had bought for a few hundred dollars on the installment plan.

The first dirt road was always plowed for the milk truck, but never the second, and in the snow you could see the tracks of wagon wheels and two narrow trails where the horses had walked. A mile down the road was the Greens' farm. Every morning they hauled milk to the pick-up station, a full silent load up to the hill, and then back, the empty returns from the previous day clanging raucously behind the horses as if in melancholic cele-bration. No one else ever used the road. If it was passable we drove to the cabin, if not, we walked, single file, in the horses' tracks, our arms full of food.

Every Friday the cheap padlock was opened, every Friday I stepped inside. A room so dim my blood turned gray, so cold I knew no human heart had ever beaten there—every line, every article of furniture, every scrap of paper on the floor, every burned-out match in a saucer filling me with desolation, depopulating me. A single room, twelve feet by eighteen. A double bed, a bureau, a round table to eat on, and against the wall a counter with a kerosene cooker. In the exact center of the room, a pot-bellied coal stove. All these objects had been watched by me in a state of advanced terror, watched so many long nights that even in the daytime they seemed to be whispering bad messages.

My mother would make a quick meal out of cans. Corned-beef hash or chili. Conversation was usually sparse.

"I have a good cottage tonight."

"I can't remember where I am. We'd better stop at the administration building."

Outside, the lead-gray afternoon slipped almost imperceptibly into twilight. Very gradually the earth moved toward night and as I sat eating I noted every darkening shadow. Jean sipped his coffee and lighted a Pall Mall. My mother arranged the kerosene lamp so she could see to do the dishes.

"Frank, get me some water."

Through the door and into the twilight, the bucket against my thigh. There was a path beaten through the snow, a dark line curving through the drifts to the well. The low sky was empty, uniformly leaden. Stands of trees spread pools of darkness, as if night came up from their sunken roots. At the well I tied a rope to the handle of the bucket and dropped it into the darkness upside down, holding the line. The trick was not to hit the sides. I heard a muffled splash. Leaning over the deep hole, with the faintest hint of warmer air rising against my face, I hauled the bucket hand over hand until it rose suddenly into view, the dim sky shimmering within like some luminous oil. Back to the house with the water. Absolute silence except for the sounds of my own movement, absolute stillness except for a wavering line of smoke from the stovepipe.

While Mother did the dishes Jean and I sat at the table. He sipped at his second cup of coffee. I fished a dime out of my pocket. "Could you get me a couple of Baby Ruth bars?"

Jean sucked his teeth and reached for a wooden pick. "The stuff is poison. It rots your teeth."

"Oh Jean, I know. It won't take you a second. There's a stand in the administration building."

"You're so finicky about food and you go and eat that stuff. Can you imagine the crap in those mass-produced candy bars? Dead roaches and mouse shit and somebody's nose-pickings."

"Jean, for heaven's sake!" My mother laughed.

"Well, he won't touch a piece of perfectly good meat and then he'll eat that junk."

"It'll only take you a second." I pushed the dime across the table.

"I know the trouble with you. You're too lazy to chew your food. You wash everything down with milk." He glanced at the coin, his eyes flicking away. "All right. If you want to kill yourself. Keep the dime." He finished his coffee and cigarette slowly, savoring the mixed flavors and the moment of rest. Since he'd stopped using the holder his smoking style had changed. He'd take a quick drag, blow out about a third of the smoke immediately, inhale the rest, and let it come out as he talked. I often made it a point to sit in such a way that a strong light source behind him showed up the smoke. It was amazing how long it came out, a fine, almost invisible blue stream, phrase after phrase, changing direction smoothly as he clipped off the words. For some reason I admired this phenomenon tremendously. I could sit watching for hours.

Jean pushed back his chair and stood up, stretching his arms and yawning exaggeratedly. Even this he did gracefully. Like a cat, he was incapable of making an awkward move. Looking out the window he sucked his teeth noisily. "Well," he said slowly, "the lions and tigers seem to be under control tonight."

I felt my face flush and quickly turned away. It was a complicated moment. My fear of staying alone in the house had been totally ignored for weeks. For Jean to mention it at all was somehow promising, and I was grateful despite the unfairness of his phrasing. He knew of course that it wasn't lions and tigers I was afraid of—by using that image he was attempting to simplify my fear into the realm of childishness (which he could then ignore in good conscience) as well as to shame me out of it. Jean was telling me, with a smile, that my behavior was irrational and therefore he could do nothing to help me, something I would never have expected in any case. I knew perfectly well that no one could help me. The only possible solution would have been for me to stay in the city on weekends with Alison, but that battle had been lost. Jean and Mother wanted me with them. Not because they felt they had to look after me but because I was useful. I drew the water. I tended the fire so the house would be warm in the morning when they returned.

"We'd better go," Mother said, lifting the last dripping dish from the plastic basin. "Frank, you dry the dishes and put them away."

I watched their preparations with a sense of remoteness. It was as if they were already gone. Mother dried her hands carefully and put on her heavy coat. Jean bent over the row of paperback books and pulled out an Erskine Caldwell. "I won't be able to read tonight but I'll take it anyway."

"All right?" Mother asked. They stood for a last moment, waiting, making sure they hadn't forgotten anything, sensing in each other the precise moment to leave. Then they were through the door and away. I followed a few moments later, stepping in their footprints to the road. I watched them walk into the darkness underneath the trees. My mother turned at the top of a rise and called back to me over the snow. "Don't forget to set the alarm!" She hurried to catch up with Jean. As they moved down the hill it was as if they sank deeper and deeper into the snow. Dimly I could make out the top halves of their bodies, then only their shoulders, their heads, and they were gone.

I went back to the house. After an initial surge of panic my mind turned itself off. Thinking was dangerous. By not thinking I attained a kind of inner invisibility. I knew that fear attracted evil, that the uncontrolled sound of my own mind would in some way delineate me to the forces threatening me, as the thrashing of a fish in shallow water draws the gull. I tried to keep still, but every now and then the fear escalated up into consciousness and my mind would stir, readjusting itself like the body of a man trying to sleep in an uncomfortable position. In those moments I felt most vulnerable, my eyes widening and my ears straining to catch the sound of approaching danger.

I dried the dishes slowly and put them away, attempting to do the whole job without making a sound. Occasionally a floorboard creaked under my weight, sending a long, lingering charge up my spine, a white thrill at once delicious and ominous. I approached the stove nervously. The coal rattled and the cast-iron grate invariably banged loudly despite my precautions. I had to do it quickly, holding my breath, or I wouldn't do it at all. Once finished I checked the window latches. There was nothing to be done about the door; it couldn't be locked from the inside and Mother refused to lock it from the outside because of the danger of my getting trapped in a fire.

By the yellow light of the kerosene lamp I sat on the edge of the bed and removed my shoes, placing them carefully on the floor. The Big Ben alarm clock ticked off the seconds on a shelf above my head, and every now and then a puff of coal gas popped in the stove as the fuel shifted. I got under the covers fully clothed and surveyed the stillness of the room, trying to slow my breathing. For an hour or more I lay motionless in a self-induced trance, my eyes open but seldom moving, my ears listening to the sounds of the house and the faint, inexplicable, continuous noises from outside. (In this state my ears seemed rather far away. I was burrowed somewhere deep in my skull, my ears advance outposts sending back reports to headquarters.) As I remember it the trance must have been close to the real thing. It was an attempt to reach an equipoise of fear, a state in which the incoming fear signals balanced with some internal process of dissimulation. At best it worked only temporarily, since fear held a slight edge. But for an hour or two I avoided what I hated most, the great noisy swings up and down. The panic and the hilarity.

At the first flashing thought of the Southbury Training School I sat up and took a book from the shelf. Escaped inmates were rare, and supposedly harmless, but I knew that a runaway had ripped the teats from one of the Greens' cows with a penknife, and that another had strangled four cats in a barnyard. I read quickly, skimming the pages for action and dialogue while most of my mind stood on guard. Book after book came down from the shelf, piling up on the bed beside me as I waited for sleep. I knew that if I left the lamp on I would stay awake most of the night, so when the pages began to go out of focus I set the alarm clock, cupped my hand over the mouth of the lamp chimney and blew myself into darkness.

Being sleepy and being scared do not cancel each other out. After hours of waiting the mind insists and slips under itself into unconsciousness. The sleeping body remains tense, the limbs bent as if poised for flight, adrenalin oozing steadily into the blood. Every few minutes the mind awakens, listens, and goes back to sleep. Fantastic dreams attempt to absorb the terror, explaining away the inexplicable with lunatic logic, twisting thought to a mad, private vision so that sleep can go on for another few seconds.

I wake up in the dark, a giant hand squeezing my heart. All around me a tremendous noise is splitting the air, exploding like a continuous chain of fireworks. The alarm clock! My God, the clock! Ringing all this time, calling, calling, bringing everything evil. I reach out and shut it off. The vibrations die out under my fingers and I listen to the silence, wondering if anything has approached under the cover of the ringing bell. (Remember a children's game called Giant Steps?)

I sit up cautiously. My body freezes. Rising before me over the foot of the bed is a bright, glowing, cherry-red circle in the darkness, a floating globe pulsating with energy, wavering in the air like the incandescent heart of some dissected monster, dripping sparks and blood. I throw myself backward against the wall behind the bed. Books tumble around me from the shelves, an ashtray falls and smashes on the floor. My hands go out, palms extended, towards the floating apparition, my voice whispering "Please . . ." Impossibly a voice answers, a big voice from all around me. "FRANK! FRANK!" My knees give out and I fall off the bed to the floor. I can feel the pieces of broken ashtray under my hands.

From the corner of my eye I see the red circle. I keep quite still, and the circle doesn't move. If I turn my head I seem to sense a corresponding movement, but I can't be sure. In the blackness there is nothing to relate to. Step by step I begin to understand. My body grows calmer and it's as if a series of veils were being whisked away from my eyes. I see clearly that the circle is only the red-hot bottom of the stove—a glowing bowl, its surface rippling with color changes from draughts of cool air. The last veil lifts and reveals an image of magic beauty, a sudden miracle in the night. I fall asleep watching it, my shoulder against the bed.

Hours later the cold wakes me and I climb up under the covers. When dawn comes my limbs relax. I can tell when dawn has come even though I'm asleep.

I woke up when the wagon went by, creaking like a ship, passing close, just on the other side of the wall by my head. Chip would be driving, I knew, with Toad in back watching the cans. They never spoke as they went by. Sometimes Chip would murmur to the horses, "Haw, gee-aw." The traces rang quietly and the tall iron-rimmed wheels splintered rocks under the snow.

It was hard to get out of bed. The air was cold. Water froze in the bucket and the windows were coated with ice. The light was gray, exactly the same quality as the twilight of the night before, devoid of meaning. I cleaned out the stove, laid paper, a few sticks of kindling and some coal, splashed kerosene over everything, and struck a match. With a great whoosh the stove filled with flames. My teeth chattering, I rushed back under the covers. I fell asleep waiting to get warm.

When Jean and my mother came through the door I woke up. They seemed tremendously alive, bustling with energy, their voices strangely loud.

"It's freezing in here. What happened to the fire?" I sat up in bed. The fire had gone out, or more likely had never caught after the kerosene had burned.

"You forgot to set the alarm," my mother said.

"No I didn't."

She knelt and relit the fire. Jean stood in the open doorway, knocking snow off his galoshes. He closed the door and sat on the edge of the bed, bending over to open the buckles. "My God, it's cold. We should have stayed in Florida."

"I vote for that," I said.

"Just get your ass out of that bed." He rubbed his stocking feet and twisted up his face. "How about some coffee?"

"Just a second," my mother said, still fussing with the stove.

Jean stood up and undid his belt. "Okay. Let's go." He waited till I was out of bed, took off his trousers, and climbed in. The heavy black and red flannel shirt he wore in cold weather was left on, buttoned tight over his narrow chest. He ran a finger over his mustache and waited for his cup of coffee.

Mother made it for him while I fixed myself a bowl of cornflakes.

"It's not very much to ask to keep the stove going," my mother said. "I never ask you to do anything."

I ate my cornflakes. The stove was beginning to give off a little heat and I pulled my chair closer, arranging it so my back was to the bed. I heard Mother undressing, and then the creak of the rusty springs as she got in beside Jean. From that moment on I was supposed to keep quiet so they could sleep.

There was no place else to go. Outside the land was hidden under two and a half feet of snow. The wind was sharp and bitter (I found out later that locals considered it the worst winter in forty years) and in any case I didn't have the proper clothes. Even indoors, sitting in the chair with the stove going, I kept a blanket wrapped around me Indian style. The time dragged slowly. There was nothing to do. I tried to save the few books for nighttime, when my need of them was greater. I drew things with a pencil—objects in the room, my hand, imaginary scenes—but I was no good and quickly lost interest. Usually I simply sat in the chair for six or seven hours. Jean snored softly, but after the first hour or so I stopped hearing it.

Midway through the morning I remembered the candy bars. Certain Jean had forgotten them, I looked anyway, getting up from the chair carefully, tiptoeing to his clothes and searching through the pockets. Nothing. I watched him in bed, his face gray with sleep, his open mouth twitching at the top of each gentle snore. My mother turned to the wall. Jean closed his mouth and rolled over. The room was absolutely silent. I went back to the chair.

They awoke in the early afternoon and stayed in bed. Although the small stove was working it was still the warmest place. Freed from the necessity of keeping quiet, I walked around the room aimlessly, getting a drink of water, rubbing the haze off the windows to look outside. My mother raised her voice and I realized she was talking to me.

"Take some money from my purse and go down to the Greens' and get a dozen eggs."

The trip to the Greens' would take an hour each way. Outside the temperature was five or ten degrees above zero and it was windy. I didn't want to go. My heart sank because I knew I had to.

Children are in the curious position of having to do what people tell them, whether they want to or not. A child knows that he must do what he's told. It matters little whether a command is just or unjust since the child has no confidence in his ability to distinguish the difference. Justice for children is not the same as justice for adults. In effect all commands are morally neutral to a child. Yet because almost every child is consistently bullied by older people he quickly learns that if in some higher frame of reference all commands are equally just, they are not equally easy to carry out. Some fill him with joy, others, so obviously unfair that he must paralyze himself to keep from recognizing their quality, strike him instantly deaf, blind, and dumb. Faced with an order they sense is unfair children simply stall. They wait for more information, for some elaboration that will take away the seeming unfairness. It's a stupid way of defending oneself, but children are stupid compared to adults, who know how to get what they want.

"Couldn't we wait until they come up with the wagon?"

"No. The walk will do you good. You can't sit around all day, it's unhealthy."

"Oh Mother, it'll take hours."

Suddenly Jean sat up, his voice trembling with anger. "Look, this time just go. No arguments this time."

I looked at him in amazement. He'd never even raised his voice to me before. It was against the unwritten rules—my mother was the disciplinarian. I could see he was angry and I had no idea why. Even my mother was surprised. "Take it easy," she said to him softly. "He's going."

Jean's anger should have tipped me off, but it didn't. Wearing

his galoshes and his overcoat I went to the Greens' without realizing why they had sent me.

It was no secret that I wanted to go along to the training
school at night, to sleep on an extra bed somewhere. For months
Mother put me off, but when she realized I would never get
accustomed to staying alone she gave in. She was tired of dealing
with me, tired of my complaints and my silences. (Alternative
unconscious motivations for her change of heart: one, she felt
guilty about me; two, she decided to show me something that
was worth being afraid of—namely, the worst men's cottage, to
which Jean was assigned the night I tagged along.)

We drove slowly down the steep, twisting road to Southbury,
our headlight beams traversing back and forth across the snow.
Jean leaned over the wheel, craning his neck to watch for the
cutoff through the black truncated trees. "It's along here somewhere."

"We have to pass that boarded-up farmhouse," my mother
said.

"Here it is." He applied the brakes slowly and the tires pulled
against the sanded road. We were entering the grounds through
the back, saving a mile. The car bumped along through the woods
for a few hundred yards and then emerged at the top of a hill.

The Southbury Training School spread below us like a toy village in a Christmas display. Small dormitories disguised to look
like suburban homes were spread evenly over a square mile of
stripped and graded hillside. Halfway down, the two administrative
buildings rose into the air, their white cupolas lighted by flood-
lights. Weaving across the hillside in every direction were the
lines and curves of a network of private roads, described in the
darkness by chains of street lights winking on slender poles.

Jean edged the Ford over the lip of the hill and the bumpy dirt
road changed immediately to a smooth, carefully plowed asphalt
ribbon. We rolled along silently, watching the powdered snow
drift across the surface of the road under the headlights.

"There it is," my mother said as we approached one of the
dormitories. "Number Twelve."

Jean pulled up in the driveway. There was a brass knocker on

the front door, and a mailbox, and a green metal tube on a stand
with "*Danbury Times*" written in elaborate lettering. I caught
some movement out of the corner of my eye. The blinds were
raised in one of the ground-floor windows and a girl stood combing
her hair with long, even strokes. She saw the lights of the car and
smiled. Half her teeth were gone. I looked away quickly.

My mother rang the bell and stood close to the door to be out
of the wind. Almost immediately it swung open, spilling a long
bar of yellow light across the snow. She lifted her hand in a
signal that could just as easily have meant we should wait a
moment as to wave goodbye, and was gone.

We drove slowly across the hill toward the boys' side of the
school. In the bad weather the roads were empty.

"It looks deserted," I said.

"It isn't. Wait till you get inside."

The tires spun on a patch of ice as we climbed the driveway to
Cottage Eight. We stopped next to a black Chevy, the only car
in the parking area. Its windshield was coated with snow.

"That's Olsen's car. He has the shift before mine."

"It's brand new."

"Some of these guys work two shifts. They make a lot of
money."

"Why don't you?"

He laughed. We sat for a moment, watching the building.
Jean took out a cigarette. "The smell is pretty bad at first but
after a couple of hours you don't notice it."

I could see small ways in which the building differed from the
one my mother had entered. There was no box for the newspaper,
no potted evergreens at the edge of the drive. Even in the darkness one could see that the front door needed painting. Some of
the shutters were closed.

"None of these people are dangerous, are they?"

Jean finished his cigarette. "They're just feeble-minded. They
can't take care of themselves."

We stepped out of the car. The air was cold and gusts of wind
seemed to pass uninterrupted through my clothes. After a few
steps the smell began, like a tangible line in space. Smells are
hard to describe. This was a combination of pine, vomit, licorice,

old urine, sweat, soap, and wet hair. Jean rang the bell and after a few moments the door opened.

I was prepared, of course, but prepared through my imagination, and I couldn't possibly have imagined the reality. First of all it was hot, really hot, like a furnace room. I began to sweat immediately. The smell was overpowering. It was useless to breathe carefully as I'd done outside; here the smell was so pungent and thick it seemed to have taken the place of air—a hot substitute filling my lungs, seeping into my blood, and making me its own creature. With the first deep breath I was no longer an air breather. I'd changed to another species.

It was noisy. A noise that raised the hair on the back of my neck. Far-out throats, tongues, and lips forming sounds that wound their independent way up and down the scale with no relation to anything. Whispering, mumbling, fake laughter and true laughter, bubbling sounds, short screams, bored humming, weeping, long roller-coaster yells—all of it in random dynamic waves like some futuristic orchestra. In this meaningless music were sudden cries of such intense human significance that I stood paralyzed.

It was as if all the saints, martyrs, and mystics of human history were gathered into a single building, each one crying out at the moment of revelation, each one truly there at his extreme of joy or pain, crying out with the purity of total selflessness. There was no arguing with these sudden voices above the general clamor, they rang true. All around me were men in a paroxysm of discovery, seeing lands I had never known existed, calling me with a strength I had never known existed. But they called from every direction with equal power, so I couldn't answer. I stood balanced on the pinpoint of my own sanity, a small, cracked tile on the floor.

"They're a little noisy now. It's just before bedtime and we let them blow off some steam."

I looked up and discovered a huge man standing in front of me, smiling. Involuntarily I took a step backward. He was all eyes, immense white eyes impossibly out of his head, rushing at me. No, he was wearing his eyes like glasses. Two bulbous eyes in steel frames. He turned his head and the illusion disappeared.

Thick lenses, that was all. His bald head gleamed with sweat. His arm was as big as my leg.

"I'm Olsen," he said.

"Where's Jean?"

"He'll be back in a minute."

There was movement behind his back. I watched from the corner of my eye, afraid to look directly. A naked man slipping into the room, hunched over like a beaten dog, a shiny thread of spittle hanging from his jaw. He cruised silently along the wall, limp fingers touching the plaster, turned, and stopped, his shaggy head facing the blank wall one inch away. Without even looking Olsen raised his voice and said, "Back to bed."

The creature lifted one leg and touched his toes to the surface of the wall as if it was a ladder he was about to climb. Below the tangle of black hair in his crotch, his veined penis and scrotum hung limply almost halfway to the knee, against the inside of his thigh. It was as if they'd been grabbed and stretched like soft taffy. His toes scratched the wall. Olsen took a step toward him, leaning over slightly, and clapped his hands smartly. "Back to bed!" The creature scurried along the wall and disappeared through an open doorway. For the first time I noticed there were no doors. Doorways without doors. From each darkened passageway the noises rushed at us. Suddenly, the sound of a crash. Olsen knew just where it came from. "Back in a second," he said.

Alone in the room, I stood by the door, my hand touching the knob. I could hear Olsen shouting in another part of the building. Far back in the corridors half-visible figures were moving in the dim light. I supposed that Jean was with them.

An old man appeared, hesitating at the edge of the room. When he saw me he froze instantly, like a highly trained hunting animal. His watery blue eyes were fuzzy spirals and his cheeks sank into his head, making hollows the size of ping-pong balls. He wore a kind of diaper from which his skinny legs, all tendon and finely wrinkled skin, emerged, half bent with age. He took a step forward.

"Back to bed!" I said. "Back to bed!" For a moment he didn't move, then, leaning his head back, he opened his mouth and revealed two gleaming pink gums, toothless, looking like wet rubber. His thin shoulders shook with laughter. When his fuzzy eyes found me he shouted across the room.

"Sonny, I've been here since before you were born. I don't even belong here. I belong in a mental hospital. Everybody knows that." He turned and left the room.

I wanted to wait outside until Jean came back. There was a large brass lock high on the door. I turned what seemed to be the appropriate knob but the bolt didn't move. Examining the mechanism more closely, I heard a noise behind me.

Something was rushing down one of the corridors, something low and fast. No bullfighter ever waited for his foe more apprehensively. To my amazement I found myself giving a short, nervous laugh, a desperate guffaw in the teeth of my predicament. Zooming into the room was a flash of chrome-man, a monstrous human machine blurred with speed, bearing down on me like a homicidal hot-rodder. A man in a wheelchair, but what kind of man? His body was tiny, like a child's, his head impossibly huge, the size of a watermelon. Flailing at the wheels of his chair like a berserk rowboat enthusiast, he backed me into a corner and threw his hands into my face.

"See my pretty 'racelet?" he said in a high voice. "See my pretty 'racelet?"

Flinching, twisting to avoid the touch of his wild hands, I tried to slip past. He slammed his chair into the wall and trapped me.

"See my pretty 'racelet?"

"What? What do you want? What?" Reluctantly I looked him in the eye. His bland idiot's features seemed small in the gargantuan hydrocephalic head. All scrunched together in the cavity that was his face they stared out at me like a fish from a goldfish bowl.

"See my pretty 'racelet?" he said, still holding his arms up. In a tantrum of infantile frustration he drummed his heels against the bottom of the chair. "See! See!"

"He wants you to look at his bracelet," Jean said, grabbing the back of the chair and pulling him away. "This is Freddie. His nickname is pinhead."

"Pinhead, pinhead! See!"

"Go ahead," Jean said. "Just look at it."

Around the creature's wrist was a cheap chrome I.D. bracelet. He held his hand motionless when he realized I was looking at it. The word FREDDIE was engraved in block letters. I touched it with my index finger. "It's very pretty. Very nice."

"Pretty 'racelet?" Freddie said, calmer now.

"Yes. Very pretty."

"Pretty 'racelet?"

Olsen appeared from one of the corridors. His big feet clomped noisily on the tile floor. "Time for lights out?"

"Okay," Jean answered, rolling Freddie away. "Frank, you can go in the office." He pointed to an open doorway.

Freddie rocked back and forth in the chair. "Lice-out. Lice-out. Lice-out."

Olsen reached out and slapped his immense dome with an open hand. "Shut up, idiot." They rolled him down one of the corridors.

The office was a small room with a desk, a chair, and a cot. There was no door to close. I sat on the cot and watched the blank wall. As Jean and Olsen progressed through the building turning out lights, the screaming gradually subsided, falling to a steady murmur like the crowd noises in a movie. It was less nerve-wracking, but somehow more ominous. The mood in the building was changing from wildness to slyness. Plans were beginning to cook in countless heads, and as a novelty, a break in the routine, it seemed to me that I would be the focus. I jumped up nervously as Olsen came in. He looked down at me, his big white eyes embedded in their surrealistic lenses. "I'm going off now. I want to show you something."

I followed him out of the office, sticking close behind. We took a few steps into a hallway and stopped. In the gloom stray rays of light collected in his glasses like fireflies.

"The boys are harmless. They're scareder of you than you are of them, so you got nothing to worry about. I want to show you this guy so you know what he looks like. A couple of times he's grabbed a broom and snuck up behind somebody and belted them. If he ever tries anything all you got to do is look him in the eye and he backs down."

"Maybe it's better if he doesn't see me."

"He won't. He can't see past the light."

There was a snapping sound and a powerful flashlight beam showed us a glowing circle of green wall. We took a few steps and the beam spilled into a small room. With a flick of his wrist Olsen found the occupant, sitting on his bed, knees drawn up to his chest, rocking slowly back and forth. (In the South they call it hunkering.) He looked young, and strong—completely normal except for his nakedness and the fixed expression of anger on his face. His eyes blinked in the strong light but he didn't look away. The creaking of the bedsprings stopped as he held himself rigid. He seemed to be looking directly into my eyes in a contest of wills. Suddenly his head jerked forward and a glob of spittle curved through the air and fell at my feet.

"Tough guy," said Olsen. "Once he threw his own shit at me. But he'll never do that again."

My eyes were locked with the inmate's. "Did you punish him?"

"Punish him!" Olsen laughed. "I beat the living daylights out of him. He was in the infirmary for three days."

"Did he understand?"

"What?"

"Did he understand why you hit him?"

"He didn't throw no more shit so I guess he did."

"What's his name?"

"Gregory."

"Can we go back now?"

"He doesn't know how lucky he is. He's the only one in the building with a room of his own. Look." He flashed his light up the hall. Beds were set up along the walls of the corridor. People were sitting up in them watching us silently. Most of them fell back as the light struck them, like dominoes in a row. To the rest Olsen yelled "Lights out! Bedtime!"

"Can we go back now?"

Olsen had gone off duty and Jean and I were in the office.

"Lovely, isn't it," Jean said sitting on the edge of the desk.

"Is there any place with a door? I'd feel better with a door."

"No, but you'll be all right."

"What about that guy named Gregory?"

"He won't do anything. He's probably asleep. They go to sleep like *that*." He snapped his fingers. After a moment he raised his head and stared out the doorway. "Isn't it incredible the way some of them are hung? They've got equipment a horse would be proud of."

"Jean, I don't think I can make it."

"It's perfectly safe." He stood up. "I've got to make the rounds."

"I can't stay here."

"Well I can't take you back. You'll just have to."

"I'll sleep in the car."

"It's freezing out there."

"I'll take some blankets. It'll be all right."

He stood for a moment without answering.

"Please, Jean."

"Okay. Suit yourself. I've got to make the rounds." He started out, then looked back. "If it gets too cold out there you'd better come back in."

"I will. Yes. Thanks." Quickly I began to strip the blankets from the cot. Then, remembering, I rushed after him. "Jean! The lock! How do you work the lock?"

So for the rest of the winter I stayed in the cabin at night. I never got used to it, but in some ways the nights were better than the days. The nights were warm fantasies of terror, Technicolor nightmares. I recognized somehow that everything happening to me alone at night in the cabin was of a low order of reality. My hallucinations, the fear itself, the entire drama came from inside my own head. I was *making* it all, and although it was terrifying, it was not, as were the days, cosmically threatening.

The days were emptiness, a vast, spacious emptiness in which the fact of being alive became almost meaningless. The first frag-ile beginnings of a personality starting to collect in my twelve-year-old soul were immediately sucked up into the silence and the featureless winter sky. The overbearing, undeniable reality of those empty days! The inescapable fact that everything around me was nonhuman, that in terms of snow and sky and rocks and dormant trees I didn't exist, these things rendered me invisible even to myself. I wasn't conscious of what was happening, I lived it. I became invisible. I lost myself.

At night I materialized. The outlines of my body were hot, flushed, sharply defined. My senses were heightened. I knew I was real as I animated the darkness with extensions of myself. If the sky was more real than I was, then I was more real than my phantoms.

But the days predominated. The flat sky. As the winter passed a sense of desolation invaded my mind. I wasn't afraid, it was too nebulous for that, but I was profoundly uneasy. Perhaps in the back of my mind was the fear that everything would go blank, that I would become the sky, without a body, without thought. I remembered the peculiarly impersonal quality of some of the screams in Cottage Eight.

In the spring I started going down to the school just to hang around, walking the four miles with a quarter in my pocket to get a milkshake at the soda fountain in the administration building. I roamed freely through the public rooms. In a scaled-down bowling alley I used to set up the pins for myself after each frame. Sometimes there were movies in the auditorium. I'd wait for a group of boys to come across the lawn behind their counselor and tag along at the end. I remember a conversation I had one day before a Gene Autry picture with a boy who attracted my attention because I thought he looked exactly like me.

"Who're you?" he asked. "Are you new?"

"No. I'm Mr. Fouchet's son."

"He takes our cottage at night sometimes. He's okay. He never hits you."

"Do the others?"

"Some of them."

(Whistles and applause as Mr. Miller, the director of the school, climbs on stage to make a few announcements before the picture. I laugh at the wildness of the audience. They're having a great time.)

"I'm going home next week," the boy says. "If you're around you'll see the car. It's a red Buick."

"We have a Ford."

"My pop's a policeman. He carries a gun."

(More whistles and cheers as the house lights go down and the picture begins. I watch the boy. There's no way to tell anything is wrong with him.)

The Southbury school affected me more deeply than I realized at the time. Most immediately it was a place in which being different was a good thing—I was different only because I wasn't feeble-minded. My general loneliness in the world was dramatized microcosmically, in terms favorable to myself.

I believed I was intelligent. For a long time that thought had been important to me. At the school I felt for the first time that my intelligence was worth something to someone else besides myself. Here was a huge organization, an immense, powerful world existing for the inmate, but existing for me as well. I was the other extreme! At last I'd found someplace where my only possession would be relevant! To picture myself as being aware of all this would be a misrepresentation. I wasn't vain. I didn't look down on the boys. In some ways I needed the school as much as they did, and I certainly felt closer to them than to the children at conventional schools.

But of course the Southbury school, except for one incident, was as uninterested in me as the world it represented. Which is as it should be. While I passed through the attenuated agonies of growing up, trying to get through to a psychologist in the library of the administration building, there were boys next door who were never going to grow up at all, boys who would starve to death without someone to feed them.

I was alone in the library reading *Life* magazine. A man stopped in the hallway and looked at me through the double glass doors. I watched him come in without raising my head.

"Hi," he said casually. "What are you reading?"

"Just this magazine."

"It's a good issue. I've read it myself." He spoke to me as if we were old friends. "You remember me, don't you?"

It came to me in a flash. He'd mistaken me for one of the boys. Perhaps the boy from the movies who looked so much like me. A bewildering array of emotions exploded simultaneously—confusion, embarrassment, a kind of childish love, apprehensiveness, but behind it all, as steady as the solid bar of sunlight across the polished table, triumph. The moment was at hand.

"Of course you're not really reading it, are you?" he said. "You mean you're looking at the pictures."

"No. I'm reading it."

"Don't you remember me? I'm Dr. Janetello."

I hesitated, trying to think up an answer, but he went on.

"Would you mind reading something for me?"

I looked down at the page. "Members of the Eighty-second airborne reserves bail out over Colorado. Four thousand men took part in a mock attack . . ."

"That's enough," he said. On the table were two books I'd taken from the shelves. He picked them up. *The Short Stories of de Maupassant* and *Pickwick Papers*. Do you read this too?"

"Yes. I liked *David Copperfield* so I thought I'd try this."

"How did you get in here?" he asked quickly. "Are you from Southbury?"

"My stepfather works here."

"You think it's clever to play me along like that?"

I didn't answer. It was going wrong. I looked up at his round face. A few beads of sweat were collected along his upper lip and his eyes suddenly seemed very small.

"Do you have permission to use the library?"

"No. I guess not."

He stood for a moment without saying anything, as if undecided whether to continue. Then he dropped the books on the table with a bang, turned quickly, and left the room. The double doors continued swinging long after he was gone.

24 Clive T. Miller

Clive T. Miller was born in Brooklyn in 1938 and was graduated from Harvard in 1959. His first novel, This Passing Night, *was published in 1962.*

◈

WHERE THEY BURN THE DEAD

There was a man by the name of Sam Babu, who used to travel from city to city with a pair of canaries. He would go to the busy hotels, and when the tourists came out he would make his trained birds perform stunts. His rivals usually promoted cobra-mongoose fights. They all stayed on the porches, waiting for the American families or elderly British matrons to finish lunch. Then they would vie loudly for the guests' attention, competing for the couple of cents the tourists generally gave—or, in the case of Apollo Corelli, the plastic ballpoint pens.

Tito Corelli did not notice Sam Babu until one day, standing on the porch of the Ashoka Hotel, looking down at a blonde girl swimming in the garden pool, he felt something brush against his leg. He turned around. There was an Indian squatting by his feet, hunched over a bird cage with two canaries in it. Tito turned back to watch the girl. About a minute later, he felt uncomfortable. He was sure the man was staring at him. But when Tito looked down, the Indian was studying his birds. Tito looked at his large oval head, and the beanie which covered the top of it. The man seemed pale for an Indian and gnome-like, hunched over in his dark green shirt.

Tito watched him unroll a dirty white rectangular napkin and place upon it a tiny baby carriage made of thin sticks. He tried to get the birds, who were wearing miniscule bonnets, to push the baby carriage with their beaks. But, instead, they just hopped about, leaving their droppings all over the carpet.

Tito saw him every day, kept passing him somewhere on the vast porch. He was always squatting on the ground: under one of the slow-turning huge electric fans, sometimes against a wooden post, sometimes with his back to a wall alive with lizards.

Once when Tito received a house call from his father telling him to get downstairs because he was wasting the entire morning, Apollo added, "By the way, there's a guy here who keeps hanging around, asking me questions, trying to get me into a conversation."

"I'm still in the bathroom."

"This character keeps offering to be our guide and show us the city. Make it snappy. I'll be out on the porch."

As soon as Tito got out of the elevator, he stopped short. There was the Indian glaring at him. He wondered if this was the man his father had spoken to him about. It was the first time Tito had ever seen him standing up. He was by the reception desk; the green shirt, Tito realized, was an olive fatigue shirt with a US Marine Corps arm patch. On the tape above the left breast was stenciled the name GLOSSOP. The Indian's white pants had been cut, crudely and unevenly, high above his ankles. Tito went to the desk and asked for the mail. It had not yet arrived. Turning away, he looked more closely at the Indian. One pants leg was frayed at the knee. The pants themselves were filthy. He must have slept in them in the streets of every town: in the stifling air of smoky Calcutta, on the pink clay of Jaipur, under a Bombay stone arch, in the dung heaps of camels, among the pilgrim lepers of Benares. He held up a small piece of paper that said MY NAME IS SAM BABU, and then handed Tito a card.

An English lady and her daughter were complaining to the clerk behind the desk. They had left their shoes by their door last night to be shined. This morning they found only one pair, with dried mud on the outside, some other stains on the inside, and belonging to neither of them.

Tito read the card:

IVORY WORKS
MANUFACTURER OF IVORY GOODS,
SANDLE WOOD, OLD BRASS
AND CURIO OLD DEALERS
AT A DISTANCE OF 400 YARDS
FROM HOTEL YOU STAY.
SAVE YOUR MONEY FROM RETAIL DEALERS.

Tito Corelli shook his head and returned the card. Sam Babu looked at the card. Tito walked out to his father scowling on the porch.

While in New Delhi, they hired a car and chauffeur on only one day, and then they did not drive into the old part of town. It happened that they had arrived just as Holy Week began, and Apollo thought it too dangerous to drive far from the hotel. Beyond was the noise, burning incense, colored water and dyes: Apollo was afraid his suit would get permanently stained.

Every day during their vacation at the Ashoka, Apollo would make wisecracks in the voice of a tour conductor: "This afternoon will be spent at your leisure." Which meant organized letter writing.

"You!" Tito would hear himself being called as he entered the salon for the stationery and free post cards with photographs of the hotel. "Hey, you!" would come the order from the old man who had forgotten Tito's name while thinking about the business back home or counting his small change. "Don't forget the envelopes!"

Tito was surprised at how often he ran across Sam Babu. When he entered a room, he usually found that Sam Babu was there, too. He saw him in the shadows or a corner, watching him. At first, even when Tito faced him, he did not make any movement: just stood there. But after a time, when he saw Tito he would hold a card toward him like a signal. When Tito handed the card back, the Indian would produce a different one—never the same card twice—and wait while Tito read it.

One evening after dinner, Tito left his father reading in the lounge and went to the bathroom on the main floor. He washed his hands and face. The Indian who offered him a towel was Sam Babu.

He left the men's room and went back to the lounge. Sam Babu trailed behind him. The towel was draped over the Indian's arm as if he were a waiter. When Tito sat down next to his father on the couch, Sam Babu remained stationary at the door.

Apollo glanced up from the English-language newspaper. "Here!" he called, signaling the Indian.

Sam Babu quickly came over.

"Do you carry Chivas Regal?"

"Chivas Regal," the Indian repeated.

Out of the corner of his mouth, Apollo said to Tito, "What, is this guy, stupid or something?" He said to the Indian, "Or Ambassador's 25-Year-Old?"

"The ambassador is twenty-five years old?"

Tito laughed. Sam Babu looked at him. "Oh, I understand," the Indian said. "The young ambassador. Very good joke."

"Who is this guy?" Apollo seemed to be in a good mood. He said to the Indian, "Do you work here?"

"Yes," Sam Babu told him. "On the porch."

He folded the towel and tucked it into the top of his pants. He sat down next to Tito. "Do you know about the beasties?"

"The what?" Apollo frowned.

"The beasties in the woods," he told Tito. There were monsters in the forests with many heads, with a thousand eyes apiece, who could never be killed and who ate up anyone that stumbled upon them.

"Do you know this guy?" Apollo said out of the corner of his mouth to Tito.

"Sure," Tito said. "This is Sam Babu."

"Oh really?" Apollo adjusted his glasses. "These gremlins, how do you know they exist?"

"I have seen them and their leader."

"You mean there's one monster bigger than the others who's in charge?"

"Yes—Beezlebub."

"And you say you've seen them with your own eyes?"

"Oh my gracious yes. They are dreadful."

"It's not just that you've heard about them."

"No. I have seen them."

"How many times?"

"One time."

"What did you do? Did they talk to you?"

"Oh my goodness gosh no. They cannot talk. They are beasties."

"Well, what did you do? Did you go up to them?"

"I ran. I ran away very fast out of the woods."

As Apollo laughed, he put the back of his hand to his mouth. Tito met Sam Babu's eyes and smiled. "You were lucky that the beasties couldn't catch up to you, that they can't leave the woods."

Sam Babu nodded and grinned. Apollo said, "You're crazier than he is: you believe him!" As he drew his arm away from his mouth, his hand was wet.

"Would you like this?" Apollo asked the Indian, holding out a pen. Tito recognized it immediately as having been stolen from the Istanbul Hilton. It was orange with a huge orange quill and gold ballpoint tip and had stood like a dart on the desk in a bright orange-and-yellow stand. Apollo waved the quill under Sam Babu's nose. Sam Babu was delighted. Apollo said, "If you carry this into the forest with you, you'll be safe from the monsters."

Sam Babu said suddenly. "I would like very much to have a transistor."

"Can't you get them here?" Tito asked.

"They cost too much money."

Apollo said, "I hate people who talk about money."

"People always promise to send me radios from America, but they never do."

Apollo said, "Money's dirty."

"If I had a transistor, I could catch Ceylon. Come. I will show you Ceylon on the great big map." Sam Babu got up and headed for the door.

"You want to come along?" Tito asked his father.

"You go. You need the exercise."

The map hung on a wall behind a wooden counter, in an alcove occasionally used as a hat-check room.

"If I had a transistor, I could listen to Radio Ceylon." The Indian removed his beanie, tossed it straight at the island. "That country," he said. "It has very good music."

Then he climbed over the counter, retrieved his cap, stuck it on his head. He scrambled back and looked up, smiling, at Tito.

Tito said, "If I ever return, I'll bring you a radio."

"You can send it. If you have a friend who intends to travel to India, you can send it with him. Tell him to give it to Sam Babu at the Ashoka Hotel. I will like that very much." He reached into his pocket and presented Tito with a box of incense sticks. "If you burn these, they are very good for keeping away the devils." He reached into his pocket again and handed Tito a card.

GUIDE FOR YOUR HAND-BAG

THE METAL IS GUARANTEED NONTARNISHABLE. THE DESIGN IS TAKEN FROM INLAY WORK OF FAMOUS HISTORICAL BUILDINGS OF INDIA. AFTER A FEW MONTHS OF ITS USE TAKE A PIECE OF THE INNER PORTION OF A LOAF OF YOUR BREAKFAST (WITHOUT BUTTER) PRESS IT ALL OVER THE EMBROIDERY AND IT WILL PICK UP EVERY BIT OF DUST AND IS THEN READY AGAIN TO GLAMOUR WITH YOU.

Without paying too much attention, Tito turned the card over before handing it back. He stared in amazement at what the shaky letters said:

THE PERSON ASK ABOUT YOUR ROOM.

Tito looked at Sam Babu, who continued smiling.
"What person?"
Sam Babu made no sign.
"A man?"
Sam Babu nodded slowly.
"What did he look like? Was he alone?"
Sam Babu nodded again.
"Can you tell me what he looked like?"
"The man," Sam Babu asked, "or the lady?"
"There were two? Were they together?"

"There was a man two times," he said. "And once there was that lady."

Tito looked to where Sam Babu was pointing. Down the corridor was the blonde girl he had watched swimming in the pool. She walked with an easy swinging gait, turned right at the corner into the lobby and toward the old couple waiting. She had the round, clean, Midwestern face of a college sophomore, of a nineteen-year-old campus football queen. Tito turned back to the Indian.

Sam Babu said, "I think she loves you."

II

Tito began to be disturbed by a feeling that he was being chased. Yet he liked the pursuit and he liked his own role as pursued. Did it matter that his father believed they were being followed only by sly beggars who were after the wallet at his hip, the Travelers Cheques at his heart? But he began to agree with the old man about the perils of night and of strangers who play on your trust. He continued to write daily to Ariadne, but his thoughts were always concentrated on his opera. He saw himself in the role of his own hero, Gino Melandri, and as other heroes, too: Radames, Manrico, the Unknown Prince who can answer all riddles. When the hired greeter in Jaipur, a blue-turbaned Sikh, inquired immediately, "Which is Corelli the Writer?" he was not surprised. He was Verdi's Filippo Secondo, Simon Boccanegra, Shakespeare's tormented kings, traveling with the old man. And Sam Babu—for when they got to the Rambaugh Palace, he was squatting at the entrance.

Sam Babu was wearily crouching on the tiles of the sprawling hotel, which had lately been one of the Maharaja's palaces. Next to Sam Babu, their heads tucked into molting yellow feathers, were the trained canaries asleep in the homemade wire cage. Apollo was ahead with the bellboys; Sam Babu offered Tito a tired smile.

And later, after their bags had been deposited in their room, which gave out on the gardens, and they were walking to lunch, Tito showed his father the advertisement cut out of the Hindustan Times and pasted on a card:

MATRIMONIAL

WANTED a Tank Kshatriya match age about 25 years for a girl appearing in Preparatory final Examination, well-versed in household. Daughter of a senior well-placed officer. Decent marriage. Apply Box 22827-IN.

"Where did you get this?"

"From Sam Babu."

"Who?"

"You remember: that Indian we met at the Ashoka. Didn't you see him when we came in?"

Apollo made a face. "What—did he follow us here?"

"Didn't you see him?"

"When I took trips at your age, I used to notice things my mother and father never saw. You'll find as you get older, when you go to work and have things on your mind, your wife will notice more than you. Girls notice things a lot. Men usually don't have time."

After lunch Tito confronted Sam Babu. He noticed the Marine Corps insignia had come off the shoulder of his fatigue shirt. Tito decided to buy the cards from him instead of handing them back.

"Who is the blonde who keeps asking about me? Do you know her name?"

"Finn," Sam Babu told him. "Becky Finn."

"And the old man and woman she's traveling with?"

"They are her grandmummy and granddaddy," Sam Babu smiled.

"They're coming to Jaipur, aren't they?"

"Tomorrow."

"What about you? You don't look too well. You need more sleep. Are you following me?"

Sam Babu knitted his brow. "No," he said, scratching his palm with a card, "I don't think so."

"I see."

Then suddenly the Indian brightened. "Would you like me to?"

"Sam Babu," Tito said amiably, "Sam Babu."

He bought some more cards.

"Would you like to know what just happened?"

"Don't tell me: You just got in a new supply of cards."

Sam Babu laughed. "No, would you like to know the future?"

"I have a pretty good idea—that I'm going to run out of money. That we're going to change places, and I'm going to become a traveling man with your birds, and you're going to be stuck sleeping with my daddy in Hong Kong and Japan."

"I have a friend," Sam Babu offered, "who is a wizard and can tell you the future. That gentleman there."

The gentleman's name was Estelle. It seemed to be his only name. He stood several yards away from them—at the end of the open passage. For an instant Tito saw him full-faced; before he quickly turned and busied himself at the mail desk. He wore a voluminous blue garment wrapped around his heavy frame like a toga, and sandals far too large for his dainty feet. Several times while Tito and Sam Babu talked, Tito was aware of Estelle sidling up to them. When Tito looked straight at him, he retreated behind one of the columns. Tito couldn't be sure whether he was trying to eavesdrop or not. He might have been merely abstracted, unaware of his own nervous movements.

That night he and Tito sat together—he wouldn't allow Apollo to join them—across a table in the intimate gardens. He shook the zodiacal dice. They were easy to read under the full moon.

"You will meet a beautiful girl with golden hair."

"Could I have seen her but not yet been introduced to her?"

"Maybe." Hunched over, he studied the dice. "You will marry her."

"How do you know that?"

Estelle leaned toward him across the delicate wrought-iron table planted firmly in the center of the lawn, in front of the trees and shrubbery and flower beds. His garment fell open, there was a roll of flesh under his breast. His thick lips parted. Tito caught the words "all knowledge accessible . . . heavenly orbs . . . conjunctive . . . incredible luck." The wizard paused to slap his thick forearm, scratch it and look around, muttering, "A terrible distraction . . . goddam bugs," before he turned back to study again the roll of the dice.

"Her first name begins with the letter 'B.' "

" 'B.' "

"Do you know anyone whose first name begins with 'B'?"

"Boris. How about 'A'?"

"The dice never lie," Estelle said. He shook them and they clattered on the table under the moon.

"You couldn't have skipped a letter?"

"No. You see what the dice say now? The last name of the bride begins with 'F.' "

Later, while undressing for bed, Tito told his father that they would meet Becky Finn.

"Usually *girls* tend to be superstitious," his father said. "But I know you—you believe that nonsense. Things like that make a big impression on you. The next thing I know, you'll be back in the institution. My God!" He put a hand to his cheek. "I don't mind throwing out the dollar for that guy to read your fortune, but to spoil a wonderful trip because of it. . . . It's not sensible to take a risk like that. You better go to sleep and forget all about it. And if you were smart, you'd get wise to yourself and cut out smoking."

"I'm not smoking," Tito said. "You've already told me you don't like to breathe in the ashes while you snore."

"So am I wrong? And who's talking about right-this-moment? Why must you always think I'm criticizing you!"

Tito could not fall asleep. He worried about the girl and the man who had separately inquired after his room. He lay awake all night under the mosquito netting, waiting for the sneakered footfall, the knife. During the next day, Apollo rushed him through the city. They scurried along dirt paths lined with bazaars, past stalls with multicolored silks hanging on hooks like the iridescent flesh of skinned animals Tito had seen in other markets. On an elephant, in a lorry, in the back of the private limousine— while his father slept—Tito sat, nerves on edge, expecting the assassin's shot. He was unwilling to acknowledge the possibility that he was merely a tourist, one of the many using the same few accessible Eastern roads and the same air routes from which they made stopovers at no extra cost.

Before Tito and Apollo checked out of the Rambaugh Palace, at seven in the morning and while Apollo was paying the bill, Tito looked for Sam Babu. He couldn't find him. He said good-bye to Estelle and asked him to tell Sam Babu that he said good-bye. Then he went to the mail desk. A lady of about fifty stood before it, complaining. In her hand she dangled a pair of green tennis shoes with knotted laces. On her feet she wore gold, embroidered Persian slippers. The toes of the slippers were curled. She accused the valet of stealing her shoes during the night. Expecting to have all her shoes cleaned at one time, she had lined them up outside her door. The only pairs that remained were the two she hadn't put out—her slippers and her tennis shoes, which she slammed on the top of the open guest-register.

Tito placed a note among Becky Finn's letters:

"You're late in arriving. I wish you'd make up my mind where we're going. Because now you're in Jaipur, but we're on our way to Agra."

Then they took to the empty road, he and his father and the blue-turbaned Sikh who had guided them around town. The Sikh drove very fast down the narrow, unpaved, bumpy road. The air was cold. Tito saw through the limousine window a few rattling carts, and fleetingly he saw a dozen women in silk veils and shawls, walking in single file, with baskets of ordure balanced on their heads. All during the morning Tito listened to strange animal noises: the cackle and screech of birds he couldn't identify. The grunting of some unseen beast mixed with the chattering of monkeys. He could not separate the sounds, and together they confused him. Once he heard something that sounded like goats bleating; but when he looked through the window, he saw instead a horde of buffaloes caked in the silt of a crowded black water hole.

He thought about his opera. He wondered what music would fit the next-to-last scene, the rumble between the hero's and villain's gangs. As he rode past the farms and patches of trees with wild monkeys swinging, past other trees full of bats asleep upside down, he listened to the words of his opera inside his head —to the flyting between the tenor and baritone:

Bandit, you stole my girl and raped her!

Melandri,
My teeth are enough for Infantino,
But I've got a knife for you.

Ugo Gondolfo,
This is our fatal hour.

Melandri, your life is a scandal and a disaster and a ruin.

You stole Adrianna and raped her!
Give me back Adrianna!

I've got a knife for you, Melandri.
I'm going to cut out your eyes and take home your heart!

Ugo Gondolfo,
This is our fatal hour.

The driver stopped the car alongside an irrigation ditch and
a pair of bullocks turning the enormous, heavy wooden wheel.
The peasants surrounded the car, peered in curiously. On both
sides of the road were their clay huts with roofs held together by
manure and mud. Flat cakes of dung were drying on the hill
before being stored for winter fuel.

At a waystation outside of Agra they ate their packed lunches.
And it was then the Sikh told them that he was commissioned
to return to Jaipur to pick up the girl and her grandparents and
transport them tomorrow along the very same road.

But they did not see her. The only person they met in Agra
was Sam Babu. He had made his own way to the Taj Mahal. He
was sitting on a marble bench, terribly ill. Across his brow there
were white, streaked markings. Behind him was the mausoleum.

"Sam Babu," Tito said, "I didn't know you were a holy man."

"You must not touch me," the Indian warned, "I have the
disease."

"What disease?"

"I have traveled all night. My birds are dying." He pointed to
the cage by his feet. The canaries slept next to each other on the
swing; under them was a molt of feathers stained with droppings.
"I have traveled all night."

"Why?"

"I ran through the woods, the beasties tried to catch me.
Where is your daddy?"

"He's over by the gate, he didn't want to walk all the way down. But he'll be here in a minute. As soon as he sees me talking to you."

"I must thank him. The orange pen which he gave to me kept the devils away. I ran through the woods with the pen and my incense sticks. Finally I rode in the back of a cart."

"Yes. But why?"

"Last night I was delirious with fever. Very hot. I painted my forehead with Brahma until this morning. I want very much to receive the Creator's Grace. You must not touch me."

His cheeks were lined, his body seemed to have shrunk. In a matter of a few dark hours he had worn himself out.

"You ripped your shirt," Tito said. The tape with the name GLOSSOP hung like a ribbon pinned to his chest.

Sam Babu stooped, lifted the cage, and placed it on the bench. Then he stood up—feverish, fatigued—and handed Tito a card.

Again Tito saw: THE PERSON ASK ABOUT YOUR ROOM.

And holding it by the edge, Tito felt an odd apprehension. Perhaps the small tips had corrupted Sam Babu, so that the slight friendly man repeated the message which had produced the greatest effect on Tito.

Tito told him, "You better go home. You should be in bed. Is there a doctor here you know?"

"Last night I painted Brahma. Today I washed him off. Now I have painted Vishnu, the Preserver. Oh, I am terrible, I am not a holy man. But I would like very much to receive Grace."

"When was the last time you went to bed?"

"I have not been to sleep since I left Delhi."

"Sam," Tito urged, "will you please go see a doctor?"

"My birds are dying and I have terrible pains. I must leave at once for the Holy City. A friend will take me in his car."

"To a doctor?"

"No, to Benares."

"Sam," Tito said, "you're not dying. Look. All you have to do is go to a doctor and get a couple of hours' sleep."

But heavy of step, clutching his cage and cap, he began to walk—away from the bench and tomb, and down the long white way of the spouting fountains—to whatever conveyance awaited him.

III

He was there in Benares. The following night, Tito saw Sam Babu wandering just outside the hotel's private grounds, in the company of several holy men and pilgrims.

"Tell me about that man," Tito asked the manager.

"He is a mad man. He has come here to die." While he spoke he ran a hand up and down the jacket lapel of his smartly pressed, white linen suit. "He tried to come in here to beg for alms. We do not allow that. Can you see the chalk marks on his forehead? He is a follower of Shiva, the Destroyer, the Reproducer."

Apollo, by their side, said, "Isn't that something."

"Sam Babu," Tito murmured.

Apollo asked, "Is that Sam Babu? How do you know?" He frowned. "Are you sure?"

"Yes."

But it was no good going to him. He was beyond Tito's reach and in the protection of those who understood him—that bewildered pale man hoping to please his gods. The group that surrounded him paced the roadway, chanting, walking him up and down as though reviving a drunk. In his hand was the bird cage, shrouded by the spotted white cloth, which he swung to and fro like a thurible. Tito sensed that whatever he was doing was as private as the act of making love; he turned away embarrassed.

By six the next morning Sam Babu was in a state of deep shock, and he lay stretched in the roadway amid the mendicant pilgrims. The name tape was finally gone from his olive shirt. Just beyond his bare feet—for his sandals were gone, too—was the bird cage.

"That man is dying."

The words, contemptuous, bitter, came from their guide. He was a teacher who aspired to write. In his spare time he made extra money by being a guide. Now he conducted Tito and Apollo into a car, directed them through the square to where their barge waited moored at the bathing ghats.

Begging along the right side of the walk that led to the river's steps, was a row of lepers.

The guide said to Tito and Apollo, "Walk on the left." He was a few yards ahead of them, facing them and walking backwards. "Do not pay attention to the beggars. No photographs."

Apollo, with his eyes straight ahead, spoke out of the corner of his mouth. "Hurry up and snap a picture."

The beggars reached out their hands. The guide said to Tito, "Move a little more to the left. They are not permitted to beg on the left. It is the law."

Apollo kept his arms stiff and straight down his sides, his hands closed into fists. He moved more to the left. A crippled dwarf, hobbling on sticks as thin as his bones, brushed against him, and Apollo instinctively raised his elbow and forearm for protection. He brought his arm down and felt inside his pockets for his checks and wallet.

The guide said to Tito, "You're walking too far on the right."

A finger scratched Tito's trousers and hooked onto a cuff. He looked down and saw a blistered stump rub across his shoe.

"Get over here!" Apollo said.

Suddenly a leper jumped up and blocked Tito's path. He stretched out a palm with only a thumb attached. Tito heard the guide shout, "Get back," but some others broke rank—grasped at the air—darted back into place. He looked for the guide, who was hidden among some bare chested Indians on their way to the river. He saw his father slip, catch himself, and turn around toward him, calling, "Hurry up!" He pushed through the crowd and caught up to his father and the guide.

They stood near a holy man who sat in a niche like an idol, wearing only a loin cloth and covered with ashes. His slender legs were crossed at the ankles, his eyelids were shut in supplication behind his censers and urns.

The guide said, "One photograph only."

They walked on the glossy stones down to the river, past the outdoor barbers shaving their squatting customers' heads. Then away from the bald Buddhist priests clad in orange and praying.

The guide announced, "Every year tens of millions of Indians come to Benares to bathe in the holy river Ganges—to be washed, to be healed, to be saved."

The three of them stepped onto the private boat. The guide navigated it a few hundred yards out to sea.

Tito stared at the shore. For a long time he saw only a mass of brown bodies moving toward him, from the top of the square to the river bank. With his arm he wiped the perspiration from above his lip. Then he sat down in the boat, holding his camera tight. He pressed the case against his mouth, feeling sick, as the bodies continued to move down the bathing ghats. He did not want to look at their faces. He tried to think of them only as various stages of suffering—an index to the descriptions of every disease known to man: The infirm, cautious blind; the amputated; the palsied decrepit; the lowing arthritic, rheumatic; the birth-deformed; the spastic, convulsive epileptic writhing and twisted; the harrowed consumptive hacked by a churchyard cough; the carbuncular lame with his festering ulcers and boils, the pus of the abscesses leaving blots on the stones. The bodies moved forward—the walkers, the crawlers, the rollers, the supported, the carried: the scourged, incorrigible regenerates inhabiting the earth—the tainted and maimed reminders of God's complex art, bereft of all but their burning, appalling belief—come now to cleanse their sores, be relieved of their pains . . . the invalided, morbid defenders of man's ultimate faith.

"Take all the pictures you can," Apollo told him.

There was a chill on the waters of the Ganges, and a pungent odor. The sun rose higher. The day dawned hotter. The bathers continued to pray in the river up to their ribs. Tito saw in the near distance the flames of the burning ghats; the hired mourners stoked the logs like cooks.

"They do not need a doctor to verify the people are dead," the schoolmaster was saying. "They do not have doctors available for everyone."

The slow motor of the boat made a guggling sound in the water. For a while Tito stared at the grease it dropped, the small waves it churned.

"Does this depress you?" he heard his father ask him. "Do you find this depressing?" There was excitement in his voice. "Thirty-odd years ago when I came here with your mother, she couldn't take the smells; some women are like that. At least this is more interesting than the average, run-of-the-mill sightseeing tour."

A few feet away a devotee washed his mouth out in the river.

"You're so damn lucky," Apollo was saying. "What other boy your age has seen this? When we get home you'll really be able to let your friends have it! We've seen everything on this trip," he explained to the guide. "We've gone from the best to the worst."

Tito said to the guide, "Those people might get hurt: the wall is cracking over there."

Apollo said, "Remind me to have that repaired."

"Do you see the sacred pepal tree?" the schoolmaster pointed.

Apollo said to Tito, "I'm really spoiling you. I hope the rest of this trip isn't an awful letdown. When you get home, are you going to be blasé!"

They were abreast of the crematory pyres. Corpses lay on the sides of the piles and on top.

The guide said, "Here are the burning ghats. No photographs."

He informed Tito that he would be willing to write a novel with him.

"I don't write novels," Tito told him, "I'm an opera librettist." He watched the puffs of smoke going up from the shore.

"You could write every other chapter in New York and mail it to me. I will write the other ones."

"The odds or the evens?"

"I will write the first chapter, because I know India. It will be a very quiet story without violence. Too many American novels have too much violence. India is a very peaceful country. The hero, however, could be an American. He is a Peace Corps worker who has come to help India. He falls in love with an Indian girl-missionary."

"But then a rivalry develops between them while they cultivate some farm."

"Yes, that is good," the school teacher said.

"Until she stabs him. And in his dying breath, he grabs her round the throat and squeezes until her eyes pop out of her head, and bounce down the bathing ghats and into the Ganges."

"That is precisely what I mean: You Americans do not know how to write a good story. No, this will be a very tranquil love story. And it will be very sad at the end, when the young hero gets transferred to Puerto Rico."

Tito noticed long black hairs spouting from the rims of the school teacher's ears.

"And in the story we can show how the Moslems make the silk and the Hindus sell it. How the Moslems and the Hindus work hand-in-hand."

"Does the Peace Corps worker represent the Hindus or the Moslems?"

"We can decide. When you return to New York, write to me and send me your photograph and briefly describe yourself and the things we have done here. So in that way I will be able to recall you and the conversation we had about the book."

"Why don't we have the Peace Corps worker represent the Moslems," Tito suggested. "He comes from America with a pair of silk underpants—in his civilian life he had been a traveling salesman of women's lingerie—and he presents the panties to the heroine as a gift. He *sells* them and she *wears* them, and you have your symbol established right at the start. The sad part comes when she tries them on and she finds they don't fit."

There was smoke in the air, a fulmination of spices and gums. In his head Tito heard a passage from *Love without Juice*, the scene when Adrianna Danise returns to Melandri after she's been raped:

> Gino, Gino,
> Hold me. . . .
> You have nothing to be afraid of any more.
>
> Gino, Gino,
> Hold me. . . .

The sun burned closer. He felt very lonely and homesick. The ache in his stomach for Aria started again.

Later that morning, from his perch on a monkey temple's ramparts, he watched the animals plucking at ticks. Down below, across a narrow dark alley, was the Temple of Gold. Lined up along the lane were the wretched beggars. The marble entranceway was splattered with mud. Tito had watched the bathers plod up from the river, barefoot and tramping, into the Temple of Gold. Now he heard them chanting inside. And even from where he was he smelled the vapors, naked flesh rubbing naked flesh, like cattle in rut.

"Had enough, buddy?" his father said, behind him. "It gets a little tedious visiting shrines."

He made his descent into the mob, with the guide in the lead and his father calling back to him: "Sonny!" He trailed behind. He hung back, they entered a jewelry shop. His father examined a carpet of gems; listened to the owner's explanation of how it had been made, and the difference between precious and semi-precious stones, the devaluing flaw which makes the star sapphire shine.

"How much would a carpet like that cost?"

"This is not for sale," the owner said. "It has been in our family hundreds of years."

"Just name a price. I don't want to buy it. But how much do you think it's worth?"

"I'm going back to the hotel," Tito said. "I've got to go to the bathroom."

"Now?" his father moaned. "Isn't that something."

"You stay; I'll meet you back at the hotel."

"Well, here's enough to pay for a rickshaw." He paused. "But don't be up there all day. When I get back, I want to see you in the lobby."

Tito left the cool shop. He shoved his way past the vendors, the hawkers, the rabble loudly bargaining—to the center of the square. Battered on all sides, perspiring, he thrust toward the ghats or temple or hotel, he did not know. Nor did he try to stop. He pressed forward on impulse—headlong, heedless—past the outdoor florists, who sat under torn black umbrellas which gave little shade and scarcely prolonged the life of the yellow blossoms already dry and exfoliating, beginning to stink, the petals heaped on the earth like bits of flaked skin. Past the fruit carts in the middle of the square, the fruits and vegetables rotting, swarming with insects. Past the dye-sellers with their tiny mounds of ochre and red pigment. He pushed onward, avoiding the bullocks roaming the alleyways—missing the girl at home, and certain that doom awaited him back in New York.

He turned into a street, wheeled into an alley in hopes that he'd find more room. It was only more crowded. He blundered against the rump of a sacred cow munching garbage. He rebounded, recovered himself in the very same stride and continued his mindless fleeing, all the time smelling the sweet excrement on his trouser leg. He pushed through the panhandlers and lame, the outcasts with their odor of fish, flung himself against all obstructions which blocked his advance until he was struck in the forehead by a plank of wood and knocked into a doorway.

And only then did he hear the halloos and shouts of the pallbearers. They shifted and floundered while trying to rebalance the weight on their shoulders, the burden which slipped and crashed to the ground, the body sliding halfway out from under its sheet. The head remained covered. Yet even without seeing what lay hidden beneath, Tito knew it must be Sam Babu. A man with the familiar bird cage stepped to one side. Another with an urn clutched in his fist looked down. The corpse lay stretched in the gutter among two dozen cards.

The pallbearers knelt down and straightened the sheet, again took up their load. And with the mourners chanting and shaking censers and colored sticks, they headed their cargo in the direction from which Tito had come, leaving him in the doorway.

He stepped into the road. He bent down and picked up the nearest card.

BEWARE OF THE OFFER

4 COLOR SLIDES

For Rs. 5.00

4 COLOR POST CARDS

For Re. 1.00

He turned it over. KISS, it proclaimed at the top in Sam Babu's infirm print. And below it the words

love
loyalty
friendship
affection
adoration
sweetness

like a list of diseases to be avoided, and he dropped it with despair.

25 Ken Kesey

❖

LETTERS FROM MEXICO

AN INTRODUCTORY NOTE
BY ED MCCLANAHAN

Ed McClanahan, senior editor of Per Se, teaches creative writing at Stanford University.

Ken Kesey is the author of the critically and financially successful novels *One Flew Over the Cuckoo's Nest* and *Sometimes A Great Notion*. He is also the former amateur wrestling champion of Oregon and one of the earliest paid-volunteer subjects (c.1958) of government-sponsored research experiments with psychedelic drugs. In the summer of 1964, Kesey, "possessor of a phenomenal bank account" after the publication of *Notion*, incorporated himself (Intrepid Trips, Inc.), purchased a 1939 International schoolbus and some $20,000 worth of movie-making equipment, gathered about him at his La Honda, California, home a group of old and new friends ("The Merry Pranksters"—during the next three years their number was to fluctuate from as high as thirty down to half-a-dozen or so of the very hardiest and most loyal souls), set them to work preparing the bus for the venture he had planned (the preparations largely consisted of coating its fuselage with spray paint in an infinite variety of colors), climbed aboard, hollered the equivalent of "All ashore that's going ashore" (about fifteen people weren't), and took off for the New York World's Fair.

Two months later Kesey and the Pranksters were back in La Honda with 36 hours of 16 mm. color film of their adventures, which they intended to edit down to a feature-length movie. They set up a cutting room in a shed in Kesey's yard, and in April, 1965, they were still editing away (Kesey's Christmas tree that year had been decorated with perhaps a quarter of a mile of cut film), when the sheriff of San Mateo County and his merry band of deputies swooped down and arrested Kesey and thirteen of the Pranksters for possession of marijuana. All were released on bail the following day, and the charges against twelve of the fourteen were soon dropped, but in December Kesey and one other Prankster were convicted. Kesey was sentenced to six months in jail and three years' probation, then released on an appeal bond.

During the seven-month interim between the arrest and the conviction, Kesey and the Pranksters (along with the then-unknown rock and roll group "The Grateful Dead") had begun to produce a series of psychedelically oriented Saturday night happenings which they called "The Acid Test." At first these events were held in Kesey's home, but as their fame began to spread and ever-larger crowds turned out The Acid Test was moved to night clubs, then to more spacious dancehalls, and finally to San Francisco's cavernous Fillmore Auditorium. On the weekend following Kesey's conviction The Acid Test was scheduled to be the main attraction of a three-day-long marathon psychedelic circus called the Trips Festival, which was to be held in the vast, tentlike Longshoremen's Hall on Fishermen's Wharf. And five nights before the Trips Festival was to open, Kesey was arrested again, this time on a San Francisco rooftop in the company of a 19-year-old Prankster named Carolyn "Mountain Girl" Adams, who later acknowledged that she—not Kesey—was the owner of the packet of marijuana which the police found on their rooftop.

Kesey, once again freed on bail, did participate in the Trips Festival; an estimated 12,000 people descended upon Longshoremen's Hall during those three days, and the Festival (owing largely to the interest generated by the tremendous amount of publicity that accompanied the second arrest) was a huge success, and is now generally recognized as the grandaddy of all the psychedelic rock dances which have made San Francisco "the Liverpool of the American music scene." (A prediction: when the musical historians come to consider the rock and roll phenomenon of the 1960's, the figure of Ken Kesey will loom exceeding large, not as composer or musician—though in fact the Pranksters once formed their own rock group and cut an LP album—but as the inventor of a new way to listen.) But within a week after the Festival, an aged truck registered to Kesey and containing a pair of fluorescent-painted shoes (a Kesey trademark) and a suicide note ("Ocean, ocean, you'll get me in the end . . .") was found parked atop a cliff above the sea along a lonely stretch of the Northern California coast. And Ken Kesey, disguised as "mild-mannered reporter Steve Lamb," was in Puerto Vallarta, Mexico.

There he remained for almost two months—"pranking around," as he puts it—until he attempted to phone his wife Faye in California, and a well-intentioned friend mistakenly mentioned the call in the presence of a newspaper reporter. "Kesey the Corpse Having a Ball!" the next day's headlines screamed. Friends frantically wired Kesey that the jig was up, and after hiding out in the Puerto Vallarta jungles for several days he made his way south to Manzanillo, a tropical beach resort town in the state of Colima, a place rarely visited by gringo tourists. Meanwhile, his old friend Larry McMurtry (the Texas writer whose novel *Horseman, Pass By* later became the movie *Hud*) and Kesey's San Francisco attorney Brian Rohan had arranged, through a Mexico City attorney named Estrella, for Kesey to be granted a temporary and somewhat shaky amnesty by the local Colima government. Within a few weeks his family and a small coterie of Pranksters arrived, bus and all, and they set up shop in a house on the Manzanillo beach and began again to work on the film, which was by this time nearly 50 hours long.

Kesey remained in Manzanillo for the next six months, an idyll frequently shattered by the sometimes real, sometimes imagined, threat of Federales, "FBEyes," or vacationing deputies from the San Mateo County sheriff's office. During the Puerto Vallarta–Manzanillo period he produced the only sustained writing he has done since *Notion*: a series of fifteen lengthy letters to McMurtry describing his surroundings, his predicament, and his state of mind. Three of those letters appear here.

In the fall of 1966 Kesey returned to the States, this time

crossing the border riding a borrowed horse, carrying a guitar, and calling himself "Singin' Jimmy Anglund." He hid out for nearly two weeks in the homes of friends, granted interviews to trust-worthy newspaper and TV reporters, and "rubbed salt in J. Edgar Hoover's wounds" until half a dozen FBI men in a car-pool chanced to spot him on a busy Bay Area freeway, gave chase, and got their man at last. Kesey was immediately released on bail again, tried on the San Francisco charge, and convicted of a misdemeanor ("knowingly being in a place where marijuana is possessed"). Meanwhile, his San Mateo County appeal failed, and in July 1967 he entered jail there to serve four and a half months (with time off for—unlikely as it seems—good behavior) of the old six-month sentence. Since his release he has been living with his family and a small, close-knit group of Pranksters on a communal farm in Oregon, where he is at work on a mixed-media book about his jail experiences, entitled *Cut the Motherfuckers Loose!*

Kesey's latest word of advice to his fellow members of what he has called the Psychedelic Mafia: "Speak swiftly, and carry a big soft."

LARRY:

Phone calls to the state min. 8 bucks a piece besides was ever a good board to bounce my favorite ball of bullshit offen, it was you. And with the light steady enough to instruct where the end of the breakwater is out across the bay, ocean calm and warm fifty feet from mine here in outside under tarp beside that cursed bus and kids asleep inside, first time in some moons I feel like bounc-ing a jubilant ball.

I feel good. Healthy, tanned, standing happily tall again after too many stooped hours ambling stiffly about fink ridden Mexico as the white-haired, bespecticled and of course mild-mannered reporter, Steve Lamb, I am chancing here a stretch or two in full daylight as Sol Almande, Prankster Extraordinaire.

Is relatively now. In between here and whatever furthest time back my pen touches lies many an experience, no small amount of achievements and a tidy sum of insights. I was never one to happen through the market place any place on this world without grabbing onto whatever my fancy and my resourcefulness could compromise upon.

cut to

(longshot right down on rooftop of San Francisco North Beach—levels, ladders, asphalt squares. At first glance almost a set—semi-symbolic University theatre clever Jewish director type of stage set—then a man and a young woman interrupt the parrallel arrangement of horizontal surfaces. On a thin and rather ragged mattress, 1½ inch foam in blue cover, shape indicates it was a pad for the back of station wagon. The man has all the usual stigmata of the bohemian in vogue at that period . . . a bohemian crowding that age when "Its time the goddam ninny stopped actin like them snotty Vietniks and dope fiends and acted his age." No longer even the argument of ideals and escape, just pure social outrage, voiced by the fleecy image of daddy-mama-and-other-dear-but-square-ones.

(He has partially balded and has been sick long enough it is difficult to know if he is 25 or 35. Hair boils wildly from his head in thick kinky blond locks. His neck and torso are thick and muscular though he is not short as those built thus usually are. His face is excited but tired, lopsided with the strain faces show after too long forced to smile diplomatically. The girl almost as big as her companion, matching his six feet in height but not his weight. Her hair is long and reddish brown; dark appearing cool black except where the light occasionally sets off the reddish luster. Her eyes almost identical hue, and quite large. Rather like the eyes of an Irish setter pup just turning from awkward carefree frolic to the task of devotion. Her face is young and pretty despite a too broadness and her manner is ornery and funloving as she and her companion banter over the plans for the forthcoming Trips Festival. Their talk concerns personalities and wiring problems.)

"With that big new speaker"—the girl is on the optimistic side of the banter—"we'll be able to wire that place so you can hear a flea fart!"

"Hasn't happened yet," the man says. Pessimism nowhere near the strength of her mood.

"With this many days to get it set up? Always before we were in the hall that night and maybe set up before we finished in the morning. We got almost a week till Friday."

"I hope Stewart gets that Albright business straight. Fillmore was enough of us getting booted out at two."

"Just when we got this system working good," she agreed, a bit too unanimously.

"Just when we got everything to where we could quit playing with wires and start playing. No more of that shit. Stewart's got to have the cops, managers, everybody cooled completely before we get so deep into it that it'll be obvious we don't plan to pull out."

"Because without the Pranksters the Festival will be just another rock and roll dance."

"Just another Family Dog."

"Right!" the girl agrees this time her tone shrewd and curt as well as confident.

The pair lie on their stomachs chins on hands looking down 4 stories to the alley below. As they talk they each occasionally scrape from the asphalt rooftop large gravels to toss down (and see?

Cut back now

See? just as the pair see a police car pull in, park in the alley, and red light in the hillside drive 50 yards to my left blinks in the dawn—do I learn anything? Or once again lie loaded and disbelieving as two cops climb 5 stories to drag me to cooler?

Oh well; a man could get piles sit too long one spot.

Stay tuned,
Kesey

LARRY: This at Puerto Vallarta not long after news leak set me scrambling.

For a long time now he had been sitting watching a fruitless surf, sitting sadly staring out with a swarm of situations and the fact that he could illiterate up a f—ing storm in the flush, flush, lush lush lush of Mexico.

He had seen a fish, yellow tail tuna's broken leap. Two times now. Both times had been good. And he hoped that he could see it leap again without turning into Hemmingway. But his hopes proved vain. For he went back and rewrote rearranged picked and changed for a full half hour when it lept the third.

And after that he was compelled to spend another ten until clang! Somebody! not just humble hermit crabs anymore but a tourist a noise a *federale?* sound of jeep. Clang Clang Clang sudden reappearance of hatted American followed by mex! roar again of jeep—then—ah—the two turn, leave. WHOP! of surf again into that crack left by the fear change of their leaving. Still around though, close. What if they should connect his sitting alone writing with the KESEY CAVORTS IN PUERTO VALLARTA headline? He opened his other pad, let the colored part show; always do a quick sketch pass off image as artist.

And beneath these everlasting the call I hear. Grit and take it. Maybe I gotta kind of grit-your-teeth-and-grin-John-Wayney sorta zen. And sometimes the third "It's all shit" followed by, slower, slyer, "but it's all *goood* shit."

Until he achieved a leveling with a three sided palm hut housing empty bottles an empty cot and doodlebug holes thick and heavy about in the dust indicating a bad year for ants. Also some of those scrawny trees with those greeny things—not coconuts but mangoes or papas or one of those tropical gizmos he hadn't got to know because he hadn't really come to believing in them yet.

"Wellsir, this place might just hold me a spell," he drawled and took off his shirt. Ten minutes later he was smoking the 3 roaches rolled together in a cone and examining with his knife one of the green gizmos as it bled meekly white in his lap. The innards were white and meek and full of pale little rabbit pills. A papaya, he surmised, and mighty young papaya to be put to the sword, let alone the tooth. He hid its remains lest some Mex uncle tom hermit come back up to his shack and see his prize papaya caught redhanded dead before its prime, unzipped his fly to let his sweating nuts air out, and leaned back into twilighting crickets to ring his planetarium, see what the next moment was going to bring.

And was suddenly alert to a rare alarm—"Ritual, Ritual," it whispered, faint. The alarm starts and startles beat an even bigger fear. That he wasn't taking care of his job. Mex returns shorts swims suspicious—maybe sketch now? And had they put out a reward for Chrissakes every f—ing peon in the *state* after his ass and 75 pesos? Okay If this is them straight out the surf over the rocks he'd checked out earlier go under turn sharp left far under as he could swim *voices!* clang clang, again this could be the show un-f—ing believable as it seemed but by god it was keep loose or get busted maybe five years five years even staying outside bars playing stacked low game as pawn not even player, five years against possibility of getting snuffed while staying loose. That pat. All the time. And he knew why. He was at last being forced to the brink of his professed beliefs. Of all that he had babbled about for years now being brought up continually for actual down-to-the-wire testing!

"OOO OOOO!" God almighty! Now some fool over the rocks there wailing like a ghost! "OOO OOO!" A signal? Door slams. Man is hot again. Shows up again take out pen and draw the f—er fast. Only possibility against true foe as well as 3rd level foe like american fink. *Draw* him. *Write* him. *Imagine* him into plot always and then believe all that crap you've been claiming about altering by accepting. Believe it! Or you are a goner, m' boy, a walking dead man for evermore fading finally inaudible like the voices mumbling litanies in the cathedral!

So having vowed thus—and having checked to find the Mex working on the road above—he resolutely dug up his stash, lit up the next to the last joint in all of Mexico, and just leaning back to embark once again upon the will of God—Ka-BOOOM!—up the hill dynamiting? Now that's a ka-boom of a different color. I'd go watch them do a little blasting. "And have every Gringo driving past" another voice interrupted "pointing at you gawking there's Ken *Kee-zee*, Mabel!"

In short, this young, handsome, successful, happily-married-three-lovely-children father, was a fear-crazed dope fiend in flight to avoid prosecution on 3 felonies god knows how many misdemeanors and seeking at the same time to sculpt a new satori from an old surf and—in even shorter—mad as a hatter.

Once an athlete so valued he had been given the job of calling signals from the line and risen into contention for nationwide amature wrestling crown, now he didn't know if he could do a dozen push-ups. Once possessor of phenominal bank account and money waving from every hand now it was all his poor wife could

do to scrape together 8.00 dollars to send as gettaway money to
Mexico. But a few years previous he had been listed in Who's
Who and asked to speak to such auspacous gatherings as the
Wellsley Club in Dahlahs and now they wouldn't even allow
him to speak at a VDC gathering. What was it that had brought
a man so high of promise to so low a state in so short a time?
Well the answer can be found in just one short word, my friends,
in just one all-welused sylable.

   Dope!

   And while it may be claimed by some of the addled advocates
of these chemicals that our hero is known to have indulged in
drugs *before* his literary success we must point out that there was
evidence of his literary prowess *well before* the advent of the so
called psychedelic into his life but *no evidence at all* of any of the
lunitic thinking that we find thereafter!

>   (oh yeah, the wind hums
>   time ago—time ago—
>   the rafter drums and the walls see
>   . . . and there's a door to that bird
>   in the sa-a-a-apling sky
>   time ago by—
>
>   Oh yeah the surf giggles
>   time ago time ago
>   of under things killed when
>   bad was banished and all the
>   doors to the birds vanished
>   time ago then.)

   And thought then "Let my winds of whatever thru and out of
this man-place paranoia be damned and into the jungle—
   "Where its *really* scary."
   The road he'd reached was a Mexican fantasy that had petered
out for the same reason his heart and lungs were working so hard
now—too steep. He sat down in the road, looking out at the sea.
No cars had been along the road—what reason? it petered out
right there? when? time ago?—since the last rainfall.
   The sky had clouded. The sun, nearing its setting, vanished
through the clouds into the sea thump! a car on the road above.

Stops. Starts. Probably the workers but—he stands, effecting a satori smile—

> If you gonna ride the
> wind
> Ride the fat and ride the thin
> Ride the soft and ride the boney
> time ago——time ago
> because there ain't no other
>   poney
> time ago agin.

. . . Someone approaching!

He waits. Long time. It creaks closer and comes out in the very last of the jungles fading light. A little honeybear of a thing. He is delighted and tries to whistle it over but it turns as soon as it senses his presence and sckuffles back. And the mosquitoes get him up and moving again.

Kesey

LARRY:

Isn't it a drag? interrupted right in the middle of the past to have to out into the world and actually *deal* with it. The past don't come The End Twentieth Century Fox and you can get up walk home and tell people who it was because it's over.

Because it isn't over. Up on the same hill I saw red lights. To shit, and while I'm at it peek over the edge see what the FBEyes are looking at this morning. *Plus* "don't forget the San Mateo Sheriff's office, a lot of them are taking vacations in Mexico for the specific purpose of bringing you in."

Is some of the news Faye brings from USA.

By the time I get sit it's full grey dawn. A slate fan of clouds rattle above the Sierra Madre Occidental. Egrets gulls and grackles rise calling from the backwater across the highway, flapping overhead to the beach behind me to earlybird the worm. Bells ring across the bay in town 20 or 30 times—mexican chime code still a complete mystery. Be able to crack it in a few weeks tho, sir; at most one month. "A *month!* By God, Mister, you think I want information of such stature in time for the *Universal Wake?* Strange vehicles sculking around the rocks not five minutes ago *who knows* they're cops American or Mexican? A manta ray cruzing the beach like a frigging doberman out of the K9 Korp, and out in the bay some brand new contrivance like never before floated water before—great rustproof triangle would cover a city block with all three points of the vessle running black and yellow steel pools big around as these tugs that went out to nose around and were waved off sticking straight into the sky 3 times as high as the hotel over in town yonder—and you tell me a month? Well, mister, you figure that bell code pronto. I need to know the time within the frigging hour or you'll be playing with those slide rules and charts up in Ancorage!"

The old captain pivots smartly and stalks off, returning the frightened salute of the younger officer who was stammering at the departure.

The horizon was coloring now in the east; it reminded the officer of paintings speed painters at Bakersfield County Fair splashed onto white fiberboard in one minute flat—3 dollars apiece 2 for five bucks—still hanging when he enlisted; A rectangular sunrise, one on each side of F.D.R.

The bells chimed again. Barely moments since the last ringing. No ryme or reason, pattern or possibility. "In an hour?" In fact, for all anybody knew, it might be the Police Chiefs Idiot daughter at the rope again. He shivered. To have to check that out again. And find an armless and legless unfortunate—result of food poisoning; the mother 2 months after conception nearly dieing from a can of bad green beans paralyzing development of the embryonic limbs and producing a, well, child with an alarmingly lovely face—features that might have posed for Leonardo's Pieta despite the fact that closer examination revealed the mouth to be but two beautiful lips sealed forever over a skull that showed no evidence of any oral opening whatsoever. Below the cute nose the bone ran in a solid fortress to the chin. A quick tracheotomy by a clever intern was all that saved the poor creature from asphyxiation moments after birth. X-rays and a 3/16 in. carpenter's auger finally afforded the infant the luxury of breathing from her nostrils instead of a hole between her collarbones, but a mouth the doctors were unable to provide. X-rays showed a complete absence of tongue, glottis, throat, or any cavity whatsoever where the mouth might be jenny-rigged.

"We're feeding the little darling through her nose," the doctors informed the grief-crazed mother (the father, so claimed those of the sisters at the cathedral, unfortunately unhampered by any oral malfunction, who just happened to be the one who had purchased the evil can of beans, expired not many weeks after the birth as a result of botulism—rumor had it he left the hospital immediately after his legless, armless, and mouthless offspring, to buy all the canned green beans the marketplace could provide, take out a large life insurance policy (which proved worthless owing to a ridiculously small mistake made in the forms by the distraught father) and lock himself in a secret out-of-town hotel hideaway eating beans, letting them set, opened, adding houseflies and horned toads, recapping them, recapping and days later eating until he either successfully bred and consumed the proper poison, or until his system surrendered under the constant onslaught of beans and flies).

"But if you disregard the child's ah deficiencies," the doctors consoled the grief-freaked mother when they decided she might try to follow her husband's lead, "she is a very very lovely child."

"*Already* she has the most expressive eyes I've *ever* in all my years witnessed," a kind old nurse added. "She'll be a beautiful girl! The two of you will do fine. God will see to it."

This was adequate to drive mother and infant from the canned goods into the nunnery, where the mother found St. Teresa and crocheting, and the child did grow into a very very lovely girl. The medical men in their haste to get a potential suicide and/or mercy killing off the hospital grounds had benevolently neglected to inform the mother that the X-rays indicated very little more space for brain than mouth, and the girl had exhausted this area by the time she was 3 or 4. After that the mother or one of the other sisters could frequently be seen pulling a wagon about the cathedral in which was propped a face that grew yearly more and more strikingly beautiful.

"Who gives a snap how *pretty* the girl is," the young officer grumbled, returning to his office in the decoding department, "when you climb ten miles of treacherous ol ladder to find her swinging on the bell-rope *like that.*" He shivered again. "I mean who cares if she's *Hayley Mills?*"

Though bulging from the simple mock-habit sewn for the girl

and torn (just like last time, by god. . . .) from neck to belly button, were two of the most inviting prizes ever to quiver at the end of a bell-rope.

"But who cares if she's Jayne Mansfield or even June *Wilkinson?* C'mere you—" Again he had to carry the creature over one shoulder as he descended the precarious ladder. And just as before her lewd buzom was forced against his cheek or—when he tried to hold her away from his sweat-soaked face—that tongueless mouth and those large eloquent eyes smiled at him so suggestively he was forced to confess some grave doubts concerning the girl's reputed imbecility.

"But what I can't phathom," he panted, "is how you get up that ladder and get *out* on that bell-rope that way."

A rung broke like a dry pistol crack; half-falling he grasped the ladder pole with one hand and lurching snatched out to secure a better purchase on his load with the other hand. Which fell full over one of the full crimson nippled breasts. As soon as he regained a solid rung once again he quickly resumed his former and more decoorous hold on his load.

He made no mention of the incident—it was an accident, a slip! —to the Mother Superior nor to the anonymous ear that listened to the mundane sins he droned into the confessional box. Nor even thought of it again himself the rest of the day as he prepared his report for the captain.

But in bed that evening, locked alone in his quarters, the discovery finally burst loudly into his consciousness. "That—her—*it* felt *back!*"

And barely slept at all that night for the listening out the window across the bay.

Little love story just for variety.

I've still heard nothing from Estrella. Plan was he'd contact me through alias at Telegrafo in Manzanillo. Don't know *what's* happening. (fear Rohan didn't send cash. Lawyers someway always suspect other lawyers being crooks. Wonder why.) But I like Estrella. He's pompous and prideful and *just* right.

Did I ever thank you?

                                                                        Kesey

26 Herbert Gold

Herbert Gold was born in Cleveland in 1924 and was educated at Columbia University and the Sorbonne. He has written seven novels, including The Man Who Was Not With It (1956), Therefore Be Bold (1960), and Fathers (1967); a collection of stories, Love and Like (1960); and a collection of essays on American literature and culture, The Age of Happy Problems (1962).

❖

DEATH IN MIAMI BEACH

The state of madness can be defined partly as an extreme of isolation of one human being from everyone else. It provides a model for dying. Only an intermittent and fragmentary awareness of others interrupts the black folding of the layers of self upon each other—this also defines the state of that dilemma known as "mental health."

There is a false madness induced by the accidents of isolation which prisoners, travelers, and the very ill may sometimes experience without giving up their return ticket. Surely you out there all know what I mean from your own troubles and painful decisions. To say that it is false madness does not soften its extremity. The mask of existence fits harshly on your skin, but it is in fact your only skin; and when harshly your skin is peeled off—beneath it you are naked and your naked isolation is no joy to you.

During a period of work on a long job of writing in the winter of 1958, I deliberately withdrew myself from all those who knew my name and traveled by automobile in slow stages through the deep South to Miami Beach, Key West, Havana, and finally back

up toward Detroit. No one asked me to write a novel, no one
asked me to go away; but I did anyway. I was tempted by the prospect of dreaming through my story amid a pleasant chaos of sun
and sea, all other responsibilities suspended, and so I arranged
it for myself.

Work is very fine, but after the day's work, isolation, silence,
and death seemed to follow me through the zazzy carnival of
Miami, the casual resort indolence of Key West, and the smoky,
blistered elegance of a tourist's Havana. In Havana, from the rooftop of the Ambos Mundos Hotel, I could see Batista's police loafing with their weapons in front of public buildings; occasionally
there were bombs; once a body happened to be left in the street
and people hurried by as if they knew nothing, nothing, nothing
at all but the next step before them.

At Key West, a few days before Christmas, I visited the turtle
slaughterhouse. It is one of the few tourist attractions on this
spot of island, "North Havana," raised far out into the sea off the
coast of Florida. Visitors take their kiddies by the hand and
lead them to see the nice turtles.

Before being killed and canned, the turtles swim in dense
kraals, bumping each other in the murky water, armor clashing,
dully lurching against the high pens. Later, trussed on a plank
dock, they lie unblinking in the sun, their flippers pierced and
tied. The tough leather of their skin does not disguise their
present helplessness and pain. They wear thick, sun-hardened ac-
cumulations of blood at their wounds. Barbados turtles, as large
as children, they belong to a species which has been eliminated
locally by ardent harvesting of the waters near Key West, but the
commercial tradition still brings them here to be slaughtered.
Crucified like thieves, they breathe in little sighs, they gulp, they
wait.

At a further stage, in the room where the actual slaughtering
occurs, the butchers stride through gore in heavy boots. The
visitor must proceed on a catwalk; a misstep will plunge him into
a slow river of entrails and blood. Because it was near Christmas-
time, the owners of the plant had installed a speaker system for
musical divertissement of the butchers, and while the turtles dried
under the sun or lay exposed to the butchers' knives, Christmas

bells tolled out, electronically amplified, "God Rest Ye Merry, Gentlemen," or the Bing Crosby recording of "*Adeste Fideles.*"

These commercial details are not intended to support a special plea on behalf of the humane harvesting of Barbados turtles. In fact, let me grant that I sought out this scene and visited the abattoir without having any proper business there at all: merely curiosity and the need to confirm my imagination about it. I should be judged for vulgarity by the man who chooses out of purity not to follow me, not by the man I saw lurking outside, with a face ravaged by the horrified fascination which makes it impossible for him to visit his dreams. What had I done which he could not permit himself? Was I filthied, was I weakened by pleasure but obscurely nourished, was I fed on coveted turtle joys after trampling in turtle blood? Had I asked permission from the butcher and plied a knife with my own hands on the belly of one of the slow, unblinking, dragon-headed, ancient sea-beasts? And did it arch its graceful dragon neck in reproach as I stabbed? He stared at me like a jealous lover, imagining my wickedness, rabid and hopeless, wanting to bury his head in the reek on my hands.

Most of us turn from the vision of death only out of weakness, and this is no turning from death. Serve up your turtle steak, gourmet friend, with no protest from me; I'll eat at your table. ("A nice rendition," one gentleman said of Bing Crosby to his wife. Turtle is tasty, somewhat gamy meat. Protein nourishes the brain—brings oxygen and freedom.)

A few days later, in Miami Beach, I participated in two trivial accidents. My hotel was in one of the oldest, therefore least expensive, parts of the town, only a short block from the sea and a short block from restaurants and therefore very convenient to my casual schedule: breakfast at Whelan's, a stretch of writing, a long swim, lunch, a pleasant bit of loafing on the beach, then perhaps some sunbaked work at my typewriter on the tar roof ("solarium"), and another swim before dinner. I had the habit in the morning of disregarding the elevator, hurrying down a back stairway of the Webster Hotel, through an alley, and so shortcutting to the drugstore. One day, wearing tennis shoes, I felt an evil slide and crunch underfoot, and knew first by the shrinking in my heart and then by simple inspection that I had stepped on a small animal.

It seemed to be a variety of cockroach. It had been perhaps an inch and a half long, longer with its wings spread, and it had strayed from the raised platform nearby where the hotel stored its rubbish. Now it lay twitching, legs scrambling in the air without moving, and a yellow ooze seeped from its body within the crushed carapace. I suppose it was already dead despite all this nervous movement. I went for a walk, told myself that this was a silly matter to be fretful about (I was merely isolated), and finally took my habitual breakfast: orange juice, scrambled eggs, toast, coffee.

An hour later the dead beast was glued by its own innards to the paving of the alley; the Florida sun was moving through the sky above it. But now there was also a row of ants leading to it, another leading away, like twin caterpillars dissembling their unity of purpose. They were not merely eating, of course, they were carrying off the meat to their hill someplace. But the dead roach still twitched, and when the tickling jaws struck, it fluttered, squeezed, blindly pushed in its place. The ants went scrambling away, each carrying its minuscule steak.

All afternoon the shell of the roach lay there. Its row of legs no longer waved of their own power, but there were still tremors as the eating ants tugged at it. Unfatigued and busy, they were determined to wipe this slate clean.

Shortly before dark I again came down the back stairway. Now the familiar arena had changed. Another foot had struck, more strange and haphazard than my own. The shell of the roach was destroyed; there were also dead ants freckling the stone; stillness and death. The ants were suddenly individual in death; the undulating columns were erased. And the work of eating was permanently interrupted for both eaters and eaten.

The next morning when I walked through the alley no sign remained. A sweeper had done her work; there were straight, mechanical striations—a friendly broom. Good. But I bent to look for some sign or memorial to the departed beast on this stretch of alley which I now knew very well. There was none. Marks of broom; new arrangements of pebbles and dust; history here had entered upon an epoch which was strange to me.

Then finally a homely death entered what might pass for society in my isolated Miami Beach—the world of the soda fountain at Whelan's, where strollers came into an air-conditioned place to shake off the sand of the beach, sip a Coke, buy lotions and plastic sunglasses, and sometimes order a quick meal.

I was taking my breakfast, according to my habit, on a stool at the counter. By this time I was acquainted with Frank, the short-order cook, who had emigrated from Second Avenue in New York twenty years ago for his health and, for sweet health's sake, still managed to cover the leathery pouched skin of age with a fierce Miami tan, despite his long hours in Whelan's service. It relieved the silence to exchange a few morning words with a man who by now knew my face: "Two scrambled light."

"Same as yesterday, Mister."

"Yes, like yesterday." (Triumph in my voice: He remembers me!) "Whole-wheat toast. You got marmalade today?"

"Marmalade." Frank knew my face and my eggs.

Other eaters, like me, were forking up eggs and grits and sipping their Cokes or coffee when the woman entered. She was blotched with sunburn, had a swollen nose, and a mouth open so wide for noise that all her features were distorted. Emitting emergency alarm signals, turning her head and staring, demanding passage, demanding attention, a shouting vehicle, she pushed a stumbling old man along with her. "Ohh," she screamed, "a Bromo! For God's sake a Bromo! My husband is dying, a Bromo, for God's sake!"

The man's face was blue and he seemed barely conscious. He swayed stiffly as she steered him toward a stool near me.

"Oh, a Bromo right now, please!" she wailed.

Frank, behind the counter, looked sideways at her, pretended the impossible—that he did not hear her—and went on making a bacon-lettuce-and-tomato sandwich on whole-wheat toast, light on the mayonnaise.

Two or three of us jumped up to support the old man. His skin had a thick purple glow that said death to all our eyes.

"Oh, have mercy, a Bromo for my poor husband!" the woman screamed. "He didn't do nothing to you! For God's sake why don't you give it to him?"

Floundering, I watched Frank finish the bee-ell-tee, slide it onto a plate, and hand it to his customer. The hotrodder bent his head to the spilling sandwich and ate as if his life depended on it, thrustingly. In the meantime, the pharmacist, a short man in a white coat, sweating profusely despite the air conditioning, came bustling from his cubicle and said, "Heart attack? You want I should call a doctor, Missus?"

"Ohh, please, dear God, a Bromo!" she shouted.

"I'll call a doctor, he'll be right over."

"Bromo for a dying man! Why don't you give it to him? Mercy, mercy!"

The pharmacist was on the telephone and the howling woman subsided in shrill spasms. Her husband swayed on the stool, his eyes shut, while his wife leaned sobbing against his back to keep him from toppling onto the ground. She refused to let anyone touch him in order to lay him out on the floor—someone's idea —as if this ministry would commit him once and for all to the hands of death. Naturally, my innards shrank from this; the layers of the self closed tight; the flower of feeling was shut, sealed. I wanted to rush in some place, rush away; strike, destroy, run; kill Frank, kill the hotrodder, because a man was dying and nobody could do anything. Thus righteousness substitutes for being straight with the world. I was sly and scared. Thus I occupied myself with rage at my friend Frank, who pretended to hear nothing and stubbornly refused to make the glass of Bromo Seltzer.

During the five minutes before the doctor arrived, the scene altered rapidly and tensely. Of course, all the breakfasters but the determined hotrodder stopped their eating. The kid in the leather jacket asked for pretzels with his Coke for sustained strength behind the wheel. The rest of us drifted, lurking behind the sick man on his stool. His wife wept and cursed and heaved out her sobs because no one would supply a Bromo.

Then abruptly the man shook himself and opened his eyes and tried to stand up. He stumbled; his wife pushed him back onto the stool. He shook his head and mumbled. Then rapidly the purple color diminished; his eyes stopped their blind rolling; he began to talk with his wife. He was returning to the living. He and his wife had a whispered consultation. She nodded rapidly at him, like a bird.

Suddenly she alighted and flew out the door. The man, left behind on the stool, said hoarsely, "Lemme have a glass of water, will you, pal?"

Frank gave him the water.

Now the doctor entered, rolling his sleeves down and carrying his black bag open. He had apparently run a block in the tropical morning heat.

"Haha!" said the formerly dying man. Just like that: "Hahaha! Hi, Doc!"

"You're the sick man?" said the doctor. "Let's see now—"

"Hahaha! Don't touch me, Doc," said the old man, leaning away. "Listen, Doc, it's a funny thing. My wife gets herself all excited—aggravated."

"You mean you're all right?" the doctor said.

"Just like a little attack was all I had, hahaha," said the old man.

"You're okay?"

"Look, Doc, I ain't been eating right, you know, enjoying myself, hahaha. A little attack. I get them sometimes. Like a little attack is all."

"Okay," and the doctor firmly, "you don't want me to look at you? Okay." He nodded briskly to the pharmacist, said, "I've got a patient in my office," and trotted off again into the heat.

The old man smiled and gazed without malice at Frank, who had refused him the Bromo. Instead of leaving a tip he left him one word of explanation before he headed off after his wife. The word was deposited on the counter behind him with an apologetic smile: "Constipation."

Eggs in the plates of all the late breakfasters were left cold and shiny. The hotrodder alone had finished his sandwich, Coke, and pretzels, and left whistling. Angry at last, I discharged an unformulated hostility on Frank: "Why the devil didn't you give the man his Bromo?"

His reply seems an obvious bit of logical disquisition at this remove, but there in the shadow of panic and crisis it struck me with the force of revelation. Rubbing a dirty cloth on the counter

—formulating and reformulating a smear of grease before me—he said, "If he was dying of a heart attack, what good would a Bromo do him? And if he was not dying, what good is a Bromo?"

"Yes, but."

"So I have to do my job, but I don't have to listen to nuts."

"But you didn't say anything! That woman was hysterical."

He looked at me with undisguised pity for my ignorance. "That's why I didn't say anything. I been in trouble for saying things before, I learned."

He went back to work; the pharmacist was back in his cubicle, counting pills into a bottle; the doctor had returned to his office. It was eleven o'clock and Frank took down the sign about the breakfast special. A man came in frightened to ask for the special, and Frank pointed to the sign, which was upside down on the counter, and said, "It's five minutes after eleven already. But I'll give it to you." The look of despair faded from the man's face.

In a few days I finished my own job and began the long drive out of the false Florida summer into the northern winter, my wheels passing over all sorts of unfelt beasties, my gullet accepting steaks and chops, my heart leaping with no better welcome to death than before. In Detroit my daughter asked me, "What's God's last name? How big is the whole world? Where do you go when you die?"

The foregoing inconclusive words were written two years ago. Now I have seen fit to return to my cafeteria-and-old-folks slum on lower Collins Avenue, and ostensibly for the same lure of cheap sun, sky, water, beach, boredom. I write, I swim. I stroll on Lincoln Road, I eat steaks and pizza, I sniff the sea with my sunburnt beak, I suck in my belly and run barefoot on the sand, I sleep, I write. In front of one of the new hotels I found a nude in plaster, beckoning, with her hand lifted as if hitching a ride. All aboard, you masturbators. Some of the fruit juice and hamburger stands have disappeared; new ones have opened. The Ellis Department Store, Here Since 1919, is closed, looks ransacked, has a box of Fruit of the Loom T-shirts spilled in the window and a U. S. Federal Court bankruptcy notice affixed to its sealed door.

I met a waitress in a restaurant which advertises nine-course dollar dinners. She has a pretty, lively, thirty-five-year-old girl's face, with all the black brightness of eye a man could want; she turns out to be Corsican and we speak French; an artillery sergeant brought her to Florida and apparently tired of her brightness of eye. She has a rattling Corsican accent, likes Edith Piaf records, and gives me extra shrimp bits in my shrimp bits salad. So some things change. Last time I heard no Edith Piaf and earned no extra forkfuls of shrimp. The sirloin steak she brings me spreads its wings and seems ready to flop off the plate. My gut talks French and I take ease in the flattery of food. I wait and at last she slips into my booth with me and sighs. It is eleven o'clock, time to begin real life. Her history is sad. I feel obliged to offer some recompense for the evil done her by men and luck, and so I listen, wondering how her eyes can remain so bright as the disasters and disillusionments unroll.

When I said good night, she replied with a funny, rapidly fiddling, diddling, twenty-one-fingered gesture at her mouth. I asked what it meant. "Fun and glee," she said, "fun and glee! *Maintenant je suis une vraie Américaine.*" Her eyes burn like stars, but like the stars, she has darkness between them.

A day and a night and another day. The first week passes.

I eat salty bagels in the sun, I listen to the teenage girls after school with their curious mixture of Florida cracker and Bronx accents. I go back into the damp of my room—the peculiar dank assault of cheap tropical bedrooms—and think my novel through once again, examining the pile of manuscript with my intentions in motion like a column of ants working over the struggling body of an insect. And when the life seems to weaken, I leave it and go out onto the beach or into the street.

Madness consists partly in an extreme of isolation? Partly. But the demented tumble down from their associations and memories into other associations and memories; they are sent away into the future with a map of the past which conforms to no agreed past and to no other map—and yet it is their only chart, their history and route, their needs which are unfailingly present. The lonely traveler also brutally inflicts absolute possession of his movements upon the endless day, and the novelty of what he sees joins him in yet another way to his deepest desires and dreads. He returns, he never lets go. There is no escape even in isolation; there is no isolation, merely interrupted and distorted association, until death claims us. Then every man is an island entire of itself.

In love, we seek freedom and purity even more than the comfort of diminished isolation. Those few fortunate ones who have the talent can bear the paradox of love. The rest of us are harassed by our contradictory demands—*join me, make me free.* With age and aging, the model of all voyages (learn and grow, diminish and weary), comes final approach to the ultimate simplicity which love seeks to confound—death. A paradox forever out of balance to answer a grave black simplicity: *we are ill used.* The facts we make for ourselves disappoint the intentions with which we make them. The opposable thumb, which is said to be responsible for civilization and history, gives us no answers here, though with it we can grasp our pens and break insects in our hands. Finally we die, opposable thumbs and all.

In the meantime, I visit my story. We exchange visits. I laugh over it, frown and worry over it, and urge it forward. Then I leave it for the Miami streets. The book follows me; it does not let me visit unaccompanied; it enters me instead and I try to shake it off as an adept at voodoo fights against possession by the importunate god. The opposable thumb is of no use in this contest; both the prize and the weapons have reached beyond tools, even tools of thinking; I am the quadruple god's horse—dream of love, hope of meaning, joy of power, relish in being. Too much burden on one soul. Who asked me to feel sorry or glad for others? They were merely pious who asked me. Why follow their orders? I decide: I *won't.* But I cannot escape my self, which also gives orders. The flower of feeling opens; the flower shuts; it obeys the freshness of weather. All emotion flowing from health or illness partakes of the pathetic fallacy, identifying moral value with the gifts of nature. My feet want to run; I am wearing Keds, and feel light on the foam rubber soles; but the heat of the sun holds me to earth.

There is a hotel on Washington Boulevard which specializes in "economical, comfortable living for the retired." It is a huge dark building like the Women's House of Detention in Greenwich

Village, but without the bars on the rooms, and there are purple
lights playing on the palm trees outside, soft music piped throughout the grounds, and the frequent blare of a loudspeaker: "Missus
Goldberg to the telephone! Missus Goldberg! *Sadie, answer the
phone!*" when the children call from New York. The streets of
the neighborhood are filled with chattering of mournful elder
statesmen, mostly losers after sixty years of continual negotiation,
men with chagrined pouches slipping sideways beneath their eyes,
women with hair bursting onto their cheeks and upper lips, as if
all at once, near the end, they have decided to make a final try at
being better men than their husbands.

To walk through the crowd during the hour following their
afternoon naps is to wade in senility. There is a deep-sea lack of
light despite all the sun and brisk resort clatter; you gasp for life
and run to look in a dusty window. Narcissus wants to be just
thirty-five, "*nel mezzo del cammin di nostra vita,*" and not seventy,
not seventy! The crowd flutters by. "She thought she could be
my daughter-in-law! A girl like that! To be my daughter-in-law!
And you know what? Now she is." "I used to be in business.
I had a good business. It was a nice store, good location. Furniture. I should have kept my location." "What does the weather
report say? Does the weather report ever say anything but the
weather?" "Moishe died. He had an attack. Well, we all got to
go."

Is it the same voice, the same rhythm? It is the same crowd—
grief, isolation, death. There almost always seems to be an ambulance pulling up or pulling away.

It is fine to tell a story, which feels like affirmation, but afterwards, after the morning's writing, then what? Writing is an expression of affirmation, power, longing, but not a proper cause of
these emotions in the writer. He is a guide into delight and dread
because he can escape victimization (he thinks); he has left a
little trail of paper behind him as he threads his way into the
maze, and can find his way back (he believes—though the roar
of the maze sets up a disarray in anything as fragmentary as his
intentions about return). He tracks the minotaur with an open
mind. "Maybe I'll like it," he says, "and maybe I won't. At least

I'll see." He initiates passion only because he has it—otherwise
self-delusion and covetous self-therapy. And so it is not good to
be alone for long, entirely alone.

But at least for a time, until they dim out, loneliness sharpens
the eyes. I feel like a safecracker; loneliness has also sharpened my
fingertips, and my entire body throughout feels the clicking tumblers as I yearn toward the combination. I come to focus, I work.
But afterwards, then what? I have retreated from the distractions
of Manhattan. There are no telephone calls. No friendship, no
duties, no hazards of pique or pleasure. I shall work till the battery runs down, frozen and stilled by this busy emptiness under
the sun. I ask myself: Can the silent column of ants reconstruct
the living roach at its leisure underground? No, only a tree can
make a tree, only a winged roach can make a winged roach. A
column of ants works by an invisible will which resides in no
one of its jointed parts, but only a swollen green ant can breed
an urgent ant.

As I walk on Lincoln Road, the smart shopping area of "the
Beach," I ogle the oglers, the sunburned sun-worshipers basted
with oil, cream, tonic, and lotion—the touts, boxers, fairies, grand-
mothers, exiled Cubans, local hotrodders and their gumchewing
molls, sportsmen, natty invalids in gabardine, drunks, stockbrokers,
antique collectors, Semites and anti-Semites all taking the air
together on Lincoln Road. Hill people, swamp people, and ex-pugs
sell newspapers flown in from all over—New York, Chicago, Los
Angeles ("Smogsville!" cackles a refugee). And New York is
harried by flu and Chicago is black with coal and damp. And
here we all are on Lincoln Road, with a delicious breeze, courtesy
of the steakhouse pumping cool air into the street. So let's buy
the hometown paper to see how miserable we might have been,
for others are.

On Lincoln Road, fair Lincoln Road in Miami Beach, the
Negroes have been freed; freed of existence, that is; only a few
black ghosts slip discreetly by. Even if they were not so discreet,
they would be invisible, though for a new reason: they are going
someplace, namely, to work, or at another hour, home. For them,
Lincoln Road is a mere artery for transit, while for the others,
Lincoln Road is parlor, sunroom, promontory into health and

beauty. For the visitors, Lincoln Road is a slow matter, a recipe for yearned-for slowness, sloth, strolling ease, delicacy of control. The cocky Broadway chapparoonies are wearing their new pleat-less "Miami-Tailored Daks." Their bellies do the work of belts, hiding the place where belts would be. Now I'm so slow I don't need a belt, the pants proudly announce; I'm just walkin' along, just struttin' down the avenue, just here and pleasant with myself, and when I take a breath, the expandable elastic waistband expands with me. In the men's room of a bar off Lincoln Road, hung with photographs of wrestlers, there is a curious vending machine which is decorated with a crown and raised scepter and submits a product called DE-LA: "Say Delay, a light lubricating ointment designed to aid in the prevention of premature climax. Odorless. Safe. Stainless. Easy to apply. Directions on package. 50¢ coins only. Machine does not give change."

Machine makes comment, however. Machine is trying to tell us something.

The Negro girl who cleans my room gets yelled at, screamed at, all morning. "Stupid, stupid, stupid! A single room only gets two towels, one face, one bath!" She smiles slyly to herself as if she knows where the manager's DE-LA is hidden. This is the southland, I am reminded, where we have grits for breakfast. But it is not quite dat ole Dixie, boss, which changeth not, nor can age alter it. It is Miami Beach. The Sholem Aleichem Literary Society ("Managed by Tourists—Managed for Tourists") has a For Rent sign on it. "Owner Will Remodel for Any Business."

I decide as I walk: I'll write my book till the battery runs down, though distraction seems necessary; other duties, friends, "real life."

The sirens of the police ambulances work up and down the Beach all day and night, announcing the news as they carry away the attacked, the fallen, the stroked, the perished. A population of the aged sheds its members at the merest trifle of an excuse—a bottle of cold pop in the sun, a skipped nap, somebody raising his voice suddenly—or no excuse at all. It touches life and someone dies. It treads carelessly and someone dies. The sirens whir and howl and Negroes courteously open the back door for the corpse. For some reason people smile at the ambulance as they stroll, sucking ice cream. Perhaps they dream of an accident, a distraction: *Siren meets white Thunderbird, boy of forty cut off in his prime, had a girl in there with him, not his wife.* Perhaps thinking: *Not me this time.*

One of those impossible coincidences. Today I met Dr. Meyer leading his blind wife. He was our family doctor in Cleveland, addicted to practical jokes, who always said he wanted to do research, and in fact he had some sort of connection with one of the important drug laboratories. When he retired from practice, he announced to my parents over a bottle of wine that now he would begin his true life's work. I had decided that his practical jokes, bought in Jean's Fun House on East 9th Street—buzzers, false flies, stomach noises, leaky cups—were a symptom of childish anger at adult responsibility. But now that he could retire from practice and try his hand at research. . . . It turned out that his wife had inoperable cataracts; she went blind fast, and he went sour, quiet, mean; and they left Cleveland for Miami Beach, where I saw him leading her, walking with the stiff, frightened step of the unaccustomed blind. He is shrunken; only today do I notice that he is a small man—when I was a boy, he was immense. At present, and forever until the very end, his life's work is to steer his wife to the beach in the morning and sit with her to describe what he sees. He has replaced both practical jokes and dreams of a laboratory with loyalty to his wife, but virtue has made him a furious runt.

Fantasies of thighs, breasts, bellies as I nap on the beach. I awaken, sticky with salt. My nose is peeling. Shall I visit the Corsican waitress again tonight? Shall I ask the Meyers to dinner? But I have made this disappearance into Miami Beach in order to avoid the troubles of others and of myself. I swim again. I doze again. I dream of sex with a woman I overheard describing the proper way to kill a chicken "so it don't suffer. You ask anyone, they'll tell you. And there's nothing like fresh-killed chicken. You can't trust the butchers."

A man in the coffee shop later said to the cashier: "I been sick, that's why you ain't seen me. Doctor said coronary thrombosis. You ever heard of that?"

"Naw. Lots of people got coronaries, but that thrombosis, that's a new thing. The docs keep finding new things so they can charge us."

"Well, I'll tell you, it left me feeling pretty weak."

I went one night to see a road company version of *My Fair Lady* at the Miami Beach Auditorium, which more frequently provides hospitality for wrestling or boxing matches. A maggoty, bored imitation of Rex Harrison, a thick Eliza without any bounce. The audience is quietly taking in the famous sight. They write on their postcards home: Tonight we saw a Broadway show, but the girl was fat.

Crazy Louie on the beach—a frantic grandfather with Latin records, maracas, castanets, silk Cuban shirts, feathers, straw skirt, rubber Halloween masks, a huge earring loosely hooked to his ear by a bent hairpin, thick glasses sliding down his nose, leathery withered legs, dancing and dancing, all sinews and grins and shakes to some inner song while the portable phonograph goes rattle-and-scrape, screech, rattle, and scrape. Amazingly, the crowd which regularly gathers on the sand nearby seems to enjoy his music; some of them shake, too, dreaming of the days when they had lust to squander on their legs. Dr. Meyer's wife smiles as he describes the scene. "Are you smiling, Meyer?" she asks. He says yes, but is lying. Crazy Louie bangs his castanet under her nose and screams *"Ole!"* and she jumps. At last Dr. Meyer smiles.

Then he tells her that sometimes the beginnings of arteriosclerosis can be detected at age twenty-five. "Cuts off the blood supply to the brain. The psychiatrists think they're smart, but they can't do anything about the histological system. The brain dries up like a scab."

"Meyer, you shouldn't use such language."

"You mean histology?"

"I mean scab, Meyer."

Crazy Louie is dancing and cackling, kicking sand. The old ladies in their bathing skirts fan themselves contentedly as he enters his Afro-Cuban apocalypse. On the beach there is a rural, village tolerance of madness. Louie doesn't do any harm. His children sent him down. He is new since my last visit.

And where are my old friends?

The cockroach in the alley is long gone, of course, and its

grandchildren unto many generations. But I have found cheap sun again for my sinus, and white ocean breaking against the distractions of Manhattan in winter, spring, summer, fall. I think of a friend, a Jewish chauvinist, arguing with his girl: "When your people were still living in trees and hitting each other with sticks, my people already had sinus trouble."

The Spinoza Forum is gone, replaced by a motel. Dr. Wolfson still goes to the beach every afternoon. But the neighborhood is changed. He has nothing to say to me except that raw beets, honey, and tangerines keep a man virtuous and healthy, no matter what his age.

The woman who knew Thomas Wolfe—did I forget to mention that last time?—and swam as if she wanted to die, and worked as a B-girl . . . gone. She wanted to reconstruct some cabin-in-the-woods dream of perfection, but she could never find the missing pieces. Life is not a jigsaw puzzle; once it has been scrambled, the old picture is gone.

The racing-car driver with whom I chatted a couple of times at breakfast—gone.

The column of ants at the cockroach—gone.

The drummed-up acquaintances—even their names forgotten.

The hotel clerk who wanted to explore in Guatemala—perhaps he is exploring in Guatemala. The new manager of the hotel has never even heard of him.

And the man who died—dead.

I know this for certain, for I have finally discovered an old friend. Frank, the gray bozo behind the counter at Whelan's, is still there. I had taken up new eating habits and did not return to Whelan's during my first week in Miami Beach, but then I did and found him, still building hamburger platters and scrambling eggs. At first he did not remember me. He never knew my name. When I reminded him of the incident about the man who died, and of our long breakfast friendship, a look of irritation captured his face—demands were being made on him—but then his cross mug creased into a smile. He did remember me! He only needed to be reminded!

"You know that old fool," he said. "Later really did die. He's dead. Later died."

There was a new cat in the store. A new special on tooth-brushes. A new pharmacist.

I had a hamburger on our old friendship, and Frank put an extra slice of tomato on the side to *prove* that he remembered me. But why should he? He had been an experience for me—the same now, with balder eyebrows—but what was I to him? For me he existed as an example of something, a moment of frightening history, a troubled memory which I had set down in words. I had needed a friend then, but he did not. I was frightened by death then, and worse, by a way of receiving death, but he was not and perhaps never admits that he might be.

Why does he stay in Miami Beach?

Yes, for a job. Yes, for the sun. But why there?

All right, then why not there?

Why do I go back?

Why did I go back? What happened to those dead and dying ones? They died and were dead; they were swept away. I thought, the first time I went to Miami Beach, that I had made a free choice to be isolated, but I discovered that everyone comes to the state of isolation in time—though not freely. What I did out of apparent health and youth, in the pleasure of work, those others did in sickness and age, in the anxiety of boredom. But eventually work is done, health turns to decay, youth turns to ripeness turns to age; feebleness and dying must precede death except for fighter pilots, who are anachronisms. Miami Beach is an extension, adult education course in how to die, pursued with great seriousness by the enrollees. The old folks work at it with deliberate and modest intensity, in group sessions, complimenting each other on their tans, their sport shirts, their postgraduate skill at finding a proper weather. The young vacationers flush in on packaged tours, immerse themselves in the ceremonial indulgences of resort hotels, eat, swim, and enjoy their honeymoon wrestling, take in Eartha Kitt or Leo de Lion, sigh with boredom and excess, buy bottles of Man Tan at the air terminal ("Arrive With Fresh Sun On Your Cheeks!"), and flee back to real life with a secret conviction that this is leisure? Strictly for the birds, brother.

That first time in Miami Beach, I was a curious observer, ob-

HERBERT GOLD

scurely moved, with the face of a man who fearfully unwinds a rope as he visits his dream of the turtle slaughterhouse. The second time (the last time!), two years' change had begun to discover my implication to me; I broke the rope; the model of death is real; the dream of dying is real. The tanned, reduced, heliotropic Doctor Meyer recognized me despite his wife's blindness ("Hannah! Look who's here!"), and when I spoke to her, she gropingly embraced me. This was why I went back—to feel Mrs. Meyer's arms hotly convulsed about my neck, as if I were still a boy in Cleveland, and to know that I was not a young man from Cleveland visiting Miami Beach as he had toured carnivals, the war, the Caribbean, Europe, and taken the boat ride around Manhattan. I was a winter visitor, tired of town, come for the sun, who had been there before.

Am I now satisfied with what I found? Which is: "Later really did die. Later died." Just as in the alley two years ago, in that swept space where there was no longer any roach and no column of ants, history enters upon new epochs which begin to grow familiar to me.

27 Albert J. Guerard

Albert J. Guerard has published six novels, including Night Journey (1950), The Bystander (1958), and The Exiles (1963), and critical studies of Thomas Hardy, André Gide, Joseph Conrad, and Robert Bridges. He is Albert L. Guérard Professor of English at Stanford University.

❖

THE INCUBUS

I

One May evening of his twenty-second year Duncan Tait, who wanted to be in touch with the world of art and literature, had an experience which changed his life. He was taken to a party in the Village. A young man from his home town, Paul Anders, took him. This was the same young man who had found Duncan Tait a job on the business staff of one of the large women's magazines.

Actually, Tait had been in New York only three weeks when he went to this party, and met the painter Sue Shelton, who was two years younger. He still had the shaved haircut and scorched distant gaze of the western small-college athlete. He had the firm handshake, looked you straight in the eye, and bore the bland depthless face of an innocent. He was six feet two and weighed one hundred and ninety pounds. It was odd for a man of that size to want to be in touch with art and literature.

On emerging from the subway the two young men, at Paul Anders' suggestion, took off their ties. Thus they would not seem to be outsiders among the artists. Mounting the dark sagging stairs,

Duncan Tait heard the weird African sounds of an esoteric record float down from the party. He became much excited. This was the kind of experience he had come to New York for.

It was a rather odd party, spread over two drab underfurnished rooms. Sue Shelton stayed in one room with half-a-dozen men of Duncan's age or younger who had moustaches and dark impatient stares. She was barefoot, coiled in a black skirt and a black blouse deeply unbuttoned, and she was the only girl at the party. She and her artist friends huddled over the phonograph and its African moans. In the other room, held back as by an invisible fence, were four older men standing in an embarrassed silence. They stared at Sue, who had invited them, through the open sliding doors. They held tall glasses and didn't know what to say or do. They were muscular men who might have been insurance sales-men, and who wore identical gray business suits. It was evident they had not met each other before this evening.

Duncan Tait found himself with these men, even though he wore no tie, while Paul Anders went off for their drinks. He too stared at Sue. In those days one long brown lock hung over her sullen right eye. A sensuous underlip stuck out. She did not have, then, the carved distressed look of the later photographs. She had a soft petulant young girl's face above the frankness of her body. Duncan stared at her bare feet and drawn-up knees, and thought he had never seen a girl so dangerous and so desirable. Then he realized she was staring back at him, with her dark eyes fixed and scornful. It was a faint smile as of recognition, a challenge. Could she stare behind his face, and even know what he was feeling? The dryness, the sudden taut desire! She turned away with a quick grin.

He despaired of meeting her. More people arrived, even two stringy bluestocking girls, and soon everyone was talking at once. But then suddenly she was beside him. She padded up to him in her bare feet and put a hand on his. She asked him to go with her to the kitchen to get something to eat. Some nuance of ex-pression told the others not to come. They stared at Tait with cold annoyance.

But they never got to the kitchen. She led him instead to the narrow landing off the stairs. She went off into the darkness and stood there, white and rather small.

"I'm Sue Shelton."

"Yes, I know."

"Come over here a little closer and tell me what you do. I'm a painter."

"Yes, I know."

"You've got to learn to say something else, if you want to keep me amused. Don't you want to keep me amused?"

He told her the name of the women's magazine for which he worked in the circulation department.

"Someday I'll get into editorial work. It's more important. It puts you in contact with creative people."

"Oh Lordy! Is that what you want?"

She stepped toward him, and put her hands behind his neck. But with an inward pressure on his ears she was, at the same time, holding him expertly away. Her body came very close and she was standing on tiptoe. Her odor was smoky and exciting.

"You aren't a very interesting person, are you?"

She said this impersonally. She might have been weighing a product in a store.

"What do you mean by that?"

"I mean I don't think you're very bright." She still held him off. "All the same I want to go somewhere with you. Do you want to take me somewhere?"

"You mean just leave, like that, without saying anything?"

"Don't they do that in North Dakota?"

"Oklahoma," he said. "Tulsa, Oklahoma. You'll have to get your shoes."

"No. I don't think I need any."

And this was the beginning of his long experience. In the taxi she sat far away from him and silent. She told him what hotel to go to, where she wouldn't need a bag or even shoes. But in the elevator she stood against him, her mouth working, ignoring the bellboy and the man who ran the elevator. She padded ahead of him down the long halls in the black skirt and blouse. And later, exhausted, Duncan remembered their first act of love as a violent combat with a brown coiling animal body as firm as his own. It was very different from anything he had experienced in the back seats of automobiles on hot Oklahoma nights, under the skeletal derricks. Sue's face turned from side to side as in loathing of him and of herself, while her hard body thrashed. At one point she began to scream.

He was frightened, even after she returned to her calm. He lay back and watched her go to the window and throw it open, stand there taking deep breaths. Yes, she frightened him. But also he felt an odd affection for this lost creature who in her drunkenness had chosen him over all her friends. So when she proposed to go home by herself, he insisted on accompanying her. She had been on the verge of going off without leaving him her address.

She lived in a cold-water flat not far from the brownstone house of the party. The floors and walls were cluttered with sketches and unfinished paintings. The work seemed to Duncan very amateurish, a child's geometric scrawl. Still it was exciting to be in an artist's messy studio. He looked at the paintings, but she began turning them over to face the wall.

"You're too modest," he said.

"This hasn't anything to do with you. You don't know anything about it."

"I'd like to," he said. "I care about it. I don't think there's anything more important than writing or painting."

"You don't?" She stared at him with her sullen lovely eyes. "How about what we did tonight?"

The remark shocked him. Still he had to answer her gallantly.

"Can I stay, dear?"

"No, you can't. The bed's already full up. And don't call me 'dear.' "

"What do you mean?"

"Come and look." She took him by the hand and led him into a dark room. He could hear someone breathing there. She turned on the light. He saw the moustached but now placid face of one Charles Clifford, who had been at the party. The sheet cut across his bare slender chest; the moustache was sandy and inadequate.

"So, Mister Tait. Why don't you say anything?"

"Well . . ."

"Why don't you offer to throw him out?"

"You mean after what happened tonight?"

She sat down on the bed and laughed. She sat there in her bare feet.

"Oh for God's sake, go home Mr. Tait. Mister Hick. Go home and get your beauty sleep."

Duncan's eyes had begun to blur. It might have been anger; it might have been a kind of terror. He rushed out into the night.

That first summer Duncan Tait spent becoming accustomed to New York. He took a one-room apartment and decorated it with impressionist reproductions—not because he wanted a place where he could bring a girl, but because he wanted to feel "established." In fact he put Sue Shelton out of mind. He was on the threshold of a career and devoted himself to that. For example, he studied the stories published by this woman's magazine and read the biographies of artists. He even talked so much about creativity and the creative process, here and there, that he found a job with a new "research institute" devoted to ghost writing and the editing of manuals. He was on his way.

He still believed in that freedom demanded by creative people. But the Sue Sheltons were not for him. In August he looked up a girl he had danced with once or twice at a college affair, Nancy Charters, only a name in an address book. She turned out to be fairly rich and also, in her pale quiet way, the kind of girl one might marry. She was blonde and unaggressive and lived with her mother at the Sherry-Netherland. Duncan had a standing invitation to drop in for cocktails. Occasionally they took him to an expensive restaurant, the pale daughter and the ageless mother, with Paul Anders making a fourth. Duncan looked at Nancy's cool, languid hands and her discreet bracelets and rings. Her body without bone or muscle lay relaxed under his hand as they danced gravely on Saturday afternoons. He might almost have forgotten Sue Shelton's clawing fingers and ribboned thighs and her ankles locking him as in a vise.

Then early one evening, walking home from the Sherry-Netherland, he ran into Sue. She was dressed with a late summer elegance, slim and lovely, with high heels and a clinging cocktail dress. She held out her hand, and looked up at him with a smile that was faintly mocking. The rich perfume hung over her, and the old smoky odor. And at once he wanted to touch her, there on the crowded sidewalk. She pretended to be hurt because he had not come to see her. And she put one hand in his as a child might, gravely, lacing his fingers softly with hers. They went to his apartment.

This time the act of love came upon him almost by surprise, so tender and quiet had she been. They had danced and listened to records and sat cross-legged on the floor, all this for hours. He was not even aware, until he felt her body beneath him, that he wanted any more than that quietness. And now, looking up, she stroked his chin softly. A faint red light winking from a store below crossed her face, then left it in shadow. He was bemused by the darkness and her tenderness.

"I love you," he said. "Why did you go away?"

"Go away?"

"I mean why did you go back to him that night, last May?"

Her thin shoulders stirred. There was a distraction of her body.

"Oh that! That wasn't important. Isn't."

"You don't love him?"

"I don't love anybody," she said. "He's my best friend, though. That's all. And he hasn't any money."

In the darkness his thoughts revolved busily over this girl lying softly beneath him.

"Come and live with me," he said, astonished by his audacity. "Leave him!"

She laughed, then slipped away. She crawled across the room and turned on the light above his desk. From that distance she regarded him.

"You want me to be respectable? A little home on east 76th?"

"I don't care what you are."

She looked about her at the Cézannes and the Degas, the inevitable rosy dancers.

"My God," she said. "It really looks like a home. It would be, wouldn't it, almost like getting married? Would you even marry me, Duncan? Would you crawl all the way down and pull me up?"

He said nothing. She was mocking him again.

But then she came toward him across the room and kissed

him gravely and he caressed her small naked back. She was changing there under his touch.

"I mean it," she said. "I'm so awful and I've done such things. I'm just something that's been dragged through the street. Only it's myself that's done all the dragging. So would you marry me, anyway?"

For a moment Duncan saw himself standing as at the edge of a gulf, and his career vanishing into it. But she was still against him, her body there, and he could not help himself.

"Yes," he said. "If that's what you want."

But she held him for only another moment. Then she broke away. She went back to the desk and turned off the lamp and stood in the darkness at the window that yet caught some light from the street.

"Oh I guess I don't mean it, really," she said. "No, I don't want to get married. But I do want a little order in my life, not just the dragging. I don't want to just kill myself."

"I know," he said. "So that's why you should come. We can try to make it stick. Other people do."

She turned and came back to him.

"No, Duncan, I couldn't work in this place. I have to have my own dirty rooms. And I couldn't have you watching me. But I will promise something. I'll come here every night."

And that is what they arranged; it seemed to him rather cold and practical. But this, he surmised, is the way things work out in New York. Every afternoon he went to her apartment at five-thirty for a drink, and there he would usually find some of her friends, even the deposed Charles Clifford. Clifford had a kindly, quiet, reserved face and the sandy, inadequate moustache. His manner was so mild and feminine that it was hard to believe he and Sue had ever been lovers. Perhaps they hadn't been? In any event Duncan was glad to talk with them, Clifford and the others, so long as he had his evenings with Sue.

Every night punctually she did come to his room. Sometimes they would go innocently to the movies, where she sat beside him tender and loving and touching his hand very gently. Or she would even curl at his feet while he did his reading on the arts. But that was one of the things that came between them. She was

soon exasperated by his talk about the creative process, the sub-
conscious and all that, and by the books he bought on modern
painting. Once in a rage she even tore down the new impressionist
reproductions. And yet she was making a real effort to carve out
a new life and to love him as gently as he wished. It was only in
the dark night, especially if she had flared up at him before, that
her body again became feverish and possessed.

Otherwise, they had their quiet time of love, their orderly
days, two weeks in all. And Duncan Tait enjoyed both the hours
at her apartment and their dark time together at his own. He
did like going to her place after his work in the chromium
office, to find her friends lounging about. He had come to New
York for this, after all; to know artists and writers. He would ask
them how they got their ideas. Did they carry the ideas for whole
paintings in their heads? This was all very interesting. Only sometimes it seemed his arrival at five-thirty interrupted their talk, and
threw a pall over the gathering. There was a silence as he crossed
the room to kiss Sue on the forehead. She would turn away and
ask him, coldly, to take care of the drinks. And she made it plain
that he was not to go into the studio where she kept her paintings.
He could only see them, her childish scrawls, through a half-
opened door. Soon it was only something he was privileged to over-
hear: all their talk about painting and the wild gossip of the craft.

Once he arrived to find only Clifford. And they had their first
real talk; things began to come out. He heard with surprise that
Clifford thought Sue was really a painter, not just a hanger-on.
And he learned that Sue Shelton, like the poor forgotten Nancy,
was the daughter of a very rich man. But she had spat upon him
and the "opportunities" he gave her. She would not go to college.
No, she would not even accept an allowance. She repudiated all
the things which, like her good looks, had come to her unearned.
What on earth didn't she repudiate? Her painting, Clifford said,
was all that she had on her own. And Duncan began to discern
it more clearly: the cage in which she lived.

Her body had its prison too. There was a life of the nerves, a
fury just beneath the surface. And this also was changing from
day to day. For the act of love was becoming a rite to be fulfilled,
a thrashing of rasped and fraying nerves, bone crushing against

bone. So it was again like that combat of the first night, a hatred and a loathing. She would leap from the bed each time and go to the window, throw it open for air and stare out at the darkness. He wondered what caused the swift dreadful changes. The time came when she would not stay with him at all, but instead dressed quickly and went back to her own place.

He would lie in bed and think of her descending very small and solitary in the elevator, and walking through the empty lobby.

And even this changing was only ten days more. Then one night she did not come at the usual hour. He fixed his own drink and made some sandwiches. She did not come until after two-thirty in the morning, and her mouth was like a scar. She stared at him scornfully.

"Take a good look," she said. "Your little sweety has been laid."

"You're drunk," he said. "You don't know what you're saying."

"Well, I know what I was doing. I was being laid."

"What happened?"

"I just told you. I was being laid."

"Who was it?"

"I don't know who. It was someone in a bar."

She was very drunk, so he put her to bed. But the next morning they had a terrible talk, and he made himself forgive her. She told him of her old need to soil and degrade everything—her face and her body and her name—all these things that were not "herself." And it had to be with these strangers, the very most contemptible men, the salesmen and hucksters and the slick shyster lawyers.

Duncan told her he would try to help her; he was indeed forgiving. But three nights later she came to him very late and drunk again, and stood in the doorway cursing him. She challenged him to reprove her. This time it had been an insurance salesman who insisted on calling her "Honey." She was sober enough to remember the experience in some detail.

The next morning, at his office, Duncan found he could not work at all. The violence of his feelings was unendurable. So he waited until three o'clock and then went back to the apartment to pick up his things. He would move out right away, vanish from her life.

But instead he found a note from her under the door. Only one sentence: she was not coming again.

So that was that. A few weeks later he called on Nancy Charters, and after a decent interval married her. It almost seemed to him the end of an adventurous youth. New York had scared him. He found himself shying away from the Village, or skirting the bars where Sue Shelton might have been found. And not long afterwards, when he was offered a position with a large company in Chicago—as adviser for the company's educational foundation —it seemed prudent to accept.

II

He was moderately successful at his work, processing applications and the like. He had his modest talent and his great desire to be helpful to creative people, now chiefly scientists. Only sometimes he regretted that he never saw the moustached unfriendly young artists any more. There was a violence he missed. And so it was for his own married life. They bought a small house in Winnetka, and Nancy came to meet his train. On Fridays she came into town, and they would have dinner at one of the good restaurants where it was possible to dance. But still she lay soft and relaxed under his hand. They were having their good quiet life with decent people. Yet he longed to have her meet him one day in bare feet, at the station in Winnetka.

And then of course, several years later, he ran into Sue Shelton, while on a trip to New York for the company. He had an hour before his train and wandered into the Museum of Modern Art. And there she was near the foot of the stairs. She looked tired and lovely in a peasant skirt and sandals and a white blouse with ruffled sleeves. And no makeup at all. She might have been an overwrought young painter from one of the arty high schools.

She was astonished. She stared at him, paralyzed, unable to speak at all. He might have been an apparition.

So he had to begin. He told her about his marriage and about the progress he was making. They went through the first rooms, without looking at the pictures, and she glided beside him silkily, just brushing against him and then gone. Finally she told him of the shock she had felt seeing him there, suddenly, for only a moment before he had entered her mind for the first time in months. It was as though he had been "sent" at that particular moment. He noticed her hand tremble. Did she drink so very much?

But she was lovely in her sullen hostile way. Audaciously he said his wife was very pretty, but never went around in bare feet. He was sorry about that.

She frowned as though making a decision. Then she laughed and took off the sandals.

"Here, you hold them for me. After all, I want to please you."

He found he was moving into depths he had not intended.

"Why?"

"I just do." She looked past him craftily. "Let's say for old times. You see I think it's my job to please you. Attract you."

"Job?"

"Why not? I mean look at the way you turned up today. I'd only just arrived and in you walk. Do you think that was just an accident?" She smiled up at him. "Anyway, aren't you glad?"

He just touched her and then took his hand away.

"You walked out on me, Sue. Just four words."

"You know why that was," she said. "Maybe I was ashamed. But let's talk about something else."

They wandered on through the gallery.

"All right," he said. "Yes. Why don't you show me your favorites here? You never even told me what painters you liked best. And I miss it, you know—being with you and Clifford and the others . . ."

She looked about her with distaste. They were alone in a room dominated by severe abstractions, her own kind of painting. And then she stared at him with the old open-mouthed contempt.

"No," she said. "Let's go out. Maybe you can buy me a drink. How much time have you got?"

"I'm supposed to take the Twentieth Century at five."

"All right. I'll walk you to Grand Central. I'll get you there by five."

There was bitterness and a desperation in her voice. She walked demurely beside him, but did not want to take his arm. She had

put her sandals back on. They strolled down Fifth Avenue, looking in at the windows.

"Are you getting on all right?" he asked.

"You mean am I still awful? Am I still a bitch?"

"I mean your work. How is it going?"

She did not answer him at all. She walked ahead sullenly. But
a few blocks further on she did touch his arm.

"I'm sorry I said that, Duncan. And I'm sorry I was so awful
with you, then."

"It's all right," he said. "It wasn't your fault."

But she was trembling again; her queer nerves betrayed her.
She took his arm fiercely and pulled him into the entrance of a
large building.

"Only I don't see how you turned up just today? Or why?"

He told her he didn't understand. And she shook her head as
if to clear it of an ugly thought.

"I can't go any further with you," she said. "Just kiss me once.
Then go away and leave me alone."

"Here?"

He looked about desperately. He was a young man with a career
to jeopardize.

"Yes, you fool. Here. Because I want you right now and I'm
not going to have you."

And he was against her, with the smoky odor all over him,
and her small mouth working. Then she pushed him away.

He walked away from her with long strides, intoxicated, his
hands and his body sweating. He walked until he came to a stop
light and then he turned and ran back to the marble shadowy
entrance way. But she was gone. And he knew that he loved her.
He realized, panting, that she was all that really mattered, she
and her disorderly way of living and her violent artist friends.
That was "life," and he did not want to be left outside.

It never occurred to him to leave his wife. But after that meeting he got into the habit of looking Sue up, over the years, on
his trips to New York. It might be once in two years, it might
be three or four times in one busy autumn; and she never refused
him. As a rule he found her in the old apartment where she had

lived with Clifford, and sometimes the quiet Clifford would be there, sometimes not. She would greet him, oddly, with a gesture of distaste or even fright, followed by her cynical sexual glance. It was as much as to say, *Good God, so here you are again!* She would look him up and down insultingly, to measure his aging and his junior executive's clothes.

But no matter: she would always accept him. He was deeply pleased in his masculine vanity that she wanted him. And always when it was over she would leap from the bed as from a task accomplished. She would rush to the window and stare out.

She was more nervous than ever, but her face and body seemed unchanged. Only Clifford had aged. The ineffectual moustache could not hide his failure. Even poor Clifford understood now that she was faithful to Duncan in some obscure bodily way, as another might be faithful in the heart. So he would make off to spend the night with a friend. But Duncan was sorry to see him go. He still longed for those wild subversive dialogues on art.

The tables in Sue's apartment were covered with odd books on psychology now, and the religious tracts of unheard-of sects. Years had passed. But there were still the paintings, which in the old way she turned to the wall. She stalked up and down in front of him in her bare feet, angry and drinking, hardly wanting to talk at all. And now the brief fierce act of love was truly a thing of ugliness and hatred for her, some kind of bitter obligation. It had become an obligation for him too. He would endure this awful frenzy for the tenderness that preceded it, the slow stroke and hardening of desire, and for the few moments of calm that followed. But it all seemed so odd, her hostility and her acceptance: odd that he could turn up after a month or a year, with no letters and no telephoning in between. And each time meeting him at the door she was a little more cynical and insulting.

Then there was a period of almost five years when he did not see her at all, and in fact almost forgot her. He was successful; the mask was hardening on his life. He served now on the drives and committees and he belonged to the clubs intended for rising young men. There was a little more fat on his bones. All the paraphernalia of success.

His life was full of cleanliness and service. And suddenly it

filled him with disgust. The fat, he feared, was really on his soul.
He needed to see her again: the lost one. And this time—looking
up Sue, finding her after a long evening of trailing her from one
address to another—he sought violence itself, disorder, the wildness and obscenity and rage.

But it had been almost five years! She opened the door and
stepped back with a cry. Her hand went to her mouth. For a
brief moment Duncan believed she must have thought it was
someone else standing in the door, her eyes blazed so with hatred.
Behind her was the smoky room and her friends, even poor
Clifford. Their eyes met guiltily. He would have liked to talk to
them all; he waved to Clifford in a friendly, off-hand way. But
Sue pushed him out onto the landing, and shut the door.

"So here you are," she said. "A few days late, I would say. Even
a few years."

"I know. But I just couldn't help myself. I had to come."

"Hey, you've forgotten. That's my speech, not yours."

"You're looking wonderful," he said. But he could detect the
few gray hairs in that light, and the lines. "Can't I come in?"

"No, you can't." She ran her hands over his face, felt for the
bones as a painter or a sculptor does. "You're older too. But your
face is still commonplace. It always will be."

"I wanted to come before," he said, relishing the old insult.
"Then I tried not to. I thought there was something a little wrong
about it. But now here I am."

"And here you are," she said. "And now you think you might
as well sleep with me as take in a movie? It's just as easy as that.
You stay away five years and then you knock on the door and say
Come on, let's go to a room, let's don't bother about dinner, let's
don't even talk over old times."

"No," he said. "I do want to talk over old times. I do want
to come in, I want to be with your friends. I don't want things
that other way."

"Well, I do," she said. "And that's the way they're going to be."

She told him where to go: the obscure hotel where she would
meet him in an hour or so.

And still time passing! He came again and again and one morning he realized with astonishment that he had spent and wasted forty years of this only life he would ever have. His wife and children were pleasant strangers, and his job would never again be new. He felt a twinge of conscience because his position was so respectable and secure. There was his good public life, and it now seemed a waste of days. A hard red core of violence was gone.

Now he understood more clearly why he had to look up Sue whenever he went to New York. The time was past when he had to exhaust any longings of the flesh. But now the very touch of her—the fact that he had to seek her out so darkly—was a communication with the glowing disorderly creative world. It was part of the game that he had to track her down in cat-ridden tenements and obscure Second Avenue bars. And wherever he found her, there were still her paintings to be turned quickly to the wall, many more paintings now. The floor and chairs were littered with quack treatises and books on occult religions. She was sick, yes—but she had escaped the corrosion of success. Hers was still the old life of darkness.

Again there were times when it was not her youth he was seeking but his own. She was obviously dyeing her hair; in the pallid light of hotel bedrooms her face would be ravaged on the pillow. But still he felt each time, as she welcomed him with her angry resignation, that something had been saved. The wasted years dropped off.

Moreover, there was always the pleasant element of risk. For he had risen still higher in the company and, within certain small circles, his face was becoming known. And he found this intolerable. Once, therefore, he took Sue to a hotel where he was well-known for his conferences with small college presidents and others seeking grants. She came with him a little drunk, wearing scuffed white shoes, slacks and a moth-eaten fur jacket. That was all he had wanted really, this time: to walk with her through the lobby to the elevator, and the loss of his good name. But nothing happened. The desk clerk nodded respectfully.

The next time he went to New York he happened to see a painting by her in one of the 57th Street windows. It was a black and white canvas in what struck him as the Piet Mondrian style, although he knew very little about styles. It did surprise him that she had actually done work which was thought worthy to be put on sale. He went inside and learned that the painting was priced at four hundred dollars. The dealer remarked that Sue Shelton was very nearly a great painter.

Very nearly a great painter? The statement was absurd. And yet it was something, wasn't it, to have kept trying all these years! A small revolution occurred in Duncan Tait's tired feelings. Sue Shelton was a person too, with her longings and despairs and this stubborn courage, and her old obscure bond with himself. And what did it all mean, really? All this time she had had her artist friends. That was one side of her life. And then there was that other neurotic devious side, that need to degrade herself with men she could only despise. But always only once: never the same salesman or lawyer again.

So where did that leave him, whom she never refused? With a hard shock and flood of shame he realized that he—he who stood between the two groups—must have been the one great romantic attachment of her life. And he had never understood! All these years she had come trotting at his call, only to receive so very few words of love. No wonder the bitterness of her welcomes.

He telephoned at once; he had to make amends. For a long minute she said nothing, after picking up the phone. Then she told him he could come at twelve o'clock. But not before: she would have guests until then.

He found her in a lovely black dress but with the bare feet of the old days, and around her the ashtrays and soiled glasses of a party. She must have driven off the last of her guests only a few minutes before. She came toward him drunkenly, white and faintly trembling. Then he saw there was something wrong with her face. The eyes were blackened as if by fists. She had lost much weight; the bones were working out.

He tried to lead her to the sofa, tenderly. But she broke off and padded away. He sat down and told her of his pride on seeing her painting in the window. He thought it showed wonderful "control."

"Oh for Christ's sake. You didn't come to talk about that!"

"No, I didn't. I want to talk about what's happening to us."

"What is happening?"

He explained to her the turmoil of his feelings of that morning. It had come to him that this old old bond between them was something more than sexual obsession. Wasn't it, really, the simpler thing, the thing poets and novelists write about?

She stared at him with hostility.

"You're drunk," she said.

"No. Let me tell you exactly how I feel."

She stalked back and forth in front of the sofa while he made his apologies. He told her of the many ways she had ministered to his needs. He had "used" her shamelessly for his devious urgings.

Suddenly she was standing over him, trembling and angry and then going off into peals of laughter.

"So you don't want to go to bed?"

"No," he said. "I want to love you this other way."

"And you're ashamed because you've 'used' me?" She went on laughing. She put her head in her hands and rocked back and forth. "Oh if you only knew! It's just the funniest thing I ever heard."

Then she was on the floor, still laughing hysterically and then crying. But when he tried to touch and comfort her she struck him away. And she was so very drunk that there was nothing for it but to leave.

From Chicago he wrote her a long letter of explanation and apology. She answered him with an unsigned postcard of half-a-dozen words. She begged him to leave her alone. So he was afraid he had come to her too late, with his apologies and his love.

And that was almost the end. Thereafter, except for one strange meeting, he had to watch her life from a distance, by making discreet inquiries of dealers in Chicago and New York. For a long time the curve of her life had been almost imperceptible. It hovered as she too bravely entered her forties. And as a painter she had begun to make her name.

But then, almost as though success were intolerable, the curve dipped sharply down.

For now, he heard, she was drunk almost all the time. She had been arrested for uttering terrible obscenities at the top of her voice in the bar of a great hotel; she was evicted from one room after another. Once, when her name even appeared in a Chicago paper, in connection with an arrest, Duncan resolved to go to New York to help her get back on her feet. But something else intervened, some other moral obligation, and the next time he went to New York she was gone. He picked up the rumor she was dying from a cancer she had refused to have examined. She had gone to New Mexico, to Santa Fe, with her poor Clifford, who had stopped painting so long ago. He had subordinated his career to hers.

A month later, while on a Foundation trip to Los Angeles, Duncan decided to stop off and see them. She would have forgotten their misunderstanding; so much time had passed. And perhaps she and Clifford would need help. Duncan rented a car at the airport, since he thought they might enjoy a drive. They could have a drive this evening and in the morning visit Taos. Now in the late afternoon he drove the last desert miles into town. The nearer mountains were yellow and the farthest black, and the town was there at the end of its high plateau. Obscurely he felt he too was coming to the end of something. He drove past the motels and into the old city, and to the La Fonda, where he took a room. There was a stillness about the place, and he began to become excited. It was like getting ready to see Sue in the old days, arriving in a hotel and thinking of her body and of the smoky odor he would detect even before they had kissed. He forgot how much time had passed.

He asked directions to their place. He drove past the motels and garages and into the open, and here with the land dropping away there was still light over the black mountains. In a row of baked small cottages theirs was one of the last in the direction of the penitentiary. It was a bare place and the grass and flowers were dying.

Clifford met him at the door. He was very surprised, disturbed in his tired frail way. He did not ask Duncan to come in.

"She's not well," Clifford said. "I think it would be better, really, if you didn't see her."

"I know she's sick. That's why I came. I rented the car because I thought she'd like a drive."

"She's not that sick. She's working. She works all the time."

"It would do her good to get away," Duncan said. "Tomorrow we could drive out to one of the pueblos."

"I don't want you to see her. She'll just get upset. She's working so hard and that's all she wants."

"I have to see her," Duncan said.

"All right then. But you're making a mistake."

Clifford led the way down a dark hall and then opened a door quietly. The light of a floodlamp fell on the canvas she was working at.

And there she was: there in the ravaged center of what had once been a living room, with her back toward them, painting, and all over the floor and against the walls were her cold disciplined canvases. It was the work of her lifetime. He looked at her gray hair and at the paintings on the floor. Through them now were wild strokes and gashes of color spattering at the edges, brilliant blues and oranges and vermilions. She must have been hacking away at her old work in a fury of correction, violating the precise cubes and planes.

And now she was working with her back to him and to Clifford, with her back to the world. Between strokes she rubbed her hands on her slacks to wipe off the perspiration and to stop the trembling. It was some minutes before she turned around and saw them.

But then it was with the sharpest cry of all their long time. Her face had fallen away; her dying eyes bulged out.

"Oh no!" she shouted, but at Clifford, not at him. "Oh it just can't be. It can't be again! It's got to let go sometime!"

It struck Duncan as the babble of a very sick woman; he was alarmed for her and distressed. He started to walk toward her, his old old friend, holding out his hands. She stared at his hands.

"Please," she said. "Don't come any closer."

"What's the matter, Sue?"

She would not look him in the face.

"Get out," she said. "I don't want to see you. I want you to go away."

She turned back to her work, trembling. She stood there before it.

He never saw her again, and four months later she was dead. Not long after that, in New York, there was an important retrospective show, and (as a trustee of one museum, as a member of various committees) Duncan Tait was invited. So he was to see them at last, those paintings she had always turned to the wall! No matter that crazed by sickness she had also turned from him as from something unclean. He could still cherish her queer loyalty of so many years.

The paintings in their chronological arrangement and monotonies depressed him. So much energy had gone into them, so much of her life! In those last paintings of the Santa Fe time the pure cold designs were gashed as by a violent claw. Yet it was before these ruined paintings that most of the visitors stood. He discovered with surprise that this was not Sue's first show. There had been half a dozen in her lifetime, even one in Paris. And he had not even known that!

At first he was lost in the dense crowd in the two small rooms. But presently he recognized faces: critics, rich people, names. There was a certain amount of enthusiasm over the paintings, and an undertone of sadness because a fine painter had died so young. He heard whisperings; she had taken dope, she had drunk herself to death. It was the grand old ruinous artist destiny of his youthful reading and dreams. Perhaps too they were speculating on her many lovers.

Then near the end of the show, and huddled by the last paintings, Duncan recognized the worn faces of her friends. And there too was the tired Clifford. The little group had set itself apart. And in a rush of affection for them, for these faithful ones, for Sue and himself, for all the distraught and betrayed years, Duncan wanted to join them. He wanted to become one of them at last. For that was what Sue had really meant. She had been his frail touch on the pulsing life of art.

Still, he waited until the others had left, the rich people and the names. The ruined paintings glared in the emptying room. Then glasses appeared and a small table, several bottles of champagne; they were waiting for him to leave. Instead he walked slowly toward them.

But he was walking into a silence. Clifford looked away in embarrassment; the others stared past. Then one of the youngest stood up. He at least could not have been at that party in the brownstone house, that first magic May evening, almost a quarter of a century before!

"It's eight o'clock. The show's over."

"I know," Duncan said. "But I want to talk to you. All of you. You were her best friends."

"So?"

"I was one of her friends, too. One of the oldest . . ."

"That's one way of putting it."

Another man spoke up. It was one of the hostile faces from all the way back, ravaged, the teeth stained and rotten.

"Are you waiting for us to offer you a drink?"

Duncan was bewildered by this hostility. He turned to Clifford for help.

"What's it all about?"

"Why don't you leave us alone?" Clifford said. "Everybody's tired. We're all likely to say things."

"But I want to talk to you!"

Clifford took him rather firmly by the elbow; he found himself moving toward the door.

"It's all over," Clifford said. "Just forget it. Forget her."

They were almost at the door. And now Duncan Tait stopped. He held his ground, his precarious place among them, with the silent group of friends still in sight.

"I don't understand. Why are you pushing me?"

"It's time to go."

"But look, there's something I have to know. What did she mean out there, when she said 'It's got to let go sometime!'?"

"I don't know," Clifford said.

"Was she talking about me?"

"Yes. Of course she was talking about you. Why don't you just forget it?"

"I can't. I want to know what she meant."

Clifford raised his calm eyes.

"She had her crazy religious ideas. All her queer notions."

"Yes?"

"And they were physical too. Let's say she was neurotic, call it whatever you want. But you understand she wouldn't let sex, all that, have anything to do with what she cared about. I don't think Sue ever slept with one of her friends, or anyone she liked at all."

"I don't believe you."

"She would have thought it a betrayal. You see, she had this awful fear, this hatred and disgust. All those men she picked up in bars . . . She had to degrade herself, she had to run herself down. But also she thought she was degrading them. It was her very contempt . . . It was her crazy way of repudiating them."

"But I was different!" Duncan interrupted. "With those men it was always just once and she never saw them again. But she always came back to me."

Clifford shook his head. And the worn circles of faces still watched, from fifty feet away.

"No, it wasn't quite that. It was always you who came back to her. At least that's how she saw it. You were, I'm afraid, one of her strange delusions. She saw you as something that had been sent, been inflicted . . ."

"Why delusion? I was faithful enough . . ."

But Clifford was almost beyond charity now. He took Duncan by the elbow again; his fingers dug in angrily. Then they were moving onto the sidewalk, out onto the dismal street.

"You force me to say things! You force me to be cruel! Why don't we just say that she hated you? Isn't that enough? She hated all you stood for, and all your talk about artists, and all your wanting to climb into her life. And it was just because she hated you . . ."

"I don't believe it," Duncan Tait said. "I don't believe it at all."

But he was talking to no one, now; and he was alone on the sidewalk, with the theater traffic burning by, and the door to the gallery closed behind him.

28 Mark Mirsky

Mark Mirsky's first novel, Thou Worm Jacob, was published in 1967. He is a member of the Teachers-Writers Collaborative and is currently teaching English at the City College of New York. He is also an actor, playwright, and director, and two of his plays are scheduled for off-Broadway production.

❖

SIMCHA

Simcha Tantsenn! There was a name to dance to. And everyone in Dorchester danced to it—though Simcha did a crooked step.

Simcha was our State Senator. Ours? Well, he was Dorchester's. I didn't vote for him. But the Jews did. So did the Colored in Roxbury and the Irish in Mattapan. Who thought they could be so stupid?

Simcha was sharp—that was known all over Boston. He had sold the jailhouse three times and the John Hancock Building twice. Simcha who never had a dime! And watch out! Because now I hear he's peddling shares in the Prudential. A check bouncer! A liar! Our Simcha—God love him! And Dorchester's favorite son.

Simcha was lately in high spirits. He had just become a State Senator. Dorchester's old one, an attorney, had just been booted up to judge. And Simcha, with the help of the bookies and undertakers in the community, had succeeded him. Simcha could never become a judge. Not that he wasn't intimate with the law, having been hauled into court continually by angry constituents. But he wasn't a lawyer. As he himself advertised, he didn't even have a high school degree.

467

Why did he advertise this?

You see, Simcha appealed to the sympathy vote. Give me the job, he told Dorchester. Otherwise I'll starve.

And it was true. There was nothing else Simcha Tantsenn could do. He couldn't add well enough to be a bookie. If you don't keep your books, the big boys in Newton get after you. So they sent him to the Statehouse to handle million-dollar budgets. That's how Dorchester thought. Keep Simcha off the streets. Put him in the Statehouse.

"My heart's in Dorchester," Simcha posters announced. And Dorchester was flattered. Who else would have the nerve to say such a thing? Everybody in Dorchester wanted to get out of there.

Dorchester knew that Simcha was a sharper, an ignoramus, and a faker. But there was one thing about Simcha that they really loved. He was a promiser. He would promise you anything. Really! Anything you wanted. From the Empire State Building to a seat right next to the Messiah on the Day of Judgment. And don't think in Dorchester there weren't requests for such.

In Dorchester—better a promise than nothing. People were even willing to pay for them. And Tantsenn would take your money with a smile.

Simcha Tantsenn knew how to collect. He had served his political apprenticeship under Mayor Curley of Jailhouse fame. Curley's stooge in the Jewish district after the Mayor's demise in city politics, Simcha blossomed into a power in his own right. A heavy man, his weight girdled into a shiny blue serge suit, Tantsenn made the rounds in Dorchester collecting money, pledges, political power, allying himself with everything cheap, rotten, or desperate.

Simcha greeted you with a grin. He waddled forward like a lugubrious penguin, shook your hand daintily, and said, beaming, "God wove you!" Simcha's smile was something. It bordered on the lewd. The fat folds of his cheeks overlapped each other in the fullness of that smile. Such a smile urged you to come out with a proposition, to ask a favor, to let him do something for you.

From table to table he went in the delicatessens of Dorchester, greeting everyone in sight. "Hellow," he lisped, bending over a table. "How are you, God wove you? How are things?" Three times a day, he made the rounds of the delicatessens, no matter what business was going on at the Statehouse. Whether Simcha knew you or not, you always got the big hello from him. His big nose would quiver over you, sniffing for a promise you might pay for. It was his business.

Now and then he made a mistake. For instance the time after the great hurricane that pulled huge elm trees along Blue Hill Avenue. Electricity all over Dorchester was knocked out. It was just before the elections. Simcha toured Dorchester with a sound truck, announcing that he had just spoken with the Edison Company and the lights would be on the next day. "I pwomise!" sounted Tantsenn with a joyful lisp. So none of the merchants bought ice for their deep freezers. Five days later, when Edison finally turned the electricity on, thousands and thousands of frozen foods were ruined. And so was Simcha—temporarily.

Why only temporarily? Well, the middle class was deserting Dorchester in a steady stream. Those who were stranded behind needed promises. You can't ruin a merchant-in-promises. Not Simcha. Temporarily—yes. After his defeat at the polls, he deserted his wife, his children—and ran off to Florida, the race track. But Dorchester called him back. Come back and promise! Back came Simcha, a little seedy and run down, but refreshed in spirit, to take office and dispense promises.

The bookies liked him. So did the crooks, the gamblers, and the undertakers. Here was a man who could be depended on. He would sell his vote in the Legislature to the highest bidder. Simcha Tantsenn when you came right down to it, was a straightforward proposition. On Beacon Hill, here was a man you could trust. Simcha was one of them, their boy. With no compunctions, they underwrote his campaigns.

And there were some who genuinely liked Simcha. You had to admit there was something of the artist in him. Something he had inherited either from Mayor Curley or from some ancestor, some phoney Zaddik in Galicia, a peddler in miracles. Who else could get the Governor to pick up a rubber check? Especially when you drop it in the State Treasurer's office. To get an Irish Pol to pick up your tab? In Boston—it was a miracle.

Maybe it was his fake heart attacks that won the heart of Dorchester. Simcha loved attention. He first tried out his act on the floor of the Legislature. That's a rough place for beginners. The Reps knew he was faking and stoned him with law books. Have you ever picked up the Legislative Acts of Massachusetts? A good book, it weighs at least thirty pounds and is a foot-and-a-half thick. A hard black binding. A regular cement block. Simcha collapsed in the aisle shouting "Heart! Heart! Heart!"

The books flew through the air. When they dug Simcha out, he went to the hospital in earnest.

His next try, he chose a better place to open. The Democratic State Convention. There are a lot of amateurs from the west and south of the state. What do they know about Simcha Tantsenns?

Nobody was paying Simcha any attention that day; his vote had already been bought. So suddenly Simcha jumps up, grabs the microphone in the Dorchester section, and shouts over the loudspeaker system, "Heart! Heart! Ayyyyyyyy!" And he collapses. He takes a real dive. Because he's standing on the head of his henchman, Cockeyed Zitzz. The boys from Dorchester and South Boston laugh and hiss. But from Worcester and Framingham and Springfield goes up a moan and a groan. "Ambulance! Ambulance!" A siren starts up. The cops clear the aisles. They take Simcha down the main aisle on a stretcher with the band from Peabody playing a funeral march. Believe me, it was impressive. It stopped the convention. It got in all four Boston newspapers. Simcha Tantsenn was known all over the state.

But the coup d'état was the St. Patrick's Day parade. Simcha was running for mayor. It was a joke. He wouldn't get enough votes to qualify. A pish in the bucket he would get. But, he would get attention. Simcha announced his candidacy early. Early enough to get a place of honor in the St. Patrick's Day parade. The Irish told him to stick a finger in his touchus. He could ride with the Sanitation Department. In the back truck. They had enough Irish Simcha Tantsenns. They didn't need a Jewish one on parade.

So Simcha, that genius of political tactic, our Simcha, hired a jeep. He got out his best tuxedo, dressed Cockeyed Zitzz up in a military uniform, and got one of the queers from downtown Boston to drive. Cockeyed Zitzz is dressed in what looks like a full colonel's uniform. And the queer is dressed like a private. Their insignia is strange. But on St. Patrick's Day, nobody is going to notice the difference. Not in South Boston where they have been drinking Jack Daniel's by the bottle since four in the morning. The parade starts. The bands begin. And unobtrusively, right in the back of the Governor's limousine, the open one, bearing the most important politicians in the parade, a jeep wheels out from a side street and cutting in front of the honor guard, begins to follow.

Guess who? Cockeyed Zitzz is standing up, in a Bird Colonel's uniform, saluting Simcha. And Simcha is waving to the crowd, to the honor guard, to the limousine with the biggest Pols in Boston in it. "God wwhhovvve you!" Simcha cries out as loud as he can. "God wwhhovvve you!"

If that had been the end of it. Listen, the Pols can take a joke. It would have meant stopping the parade and getting a Sherman tank to dislodge Simcha from his position. "Let him have a little fun," said the Governor. "What the hell." Let him get a hand in Boston. What good would it do him?

And then, right in front of the grand reviewing stand, right in front of the huge platform hung with red, white, and green bunting, where the Lord Mayor of Dublin is standing with his long shillelagh, looking at the great sight of the whole of the Boston Irish strung out for miles in every direction, where the crowd is thickest and the brass is shiniest, Simcha Tantsenn picks up a military loudspeaker and yells, "Heart! Heart!"

Oy vey! Catastrophe. Cockeyed Zitzz catches Simcha as he falls. The queer runs the jeep into the reviewing stand. The ambulance starts screaming. The parade jams and grinds to a stop. The band on the stand starts to play, to cover it all. The honor guard lowers its bayonets. All over Boston, noontime whistles shriek. And nobody has told the Lord Mayor about Simcha Tantsenn. Gathering the skirts of his robes, he has hurried down the steps of the stand. Looking over the stricken politician, he orders the cops to lift him to the stand. So they carry Simcha to the place of honor, right next to the microphone. Simcha revives. The Lord Mayor whispers, "Praise God!" And it carries into the mike. Down the length of South Boston it echoes, "Praise God!" in a thick Irish brogue. Well—the cheers are deafening. And Simcha, taking hold of the Lord Mayor's shillelagh, raises himself up and whispers into the mike to a million Irishmen—"God wwhhovvve you."

What can I say? It was a historic moment. Not only did all the papers in New England cover it . . . but it was on national television. Simcha Tantsenn had stolen the St. Patrick's Day parade. He came close to being mayor.

29 Jay Neugeboren

Jay Neugeboren has published two novels, Big Man (1966) and Listen Ruben
Fontanez (1968). He was born and brought up in Brooklyn.

❖

LUTHER

Luther arrived at Booker T. Washington Junior High School
(Columbus Avenue and 107th Street, Manhattan) in September
of 1955, six months before I did. I met him at the end of February, the third week I taught there, when one of the assistant
principals asked me to cover the cafeteria during fifth period for
a teacher who had to be at a conference. "Good luck with the
animals," I remember him saying.

I was on my guard when I entered the cafeteria; perhaps even
a trifle scared. The stories I had been hearing in the teachers'
lounge had prepared me to expect anything. During the winter
months the students were not allowed to leave the lunchroom
and the results of keeping them penned in—the fights, the food-
throwing, the high-pitched incessant chattering in Spanish, the
way the Negro and Puerto Rican boys and girls chased each other
around the tables—such things did, I had to admit, give the room
a zoo-like quality.

The day I was assigned, however, was a Catholic holy day and
many of the students were absent. Those who remained filled a
little less than half of the large room and though they were noisy,
it was relatively easy to keep them in order. Luther sat at a table
by himself, near the exit to the food-line. Occasionally, I noticed,

a few boys would come and sit next to him. The third time I patrolled his area, however, his table was empty and he stopped me.

"Hey, man," he said, poking me in the arm to get my attention, "you new here?"

He had a stack of about ten cookies in his other hand and he put one into his mouth as he waited for an answer. When I told him that I was not new, he nodded and looked at me. "You have any trouble yet?"

"No," I said, as sternly as possible. Despite my feelings of sympathy for the students, I knew that if I ever hoped to get anywhere with them, I had to appear tough and confident. "No," I repeated, almost, I recall, as if I were challenging him. "I haven't."

Luther cocked his head to one side then and smiled slowly. "You will," he said, and went back to his cookies.

In the teachers' lounge, the first time I told the story, somebody asked if the boy who had stopped me was a little Negro kid, very black, with a slight hunchback. I said he was. The teachers laughed. "That's Luther," one of them said.

"He's batty," said another. "Just leave him be."

I repeated the story endlessly. It was the first anecdote of my teaching experience that excited admiration and some sort of reaction from those I told it to, and this was important to me then. I had no more direct encounters with Luther that term, though I did see him in the halls, between classes. I always smiled at him and he would smile back—or at least I thought he did. I could never be sure. This bothered me, especially the first time it happened. Through my retelling of the story, I realized, he had become so real to me, so much a part of my life that I think I took it for granted that our encounter had assumed equal significance in his life. The possibility that he had not even repeated the story to a single one of his friends disturbed me.

Once or twice during the term I spotted him wandering around the halls while classes were in session, slouching down the corridor, his body pressed against the tile walls. When I asked the other teachers if he was known for cutting classes, they told me again to just leave him be—that the guidance counselor had suggested that the teachers let him do what he wanted to. He was harmless, they said, if you left him alone. Those teachers who had him in their classes agreed with the guidance counselor. Left alone, he didn't annoy them. When he wanted to, he worked feverishly—and did competent work; but when he did not want to work he would either sit and stare, or just get up, walk out of the room, and wander around the building. He was, they concluded, a mental case.

I returned to Booker T. Washington Junior High School the following September, and Luther turned up in one of my English classes. He had changed. He was no longer small, having grown a good five inches over the summer, and he was no longer quiet. When classwork bored him now he would stand up, and instead of leaving the room, would begin telling stories. Just like that. He had his favorite topics, too—his cousin Henry who had epilepsy, Willie Mays, what was on sale at the supermarket, the football team he played on, the stories in the latest *Blackhawk* comic book. When he ran out of stories, he would pull *The National Enquirer* out of his back pocket and begin reading from it, always starting with an item in the "Personals" columns that had caught his eye. I never knew what to do. When I would yell at him to sit down and be quiet, he would wave his hand at me, impatiently, and continue. Moreover, no expression on his face, nothing he ever said, indicated that he thought he was doing anything wrong. An hour after disrupting a class, if I would see him in the corridor, he would give me a big smile and a hello. After a while, of course, I gave up even trying to interrupt him. I listened with the other students—laughing, fascinated, amazed.

I tried to remember some of his stories, but when I retold them they never seemed interesting, and so I purposely gave Luther's class a lot of composition work, trying to make the topics as imaginative as possible—with the hope, of course, that he would use one of them to let loose. But all of the topics, he declared, were "stupid" and he refused to write on any of them. Then, when I least expected it, when I assigned the class a "How To—" composition, he handed one in. It was typewritten on a piece of lined notebook paper, single-spaced, beginning at the very top of the page and ending just at the first ruled line. It was titled: "How To Steal Some Fruits":

How To Steal Some Fruits, by Luther
Go to a fruit store and when the fruitman isn't looking take some fruits. Then run. When the fruitman yells "Hey you stop taking those fruits" run harder. That is how to steal some fruits.

The next day he sat quietly in class. When I looked at him, he looked down at his desk. When I called on him to answer a question, he shrugged and looked away. At three o'clock, however, no more than five seconds after I had returned from escorting my official class downstairs, he bounded into my room, full of life, and propped himself up on the edge of my desk.

"Hey man," he said. "How'd you like my composition? It was deep, wasn't it?"

"Deep?"

"Deep, swift, *cool*—you know."

"I liked it fine," I said, laughing.

"Ah, don't put me on, man—how was it?"

"I liked it," I repeated, my hands clasped in front of me. "I mean it."

His face lit up. "You mean it? I worked hard on it, Mister Carter. I swear to God I did." It was the first time, I remember, that he had ever addressed me by my name. He stopped and wiped his mouth. "How'd you like the typing? Pretty good, huh?"

"It was fine."

"Christ, man," he said, stepping down from my desk and moving to the blackboard. He picked up a piece of chalk and wrote his name, printing it in capital letters. "How come you so tight? Why don't you loosen up? I ain't gonna do nothing. I just want to know about my composition. That's all."

I felt I could reach him, talk to him. I wanted to—had wanted to for some time, I realized, but he was right. I was tight, uncomfortable, embarrassed. "Where'd you get a typewriter?" I offered.

He smiled. "Where I get fruits," he replied, then laughed and clapped his hands. I must have appeared shocked, for before I could say anything, he was shaking his head back and forth. "Oh, man," he said. "You are really deep. I swear. You really are." He climbed onto my desk again. "You mind talking?"

"No," I said.

"Good. Let me ask you something—you married?"

"No," I said. "Do you think I should be married?"

"It beats stealing fruits," he said, and laughed again. His laugh was loud and harsh and at first it annoyed me, but then his body began rocking back and forth as if his comment had set off a chain of jokes that he was telling himself silently, and before I knew it I was laughing with him.

"I really liked the composition," I said. "In fact, I hope you don't mind, but I've already read it to some of the other teachers."

"No shit."

"They thought it was superb."

"It's superb," he said, shaking his head in agreement. "Oh, it's superb, man," he said, getting up again and walking away. His arms and legs moved in different directions and he seemed so loose that when he turned his back to me and I noticed the way his dirty flannel shirt was stretched tightly over his misshapen back, I was surprised—as if I'd noticed it for the first time. He walked around the room, muttering to himself, tapping on desks with his fingertips, and then he headed for the door. "I'm superb," he said. "So I be rolling on my superb way home—."

"Stay," I said.

He threw his arms apart. "You win!" he declared. "I'll stay." He came back to my desk, looked at me directly, then rolled his eyes and smiled. "People been telling stories to you about me?"

"No."

"None?" he questioned, coming closer.

"All right," I said. "Some—."

"That's all right," he said, shrugging it off. He played with the binding of a book that was on my desk. Then he reached across and took my grade book. I snatched it away from him and he laughed again. "Oh man," he exclaimed. "I am just so restless!—You know what I mean?"

He didn't wait for an answer, but started around the room again. The pockets of his pants were stuffed and bulging, the cuffs frayed. The corner of a red and white workman's handkerchief hung out of a back pocket. He stopped in the back of the room, gazed into the glass bookcase, and then turned to me and leaned back. "You said to stay—what you got to say?"

The question was in my mind, and impulsively I asked it: "Just curious—do you remember me from last year?"

"Sure," he said, and turned his back to me again. He looked in the bookcase, whirled around and walked to the side of the room, opening a window. He leaned out and just as I was about to say something to him about it, he closed it and came back to the front of the room. "Man," he exclaimed, sitting on my desk again. "Were you ever scared that day! If I'd set off a cherry bomb you'd have gone through the fan." He put his face closer to mine. "Man, you were scared green!"

"Was I scared of you, Luther?" I asked, looking straight into his eyes.

"Me? Nah. Nothing to be scared of." He hopped off the desk and wiped his name off the blackboard with the palm of his hand; then he started laughing to himself. He looked at me, over his shoulder. "Bet I know what you're thinking now," he said.

"Go ahead—."

"You're thinking you'd like to *help* a boy like me. Right? You're getting this big speech ready in your head about—."

"No," I interrupted. "I wasn't."

He eyed me suspiciously. "You sure?"

"I'm sure."

"Not even with compositions? Oh man, if you'd help me with compositions, before we'd be through with me, I'd be typing like a whiz." He banged on a desk with his palms, and then his fingers danced furiously on the wood as he made clicking noises inside his mouth. "Ding!" he said, swinging the carriage across. "Ain't it fun to type!"

"Okay," I said. "Okay. Maybe I was thinking that I would like to help you."

"I knew it, man," he said, to himself. "I just knew it."

"You have a good mind, Luther—much better than you let on."

"I do, I do," he muttered, chuckling. I stood up and went to the closet to get my coat. "Okay. What do I get if I work for you?" he asked.

I shrugged. "Nothing, maybe. I can't promise anything."

"I *like* that, man," he said.

"Could you call me Mister Carter?" I asked, somewhat irritably. "I don't call you, 'hey, you'—."

"Okay, Mister Carter," he said. He took my coat sleeve. "Let me help you on with your coat, Mister Carter."

We walked out of the room and I locked the door. "You ain't a *real* social worker like the others," he commented as we started down the stairs. He held the door open for me. "I do like that."

I nodded.

"Playing it close to the vest again, huh? Tight-mouthed."

"Just thinking," I said.

When we were outside he asked me what he had to do.

"For what?" I asked.

"To get you to help me to be somebody, to educate myself— all that stuff."

"Do what you want to do," I said. "Though you might start by doing your homework. Then we'll see—."

"I know," he said, cocking his head to one side again. "If I play ball with you you'll play ball with me. Right? Okay, okay. I know."

Then he was gone, running down the street, his arms spread wide as if he were an airplane, a loud siren-like noise rising and falling from him as he disappeared from view.

The next few months were without doubt the most satisfying to me of any during the eight years I've been a teacher. Luther worked like a fiend. He was bright, learned quickly, and was not really that far behind. He did his homework, he paid attention in class, he studied for tests, and he read books. That was most important. On every book he read I asked him to write a book report: setting, plot, theme, characters, and his opinion of the book—and once a week, on Thursday afternoons, we would get together in my room for a discussion. During the remainder of the term he must have gone through at least forty to fifty books. Most of them had to do with sports, airplanes, and insects. For some reason he loved books about insects. All the reports came to me typed, and on some he drew pictures—"illustrations" he called them, which, he claimed, would be a help to me in case I had not read the book.

When we would finish talking about books, I would help him with his other subjects, and his improvement was spectacular. I looked forward to my sessions with him, to his reports, to just seeing him—yet from day to day, from moment to moment, I always expected him to bolt from me, and this pleased me. Every time he came to me for a talk I was truly surprised.

When the term ended he asked if I would continue to help him. I said I would. He was not programmed for any of my English classes during the spring term, but we kept up with our weekly discussions. As the weather improved, however, he read less and less; I didn't want him to feel as if he *had* to come see me every Thursday, and so, about a week before the opening of the baseball season, I told him that I thought he had reached the point where he could go it alone. "When you feel like talking, just come knocking—" I said. "We don't need a schedule." He seemed relieved, I thought, and I was proud that I had had the sense to release him from any obligation he might have felt.

Then, suddenly, I didn't see him anywhere for three weeks. I asked his home-room teacher about him and she said she hadn't seen him either; she had sent him a few postcards, but had received no reply. That very night—it was almost as if he had been there listening, I thought—he telephoned me at home.

"Is this Mister Carter? This is Luther here."

"Hi, Luther," I said.

"I looked you up in the telephone book. You mind me calling you at home?"

"No, no. I don't mind."

"Okay," he said, breathing hard. "I just wanted to let you know not to worry about me because I'm not in school. Okay?"

"Sure," I said. "Sure."

"I had some things to take care of—you know?"

"Sure," I said.

"Man, you *know* you're itching to ask me *what?*" He laughed. "You are deep. I'll be back Monday."

That was all. On Monday, as he had promised, he returned to school and came to visit me in my room at three o'clock. We talked for a while about the way the pennant race was going, and then he said, "Okay, let's cut the jazz, man. I got something to say to you." He seemed very intense about it and I told him that I was listening carefully. He pointed a finger at me. "Now, we stopped our sessions, right?"

"Right," I said.

"And the day after we stopped, I began to play the hook for three straight weeks, right?"

"Right."

"Okay. Now you can tell me it ain't so, but I'll bet you'll be thinking it was your fault. It ain't. If you want the truth, I ain't done a stick of work all term for any teacher—so don't go thinking that I stopped being a good student cause we stopped our meetings."

He let out a long breath. "I'm glad you told me," I said.

"Shit, man," he said, getting up and going to the door. "Don't say anything, huh? Why you got to say something all the time?" He came toward me. "Why?" He was almost screaming and I slid my chair back from the desk. He shook his head frantically. "Why, man?" he said. He reached into his side-pocket and I started to stand up. Abruptly, he broke into laughter. "Oh man, you are deep! You are just so deep!" He clapped his hands and laughed at me some more. "Ra-ta-tat-tat!" he said as he banged on a desk. "You're real sweet, man! Just so sweet! Ra-ta-tat-tat! Comin' down the street!" He sat down in one of the seats. "But don't you worry none. I got seven liberry cards now and books growing out the ceiling. I got a liberry card for Luther King and one for Luther Queen and one for Luther Prince and one for Luther Jones and one for Luther Smith and one for Luther Mays and one for Luther B. Carter." He banged on the top of the desk with his fist, then drummed with his fingers again. "But don't you worry none—ra-ta-tat-tat—just don't you worry—."

"I'm not," I said.

"That's all," he said, and dashed out of the room.

He attended classes regularly for about two weeks and then disappeared again for a week. He returned for a few days, stayed away, returned. The pattern continued. In the halls when we saw each other he would always smile and ask if I was worrying and

I would tell him I wasn't. Once or twice, when he was absent, he telephoned me at home and asked me what was new at school. He got a big charge out of this. Then another time, I remember, he came riding through the schoolyard on a bicycle during sixth period, when I was on patrol. "Don't report me, man!" he yelled and rode right back out, waving and shouting something in Spanish that made everybody laugh.

Near the end of May, the assistant principal in charge of the eighth grade called me into his office. He knew I was friendly with Luther, he said, and he thought that I might talk to the boy. For the past six or seven months, he told me, Luther had been in and out of juvenile court. "Petty thefts," the assistant principal explained. I wasn't surprised; Luther had hinted at this many times. I had never pressed him about it, however, not wanting to destroy our relationship by lecturing him. The assistant principal said he didn't care whether I said anything to Luther or not. In fact, he added, he would have been just as happy to get rid of him—but that before he was shipped off to a 600-school or put away somewhere else, he wanted to give me an opportunity to do what I could. More for me, he said, than for Luther.

About a week after this, on a Friday, Luther telephoned me. "How've you been?" I asked.

"Superb, man," he said. "Hey listen—we ain't been seeing much of each other lately, have we?"

"No—."

"No. Okay. Listen—I got two tickets to see the Giants play tomorrow. You want to come?" I didn't answer immediately. "Come on—yes or no—tickets are going fast—."

"I'd like to," I said. "Yes. Only—only I was wondering where you got the money for the tickets?" I breathed out, glad I had said it.

Luther just laughed. "Oh man, you're not gonna be like that, are you? You been listening to too many stories again. That judge from the court must of been gassing with you. Tell you what— you come to the game and I'll tell you where I got the tickets. A deal?"

"A deal."

"Meet you in front of the school at eleven o'clock—I like to get there early to see Willie go through batting practice. Batting practice—that's more fun than the game, sometimes. You know?"

He was waiting for me when I got there a few minutes before eleven the following day. "Let's go," he said, flourishing the tickets. "But don't ask me now, man—let's enjoy the game first. Okay?"

I did enjoy the game. The Giants were playing the Cardinals and to Luther's delight, Willie Mays had one of his better days, going three-for-four at bat, and making several brilliant plays in the field. For most of the game, I was truly relaxed. Along about the eighth inning, however, I began to think about the question again—to wonder when would be the best time to ask it. Luther, it seemed, had forgotten all about it. The Giants were winning 5–2.

"Oh man," he said. "If only that Musial don't do something, we're home free. Look at Willie!" he exclaimed. "Ain't he the greatest that ever lived. He is just so graceful! You know? How you like to see a team of Willie Mayses out there? Wow!" Wes Westrum, the Giant catcher, grounded out, short to first, and the eighth inning was over. "One to go, one to go," Luther said. Then he jabbed me in the arm with his finger. "Hey listen—I been thinking. Instead of an All-Star game every year between the leagues, what they ought to do one year is have the white guys against our guys. What you think?"

I shrugged. "I don't know," I said.

"Sure," he said. "Listen—we got Willie in center. Then we put Aaron in right and Doby in left. He's got the raw power. Some outfield, huh? Then we got Campy catching and Newcombe pitching. You can't beat that. That Newcombe—he's a mean son of a bitch, but he throws. Okay. I been thinking about this a long time—." He used his fingers to enumerate. He was excited, happy. "At first base we put Luke Easter, at second—Junior Gilliam, at short—Ernie Banks, and at third base we bring in old Jackie Robinson just to give the team a little class—you know what I mean? Man, what a line-up! Who could you match it with?"

When I said I didn't know, Luther eyed me suspiciously. "C'mon—Musial, Mantle, Williams, Spahn—you name 'em and

I'll match 'em, man for man, your guys against ours." He stopped and cheered as a Cardinal popped out to Whitey Lockman at first. "What's the matter—don't you like the idea? Ha! Face it, man, we'd wipe up the field with you. Swish! Swish!" He laughed and slapped me on the knee. "Hey, I know what's bugging you, I bet—." He leaned toward me, cupping his hand over his mouth, and whispered in my ear. "Tell the truth now, would you have ever offered to help me if I wasn't colored?"

"Would I—?" I stopped. "Sure," I said. "Of course I would. Of course—."

Luther smiled; triumphantly, dubiously. "Look," I said. "As long as we're asking questions, let me ask you something."

"About the tickets, right?"

"No," I said. "Forget the tickets. No long lectures, either. Just a question. Just one: how come you steal?"

"Oh man," he said, laughing. "That's an easy one!—Because I'm not getting what I want and when you don't get what you want, man, you got to take. Don't you know that?"

I stared at him, not sure I had heard right. He winked at me. "Enjoy the ballgame, man! Say hey, Willie!" he shouted, as Mays caught a fly ball, bread-basket style, for the second out. "Ain't he the sweetest!"

A minute later the game was over and the players were racing across the field toward the clubhouse in center field, trying to escape the fans who scrambled after them. "They won't get Willie," Luther said. "He's too swift, too swift."

When we were outside I thanked Luther and told him how much I had enjoyed the game. "How about a Coke or something?" I offered.

"Nah," he said. "I got things to do." He extended his hand quickly and I shook it, the first time we had ever done that. "Okay. You go get spiffed up and get a wife. Time you were married." He tossed his head back and laughed. "Ain't you married yet? No, no. *Smile,* man—how you gonna get a wife, never smiling." He started away, through the crowd. "Stay loose," he called back. "Don't steal no fruits."

I never questioned him again about stealing, but even if I had wanted to, I wouldn't have had much opportunity. He did not come to see me very often the rest of that year. When he returned to school in September of 1958 for his last year of junior high school, he had grown again. But not up. He never did go higher than the five-five or five-six he had reached by that time. He had taken up weightlifting over the summer, however, and his chest, his neck, his arms—they had all broadened incredibly. Instead of the dirty cotton and flannel shirts he had worn the two previous years, he now walked through the halls in laundry-white T-shirts, the sleeves rolled up to the shoulder, his powerful muscles exposed. There were always a half-dozen Negro boys following him around now also and they all dressed the way he did—white T-shirts, black chino pants, leather wrist straps, and —hanging from their necks on pieces of string—miniature black skulls.

The guidance counselor for the ninth grade came to me one day early in the term and asked me if I could give him any evidence against Luther. He claimed that Luther and his gang were going around the school, beating and torturing those students who refused to "loan" them money. All of the students, he said, were afraid to name Luther. "The kid's a born sadist," he added. I told him I didn't know anything.

The term progressed and the stories and rumors increased. I was told that the police in Luther's neighborhood were convinced that he and his gang were responsible for a series of muggings that had occurred. I tried not to believe it, but Luther all but gave me conclusive proof one afternoon, right before Christmas. He came into my room at three o'clock, alone, and said he had something for me. He said he trusted me not to tell anybody about it or show it to anyone. I said I wouldn't.

"Okay, man—here it is—." His eyes leapt around the room, frenzied, delirious. He took a little card from his wallet. "You might need this sometime—but don't ask me no questions. Ha! And don't you worry none. I'm doing okay. Expanding all the time. Don't you worry." I took the card from him. "See you now, Mister Carter. See you, see you."

He left and I looked at the card. Across the top was printed: THE BLACK AVENGERS, and below it was written: "Don't touch this white man. He's okay." It was signed by Luther and under his name he had drawn a skull and crossbones. I put the card in my wallet.

In January, to no one's great surprise, Luther was sent away to reform school in upstate New York. I was never exactly clear about the precise event that had led to it—the policeman assigned to our school said it had to do with brutally beating an old man; Luther's friends said it had to do with getting caught in a gang war. They claimed the fight was clean but that the cops had framed Luther. There was nothing in the papers, Luther had not contacted me, and I did not find out about it all until he had already been shipped off.

I received a postcard from him that summer. It was brief.

I hate it here. I can't say anymore or they'll beat shit out of me. I hate it. I'm reading some. I'll visit you when I get out and we'll have a session.

I answered the card with a letter. I told him I was sorry about where he was and that I'd be glad to talk to him whenever he wanted. I gave him some news of the school and included some current baseball clippings. I asked him if there was anything he needed and if there was anybody in his family he wanted me to get in touch with. I told him that in return for the time he'd taken me to the baseball game I had ordered a subscription to Sport magazine for him.

He replied with another post card.

Visiting day this summer is August 21. I'd like for you to come.

When I arrived, he seemed glad to see me, but I remember that he was more polite than he had ever been before, and more subdued. I wondered, at the time, if they were giving him tranquilizers. I was only allowed an hour with him and we spent most of that time just walking around the grounds—the school was a work-farm reformatory—not saying anything.

The visit, I could tell, was a disappointment to him. I don't know what he expected of me, but whatever it was, I didn't provide it. I wrote him a letter when I got home, telling him I had enjoyed seeing him and that I'd be glad to come again if he wanted me to. He didn't answer it, and I heard no more from him for a year and a half.

Then one day in the spring of 1961, just about the time of the Bay of Pigs invasion of Cuba, I remember, he popped into my room at school. He looked horrible. His face was unshaven, his clothes were filthy and ragged, his eyes were glazed. Underneath his clothes, his body had become flabby and he bent over noticeably when he walked. At first I didn't recognize him.

When I did, I was so glad to see him, I didn't know what to do. "Luther—for crying out loud!" I said, standing up and shaking his hand. "How the hell are you?"

He smiled at me. "I'm superb, man—can't you tell from looking at me?" He laughed then, and I laughed with him.

"You've gotten older," I said.

"Past sixteen," he said. "That means I don't got to go to school no more—"

He waited, but I didn't offer an opinion. "How about going down with me and having a cup of coffee? I'm finished here for the day—just getting through with mid-terms."

"Nah," he said, looking down and playing with his hands. "I gotta meet somebody. I'm late already. But I was in the neighborhood so I thought I'd come let you know I was still alive." He came to my desk and looked down. He shook his head as if something were wrong.

"What's the matter?" I asked.

"Don't see no wedding ring on your finger yet." He looked straight into my face. "Hey, man—you ain't a fag, are you?"

"No," I said, laughing. "Not that I know of—."

He laughed, his mouth opening wide. "Okay. That's all the gas for today. I'll see you, man."

During the next few months he visited me several times. Sometimes he looked good, sometimes bad—but I never could find out what he was doing with his days. He never gave a straight answer to my questions. More and more, I felt that he was asking me for some kind of help, but when I would touch on anything personal or even hint that I wanted to do something for him, with him, he would become defensive.

I didn't see him over the summer, but the following fall he came by periodically. He seemed to be getting a hold on himself, and sometimes he would talk about going to night school. Nothing came of the talk, though. In November he was arrested and sent to Riker's Island—to P.S. 616, the combination prison-school for boys between the ages of sixteen and twenty. His sentence was for eighteen months and during the first three months I visited him twice. Both times all he wanted to do was to talk about the English class we had had, and the stories and compositions he had made up. He said he was trying to remember some of them for the English teacher he had there, but couldn't do it all the time. He seemed to be in terrible shape, and I didn't have much hope for him.

So I was surprised when I began getting postcards from him again. "I am studying hard," the first one said. "There is a Negro who comes here to help me. I like him. I will be a new man when I come out. Yours sincerely, Luther." It was neatly and carefully written. The ones that followed were the same and they came at regular intervals of about five weeks. He told me about books he was reading, most of them having to do with Negro history, and about how he was changing. "Improving" was the word he used most.

I answered his cards as best I could, and offered to come see him again, but he never took up any of my offers. When his eighteen months were up, I expected a visit from him. He never came. Sometimes I wondered what had become of him, but after the first few months passed and I didn't hear from him, I thought about him less and less. A year passed—two since we had last seen each other at Riker's Island—and then we met again.

I spotted him first. It was a beautiful summer night and I had gone up to Lewisohn Stadium for a concert. It had been good, I was relaxed and happy as I walked out of the stadium. Luther was standing at the corner of Amsterdam Avenue and 138th Street. He was wearing a dark blue suit, a white shirt and a tie. He was clean shaven, his hair was cut short and he looked healthy and bright. He was stopping people and trying to sell them newspapers.

"How are you, Mister Carter?" he asked, when I walked up to

him. His eyes were clear and he seemed very happy to see me. "Interested in buying a newspaper to help the colored people? Only a dime—."

"No thanks," I said. The paper he was selling, as I had expected, was *Muhammad Speaks*, the newspaper of the Black Muslims. "You look fine," I added.

"Thanks—excuse me a second." He turned and sold a copy to somebody. People snubbed him but this didn't stop him from smiling or trying. I waited. When the crowd had gone, he asked me where I was going. "Home," I said. "Cup of coffee first?"

"No thanks," he said. "Thanks, but no thanks."

"When did all this start?" I asked, motioning to the newspapers.

"At Riker's Island," he said. He put up a hand, as if to stop my thoughts from becoming words. "I know what you're thinking, what you hear on TV and read in the newspapers about us—but don't believe everything. We're essentially a religious organization, as you may or may not know."

"I know," I said.

"And it's meant a lot to me—I couldn't have made it without their help. They—they taught me to *believe* in myself." His eyes glowed as he twisted his body toward me. "Can you understand that?" It seemed very important to him that I believe him. "*Can* you?" He relaxed momentarily and shrugged. "I don't believe everything they teach, of course, but I follow their precepts: I don't smoke, I don't drink, I don't curse, I don't go out with women who aren't Muslims—I feel good *inside*, Mister Carter. Things are straightening themselves out." He paused. "It hasn't been easy."

"I know," I said, and smiled.

He nodded, embarrassed, I thought. "I'm going back to school also—."

"I'm glad."

"Even my body feels good! I'm lifting weights again, too," he said. Then he laughed and the sound tore through the warm night. His eyes were flashing with delight. "Oh man—someday I'll be the head of a whole damned army! Me and my old hunchback." He laughed again, pleased with himself. Then his laughter subsided and he patted me on the shoulder. "Oh man, you are still so deep, so deep. Don't worry none, Mister Carter. I don't go around advocating no violence." He chuckled. "I've got to go," he said, extending a hand. "It's been good seeing you again. Sure you don't want to buy a copy?"

"I'm sure," I said, shaking his hand. "Good luck to you, Luther. I'm glad to see you the way you are now—."

"Thanks." We looked at each other for a minute and he smiled warmly at me. Then I started toward the subway station. When I had crossed the street he called to me.

"Hey—Mister Carter—!"

I turned.

"Let me ask you something—do you still have that card I gave you?" He howled at this remark. "Oh man, I'd save that card if I were you! I'd do that. You never know when you might need it. You never know—."

I started back across the street, toward him. He tossed his head back and roared with laughter. "You never know, you never know," he repeated, and hurried away from me, laughing wildly. I stared at him until he disappeared in the darkness. Then I just stood there, dazed, unable to move—I don't know for how long. Finally I made myself turn around, and as I walked slowly toward the lights of Broadway all I could feel was the presence of his muscular body, powerful, gleaming, waiting under his white shirt, his clean suit.

3⓪ Irvin Faust

Irvin Faust is director of guidance at Garden City High School in New York. He has published a collection of stories, Roar Lion Roar (1965), and a novel, The Steagle (1966).

❖

WOBBILLOBBY MOBBAYS
(FROM *THE STEAGLE*)

On the morning after Kennedy blockaded Cuba, Dr. Harold Weissberg sat in his classroom and stared at his twenty-two pages of notes for the first lecture of the day. Lifting the pages as if they were counterweights, he checked off fifty-seven footnotes, which was a new record for him, with two pages all footnotes, another record. So, he thought with a little sigh, on the day the world goes with a bang, not a whimper, they will all suck in my notes like always, the sweaters and the lumberjacks, suck in and blow up like old Hoover vacuums, the ones with the belly-bags. If he stuck in a pin . . . footnotes all over the ceiling. . . . He sighed bigger for them, for himself, sitting in the last row, drinking in knowledge (which was power) as Pearl went up in smoke. All those glasses and pimples and dirty shoes; on this day—bigger and better than Pearl—they should *all* have it better (on a campus they should be anyway, with greenswards and field houses and college widows, the kind Groucho Marx used to goose). Oh no this above all days they should definitely have it better. He crossed out twelve footnotes. . . .

He leaned forward and watched them file silently in, glasses smudged, foreheads blooming, IQs zooming far over the 125 cut-off, tight with their A pluses and authoritative term papers and the hell with anything less, like destruction. He shuffled papers and waited. Loretta Greenbaum, the little junior with the pointed nipples, slid into position, her face very pale, hair pulled back so tight that her eyes were wide and interested . . . Rose Pensky's eyes and doorknobs she had, and that confidential head-bob. He tucked Rosie into her space. Twice a year, mid-term and final they had scraped knees, he and Rosie . . . Today the little junior's legs didn't tuck under; they were floppy and absent-minded. Taking my picture, he thought. So. This was Rose, way up there, with all that gleaming white, while 146 IQ Heshy Weissberg debates two years whether to drop his pencil and cop a gander. All that scholastic aptitude and he could never figure the right angle for a dropped pencil. . . . Standing, he carefully fingered his glasses and put them on. He cleared his throat and gave it the mysterious smile. "Today's topic, as you know," he said, "concerns the mystique of the hero in Elizabethan literature as reflected in existing socio-action terms. We . . ." He took off his glasses and gazed at the thousands of ants covering the page, then looked up again and focused on the gleaming white, far up in the back row. Next to her a pair of smudged glasses sitting stiffly aloof. And all the while, he thought, the ships are steaming, right for that port. Over his head he saw in exquisite detail a dirt-caked finger-nail drooping for the button in Loretta's sweater. Screwitall, he whispered to himself and walked around his desk, leaned back and folded his hands. They lifted their pens. "The thing I can't understand, and never will if I live to a hundred," he said, "is why Willie Mays did not get the most valuable player award this year." The pens plunged. He slapped his desk hard. "Or for that matter," he said, "last year or the year before." He began to pace back and forth in front of the room, his hand folded behind his back, while they scribbled furiously. "Howinhell anyone in his right mind can overlook this man is completely incomprehensible to me." The pens ran with him; he stopped, they stopped. They sucked in breath as he faced them, holding up one finger. "Look," he said quietly. "Just look at the goddam record. Home-run king of the majors with forty nine." He lifted the next fingers and they swung up and down into notebooks. "One forty two ribbies, 304 average, one twenty runs scored, nineteen thefts and . . ." Stopping abruptly, he walked to the first row and poked his hand at Sheldon Wordman, whose glasses were always shiny, "Whoinhell can touch that glove, eh who?" Sheldon hunched his shoulders and shook his head. "That magnificent glove that sucks in everything except your lumberjacket in the goddamn bleachers." Sheldon nodded happily and wrote quickly. Weissberg retreated and looked up at the little junior; her knees clapped and snapped his picture twice. He smiled. "Ah but that," he said thoughtfully, "that is all terribly, coldly statistical, though certainly very impressive, oh yes impressive, that 312 lifetime average, 368 roundtrippers in only nine and a half seasons, four times forty or more circuit clouts, more basepath larceny than any colleague in the senior circuit, batting king in fifty four, fifty one homers in fifty five, before expansion made a mockery of such a performance." His eyes bored into Sheldon Wordman. "Forget it, man. Forget the book." Sheldon nodded. "Look at Mays, the complete performer, the heart, soul and guts of the Giants. Just look at that." He smiled coldly and Sheldon smiled back. "My God," he said, pacing, "where would this club be without him? Where?" He spun around. "This man faints because he reaches for more than exists, he slides off the bench, he is carried away and is out for a week and they fold, blow sky-high, and if you will take the effort to look it up you will find this true in every game he missed since coming up from Minneapolis. . . . So OK OK, he comes back and what happens? He merely bangs them into the playoffs with a ninth inning blast. Then takes charge so no johnny-come-lately Cepeda or McCovey can foul up the works . . ." He stopped, ran his hand through his hair, and stepped up the aisle. "Who else," he asked in a voice that sliced the tension, "has Ford in his hip pocket?" The glasses swung up and blinked.

"NO ONE," he said.

Glasses blinked and swung down. That one might be on the final . . . Weissberg walked back to his desk and sat on it. "There is no question," he said softly, "that Wills is a dynamic, even an important player, and so are Groat and Robinson and Pinson, et cetera et cetera. But, and this is the point, that team is nothing, I repeat, *nothing*, without this man, who, I suggest has been denied recognition by a vicious, petty, envious claque of anti-New York writers. Oh yes, anti-New York, make no mistake, my friends, because Mays, of course, is and always will be a New York product. A stickball player. A three sewer man. Only here is his artistry appreciated and savored; yet even when transplanted to an alien culture he produces, and *this*, I suggest is the true mark of the man." He paused and drew a deep, refreshing breath. "Take Mantle." He leaned back and grinned. "Surely a fine player, magnificently endowed. But the temperament, my friends, yes the temperament is not quite with it." He loomed over Sheldon, who sat up, pen poised. "And Mantle," he said, with a little sneer, "HAS BAD WHEELS." The sneer filled the room and closed the little junior's legs and threw Sheldon at his notebook. A hush. Engulfing them all. Leaning far, far back then, loosening his tie and closing his eyes, he said gently, "Oh the Giants were so named because old Jim Mutrie, who preceded McGraw, looked up one day and said 'oh aren't they wonders, though, my Giants,' and so my friends they were, before the turn of the century and then into the early decades of this one when they meant greatness and Larry Doyle said it for us all when he crowed 'IT'S GREAT TO BE YOUNG AND A GIANT,' for there was only one team then and only one little Napoleon who drove them to the heights with Matty and Iron Man Joe and the Eleven Thousand Dollar Lemon, who wasn't, and Bonehead Merkle, who wasn't really at fault because the third base coach was asleep, but there they were, oh it's true, drawing their pants on one leg at a time, which of course did not seem the case to the Robins or the Cubs or the Bucs, and still the legend flowered despite the Ruths and the Meusels and the Chases and the other interlopers, because you see the flame had been passed on from Big Six to King Carl and Prince Hal and Fat Freddie and tough Blondie, who said in that magnificent telegram 'CAN'T MISS, AM ON MY WAY,' and naturally they didn't miss, under Memphis Bill copping all the marbles in thirty three and gonfalons again in thirty seven and thirty eight, and on then even into the lean years when they were still the dynasts, yes even with crazy Danny and Nappy Reyes and Mercury Myatt and Hooks, under Master Melvin, who was always class, but as Leo said so succinctly, nice guys do finish last and then proved it with the Barber and Larry and Dusty and Bobby and the shot heard round the world, and with Willie laughing to keep them loosey goosey and outrunning his cap they copped again in fifty four and bombed the Indians four straight, from which, incidentally, the Tribe has never recovered, Willie administering the coup de grace, and I do mean grace, with highway robbery on Vic Wertz' drive to furthest dead center, which if one were there one will never forget . . ." He stopped.

"AND THEN THEY TOOK THEM AWAY."

His fist was pounding now; the class cowered. "They took them away," he said, brushing the moistness from his eyes; the little junior brushed, too. "These robber barons, who for six generations gulled us," he said. "AND I PROTEST." He slipped off the desk, walked into the well between the class and his territory and firmly planted his legs and raised his arms. "With all that is in me, for all of us, the unvocal millions, from St. Louis to Philadelphia to Boston to Bensonhurst to Harlem, *I protest*." Overheard, near the cracked ceiling he saw the ships steaming and his voice grew strong and deep and new. He reached far back, to stickball, saloogie, simplicity, sense and triumph.

"YOBBOU OBBAND MOBBEE HOBBAVE BOBBEEN COBBONNED, BOB-BILKED, SCROBBEWED BOBBYE THOBBEE BOBBOSSOBBES, THOBBEE GROB-BEAT SPOBBORTSMOBBEN THOBBAT TOBBOOK OBBOUR CLOBBOSEOBBEST FROBBIENDS FROBBOM OBBUS. OBBAND THOBBEN ROBBEACHED THOBBEE SOBBINOBBISTOBBER OBBEND WOBBITH THOBBEE KOBBIDNOBBAPPOBBING OBBOF THOBBEE GROBBEATOBBEST OBBOF THOBBEM OBBALL WHOBBOO OBBIS OBBOUR WOBBILLOBBY, YOBBES GROBBEATOBBER THOBBEAN COB-BOB, SPOBBEAKOBBER, WOBBAGNOBBER BOBBIG SOBBIX, BOBBIG TROB-BAIN, ROBBAHJOBBER, OBBOTT, JOBBO DOBBEE, TOBBERROBBY, STOBBAN, TOBBED, JOBBACKOBBY, YOBBESS MOBBY FROBBIENDS, OBBEVOBBEN THOBBEE BOBBAMBOBBINOBBO, FOBBOR OBBI SOBBAY THOBBAT WOBBIL-LOBBY OBBIS WOBBITHOBBOUT DOBBOUT THOBBEE BOBBEST, THOBBEE TOBBOP, THOBBEE ZOBBENOBBITH, OBBOF THOBBIS OBBOR OBBANOBBY TOBBIME, OBBAND OBBI SOBBAY WOBBITH OBBAL THOBBAT OBBI POB-BOSOBBESS. YOBBOU OBBOUT THOBBERE, BROBBING MOBBISTOBBER MOB-BAYS BOBBACK TOBBO OBBUS OBBIN THOBBIS TOBBOWN THOBBAT SPOB-

BAWNED HOBBIM. THOBBAT KNOBBOWS HOBBIM, OBBAND OBBI SOBBAY
FOBBOR OBBALL OBBOF OBBUS THOBBAT DOBBEMOBBAND THOBBIS,
SCROBBEW YOBBOU OBBALL."

The class rose and for ten minutes cheered, whistled, stamped
and applauded and Weissberg smiled and waved back and clasped
his hand over his head and turned and walked out. With the
excitement still buzzing, he saw Dr. Florence Maguire, tall, full-
chested, prim, aloof, walking toward him, her eyes fixed on prob-
ability equations. With the ships steaming, with the finger sagging,
with nothing, absolutely nothing to lose, he walked up to her,
his hands cupped to receive her breasts, his smile charming and
irresistible. Everything goes, he said to himself, blessing the goddam bomb. Everything.

31 Leslie Fiedler

Leslie Fiedler, who was born in Newark, New Jersey, in 1917, is one of our most perceptive and sympathetic critics of contemporary American fiction. His books of criticism include An End to Innocence (1955), Love and Death in the American Novel (1960, revised 1966), No! In Thunder (1960), and Waiting for the End (1964). He has also written four books of fiction, Pull Down Vanity and Other Stories (1962), The Second Stone (1963), Back to China (1965), and The Last Jew in America (1966).

❖

NO! IN THUNDER

That the practice of any art at any time is essentially a moral activity I have always believed; indeed, I do not know how to begin to make a book or talk about one without moral commitment. Yet for a long time I tried to keep this secret from myself as well as from others, since in the critical world in which I grew up, a "moralistic approach" to literature was considered not only indecent but faintly comic. Most of my best literary friends, at any rate, considered it strategically advisable to speak of novels and poems *purely* (the adverb is theirs) in terms of diction, structure, and point of view, remaining safely inside the realm of the formal. But an author's choice of—or a critic's preference for —one point of view, or type of diction, or kind of structure, or even his emphasis on one of these elements at the expense of the others, involves a judgment of the experience he is rendering; and such a judgment is, implicitly at least, a moral one.

One of the special strengths of modern fiction has been its awareness of the moral dimension of form; and the seminal greatness of Flaubert lies in his willingness to entrust judgment primarily to style: to transform style, in effect, from a social grace to a tool of ethical analysis. The author of *Madame Bovary* seldom comments directly on the social concerns which most deeply vex him; he has, indeed, an almost fanatic resolve *not* to admonish or preach, but his style is his surrogate in this regard. And his style judges—judges Emma and Homais, the clichés of Romanticism and Revolution, the formlessness and falsity of bourgeois life. By the same token, that style judges and condemns, as all serious style continues to judge and condemn, the literature of the market place and those misguided books dedicated to anti-style.

There are, of course, certain counterfeits of style, quite unlike Flaubert's, which are symptoms of the decay of their world rather than judgments of it; for there can be no neutrality in the area of technique. The form of a book represents either a moral critique of man and society, or a moral surrender. The pseudo-styles— which are called, a little misleadingly, "naturalist" and which have been practiced from the time of Émile Zola to that of James Jones—have represented such capitulations before the collapse of discrimination and sensitivity in the world around them; even as earlier Scott's manly carelessness and Dickens' hasty improvisations represented a retreat from moral engagement, and the ecstatic schoolgirl anti-style of Jack Kerouac projects a more recent sort of cowardice. Such writers as Zola, Jones and Kerouac are guilty not only of moral weakness but of hypocrisy as well, for they proffer their sloppiness and their submission to the decay of language as token of their sincerity and belongingness. To seem "one of the boys" is especially an American temptation, eternally offered and eternally accepted. But it is not only the principled anti-stylists, populist or Beat, who stand condemned in the court of high art for flagrant immorality, an immorality of form which all their avowed (and guilt-compelled) dedication to quite moral ideas and causes cannot mitigate. Those responsible for books like *Exodus*, or *Advise and Consent*, or whatever improbable contender is currently fighting its way up the best-seller lists, must also be adjudged guilty, since ignorance is no excuse, and good will merely aggravates the crime.

In the realm of fiction, to be inept, whether unwittingly or on purpose, is the single unforgivable sin. To be inept is to lie; and for this, time and the critics grant no pardon. Yet the contemporary audience forgives the liar in art, even adulates him. It knows he is lying, but it needs his lies. In our Do-It-Yourself Age, when no one can really do anything for himself unless provided a kit and instructions, men are plagued by the failure of self-deceit itself, afflicted with a fatal incapacity to believe themselves happy. If happiness is, as Swift insisted, the faculty of being well-deceived, most men can no longer achieve it on their own. They must be lied to every day, and they are willing to pay well for the service.

Our culture is organized around the satisfaction of this demand, and the moral artist, who is the truthteller, is subject (not invariably, but with distressing frequency) to one of two indignities, the first of which is called success, the second failure. Either he is admired, like Faulkner, for the wrong reasons: bought and unread because he is a living "classic" (in the United States, everything is speeded up to a bewildering tempo), his works posthumous before he is laid in the grave; or he is even more enthusiastically bought and misread—like Pasternak, whose *Doctor Zhivago* became the very symbol of being one up on the Russians, or like Nabokov and D. H. Lawrence, the happy authors of once-banned books! Or the moral artist may be condemned out of hand, like Pasternak in Russia or Lawrence in the United States (until only the other day).

The customary charge leveled at the serious writer, until he is ripe for the even more deadly one of being a classic, is that of having written a dirty book. The Russians apparently believe this of all successful American writers who do not sympathize with Soviet objectives; but ironically, the charge is also believed in America of many of the same authors. It is, indeed, part of what has almost assumed the status of a ritual—the standard initiation of the truthteller into the culture of his country, inflicted at the moment when his truth still hurts. One is not startled, perhaps, to discover that Walt Whitman was once called "the dirtiest beast of the age," but it is a little disconcerting to learn that Hawthorne's *The Scarlet Letter* was accused of representing "the beginning of the era of French immorality" in American letters.

Yet it will not do to ignore the difference in the level of hysteria with which such charges were leveled at serious art one hundred years ago and that with which they were made of the first great books in the "modern" tradition at the point when the first of the Great Wars was about to begin. Whatever offense great art has always given and given with particular effect in America seems to have been compounded when, in what is still called, after nearly fifty years, "modern art," that offense was confessed in nonconventional form. Apparently the common man can more easily forgive an attack on home and mother than a flagrant disregard for harmony, or punctuation, or representation. Perhaps it is simply because technical offenses are less easy to overlook or to cancel out by misreading.

I have a clear memory of myself at fourteen or fifteen, struggling for an education in the public libraries of Newark, New Jersey, and having to fight to get Joyce's *A Portrait of the Artist as a Young Man* out of a locked room where it was kept with other dangerous material. Proust's *Remembrance of Things Past* was on the open shelves, but it was no easy matter to get it past the vigilance of a certain librarian who, in her spare time, went through the photography magazines stamping all female nudes three times with the official library stamp (to keep, I suppose, the minds of adolescents pure) and who regarded me as a special challenge. This experience has always seemed to me an archetypal one, my personal myth of The Intellectual Life as Moral Combat; for certainly (to a temperament for which, and in a time when, struggle seemed as necessary as eating) the library became for me an arena in which my morality was pitted against theirs in a war to end all wars! It was not dirty books I was after, I wanted to protest; it was. . . . But I did not know how to explain what it was I sought.

Only a long time afterward did I realize that I had been completely misled by the rationalizations of the guardians of the library, that it was not really the "dirtiness," the frank sexuality, of certain novels that irked the censors, but something quite different. Best sellers—in our country at least—have always been books which exploit sex as far as (and a little farther than) contemporary taboos will permit. From *The Monks of Monk Hall* to

Peyton Place or the latest paperback by Richard S. Prather, the really popular book has talked of sex on the level of broad suggestion; it has spoken the last common language bearing on the last link (as Moravia has argued) between us and the world of nature. It seems to me now that what must be insisted upon is that even a good book can be a popular success if it can be thought of as dirty, like Nabokov's *Lolita* and Faulkner's *Sanctuary*.

No, the problem of the nonacceptance of serious fiction lies elsewhere: in the fact that *to fulfill its essential moral obligation, such fiction must be negative.* There is a dim sense of this in the popular mind, reflected in the over-the-bridge-table charge that certain great books, whatever their merits, are too "morbid" and responded to by the publishers' defensive assurances on the book jackets: "But beneath the shattering events of that book . . . lies a passionate affirmation" or "This is a book of great themes, of life, death and regeneration, of the dignity and triumph of man." Like the more particular religious reassurances of another age, these vaguely pious assertions are rooted in a profound distrust of art itself; and before them I am moved to resentment and anger. I can never read one without remembering a favorite anecdote of my old teacher, William Ellery Leonard, about how, one night in an inn, he had to share a bed with a man whom he had never met before. He felt no qualms until his bedmate kneeled down beside the bed to pray. "At that point," he liked to say, "I grabbed my wallet and ran!" So I before the book whose jacket assures me that the author is committed to affirmation, or love, or a belief in the dignity of man.

Insofar as a work of art is, as art, successful, it performs a negative critical function; for the irony of art in the human situation lies in this: that man—or better, some men—are capable of achieving in works of art a coherence, a unity, a balance, a satisfaction of conflicting impulses which they cannot (but which they desperately long to) achieve in love, family relations, politics. Yet works of art are *about* love, family relations, politics, etc.; and to the degree that these radically imperfect human activities are represented in a perfectly articulated form, they are revealed in all their intolerable inadequacy. The image of man in art, however magnificently portrayed—indeed, precisely when it is most magnificently portrayed—is the image of a failure. There is no way out.

The self-conscious writer, realizing this irony, feels a demand to make explicit the essentially negative view of man implicit in his work insofar as it is art at all. He is driven to make his avowed attitudes and allegiances congruous with the meaning that his techniques cannot help declaring. Especially in recent times, when the obligations of self-consciousness are imposed on us with a rigor unheard of in the past, the writer becomes aware that his Muse is more like the *Daimon* of Socrates (who appeared only to say *No!*) or the God of Job than like any of those white-draped Ladies of the genteel mythologists. The spirit which speaks to him conveys no reassurances or positive revelations; only the terrible message that what his best friends—in newspaper offices, or the pulpit, or Congress—have been, like Job's, telling him is "the thing which is not right." And that spirit addresses him from the whirlwind, directing his attention from himself to those absurd beasts, the Behemoth and the Leviathan.

Demonic, terrible and negative; this is the Modern Muse— "Bluff'd not a bit by drain-pipe, gasometers, artificial fertilizers," as Walt Whitman had the wit to see; but in his euphoric, comic vision the sense of terror is dissipated. It is to such a writer as James Joyce (who chose for his slogan the device of Satan himself: *Non serviam*, "I will not obey!") or to Henrik Ibsen (whose final words were "On the contrary . . .") or to Whitman's contemporary, Herman Melville, that we must turn for the decisive clue. The secret motto of *Moby Dick* was, Melville once confided: "I baptize you not in the name of the Father, the Son and the Holy Ghost, but in the name of the Devil." Even better, perhaps, because less theatrically gothic, is the phrase Melville attributes to Bartleby the Scrivener, his portrait of the writer in the modern world—a phrase in which there is already implicit Bartleby's insanity and death: "I would prefer not to." Most explicit of all is the comment in a letter to Hawthorne, in which Melville pretends to describe the essence of his beloved contemporary's art, while in fact revealing the deepest sources of his own:

There is the grand truth about Nathaniel Hawthorne. He says No! in thunder; but the Devil himself cannot make him say yes. For all men who say yes, lie; and all men who say *no*—why, they are in the happy

condition of judicious, unincumbered travellers in Europe; they cross
the frontiers into Eternity with nothing but a carpetbag,—that is to
say, the Ego.

It pays to be clear about the nature of the "No! in thunder,"
which is quite different from certain lesser no's in which a thriving
trade is always done: the no in newsprint, for instance, and the
no on manifestoes and petitions. A play written in the 1950s about
the Salem witch trials, or a novel of the same period celebrating
the revolt of the Maccabees, despite their allegorical intentions,
are cheats, exploitations of the pseudo-no. Even the attack on
slavery in Twain's post-Civil War *Huckleberry Finn*—or, for that
matter, in Mrs. Stowe's pre-Civil War *Uncle Tom's Cabin*—like
an anti-McCarthyite fiction in the recent past or an excoriation
of segregation right now, carry with them a certain air of presumptive self-satisfaction, an assurance of being justified by the
future. They are Easy No's, merely disguised yes's, in varying
degrees sentimental and righteous; they are yes's by anticipation,
tomorrow's yes's. The "No! in thunder" remains a no forever; like
the no implicit in the whole work of the Marquis de Sade, or the
deeper no of *Huckleberry Finn*—Huck's no to womankind, the
family and organized society, which remains to this very day a no.

The "No! in thunder" is never partisan; it infuriates Our Side
as well as Theirs, reveals that all Sides are one, insofar as they are
all yea-sayers and hence all liars. There is some evidence that the
Hard No is being spoken when the writer seems a traitor to those
whom he loves and who have conditioned his very way of responding to the world. When the writer says of precisely the cause
that is dearest to him what is always and everywhere the truth
about all causes—that it has been imperfectly conceived and in-
adequately represented, and that it is bound to be betrayed, consciously or unconsciously, by its leading spokesmen—we know that
he is approaching an art of real seriousness if not of actual
greatness. The thrill we all sense but hesitate to define for ourselves—the thrill of confronting a commitment to truth which
transcends all partial allegiances—comes when Dante turns on
Florence, Moliere on the moderate man, de Sade on reason,
Shaw on the socialists, Tolstoy on the reformers, Joyce on Ire-
land, Faulkner on the South, Graham Greene on the Catholics,

Pasternak on the Russians and Abraham Cahan or Nathanael West on the Jews. What people, what party, what church needs an enemy when it has a great writer in its ranks?

Unless he bites the hand that feeds him, the writer cannot live; and this those who would prefer him dead (so they can erect statues of him) can never understand. I remember Faulkner's coming once, rather improbably, to Missoula, Montana, and getting engaged in conversation with a lady Montanan, who cried out at one point, "Why can't So-and-so write a novel that would do for this part of the world what you've done for Mississippi? He *loves* Montana so!" To which Faulkner, of course, answered (maybe I only dreamed it; it all seems so pat), "To write well about some place, you've got to *hate* it." A pause, and then, "The way a man hates his own wife." But this is scandalous in a way with which the righteous cannot seem to come to terms. Not only the Great Audience but also, and even especially, the Little Elite Audiences demand of the writer its disavowal in the name of a kind of loyalty which is for him death. The first attack on me as a critic ever to appear was launched because I had made some rather drastic qualifying remarks about, I think, Thomas Mann— a small god, at any rate, of the avant-garde church to which I was presumably applying for admission. "Aid and comfort to the enemy" was the implicit charge; but this charge the sayer of the Hard No must be willing to face; for he knows that the writer who rejects the negative obligation perishes even as he pleases, perishes though he please only a handful of the very best people—those, for instance, whom he has begun by admiring and whom he never ceases to admire.

It has not always been necessary for the writer to be aware of his denial; his work will do it for him anyhow, if it is honest work. Indeed, at certain periods in the past, its seemed almost better that the writer deceive himself as well as his contemporary audience about his intent: that Dickens, for example, believe himself to be glorifying the purity of woman and the simple heart of the child, while giving us in fact his mad, black-and-white nightmares, in which things live the life of men, and men perform with the lifeless rigidity of things. In the same way, Dostoevsky could think himself the apostle of a revived orthodoxy, and Samuel Richardson considered his essential task the defense of bourgeois virtue. But these days the writer cannot afford to lose for an instant his sense of himself in opposition to the world; let him pretend, however briefly, that his no is a yes, and he will end up writing A *Fable* or *The Town*, travesties of his own best work.

Naturally, not all writers in our time accept the negative obligation; and, indeed, its rejection separates the purveyor of commodity-fiction from the serious artist in the novel. There are certain pseudo-novels which are, in fact, transitional stages on the way to becoming movies or substitutes for going to the movies; and these books are obliged to be cheerful, positive, affirmative: to sustain the belief in endurance, piety, hard work and a deliberately maintained blessed stupidity. Here is the giveaway! Nothing can, after all, be wholly positive; and even the most affirmative of subnovels (say, *Marjorie Morningstar*) must end by denying something: dirt, disorder, eccentricity, non-conformism, skepticism, intelligence—in short, the negative obligation itself! Conversely, the nay-saying writer is not wholly negative; he is in favor of one thing by definition: telling the truth (*Madame Bovary* will do as the counterexample) and accepting the tragic implications of that truth, the vision of an eternal gap between imagined order and actual chaos.

But it is not enough, in our time, for the serious writer to confess *in general* the inevitable discrepancy between dream and fact, between the best man can imagine and the best he can achieve. The artist must be willing specifically to comment on the defeat of a particular dream. The anti-artist, on the other hand, incurs only the most general obligation; despite the particulars in which he apparently deals, he is in fact composing parables, pseudo-myths, to express not wonder and terror but sentimental reassurance. What life refuses, the anti-artist grants: the dying catcher hits a three bagger, and everyone loves him; the coward, at the last moment, finds the courage to fight the segregationist and his hired thugs; the girl in the office takes off her glasses and wins the heart of the boss's playboy son. That these are prefabricated, masturbatory dreams almost everyone (including, I suspect, the authors) would be prepared to admit, yet they do not stir in most of us the moral indignation we feel at the distribution of other habit-forming drugs. They seem more benign than marijuana, which is banned, or tranquilizers, which may soon be sharply regulated; because we accept the fantasies they promote as finally truer than those born of "pot" or happiness pills. Assuring us that man is OK, that men are OK, that we are all—despite our mistakes and the machinations of others—OK, they feed into (at least they do not contradict) the last widely held *Weltanschauung* of the West: the progressive and optimistic, rational and kindly dogma of liberal humanism.

Yet, as some of us are rather disturbedly aware, many if not most of the eminent writers of the twentieth century have found themselves in conflict with this dogma, not always *despite* its nobility, but often because of it. The fact that such otherwise ill-assorted writers as Shaw, Joyce, Faulkner, Yeats, Pound, Eliot, Wyndham Lewis and Samuel Beckett are arrayed against the liberal tradition indicates that it represents for our age the belief against which the serious artist must define himself, the official "Yea!" to which he must say his private "Nay!" As earlier poets had to say "Nay!" to the fifth-century Greeks' belief that their world was really explicable in terms of the Homeric gods, or the Christians' assumption that their society was Christian, or the Enlightenment's conviction that its passion and politics were finally rational, so the artist today must deny the liberal view of the possibilities of man. But liberalism is essentially different from earlier official faiths, religious or secular, in that its ideal is "openness" rather than orthodoxy; and the writer striving toward the Hard No is likely to discover that his most ardent denial is met with a disconcerting "Yes, yes, though all the same . . ." or "I don't finally agree with you, of course, but still . . ."

Nietzsche's assertion that God is dead once shook half the world, and Ibsen's attack on marriage left northern Europe trembling, but they find us merely confused or indifferent—or, as we say when confusion and indifference reach their highest pitch, "tolerant." Only an assault on tolerance itself is able to stir us as Goethe's assault on the ban against suicide once stirred his readers. The very advocacy of adultery, which from the time of the troubadours to that of D. H. Lawrence possessed an almost magic potency to provoke, has now become fashionable and meaningless.

The recent redemption of Lady Chatterley's Lover in the courts represents not a triumph of literary taste over taboo but a failure of the moral imagination; and Lillian Smith can suggest in her novel One Hour, an essentially middlebrow book, that an Episcopalian priest's moment of vision and truth comes when he is in bed with his friend's wife. Who can épater la bourgeoisie when the bourgeoisie regards even the grossest scandal as a test of its capacity for understanding and forgiveness?

Yet there is finally a liberal view of man, to deny which is to risk blasphemy: an image of the human situation which persists very like a dogma beneath the undogmatic "openness" of which contemporary society is so proud. This view sees man as the product of a perhaps unplanned but rationally ordered and rationally explicable universe, a product which science can explain, even as it can explain the world which conditions him. The first fictionists who accepted this view of man thought of themselves as protoscientists and of their books as scientific reports on how vice and virtue are produced in the great laboratory of society. Such books, with their blend of rationalism, determinism and quasi-scientific objectivity, were variously hailed when they appeared as examples of Realism, Naturalism, Verism, etc.; and whatever the inadequacy of their styles, they performed in the beginning the essential function of art, the negative one of provocation and scandal. Novelists like Zola and de Maupassant—in America, even so belated a representative of the school as Dreiser—horrified the genteel by exposing the self-delusions of sentimental Christianity. They soon fell victim to the fallacy of imitative form (realism-naturalism did not have to eschew style, as the example of Flaubert should have made clear) and proffered anti-style as evidence of their honesty. But even their very bad writing served temporarily a good cause, exposing the pretensions of academic rhetoric.

Purveyors of the old realistic article still circulate among us (James T. Farrell, for instance, and Nelson Algren), but they tell no truths that are not clichés, and they give no valuable offense. Indeed, they have become indistinguishable from the producers of chic Italian movies and from TV entertainers like Paddy Chayefsky—second-rate artists, purveyors of the scandal of the day before yesterday. The day is gone when the tradition of realism-naturalism was so deeply accepted as *the* mode of serious literature that a mannered and artificial stylist like Hemingway, or an exploiter of backwoods rhetoric and gothic nightmare like Faulkner, had to pretend to be a "naturalist" in order to seem respectable. In the first place, realism-naturalism has become an academy itself, sustaining a triumphant orthodoxy instead of challenging one; and meanwhile, certain contraband, smuggled into the presumably objective laboratory report from the beginning, has come to seem more and more essential: political propaganda, heavy-handed symbolism, righteous pornography and sentimentality.

The latter two especially have assumed a disheartening importance in the standard subforms of post-realism, first clearly defined in the United States in the 1930s: the Popular Front Novel, on the one hand, and Regionalist or Protest Pornography on the other. John Steinbeck is the father of the first, having established in *The Grapes of Wrath* the prototype of the pious tract disguised as a sociological report, in which the cruel exploiters of labor are contrasted with simple and kindly men who give candy to children, and women of the people who offer their swollen breasts to the starving unemployed. Erskine Caldwell is the founder of the other, having created in *Tobacco Road* a genre capable of providing all the forbidden thrills of a peep show together with the conscientious satisfactions of deploring the state of the (more exotic) poor. It is hard to remember that Caldwell was considered a serious "proletarian" writer before he became a paperback best seller; one reads with surprise the accounts of his current reception in places like Turkey, where he is still regarded as a pattern for "village literature." In this country, his example has occasioned lately only such bootleg high-school literature as Grace Metalious' *Peyton Place*.

Steinbeck's prototype, however, continues to provide inspiration for the prevailing upper middlebrow form of our time: the serious pseudo-novel as practiced by certain not-quite-first-rate authors, committed equally to social conscience and success, and sure that these are not mutually exclusive goals. There is scarcely a moment these days when such authors of the Sentimental Liberal Protest Novel as Irwin Shaw, John Hersey, Budd Schulberg and James Michener are not fighting for slots on the list of best sellers; since in our time left-of-center politics has become, by virtue of converting all its political content to sentiment, the reigning belief of the educated middle classes. In our genteel age, the class struggle has been translated from a confrontation of workers and bosses on the barricades to a contest between certain invisible or remote exploiters and all the rest of us—a contest in which more tears are shed than blood. The writer dedicated to portraying that struggle is no longer the man in the work shirt rolled to the elbow and open at the neck, but the man ashamed of his gray flannel suit—the searcher out and defender of Victims. For the image of man which possesses the genteel conscience is the image of the Victim: the snubbed Jew, the oppressed Negro, the starving Chinese, the atom-scarred Japanese, the betrayed Hungarian, the misunderstood paraplegic. For each Victim there is an appropriate book, a last indignity: *Gentlemen's Agreement*, *The Wall*, *The Bridge at Andau*, *The Last Pebble*, *One Hour*. Even the War Novel is recast in the prevailing form, captured, like *The Young Lions*, for piety, protest, and self-pity. In the end, we are left with the sense that wars are fought and armies organized (in representative platoons, with all minorities duly represented) so that the persecuted Jew or tormented Italian can shame his fellows by proving his unforeseen valor in the end.

Having only a single theme, of a rather simple-minded sort, the Sentimental Protestors are driven to eke it out, to conceal its stereotypical bareness with up-to-date details and topical references. Their eyes are constantly on the headlines; and before the ink is dry, Michener and Hersey are already embarked for the scene of the latest indignity—or at least racing for their type-writers! It is a somewhat comic contest, with the whole reading world breathlessly waiting to discover who will get Little Rock first, who the Puerto Ricans. But what is the ersatz morality which sustains the protest fictionists, from Hersey-Shaw to Jones-Algren, from the soft-sell defenders of the dark-skinned peoples to the tough apologists for maximum security prisoners and minor hoods? It is the theory that the "Little Man" must be defended against the great and powerful merely because he is little and "wants only to be let alone." Little! Surely no more degrading label has ever been invented for the exploited, none which has so combined pathos and condescension: the little Jew, the little shopkeeper, the little mixed-up kid, the bewildered little pusher of dope, the little pimp trying to establish himself against the competition of the big operators. . . . Against so abject a surrender to sentiment, one wants to cry out in the terrible words of the Old Testament, "Thou shalt not honor the poor man in his cause." But who could be heard over the voices of those storming their book counters for copies of *Exodus* and *Hawaii?*

What, then, of serious literature in our time? What counterimage of man does it proffer? Not, as so often in the past, an image of man struggling (and failing) to fulfill some revealed or inherited view of himself and his destiny; but of man learning that it is the struggle itself which is his definition. In a time when answers are the business of professional answer men (cheats and delusions carefully rehearsed before the show is put on the air), we have been forced to learn that our humanity is dependent not on the answers we hope for but on the questions we are able to ask. Like Job, we are granted no response except from the apparition which tells us it is time to be still, time to know that man is he who asks what man is. And like Melville's "unencumbered travellers," we must be prepared to leave our Encyclopedia Britannicas and Oxford English Dictionaries behind us, to cross the frontiers of Eternity with no baggage except the Ego. This the most serious writers of our day have taught us, insisting that we endure uncertainty, not as a stage on the way to knowledge, but as our essential condition. Now we see as through a glass darkly. There is no "then."

This view of man opens into a world not of melodrama but of ambiguity, not of the polemical but of the problematical. Saul Bellow's *The Victim*, for instance, will survive *Focus, Gentleman's Agreement, The Professor's Umbrella* and all the other earnest and humane tracts on anti-Semitism because, despite its title, it is not a protest novel at all. In Bellow's view, both Jew and gentile are simultaneously Victim and Victimizer; he renders their mutual torment in terms of their common desire to discover what it means to be human, their common need to *be* what is human. Our Jewishness or gentileness, Bellow leaves us feeling, is *given;*

our humanity is what we must achieve. There is no more room for sentimentality in such a travesty of the liberal Jewish novel than there is in Robert Penn Warren's similar recasting of the political novel, or Malamud's of the novel about baseball, or James Baldwin's of the standard Negro novel, or Mary McCarthy's of fictional protests against the restriction of academic freedom. Reading, say, *All the King's Men*, one need only think of *The Last Hurrah* or *Advise and Consent*—or picking up *The Natural*, one need only recall Mark Harris' *Bang the Drum Slowly*—to realize how we ordinarily lust to be lied to, and how seldom we are granted the privilege of hearing the truth.

Ambiguity is the first resource of the serious novelist, tempted like all the rest of us to clichés of simplicity; but to say that the good novel is ambiguous is not to say that it is difficult and confused (this is optional), merely to insist that it is *about* moral ambiguity and that it cannot betray its theme. I distrust the writer who claims to know black and white, left from right, Hip from Square, Them from Us—no matter which of the sides he chooses. And I distrust especially the characters in whom he embodies his presumable insights. The protagonists of the best recent books are not self-righteous, long-suffering, diminished prigs, who want only to live in peace and are sure they know what peace is. From the most sympathetic to the least, they are troublemakers like their authors, who will not let the world rest until it acknowledges that they exist. We have by now quite a gallery of such types, including Joyce's insufferable Stephen, too stiff-necked to grant his mother's deathbed wish; Kafka's K., guilty as charged though no one knows quite what the charge is; Nathanael West's Miss Lonelyhearts, trying in vain to be the Christ in whom he does not believe; Ralph Ellison's Invisible Man, vainly striving to escape the myth of his color; and Faulkner's Popeye, counterfeiting manhood with a bloody corncob.

The contemporary novel through which such characters stalk—bringing harm to those around them, even as they court destruction for themselves—is terror-ridden, dreadful; but it is not humorless. In the midst of Faulkner's grimmest book, *Sanctuary*, a couple of rustics play out a humorous scene in a whorehouse. West's bleakest novel is his funniest, *A Cool Million*, whose title

comes from the "Old Saying": "John D. Rockefeller would give
a cool million to have a stomach like yours." Kafka, we are told,
used to laugh until the tears ran down his cheeks, reading aloud
from *Amerika*. Joyce, one sometimes feels, would do anything
for a laugh, and Beckett has thought of some things to do which
even his master could not imagine; Bellow can be a clown; Mary
McCarthy insists on compelling our titters in the midst of our
deepest shame; and the British "Angries" have us guffawing like
a pack of fools. In this sense, Mark Twain is the true ancestor of
the modern writer, and his *Pudd'nhead Wilson* a storehouse of
the sort of humor which is not dated by changes of fashion.
"*October 12, the Discovery*. It was wonderful to find America, but
it would have been more wonderful to miss it." This is our kind
of joke, proper to a world in which we may all die laughing—as
we like to say.

Such humor is not incompatible with negation, or even terror,
for it is not party or factional humor, with which the *in*'s satirize
the *out*'s, and the "normal" put the eccentric in their places. It is
total humor, through which men laugh not at their foibles but at
their essential selves. The vision of man shared by our greatest
writers involves an appreciation of his absurdity, and the protagonists of our greatest books are finally neither comic nor tragic but
absurd. To the modern writer, the distinction between comedy
and tragedy seems as forced and irrelevant as that between hallucination and reality; his world partakes of both, and he would
be hard put to it to say where one ends and the other begins.
The conventional definitions of the comic and the tragic strike
him as simplifications, falsifications of human life, appropriate to
a less complex time. To insist that we regard man, even for the
space of three acts or five, as *either* horrible or funny; to require
us, through four or five hundred pages, *either* to laugh or to cry
we find offensive in an age when we can scarcely conceive of
wanting to do one without the other. For us, the great works of
the past are those which occupy an intermediate position between
comedy and tragedy: the *Bacchae* of Euripides, the *Misanthrope*
of Moliere, Shakespeare's *Measure for Measure*, Ibsen's *An Enemy
of the People*, Twain's *Pudd'nhead Wilson* and Melville's *The
Confidence Man*. And the writers of our own time whom we most

admire—West, Faulkner and Beckett, among others—pursue a third genre, which suggests that the ludicrous is the source of pity and terror, and that pity and terror themselves are the heart of the ludicrous.

The vision of the truly contemporary writer.is that of a world not only absurd but also chaotic and fragmentary. He tries in his work to find techniques for representing a universe in which our perceptions overlap but do not coincide, in which we share chiefly a sense of loneliness: our alienation from whatever things finally are, as well as from other men's awareness of those things and of us. Rapid shifts in point of view; dislocations of syntax and logic; a vividness more like hallucination than photography; the use of parody and slapstick at moments of great seriousness; the exploitation of puns and of the vaudeville of dreams—these experiments characterize much of the best work of recent decades, from Joyce's *Ulysses* through Djuna Barnes' *Nightwood* to Wright Morris' *Field of Vision*, whose winning of the National Book Award so incensed the guardians of middlebrow standards. At the present moment, Morris is almost alone in the United States in his continuing devotion to the themes and techniques of the negative novel. (There is, to be sure, the young novelist John Barth, strangely ignored.) For we have been suffering a general loss of nerve, or a waning of talent, which has persuaded writers of such different origins and generations as Hemingway, Faulkner, Saul Bellow and Mary McCarthy to pursue affirmation in the place of art—disconcerted, perhaps, as they pass from being ignored to relative degrees of fame and victimized by a perverse sort of *noblesse oblige*.

The unearned euphoria of *Henderson, the Rain King;* the shapeless piety of *A Fable;* the sentimental self-indulgence of *Across the River and into the Trees;* the maudlin falsity of *The Town;* the heavy-handed symbolism and religiosity of *The Old Man and the Sea,* destined from its inception for the pages of *Life*—such failures make over and over the point that the contemporary American writer can abjure negativism only if he is willing to sacrifice truth and art. For major novelists and minor, the pursuit of the positive means stylistic suicide. Language itself decays, and dialogue becomes travesty; character, stereotype; insight, sentiment. The Nobel Prize speech destined for high-school anthologies requires quite another talent from that demanded by the novel; and the abstract praise of love requires another voice from that which cries No! to the most noble temptations, the most defensible lies.

Yet one must not forget, in the face of their recent decline, the successes of Bellow and Hemingway and Faulkner: the terrible impact of *The Victim, The Sun Also Rises* and *The Sound and the Fury*. The last, in particular, remains the exemplary American novel, perhaps the greatest work of fiction produced in the United States in the twentieth century. And it is no accident that its title comes from the bleakest passage in Shakespeare, or that its action begins inside the mind of an idiot. The point is insisted upon bluntly, almost too obviously: life is a tale told by an idiot, full of sound and fury, signifying nothing. Here is the ultimate negation, the Hard No pressed as far as it will go. Yet "nothing" is not quite Faulkner's last word, only the next to the last. In the end, the negativist is no nihilist, for he affirms the void. Having endured a vision of the meaninglessness of existence, he retreats neither into self-pity and aggrieved silence nor into a realm of beautiful lies. He chooses, rather, to render the absurdity which he perceives, to know it and make it known. To know and to render, however, mean to give form; and to give form is to provide the possibility of delight—a delight which does not deny horror but lives at its intolerable heart.

1960

32 John Lennon

John Lennon, actor, author, and Beatle, was born in Liverpool in 1940 and attended the Liverpool College of Arts. He has written two books of Liverpudlian nonsense poems and stories with his own illustrations, In His Own Write (1964) and A Spaniard in the Works (1965).

◈

RANDOLF'S PARTY

It was Chrisbus time but Randolph was alone. Where were all his good pals. Bernie, Dave, Nicky, Alice, Beddy, Freba, Viggy, Nigel, Alfred, Clive, Stan, Frenk, Tom, Harry, George, Harold? Where were they on this day? Randolf looged saggly at his only Chrispbut cart from his dad who did not live there.

"I can't understan this being so aloneley on the one day of the year when one would surely spect a pal or two?" thought Rangolf. Hanyway he carried on putting ub the desicrations and muzzle toe. All of a surgeon there was amerry timble on the door. Who but who could be a knocking on my door? He opened it and there standing there who? but only his pals. Bernie, Dave, Nicky, Alice, Beddy, Freba, Viggy, Nigel, Alfred, Clive, Stan, Frenk, Tom, Harry, George, Harolb weren't they?

Come on in old pals buddys and mates. With a big griff on his face Randoff welcombed them. In they came jorking and labbing shoubing "Haddy Grimmble, Randoob." and other hearty, and then they all jumbed on him and did smite him with mighty blows about his head crying, "We never liked you all the years

515

we've known you. You were never raelly one of us you know, soft head."

They killed him you know, at least he didn't *die* alone did he? Merry Chrustchove, Randolf old pal buddy.